H

THE KISSING GATE

Also by Pamela Haines

TEA AT GUNTER'S

A KIND OF WAR

MEN ON WHITE HORSES

Pamela Haines

The Kissing Gate

1981

DOUBLEDAY & COMPANY, INC., GARDEN CITY, NEW YORK

All persons in this book are fictitious,
and any resemblance to persons living or
dead is purely coincidental.

ISBN: 0-385-15309-0
Library of Congress Catalog Card Number: 79-6581
Copyright © 1981 by Pamela Haines
All Rights Reserved
Printed in the United States of America
First Edition

For Charlotte and Paul, Lucy, Nick,
and Emily,
with my love

A very big thank-you to all those, too many to mention, who during the writing of this book answered queries, opened archives, and generally gave of their time. A special thank-you to Catriona Dunbar (now McDermott) for the loan of her lovely name, and as many thanks to Jessica Lebon as she cooked hot dinners during my last hectic weeks of typing. Last of all, thank you to Peter Hole and Jim Hesketh, both of Barclays Bank, without whose help this book would not have been possible.

THE KISSING GATE

PROLOGUE

1820

Sarah Donnelly, thirteen years and three months, and on an errand, walks along the last mile of the road home to Downham. If you can call Downham her home—since really it's only the place where she works. Hawes is the town where she was brought up and where her mam lives now (and her da *used* to). Her mistress had promised Mam that this, her first post, where she will learn to be a real maid, would be a second home for her. It is in Wensleydale, in Yorkshire—like her real home. But it hasn't *seemed* home. Mrs. Mumford has too rough a tongue for that, and a heart not quite warm enough to offset it. Today:

"I'll have two dozen of the eggs, all on 'em to be fresh, still warm if he can and the butter to be packed either side of t'basket and nowt to pay while he's owing me . . ."

Sarah walks. Downham Bridge, humpbacked, is just in sight. The sun is shining on this May afternoon, the first fine day for a week, and a light breeze is making the clouds race. She walks but she'd much rather run: or best of all, skip. But there can be none of that—not with a basket on her arm, and such a precious load. And such possible wrath to come. Just one egg broken would take a lot of explaining. Twice she's stopped on the way to lift the cloth and see if they're all right. Except that: just looking at them could break them . . .

When I get back, she thought, when I get back, and when I've prepared the tea and vegetables and washed the dishes and done the plate and trimmed me lamps, then I'll maybe . . . in her tiny cupboard of a room under the eaves, there might be just enough light to make out the words that went with the pictures in her rhyming book. But even if there were, she rather feared she might just yawn and yawn and yawn—and then not remember anything at all till gone half-five in the morning.

Although she had to be up so early, it was surprising how noisy it often was by the time she came down. Mrs. Mumford's cottage was just next to the rope-works, in an alley turned off from the market square, on a line with the Castle. They started early enough at the rope-works. She'd often see Samuel Rawson, "young Mr. Rawson," come clattering into the yard well before she'd finished her front doorstep. He always passed the time of day—once he even said that she should come in and see how the ropes were made.

"We've space for a little lass, and I'll not let old Marchant tie you in knots . . ." But she had never dared to go in—and anyway she was afraid of old Mr. Marchant, who had a beard like the Giant in Jack the Giant Killer. Young Mr. Rawson looked after the whole works: he owned them now, even though "old Mr. Rawson," or "Old Jacob" as they called him, wasn't old at all but still a man in his prime. But not so many years ago, after spending no more than five shillings, he had won the largest sum of money she had ever heard of: *ten thousand pounds*, in the Great Yorkshire Sweepstake. Now Old Jacob no longer needed to work, but lived in a fine house he had built, standing in its own grounds off the market square, at the top end. He had called it Almeida House, after the name of the horse.

It was said that he wasn't very generous with the money and that he hadn't given any to his family at all. They said too that he gave himself airs, and fancied himself quite the equal now of the Ingham family (who were *really* grand people and lived in Downham Abbey and had used to own sugar plantations right the other side of the world . . .). And the very proof that they lived in the Abbey was that now as she came nearer to the bridge, she could see some of them.

Ahead were a plump nursemaid and four children, coming along the path which led from the Abbey to the main road, past the church which they called the kirk, and past the Kissing Gate (except that it wasn't *really* a kissing-gate: Mam had said, when she saw it: "That's never a kissing-gate . . ."). The nursemaid was carrying the youngest Ingham, a bonneted bundle. A little girl of about seven or eight walked alongside her, while the eldest boy—Charles, they called him—was running ahead of all of them, dressed in a heavy velveteen suit. He had reached the Kissing Gate already.

Sarah thought he might go through the Gate and into the churchyard—the kirkgarth as she called it—because there were often stray lambs grazing there in the spring. He was certainly up the steps and pulling at the iron bars. But he only gave the Gate a shake, and then ran on.

He would have had to go in that way, though, to get to the kirkgarth, since one wasn't allowed to use the main kirk gate (even though it was much much nearer the town), except on Sundays—or if you were the parson. Mrs. Mumford had told her that, so it must be true. If you came into the kirk through the wrong gate, then you were likely soon enough to be *carried* through the Kissing Gate—in your coffin.

There were lots of beliefs like that. But the new young vicar, Mr. Cuthbert, he must not think very much of them, for only last Sunday he'd given a very stern sermon about what he called "the evils of super-stition." Mrs. Mumford didn't suppose anyone would pay much atten-tion . . . "He's from a university," she said. "What'll he know?"

Sarah had to go with the Mumfords every time they went to church. That was why she now was able to recognise the Inghams: they had their own box pew in church, up some steps, so that once they were in-side you could not see what they were doing. She often imagined them pulling faces at the dreadful scraping noise which George Mumford made on his violin when he played with the musicians. She liked the look of Squire Ingham—he was what she imagined a squire *should* be, large and jolly and kindly looking (although she knew she'd be quite terrified if he should actually speak to her . . .). Mrs. Ingham was said to be very weak and delicate and was at this moment still very ill from the latest baby.

Sarah could see that carrying this baby was what was making it difficult for the nursemaid to keep up. Sarah saw now that the little girl was ahead as well, although not very much. Besides the baby, the nurse had also a little boy in a red frock pulling at her skirts. That was George Ingham. Charles was a long way on now—Sarah heard the nurse call for him. But he didn't answer or even turn round. Just went on running, the Abbey far behind him.

Just as the Kissing Gate wasn't *really* a kissing-gate, the Abbey wasn't really an abbey, but rather was the Inghams' private house, and very splendid indeed. Once, though, there had been monks there—they had been famous for breeding white horses. There were some ruins still: the lovely Abbey gateway, but mostly the church—fragments of walls, grave slabs, some stone knights in chain armour . . .

She paused a moment—she was right by Downham Bridge now. If she hadn't the load and the hurry to be back, she'd have liked to linger, watching the swiftly flowing river—clear brown water over the white pebbles. After the gales of last week the river was very swollen, and it had risen to quite a height; she imagined that under the bridge it must have quite covered the mossy stones at the side and the lichen on the arch.

Charles Ingham had run straight out onto the road now, not looking out at all for carts and carriages. She wondered if he would try to climb the stretch of new dry-stone wall on the other side. Beyond it was the meadow and the river.

"Charles, Master Charles!" called the nurse. She and her charges had only just reached the Kissing Gate. The girl had fallen back and was picking some flowers that grew by the edge of the gate.

Oh, but it all looked so lovely. The Abbey and the river and the bridge all cradled in the hills and the moors. Gentle green in the pastures below, and then above, in the summer, great stretches seeming to hang over. It had been the first lovely thing she'd noticed when, eight months ago now, Mam had brought her over to that terrible interview with Mrs. Mumford. Jogging along in the carrier's cart that day, her heart had lifted when she'd seen the view, and stayed up all the way into Downham. They'd both been afraid that Mrs. Mumford would ask questions about her da (and perhaps not even believe that she *had* a father). "He's gone back to Ireland," Mam had had to admit in the end, but you could see that Mrs. Mumford wasn't at all sure. "You can ask in Hawes about John Donnelly," Mam had said proudly.

"Charles, Master Charles, *please* now!" Master Charles had climbed the wall and gone right into the meadow. As Sarah began to cross the bridge, she glanced down. He was playing about not on the grass but by the water's edge. Scrambling among the branches of an alder tree, pushing them aside. That won't do his fine suit any good, she thought.

And then—the suddenness of the splash shocked her. For a second— it was only a second—she stood rooted like a tree. Then she glanced quickly the other way. The nursemaid was nearly at the road now. She had seen. Her scream rose. Clutching the baby to her she began to run awkwardly—always screaming.

Sarah moved. She ran back to the other side. She thought quickly: the current will pull him under the bridge. I must . . . Her legs wouldn't move fast enough. Down over the flat white stones to the water's edge. The frothy, angry, swollen river. And then—in.

She tried to swim, because she could a little—only it wasn't possible. It was possible only to fight the force of the water, to keep above the brown swirl. If she did not reach him, he would be dashed onto the jagged stones in the centre. *She* would be dashed onto the jagged stones! . . . The water was a furious torrent now, until—Our Father which art in Heaven, oh thank God—she was near him. Then she was touching him, losing him—clutching at him again, getting hold, grabbing wet velvet.

She had him. But even as she pulled, he pulled back. He was clinging to her. Trying to drag her. Panicky, frantic grabbing. She realised with horror that he might pull her down . . . His hands were in her hair, her bonnet pulled over one eye. Now he was pushing down on her shoulders.

Against the rush of the water she fought him. She was swallowing great gulps of liquid. He was unbelievably strong. Only a small child—and in his deathly fear he was stronger. He shall not—we must—*we shall both be lost.*

Then suddenly—so suddenly—it was all right. She felt him go limp against her. Now she could pull him, drag him, swim as best she could —and make for the land. The river's edge was near, *must* be near now.

Seconds after she had stumbled onto the flat boulders. Charles clinging limply to her now, she felt strong arms grasping her. She fell against the stiffness of a man's coat. Her eyes, sore, buffeted, could hardly see.

On the other side the nursemaid screamed still, but weakly now, from hysterical habit. The other children had joined her. Thin little wails of terror.

She saw then that the man was young Mr. Rawson. Charles had his eyes shut. "Is he—?" she began.

"He'll live," said Mr. Rawson. And indeed Charles, already leaning forward retching violently, a great spout of muddy water, was plainly alive.

"You did well," Mr. Rawson said. "There'd not have been much I could do, time I'd sighted him." Then he said to her, "Wait there a minute."

His trap had stopped just by the bridge. He went and came back with an old blanket and a piece of sacking. First he wrapped up Charles and then Sarah. He placed them both in the trap and they set off at once. They crossed the bridge and then turned right towards the Abbey. When they came up to the Kissing Gate, the nursemaid and her charges were standing there. He took them up too. There was scarcely room. The nurse was whimpering now. Charles was white and still.

They went through the Abbey gateway and up to the front entrance. Sarah was surprised that he didn't go round to the back. But bold as could be, and carrying Charles wrapped in the blanket, he was going to the front door. The nursemaid, teeth chattering as if she'd been the one in the water, said to him as she climbed out of the trap: "I'll tell the Master—someone'll tell the Master. You've been good . . ." She sobbed. "It's Mr. Rawson, Mr. Samuel Rawson, isn't it, sir?"

"That's it," he said shortly. "But it's not much *I've* done . . ." Then as she had trouble getting the little boy out: "On with you, quicksticks . . . I've this little lass here to fetch home."

Just then the front door opened. A footman took Charles from his arms. The nursemaid had begun crying again. Mr. Rawson came back to Sarah.

"Now we'll away to the Mumfords," he said, "when we've thanked God." He told her as they drove along that she should pray at once, a prayer of thanksgiving that the Lord had saved *both* their lives. "It might not have been," he said. "A river in full spate—there's been some luck there—*and* pluck . . . Let us pray," he said. " 'I will alway give thanks unto the Lord: His praise shall ever be in my mouth . . .' "

They were already almost at the market square in Downham, when she remembered the eggs.

"I'd a basket—" She'd begun to shiver. She pulled at his sleeve: "My basket—the *eggs!*"

"What's that?" But when she told him he just gave a shake of the reins and said firmly, "She can whistle for them, can Mrs. Mumford. We'll not go back. You're like to have a bad enough chill—if we don't have you home soon."

When they were coming by the market cross, he said: "The Squire'll be wanting to thank you, I don't doubt . . ."

She was shaking still. "No. I'd liefer not—"

"Why's that? You'd have nowt to fear. He's good with childer, is Squire. Kindly." They turned off the square and up towards the alley. "And for all he's a wencher—God forgive him—a *fine* man . . ."

"What's a wencher?" asked Sarah.

"Aye, well . . ." He lifted up his head. " 'But whoso committeth adultery with a woman lacketh understanding: he that doeth it destroyeth his own soul,' Proverbs six . . . Aye—well, you'll not need to know that . . ."

At the house he didn't just set her down but actually carried her in. So that Mrs. Mumford, come to the door in her apron, was quite taken by surprise. "Whatever next, what's she done now?"

Mr. Rawson explained. And he made her promise that Sarah should have hot brandy and milk and a seat by the fire and her bed warmed, and no more work that day.

"She did well—very well like. He'll be more than grateful will Squire."

But of course it didn't work out quite like that. I knew I'd catch it, she thought. She had the hot drink (without the brandy), and even the warming pan in her bed—but she got the reproaches as well.

"I'm sure I don't know what I'm to do. Twenty-four eggs the less. And I'd the custards to make. You didn't take care, did you?" She warmed to her subject. "Didn't think—not to put them down careful

like afore you run in the water. *No thought,* I don't doubt . . . It'll be
the Irish in you. God knows your mam, she seemed a hardworking,
God-fearing Yorkshire woman. Minding what she's doing. Except
mebbe when she tied herself up with a murphy . . ."

But that's not fair, Sarah thought later. All I want is my da back.
(And certainly her mam did . . .) There seemed always someone to be
rude about him—almost as if there were something bad about being
Irish. Maybe some of them that came over in summertime, to help
bring in the hay, maybe *some* of them weren't as good as others. But
Mam, when she'd been a girl on the farm in West Burton—not so far
from here—and had used to take out pints of beer to them in the fields,
she said they were all, or almost all, fine fellows. A bit rough maybe,
but her da he'd been the best, and the one that sang and danced like
none of the others.

So Mam had ended up keeping company with him, although her father hadn't been at all pleased, Mam said. The next summer he'd come
back, and this time he stayed on in Yorkshire so they could be wed. Her
family had been very angry, and wouldn't have anything to do with her.
Sarah had never seen any of them. Da had got work helping build the
dry-stone walls they were putting up all over the dales, to divide off
what used to be common land (Enclosure they called it. It was the
law). Sometimes he had to travel with the work, but not too far.

He hadn't taken Mam back to Ireland because he'd said the living
there, it wasn't as good as Yorkshire. Only, she thought often, how
beautiful it sounded—just the name, Connemara. His little town was in
Galway county, not far from Lough Corrib. They called it Carrownacally. Da used to laugh when she tried to say it. They spoke a
different tongue over there, he said, and when she was small, and right
up to her last memories of him, he would sing to her in that language.

> "*Sheohin, shioho, mo stoir is mo leanb,*
> *Mo ghia gan cealg, mo chuid den t-saol mor . . .*"

he sang for her at night. And *mo pheata* he called her always, *mo
pheata.* Even when he spoke English it sounded so different, quite
different from everyone else she knew.

She only wished now that she could sing and dance as he'd done. She
remembered his feet, and how fast they would go. She had no music in
her—she wasn't like him in that way at all. But she was small like him
(even for thirteen she wasn't very big), and wiry, and she had the same
sandy-coloured hair. Mam's hair was black with a curl to it, and she was

very large, so that when she hugged Sarah, which was often, it felt lovely and so, so safe. But Da had sat her on his knees—they were very bony—when she was small, and bounced her up and down, up and down. And told her stories of *bean si*, the fairy woman, and *gruagach*, the giant, and *puca*, the bad fairy . . .

Then suddenly he wasn't there. She couldn't have been more than six or so. He'd wanted to go back to Ireland, Mam said, just to visit—and then he'd return to Yorkshire. Only he didn't come back. Not another word had they heard. Mam had got more worried each year. She'd got someone in Hawes (where they'd moved to when Sarah was four or five) to write to the priest in Carrownacally. But there'd been no answer. Mam had thought perhaps the priests had found out he'd been wed in the wrong church and they were vexed with him . . . It wasn't as if he hadn't a big family over there—*twenty* brothers and sisters he'd spoken of, to say nothing of all the other relations . . . They're my family too, Sarah would think. She was all alone, just her and Mam, although now they hadn't Da, it was good, Mam said, that she'd lost her other children. "*Five* bairns I should have . . ."

"We've to forget about him," Mam had said in the end, when they'd given up hope of news.

"But he's my *da*," Sarah had protested, crying then. "I want to go where he lives," she'd told Mam.

"We couldn't," Mam had said. "And how'd we pay? You've just to remember you've a family there, and you're *half*-Irish. And your childer, they'll be one *quarter*. You're Donnelly, and mebbe one day—but for now, put it all out of your head . . ."

Mam had got work in Hawes by then, the best she could, and as soon as possible Sarah was to also. (Although in the end Mam hadn't let her go till she was twelve . . .)

Sarah liked living in Hawes: it was so high up, with mountains around. The name Hawes *meant* a pass between mountains. Their home was at the lower end of the town where the houses were all higgledy-piggledy. Not far away from Hawes, where Hearne Beck and Fossdale Gill met, there was a huge waterfall. The stone scar stuck right out and the water fell from it one hundred feet. She had liked to stand behind it and watch it go over.

But although it was so splendid, she couldn't *love* it the way she loved the little waterfall by the Kissing Gate. For when you went through the gate and up to the kirk, and the graveyard with its elms and yew and birch and the beck running along gently, you had first to go along a path with a bank on the right, all grassy, where daffodils grew now. But on the left it was dark and ivy-covered, with a wall all covered with moss, going on up and dividing the other bank from the graveyard. And through a hole in the wall the water from the beck came rushing, cascading down, a great torrent. It didn't fall like the other one—only the height perhaps of two men—but she loved the *sound* of it, sometimes louder, sometimes softer, before it ran away under the Abbey road and into the river Down.

Just inside the Kissing Gate, before the grassy bank really began, was where people buried charm bags. Mrs. Mumford had told her about those. If you wanted to protect somebody, or bring them back, or whatever, you had to put something of theirs in a little bag and bury it. And because it was near the Kissing Gate it would bring you good fortune. Sarah had found the remains of a little rag doll her da had made her once, and she had brought it back with her after her first visit home at Christmas time. Then she'd cut off a piece of it, and made a little bag and buried it—and then she had waited . . . But she didn't have much hope. It was just best to do all you could. And if she hadn't done so, she would always have wondered if . . .

She certainly believed everything they said about the Gate. It must be very important, she thought, to everyone in Downham if the Reverend Cuthbert needed to preach a *sermon* about it. And indeed Mrs. Mumford had been quite vexed with him last Sunday.

"Too clever by half, and only a young lad at that," she said. "It's flyin' in t'face of what's known. He should let well alone . . ."

But then when Sarah had asked her once why it was called the Kissing Gate, if it wasn't a kissing-gate at all, she had answered quite indignantly: "I don't know." Grumbling then: "Using your head for thinking up questions when you could be minding your own business . . ."

Although she'd been quite happy to tell Sarah about the odd fragments of ribbons or thread or lace or hazel thongs which Sarah had seen there at different times, fastened low down on the railings. They were messages, Mrs. Mumford said, between people—especially those keeping company . . . And she was willing enough to talk about the Gate. For instance, Sarah had never thought of swinging on it until Mrs. Mumford told her she mightn't. Never, *never. Ever.*

"It's well known," she'd said to Sarah, "what they say . . . 'Them as swings on t'Gate, swings on t'gibbet . . .' "

Just to think, Sarah had told herself, just to think that swinging on the Gate, no more, could mean your ending up *hanged*—as a criminal. She shivered as she heard. Ever after, though, to swing on it had been the most terrible temptation to her. She could hardly pass the Gate but she'd want to lift the latch, put her feet on the bottom rail, and swing and swing and swing . . .

Although Mrs. Mumford was rough-tongued, she wasn't *always* bad-tempered. She liked to talk a lot, and when she had Sarah as an audience she could be quite kind. Mondays, while they did the weekly wash together, standing in the stone-flagged kitchen with their hands plunged in the tubs, was a favourite time for talking.

And that was why Sarah knew so much about the Ingham family: the names of the children, and their ages, and about the Abbey not being an abbey, and so on. Mrs. Mumford really liked to talk about them. The Rawsons, on the other hand, she hardly bothered to speak of. For a start, she didn't think much of Jacob Rawson—and the sweepstake, and the horse, Almeida, and the big house. "He's a nothing, is Old Jacob." But the Inghams, that was quite a different matter. They were *carriage* folk, she told Sarah, and very grand . . .

Sarah had not really expected anything from the Squire, although Mrs. Mumford had suggested that perhaps he would want to give her a little piece or two of silver to say thank you ("But I'd be better pleased if he'd pay for t'eggs. Mr. Rawson may have fetched up t'butter, but them *eggs* . . ."). Sarah hoped really that everything might just be forgotten, so that she was made very nervous when two days later a servant from the Abbey brought the message that the Squire would like to see Sarah Donnelly.

Such a washing and brushing and giving of good advice by Mrs. Mumford . . . And then the walk up through the town, with her best boots pinching (I must have grown, just a little, she thought—but Mam mustn't know. How'd we buy new ones?). Then turning up the Abbey road and past the Kissing Gate. Touching it for luck, but not wanting at all to swing on it now. Walking through the archway and up the drive . . . She had been told to come to the front door, but she would much rather have not. The house so large and square, with her standing there on the step for anyone to see. Behind her, beyond the drive, fenced off, green stretched out to where the hills began. The ground dipped a little, just near the house. That was where the monks had had their fish pond, Mrs. Mumford said, when the house was an Abbey.

She tried to think about that now, waiting for what seemed an age until the door was opened. Bad weather too, coming on. Spitting rain.

That was the first thing the Squire remarked on when she was shown into the big room, with the fire brightly burning, and the great man sitting there in an enormous leather chair. She was trembling, not just from the outside cold, but nervousness too. She tried to remember Mrs. Mumford's words of advice ("And if it's *money*—brass, he give you—

then I'll want for to see it. It's to be for your poor mam that's been left by a no-good Irishman. And don't hang your head—you've not to hang your head . . .").

At once on coming in she felt her head go down. She could not stop it. She stood waiting just inside the doorway.

"The child, sir, Sarah Donnelly, sir," the manservant said, leaving her alone.

"Well, Sarah?" The Squire rubbed his hands. "Well. I've brought you out on a cold day. Who'd have thought we were in May—" He paused. She still didn't dare to look up. His voice seemed much louder than she'd thought. "I waited," he said, "I waited to see you, so that you should make a complete recovery." She lifted her head up just a very little. His eyes were a startling blue, and looking straight at her. I will be brave, she thought.

"You *have* made a full recovery, Sarah, eh?"

"Yes please, sir, I'm nicely sir, thank you."

"You're a very brave little girl, do you know that? V*ery* brave . . . Mrs. Ingham, she'd particularly like to thank you. Unfortunately she's confined to her room—her health is not good. Charles now, we shall see him presently . . ." He frowned, but kindly. "Come a little further into the room. There—if that's not better."

There was a big yellow dog lying in front of the fire, wearing a brass-studded leather collar. She was afraid to come any nearer.

"You know you risked your life? It's a bad river when it runs so high —you realised that?"

"Yes, sir, no, sir—"

"The word has gone round already. You are quite the little heroine. And well deserved—" He paused. "Did you ever read a book called—I forget the name, but little Lucy the heroine—" he broke off. "But of course you wouldn't. Forgive me." He smiled then to himself.

"I might have done," she said, speaking up suddenly, "I might. I read *any* books. Any I can get to see . . ."

"Do you now? Upon my soul." He said it again: "Upon my soul, do you? Well then, come a little closer. I shan't eat you." He reached over for a large box with a wooden lid. "Would you like one of these, eh?"

She took one. It was a sugar plum. But—should she eat it now? (Mrs. Mumford had said, "And mind your manners, and don't go showing your teeth. They're not your best . . .")

"Go on, eat it." He raised his eyebrows. "You're not saving it for starving brothers and sisters, are you? Do you have brothers and sisters, Sarah, that are in need?"

She said indignantly, "There's only me—and I want for nowt."

He paid no attention to her outburst, but asked calmly, "And where you are now, your place at work, are you well fed there?"

"Yes, sir," she said loyally, "it's a good meat house, sir." Her flare-up had died down.

"That's an Irish temper you have," he said, smiling. "You *are* Irish? The name . . ." He looked across at her: "Why don't you sit down? I shouldn't keep you standing."

Which chair and where? She chose the wrong one, of course. It wasn't even a chair but was meant for feet. Her knees came up to meet her face. She saw that he was laughing at her. She thought then that she might cry. Don't let me, please God. But his face was serious again, and the eyes kindly.

"Your mother, Sarah, is she Irish?"

"No, sir, she's from West Burton, sir. New here, sir."

"And your father?"

"He's away now—he went home to Galway, sir. That's t'other side of Ireland. They call his place Carrownacally, sir—"

"Do they indeed?"

"He builded walls, sir, t'new walls. But first he were here for t'hay, when he were nobbut a lad and . . ." Out it came then—the whole story. Even down to Mam getting people to write to Galway. Everything.

"There'd 've been five children Mam said—" She stopped then, horrified at realising how long she'd spoken for.

But "Hmm" was all he said. "Hmm." Then: "I expect he'd have been very proud of you, Sarah—don't you think that now? Proud to be your father, eh? And I expect he'd think too that you deserve a reward." He rubbed his fingers together thoughtfully. "Don't *you* think you deserve a reward—eh?"

In the middle of last night she'd thought: perhaps he might give me a *whole gold sovereign*—that I could take home and surprise Mam . . . Then she remembered:

"The eggs, sir," she said now. "I dropped 'em, broke 'em like when I went in t'water. Mrs. Mumford's eggs they were, sir. If I could ask for t'price on 'em, sir." She hesitated. "Else Mrs. Mumford, she'll scold me, sir. She's vexed I weren't more mindful . . ."

When she'd said all that, she trembled. Accepting something, a little something, that was all right. But this was *asking* . . .

"Of course, of course," he said hastily, as if it were of no importance. "It'll be seen to." He reached out and pulled the bellrope. "Well, well," he said. "Built walls, your father, did he? And you—what do you hope to do?"

"Sir?"

"When you've finished with Mrs. Mumford, what do *you* hope to become?"

"Into service, sir. Mrs. Mumford she said, sir, as she knows someone is housekeeper at a big house, Ripon way, sir—happen I might get a place there like—"

He interrupted, "You can read, though? Is that right? You told me you could read—"

"Yes, sir, I learned myself to. I read all sorts, sir, whatever I can make out—what's lyin' aboot. I *can* read, sir," she finished lamely. As if he'd questioned it.

A manservant came in, a different one. The Squire took out a gold sovereign from a small leather case.

"This to Mrs. Mumford, please—next to Rawson's rope-works. Send Webster. This is to pay for the eggs she lost. And any expenses when the child was cold. Tell her she'll have her little maid back in time for tea."

That done, he sat quite still, just looking at her. Silence. She could hear the fire crackling. The big yellow dog got up slowly, stretched and sighed. Then he crossed over to be patted.

Fondling the dog's ears, the Squire said slowly: "I think what we shall do—because you like books so much, and learning—what we shall do is . . ." He looked up at her.

But she must have missed the next bit. Because although she was listening so eagerly, too eagerly maybe, the words seemed to run together —and the next thing she heard was: ". . . school. So—instead of away into service, away to school. How do you say to that, eh?"

But she could not. Could not speak at all. Her mouth open, but no sound coming out.

"Come now, Sarah, you must think *something* of the idea?" He paused, then as if thinking aloud, "I wonder—you know Mr. Paley?"

"No, sir."

"The vicar here at Downham, Sarah. Before Mr. Cuthbert came. He lives off the far side of the square—and he takes pupils. You would not be ready to go to school *immediately*, would you? There might be things you should learn—I would not risk your being a fish out of water. Mr. Paley—a good soul—you could take lessons with him, maybe for a year or so. His daughter Matilda is nearing middle-age—I know she requires a maid-companion. She, and he, they will see that you become quite the young lady—and able to go to school . . ." He stretched his legs before the fire. "Well—and what do you say *now*? Still no opinions, eh?"

"Please, sir, thank you, sir." It was too much. She was shaking. He said: "And afterwards, you could become perhaps—a governess? Who knows?" He pulled again at the bellrope. When the servant answered: "Master Charles," he said. "Downstairs, please." Then he asked: "Is Rawson here yet?"

"No, sir."

"Send him in directly, would you?" He turned back to Sarah. "He'll wait till the day's work is done, and not come before—if I know Sam Rawson. That's someone not a chip off the old block . . ." He paused. "Where were we, Sarah?"

"At school, sir. I mean, at Mr. Paley's, sir . . ."

The nursemaid brought Charles down. It wasn't the confident child of two days ago. But nor was it the white-faced, trembling one who had retched up at the water's edge. He looked pale but tidy. His hair, beautifully combed, shone black, glossy. His face had an odd expression, almost defiant. He came into the room reluctantly, pulled by the nurse.

"Leave us, please," the Squire told the nurse. Then, "Charles," he said, "here is Sarah come to see you. Sarah Donnelly." Charles had his head turned away. "You remember Sarah?" Then when Charles didn't answer, "What do you say, sir?"

"Yes, Papa." He said it saucily almost.

"Very good, Charles. And now, I want you to say *thank you* to Sarah. She saved your life—"

"Shan't," he said sullenly. Then at once began jumping about, shadow boxing, as if no one else were there. Suddenly full of energy, reminding Sarah of his capers two days ago.

The Squire said, "I think your nurse—perhaps sometimes your mother—they are not stern enough with you . . . Did you hear what I asked you, sir?"

Sarah interrupted, "Let him be, sir. It's no matter, sir."

"A difficult lad, my son. No, you shall have a thank you, Sarah. *Now*, sir—"

But it was *she* grew afraid. Charles did not seem to mind at all. She saw God the Father speaking, this great strong man, angry, red in the face, the veins showing above the white of his necktie.

"Thank Sarah, please. *At once, sir.*"

Then Charles, in a low sulky voice, scarcely to be heard: "Thank you . . ."

"Thank you, Sarah, for saving my life—" said his father.

Charles looked up, then spat the words out, surprising her with his violence.

"ThankyouSarahforsavingmylife—and now, *can I go?*" He didn't look

at her at all, but a moment later, when he was at last allowed to leave—
as he was going out of the room, he flashed her a haughty look: I despise you, he seemed to say.

But the Squire's anger was over. Only a little after Charles had gone,
he was jolly again, and smiling.

"We have to be firm," he told Sarah. "A parent must be firm." Then
rising up from his chair, a little stiffly, and looking at her kindly:
"What do you say now—should you like perhaps to see something of
the Abbey?"

"It's wetting still," she told him, when he asked if they should go
outside and look at the stone knights and the arches.

"Is it now? Well, we shall look only *inside* today, then. But outside,
you know, we have some of the abbey walls still—the north transept,
two lancet windows . . . You know that there were monks here until
the sixteenth century? But we, we have been here only since the reign
of Queen Anne. This house was built in 1700. Quite new . . ."

She would have liked then to have asked him something about the
days when the family had had sugar plantations—because of a story
Mrs. Mumford had told her once—but she was afraid to mention it, in
case it was something the Inghams did not speak of . . .

It was quite her favourite story, though—all about a black servant the
family had had ("blackamoors," they were called, Mrs. Mumford said,
and many people in London had them). This servant came from their
plantations, and had been with them for five or six years, when he'd
won quite a lot of money and a little fame in a prize fight held near
Downham. Although it was all *well* before her time, Mrs. Mumford
said, she'd heard tell that he'd been very magnificently built. But not
long after he'd won, he had had a quarrel with the other servants at the
Abbey—"Happen they were jealous," she told Sarah. "It's not known,
exactly. But the cause were t'fight, and t'big prize." The quarrel was so
bad evidently, and the other servants must have frightened him so
much, that he ran away. He didn't go much further than the other side
of Downham, though, where he was taken in by a tinsmith and his family. They hid him for three or four months, and said nothing, even
though there were notices posted up saying that he was missing.

But then one of the tinsmith's daughters found that she was going to
have a baby ("Ought I now to tell a small one these tales?" Mrs. Mumford had asked, that wash-day, the soap white up to her elbows . . .).
The lass's father, because he was certain whose bairn it was, had *killed*
the darkie in a fit of anger. But he'd never been brought to justice, Mrs.

Mumford said—and that was quite right. "Each must look after his own . . ."

The bairn had been a little girl and when she grew up, the Inghams, who knew the story by now, had wanted to be kind to her and had taken her on as a servant. Twenty or so years ago that had been—when the present Squire had been only a lad. But the girl hadn't stayed there very long: leaving in less than a year to marry Joseph Marsett, a wheelwright in Leyburn. And that would have been that, and the end of the story, if it hadn't been for Becky . . .

Becky was the eldest of Mrs. Marsett's children. Mrs. Mumford had pointed out Mrs. Marsett once to Sarah—on market day in Downham. She had not looked very dark except for her hair, which was rather tight and woolly—the bit that showed in front of her bonnet. And there was maybe something about her lips that was different. She looked plump and kindly, Sarah thought.

As early as her second week with the Mumfords, Sarah had heard the gossip about Mrs. Marsett's daughter Becky—but she hadn't known who she was then. It appeared that Becky had left home, run away— just as her blackamoor grandfather had done—suddenly and without explanation. Now she was living quite high up on the moors towards Little Grinling, in a disused cow house—which could not, Sarah thought, be very comfortable. But no one had been able to persuade her down— so there she stayed. And was like to stay till the end of her days. Or so Mrs. Mumford said: "Queer allus stays queer . . ."

Inside the Abbey, Sarah did not see it all, of course. They did not go up (which she would have liked best) to the bedrooms, but went instead into the drawing-room, which looked out on to the drive and the lawn with its stately beech trees. The room was large and empty— although she supposed it was full enough of objects. The Squire pointed out some of them: lovely candlesticks of porcelain, a figure of a man holding a basket of fruit.

"Coalport," the Squire said. Then, "We are not so often in here. Mrs. Ingham is not able to come downstairs . . ."

They went from the drawing-room then into the dining-room. Sarah gasped. This, she thought, must be fairyland . . .

"You like it?"

Yes, yes, yes! Everything: chairs, fireplace, walls—all were painted. And what pictures . . . On the backs of the chairs, dragons clawed and breathed fire. On one wall, the sea roared and thundered against great cliffs. On another, autumn trees, their leaves reddening, bent in a northern wind (she would have thought it the moors above Little Grinling, except that there were strange buildings like churches standing out against the skyline). On yet another wall was painted, exactly, the Abbey grounds—except that fir trees had appeared from nowhere, and rocks. Little wooden bridges too over tiny streams, with people in old-fashioned clothes crossing them . . .

"All done in my grandfather's time, Sarah. Very beautiful, is it not? The work of one Vanessen. And painted in only eight weeks—"

He let her stand there a long time, just looking at it all. Then taking her by the hand—his was so very big that hers was nearly lost—he said: "Well, now you have seen all this. Is there anything you would like to ask me?"

"Yes," she said, suddenly bold. "Please sir, why isn't the Kissing Gate a real kissing-gate, sir?"

"My word," he said, and laughed, "my word." He gave her hand a squeeze. "Let us walk back to the fire, shall we?" On the way he asked, "What *is* a kissing-gate, Sarah?"

"I don't know, sir."

"A little U-shaped gate, that swings, Sarah, and which only one person may enter at a time—and with so little room that two people are easily trapped together . . . You understand?"

She said: "Yes, sir," even though she wasn't certain. Then as they walked along the corridor together, he went on: "But this gate, *our* Kissing Gate—the story is quite different . . . You know, Sarah—you are from Yorkshire, are you not? You know that here 'gate' can mean also 'road' or 'way' . . . And you've heard too of a 'kist,' have you not? You had a chest, a *kist*, with all your belongings, when first you came to Downham, eh? Well, a kist now—it can mean also a *coffin*. You'll have heard them speak of a 'kirkgarth kist' for a coffin, isn't that so? Eh? And then we have 'kisting'—which is placing the body in its box, and having the funeral wake after . . . You know all that?"

She nodded again. They were standing in the hall now. "Are we not grown melancholy, the pair of us, eh?" he said, guiding her back into the room, to the fire-side. He talked all the while. "And so, Sarah," he said, "we have the 'gate'—or 'way'—that they used to carry the kist, the coffin, along. And the gate too that they must pass through to reach the church . . . We are none of us sure which was meant, but we do know that the 'Kisting Gate' was its first name." He paused, resting his hands on his knees. Then, looking straight at her: "Only—folk don't like death, do they, Sarah, whatever the Bible may say? *Kissing*—that sounds much better, does it not? And kissing itself—that is a fine game, a fine game, as you'll discover for yourself one day . . ." He finished:

"And so, Sarah, you see, it wasn't long before the folk around were calling it, instead, the *Kissing* Gate . . ."

"Yes, sir. Thank you, sir." She wondered if she dared to stroke the yellow dog.

"And now," he said, rising from his chair, "last of all, we shall have this—" Taking from a shelf a mahogany box with brass feet like claws, he opened it and began to turn a handle. Lovely, jerky music came out.

"Our little barrel organ," he told her. "And see here in the lid—here are the names of the tunes. 'Golden Fair,' 'Waterloo Dance.' But you can read them, eh? Eh? What do you say to something *Irish*? Look here—we may have 'The Sociable,' or 'Paddy Carey' . . ."

Young Mr. Rawson, Samuel Rawson, was walking through the Abbey gateway just as she came out.

"Well now then," he said. "Good day to you, Sarah. And how are you?"

"Getting on gayly, thank you—" She thought he must notice how excited she was, how full of herself.

"The Lord is good, Sarah. If you hearken to His word. I'll maybe see you—you'll come in then to the rope-works?"

"Aye—mebbe."

She had to hurry on. Her pinching boots forgotten, she skipped past the Kissing Gate, on her way back into Downham. She had something to tell Mrs. Mumford.

PART ONE

1846–1855

ONE

"Lord, my heart is not haughty, nor mine eyes lofty; neither do I exercise myself in great matters, or in things too high for me. Surely I have behaved and quieted myself, as a child that is weaned of his mother; my soul is even as a weaned child. Let Israel hope in the Lord from henceforth and for ever . . ."

It was icy cold in the room. Even the thick curtains drawn against the frosty November evening had little effect.

Sarah Donnelly had grown up, married; and although for all the twenty-two years of her marriage, evening prayers in the Rawson household had always been held here, a fire was never lit. Sam would not allow it. Sarah, watching the finger tips of her mittened hands lose colour, expected the breath from her husband's mouth, as in a firm prayerful voice he read from the psalms, to come out as a white cloud in the freezing air.

She moved one leg against the other under her full skirt, just as she had done in the old days, in her cold attic at Mrs. Mumford's, rubbing the woollen of her stockings. Her daughters, Ann and Eliza, seventeen and sixteen now, had their heads bowed. Both their noses were red-tipped. Their brother Ned was watching them, his eyes darting from one to the other, and then about the room. At nearly nineteen, he was as restless still as when he had been a small lad. Now he was tapping his foot—but quietly, so that his father would not notice. His pale brown hair, almost as sandy as hers, his gentle features, his kind heart: she was annoyed with herself that he should annoy her, even so little. (Although that was as nothing, she supposed—since she did not even *like* her youngest son, Walter. True enough, thirteen years ago he had nearly killed her coming out—and he was cocky too, and greedy and sly. But still . . . I will try, she told herself. When he comes back from

Richmond School, I'll try.) It seemed that only John, her firstborn, never ever irritated her. *Never.* She wasn't sure really why that should be, but it *was* . . . And let me be thankful and God keep him from harm in Edinburgh, she said to herself.

Ned blew his nose loudly. Sam looked up.

"'. . . Surely I will not come into the tabernacle of my house, nor go up into my bed; I will not give sleep to mine eyes, or slumber to mine eyelids . . .'"

He doesn't need to blow his nose, she thought. It's just for something to do. *I* was never a fidget like that. And at *his* age—why, I had already one child and expected another . . .

Expected another. And that reminds me, she thought . . . Under guise of adjusting her collar, she turned her head just a little (now it's me being restless . . .) to see if their servant Hannah was sitting behind.

She wasn't. Over the last two or three months, Hannah had become increasingly a cause for worry. And now this evening, she had asked leave to go up to her room after cooking the meal. She had eaten something which disagreed. Terrible stomach cramps, she had. "I'm badly wi' 'em . . ." she told Sarah.

"Come to prayers if you can. The Master likes to see everyone."

Only she hadn't. Well, Sarah thought, in a few days I shall have to speak to Sam. I shall have to tell him my suspicions—whether he wants to discuss it or no. Although he was a caring person, if the matter was an unclean one—then she'd do as well to be silent.

"Let not such things be so much as named amongst you . . ." When a few weeks ago she'd tried, saying hesitantly: "Sam, just suppose we'd the trouble Mrs. Cummings's got—with her servant Daisy going off to wed. *Having* to wed . . ." Daisy had been with the man who chopped the wood and brought in the coals for Mrs. Cummings. Everyone knew about it. But Sam had just said, "If there's any of that here—*out* . . ." And then had refused to say more.

"Let not such things be so much as named amongst you . . ." Well, she thought now, I should have spoken to someone. If for instance, I'd got on better with Hannah, hadn't always felt she was judging me . . . And yet I'd used to think, I know what it's like to be a servant, I will make it easier. Only she didn't let me. She wanted no help or kindness. A great heavy carthorse of a girl. And she worked hard, conscientiously. When first she put on weight at the end of the summer, I didn't think anything more of it than that she was growing up. Perhaps she hadn't had enough to eat at her own home. The Greaveses were a large family, and poor, with a father who drank heavily. Some of the children came up to the house to see Hannah—especially her youngest brother, Arthur, her favourite. He was almost a humpback, with one shoulder very much higher than the other, and had Hannah's staring, sullen manner in a foxy face.

It was that staring, sullen manner in Hannah that had made it in the end so difficult to ask her. Sarah had postponed and postponed it . . .

". . . that our oxen may be strong to labour; that there be no breaking in, nor going out; that there be no complaining in our streets . . ."

Muzzy, the tabby cat, who must have been hiding under the table, mewed to be let out. Sam's voice did not falter. In a moment, Ned was up to open the door.

I should have asked *John* about Hannah, Sarah thought. After all, he is to be a doctor. But she had felt awkward about it, and left it too late. Now he was in Edinburgh for a course of lectures and would not be back till December. By then . . .

Even when she *had* spoken to Hannah, she'd blundered. Not known how to phrase it. "Are you certain," she'd said, "certain, Hannah, that nothing's happened to you lately?" I can use the same word for two things, she'd thought: "Certain—there's been no—" she hurried over the word, "irregularity, Hannah?"

"Ma'am, I don't—that word, what's it mean?" She had stared at Sarah very boldly, her hands folded in front of her.

"I'd thought—well, wondered if maybe there was a natural cause for your increase—your *stoutness*, Hannah." Now she had said it. She added then, "You can speak to me, you know."

She would have liked then to be warm to her. To be the kind of person to have thrown her arms about Hannah (just as so many years ago she would have liked Mrs. Mumford to have, even once, comforted her). But Hannah was not one who had *wanted* comfort. She had stared back insolently.

"It's me clothes . . . Now t'summer's at back end and it's cold, I've to wear more. And—I've ate." She said slyly: "Is there 'plaining then as how I've ta'en too much on yer food?"

"No, no, no . . ." There was nothing more to be said. And so for the moment she had stopped thinking about it. *Soon*, she would speak again. Maybe to Mr. Whitelaw, the surgeon? John was, after all, apprenticed to him, and was he not a friend too?

". . . thy kingdom come, thy will be done on earth as it is in heaven . . ."

Nearly done, now. And mercifully her feet had numbed . . . Although I oughtn't, she thought, I oughtn't to mind the cold. Not when I think what is happening in Ireland. In *my own country*. To be cold is bad enough (and soon I shall be warm), but to be without food. To be *starving*. It seemed to her that people did not care enough. It was only something to be mentioned in the newspapers. The potato crop ruined by blight—and not for the first time either, but this sounded to be the worst ever . . . And I have family there, Sarah thought. People sharing my blood, they may be starving to death. And I cannot do a thing . . .

"I'm tired," Sam said. And he yawned, sitting back, stretching out his legs. He was only a little stouter than when she had first known him. But more wiry—knotted almost. She had used to think it was the ropes . . .

"I'm tired, lass. Read to me."

As a household they did not stay up late. Both Sam and Ned had to be at the rope-works in the morning. Sam was there often by half past seven—even six in the summer (just as in the days when he had passed her cleaning the front doorstep at Mrs. Mumford's).

They sat by the fireside. Ned had gone out, or upstairs, she didn't know which. Certainly at this time of night he wouldn't be up with his adopted friend Becky (that crazy one, Sarah thought), up in her tumbledown home on the moor. I *know* he steals food for her, Sarah thought. I've seen it hoarded in his room—and he's not a greedy one himself: it's just that he thinks my potted trout or my peppercake will make a rare treat for the darkie's granddaughter . . .

The girls were doing their embroidery. It was time already to think of Christmas gifts. They both sat on the horsehair sofa. Usually Muzzy would sit between them, nose to tail, sleeping. But this evening his place was empty.

"Read to me, lass," Sam said again.

Eliza, who was always the dutiful one, already doing good works outside the home, fussed over Sarah always in a fierce way, protective. She had Sam's dour features—and when she was bent over a task you could see the same concentration . . .

"Mother's tired," she said now. "I could—"

"No, let be," Sarah said. "I'll do it." She was proud of her reading. She read aloud well—that was something school had done for her. She used to go up to the Abbey and read to the Squire . . . She ran her eyes now over the inside pages of the newspaper. She had just this last year to wear little spectacles to see the small print.

In the silence there was a yowling sound. A cat surely. And then again. Ann glanced at the empty space between her and Eliza. She smiled. "Muzzy. He's a noisy puss . . ."

Seeing her bent over her embroidery, Sarah wondered if she was thinking about her Frank. Frank Helliwell, the schoolmaster's son. To-morrow was his evening for calling. She supposed it was only a matter now of his setting himself up as a schoolmaster too—and then Ann would be away . . .

Ah, dear God. But here was something about Ireland again. Letters, letters. Always someone writing their opinion (". . . the congregation of peasantry in large masses on the roads is a great evil . . . if there is rioting, all England's disposable army would be inadequate to protect . . ."). Was no one actually *doing* anything? More deaths reported in Skibbereen, in County Cork—but no food depots had been opened . . .

She burst out: "Sam—if they have it so bad there, how'll it be with Connemara—with Carrownacally?"

"Now, now," he said. "We mustn't be trusting the papers always . . . And any road, it's all over Europe, the bad harvest. There's plenty of poor *here*—without you worrying about Ireland . . ."

She felt the familiar prickling, the rush of blood to her face. Worry, irritation, helplessness. What can I *do*?

Ann said, "Really—there goes Muzzy again. Do you hear him?" She put down her embroidery. "Will I see if he's got in the coal cellar? A heavy door like that—it closes itself. He'll not be able to—"

"Leave him," Sam said shortly. "He'll be back up."

Sarah said, "John says his professor, at Edinburgh, he read them a paper on the potato blight—"

"Well, they'll have it there too, in Scotland. There's potatoes gone lost in the Highlands, and famine too, I don't doubt."

She felt the horrid unbidden tears. And in front of her daughters too. She didn't mind Ann, but Eliza—she was so strong. But Sam had seen.

"What is it, then?" He said it kindly enough. Leaning forward, rubbing at his trouser leg above the ankle. "Is it your dad's family, is it them you have in mind?"

"They're kinfolk, then, aren't they?" She turned to her daughters. "Eh Ann, Eliza?"

Again, as always: their polite interest. They hadn't known her da, hadn't even known Mam. None of her family. They thought of themselves as all Rawson . . .

"Fretting," Sam said. "That'll do nowt for them."

"I wrote, back in August—to the priest there."

"Well," he said, "you'd maybe best write again." She wondered if he were losing patience with her, and her worries about Ireland. He added warily, "Don't fash yourself so. You don't know any Donnellys now . . ."

"I had that letter—twelve years since."

"Aye," he said. "And, if I mind right, not much was said . . ."

"It was a good letter," she said defensively. "The priests there—they're able to write." (But Da, her da—*he* hadn't been able to write . . .) She felt alone, as if she were defending the whole of Ireland.

"I'll not dispute that. But it'll have been to settle your mind, that he wrote. And he said only, there were Donnellys still about . . ."

She remembered the letter especially because it had come in the bad days after Walter's birth, when nothing had meant anything. "God forgive me," the priest had written, "forgive me lady an old man's writing that has too much to do for God and his people—there's known to me two families of Donnelly but I've had the christening of none many years now. They'll be . . ." But she had had to give up, been unable, *no one* had been able, to read the rest of the wavery crabbed script.

For the moment now, she sat quite quiet. Sam was kind enough, had always been so, about the part of her that was Irish: the part of her that had never really got over losing her da. She thought of those long ago days when, living at the Paleys and waiting to go away to school, she had told Sam ("young Mr. Rawson," as she'd thought of him then) all about herself. Visiting the rope-works, as he had suggested, and then telling him the whole story. About Da. About what Da had said, and promised . . . Sam had been very patient then. She had said to him again and again: "He'll come back, my da will come back. He *said* he would . . ."

What she hadn't been able to tell Sam, though, was about the little piece of rag doll she'd buried. She'd known even then that he would never have approved. His religion, it didn't allow of *any* superstition. He had no time for the Kissing Gate. She had been glad too that she hadn't said anything—because only a month or two later, after all those years of waiting, a letter *had* come at last. From her da. She had showed it to Sam proudly—gone round to the rope-works with it. She had wanted to say: it was because I buried a charm bag by the Kissing Gate . . .

It was only a letter, of course. It wasn't Da himself (as she had asked, and prayed, and *prayed*). It wasn't even his writing either. The priest in Galway, in Da's village of Carrownacally, had written it for him. But it had been Da speaking, or almost: Da must have told him what to say.

". . . the Father will write now as I speak, I love you, alannah, there's never a day I don't think about my little one. I was to have sent word, alannah, but it's been a bad time, there's bad times here. Four of my brothers dead—and many that are related. A great sadness. They are *hard times* here and I fear not done yet. Michael, that was your uncle—

he died of the fever, but he'd a cough on him first—there were the eight
little ones. I'd to help there, alannah. We'd only the little to eat and
drink, not like the fine farm house where your mother came from. Your
good mother and my dear wife, God bless her, I know her own will take
care of her—and you, alannah. The cough now, that sickness, I have the
same, it's been a year now. I wanted to be back with you but I'd to wait
—it's only now a little while surely till the Lord takes away my sickness,
then I'll sail again for Liverpool, and I'll be making my way over the
moors the way I was before—till I come back to my little one in
Yorkshire. Inside this letter, alannah, the Father will place a little leaf
that grows only in Ireland. The shamrock, *mo pheata*, that's to promise
I'll be with you again—though you'll surely be too old now for tales of
gruagach—the giant wasn't it now? I missed you these many years and
why wouldn't I—the Father will leave a place and I will make my
mark . . ."

How she had treasured that little cross at the bottom, that *he* had
written. And how she had treasured too the pressed shamrock wrapped
in the folds of the thin paper. It had been Sam who had taken it for
her to the glazier in the town, making it safe for her between two fragments of glass—and then later making it into a little framed leather-
edged circle, that she'd hidden away: taking it out only occasionally to
look at, and sometimes, to cry over.

For of course he had never come. Her da had never returned. She
could not be quite certain when it was she had finally given up hope.
Certainly just before Mam's death she had written—to the priest—
pleading for, if not Da himself, then at least *news*. But that letter had
never been answered. And the next she had received, nearly thirteen
years later, after Walter's birth—had been from a different priest . . .

It seemed to be just this last summer: since she'd read the news of
the spoiled potato harvest, and the famine which was surely to follow,
that she had had this strange feeling of belonging almost as much there
as here in Yorkshire. She could not explain it—but she would suddenly
remember, as if it were yesterday, Mam saying to her: "You're *half-
Irish* . . . You're Donnelly, and mebbe one day . . ." She would feel
then these great waves of *not belonging*. All these years in Downham,
but: I am amongst strangers, she would tell herself. My people . . .
And when she read the newspapers, with their accounts of the famine
to come: my people, she would say.

Da was dead. Of that she had no doubt. Of consumption if of nothing else—she realised that now. But what of all the other Donnellys?
She remembered now how passionately she had once wanted to go over
there. How as a child she had wanted to *see for herself*. Now it was too

late. At thirty-nine, mother of a family, she did not see herself setting out. And yet, she thought, if *only I knew* . . .

She tried to read again now from the paper. Her voice was shaky, though. She turned then to Ann.

"You can read to your father. My voice—it's *tired*."

They did not stay up late. Sam went through to the back with a lamp to check the outhouses. She and the girls took their candles. She said to them, "I'll look for Muzzy." The girls went ahead of her. She stopped for a moment, picking up a ball of thread which had caught and rolled behind a chair. She followed it round.

But what was this? The tabby cat, Muzzy, lay firmly asleep, just under the chair. A complete circle, head to tail, tail curled over his face. He stirred luxuriously when she gave him a little push with her hand.

Standing up again, she found she was trembling. Her heart had begun to race and thud. She could feel sweat prickling. A thought, so terrible that she could not countenance it, came to her mind. Please God that I may not be right. She trembled at her vivid imagination. The Irish in her. *That* could not have happened. It *could* not be . . .

Now what do I do? Wait till morning, her common sense said. It said too: and then you'll see what fairy tales you've been weaving. Go to bed.

But she did not sleep well. She heard Downham church strike one, two, perhaps three—with that ominous little pause always before it struck the hour. She turned and tossed, fearful of disturbing Sam, till sleep crept up on her. In her dreams she spoke to Hannah, more in sorrow than in anger. "All those starving children," she was saying to Hannah, "there are bairns dying in Ireland on your account. Because of you . . ."

She woke very early. It was the rooks. They left their roosts high in the elms, in the garden of the surgeon's house, at the first light of day. Angry, energetic cawing. She did not expect more sleep.

It was a surprise, eerie almost, to see when she descended to the kitchen, Hannah at the table peeling potatoes. Little Bertha, who came in only for the day, was standing in the middle of the floor with a bucket. She skipped in a frightened manner out of the way.

"Light the lamp, Hannah. You can scarcely see to do those."

But even in the poor winter light, the servant looked ghastly. Her voice was sullen: "I can see well enow—"

"And you are better? Your—stomach, Hannah?"

"Aye."

As she made the arrangements for the day she felt deceitful, soiled. Bertha scuttled about, frightened, almost as if she knew something.

"Miss Paley calls today, Hannah . . ."

Thursday. Matilda's visiting day. With her woolly, now white hair and her long, earnest, kindly, rather vacuous face, Matilda Paley had been christened The Sheep by the boys. Now, every Thursday morning, she was to be found at Number Three, Hillside—the Rawson house— sipping Madeira and gossiping, gossiping, gossiping. She arrived always at the exact hour of half past ten, drank a glass of wine, or two or three, and left—later and later. Often nowadays she could be got out only in time for when Sam and Ned came for their dinner. The genteel faded woman (whom the little maid Sarah had been boarded with, companion to, in those days when although she *thought* she could read, it was found she couldn't pronounce the words properly . . .), part of Sarah's past, could not be shaken off. "And I suppose," Sarah thought sometimes, "I *am* grateful. Matilda had been a busybody then, but *kind* . . ."

"When you have the tray laid, Hannah, I'd like you to go up to Mr. Barrington's the chemist—with a bill. It should have been taken care of yesterday—"

"Yes, ma'am. Aye."

She felt wicked (why are my suspicions so terrible that I cannot voice them directly?).

"And take care how you tread—there's icy ways. Those cobbles."

Later, she watched Hannah leave. Saw her walk slowly, heavily, clutching her shawl to her. Saw her turn the corner and into the market square.

"Bertha," she said urgently. "Get up there quick to do Mister Ned's room." A moment later, Bertha, armed with brushes, was scuttling past her.

She had perhaps only fifteen minutes before Matilda's arrival, before Hannah's probable return. Bertha she did not fear. Going down the narrow stairs to the kitchen and Hannah's room, she was shaking. Muzzy following her down, rubbing his head against her ankles, nearly tripped her.

Hannah's room was small and intensely cold. The tiny window did not fit well and an icy wind would come off the high land behind the house, down from the moors. Sarah remembered her own dark little room under the eaves at Mrs. Mumford's and thought that perhaps she had not learned much from her own discomfort. Today the room was colder even than usual. She saw why, now. The window had been thrown wide open and an icy gust blew in. She shut it, and shut the door against the cat, then her gaze went quickly round the room. On the bed table a pin cushion, frayed. A comb with broken teeth. A motto: "All ye works of the Lord, praise ye the Lord . . ." The bed had been hastily made. It looked lumpy.

She opened drawers—God forgive me, she thought. The paucity of Hannah's belongings, their threadbare neatness. Two of the drawers were empty. She looked next in the chest, or kist, covered now with a cotton rug, in which Hannah had brought her effects two years ago now, over from the village of East Burton. But except for two summer aprons and print dresses, it was empty.

She thought again, I must hurry. Lifting the counter-pane a little, bending down, she looked under the bed. Not even a chamber pot. Much fluff. But then to one side, a laundry bag, damp, heavy. She brought it out. Inside were wet underskirts, in a bundle: they were covered in pale rusty stains. Hastily rinsed.

Her fear grew. Any moment Matilda would arrive, Hannah would return. She pushed the bag back. In the shadow she thought that the bed springs bulged, fancied that the line was uneven. She thought . . . But no, let it not be. No. Lifting with frantic haste the flock mattress and then, underneath, *dear God*—the naked coal-dust-smeared body. A baby. A *new-born child*.

Her legs would scarcely take her up the narrow stairs again. She washed her hands. They shook as she rubbed them again and again with the linen towel. Meeting Bertha, she avoided her gaze.

"Please, ma'am, Miss Paley's here, I showed her—"

"Thank you, Bertha."

Matilda, leaning forward in her chair, sheep's curls shaking, her gloved hand clasping the glass of Madeira (her second already): "My *dear* . . . Now about the vingt-et-un on Tuesday . . ." Her voice wavered always. Sarah thought, I want to hear a *man's* voice. I want a *man* to help me . . . But it was two hours nearly till dinner time, and Sam was anyway over at Leyburn this morning. Ned was at the works, but how could she rush up and frighten Ned? Ned was not for leaning on.

John. That would have been the best. *If John could have been there.* Almost a doctor—he would have known what to do.

". . . I have been going to ask you if you have any news of the dear boy, of John? Scotland is such a wild country . . ."

Sarah recollected herself. She said patiently: "He stays in Edinburgh, in the capital. I don't doubt they're very civilised there—"

Matilda's voice was a bleat: "Sarah dear, I had quite forgot." She held out her empty glass. "If I might—?" Then, "You have had a letter?"

"Yes, yes. He speaks of an operation. He is to see one soon. He must. And he dreads that, he tells me."

"I am sure they are very grand, these lectures, Sarah. Perhaps he will get fine ideas and not wish to come back to finish his apprenticeship with Dr. Whitelaw . . ."

"No, no. It was Dr. Whitelaw first suggested Edinburgh. It was with his blessing. He is from Scotland himself, you know."

"I hear that he plans to retire there. He is quite an age—and out in all weathers."

"It is for that John will certainly be back. Old Jacob Rawson helps us. We are to buy Dr. Whitelaw's practice for John—"

"Then the little rumour I heard is *correct*. Sarah, what a sly one! Am I to tell?"

I will give her some gossip, Sarah had thought, so that I do not reveal *this* to her. Hannah would have been back by now, a long time. I must tell someone. And it *must not be Matilda*. She dreaded that as she sat there she would blurt it out.

"It was always intended, Matilda, that he'd have the practice at the finish—"

She could smell the dinner cooking. Roasting meat, vegetables boiling, wafted up from the kitchen. She would not be able to face Hannah, would not be able to look at her at all. She could hear her own voice going on, talking, talking.

She did not know how she got through the remainder of Matilda's visit. Afterwards, she had no recollection of it. When Sam came in, his hands clasped together, stamping feet with the cold, she rushed up to him, saying, "Quick. At once. There's something I have to tell you. There's something you have to see . . ."

Hannah said, "Aye, ma'am, aye." It was Sam speaking to her, but she answered as if it had been Sarah. She looked at Sarah too—when she looked at anyone. Mostly her eyes were downcast.

They were in the dining-room. Bertha had already laid the dinner. It was a room where, when not eating, no one could feel at ease. The window faced to the back; what little light there'd been today was fading already.

"It's true, then?" Sam said. "You'll not deny it?"

Sarah, seeing how she looked: the greyish pallor, the dark circles under the sunken eyes, said: "You'd best sit down, Hannah. That chair

—there." She could hear Ned's voice outside, his light step. His head came round the door.

"Not now, son," she said before Sam could speak.

"Aye," Sam said. "Eating'll have to wait on this. Tell your sisters then." He had picked up a Bible and was waving it back and forward with a see-saw motion. His brows were knit.

Sarah thought: I've let a life be lost. Last night—I let it. Why did I not act yesterday—weeks before—on my suspicions? Death has come through me. *It is my fault.*

"We're sat here then, Hannah, till the truth's out. What do you say, eh?" When Hannah didn't answer, he brought the Bible down with a crash onto the table. The glasses, the silver rattled.

"Hannah—'there is a shame that bringeth sin, and there is a shame which is glory and grace'—Ecclesiastes. Will you tell us, then? Hannah, Hannah—'Seek ye the Lord while he may be found, *call ye upon him* while He is near . . .'"

The poor little corpse, blackened with coal dust, a vivid red mark clearly visible on its neck, had been wrapped in old sheets. And it had been Sam who had done it, while a frightened Bertha sobbed in the kitchen, attending to overcooked potatoes.

"Hannah—if you'll not speak to me, then to your mistress—eh?" He paused. "I've sent word. You know that, eh? I've sent word already. They'll be here before long. They'll likely take you into Leyburn."

Hannah spoke then—almost for the first time: "What'll they do to me then?"

"That's for the law to decide. But God is just. God *is* the law, Hannah." There was silence for a moment then, "I've sent for your father," he said.

Of what use was that? thought Sarah. Greaves was known to be a drunkard. If he could be found in a fit state to speak to anyone, Hannah could not want to see him.

"And Hannah, would you want your little brother—Arthur, is it?—would you want him knowing all this?" Hannah's head had gone down again, chin into her chest. "Hannah, please listen carefully, lass. Was it—was what your mistress found this morn—you've to answer me straight—did it live?"

No answer.

"I repeat, Hannah, *did it breathe?*"

When she shook her head very slightly, Sam said, "I want you to hold this Bible, Hannah. Come now, *take* it . . . I want you to hold this Bible and say *before God*, 'I swear that my bairn never breathed . . .'"

She didn't speak, and he said then: "They'll find out. The law'll find out. They've ways—"

"I swear," she said in a faint low voice, her eyes still down.

"Louder, Hannah. And—you've to stand up for this."

"Sam, love," Sarah protested. But he lifted a warning hand to her as if to push her out of the way. Hannah rose with difficulty. She leaned against the table edge.

"I swear as t'bairn," her voice could scarcely be heard, "I swear as t'bairn—never breathed . . ."

"Say now—'so help me God.'"

"So help me . . ."

"Well now," Sam said, rising. He took the Bible from her. "That done—we'd best have our dinner . . ."

The news travelled fast. It was at the Black Swan (T'Dirty Duck) Inn, just a few yards up Hillside and round into the market square, within the hour. By the next day it was all over the town. Sarah knew that Matilda must have heard and she dreaded a sympathetic visit from her. Ann and Eliza had had to be told. Ann had burst into tears, while Eliza had gone very white and then asked practically if there was anything she could *do*. Ned had seemed both upset and shocked and, she would almost have said, frightened. But he had said only: "What'll they do to her?" his face creased with anxiety.

"Take her before her betters, I don't doubt." She hadn't wanted to add: "And when they do—when she goes to court—she'll hang." Not just because it would distress him, but because she didn't want to think about it herself. She stayed in the house all that next day, not wanting to meet people, hoping there'd be no callers, and found that she could think of nothing else but Hannah—and her probable fate.

Just before going to bed she remembered suddenly the time that, two or three months ago now, Hannah had walked around for several days sullen, and with red-rimmed eyes. She would not answer Sarah. In the end Sarah had asked Bertha, "Has she bad news?" And Bertha had said in her little, scared voice, "Nay. It's an upset. It's—she says she's brought ill luck on herself. She went into t'kirk, but she—she didn't go in by t'Kissing Gate . . . She were pressed for time—visiting her auntie's grave, she were—"

Sarah had protested, "You know what Mr. Cuthbert said, three Sundays past. And not for the first time either. It's all fancy, that you must go in by the Kissing Gate. *Superstition*, that's what it is, and—"

But Bertha had interrupted, warming to her subject, not scared now:

"And she says as how t'Kissing Gate, it always win. God hasn't—the Lord's got no power there."

"That's nonsense," Sarah had said sharply. "And I've a good mind to tell her so . . ." But she had not in the end said anything (perhaps because she was so superstitious herself). And now too late she realised that it must have been something much more serious bothering Hannah then—that probably about then she had realised finally, irrevocably, what had happened to her . . .

As yet no word had come to them from old Jacob Rawson at Almeida House. That at least was a mercy. Although he would be bound to know, and sooner or later would be sending for one of them—she hoped Sam—to listen to his views on the matter. (Sarah marvelled always how he heard any news at all, since he went nowhere and saw practically nobody—but hear he did, without fail.)

The Squire would know, of course. He might send for me, Sarah thought. But that she did not fear. He had been her friend always. Remained so. And although she saw him now only two or three times a year, he showed still the greatest interest and concern in her and hers. (Indeed it was that very concern which often prompted Old Jacob to some of his few generosities. He could not abide the thought of being outdone by the Inghams in anything.)

The Squire had not married again, although his ailing wife had died only a year after Charles's rescue, when the youngest child was still a baby. Sarah knew, though, that he found solace just as before—after all, he was famous for wenching (to think that I tried once to ask Sam what it meant!). Outside Downham, of course. Although it was rumoured lately that with age he had grown more sedate. Certainly his popularity was as great as ever.

Charles had not inherited it. He had grown up handsome enough, but with an arrogance of manner which she, at least, found very unattractive. Nor had she ever heard word spoken of any kindliness or good humour, or thought for others. She knew too that he drank more than his father liked. But at least he had married to the Old Squire's satisfaction: a very young and very elegant beauty whom he had met in London and by whom he had already three children. Georgiana Ingham. Sarah thought her rather too set up with herself. She would see her walking up to the family box pew on Sundays, a haughty expression on her face . . . A fit partner for Charles.

Sarah had preferred always the look of the second son, George. He had seemed a very gentle person, and had had the Squire's eyes so that she'd imagined he ought really to inherit. But that would never be possible. He had gone into the Army (perhaps to escape his brother?), and four or five years ago now had been killed in Afghanistan, at Kabul. The eldest girl was a Mrs. Ballantine now and lived in London. She would be seen occasionally in the box pew.

No, Charles was not liked, but would inherit the Abbey. Although it would be good for his pride, Sarah thought, to realise that Downham was becoming a place of less and less importance, now that the neighbouring market town of Leyburn was increasing so in size. There was even talk of bringing the *railway* there, and in fact inspectors had already toured the area, Downham as well, to assess the traffic. Meeting him on the road, they had asked Fred Pullan, the sixty-year-old saddler living in Castle Alley, "Well, my man, and where do you come from?" and had received the answer proper to a stupid question: "I come from home. And I'm goin' back to't . . ."

The two big fairs, however, in spring and autumn, they made Downham still feel quite important. People came from far afield for them and for a week or more there was so much life and excitement. All the unbroken colts which the gypsies sold, reared and snorted and whinnied, and in the early evening shaggy ponies, excitable, clattered up and down the road to the square. At night the drovers, down from Northumberland and Scotland, slept on the cobbles, wrapped in their plaids, round a large bonfire. Or sang or talked. Often it was very noisy, with a lot of merrymaking.

It had been at one of these fairs that Hannah had had her misfortune. Sarah, visiting her at Mrs. Greaves's request, learned this. (She told herself that, *yes*, in the end she would have gone to see her of her own accord . . .) Hannah had told her mother: "I'll speak to Mrs. Rawson now." And Sarah had heard then a sad tale of music and a little dancing, and a great deal of drink . . . Hannah, in her prison cell, did not once look at Sarah as she spoke, except at the very end of her story, when she said dully: "If I saw him now—the one that did it—I'd not know him again—which he was . . ."

But then, just as Sarah was leaving, she said, her voice a little uncertain: "Arthur, our Arthur—he's only a small one, ma'am—but it's made him in a fair rage, that they've put me here for what I done. And that— and that there's maybe worse to come. That I might—" she hesitated. "That I might—swing. He's in that much of a rage with *you*. Wi' *all* you Rawsons. 'If I'd my way,' he said to me, ma'am, 'if I'd my way—I'd finish all of them. All of them. An eye for an eye . . .' he said, ma'am. He were in such a *passion*. I were nearhand afraid of him myself . . ."

"But Hannah," Sarah began. She was afraid then she was going to cry. She wanted to say to her: "I'm sorry. It's *my* fault, Hannah. I could have helped . . ."

Hannah spoke again. She was saying more, Sarah thought, than in all her months as a servant with them. Although her tone was still sullen, it was impossible to miss the emotion lying underneath.

"Ma'am—he'll sorely miss me, will Arthur." She said it hesitantly: "I know to look at he's not much—wi' his poorly shoulder, and all . . . but as far as his head goes, well, he's as sharp as any of them. You'll not find a cleverer. There's nothing missing there . . . So, ma'am, if ye'd maybe look out for him—if I could think as how when he's a bigger lad, you'd maybe help him. If I could think—as how he'd be *all right* . . ."

"Yes, yes, Hannah." She would promise anything. Wanted only to dull her guilt, the guilt of her whole family—all the Rawsons. "We'll help him. And meanwhile, you—get what rest you can. We're arranging to send in a few things. And your family, there's something gone to them too . . ."

She would have to tell John. Home again that evening, she recounted the visit to Sam,

"It's really shaken me. I should've—the *poor* lass—"

"That's as may be," he said. He was looking for his place in his Bible. He took the markers out of three other pages and said: "John, now. You'll let the lad know—of the mishap?"

"Yes," she said, "of course." Sam hated holding a pen except for the painful and necessary keeping of accounts.

But when she tried to write to John, not a word would go on the paper. She did not know even how she should begin. He would worry for her, in case all of it was making her ill (and in truth, it was . . .). She regretted already that in her last letter she'd told him she fretted about Ireland. Now he would worry about that too . . .

In the middle of the night she woke suddenly, trembling, sweating, leaving behind a nightmare she could taste but could not remember. She knew then that it was her negligence which had caused the whole tragedy. She had not been a proper employer, had not spoken to Hannah when she should, had not persisted. And God had seen that she had hidden her face, that she had left undone those things which . . . It was *she* the wicked one. And as a punishment God would not look with love on her and hers. The sins of the father . . . *her* sin would be visited on *her* family. Not on the Rawsons—(I am not after all, in the end, a *Rawson*)—but on those unidentified, those random Donnellys about the village of Carrownacally! Ghostly unseen figures—her imagined cousins, uncles, aunts, even perhaps half-brothers and sisters? *Her own blood . . .*

you've little time—would *you* write to John for me? About Hannah . . ."

That afternoon she went to see the Squire. It was best he heard as much as possible from her. As she came out of the Abbey and onto the road, the light was going fast. She thought she would walk back through the Kissing Gate and the kirkyard. But just as she came up to the Gate, before she could see it, she heard its creaking sound.

Arthur Greaves, straddled across the bars, head down, was swinging it vigorously to and fro. Other boys did it. They shouldn't, but they did. She had told them off before now.

"Give over," she said. "It's Arthur Greaves, isn't it? You've not to do that. You know what's said." She tried to forget the horrid saying: "Them as swings on t'Gate, swings on t'gibbet." "And besides, it's bad for the Gate." When he didn't stop, she said, "And I'd like to pass, if you please—"

He looked up then, but still without stopping—to and fro, to and fro. He looked at her, hard. At once she turned her head away. She had been going to say, in a moment, something about Hannah. Something, anything, *kind*.

But she could feel even when she wasn't looking that he stared at her still. And it was with dislike, not curiosity. Even perhaps hatred. Had not Hannah said as much?

"I can't say kind words now," she thought, turning away, deciding instead to walk the road home. Another time, she told herself. Sam shall help . . .

She went to see Dr. Whitelaw. Balding, sandy-haired, w
mous paunch on which his hands rested in a most reassurii
he had always been a good friend to her. (She had dared to
five years ago now, "John wants to be a surgeon, and
sure . . ." afraid he might laugh, only he had said at once: "S
to me, send him to me . . ." And Old Jacob had paid, of cour
promptly too. He set great store by eldest sons of eldest sons. An
he had heard that she had been visiting Squire Ingham wit
news . . .)

Now she wanted Dr. Whitelaw's help. But first:

"What'll they do?" she asked. "About the bairn, and Hannah .

"There has to be a post-mortem. There *must*. That way they can fi
out if it lived—even for a little."

Sarah said dully, "I heard its cry. I never said to Sam. The girls, the
thought it was the cat . . . Hannah swears, but I *heard it*. She thought
no doubt it was the place farthest away from us, but all the same—it
wasn't far enough, the coal cellar. And I heard. I don't know really
what I was about . . ." She paused a moment, then she asked: "Will
she—" and hesitated.

"She'll hang. Aye. If it's proved alive. There's no jury can give any
other verdict . . ."

I killed that child, she thought.

". . . The law says so. Mind you, the law is not right. Women are
not themselves after childbirth. God knows what I have seen. And you
yourself . . . But God is merciful, Sarah. He sees into men's hearts . . ."

He lifted his hands for a moment, then clapped them heavily onto
his knees. "Well—and how's that lad of yours? Have you news from
Edinburgh?"

"He's to see an operation . . ." She could think of no other news.

"Yes, indeed. He's been fortunate here. Nothing too bad . . . He'll
not like it, we none of us do. But there's talk of some experiments, of a
fine substance which will send the poor patient into a deep sleep." He
paused. "It's to be hoped they'll wake again . . . And you, how are
you?"

"Did you read the news then of Ireland?"

"Why do you answer me Scotch fashion? Eh? And you a Yorkshire
woman . . ."

"It's the politics of it all—they talk about relief works, but they don't
send *corn*. There's folk starving . . ."

She must have been with him half an hour that morning, maybe
more. Just as she was leaving, she said to him: "Would you—I know

TWO

Ned wondered if it was something to do with the ropes, with the hemp. He imagined tiny fragments, could almost see them, floating from the cords, dancing in the air—making directly for his nostrils. He would breathe them and then: some days it was all right. Nothing to bother about at all. But, sometimes . . . And the first sneeze was no relief. It led only to another and another. He would feel he couldn't breathe. On bad days, like this morning, as he paced the rope-walk—wooden top in hand, keeping the strands of yarn separate—thick ribbons of mucus would force their way out, to be brushed away angrily at the next pause.

The apprentices, Walsh and Rider, were turning the twisting machine vigorously for him as he walked to and fro. Seventy-year-old bearded Mr. Marchant worked away quietly at the back. In a day, Ned thought, I can walk as much as eight miles. He had calculated once. Each journey was longer or shorter according to the length of rope, but began always where the three or four hooks holding the rope strands hung from the twisting machine. At the other end was the sledge with one hook on which the other end of the yarn hung. The ropes already made up today waited on the side in four-yard lengths, to be made up into halters for a horse-dealer. From cotton, manila, hemp, sisal, cotton waste (which snicked the fingers) they made as well, plough lines, waggon ropes, tethers, ties, even rabbit snares.

There was a banging on the outer door. He didn't answer it. Let Walsh or Rider . . . He reached the end of the rope-walk, and realised he'd been dreaming as he paced. He shouldn't. He'd been told that. Years ago through not taking care Mr. Marchant had lost a finger . . .

Again the banging on the door. Then just as he was bending over a bale of cotton, a hand on his shoulder: "Ned!"

Unwelcome. Always unwelcome. Charles Ingham. Young Mr.

Ingham, Squire's son. For a moment Ned didn't speak. Charles said, "Your nose, my dear fellow."

Ned said angrily then: "I have to finish this—knot . . ." He pulled at one of the halter ropes. Then he called to Walsh and Rider: "Give a hand there to Mr. Marchant . . ."

"But don't let me interrupt," Charles said, with mock courtesy, leaning back against the wall. He lifted an eyebrow: "You know the goodwill with which I call. I had business over in Leyburn—if you can call anything I do business—and it came into my mind as I rode back: I shall visit Ned." He paused and when Ned didn't answer, leaning further back, crossing one leg, he said slowly, "I often think, what you do there, how it would suit me. I rather envy you—workmen."

Ned had felt safe from a visit today, since there was hunting. Barely masking his impatience, he said, "You don't go to the Meet?"

Charles ignored this. "I am often sorry, watching you so industrious, that we are no longer plantation owners. I see myself . . . caring about crops rather larger than those which concern me here, master of thousands of hands, monarch of all I surveyed. A pleasant dream . . ." He pursed his lips.

Ned said, "You called for some special reason?" He could not keep the irritation out of his voice. He thought then: "Perhaps if I am silent, he will just go . . ."

"Why the sullen looks, Ned, eh? Don't you care for me to call? I had thought . . ." He pulled idly at the lengths of rope, sent them swinging. "It's not every workman who can boast of visits from, no, the *friendship* of—the son of the manor."

"I can get on, and well you know it, without visits from you—"

"Ned, Ned—you know those aren't your feelings, eh? That's not how you feel about Charles—eh?" His tone was wheedling.

At least, Ned thought, he hasn't been drinking. For although Charles's visits weren't frequent, they were quite often enough. Usually the smell of brandy would be overpowering. Why does he have to pester me? Ned thought, wondering what it was he had done five years ago, to cause this attachment: for certainly he could not seem to shake off Charles.

Aged fourteen that summer, and walking up on Downham High Moor (his place, private, where he met with few people, where he could play his flute as much as he liked—the only other sounds the cry of peewits, sheep bleating, their bells. Or as that day, larks hanging high in the summer sky . . .). Then the figure that had seemed to appear from nowhere, grown man dismounting, walking over to him where he sat in the heather—a figure recognised but not really known, belonging more to church on Sundays . . . Saying to him, "You're the Rawson lad, the younger—eh?" Then when Ned had mumbled "yes" (wondering a little after about the "sir"), Charles had stood quite still, staring at him. Then: "You're the one visits old *Becky?*" Ned had not thought of her as old. He replied daringly, impudently even: "And what if I do?" "You may do as you please," Charles had said then, easily, carelessly, "but if you would take advice from an *older* fellow—" and he had come then and sat beside Ned on the ground, putting one arm round Ned's shoulder. Ned had hated that. Then, his lips so near that Ned could feel the heat of his breath: "If you would take advice—for you're a fine lad," his grasp tightened, "fine to look at too . . . Listen to me eh when I say, don't meddle where you don't understand." He pulled Ned towards him. "Is it likely, do you think, she would live alone if fit to live with other human beings? Eh? Bad blood, black blood, Ned—it is *Ned?*" His fingers played on Ned's upper arm. "You so fair—mixed up with a darkie. You know the story? eh? Be a sensible fellow . . ."

Ned had hardly felt able to speak the while, wondering what happened to someone who pushed away, even knocked over, an Ingham? (It would reach the Squire. And then Mother would know, and *Father* . . .) So he had stayed like that, while Charles, arm still encircling him, asked him about himself. The very, very little that he gave away, he regretted almost immediately (even more so, in the years after, when again and again he would meet Charles—perhaps in the market square, outside church or worst, when he visited the works . . . then he would think, I wish I had been completely silent. Given him *nothing* of myself . . .).

But at last it had been over. Hand clapped lightly on his thigh in farewell: "Be a sensible fellow, Ned, eh?" and he was gone.

If only he would go today . . . But here he was, leaning back again languidly, crossing now the other leg.

"Still paying those perilous visits to Becky, eh Ned?"

"I might be—"

"Really, I marvel that she can stand this time of year. The cold. I think there is no proper roof, little . . . and what does she eat? I wonder sometimes, because it is after all part of our moor, if I should not maybe—pay her a call?"

"Please yourself."

Charles spoke suddenly, sharply: "What makes you think you can speak to a fellow like that—eh, Ned? And your superior too . . . Hoity Toity, eh?" He lifted his whip: "What I'd like—I've a damned good notion to take this to you. Insolent—"

Ned didn't move. Then he pushed his sleeve across his face, wiping away the mucus. Charles turned away in disgust. A few moments later his horse could be heard clattering out of the yard. Ned went through to tell Walsh and Rider to go for their dinner.

It was a short walk home. Only a little way along the alley (past the cottage where Mother had been a little servant maid), then down the street to the market square, and past Linden House—Dr. Whitelaw's: large, creeper-covered, with a big garden behind full of elms and, in front, fourteen windows at a glance. (One day it might be John's . . . My clever brother, he thought half-affectionately, half-angrily. Grandfather paying up for everything too . . . Because of John's decision he, Ned, had quite simply gone straight into the rope-works from Richmond Grammar. No one ever asked me, he thought, if I wished different. And what *had* been the plans, the hopes of his sixteen-year-old self? Whatever they might have been, they seemed to have passed him by. They cannot have been very important, since no one had wished to hear them. God had spoken about the rope-works. "It's your duty, son. Honour thy father—and you honour the Lord . . .")

He turned right, past the Dirty Duck to where the road sloped down, leading out of Downham towards Leyburn. Their house was the third on the right—Number Three, Hillside. White front railings, a small front garden; a low front door painted black. Here were only six windows on view, and two of them half ones . . .

At the smithy opposite, the blacksmith's apprentices were just coming out for dinnertime. An oxen-drawn waggon rumbling by obscured them from view. The sun had come up, a watery midday sun, clearing the last of the winter mist.

The meal was already on the table when he went in. There was knuckle of veal with mashed turnips, and a batter pudding with damson sauce—he knew, though, that they'd had to send out for some of it at least, to the cookshop. They hadn't yet settled in a new servant—Mother wasn't up to it—and Bertha could not really cook. Only potatoes. Mother had been in bed a week now, although she came down sometimes in the afternoons. The Hannah business had made her quite ill—she could eat very little and had to take strong sleeping draughts. When he went up to see her, though, she would talk as much about Ireland as Hannah. She had asked the Reverend Cuthbert to be sure to request prayers for Ireland from the pulpit, even if she could not be there . . .

Sad as it was, it was all very far away and Hannah a more present distress. He couldn't really believe in Carrownacally and Donnellys—

Ireland did not seem very real anyway. But Hannah . . . He did not want to think about that (at least, *at least*, Charles had somehow not mentioned it . . .).

This was a workaday dinner, so there was little conversation. Father was there but would be out again in the afternoon, and not at the works. Ned wondered if perhaps he could sneak out to visit Becky; he had not been for two weeks now. He would spin some yarn to Mr. Marchant. And go up there before the light went. Saturday afternoons, when he *sometimes* got off early enough to see her, were often taken up with the dread and obligatory visits to Grandfather Rawson at Almeida House.

"Eat up, lad. You'll be late . . ." Father taking out his watch. Ann and Eliza wiping the damson jam from the corners of their mouths . . . Nothing for them this afternoon but sewing, or visiting the poor and sick. "And while you're about it—I've shoes at Haygarth's. They'll want fetching back, and I've not time—I'll not be home while eight . . ."

Yes, yes, yes. He'd do it as he came back from Becky's. He went now to tell his lie to Mr. Marchant (O God who sees into the secrets of our hearts, bless Thy servant Becky . . .) and began the journey up the moor. He went from just behind the house, through a gate or two, some fields, and then—over the hills and far away.

Climbing up, he took great gulps of fresh air. His head, his nose cleared miraculously. He moved quite quickly even though the pockets of his cloth coat were weighted down. The scenery changed: red-brown gold of damp bracken now. Higher up too, so that he could feel the wind blowing across the sparse grass and bent. The colour had gone from the heather. The whole of the moor wore its bleak winter face. Soon, if the wind continued from the northeast, there would be snow. When it was really bad he could not get up to see her at all.

A crumbling length of dry-stone wall with the beck running not far away. And then with the best of the afternoon already gone, he saw the tumbledown cowhouse come into view. The first sound he heard was the excited yapping of her new puppy. The dog's friendliness was overwhelming. As soon as Becky opened the door to Ned, he was all over him, leaping up, licking his hands, his gaiters, his boots.

"Out wi' ye, out!" Becky said, pushing the puppy with her foot. A push not a kick. She said with pride, "Bye—there's life in that one an' all . . ."

"You'll have to name him," Ned said. "Three months he's been with you, and you don't call him anything."

"That's for ye to do, Ned . . ."

The puppy scratched at the door. "When I'm back next time, I'll fetch him a name . . ." He was emptying his pockets of gifts. Some vinegar toffee, some sugar biscuits, a bottle of Indian syrup, another of elderberry wine, half a dozen apples—things that he had stolen and hoarded in his room against a visit up here. A copy of the Wensleydale *Advertiser* . . .

It was chill inside. Acrid smoke rose from a recently lit fire. The kindling was mostly bracken. Often she would keep a turf fire in for days, even weeks, depending on her supply of fuel. Pieces of straw from the puppy's bedding were scattered about the earth floor. He sat down on an old broken chair, its front legs shorter than the back. He tilted it hard, hoping that in time the longer back legs would sink into the floor. "Well," he said, "this smoke. I couldn't play my flute—"

Becky was putting away the food out of the puppy's reach. "Read to me, then—if ye can see to spell it out . . . And—ye can let him in now . . ."

She looked at him quite fiercely, but it was the fierceness of affection. He'd grown used to her ways over the six years he'd been visiting. Used to her looks too: the mass of greying locks, as unkempt as the rest of her, the dusky tinge to her skin, the large, dark, often worried eyes which became gradually for him the most remarkable feature of her face. A face surprisingly plump and round cheeked for one who at first sight had seemed so haggard.

At first sight . . . He'd been frightened of her as a child—the idea of her. He'd known about her, as who had not? But nobody saw her and, up on the moor as he grew older, he had been afraid that, witchlike (didn't the boys of the town, and others, call her a witch?), she might be lying in wait to spring on him . . .

But in the end it had been he who had come upon her. And not up on the moor at all. It had been in a field, not far from the road, between the village of Little Grinling and Downham. His first holidays from Richmond School, and walking by—he could not remember now on what errand—he had heard from behind the dry-stone wall near the road's edge, the sound of shouting. And then one high-pitched scream . . .

It was a group of boys, five or six at the most, but some of them much bigger than Ned. "Witch, witch . . ." they were chanting. "Witch. Yark Owd Becky for a witch. Yark her . . ." One boy had a stone in his hand, and as Ned drew near, he threw it. It hit what looked at first sight a bundle of rags, huddled on the ground.

"Yark her. Yark her . . ." Ned made for the first boy, but even as he tackled him, another one, picking up a larger stone, made as if to throw it also. At once Ned picked up the largest of the boulders around, one belonging to the wall, and staggering with it in his grasp, he called out: "The next to lift his hand—gets this. *And* I'll have the Squire after you . . ."

He did not know, could not think afterwards, where he got the courage. But within minutes, they were gone. Only the bundle remained on the ground—motionless. He had approached with caution. She breathed. Relieved, he said gently: "It's Becky, isn't it? Are you all right? They've not hurt you?"

He wondered why she had come so far from home. Later he had learned that it had been to do with her food: that it had not been in the usual place and that, anxious, she had come looking: venturing down for perhaps the first time in more than twenty years . . . Looking at her now, to see if there was any visible damage done to her, he saw that she had pulled some of the rags she wore over her face: the skimpy ones left revealed thin white legs rising from cracked, flapping boots.

She let him see a little of her face, but she seemed frightened of him —and quite defenceless. He was angry still with the boys. If it had been an animal they had attacked, that would have been bad enough. But this was a *person* . . .

She allowed him then to help her up. She seemed dazed—her greying hair, unkempt, hid most of her forehead. But strangely, although she would not speak, she pressed his hand. He took that for "thank you."

"Will I walk you back? Will I see you safe?" But she had turned away, shaking her head. He had followed her then for a while—she seemed all right, but he was worried still . . . Then just as the ground became steeper, and the going more rough, she had given him a quick, shy look. To him it had seemed that she wanted to be friends, but it was she who was frightened. Seeing the expression in her eyes, he had thought: No one should have to live like that. Quite alone. And without a single friend. I shall take care of her. (He vowed then and there.) I shall be her protector.

It had been easier said than done. When she had seemed eager for him to leave her, he had turned again for home. But a few days later, he had made his way up on to the moor, together with his dinner, and his flute. The weather was very hot, and not far from where he knew she had her home, he had come upon her. A small dip in the ground— she lay asleep. The fierce barking of her dog, though, woke her. And frightened Ned.

She'd looked trapped then, when first she saw him. She wasn't sure even that she recognised him . . . The dog, a grey wolflike animal, had put one paw on her chest as if to protect her. Lips drawn back, he snarled at Ned. And then made as if to pounce. Ned had felt even more frightened . . .

But he hadn't run away, although he didn't think of himself as a brave person. Instead he had thought of giving her a present. Everyone liked gifts. His mother had said that once. And he had seen people's faces altered by gifts. Signs of love.

He opened his dinner bag and took out a meat pasty, thrusting it at her. Surprised, she'd looked at it for a moment, then the dog, pouncing, had had it in two gulps. She had seemed to him then so forlorn, so disappointed, that he'd said at once, "I've not another now—but will I fetch you one tomorrow?"

She hadn't answered him, but he had brought it just the same. Rapping on her ill-fitting door, his heart in his boots—but there had been no answer except the fierce barking of her dog. Then when he tried to push at the door, he could feel that she'd put something against it. He shouted through one of the cracks: "It's a pie—another of those pasties." The dog growled menacingly. After a while, he just left the pasty on a flat boulder nearby, calling again through the crack, "It's just outside, then . . ." Probably the dog had it.

He was not sure afterwards why he persisted except that he had vowed. But that summer he was up as often as three times a week, always bringing small gifts and always wondering if it was the dog or she who had them. Once when he'd left a Wensleydale *Advertiser* weighted down, it was gone the next time. "Does your dog eat paper, then?" he'd called through the door.

Of course he was up on the moor anyway, practising his flute. At home the noise was mocked—and he could not blame them. The flute *was* difficult, and for him then it would not come right, his fingers would not behave. It was a conical flute, widest at the blowing end with six finger-holes but only two keys. (He'd heard that a new and easier one had been invented, but that was little help for now . . .) He'd taken to playing outside Becky's home—trying to charm her perhaps with his awful learning sounds. The dog howled. Until one afternoon: slow opening of her door. Then she was standing there, watching him. The scowl that was almost a smile. The sugar cake taken from his hand (he might have been coaxing an animal), not eaten then and there, but taken away, *accepted*.

After that it had been only a matter of time. Slowly, very slowly, a relationship growing. At first they'd hardly talked—to be allowed inside her home at all had been progress enough (and so awful did he find it in there that he nearly gave up the whole business . . .). He was afraid of the dog too. Although talking about him turned out to be their first real conversation . . .

His name was James and she'd found him as a stray three or four years before. "He nivver worrit a sheep," she told Ned proudly. He brought her rabbits and sometimes other game. What did she do, then, about food and other provisions? She'd an aunt, she told Ned, and a nephew, and once a month they left her a big tin box with oatmeal and lard and tallow, and sometimes eggs and cheese. Also wool for the knitting she did, which they sold. The box was left always in the same place by the dry-stone wall and she'd return it empty.

Her cooking looked very simple. Mostly oatcakes and porridge. Some potatoes. She liked a cup of tea, she said. There was a stew pot, but the bones which he often saw scattered around the fire and had thought might be from her meals, he learned were James's finds. He was surprised at first at how much she talked—once she began. It had been only to turn the disused and at first stiff wheels.

The only subject she never liked to talk about was the Inghams. Which puzzled him because the incident of her grandfather was so long ago now, and the present Squire's family had been kind to her mother. But she'd said only: "Them Inghams—they're *wicked*. Becky thinks so . . ." Then she had become very agitated. "Becky says they're wicked . . ." He'd thought she was going to cry, maybe even have some sort of fit. It had frightened him, so that usually now he was very careful.

Her using the word "wicked"—that had upset him too, because that summer had been when he'd also discovered a most wonderful and secret pleasure which, hot-faced, he had later realised (from the warnings in veiled terms of his elders) was wrong—more than wrong, it was wicked, a dreadful sin. Although every boy could do it, only the wicked and the mad actually did so (indeed that was quite probably the cause of their madness, being wicked in that manner . . .). So that when yet again he fell, and joy and relief turned to remorse, he would say to himself: I have been wicked. It was no matter he learned later that the other boys spoke of "paw-paw tricks"—for him the word was forever coloured. When he heard as so often in church or at prayers with Father—". . . and the *wicked* shall . . ." then the blood would rush to his face.

Another time he had seen Becky really upset, had been earlier this summer—when James had died. Very grizzled now but no less fierce and wolflike, James had taken some sort of fever, dying within two days. Ned had arrived to find Becky sitting by the corpse, rubbing her hands together as if they were deathly cold. "It's all ower wi' him. But

Becky'll keep her pluck up . . . She nivver thought as he'd go—he were a bit out o'fettle, nowt more . . . but Becky'll keep her pluck up . . ." And then she had begun to cry, appalling him. "Gert bessybab," she had said scornfully of herself, not bothering to wipe the tears away.

The remedy hadn't been difficult. Within the week he had heard of a litter of mongrels about to be drowned. He secured remission for the best looking, paid for it to have its mother's milk (the owner told him, "a feeding bitch, she'll eat as much for one as ten . . ."), and when it was some eight weeks old took it up to Becky. All through the month of August, he'd been up three times a week after work, bringing it skim milk which she mixed with her oatmeal. Now the puppy was almost full-grown—and a champion rabbiter in the making.

It was today, after reading to her for a while in the poor light ("Becky, here's a family poisoned eating stew from a dead calf—found on the low moor. Like to die they were. Don't you ever do anything daft like that . . ."), that he made his mistake. Fondling the puppy, pulling at his ears, he said unthinkingly into the companionable silence: "Squire's son, he came by today. The daft nuisance. Right when I'd work to do—"

She shook. He'd seen it before—but still it frightened him. Just sitting there, shaking. And shaking.

"I'm sorry—Becky, I'm sorry now." He felt a fool, and angry with himself. Then as the trembling grew less: "We'll not speak of them again. Ever."

"Becky doesn't like it. They've been wicked—ye ken that?"

He didn't know, but at *that* word, *wicked*, he felt the hateful colour rise . . . He took out his watch, tried to make out the time.

"You're a good lad," she said suddenly. They sat quiet for a few minutes, the awkwardness over. He thought of the chill walk back. Picking up the Wensleydale *Advertiser*—she could make out her letters and he didn't want her to see about Hannah—he held out his other hand for the puppy to lick.

"Becky, I'll have to be away now. But next time—that one, I'll fetch him a name . . ."

Haygarth wasn't their usual shoemaker. But Smales, the previous one, had made Father a very poor pair of boots (his son had inherited the business), so now they were to try another. A simple repair job first. The shop was in a yard not far from the Castle, and Ned went there as soon as he'd come down from Becky's.

He'd never been in before. The shop was warm but poorly lit—just a small oil lamp and a few candles—and the smell of leather, which he loved. He thought that he would like to watch how the work was done. A craft. But so different from what he did each day. Ranged neatly on an oak-framed rack were all the customers' lasts. Another rack on the dresser held all the tools. Leather patterns lay about.

"Rawson. Aye, they're done."

"How much?"

"One and six." Mr. Haygarth held them up against his worn leather apron. Ned handed him a florin then while he searched in a bag for change.

"Can I watch awhile?" he asked. "If it'll not bother you?"

"Aye. If ye want. Sit on t'bench." He pointed. Friendly but not particularly interested, bending again over his work, stitching a welt. Ned continued to stand. He watched the needle going in and out—thought that he'd like to ask a few questions, and began: "Do you—" when he heard a door at the back open.

A girl stood there. She had her hands on her hips. "Well, our dad," she said. "Your tea's made ready." When he didn't answer at once, she said it again. Then she saw Ned. "Who's *he?*"

"That's no way of talking," said her father, but without looking up from his work. "It's Mr. Rawson. The young 'un. Ye ought to ken. Ropes . . ." Then, "This'll be my lass, Nanny," he said, looking for a moment at Ned.

"I can't know every bit folk, can I now?" She leaned back against the doorpost. Her features were small and very neat: light from the oil lamp showed an upturned nose. Her mass of curly hair looked uncombed. "*And* when I'm from home too . . ."

Ned stood awkwardly. He thought it might seem rude just to leave now suddenly.

Nanny crossed one leg, and slid a little down the doorpost. "Only for —I'm back agen now," she said, looking straight at Ned. "Sent home. Wi' fifteen shilling in me pocket. I'd a place Aysgill way—no good it were."

"Ye *lost* it and no two ways about it," her father said. He didn't look up, but his voice was angry. "And for all ye've fetched home fifteen shilling—they're soon spent. And there'll be no character come to you—"

"It weren't my fault," she said pertly. "I'd a tongue in me head and used it—an' that's all about it. It's no bad thing, a tongue—is it, then, Mr. Rawson?"

Ned took fright when she turned suddenly and stared at him.

"It when to use it you've not learned—" said her father. "I've told you . . ."

She was staring at Ned still. He tried to avoid her gaze. Next to him was the flat lapstone they used for beating the leather, to make it close-grained. He fixed his eyes on this now . . .

"That caps all—ye can just get me a better place, the next—"

"Off," said her father. "Out wi' ye." He said it resignedly.

"And yer tea?"

"When I'm done—she knows that."

Ned thought the girl would go then. But she stayed on by the door, not moving at all, looking at him. Then she ran her tongue over her lips twice. He felt inside himself a stirring, a growing—oh, but he must not . . .

"I'll have to be away. Thank you greatly." He spoke to her father. The smell of leather, of the workshop, filled his nostrils. He turned towards the door.

"Goodbye. Don't you say goodbye, then?"

Again the stirring. Water, fire—oh, but this was familiar. In thee O Lord do I put my trust let me never be put to confusion deliver me in thy righteousness and cause me to escape for thou art my rock and my fortress . . .

Coming back down into the market square he remembered that he had left behind the shoes.

THREE

INDENTURES

It is contracted and agreed betwixt Mr. Benjamin WHITE-
LAW Surgeon-Apothecary of Downham Yorkshire and John
RAWSON also of Downham Yorkshire an apprenticeship of
FIVE years during which space the said John RAWSON
binds and obliges himself to serve the said Mr. Benjamin
WHITELAW faithfully and honestly by day and by night
holyday and workday and shall not reveal his master's secrets in
his arts nor the secret diseases of his patients and shall not play
at any games and shall not be drunk nor a nightwalker nor a
haunter of debauched or idle company and that he shall not
disobey his master's orders upon any pretence nor be guilty of
nor accessory to raising any tumults or uproars in the town of
DOWNHAM.

SIGNED AND SEALED this first day of May in the year of
Our Lord one thousand eight hundred and forty-two.

> John Frederick Rawson
> Benjamin Andrew Whitelaw

John had arrived early to get a good seat for the operation. For all the
world as if I were going to the theatre, he thought. (And did they not
call it just that, a theatre?) The seats were tiered and he had one not
far from the front: the one beside him he was keeping free for his
friend, Robbie Buchanan. Robbie, who had been invited out carousing
the night before, had feared he might be late.

John was rarely late, for anything. Punctuality was a point of honour

with him, and it was a trait which old Dr. Whitelaw had encouraged.
Although, he thought now, the cold this morning was enough to make
one turn over in bed for just another five minutes. When he had leaned
out of his window after dressing, the other side of the street had been
shrouded in damp early morning mist, up from the river Forth. The
"haar" as they called the mist here. And what wasn't haar was often a
pall of smoke. It was not for nothing that Edinburgh had been christened "Auld Reekie." Most days, smoke covered the lower part of the
rock on which the Castle had been built.

Robbie, slipping into the seat beside him. "My dear fellow. Every
thanks. The crowd—I had quite to fight my way." His fresh, open face,
chubby almost, was eager, grateful. It resembled at such moments his
sister's.

"These are unpleasant affairs," he said now, looking down below
them to the operating table, "but one must. You had heard of this
ether? In America last month—a Yankee surgeon has performed an operation with the patient completely unconscious."

John said, "Is it not to be tried here?"

"We shall see, we shall see. There are difficulties, I understand."

The table was dark and heavy and leather covered. Soon someone
must suffer horribly on it. John thought, I am only a spectator and
must be brave. And God knows, with Whitelaw I have seen some
sights, heard some sounds . . . But this: it was the deliberate, theatrical
nature of it all. And yet it is something I have to do, if I am to become
a good doctor. The pain is to be inflicted in a worthy cause, it is not?
To *save* a life. And was it not just that, the thought of saving life,
which first set me on this path?

For that I refused the family business. To Father, I know, it seemed
very odd. He was born almost with the rope-dust in his nostrils and because of Grandfather's great win, took over the works very early. He expected me in (I remember him showing me off: "This is my lad, John,
who'll take over the business . . ."), but I knew always that I must handle people, and not ropes. I felt certain that I could heal.

I remember that I thought at first it would be by touch. Because
when I was seven or eight I had diphtheria, and Mr. Whitelaw visited
me every day. His hands were just ordinary hands—and he an ordinary
person—but when he touched me, I was no longer afraid. I knew then
that I wasn't going into the darkness after all. I had heard about the
darkness. Although they told me Jesus would come to take me there,
and into the light of Heaven, I did not want to go, I was afraid. But
Mr. Whitelaw saved me. *I want to do the same.*

"It is a girl," Robbie was saying. "A young girl. I had feared that."

Above them in the roof, a great glass dome letting in light. Down on the table an assistant was applying a tourniquet to the body, tying it round the thigh.

John fingered restlessly the letter in his pocket. He could have wished it had been from Mother. Then he would have known that she was all right. Mr. Whitelaw's words were reassuring, but it was not the same (". . . she has had a great shock—most unsavoury business—some degree of nervous prostration inevitable . . .). Was she not worried enough before, in all conscience, over this Irish business? And the news about that was not good . . . If only the priest in Carrownacally would scrawl even the hastiest of lines. And now the Hannah affair (why did *I* notice nothing?), the worst had happened there. The report of the inquest. Mr. Whitelaw's words: "She will hang, no doubt of it—the postmortem shows conclusively the babe was alive—pieces of its lung, chopped, floated in water, proving that air had been taken in, that the child had lived and breathed . . ." I should have gone home to help Mother, he thought. I could go even now . . . But Mr. Whitelaw had thought of that too. ". . . the best you can do, laddie, is to learn all you can and make her proud of you. Home at Christmas, when the worst will be over . . ."

Down below, the surgeon had cut in already. He saw then the blood come spurting out, splashing the floor. The girl screamed. Ah God, she screamed. Screaming, screaming—he did not think he could stand it. And for her? Now, her short, sudden, exhausted gasps. And in the stillness of the theatre the grating sound of the saw, harsh, going through bone and marrow. Then again, her groans . . .

I must manage, he thought. Nausea, sweating, shaking. It would not do to pass out. *He must not.* Desperately, he tried to remember words from John Goodsir's lectures. Chanted to himself the dry names of anatomists: "Muller, Retzius, Eschricht, Hyrth, Schwann, Vrolik . . ." From the world of Europe, beyond Edinburgh . . .

The leg was off. It was thrust unceremoniously under the table. The girl, he saw, was now unconscious.

"Well," said Robbie, "perhaps it was not *quite* so bad after all—"

"You are used to hospitals and operating theatres and mortuaries—the whole grisly business. I was damnably afraid. I am used to seeing people alive and warm and in their own homes—or but very lately dead."

"It cannot be so idyllic in Downham—"

"It is different."

"Of course it is different because it is your home. Just as Edinburgh is mine. Own now that it was not so *very* bad . . ."

"It was not so very bad—"

"Capital. And now where shall we drink? Fortune's?"

The beer frothed over in its pewter cans. Robbie was saying, "You look as if you need a change of air, and company? Why not visit us this evening? You know you are always welcome—"

He had been before twice. Had been made to feel thoroughly at home both by the kindly parents and by Robbie's sister, Kirsty—to say nothing of a trying small brother (although not quite so trying, he thought, as Walter had been), known as "wee Bruce."

"I had meant the invitation earlier—but there was a change of plan. We *had* hoped my mother's great friends the Dunbars would be there; but it seems that two are sick. I spoke of them before, I think? He is accountant for some great railway scheme—to open up the Western Highlands. A great man for business (altho' I must say in confidence— 'I do not like thee, Doctor Fell . . .'). His *lady* is rather a poor thing, always moaning—but my mother is good with her and there seem bonds of friendship. I was at school with Jamie and there is another son —but it is the daughter Catriona who is Kirsty's great friend. They have been inseparable from childhood. She is charming. To me almost another sister. I should like you to meet her—"

"I should like it too."

He enjoyed visiting Drummond Place, where the Buchanans lived. It was in what was known as the New Town, which had been built over a very short perod of time earlier in the century. It had been spaciously and graciously laid out, stretching behind Princes Street in long streets, circuses, gardens, crescents, mews. All planned: not a random growth like the picturesque but dirty Old Town above the Castle.

His lodgings were in the Old Town, in Lothian Street. As lodgings went, he supposed they were not bad. A young man from a Yorkshire country town, knowing nothing of Edinburgh, might have done worse. And he liked both his fellow lodgers. Finlay, an orphan, had been brought up in Edinburgh, but Dugald was from the Highlands—a "teuchtar." Both worked as anatomical assistants at the Royal College of Surgeons Museum. It was the landlady, Mrs. Dowell, the fly in the ointment. She was fat and blowsy and in a permanent state of outrage. The three lodgers could do no right. Willie, her plump son, was equally ready to catch them out. There was a daughter, Jeannie, too, who could be glimpsed sometimes around midday but always in night attire. She needed extra sleep, Mrs. Dowell said—but Finlay told John that it was well known that Jeannie worked hard all night satisfying customers . . .

But if he were to have looked for new lodgings, it would have been on account of Tammie. Tammie, a pet monkey who wore a little jacket of the tartan, belonged to Willie Dowell and in the evenings would sit warming himself in the kitchen, squatting over the potato pot or stew pot when it was removed from the fire—enjoying the steam as it rose. Since he farted freely at other times they supposed he blew off with equal ease while warming himself. (In fact John and Dugald discussed often whether it was sufficient to remove the jackets from the steamed potatoes—John maintaining that the miasmic air penetrated to the very heart.)

His very first evening John had gagged over butter beans on which he had seen Tammie warm his haunches—the three of them had then chased the monkey round the kitchen with a rope and a cloth: Dugald said he should be smothered. "Burke him, Burke him!" cried Finlay, using the crowd's cry for a notorious murderer, but Tammie was too quick for them. He sat in his little winter jacket watching them from the rafters gleefully. Dugald was just taking a long stick to him when Mrs. Dowell came in:

"I'll have Wullie on ye," she shrieked, "where's ma Wullie?" Then, "*Puir* wee Tammie. Here, wee Tammie . . ."

Since they had this formidable bond of hatred, he thought, it was no wonder he had made friends with the other lodgers.

"So you will come tonight?" Robbie was saying, "You will come, dear fellow? About seven?"

He did not really want to go out. As he dressed that evening he thought that pleasant as the Buchanans were—and Kirsty seemed particularly welcoming—he would rather have spent the evening in less demanding company. Perhaps with Ellie. Or he could have just stayed in his room and written home. Squire Ingham—he had thought of writing to him. The Squire would surely fuss about Mother (his gratitude seemed boundless—far in excess of Charles's worth . . .) in a way that Father would not. Perhaps *he* could find out more about Ireland for her?

The Squire was to him almost like another father. A father for special occasions. One of his very first memories was of Mother taking him up to the Abbey, and the Squire swinging him by the leg. He had not cried. And then one Sunday, a special treat, he had been invited up to the family pew, for church. Aged nine. Behind the high wooden walls there had been a roaring fire and a cupboard from which as soon as the service began, the Squire had taken glasses and wine: and for John and the other children, cordial. During the sermon the Squire had snored peacefully, his feet before the fire . . .

Of course they do say, John thought now, that he is or rather was, a great wencher. Even Mr. Whitelaw, who was not given to gossip, had hinted that this was so: but that he had always taken his pleasures outside Downham. Mother, of course, would hear nothing against him. He himself found it hard to think of the Squire as anything but an elderly, kindly man. Not that wenching was something to be ashamed of—quite the contrary. Father might not agree, but most people when they spoke of such things had in their tongue a hint of respectful envy.

I do not think really that I can be described as a wencher, he thought. Although here in Edinburgh he had not wasted time: it was just that in settling for only one person he showed himself to be not really "a lad." He was content, though. With Finlay's help and advice he had met up with Ellie—and was at one with her frequently.

She was brown-haired, with a giggle, a front tooth missing, and no demands other than the (small) sum he paid her. He hoped she was clean (strangely he did not link her in any way with other prostitutes, never thinking of her in the same breath as Jeannie Dowell . . .). She had two children and was married to an elderly man who never came from work before ten of an evening. She spoke of him always good-naturedly. "I'd the two weans to him," she told John, "he'll no bother me again." She did not like it when John worried about his returning early: "Och, hen, dinna put yoursel' to any fash aboot him . . ."

I would rather be with her this evening, he thought. She is just what I need. He toyed with the idea of skipping Robbie's invitation.

And yet it was not his heart engaged. He was not in love with Ellie. Certainly, he did not need anything of that sort—I am heart-whole as a biscuit, he thought proudly.

FOUR

I have a family now, Sarah thought. I am a *Rawson* and I must cling to that. I have a son too that I love dearly: and he is home with me again.

She sat in the over-heated bedroom—she could not get warm—the coal-fire stacked high, and pulled her shawl more tightly round her. Her crochet lay on the table beside her untouched. John, sitting opposite her in a basket chair, listening to her sympathetically.

"Palpitations," she told him, "they're what alarm me now." She felt that she shouldn't be worrying him. But was he not to be a doctor? "All this nausea and dizzy turns. It's just since—Hannah." He nodded understandingly. "Though I'd been fretting in the summer about Ireland. And worse since back end, with all the bad news. But you knew that, son—"

"Yes. I worried."

"Ned didn't. He's not over-caring." She had an urge to confide, but thought, I don't want to split the brothers. "Odd, he is sometimes, daft almost. 'Over the hills and far away . . .' " She heard her voice quaver when she sang. Tears came suddenly and she blinked them away: "Maybe he has blood from my da—who knows?"

John said, "You don't have to be Irish to make up stories or be musical—"

"But Yorkshire folk, they're not fey—"

"What? With hobs, and the suchlike—what are they but fairies? And as for the *Kissing Gate*—well, folk who can believe all that."

"Aye, well," she heard herself sound more Yorkshire, "that's one more of my worries, son—"

He said laughing, "What have you been up to, then? Defying it? Proving it all nonsense?"

Hannah, always near the surface now: "She'll hang, you say—won't she? And she'd been through the kirk gate just the week before. It worried her. She thought it brought the—bad thing about."

"Mother, really—" He shook his head.

"And that's not all. It's what *I* saw, son." She felt foolish telling him. "Just a week after it was. 'Them as swings on t'gate, swings on t'gibbet.'" She said the words slowly. "That little brother of hers—I know other bairns do it, but he was swinging away on the gate—and he'd such a face on him. *Serious* . . ."

"If I remember right, he'd *be* odd-looking. It'll be *that* that alarmed you. That and the deformed shoulder. He's—forget it, eh? For me?" He leaned back and stretched his legs. "What about some of that tea now?" He pointed to a tray laid ready, the pot covered by a cosy.

She poured him out a cup, and then one for herself.

"You're worried," he said. "It's the Irish family too."

She heard her voice tremble. "You can't get any truth from the newspapers. It *is* bad there—worse than they let on, I don't doubt."

"Perhaps not," he said, in reassuring tones. "The reports, they could be exaggerated. Work *is* provided, after all, and money for it. It'll be mainly the idle, the feckless, in real want—"

"What if ours, the Donnellys, are feckless—*have been*—what then?"

He said thoughtfully, "The people who are really helping are the Society of Friends. Some, I think, have been on an expedition. Should I try to get someone from there to make inquiries?"

Quakers, they were good. Odd, but good. "Perhaps they could send money over from us? And clothes—and food of course, on the chance. Yes, son, yes," she said. Then: I must ask him about himself, she thought. Forget myself a little.

"That teacher now in Edinburgh that spoke on the blight—he is good, is he?"

"John Goodsir? He is very popular. Though he has no smartness of manner. And little rhetoric." There was admiration in his voice. "He does not try to win favours of the class and yet does so—"

"Perhaps you'll get grand ideas. Be the one to discover something in medicine."

"I don't think so—"

"Nonsense, son. If you've a mind to." He could do anything, she thought. Anything. She went on: "A city like that—you've made friends? Buchanan—is that the name? Robbie, and Kirsty." She paused, hesitated, did not want to say the name: "And how is she, then, this—Kirsty?"

"Very sweet, very gentle."

"And you like her, son?"

"Both of them—all of them, they have been like a second family to me."

One day he will marry, she thought. I have to face that also. She tried not to wonder, yet again, if he had been already with a woman: *I do not want to know.* She felt the colour flooding her cheeks. I will not think about it. But if not yet, her mind went on, then later—when he marries. She could bear that least of all. The thought that he, her beloved John, would one day do to some young girl what, all those years ago, Sam had done to her.

"*What are you doing?*" She could hear her own voice still. "What are you doing?" But he had not answered. He had not spoken at all. She had been asleep. It was the middle of the night that first time (and it seemed, every time afterwards). Her voice to begin with had been even a little saucy—she was so self-confident, proud of herself: she had, after all, just married Old Jacob's eldest.

"No—no you don't!" But it was darkness, complete darkness. She might have been with anyone. He was a stranger. "Sam, what's up? Let me—" But a hand had come over her mouth, *in* her mouth. She had been lying on her side away from him when he woke her. He attacked me from the back, she thought now. She had seen animals— yes, dogs, cows, sheep—she remembered: something like that, from behind.

But the pain, that was the worst of it. And the shock. "What are you doing?" She had not known. Nor had she known of the consequences. Nine months to the day (and only for four of them had she known what was to happen), the first, Walter, who had lived only six weeks. She had heard, *he* had read to her from the Bible that a woman forgets her travail rejoicing in the birth of her child. She had not forgotten her travail, and when later the sickly babe, which had never been able to feed (mouthing half-heartedly as if it had lived already too long, grasping the nipple only to let it go), did not wake one morning, her grief had been not untinged with anger.

It had shamed her, the anger. She caught herself saying: "If you did not mean to stay, if you could not be bothered to stay—*why all that pain?*" But then the dreaded, the expected, happened. No sooner was the tiny infant buried, the hard breasts with their unwanted milk bound tightly, than Sam was back in the big bed with her. That dread waking in the night. *What are you doing?* A few months later, a miscarriage. And then—nothing. For nearly six months.

It had seemed to her very long. He wanted another son. But to her it was all of it pain. The same pain. Pain before conception, unbelievable pain at the end. All part of one terrible whole. And oh, those disturbed nights. If only, she had thought, it could be got over with at once, at bedtime, before she settled for the night . . . But no. Sometimes it was twice, even three times in the one night. She would hold her breath, clench her teeth, bite the pillow (it would always be painful, she could not imagine how it might ever be *not* painful), and wait for it to be over. And yet at first, no child. But she was never able to feel relieved, since she was ashamed: *she* must be doing something wrong since plainly he was doing all that was necessary, what had brought about the other two. Gradually although not in any way a holy person, she had prayed while he did it. Saying through her tears, "O Lord God, give me a man child. Soon." (All those women that Sam praised in the Bible, did not they all keep a good house, give birth to men children, become prized above rubies?) "Lord God, who had mercy on your daughter, the barren Sarah . . ." Her namesake in the Bible.

But those were the night times. The days were quite other. Then it was as if, for Sam anyway, it had never happened. The respectful touch, the kiss on the forehead, hands clasping her head, the fatherly pat on the shoulder—they were words of another language. She could understand that language—but talk of that sort did not make children.

What miracle had it been, then, what answer to prayer, that in the end those nights should have brought her—John? *My* son. But that had been the wicked thought, no doubt of it: that from the beginning she had fancied that he was hers alone, and that he looked—now like her da, now like her mam, now like some uncle she'd seen once. She had been able to tell herself that this baby, this longed-for, *living* son (and unbelievably year had succeeded year and he had survived and thrived), had grown inside in answer to her prayers. And was nothing to do with what happened in the night. At any time, except in the small hours of darkness when it happened again, she could deceive herself about this . . .

"You're dreaming," he said, "and not pouring me more tea." He brought over his cup. "You know I was speaking just now of Mr. Goodsir? Well," he said, laughing, "before he did medicine, they say he was apprenticed to a dentist, and had to take out a wisdom tooth from Daniel O'Connell—the great Irish agitator himself. And that he was mortally afraid, but that when he came into the room Great Dan opened his mouth for him, just like a child . . ."

She sat up suddenly, bolt upright. She had had an idea: for the first time in weeks she felt confident, that she had a purpose. She could not wait to speak.

"Will you go—for me?"

"Go?"

"Over there. To Ireland, son."

"But what can I—how can I?"

"Go there *now*, before you've to be back in Edinburgh." He seemed taken aback still, and she went on: "You've three weeks, haven't you? More like four . . . You'd have to be away soon—but there's time . . . If you could go to Galway, son—to *our* place, to Carrownacally. You could see *for yourself* if there're any Donnellys. Take food and clothes and money. Those Quakers you spoke of. You could—"

He interrupted. He sounded appalled. "I cannot see how I—" he began, and stopped.

She said then: "My chest of drawers, son. The top one. Open it." When he was there: "You'll find something in the corner, wrapped in silk."

It was the shamrock, the one Da had sent. She had shown it to John once before, when he was a small boy. She unwrapped it now carefully, safe behind glass with its thin leather frame.

"Look at this again, son," she said. "It came from your grandfather. And he—he was to have come after. But we'd never word again. They were hard times then. They'll be harder by far now. He'd want, wouldn't he—that we do what we can. In memory of him, and his. It's *family*, son . . ."

He hesitated. "It would be difficult—" he began weakly. But she knew already that she had won. It would be all right.

"There's little time, then, before you should be away. You can arrange something with your father. He'll find the money I don't doubt. I shouldn't try Old Jacob—that grandfather. If there's any difficulty—well, you've only to speak to Squire . . ."

Confidence, hope, soared in her. "That's settled, then," she said. "You'll do it for me?"

FIVE

He did it—for her. Yes. But it was all of it much much worse than he could have imagined. Indeed nothing he had heard or read could have prepared him for what he saw: again and again during that Irish visit he was to stop and ask himself, not—am I awake, is it real? but—why did I come, *how can I endure this?* And then was immediately ashamed. John Rawson, who was so soon to become a doctor.

But as to the practicalities—the preparations, the arrangements to go —they could not have been easier, more pleasant. He had in the end been to see the Old Squire not for money but in the hope that he would know of a possible companion, someone who, would in his turn get him letters of introduction. The old man was delighted to see him. Tender enquiries after Mother and then: yes, he knew who should be asked; and *that* person by the happiest of chances knew someone who was planning just such a journey. Forty-eight hours later John was driving to York to meet one Frederick Watson. Three days after, and they were setting out.

He was fortunate in his companion. Frederick Watson was a man of perhaps thirty-five, a Quaker, unmarried but engaged to be wed at Easter. With his square face, sharp-cut features, and open warm manner, he seemed from the first the ideal person to accompany him. They talked easily from the first meeting. When John told him the story of his mother's family and of the errand on her behalf, he said solemnly, "It would be at the best of times—and we have not those now—very difficult, *impossible* perhaps. But we shall *try* . . ."

They were to cross from Liverpool. But even the weather had conspired to make everything worse for the Irish. Over there snow was falling and a raw north-east wind blowing directly from the Russian steppes. In the West of the country the inhabitants were used to mild wet winters; when the season was over for tilling their potatoes they could stay inside, warm in their turf-heated cabins. But this year, cold and hungry, they were outside working, or seeking work from the Board of Works—and even then the money received was not enough to buy food, so high had the prices risen. With Erse their native language and little or no understanding of English, they had no real idea of what was happening. They knew only that they were starving.

Frederick, angry with his country over the whole Irish question, the whole handling of the potato failure, exclaimed: "How *in God's name*, in common humanity, when we spent—what was it, something like *ten* millions on emancipating slaves? Now, for this, we reckon in paltry thousands . . ."

The more John heard the less he wanted to go on with the enterprise. Now, already at Liverpool, he thought: I have had enough. In spite of fears already voiced about famine fever, no precautions had been taken. The Irish paupers were coming over in their hordes: the numbers here in Liverpool appalled him. Frederick explained, "Even if they are sent at once to the workhouse, they will get *at the least* a little meat, and tea, and some bread. To them—*riches*."

For most of the crossing John slept, as if fear or the anticipation of it had produced in him a great exhaustion. He felt grey with apprehension: could not tell if his nausea arose from the pitching of the boat or from cold or from the dread growing every hour in his mind. I am to be a doctor, he kept thinking, and I *cannot even do this*.

There were a lot of soldiers on board. They were very noisy, drinking porter, shouting, singing. Moving in his sleep, half-waking, John could hear them above the growling of the steamer. Once he tried to go up on the quarterdeck but he was driven back again, battered by the spray. Fear, sick fear, returned to him.

They landed at Kingstown at seven in the evening in icy sleet. Their Dublin hotel was the Imperial in Sackville Street. That night he slept badly. He had slept perhaps too much on the crossing. The next day Frederick, who had several letters of introduction, arranged for a car and the two of them went about meeting people—Mr. X of the National Schools, Mr. Y of the Board of Works. The second night they dined with a doctor and his family.

The talk was always of the famine. John told his story while Frederick outlined his plan for travelling as fast as possible to Connemara. He had authority to offer money for a boiler and the setting up of soup kitchens. He would visit and inspect the workhouses—many of them subsidiary ones taken over from deserted private houses, deserted distilleries. They would make for Carrownacally; perhaps in the West of Ireland the snow would not be so evil, so thick. Then if all went well, or if he had at the least discovered as much as possible, John could make his own way back across the country. It was not for him, not part of his undertaking to face up to or report on the varied sights. Hearing this, John felt his sick apprehension grow and grow, tinged now with impatience to be off—*to get it all over.* (Mother, Mother, he thought, what have you asked?)

Afterwards he remembered little of the journey. Images merged to desolate him in memory but always in black and white. As if he saw a moving etching. The scenery: villages, which in the distance even in the grey winter daylight beneath a sky heavy with sleet or snow had a kind of frail beauty; flanked by mountains, their lines were a satisfaction to the eye until arrived at, when they were seen to be as rotten inside as the blackened blighted potato.

Travel was in any case difficult. Not only because of the weather, the sleet, the snow, the impassable half-made roads (convenience roads built by the Public Works to give employment—roads leading from no-where to nowhere . . .), but because they had so often to change trans-port—from car to horse and back again, often they had to get out and walk. And always but always there were the beggars. He had heard about riots, read of them, and it was these he particularly feared. Before leaving Dublin he had bought himself a pistol, double-barrelled, costing one guinea.

Beggars. At first they spoke some English, not very intelligible, a blurred moan, a wail only. Asking, asking: "Ye honour, God save ye, God save us, Jaysus, Jaysus, for the love . . ." Whenever he and Fred-erick stopped, as so often they had to, then it would begin again. Throwing money, pushing the skeleton figures aside—it was nothing, it was usual to be touched, pulled at. He had bread with him that he was saving for Carrownacally—what sights might he not see there? He had brought, too, quite a lot of money, bags of pence, of groats; he wanted to give money to the Donnellys when he found them, if he found them —but he discovered now that it had to be used, must be used to scatter to these beseeching scarecrows. It was the way they flapped, the wild frightened flapping of their torn rags, which reminded him—spectres which had frightened him in the fields of his childhood.

And they were everywhere. Once during a halt in the journey while they were eating in the house of the schoolmaster, a family had moaned and scratched at the window outside, wailing, wailing. He could scarcely eat—and *by what right should he do so?* In Dublin, evidence of the good life had appalled both him and Frederick. It was the season:

balls as glittering as those happening in Edinburgh; hunting when the hardness of the ground permitted. The day they had left, their coach had passed the hunt in the country outside.

The travelling knocked him up. He told himself it was that. As they moved across Ireland he was tired all the time, day and night. Always exhausted, always afraid, with a nervous tiredness as if a lamp inside burned too brightly. At night he slept only fitfully, waking up suddenly in a panic thinking: where am I, *where should I be?* then remembering. Lying back on his pillows again, his heart still hammering. I have to go through with this, I have been found wanting yet I cannot escape. The small sleep he had was filled with dreams, dreams which made no sense to him, terrifying him only. Anxious, his body stiffened with terror, he would be hiding, pressed against the embankment while a train thundered by—a train he had missed. And the country, the world of which he dreamed grew nightly narrower, darker, more and more confined. When he woke: the stench in his nostrils, death and decay with its sweetish rotten smell, and not imagined but real—since wherever they lodged it seeped through the very walls.

He had not, in spite of Frederick's many explanations, the wide grasp, the bird's-eye view of the situation which alone could help. The immediate horrors swamped him. Children. It was *that* he could not bear, although he did not think of himself as a child lover: he was never at ease with them. Unless of course it was to heal, if they were in pain and he could touch. Now perhaps it was just because he could not touch, could *do* nothing. The healer in him was frustrated, powerless before these bags of bones carried by their mothers, their fathers, since so often their sticklike legs would not hold them up. Those black bruised spindly legs. And the great swollen bellies filled with nothing, the caved-in sunken faces on which hair grew thickly, monkeylike. They were scarcely human. The adults too were animals. It was best to think of them all as animals, and this daily he resolved to do. (But for that he must avoid the eyes—especially the eyes of the children. They were so old, even he thought with dread, wise.)

He saw Frederick as a safe haven, a talisman. They talked as they journeyed. They talked in the evenings. Whiskey and water and talk. John spoke of Goodsir, of why he admired him, of his own plans, his ambitions which seemed now to belong to another person so far away had they gone. He spoke to this eager yet solid, essentially *good* man. Hated to be separated from him. Now as unaccustomed horror piled upon horror, he leaned on him all the more, all the while suspecting there was worse to come. And Frederick himself, visibly appalled, hinted as much.

"Shall I not write *at once?*" John asked (to Squire Ingham, the Prime Minister, the Yorkshire *Gazette*, his professor in Edinburgh . . .). "Shall I not write?" he asked again and again.

"The posts are out of all scotch and notch at present," Frederick said, "it would be better to wait. When you are back—and you will be back before me—say what you will then, say what you *can* . . ."

Connemara. They were to spend the night in the town of Galway where they had letters of introduction. John thought, here on the coast surely there would be fish to feed the starving? But they learned that the fishermen could not afford salt to preserve their catch. Along the coast, no seaweed: all had been eaten. Walking the steep dirty streets of the city at night, making their way to two appointments, he and Frederick talked as ever of what could be done, of what *must* be done. And of their plans: as well as Carrownacally, Frederick would visit the town of Clifden to see the Quakers there.

In the morning they were to leave Galway very early, travelling first by car to Oughterard, on Lough Corrib, where they would leave their luggage, and then on to Carrownacally on horseback. As well as money John would take with him this time brandy, laudanum, chlorodyne, and of course biscuit and bread.

Fearful, he dreaded waking in the morning, but in the event there was scarcely time to worry. The Boots at their hotel had written the wrong hour on his slate and they were called only a few moments before their car arrived at six. They set out in the cold early morning dark, flustered and hurried, without even a mug of tea.

The sky when the light came was a clear winter blue, the first they had seen. Stillness of frost and snow. Silence. Difficult, stony countryside. They passed lengths of ill-made dry-stone walls (it would not be necessary to pull stones out in winter to let through livestock: they would have fallen naturally). He thought of his grandfather's work. *My grandfather*. In this strange land he began to feel half reluctantly the stirrings of kinship. Blood flowing more thickly than water.

At Oughterard there were extensive government works. They saw there some officials, left their luggage and began the ride to Carrownacally. Fuchsia hedges, colourless in winter, snow-flecked brambles whose fruit had been in September for many the only food. On Lough Corrib the icy wind ruffled the surface of the lake, then whipped it up savagely. The sky darkened and grew full of sleet. Then the snow began to fall, biting on eyes, cheeks. The horses, with little mettle, moved dejectedly. John thought, what distinction now between animals and humans, *who is made in God's image?* (And who would grudge these animals food, for what human now could be so useful as a horse?)

They were almost at Carrownacally. The moment had come. Dread like dark wet flakes of snow fell on him. The town as they entered had about it the terrible air of decay and hopelessness they had come to recognise. Mother had addressed her letter: "To the parish priest of Carrownacally." His name, it appeared, was Father O'Driscoll, but he was not about when they arrived. They were told he would be at the schoolhouse.

The schoolhouse was in use as a hospital. The schoolmaster, unshaven, gaunt, came hurrying out to them: crying almost, clinging first to John and then to Frederick. "Jaysus sent you, did Jaysus send you?" At the same time trying to push away the beggars, the suppliants who were already gathering round. John flung some coins and then as the scrabbling began hurriedly followed the others inside. There he was hit once more by the stench, never very far from their nostrils. Waves of nausea rolled over him so that his legs trembled.

By contrast with the schoolmaster, the priest was an angry, vigorous man, moving with purpose across the room to them, making his way past the bodies, bodies, bodies. Crowded into a room meant for only half that number, they were everywhere: lolling against each other, propped against the wall, unable to support themselves, without room to lie. Moaning, sighing sounds rose and fell like a tide ebbing and flowing.

Frederick told the priest, "I am from the Society of Friends—the Quakers. Mr. Rawson is here for another purpose." He explained first his own mission: he was empowered, he said, to install a boiler and provide money for a soup kitchen; it would be arranged through Clifden.

To their horror Father O'Driscoll waved away the idea. "No, sir. No thank you, sir," his manner definite, final. The schoolmaster set up at once a wild sobbing. "What would we want wi' that, what now?" the priest continued. "Sure and wouldn't we have every beggar come to Carrownacally, every soul that lives as far ever as sound goes . . ." He frowned, then: "Isn't it too little then, too late, isn't it?" he queried aggressively.

Frederick—and John marvelled at his calm—said only, "As you wish . . ." Then changing the subject at once, he explained John's presence.

But impatiently, as if hardly able to spare the time, "I had no letter, no sir," the priest said, "I've had no letter now—" He spoke a moment with the schoolmaster and then: "Sure, and *he'll* ask—"

The schoolmaster, who was named Flanahan, called out, asking were there any Donnellys, speaking to everyone in Irish. He sounded still as if he were crying. No one answered. He asked again—but still no one answered. The moaning barely ceased.

"I had no letter at all," the priest said, as if to finish with the matter.

"The posts are quite mad, quite mad," commented Frederick, "you could not have been expected . . ."

The priest took a pinch of snuff; John noticed all down his worn sleeve the tell-tale stains. But he seemed to be using it not as a pleasure, a soothing habit, but rather as an irritable, hopeless gesture for which he scarcely had the time. They went outside. Frederick had asked about the countryside around: cabins could be seen dotted towards the mountains, away from the sullen waters of the lough. The schoolmaster, his head shaking now, the sob still in his voice, pointed about a mile west. "Was it that way some Donnellys went now, was it?" He and Father O'Driscoll conferred together. Then the priest said with sudden resolution: "I have to visit. Sure and I'll come wid' ye—I have to visit."

As they made their way, he shouted constantly at the crowds that followed them like a pack of wolves (but without the strength and stamina): "Away wid' ye, away wid' ye!" He told Frederick and John, "I've a stick, ye must use a stick." His anger came through all the time, the anger of despair. Once perhaps, he had been able not just to love his parishioners, but to do something for them.

Attacking the snuff again: "If ye'd said now ye was coming . . ."

John said, "We sent word."

"Artn't the posts mad—didn't you say?"

He spoke frequently on the journey. "You're not Catholics, then? no, Quakers—ye said now. Quakers. And sure, they're good folk . . . Now wertn't there Donnellys this way, now? McCormack, Giloolys—arrah, I don't know at all . . ."

The road was deserted. The snow had stopped falling. It lay freshly, pall-like, concealing how many dead bodies beneath? The stench of decay hung ever present in the cold air. John thought yet again of the hopelessness of his errand. Certainly he would have nothing to tell Mother. Nothing for her comfort (but what he *had* seen, what he had borne witness to, how ever was he to recount that? How to commit the smell of death to paper? *How* to speak of it?).

In his anger, Father O'Driscoll talked on. Where did he get the energy? Only the colour of his skin, the drawn quality of his flesh, the trembling of his hands betrayed that he, too, scarcely ate enough.

". . . and if we can't help one another it's as aisy as that . . . for everyone now we do something for, there's twenty will . . . the English, sir, you're English . . . Indian meal they call it, if they give us *that* . . .

and ye'll have heard, sir, of those that grow their crops and sell for food
. . . sure now and the people don't look as God made them—" Then as
if suddenly remembering John's request: "And if I *had* a letter, when
would I write—when would I be writing letters to England?" And John
felt ashamed, wrong, guilty that Mother should ever have pestered or
tried to pester this man—expecting him to sit down of an evening and
account in leisurely fashion for events of fifteen, twenty years ago.

". . . and some say 'tis the punishment, the judgment now for those
that broke the pledge to Father Mathew. Are ye drinking men, now?"

They had almost reached the group of mud cabins. Ahead of them
the mountains stretched, grey, desolate. Already the light was going.
The priest said uneasily, as they came up to the first cabin: "Sure and
these'll be empty." There was no smoke coming from them, no signs of
activity, of life. A ghost settlement.

"Sure, and these'll be empty . . ."

Frederick stepped forward. "We shall go in." John, behind him, hesitated. Then almost at once as Frederick went through the door, before
John following could see into the gloom, he had turned. Coming out,
he collided with John. Eyes down, his voice trembling, "Indeed there's
life in there . . . there has been life recently—" To the priest he said,
visibly shaken, "Your rats grow plump on carrion . . ."

"If we'd hold of them now, they'd be eaten theirselves . . ."

John, stepping away from the two of them, pushed forward to the
next of the cabins. The ramshackle door was slightly open. To overcome, kill his fear, he crashed in noisily.

Sickly, suffocating smell—the remembered stench, but overpowering
so that waves of nausea swept over him. There were no windows and it
was a few seconds before he could make anything out. A terrible
stillness. Fear caught at his bowels. What looked like heaps of rags were
nearest to the door. Persons. Gradually as his eyes grew accustomed he
saw them, huddled together. There must have been four, five people.
He could not tell the wasted limbs one from another. They were not
real. He said it again to himself quickly, *they are not real.*

And then from somewhere else, the other side, the darker corner—a
hissing sound.

"Good God—Frederick, *here!*"

He had thought it a rat. But it was a wasted, scarcely living cat, tearing now savagely at the naked body of what had once been a baby.

He brought out his pistol. Fired twice. Stillness.

Frederick walked in. "My God—" Then he assessed the situation:
"Good fellow," he said, "good fellow." He took from him the still
smoking pistol. Father O'Driscoll was behind him now.

But John only wanted out. Not to see the other corpses. In the far corner, a bundle, a pile of rags—or a body—what matter which? Then as he looked, he thought . . . He went nearer. "Quiet," he said. Then:

"Get a light—have we a light? Light a taper." His voice felt, sounded, loud with authority. Beneath the tattered material something stirred. He was afraid at once, deathly afraid.

He stepped forward to touch. Rummaging, drawing the rags back: vomit to his gullet, and up bitterly into his mouth. In the light of the taper he saw what it was. A child. What had been a child. Beneath the nearly hairless scalp, eggshell thin, a dark downy face, the eyes closed. Cold to the touch. He took it in at a glance as he uncovered the frail swollen belly, the wasted sticks of limbs. He felt for the heart, fingers touching lightly.

"Someone, it's—someone here's alive," he said, his voice choked. Frederick came up behind him, the priest at his side.

"The *fayver*, have they the fayver?" the priest asked, pushing about the straw on the mud floor with his stick.

"I don't know," John said, surprised at his own calm. He had taken off his cloak and lifting the child gently, enclosed it. It was light, like a feather.

"Let us go back," he said to Frederick. "For God's sake, *let us go back—*"

Frederick said again only, "Good fellow—" putting a hand on his shoulder. Together they all stood outside. Other cabins could be seen ahead in the darkening afternoon. Frederick said firmly, practically, "Well, what shall you do?"

John paused, hesitated. The priest, moving about angrily: "Wouldn't there be an inch or two now in the schoolroom? For *ye*, sir, Mr. Flanahan, he'll find a corner . . ." He beat his stick hard, pushing through the snow, hitting at the frozen ground. John thought with compassion, one day I shall leave this nightmare, shall wake up from it. *He* never will.

"I take the responsibility," he said suddenly.

Both Frederick and the priest stared at him.

He said to Frederick: "I shall go back—to where we have our luggage. I think I shall then take your advice—shall do as we planned. I shall go back to England directly."

Frederick looked at the bundle in his cloak. "With—that?"

"With her, yes. With the little girl . . ."

Afterwards he was never to know how he did it. That first night, even though he still had Frederick's support, was perhaps the worst. Soon after returning from the cabins they had left Carrownacally—and its angry priest, its crying schoolmaster. Father O'Driscoll had again offered to take the child into the schoolroom-hospital ("And maybe now they *were* Donnellys—I don't know at all . . ."). And Frederick, looking grave and thoughtful, had said: "Perhaps we—you should accept, John? It would be wiser, I think. Not *better*, but wiser . . ."

Back at the inn, he asked, "She lives still?"

"Yes." Twice on the ride back to Oughterard, although there had been no sound, no movement—only the pistol shot it seemed had affected her—he had felt again for her heart and pulse. Both had surprised him. Once he had stopped and put a finger to his brandy flask and then to her mouth, half afraid, though, that she might suck, for so delicate and thin would her jawbone be that any sudden movement could force her tongue through the roof of her mouth.

He said to Frederick now, "I will see you downstairs." Then, carrying the bundle up to his room, he laid it carefully on the bed. He left it there for a full five minutes while, standing over by the window, he tried to compose himself. Queasy and nervously exhausted, he felt his legs tremble.

Bending over the low bed, he unwrapped the cloak gently. He asked himself, *what age?* trying to relate this monstrosity to any child he had ever examined. Indeed, by appearance anything from six to sixty. Certainly the face was old, old, old.

He took the pillows from the bed and laid her on them like a mattress—he could have wished them softer. Lying so lightly on them she looked even more vulnerable, her eyes still closed. What have I done? he thought. *What am I doing?* His hands shook with fatigue and irresolution—it was still not too late to change his mind. He had made no promises, merely spoken an intention . . .

His cloak was soiled, stinking. He sponged at it with water from the jug. Apart from the stench and who knows what possible contagion, it seemed to him quite unwearable. He could not imagine using it again.

Later, he thought, I will wash her, sponge her gently. If he could do it without shocking: imagining already the distended belly puncturing, the stick limbs snapping. Tomorrow, he told himself, *if she is still here.* For now, he took one of the thin worn towels from the washstand, tore off part of it, and wedged it between her legs—at the same time he thought, What is there to come out when nothing has gone in?

Next he covered her with a slip from another of the pillows, and over that his travelling plaid. A fire had been lit just before he came up, but the air still felt cold and damp.

Looking at her, "Do you want to live?" he asked suddenly, surprised that he had said it out loud. Little finger dipped in brandy. This time he felt a response. And again. He was afraid she would open her eyes, and look at him. Afraid too that she might not—ever.

Later that evening, back in the room again, he soaked a little bread in water, heating it over a spirit flame. When it was lukewarm he fed her again from his finger. That night he spent in the chair by the dying fire, half-hoping that by the morning it would all be over. Part of him, though, willed resurrection—in the intervals of fitful sleep, listening for her breathing, sending across the room some of his strength.

That was the worst night. The next day he knew by the vigour of her response—although vigour was too strong a word for anything relatively so feeble—that he had won. After taking breakfast, he and Frederick parted. Frederick pressed on him more money, some letters of introduction that might help, advice, and blessings.

The journey back. It was the same horrors in reverse, but although they were none the less, he felt removed from them if only because he was fully occupied, no longer the spectator, his ingenuity now taxed continually. He had become determined to win. Before he had been helpless in the face of all the suffering. Now there was *something* he could do.

But it was difficult. Good God, it was difficult. Sometimes he was lucky: twice on the journey he was able to buy a little goat's milk (and this was the contradiction, that one place should be as bad as Carrownacally, whilst another although not good had at least some of the trappings of life left). Thankfully, although she waved her limbs feebly now and then, she did not seem to wish or be able to move much. But she opened her mouth for him now. She was like a little sparrow, opening and shutting her beak—the skin of her face pale and thin like muslin. A little white sparrow. He remembered that in Edinburgh, in George Square where John Goodsir lived, he had seen a white sparrow perched on the railings—a portent of good luck he had been told . . .

In the hotels and inns he would not let the servants in his room. "Bring me some milk for my stomach," he would order hopefully, or if that was not possible, pap. Always he concealed her existence. The third night he was offered only some stirabout, of coarse Indian meal. He could not eat it himself. He could not offer it to her. Instead he asked for hot water and soaked some of his now small store of dry biscuit. She took drops of brandy frequently. Wondering always if he was doing right, he wished that Mr. Whitelaw were with him.

In Dublin he didn't take up the letter of introduction. It was to an engineer. He was afraid that finding out what he had done, they would try somehow to take the child from him. Although he thought later that evening, it was odd that he should fear that—for in the last two days of travelling he had grown almost to dislike her. He was ashamed of the emotion. But the more he became angry with himself, the more distaste he felt for her, the more irritation. Those eyes, colourless, expressionless, which never focussed on him (yet would he have wanted them to?). That mouth—little white sparrow wanting to be fed—opening, opening, opening. And how to find the right food? What best to do?

He could not be rid of her: taking all his energies, causing him so much anxiety, robbing him of his night's rest. And always the need to conceal her as if she were stolen goods . . .

What will Mother say? he thought yet again in the intervals of a sleepless night. He slept scarcely at all now. He dare not—as if he kept her alive by keeping awake. Although—*might it not be better if she did die?* Better for her, better for all, for might she not be an idiot, or diseased beyond remedy? He thought of that often in the night. A bad person perhaps, bad blood. And who *was* she anyway? He could not truthfully say to Mother: "I have brought you back a Donnelly . . ."

Arriving in Liverpool late on the twenty-third, he telegraphed to Leeds, "Home Christmas Eve." His journey was nearly over. That night he dreamed, in a short nap of perhaps only fifteen minutes. He was buying the child, for gold. Dark men with crafty faces whom he had never seen before were receiving the great bags of coins. And she, although her body, her physical state had not changed at all, was laughing and talking—but not with him. With everyone, everyone else. "My name is *Kate*," she told them all. "I am Kate Rawson."

SIX

"'. . . For wickedness burneth as the fire: it shall devour the briers and thorns . . . Through the wrath of the Lord of hosts is the land darkened, and the people shall be as the fuel of the fire: no man shall spare his brother. And he shall snatch on the right hand and be hungry . . . they shall eat every man the flesh of his own arm . . .'"

As he read, Father's face grew darker and his voice, his special "Prayers" voice, took on a deeper and deeper tone. He slowed the pace with relish.

The Book of Isaiah, Chapter Nine: "I shall read from Isaiah," he'd announced, "it's apt today—Christmas Eve. 'For unto us a child is born, unto us a son is given . . .'"

Yes. But the remainder, Ned thought, how could the remainder be thought of as Christmas fare?

"'. . . And he shall snatch on the right hand and be hungry, and he shall eat on the left hand, and they shall not be satisfied: they shall eat every man the flesh of his own arm . . . For all this his anger is not turned away, but his hand is stretched out still . . .'"

The voice went on. Ned moved uneasily. Restlessly. He had been restless all day. He thought perhaps he had caught it from Mother. Ever since the message from John had arrived she had been excited, almost overwrought, unable to remain still, rushing about as if a great load had been lifted from her mind. As indeed it must have. They had all been worried about him. Father, though, when he heard, had said merely, "Well, that's a mercy," with a satisfied sigh, as if letting out pent-up worry—and then had not referred to the matter again. It was Mother who had insisted word should be sent round at once to Mr. Whitelaw who had called three times in the past week, asking for news—and praising John. John was good, no doubt of it. And his return—perhaps because it was Christmas time—would be like that of the Prodigal Son (although he was anything but that . . .), with the fatted calf appearing as roast goose with all the trimmings. Preparations had been going on all day to make something special of his safe return.

"Lo, children are an heritage of the Lord: and the fruit of the womb is his reward. As arrows are in the hand of a mighty man, so are children of the youth. Happy is the man that hath his quiver full of them . . ."

Oh, but it was cold in here today. He shifted his position, tried to rub his hands together surreptitiously. Ann and Eliza were keeping so still. They were *good* too. Pinching his frozen fingers, he glanced over at the usually restive Walter. Even he was on his best behaviour.

The Squire had been worried for John too—or rather for Mother's sake he had been worried. He had sent a message twice asking if there had been any news. And only yesterday Mother, wringing her hands, had said to Matilda Paley, "Not a word from my son, not a word. I should never have sent him. Never. They'll maybe shoot him. Hungry people—*anything* could happen. And not a word . . ." And then Matilda of course had bleated, sheep's hair trembling, "*Poor* little Sarah! But you still have *two* fine boys *whatever* may have happened. I know nothing has. Although I *did* hear the other day—Mrs. Derrick was saying at the card game, she is quite an authority on these matters—the gales in the Irish sea, they are likely to be *very terrible* . . ."

" 'Lighten our darkness, we beseech thee, O Lord,' " prayed Father. " 'And by thy great mercy defend us from all perils and dangers of this night . . .' " The bell outside clanged, loudly, over and over again. Then the sound of feet scurrying across the hall. Surely Father would stop now, release them all to rush out in welcome? Mother had stood up already, was moving towards the door.

" '. . . we beseech thee with thy favour to behold our most gracious Sovereign Lady, Queen Victoria, that she may alway incline to thy will . . .' "

The door was flung open. Father halted in mid-sentence. The heads of everyone turned round. Mother was there the first. No ceremony: John standing there, leaning against the door post, clutching a bundle wrapped in a plaid rug.

"Look at the lad. Oh, thank God—thank *God* . . ." Mother, beside him, touching him. Then, "John, *what—*?" John was swaying with weariness, the bundle held close to him. Father said crisply, "Get a chair. Some brandy. Brandy for the lad. Quick." Mother, shepherding him to sit down, clung to him anxiously. Ann and Eliza and an excited Walter were beside John now, Walter prodding at his cloak. But it was Ned who stepped forward and removed the bundle from his arms at the same moment as John was handed his brandy.

"Drink up, son. Explanations will wait . . . There—we'd best get you in a warm room—"

The bundle was so light. From the way John had been carrying it, Ned had thought: well, twice the weight. But this was nothing. Folds of shawl peeped out from the loosely wrapped travelling rug. Ned pulled at them. Behind him, Ann and Eliza peered, Eliza coming a little too near, her chin nearly on his shoulder. Dear Lord—*but what was this?*

"Done up," John was saying. "I'm quite done up. And then the journey—"

"But of course we'll see to it," Mother was replying. "You did *right*, son, absolutely right. No need to fret."

Father now: "Right. Right indeed. It was the very least. Any God-fearing man . . . 'I was hungry and you gave me to eat . . . whatsoever you do unto one of these little ones . . .'"

"Oh, heavens, take care, Ned," Eliza said. "Take *care* now." She thrust a finger out hesitantly.

It could not be that it was a child. *It could not be.* His stomach contracted. He could hear the voices going on around him. He wanted to look now—and yet not look. A little cry, the child gave a little cry as he pulled back the shawl. And then, slowly, he took in pale, frightened, lifeless eyes staring out at him from above sunken cheeks. Such an ugly, hairy, little animal.

John was saying, "We must have Mr. Whitelaw at once—this evening. Even though it is Christmas. I have done all *I* can. My best. But, to be sure . . ."

"Just look at it," Eliza said. "Ann, look. Walter—"

Such ugliness. Ned thought only, I don't want to go on looking. And then suddenly, the lips bared.

"Oh, look now, look at that, Eliza," Ann said. "That's a *smile*—"

Ned's heart, skipping a beat, set up a wild thumping. He was afraid and excited at the same time. This precious bundle that no one had thought to take from him. Very gently, he touched with one finger the furry skin.

John said, "Her name is Katharine. I will explain. Later—"

"Of course, son . . ."

"Let us pray," Father said. "'Yea the sparrow hath found a house, and the swallow a nest for herself . . .'"

There was scarcely flesh on the bones. Ned prayed: O Lord, let *me* love her and take care of her.

"We must thank God," Father said. " 'Almighty God, Father of all mercies . . .' "

Ned could not still the rapid wild beating of his heart. Unbelievable, terrifying joy.

" '. . . And the angel said unto them, Fear not: for behold I bring you good tidings of great joy . . . *And suddenly there was with the angel a multitude of the heavenly host praising God, and saying, Hosanna in the Highest . . .'* "

SEVEN

"Poor bairn, the *poor* bairn," everyone said. Meeting Sarah in the town or coming to the house, they said it. Anyone who had heard the news. Mr. Whitelaw, seeing the child that first evening, he said it, shaking his head sadly. "I fear she'll not see the spring." Telling the whole family assembled: "We can but do our best . . ."

And so we did, Sarah thought now—spring already in sight—so we did. All over Christmas and into the New Year, hoping. Mr. Whitelaw had come regularly, sometimes as much as twice a day: but for Kate, not for Sarah. *She* had no time now to feel ill. Long days, short nights—they didn't worry her. Indeed it annoyed her when Sam suggested that care of this little one might be tiring her, might be too much. For she could not tell him (could not even *imagine* telling him), and certainly he would not see for himself, that the child, that little Kate had been *sent* to her from Carrownacally—for her redemption.

It was surely that. How else to explain such a miracle? John's mission: it had been in the hope only that he might bring back even a scrap of news. Instead, this scrap of humanity. And hers—*her* responsibility. All the while that she had feared some sort of punishment, because of Hannah—that she had done no better for Hannah—here instead was, not a punishment at all, but her chance of salvation.

" 'I was hungry and ye gave me meat; I was thirsty and ye gave me drink; I was a stranger, and ye took me in,' " Sam had said that. And he had said it again many times since. But that did not take from its truth. God has spoken to me, she thought, given me work to do. Not an avenging God—but a loving Father . . .

She felt almost too well, too full of energy. She could not stop. She had a battle to fight—and to win. "There's no time to feel badly," she wrote to John, now back in Edinburgh. And indeed if she were to worry about anyone's health it should be *his*. To have gone back to Scotland so soon. She could not believe him fully recovered.

She tried now to forget that in the second week of his Irish trip she had been so worried, so frantic in every way (everything seeming to come together—all wrong, her second state worse than her first. *I should never have sent him*, she had thought), so desperate that she had walked out of the house early one evening, without saying where she was going, and buried two charm bags in the earth just the other side of the Kissing Gate. (Her greatest fear, that she might meet the Reverend Cuthbert.) In one bag she had put some of John's baby curls, just a few strands, so dark and fine, and in the other a button from one of his shirts. Standing there in the half-light, the owl-light, looking at the black outline, feeling the cold iron of the Kissing Gate, she had felt a thrill of fear—and hope. She thought of generations before with their wishes and their charm bags, and their trust. Suddenly the Gate had appeared to her not sinister, but a friend. And, she thought now, John *had* returned safely . . .

They hanged Hannah, early in the year. The day, a bitterly cold one, came and went—Sarah was so busy that she did not think of it till all would have been over. She prayed then for Hannah's soul. But she no longer felt so wicked herself: she was only Sarah Rawson, a sinner like any other. And had she not been sent the means of salvation?

She worried a bit about the lad, though, Hannah's brother. Arthur Greaves. She saw him once or twice in the New Year, and then again in late February, just before the snowdrops. He was wandering about the churchyard. He stared at her, and went on staring. She could not bear that. Like the day she had seen him swinging on the Kissing Gate. She felt badly about him—it was the only matter not sorted out.

She spoke to Sam. "It's our duty," she said. "We've to do something for him. It'd be for the family—and for Hannah. I gave my word." She pleaded: "It'd be best . . ."

But Sam said at once that next spring—in a year at the most—he'd need another apprentice for the ropes. "I don't doubt they're a hard-working family, the Greaves. I'll take the lad on, without he pays indentures. And we'll say no more about it . . ." She had known then, that whatever happened in the middle of the night (and pray God it will *never happen again*), Sam was *good*.

And meanwhile, little Kate lived. By some miracle, another miracle, she even slowly began to thrive. The hours of loving attention—hers, and Ned's, for Ned was brother and sister rolled into one—were beginning to be rewarded. On the tenth of March, Sarah wrote to John:

"You will be pleased to hear that the little one ate today, two fingers

of sand cake, specially baked for her by the Helliwells—and signed for
more! Eliza is to sew her a little red cloak . . ."

Both the girls were keen and eager to help. It was not just Ned. A
common aim, a common challenge, it bound the family wonderfully.
And they were all to be aunts and uncles (they had thought first of
being called "cousin," but at the finish it had not been thought so caring as "aunt" and "uncle"), all that is, except Walter. She had thought
afterwards that perhaps it had been a mistake. Might not the unaccustomed dignity and status of "uncle" have made him behave better? It
seemed to her possible that he was already a little jealous—almost as if
Kate *were* a new little sister, a rival to his position as Benjamin. Twice,
before going back to school at Richmond, he had been caught out in
petty acts. Once, putting his tongue out at Kate (and waggling his
ears), as she lay in the little padded cot they had made her. Another
time (worse, this, Sarah thought) stealing a whipped jelly cream, made
especially for her and standing on the side. But then he had always
been greedy . . .

She longed for the day when the child would speak to *her*. Often
when she was feeding her she thought there was some special response,
but then she would realise that it was no more than an animal's welcome for the hand that feeds it. She spoke a little now. The sounds
were gibberish, mostly. A strange tongue. Irish or Erse as it was called.
It would be that. My da's first language, Sarah thought. She listened
then eagerly for the baby words she had known, the few that he had
taught her. But in the muttered stream, she could not distinguish them.

Once she tried to remember, and to sing in her poor voice, always a
little cracked sounding, the songs he had sung her. But she was not sure
of the melody (although she could *hear* the tune in her head). The
words she could scarcely bring to mind at all. *Her* version was probably
gibberish. Certainly for Kate it seemed to have no meaning. Her eyes
would look blank. (But never again so blank as that first terrible
night . . .)

She had not thought truly, then, that Christmas Eve, that the child
could live. Although if she had survived not only the privations before,
but the terrible journey, might not she be stronger than they thought?
Will she *remember anything*, Sarah would ask herself. Will she remember anything at all of her nightmare journey—more important perhaps, anything of *her life before?*

Kate would have to learn to talk all over again. Be born anew almost
—as a Rawson. Whether she is a Donnelly or not, Sarah told herself,
whether she is any blood relation at all—it is of no consequence. They
would make her one of them. Soon, very soon, all the terrible past

would be wiped out. She would be Kate *Rawson*, through and through and through.

But if she, Sarah, loved and worried about the child, it was as nothing beside the love and care lavished on her by Ned. Sarah was astonished, and touched too—for he was an odd lad, had always been odd, but this exceeded everything in loving-kindness and dedication . . . (Although she supposed that anyone so ready to spend his spare time with an outcast up on the moors would be as capable, more so, of devoting himself to a child.) Every evening straight from work he would rush to see Kate. Whenever he was free he would sit with her: she was meant to eat a lot of rich food even when she had no appetite for it, and he would take on the task of tempting her. He made toys for her too at the works. The thinnest of ropes twisted into patterns and shapes and loops, a rope dolly ("and later when you're able, I'll make the best, most bonny skipping rope ever . . ."). Her little clawlike fingers pulling, grasping at his toys would suddenly go limp.

Sarah had said to him once, "You've not played your flute awhile—"

"I've been busy with her," he said, "the little one. And the practising, the noise, it might disturb her."

Sarah said, "Had you tried?"

"What's that—disturbing her?"

"No. *Nay*—you daft one. Letting her hear it, I mean. Maybe she'll like it . . ."

And she had. It was astonishing how she liked it. No smiles at first, no movement, just her eyes. No longer lifeless, they gazed at Ned all the while. Then when he stopped, she asked for more—or rather, it was her hands which asked for more. Then a day or two later she made a cry, a word perhaps, which would pass almost for the sound of a flute. Another time when he stopped, her protests, her pleading, amounted nearly to a tantrum so that Sarah, watching, had grown afraid. One night when Kate would not settle to sleep but kept crying out, she sent downstairs for Ned. Soon, it became a habit: her flute lullaby. "Golden slumbers kiss your eyes. Smiles awake you when you rise. Sleep, pretty baby, do not cry . . ."

Kate began to grow wonderfully, month by month. She did not so much grow as flower. And now that spring had come, Sarah realised that the battle had been won. Not only would she live but, given more time, would become an ordinary child (No, never ordinary. Ned had not liked it at all when she had used that word). And by Easter when John came home, the miracle (and what else was it?) would be almost complete.

The town had shown great interest, and from farther afield, Frederick

Watson had called twice to enquire after her progress. The Reverend Cuthbert came regularly, and had asked in church for special prayers the first three Sundays. There were polite, concerned enquiries at whist-evenings, suppers, at any gathering of the Downham ladies; after Sunday service and Evensong. Mr. Whitelaw was often asked about "that poor little Irish bairn . . ."

One unusually warm day in late March, Sarah and the girls took her out in a little cart up by the Castle, then back up through the town towards the Abbey. They were seen by Georgiana Ingham, Charles's wife, who stopped her carriage and stepped out to speak to them. She was as finely dressed as ever. With her she had her eldest, Richard, who was in a velvet suit of a rather lurid green. He had ringlets and a small pale, frightened face. Mrs. Ingham was lively and gracious. Sarah decided to be subdued and respectful, although she said to herself, "Even for someone supposed to come from such a fine family, she gives herself great airs . . ."

"Oh, but let me see," said Mrs. Ingham, "pray do. Is this *she?* Oh, but the dear little—" Then, "She is quite human," she added with surprise. Sarah bridled then, but said nothing. She used looks only, but did not hope that they were noticed.

"See, Richard," Mrs. Ingham said to the little boy, pulling at his hand, turning to make sure he was still there, so half-hearted was his hold on her. "Here's the little Irish thing I told you of—from the place where all the potatoes died." She turned to Sarah: "He stammers, stutters horribly. They are of an age, the two children? I hear she cannot say much as yet—no doubt the fright of it all has tied her tongue." She said to Richard, almost severely, "You see, you are not alone?"

He looked away from his mother, but a moment later, lifting his head, he caught Sarah's gaze. She would have thought him a poor thing —if it had not been for his eyes. He turned on her the old Squire's eyes, in a child's face (that particular shade of blue, that she had never seen on anyone since). Just as she remembered them that long ago afternoon, when he had told her she was to go to school: playing with the musical box, being shown round the painted dining room.

And indeed within only a few days of that meeting, she was sent for up to the Abbey, to take Kate to meet the Squire. He had sent delicacies for her in the early days, but had not yet spoken to her.

He lifted her high, and dandled her. "Little bundle of feathers, little bird," he said. Then, "Smile for me." But she would not. He asked Sarah about the boys: "You should be proud of John. You are, eh? We lost a fine lad, when we lost George. Charles, he's not—" But he must have thought better of it, for he did not finish the sentence but said instead: "Seen little Julia, have you? Plump little puppy—it's good to have grandchildren. And your turn next, eh? Any news of courting?"

She was always just a little bit afraid, a little bit on her best behaviour. How could she ever be quite at her ease? But proud too. I am the Squire's friend.

The eyes were quite faded now. She noticed it for the first time. The grizzled hair sparse. His hands had a fine tremor too. She saw it when he brought out for Kate the barrel organ.

"I think we have here an Irish tune still. Sarah, you turn the handle. 'Paddy Carey,' what about that, eh?"

But Kate had not liked the music. It may have been the pitch, or the rhythm, but whatever—she had whimpered and closed her eyes.

Sarah said, "She's tired maybe. It's an odd thing. Now, Ned's flute, that he plays to her each night—she loves that—"

The Squire said, stroking the child gently, "It'll just be that she prefers a lively young lad serenading her. Here, you see an old man . . ."

Ned had to visit Grandfather. He did not love Old Jacob, and privately wondered who could—also, although it was his duty to go he would so much rather, so *very much* rather have passed the afternoon with Kate. Only yesterday evening he had been certain she understood at least *some* of what he sang to her:

> "When I was a little lass,
> About six year old,
> I hadn't got a petticoat,
> To keep me from the cold,
> So I went into Downham,
> That bonny little town,
> And there I bought a petticoat,
> A cloak, and a gown . . ."

So it was in a bad mood that he crossed the market square towards Almeida House. It was a very cold day, with a biting east wind. Then as he neared the house, he thought again what a fine place it was: Grandfather had done well for himself. He had to admit that.

And how much Grandfather enjoyed the power it gave him—promising to bequeath it, according to how he felt that day, to different members of the family (so long as they were not women). Only last autumn Ned had heard *he* should have it, except that Walter, departing for school, had been very cock-a-hoop: "In the case you've not heard, I'm to inherit—" It was impossible to take seriously, and yet for a moment Ned had thought: Becky shall come to live with me. I shall give her apartments quite of her own, comfortable, warm. She need not see anyone unless she wants it (Charles, coming to mock, would not have access: he would tell the servants, "Young Mr. Ingham is not to be admitted").

The gates, always kept closed, were very stiff to open. Then you had to walk up the drive and right round to the left, where the front door was hidden. It seemed somehow typical of Grandfather that his front door should not face the square like anyone else's, but instead face directly a blank wall . . . With resignation Ned pulled the bellrope.

Old Jacob lived simply, with only two servants, and a daughter Minnie to keep house for him. Sitting in most of the day, seldom going out, he behaved always as if enjoying a well-earned rest. He seemed moderately proud of his sons and grandsons, but daughters he had not thought very important. This feeling had communicated itself to his own three, so that the two who had married (one going as far afield as Chester, another to Richmond) had found men who thought as little of them as had their father. No alteration in their view of themselves had been necessary. After the death of her mother in 1824, Minnie, unmarried, had settled down to be his housekeeper. Her mother, Jacob's wife, had been pale and pretty in a quiet apologetic manner. If she had had anything to say, no one could now remember hearing it.

Aunt Minnie came now into the hall to greet Ned, her eyes popping with apprehension. She moved in her daily life from agitation to agitation. Fear and the extreme desire to please warred in her. Ned, seeing her, recognised the high-cheeked anxiety: she seemed to have forgotten to blink, her mouth slightly open. One hand grasped Ned's arm, the other, fingers up, was before her mouth.

A voice bellowed from the door on the right: "What's up, eh? *Who's that?*"

She said in a loud whisper, "He has no idea of your coming, Ned. I've forgot to tell him." She added: "He would sleep. When it came to my mind—too late."

"*Who's there?*"

Ned walked reluctantly into the room. Old Jacob sat the winter through (and much of the summer) in an enormous hooded chair facing directly the roaring wood fire. Those who wished to talk with him had to take up a position to one side—a very uncomfortable one usually, so near was he to the fire.

Ned appeared now round the side of the chair. "It's Ned." He said it again louder. "It's *Ned.*"

Staring at the fire all day had not improved Old Jacob's sight. Together with his hearing it had been failing for some time now. (Of the five senses only touch seemed still keen. On his rare visits to the works —"They'll be no concern of mine these days"—he would run his bony fingers over the rope, the hemp, the bales of cotton waste, the twine, rubbing, sniffing, searching . . .)

"Aye, well, Ned—I never sent for ye." He turned back to the fire. A strong smell clung to his clothes. His jacket front was foxy coloured with spilt snuff. Suddenly he bawled: "Minnie! Where's t'wine and cake? Lazy skivvy," he went on, to himself, "I'll not have it. Lazy she were from day she were born." He reached for the handbell on the table near him and rang it with such violence that Ned jumped. "Ring kitchen bell, lass, and let's be having t'wine and cake." He muttered: "Now I've to pay dogs, and bark myself . . ."

There was nowhere for Ned to sit. Any seat placed in Grandfather's sight would be too hot. In any case attempts to sit down were usually greeted with, "What's wrong wi' legs today? What's in 'em, eh? *Cotton*, is it?"

The wine and cake came. Aunt Minnie took a tray from a trembling servant. She had now the right to cross the room and come nearer— even to sit down: behind him (since she was of such little consequence, she was not expected to have legs stuffed with anything substantial).

Old Jacob had a wiry frame, reared as he had been on oatmeal and milk, raw bacon, good cheese—and on his own, beer was still his only drink. Porridge and oatcakes and fine local ham were, he swore, the only dishes that stuck to a man. But once he had learned that the gentry offered wine and cake to afternoon callers—well . . .

He held his glass now in a not too steady hand and drank the wine as though it were beer. "Ye can fill it up now, lass," he commanded, thrusting it behind him at Aunt Minnie. "And cake—I'll tak some o' that." The plate rocked dangerously on his knees. "Eh, bring table round, lad!"

Where Ned stood the heat from the fire grew more and more intense. His nose throbbed, helped by the wine, his eyes watered from the smoke. Fortunately he did not have to listen too closely—most of Grandfather's monologues he had heard before.

". . . I reckon to put summat in 'osses—there's brass there right enow. I might tak t'Gold Cup at that. Nay, I'll not. Too easy like. Any road—" Alcohol (he was on his third glass now) had flushed his features. "I'm as good as Inghams. What's he, then? Old un, young un— *and* old un afore that—never done a day's work in their lives. And them fancy plannytations—they couldn't keep 'em. T'black lad. Darkie. They couldn't keep him neither. That were a sorry tale an' all. I don't say owt o'that afore womenfolk. But I reckon now if he'd not been bad treated, he'd not have run off like—that way there'd of been no lass friending him—and at t'finish no mother to that Becky . . . Becky they called her eh? eh?" He turned to Ned as if memory jogged something. Then he laughed, "*There's* a tale! There's them as *knows what they know*, but don't say owt—" He stopped suddenly. "What's this fancy food, eh? Rubbish it is, rubbish." He brushed the remains of the cake irritably from his knees. "That's Ned there, then, is it? Eh? Not that John? Why doesn't that fool Ned fill my glass, eh?"

Aunt Minnie, her cake untouched, was nervously clasping and unclasping her hands. Ned looked at the clock. Round and friendly, known from childhood, it said half past four. He would be allowed away at five.

"Does that daft embroidery all day, Minnie does. Gert fool for a daughter. Backs of chairs, lumps of cottons, aye, sticking into us—I don't doubt she leaves pins in it. Won't read to me neither . . ." The voice grumbling, went on: "And when she do, I can't hear owt. I'll have that *Ned* read paper. Fetch one here then—get moving!"

Ned took a Wensleydale *Advertiser* from a pile near the fireplace. It was yellowing and well thumbed. The date was over a year before. He read out at random an account of a trial at the local assizes for sheep stealing. Grandfather continued talking throughout, but whenever Ned paused it would be: "Get on then, lad—can't read, eh? Now he can't *read* . . ."

Ned found next an item about a chimney sweep—one of the gang of sweeps and their boys who lived in Downham Castle ruins. The sweep hadn't wanted to pay the penny toll for crossing the new bridge between Downham and Leyburn, so had put his boy in a sack and carried him over. At once Ned imagined how it must have been in the coal-dusty darkness, bumping against the rough sacking. Although no worse surely than their terrible lives up people's chimneys? Skin scraped raw, always in danger of suffocation or—worst of all—a fire lit beneath them. And yet—this surprised him—glimpsed in the Castle grounds, brass plates on the front of their caps proclaiming their ownership, they *seemed* a merry enough bunch . . .

He had finished the paragraph. Hastily he began to look for something else.

"*Speak up*, lad, eh—I can't hear owt. He's here for t'wine, Ned is. They're all t'same. All on 'em. All after brass . . . I heard Squire's sent to see that *new* one o' Sarah's. It'll be brass she wants there. She's not fetching her *here*. T'bairn's nowt but a murphy—I hear it's fit to put in a circus." He raised his voice: "There's no brass to come for Popish bairns. Ned—is it, there? Sarah?" He grumbled, "Paddywhacks, I've seen 'em. Drink it all away they do. Haytime. I've seen 'em. *Paddy-whacks.*"

It was over at last. The clock had struck. Grandfather, still talking to himself, had reached for his snuff box.

"I'm going now, Grandfather." Let him try to stop me, he thought. Just time to kiss Aunt Minnie goodbye—she patted his hand agitatedly ("He's so *difficult*, Ned dear . . ."), and then hurying down the drive and into the square.

He could hardly bear to wait till he should be back at the house—and Kate.

EIGHT

And then I chanced upon a goodly town
    . . . And there was I disarm'd
By maidens each as fair as any flower:
But when they led me into hall, behold
The Princess of that castle was the one,
Brother, and that one only, who had ever
Made my heart leap . . .

TENNYSON, *The Holy Grail*

Mrs. Dowell brought John up some water unasked. Coming into his room without knocking: "I ken fine ye're going oot," she said. "When are ye in?"

John thought that she must have heard him tell Dugald that he was away to Drummond Place. He was invited for this evening, to meet the Dunbars, of whom Robbie had already told him so much. (It appeared they were much more well to do than the Buchanans. "They have a fine house in Blacket Place—there are wide gates at the end of the road, shut at night as if it were a park . . .") He had to tell Mrs. Dowell now that he would be in late.

She looked at him belligerently: "There's been noise already the day, Mr. Rawson—was that you? And puir wee Jeannie needing her rest. That canna sleep nights—" She set the water jug down with a clatter. "I warn ye—if ye're late back and I so much as hear ye tak a breath— ye're for oot . . ."

When an hour later he set out in the January darkness, it was with more than half a wish to stay indoors. The weather was cold enough for snow, and he never relished the streets of the Old Town after sunset: not liking to pass the openings to the small alleys—or closes as they were called—and especially the one where the murderers Burke and Hare had actually lain in wait for their victims. As a medical student, he found it particularly hard to dismiss them from his mind, for it was not so very long ago since the shortage of bodies for dissection had been the mainspring of that grisly trade: the robbing of fresh graves to sell to anatomists. Although to be a "Resurrectionist" was both a skilled and for a time an honest enough trade, two men here in Edinburgh had thought to bypass the whole fraught business of marking graves and robbing at full speed (while evading both churchyard guardians and other robbers) by quite simply producing their own corpses. Waylaying the unwary, luring them back to their house, filling them up with drink, and then smothering them . . .

In fact it had been to John Goodsir's predecessor, Robert Knox, that the two men, Burke and Hare, sold their victims' bodies (when the crimes came to light, Knox, who'd bought in good faith, was unfortunate enough to have had one in his room. It had not been good for his career). After Burke had been hanged his body had lain in state at the College of Surgeons ("Burke him!" the crowd had shouted—as now, he and his friends shouted at Tammie . . .), and two students had stolen some skin from the neck and right arm, and had had made a pocket book from it: brown, with the mark of the rope quite clear on it . . .

He was passing now just near where Ellie lived. He would have liked to go in. For tonight, he felt more like old acquaintance than new: he was not over Ireland yet. A weakness of the nerves still, as if any too great effort exhausted him. He had not told Robbie, or indeed anyone in Edinburgh, of his Irish visit. Later perhaps. But for now he was glad. He could not have borne that tonight he should be the centre of questioning.

It was Kirsty he saw first, coming across the room to welcome him. Her eager little face, hands open in welcome. The room seemed full of strangers. Suddenly shy, he saw them as if through a mist.

But now it was Robbie, a friendly hand on his shoulder. Then his host and hostess. Mrs. Buchanan, plump and motherly, and Mr. Buchanan of the bushy eyebrows, raised at this moment in greeting: "We had thought the cold weather might keep you indoors, sir . . ."

John was not looking his best. He felt certain of it. His cravat clumsily tied, the spot on his jacket which rubbing with cold water had only made worse. But gradually he was being put at his ease. And the strangers: perhaps it was not so bad, since he might meet them one by one.

There was an elderly aunt from England. She was very deaf—Robbie leaned close to shout the introduction. What did John think of the Scotch? she boomed at him. Instead of an ear trumpet, she wore "Wellington Ears" under her cap. Of silver papier mâché, with ribbons attached, they gave her the air of an uncertain spaniel. She did not hear his answer.

Then next, the Dunbars. First the father, whom Robbie had confessed to disliking. Burly, confident, with a forbidding cast to his mouth, he summed John up quickly and, presumably not finding him a useful acquaintance, rapidly dismissed him. His wife, on the other hand —angular, gauntly dark, her ringlets drooping despondently as she spoke —attached herself at once.

Her voice came out high and plaintive: "And how are you arrived here, Mr. Rawson? How do you come up North? Not the Coach these days, I fear. The steamer—I hope, Mr. Rawson, you did not come by *rail?*"

"Mama. Please—"

The daughter, of course. Kirsty's friend: Catriona. He could not believe his eyes. Absolutely he could not.

He was introduced. She gave her hand. But he could not look. Yet nor could he look anywhere else. Her presence, suddenly, had filled the room.

He fell over his words. "Miss Dunbar, I—" Catriona, he thought. Katharine. The same name. His dream in Ireland when he had christened Kate. It was an omen.

That brash man, that whining woman. To think that this was their daughter. So alive: it was as if she were all colour. Against the pale yellow velvet of her chair, the darkly exciting profusion of her black hair. Her vivid colouring. And all I can do, he thought, is behave awkwardly . . .

He noticed then the man beside her. Alan Dunbar; he introduced himself. He, too, John disliked. He supposed him to be one of her brothers. Straw-coloured hair receded from an enormous forehead. The face was assured with thick lips. He wore an Albert cravat, the satin rich and heavy (no agonising for him before a fly-blown glass). Catriona, highlighting some remark, touched his coat sleeve—what intimacy, who would not be a brother? her face turned towards him. And all *he* had to say was, "You have it wrong again, Pussy . . ."

Now, addressing John: "And you are to be a sawbones too?" he asked, carelessly.

"I hope so—"

"I was but just talking to Robbie about my experiences with a surgeon up in the Western Highlands. He kept a golden eagle, and the sight of it having a meal was sufficient usually to cure any disease one might have called with. The worst was a cat. *There* you would have seen dissection. Poor puss paralysed with fear and then crushed in those talons. Old Grant said to me as the entrails came out, 'He swallows those as a Neapolitan swallows spaghetti . . .'"

Catriona interrupted, "Mr. Rawson can never wish to hear such a tale, Alan. Really—"

John ventured: "I trust your brother doesn't allow *you* to see any such sights, Miss Dunbar."

"My brother?" She looked puzzled. "My brothers are neither of them in Scotland, Mr. Rawson." Then, "Oh," she said, "you think Alan and I brother and sister? But we are—"

"Cousins," Alan said. "Second cousins. You see, she would like to be first in my heart, but must be content to be only second." He turned. "Is not that so, Pussy?"

John thought, if I could merely sit and look at (and listen to) her. But if he gazed for more than a second or two, he would feel a blush begin (he could not be the same person who was so bold—so at home both outside and inside Ellie . . .). His eyes might rest only lightly on her bodice, with its tight V and its hundreds of little tucks; her silky flounced skirt with its pattern of autumn leaves (only someone so vivid could look well in that muted brown—poor Ann or Eliza, he thought, would look like little hens . . .).

Wee Bruce, the youngest Buchanan, hovered now round the edge of the company, Kirsty holding his hand. Mr. Buchanan was saying to John: "You are fortunate in your professor—Goodsir is more than good, sir. He is excellent . . . It was Monroe Tertius I had a small acquaintance with—and Barclay before that. They still speak of Barclay?"

"Indeed, sir. There is some of his dissection in the Museum. A hand—"

"Barclay, poor Barclay. In my youth, you know, they said here that the very dogs of Edinburgh avoided him—for fear he should dissect them . . ."

Bruce, pulling loose from Kirsty, tugged at John: "When they cut bodies up now does a lot of *blood* come out?" Kirsty told him fondly not to be foolish. But he persisted: "Is it *black*, the blood? And the bodies—are they always fresh now? I had this pet squirrel once and when he was buried I wished to disin—disinter him to show my friend how big his tail had been, but when I undid the box—ugh! Och, it was like the drains at my auntie's—"

"Bruce now—we haven't to be speaking of *drains*." A sugar plum was put in his mouth by an indulgent sister. Then she turned back to John, her anxious little face asking him all about his news. He had said before Christmas, had he not, that his mother was not well . . .

The tea tray was brought in. There was black or green tea. "What like is the black?" asked Mrs. Dunbar, and on hearing that it was Pouchong: "Och, I dote on that—so stimulating, so restful." John drank green tea because Catriona chose it.

"I had meant that for the men," Mrs. Buchanan said. "It is young Hyson, Catriona dear. Dalrymple's tell me it is fully the equal of Gunpowder."

Bruce was pestering his father: "Papa, Papa, can you ever guess—why is a postage stamp like a naughty boy? Guess!" And then: "Because he is licked, and put in the corner to make him stick to his letters . . ."

Exit Bruce.

During supper, an hour or two later, she smiled at him. He could do nothing then but curse the blood which rushed to his face: because certainly she would notice it—and dismiss him for the gauche fellow that he was.

The meal was delicious. He discovered that it was possible to watch Catriona, hopelessly—and to be hungry. She was a lively eater, speaking often when she should be feeding: her laden fork arrested halfway to her mouth. They ate a meat pie of raised pastry, and later there were jellies in varied colours made from the juice of fresh China oranges, which they ate together with some whip syllabubs that Catriona said were particularly from Scotland.

During the meal, Alan (the cursed Alan—for *he* was near her too) said to him, in the same insolent tone: "You are apprenticed, I take it?"

"Yes."

"To whom, then?"

"A surgeon in Yorkshire. A Scotchman. In the small town where I live—"

"And where is that?"

Catriona protested. "But Alan—why question Mr. Rawson so?" (How he loved her defending him . . .) She turned to John: "Alan will only know where this town is if it is near a race course—"

"*Touché* then," said her cousin.

"Is racing a great interest?" John asked. "Are you often fortunate? I never—"

"Frequently. Would I do it otherwise?"

Catriona said, "He knows fine he can do no other. Nag, nag, *nags* are the thing . . . But you were not so fortunate, Alan, with that very famous race—at Doncaster."

Mr. Dunbar, who had just joined them, added bluntly, "You didn't take good care of your money, sir. You failed to spot Sir Tatton Sykes. Only a fool would have backed Sweet Eringobragh—"

Alan said lightly, "But I stood to gain. Thirty to one. He ran shocking bad—I think drowsy syrups may have been to blame."

"Drowsy *stirrups*, more like." Although he joked, Mr. Dunbar's manner was still grim. They had been joined now by Robbie and Mr. Buchanan. The conversation became more serious. They spoke of the unrest in Europe. "We cannot but feel it here . . ." Of France. Then of troubles nearer home. "Industrial unrest—so confounded contagious . . ."

"Och, politics," said Catriona, pulling a face.

"Join your mother, then, as you should," said her father. He had chosen a bad moment, for Mrs. Dunbar was just then coming towards them. Her husband took no notice of her. Mr. Buchanan was saying, "The British Lion has been using his claws pretty effectually against the Kaffirs. I read . . ."

A servant coming into the room crossed over to Mr. Dunbar: "A Mr. Wilkie is here, sir—he needs to see you urgent." Mr. Dunbar got up immediately, not stopping even to make his excuses. Catriona said, "Och, that is his business face." Her mother was wagging a finger after her husband. "That Mr. Wilkie—" Then as if recollecting herself, she said to John: "My father is accountant for this railway company that's to build in the West—just where Alan's family have a house. But it is such an affair. Sometimes, you know, they must pay perhaps a hundred thousand pounds for private property that is worth five pounds because to go around it would cost more—and then there are hills too steep, and tunnels that fall in . . ."

But she had caught her mother's attention: "Catriona, to talk of railways! How I detest the horrid things—if only we might *fly* to our destinations and be done with all the noise and danger. Only the other day I heard of the most horrible—a poor lass took her canary in its little cage on the railways, and when she had alighted and been gone some yards what did she remember but that she had forgotten her songbird, so she went back, you know, and hurriedly opened the carriage door, but as she began to climb the train moved and she caught her leg and was trapped completely. I shudder to tell the tale—and then when she lay dying, 'Oh, little canary,' she said, 'you have cost me my life . . .' It was *very* affecting—"

Mrs. Buchanan, coming over just then, said cheerfully: "All this talk about canaries. Could we not have a song just now?"

Kirsty was first. Her voice was small and true. She sang "Meet Me in the Willow Glen" and "I'll Not Throw Away the Flower." When they had all clapped, John complimented her, saying, "That was really excellent," and she coloured prettily and bit her lip.

Alan sang next, a humorous duet with Mr. Buchanan, full of gesticulations and grimaces and obviously familiar to the audience, who applauded him loudly. Even the Wellington-eared aunt seemed to enjoy it.

"And now Catriona must sing," Alan declared. She protested: "But I sing quite horribly—" She was persuaded, though. And the sounds *were* horrible. She sang first *"Voi che sapete"*—trying and failing to hit the high notes, trilling unconcernedly. It did not seem to worry her. "Encore," somebody called, and she went at once into "Home Sweet Home."

Oh, God, she was beautiful. He thought if even for a moment anyone were to laugh at her singing. But she was among friends—even that dreadful cousin didn't mock at the end.

He was very late back at his lodgings. Tammie, lying in wait at the foot of the stairs, leaped up at him, giving a little cry. Almost at once Mrs. Dowell appeared at the stair head: enormous in her night attire, nightcap almost down to her eyes. She thrust the candlestick forward as if to strike him with it.

"Waking honest folk agin ; . ." She saw the monkey. "And puir wee Tammie—did they wake *ye* the noo?"

John thought, I am a person obsessed. In the days that followed, Catriona's image seemed to have taken him over utterly—vividly. The walls of his room, bare, even sometimes running with damp, were covered now with moving pictures. Just one face. Dancing black ringlets, red lips—it was her mouth he saw most clearly. Catriona. Pussy. He would let himself imagine some time in the future, some miracle, which would allow him to call her that . . . Even in the dissecting room (the cadaver an aged man, ossified with arthritis), even there she danced—appearing unheralded, only to disappear as she had come. "I can summon spirits from the vasty deep," he thought, back on a schoolroom bench. He was a man haunted. And Ellie did nothing to assuage this—she brought him only shame now.

But the real Catriona Dunbar—how to see her again? He could not bring himself to confide in Robbie. (And yet the one person he could have done never to see—Alan Dunbar—he had glimpsed already three times. Once when he was with Dugald in a tavern, another when he

was with Robbie so that he had had to go over and exchange pleasantries, then again in a wine shop . . .)

Then one day towards the end of that week, Robbie—walking the
wards at the Royal Infirmary and not met with so often now—asked
John would he take a message for him to Drummond Place? "If you are
free, that is, and would be so good."

He had another errand near Holyrood. About half past three he came
down from the Old Town and into the broad expanse of Princes Street.
On his left the Gardens, deserted in the January afternoon. Past the
new monument to Sir Walter Scott—all pilasters and little balconies
and twisted turrets—and then across to where the shops were and some,
not many, private houses. He was propelled forward almost by the
crowd. It was the time for people to be abroad.

Looking ahead of him he saw, framed black against the afternoon
sky, the Castle. The sun hung above it, an orange circle. Feathery
clouds trailed across. Arrested by the beauty, he stood still a moment,
allowing himself to be jostled. A voice said, "Why, Mr. Rawson—it is
Mr. Rawson? You are in a dream, sir!" He turned from one vision of
beauty to another, his mouth opening in shock. She was with her
mother. "And what is—where are you off to, Mr. Rawson?" Archly almost.

"I go to the Buchanans."

"Then pray remember me to *Miss* Buchanan and tell her I have the
blue ribbons—this very afternoon."

"Catriona!" said her mother. "Mr. Rawson is not your messenger
boy."

"It will give me great pleasure, Miss Dunbar." He could not look at
her properly and yet was unable to keep his gaze away. The result was
shifty-eyed. He stared instead at her hands, tucked neatly into a velvet
muff.

"Edinburgh," Catriona said now, "are you grown attached to our
city?" When, uninspired, he answered "Yes," she continued: "And like
everyone else these days, you have some comment to make on our monument to Sir Walter?"

"Only—I have no head for heights."

She laughed prettily, showing large fine white teeth. He said: "I have
just been admiring Princes Street. The finest—one of the finest in
Europe—"

"And which is *your* favourite? Which have *you* found the finest?"

"I have never travelled." Shameful admission. Dublin did not really
count. He spoke awkwardly—he had turned to wood. He saw her smile
and then suppress it. He felt as if she had hit him.

"Those hateful railways—better not travel!" exclaimed Mrs. Dunbar. "Here too, you know, they go right through the Gardens now. There is no staying them. Of course it was allowed only on the condition an embankment was built high, so that those living on Princes Street need not see from their drawing-rooms. Very fine indeed! Especially as we are still to have the noxious fumes, to say nothing of the danger . . ." Her voice had risen.

He had not dared to look at Catriona during this outburst. But now he saw that she was thoroughly impatient. Mrs. Dunbar, recalling herself suddenly, said: "Catriona—we must away."

He said quickly, inspired, "How far do you go? Perhaps I can escort you—I am in no hurry."

"The carriage picks us up at Mitchell and Heriot's, Mr. Rawson. My daughter has an appointment for a dress."

But it was so beautiful, the dress she wore now—and the bonnet, how was it that he had not noticed her bonnet? Green velvet, lace-trimmed, cherry-coloured lining against her dark hair, her face becomingly bright with the cold. And those eyes—might they dance yet again on his wall tonight . . .

The journey was not a happy one. Mrs. Dunbar spoke all the way as if he were not there. Her voice running on: "I hope, indeed I do, I hope you suit the dress, Catriona. You would have your way with it, I never knew a girl so wilful . . ." Her voice was petulant. Her head was turned towards her daughter. John, having her on his right, could not see Catriona. "And och, while you are in Mitchell and Heriot's, Catriona, it is important with a gentleman such as Mr. Mackenzie—the *Honourable Iain*—it is important that your dress be smart but not, och, what shall I say? Shall not give ideas. Your manner is already impudent . . ."

It was clear to him that Catriona was to impress someone influential if not rich. A possible match? Certainly it was not he who was to be impressed. He was invisible—furniture, footboy. And yet, when they reached the shop in George Street, Catriona thanked him so prettily that it was worth all the feelings of humiliation.

". . . And my message to Miss Buchanan. I trust you."

But then as head down he made for Queen Street: the dull thud of realisation. Even if, unlikely event, she were ever to encourage him, his suit would not be welcome. He was of no account. And how anyway would he set about it? Somehow even this afternoon he had done it all wrong. He did not know how to conduct himself in these matters—it was as simple as that. *Ellie* was no help—perhaps even a hindrance. No, the truth was that nothing in his life—not all the secret knowledge of pills and potions and, lately, of bones and blood and muscle, had been any preparation. Not even the secrets of women's insides (those once mysterious regions, moon-directed, caves in which could flourish healthy plants or great choking weeds), not even those could help him . . .

In three months it would be April. And then? No doubt, he said to himself, no doubt but that I should put all idea of wooing her out of my head. The whole useless obsession, excised. Clean, swift surgery. He hurried himself on with the notion: today, tonight, tomorrow? But like all surgery, he reminded himself, a dirty, dangerous business . . . Might not, would not, the wound suppurate?

NINE

10th January 1847

Dear Journal,

At last! I have intended for *so long* to write in you. Ever since I became seventeen in August and received you as a handsome present from Aunt Charlotte. Now I have begun, I shall write in you *regularly!*

Well—here I am, *Catriona Dunbar*. And what shall I say about myself? (I write only for my own eyes—I should not like *anyone* at all to see this and to that end I shall keep you in my little rosewood box to which only I have the key!) And why do I propose writing what I already know so well? *Because*, dear Journal, if I write all this then perhaps (*perhaps!*) in ten years' time it will be like reading what someone else has to say about me—

I am of more than medium height and of more than medium beauty (this I *have been told*, although I have been told also that I should *not* have been told, because all is vanity—Vanitas Vanitatum—but without doubt to be tolerable looking and perhaps rather a beauty *is* a help!). I should perhaps paint my own portrait? For that one must sit in front of the glass and keep glancing—

Here I am, seated at the glass! I have a deal of very dark (almost, yes, black, *raven!*) hair and my eyes are blue. In spite of that a visitor said once, "One might almost fancy she has Spanish blood in her!" But I have seen many Scotch girls like myself. My looks are not *out of the ordinary*. I have a rather large nose except that it is not coarse at all but fine, a *little* hooked perhaps and (this is the first time I have noticed it!) not exactly the same both sides—I am having difficulty keeping my mouth still in order to write this—if I press it hard together then naturally it is still but it is no longer *my* mouth. At any rate I have a moderately wide, moderately large mouth and I would rather smile than appear vexed, but alas I am only too often put out! I am *very* easily made cross, dear Journal (and anyone who had Mama for their mother might be just the same and that is for certain!), so some days I am *not* a very pleasant person—BUT *I would like to be good.*

Now for an account of Catriona Dunbar's early life. She was born on the 27th of August 1829 in Edinburgh. She is the youngest of only three children. She had already two brothers, James and Ewart. At first she liked Jamie the best but he left for Canada when she was twelve. Ewart is a soldier—he enlisted only nine months ago. She misses him a great deal too (I fancy, dear Journal, he enlisted mainly to escape Papa?).

Catriona was educated at home and then at Miss Fraser's Academy, where she learned a little Latin but no Greek. She plays two instruments—the pianoforte and the harp. She draws and water-colours tolerably, and sings atrociously—the family have never told her so but *she* can hear!! She lives at home where she is waiting until a suitable marriage is arranged—at least that is what is *thought* (and certainly Mama has already made *her* decision in that matter!). But *she* knows that she is waiting for the Beloved to appear, her Hero, whom she has not yet met (but she will know Him when she does. *Certainly* she will!). Then she will live happily ever after. But I *have* to say, dear Journal, that occasionally I do think, so dreary is it with Mama—and the waiting may be so long—that I may yet weaken, and settle for what is felt to be the *right* person (my Hero may not be "right" at all!). Dear Journal, away with such thoughts! I *must be strong.*

To return—this is the manner in which Catriona spends her days. At eight she rises. Breakfast with Mama and Papa. Papa is always down first. He reads the newspaper and eats porridge with salt only and a little cream, a cup of tea, two coddled eggs, and three slices of toast and butter. Mama and I eat only porridge and toast, but sometimes marmalade also. I drink (correction, *she* drinks!) chocolate of which her Mama disapproves (I shall end the pretence. It is easier to write in the first person and will be *just* as interesting to read henceforth).

Papa opens his post after first laying aside his spectacles and then replacing them. Mama all the while has been talking. He pays no heed. Papa receives a great deal of post but tells us nothing of the contents. In the morning after I have read from the Scriptures (I am meant really to do this *before* breakfast!) either I go out with Mama or sometimes Aunt Charlotte (who is much, much nicer, dear Journal!) to the shops in Princes Street or George Street, or else I draw, study French, do needlework, write letters, or play my harp. And then we eat, and afterwards I must rest (why should I rest when I have *done* nothing?

Rest is the reward of labour, we are taught). And yet often I feel very fatigued then. It is only the thought of the *evening's* possibilities that enlivens me (and I am to be truthful often very late abed!). Now see— it is almost *half past eleven!* I shall leave you, dear Journal, for tonight and continue tomorrow evening exactly where I left off—

11th January 1847

Today I saw a *terrible* sight! Awful. (Awful = awefull.) I was with Aunt Charlotte and we had just come out from Kennington and Jenner's when a brougham came right across and up the wrong side of Princes Street directly into the traffic. Aunt Charlotte and I and others we stepped back at once into Jenner's doorway. I heard myself scream, I thought the horse was coming directly for us. The driver was pulling on the reins—I fancy perhaps the runaway horse was mad, he foamed. I saw him so near—and then I was no longer frightened for me but rather for an old man who was on the edge of the pavement. He had put his hands up. And then suddenly *everything* seemed to go UP—I was afraid to look but I *made myself* (I had to, I am not certain why)—Aunt Charlotte had tight hold of me (how glad I am it was not Mama with me! She would have had the vapours and been quite prostrate for days!). The sight is with me still. The horse was mad with fright. His nostrils dilated, and those great hooves. He reared up so *high*—and it seemed all a confusion of reins and hooves and legs and screams and whinnying. The old man was down by then—and the BLOOD. I was so afraid, dear Journal. I have never seen blood before except for a cut finger (and a certain *unmentionable* which I first "saw" last year!!) and never like this. Some of it *black*—oh the noise and the confusion, the smell and the terror—I am not certain who was the most terrified, horse or victim (I think it was probably a tramp or beggar such as one sees occasionally in the Lawnmarket. *Poor* man!).

And now, dear Journal, to continue my account of a *typical* day (today could hardly be called that!). In the afternoons it is carriage exercise—we often call on friends. If it is a Monday, Kirsty and Mrs. Buchanan come to call (If it is a Thursday, Mama and I call on *them!*). Occasionally if I have an appointment with the milliner or dressmaker (as I have tomorrow!) we do that of an afternoon. Sometimes I must help Mama if she is preparing a charity sale or the suchlike. Then we eat again about six or half-past. *If* we are not going out I sit with Mama until nine o'clock and do my cross-stitch (I am at the moment making a cushion with a spaniel's head on it, it is Alan's spaniel—or *meant* to be!). Sometimes I try my hand at making wax fruit. Mama may read aloud. She does this very badly, and *always* Walter Scott—

The best is when we go out for the evening and Alan is there (the next best is when *he* comes *here*). However exciting the possibilities it is always happiest if Alan is there too; the truth is that I am *most happy* when I am with him. Is not that strange, but I cannot account for it except that we share blood (I did not think I had been able to write that word so soon!) and *blood* is thicker than water. Dear Journal, I hope that my future life will always in some way include Alan. Indeed one test for HIM (= the Beloved! My Corsair—for those who have read Lord Byron—Conrad the pirate, truly the most wonderful HERO!!) is that he shall like Alan—

On Tuesday evening, though, what a mood Alan was in, dear Journal! I know he felt that way because he had lost money. Papa is very critical of him. (He, Papa, is always *finding* money—or so it seems, since we apparently grow richer and richer. Although it is not done to say so!) Alan is always either excited or morose. A weather-vane no less. I would like to tell him he is quite foolish to *gamble*—Papa is quite right.

But in the summer, dear Journal, when we are at our beautiful white house in the Western Highlands, in Wester Ross, then Alan is *quite different*. I should like those who criticise him to see him there, behaving so naturally and easily—it has been so ever since my first visit (I was seven, and he seventeen!) even though it was *his* house—or rather, Uncle Alexander's, his father!—I always felt that Jamie, Ewart, and I belonged and were *welcome*. Oh, those carefree days! How I *long* for them each year! Dear Journal, we are so happy, with our luncheon alfresco on the heather, or on the great white sandy beaches—and all around us a wild, wild land of crags, and deep lochs and empty moorland and dense forest. Truly it is a *wonderful* sight (and all ours—since none of our friends or acquaintances here in Edinburgh have so much as visited there—at which I am not surprised, since the journey *alone* is the most tremendous adventure, and not for the weak-spirited! Mama takes always some special powders and draughts and trusts that she will remember none of it—they keep her mercifully silent).

We play such games amongst the rocks and the heather and are in *such* high spirits. It is *quite another world*. Once two summers ago I tripped over a stone and twisted my ankle, and then Alan, the dear person, he carried me all the way back and (I can write this here, dear Journal, because you are kept under lock and key!) it was then that I had the *most strange* feelings! I was alive, but not in the usual manner that one is alive—while he held me, it was as if I had some kind of life *inside me*. It was *so much so* that it was almost unpleasant. I *cannot ex-*

plain. Anyway, he is my very very dear cousin and when I have married my Corsair *He* will certainly allow us to meet every year since He and Alan will get along so famously (I fancy I have written something like this already this evening! I am becoming repetitious like poor Mama—).

And how embarrassing she was on Tuesday, when Robbie brought Kirsty's Hero to Drummond Place. She shamed me positively with her incessant talk about railways and her absurd fears. I thought she would *never* cease! In fact the entire evening was not a great excitement for me—although I shall *not* tell Kirsty how little I was impressed with her Hero. It would not be kind, when she is my dear friend. She had told me so much of him, and how for her he is THE ONE (how many hours have we not spent together over the years, *sisters* almost, drawing imaginary portraits of our perfect loves! I thought we were of one mind —and now this!). There is so little hope too—I think he scarcely noticed her at all except as dear Robbie's sister. (Yesterday, she said to me: "If he were to want—if he did love me—perhaps then he would be *afraid* to say—?" She hoped that I would agree. But I was forced to be honest and say that it was only possible, but not *probable*—since it is not. And then, at that, she said with a great sigh, "I wish you'd marry Robbie—" This was so that we might become sisters *really!* But I told her that could *never* be—dear Journal, it would be like a brother, or a cousin—it would be as if I were to marry *Alan,* say!)

Well, dear Journal, you may ask, what is it about Mr. Rawson that makes him not a Hero? Firstly, he is very shy (*she* finds that endearing —but a Hero should be masterful), he blushes readily (*she* finds that touching), he is not particularly well turned out (a Hero should look almost perfect! She would say, *if* I were to mention it, that perhaps he has not a. much money, b. is other-worldly, and c. lives for things of the mind! And that would be all right, if *the rest were.* I think really that she had spoken *so much of him* that I expected something quite perfection!). He is to be a surgeon in his home town. I think he is kind and good—but, dear Journal, that is not enough, *that* is not what makes a HERO!

Enough. My candle is guttering and I have just yawned most unbecomingly with no hand in front of my mouth *three times!*

To bed, then—to dream of HIM.

> He walks in beauty, like the night
> Of cloudless climes and starry skies;
> And all that's best of dark and bright
> Meet in his aspect and his eyes:

Thus mellow'd to that tender light
Which heaven to gaudy day denies—

(With apologies to Lord Byron!)

13th January 1847

How very strange, dear Journal—just when I had been writing of Mr. Rawson last night, whom should we meet in Princes Street this afternoon, but the very same! And so awkward and embarrassed. I suffered, dear Journal, for him—since whatever I said and however well meant it served only to throw him into a greater confusion! He looked up and he looked down—anywhere but *at* me. It is a pity, dear Journal, since I can see that if polished up a little he might be very tolerable looking—and he *means so well*, which does not count for nothing. I wish only that I might have said to him, "Mr. Rawson, you may have Miss Buchanan for the asking—and I would *advise you to do so*—" Can you imagine Mama's face, dear Journal?! (She was at her worst and quite adding to the poor man's discomfiture with her talk of the Honble Iain and ball dresses. Daily I grow more certain that she intends to make it *the* match of 1847. She is enchanted of course by his blue blue blood— Robert the Bruce or Patrick Spens at the least, to listen to her—just as *he* is enchanted by Papa's money. However he *does* have a beautiful castle in the Highlands, dear Journal!) Since then I have heard, this evening, that poor Kirsty has a fever so that she was not able to receive her Hero when he called. O cruel fate!

I am writing this in my sitting room—the old school room. There is still a globe standing on one of the tables and a chart of Scottish history still hangs on the wall. It is here, dear Journal, that Kirsty and I meet every Monday afternoon (while Mama and Mrs. Buchanan take wine and cake—and talk about what?), and it is here that we talk about LOVE.

Now I must return to my water-colour of the house at Wester Ross (the hour is very late!) which I am doing *quite from memory* as a birthday gift for dear Alan!

12th February 1847

Dear Journal,

I have not written in you for *four whole weeks* at least—this will not do. My resolve is to be much much better. I shall write something *every* week without fail.

But nothing is worse, dear Journal, than to feel dull, and so I am at the moment—my spirits as my looks downcast. Why, dear Journal? Am I crossed in love? Not at all—I am not even *in love,* nor do I see any prospect of being so. It is quite unbelievable how I meet week after week the same persons (men!) and not one of them HIM. And why should it *ever be otherwise?*

Dear Journal, the truth is that I do not think I can endure the prospect of months and months (perhaps even *years and years!*) of arguing with Mama over the suitability of Mr. Blank and Mr. Whatever—in truth, the prospect of continuing to live with her. There are *undoubted attractions* in being a married woman, since I should have then a kind of freedom I now only dream of. And it *would not* preclude, dear Journal, that still one day HE might come into my life (I am not sure how this would be arranged but with LOVE *everything is possible*). I should of course try very hard to be a good wife (and I do not think that would be very difficult since I have been taught all the accomplishments). I am not a *shallow person,* I have *nothing of the coquette* in me. Nor is it that I am *denying* or being unfaithful to my *ideals* and *longings.*

The truth is, dear Journal, that I *must escape.* I have had more than enough of Mama. No one who has not lived with her (not even Papa—since he is from home all day) can imagine how it is. And it can only *get worse.* Even Aunt Charlotte, who is the dearest and most gentle of persons—*and* her sister, and most proper as to these matters—even *she* ventured the other day that I must be a saint (her words!) to be as patient with her as I am—

But now, as to what has been happening. Alas, we have been seeing a great deal of Mr. *Wilkie.* He is often at the house which I cannot see the reason for since he is only the Registrar I think they call it for the Company. And Mama grumbles that business matters are now brought into the home where they are *already too much* (for once she and I are actually *agreed* on something!). It is all hard to understand especially since he was once upon a time employed by Papa and *dismissed* by him. But now they are so friendly. It is indeed puzzling—he is an obnoxious little man, and anything which makes Mama worse I cannot but deplore. She has only to *see* Mr. Wilkie (he must needs come to meals some days when Papa and he have been working together), "Oh him," she says, "we shall have railroads now for our tea and our luncheon and no doubt our dinner too, why could I not be married to a lawyer say or some such profession, or even just a *gentleman*" (her mind returns always to the Honble Iain!), but Papa says, "Perhaps if you but wait, we *shall* live like that—" (This railroad is to make fortunes for us all—we must trust that they do not find pieces of rock they cannot cut through or pieces of land it would cripple them to buy.) He is doing so well that he hints even that we might live somewhere "more exciting" than Edinburgh. I cannot think what he means, nor can I believe in it. By then I shall be a married woman—if my present mood is anything to go by! And indeed that is what Papa expects. "A fine dowry," he said the other day, "in exchange for a *fine name*" (he *too* has been thinking about the Honble Iain—).

Of Jamie there has been news. His letter for Christmas arrived in the middle of January—he says that he is doing well and that his work is to do with *logs*, and that it is very hard but that he likes it to be so. Also he is often homesick because the scenery in that part of Canada reminds him very much of *Scotland*. I think what I should really like is for him to come back, *very rich*, and to marry Kirsty!

Ewart is now in *India* but we have had no news as yet. Papa says that is typical—he has never thought well of him—in the last days before Ewart left he made quite a hobby of belittling him which was *not right* (when I have sons I shall praise them *always!*), so that poor Ewart was I think quite glad to be gone. Of course he is not at all *vigorous* like Papa and Jamie but has something of Mama both as to looks and manner (but *none* of her trying aspects!). *I* believe, dear Journal, that he will be a brave and true soldier.

And now, all about the Ball last week! Poor Kirsty could not attend—she is still too weak from the fever she began last month. I was *so sad* for her, dear Journal, and I shall explain in a few moments (or pages!).

Well, it was quite an affair, *everyone* was there. And such finery! Kirsty, dear Kirsty *was* to have worn pink tulle with five skirts and all beautifully bordered with pink bluebells (only in *shape* of course are they *blue*bells—). She would have looked very well since pink does her great justice. (I write this, dear Journal, because it will be so interesting and I think amusing to read in years to come of what we wore—the dresses themselves being then quite forgotten!) I looked very well in *my* new ball gown. It is of white crepe with two skirts over a white moiré slip, the skirt embroidered with flowers and gold net work. Its bodice is looped up at the shoulders with bows, the sleeves *very* small and quite the latest thing! On my head I wore a wreath of eglantine flowers mixed with gold and silver daisies—the dearest headdress I have had yet!

But for me the evening was nearly ruined at the start since Mama was in such a flutter for fear that I would not pay the right sort of attention to the Honble Iain—telling me all the while just how I should behave, and hinting that something might happen by the end of the evening—although the Assembly Rooms are hardly like a country house with perhaps a conservatory where certain questions may be asked! But I run ahead of myself and I *quite forgot to say* he has scarcely more than a few pennies to his name—just his *name!* and naturally the draughty property which he needs money to keep up. Mama and Lady Mackenzie sitting together and *watching* me—I declare it was not very pleasant! *She* is very stout and moves with difficulty, she has the appearance of a very old woman. *He* is thirty-five and only just comes up to my height and has already lost a great deal of his hair—*but*, dear Journal, he can be *sometimes* quite amusing and is very very kind. Although I must say here that I find it *very* wearying the manner in which he picks up my every word and contrives somehow to turn it into a stiff compliment—it is wearying too to be told at every turn that I am fascinating, graceful, dulcet-voiced, witty, charming, and with bewitching orbs!!

But taken all in all it was a *very successful* evening. My only sadness was that dear Kirsty could not be present (we shall see why the sadness in just one moment!), although it was a delight as always to see Robbie with his dear face shining good humour and kindness to *all*—it is impossible, dear Journal, not to love him! *But* can you not guess now *who* he had with him and why I should have been so sad? Yes, it was Kirsty's great love, the indentured surgeon-to-be from Yorkshire. I was never so surprised! It will be Robbie secured him an invitation since he will not be known to the subscribers, but I *have to admit*, dear Journal, that I *rather fear*, alas, that he came on *my* account (I hope this is only a fancy born of my vanity, but suspect that it is not). However, we can but hope for the best—certainly I tried to plead Kirsty's cause whenever possible during the two dances I granted him ("only one to each gentleman, mind, Catriona!" Mama warned me *as usual*—making an exception of course of the Honble Iain! I took Mr. Rawson just to spite her!).

He was quite talkative for one so shy, and even at times quite amusing. While the musicians played "A Rosebud by My Early Walk," he revealed to me that before coming up for these lectures, he *made pills*— "for," he said, "when I have my own practice I must be able to prescribe and know what I am doing. Now that there is a younger apprentice he of course does it all—my hands no longer, I trust, smell of them" (Dear Journal, I could hardly ask him to take off his gloves!), "but pomfret cakes are quite tasty after all," he said, "if you like a liquorice flavour. And an apprentice may have all he can stomach—and then there are tamarinds and the run of anything you may care to try, and at the end, the pleasure of the task well done. And" (he said this so drolly, dear Journal!) "the *very real pleasure* that one does not have to *take the pill—*"

I asked what he should do when he had finished here and he told me of the practice that he means to buy himself—or rather that his grandfather will buy. "I do not know Yorkshire at all," I told him, "but this Easter I am to stay with some racing friends in a town called *Richmond*." At that he grew *greatly* excited and told me that where he lived was less than twenty miles away and that he had been at school at Richmond and knew it *very well*. I could hardly staunch the flow, and I could see Mama look most *disapproving* (Lady Mackenzie still beside her!) as if I had over-excited him—as indeed I had because when Robbie joined us immediately after, he said to him, "My dear fellow, just *imagine* now!" and said it all again!

When I waltzed then with Robbie, he told me that Mr. Rawson was lately in *Ireland*, just at Christmas time. He went there for the whereabouts of some of his family and had a very distressing time (*he* of course had told me *nothing of that*—I think he must be a very modest person) and that he has brought back from there one of the *starving children*. They wonder very much still if it will live. Dear Journal, *how sad*.

Well, eventually the evening came to an end—but not before I had seen a great deal more of the Honble Iain, who paid me *marked attention* (to Mama's great delight!). So that when they played the air, "Lord Rosslyn's Fancy," I had to endure a *very poor word-play* of his making, and at my expense!!

Now I must say Goodnight, dear Journal. Tomorrow I shall see my dear Alan—he will return to Edinburgh from London. That is something *really* to look forward to—I have so much to tell him!

Goodnight!

Post scriptum. Prayer. Somewhere dear Corsair Beloved Hero, somewhere, wherever you are, if you are not to be too late—come and claim me *soon! Soon!!*

Catriona Dunbar scripsit
42 Blacket Place
Edinburgh
Scotland
Europe
THE WORLD

TEN

It was Lent but soon it would be Easter. And the sun shone. Ned had fastened Kate in front of his saddle as he rode over towards the Abbey and Downham church. No dead to visit particularly: his uncles and one aunt, their graves were well tended. And it was not until next week, Easter week, that the graves would be decorated. He did not expect many people to be about: he would let Kate play amongst the gravestones in the churchyard, the kirkgarth. By next month, there might be the stray lambs to watch . . .

On the road out of the town, he talked to Kate all the time. Today it was about Becky. "No one likes me going there, my little one. I shall, though—I always shall. There's no one really to care for her. She hasn't the fuss we make of you, my cockyolly bird . . . I'll not take you up yet to see her—but I've told her of you. 'There's *Kate* lives with us now, Becky,' I said." He did not think that she understood much—if anything. But one day . . .

He sang to her too as they turned into the road near the Kissing Gate:

> "I peeped through the window,
> I peeped through the door,
> I saw pretty Katie
> A-dancing on the floor.
> I cuddled her and fondled her,
> I set her on my knee,
> I says, Pretty Katie,
> Won't you marry me?"

He tethered his cob, then lifted Kate down. Standing by the Kissing Gate, holding her: "That's where Mother, Sarah-Mother saved the little boy," he explained, pointing to the river Down flowing creamily in the spring sunshine. On the opposite bank the wild garlic, the Jack-by-the-hedge, was already out. Dry catkins hung on the alders. Because the water was low, the lichen showed clear under the bridge.

Inside the churchyard he set her down, and wrapped her rug about her—although it was warm and the air soft, he could never take enough care. There was no one about among the graves: some new and gleaming, some overgrown—illegible, the stone tilted. A blackbird hopped onto the flat tombstone of Josiah Rawson and stayed to preen itself. Ned looked over at Kate—and thought of the miracle of her hair. For now, where once it had been so dark—so much part of the black furry covering which had so disfigured her limbs, her body, in those early days—now, beneath her bonnet could be seen the soft, curly beginnings: new hair, red, deepening already in some lights to auburn.

The main gate to the churchyard opened. He heard but did not see. When he looked round, the girl, carrying daffodils, was familiar. He coloured even before he recognised her, as if she was part of some shameful memory. (And what was she doing walking in so boldly, *not* through the Kissing Gate? Her father, the shoemaker, was Chapel, he remembered, and she had never appeared in church—but that was no reason for defying custom . . .) At first she took no notice of him, walking straight over to one of the graves with her flowers. He thought perhaps she wouldn't remember who he was. But then casting a curious look over at Kate, she turned towards him. She walked, her head tilted in a manner he could only call saucy, staring at him all the while. Should he address her as "Nanny" or "Miss Haygarth"?

But it was she who spoke first: greeting him, not using any name, just saying (as if it had been yesterday and not five months ago they met), "I got another place." Then when he didn't answer at once she added: "That's why you've not seen me about." She paused. "I'd no trouble—to get missen a place. No trouble at all . . ."

There was an awkward silence. Awkward only for him. She had sat down on a tombstone quite at her ease, legs a little apart. She looked down at her boots, then with a jerk of her thumb, pointing at Kate.

"Is that *it?* T'bairn your brother fetched back?"

"It is." Maybe she would ask more? But instead she remained quite silent, rubbing at her nose occasionally. He said in a rush: "Is it a nice place they found you?"

She shrugged her shoulders. "It's right enow . . . Two old ones it is, ladies. Very fond o'me they are. I've even to wind t'cotton when they do fancy work like . . ." The conversation stuck, but still she didn't move. He asked gently, whose grave she'd come to tend?

"Me mam's." He should have known that. He had heard Father once discuss the family, after they had decided that in future their boots would be made there. "Me mam," Nanny said now. "She were only one I minded. I do what I will now—I'll not tak word from anyone other . . ."

"If she's gone, who takes care?"

"Me Antie Em. She takes care of me dad, and t' little bairns—me sisters." All the time as she spoke, she stared at him. He wasn't sure what to do with his own eyes. The boldness of her expression was strange to him. And oh, but she was pretty! No, not pretty—it was something else. Perhaps the slanting eyes, the small tongue which she ran continually over her lips. She was pert.

And with her he was so uncomfortable. It was as if somehow no time had passed since that chance meeting in the shop—she had certainly expected him to remember—while what he *really* remembered was the feeling. The shame perhaps. And now to feel those stirrings again, here in a graveyard, close by a church—to know himself restless in *that* part of him. The whole of Lent, and he had not been wicked once. Nearly six weeks, and I have not been wicked once . . .

She said, "I'm home just for Easter, like." He heard suddenly his horse whinnying, and although it was nothing to do with Kate, he thought of her at once, that he had not been watching for her. He panicked. When he couldn't see her immediately, he began to shake, his legs trembling. He could think only—*the water.*

He moved quickly, distractedly. But she was not far at all. She was exploring only, pulling at blades of grass, clutching them in her fist—hidden behind a great square tombstone. When he reached her, he lifted her up at once, pulling her to him. "My little cockyolly bird . . ."

Nanny had come up behind him. "You are an old woman," she said, half angrily, half tauntingly. He blushed, but didn't answer. Then:

"I have to go back," he said, unhappy, awkward, wanting only to be rid of her, so that he could be rid too of his feelings—which were not really him, which he could not order to go away. The outing had been spoilt completely.

Walking, hurrying now back to the Kissing Gate, he felt certain that Nanny stood there still, watching him, mocking. As he went down the path, he clutched Kate to him.

If I look round now, he thought, if I look round now. A pillar of salt.

ELEVEN

"Have ye got a lass, then?" Grandfather shouted. But before John could answer, he announced: "I were thinking of building."

"Going to rival the Abbey, are you, Grandfather?"

"What's that? He talks so soft like, that'll be t'Edinburry folk. I *don't hear*, John—"

John moved nearer. Grandfather was glaring at him, but it was the fierceness not of anger but of affection. John had come to recognise it.

"Nay. I've nowt to do wi' Abbey. I thought as mebbe I'd have t'front door more toward market place. Bloody tucked in t'corner I am."

He was used to Grandfather's plans for extending the house; certainly a front door facing a brick wall was not ideal. But for all the traffic through it, it could not be called a matter of urgency. He did not expect to hear more of it.

Grandfather farted loudly, a series of five or six. "Let's have beer. Get that Minnie. Minnie!" he shouted.

John said, "I'll get it." When he came back, Grandfather explained, "I'd a mind to drink t'owd stuff—none on that fancy wine. It's Minnie as chooses that—" Having decided to forsake, for an afternoon anyway, his wine-drinking pretensions, he set about drinking ale to some purpose. In a few moments he'd asked for his mug to be refilled.

"Aye, that's better, that's good—a pot o' t'best." He said then: "That lass, t'one you fetched back from Ireland, folk say she's shaping up well. Squire's lady, she were seen looking her over in t'town."

"Mrs. Ingham's gone—many a year now, Grandfather. You'll mean Mrs. Charles—"

"Aye. Bugger t'lad. I've not time for any Charles. They say he's not t'man his dad were—" He stopped and chuckled, "Aye, there were allus talk. Folk had allus summat to say of Squire." He was amusing himself vastly: "The tales—they said as no lass were safe. That were back in

Bony's time, in t'Great French War. A right lad, Squire was. If I'd a pound for every time as he's had it out . . ." He leaned forward, slopping his drink, cackling to himself.

"Have ye got a lass, then?" he asked again suddenly.

He could not mean Ellie, John thought. And anyway, that was finished. And Catriona was not his lass (although *if wishing could make it so . . .*).

"It'll be time you got wed—is there none on them as'll have ye?"

John said stiffly, "I do know—girls."

"And you fancy none? That's a tale. Fill up t'beer pot, and tell me summat more likely."

"I'm in no hurry—to be wed."

"You do right, lad. Lasses—who wants a lass round t'place?" He frowned. There was beer froth on his lips. "I'll tell you summat. If it's brass that's stopping ye, and you've a mind to be wed—to get it ower with—" He clattered the mug down, still full of liquid. "Lad's daft," he mumbled, "nobbut a fond bugger. Wanting to get wed . . ."

John was silent. It was useless to argue with statements directed at oneself—even more useless to comment on those directed to the room at large.

"I'll tell ye this—there's brass. Nowt as'll spoil you—but brass when ye wed. There'll be one thousand pound—that'll be two times five hundred and ten times one hundred and five time two hundred pound . . . All that to come on ye when ye wed . . ."

Why not? John thought suddenly. Why not? Catriona: he had never asked her. So dragged down had he been in his hopeless passion—he had never thought that to succeed, one must try. Yet he had done *nothing about it whatsoever.*

Afterwards he could not see why the news of the money should have been of anything more than practical help towards his plans. But it was as if it had unlocked some door. The races at Catterick in ten days' time: she had said at that Ball in the Assembly Rooms that she would come up to friends in Richmond—that she would go to the races. It was not enough just to think longingly of her only twenty miles away: it was necessary to go there. And once there to try and see her. And then—why should he not at least *ask?*

I will do it.

Grandfather reached out a hand, pulled at John's coat sleeve. "I'll have a piss, then. Get t'pot. I'm buggered if I'll move." He shouted loudly, "Minnie, get piss pot for t'lad—"

Aunt Minnie fetched it out of the cupboard. She handed it to John covered in a cloth.

It was the same one remembered from his childhood—and it had been several years old then. A wartime pot, it had in its bowl not just a picture of Bonaparte but his face in relief. (It must in a time of fear, John thought, have been very consoling.)

"I'll have his nose first," Grandfather said. John held the pot steady. A stream of urine hissed and frothed and covered the Emperor's face.

A man was crying the lists at the races. "Correct card, gentlemen— names, weights, colours o' t'riders . . ." The sun was trying to break through, although April showers looked likely.

John's plan was to come over for each of the three days of the Races. Then he would be *certain* to see her. He wondered why he had not tried to make some definite arrangement. Instead he had done no more than send a foolish message, through Robbie: "Tell Miss Dunbar I may perhaps see her at Catterick Races . . ." (And however was he to be alone with her? What madness had led him to think that he would have even the *opportunity* to propose?)

He was staying at Richmond. He had decided not to be with his aunt there, but instead with an old school friend, Cyril Pullan. He needed an ally and someone to confide in.

"Far above me," he told Cyril. "And yet I am hoping—no, I am *trusting—*"

Robbie he had never really wanted to worry with his obsession—if only because he had said, more than once: "Kirsty is *very* fond of you, you know." If it were only *there* he had lost his heart, how easy it would be . . .

When he saw her, it was with a sense of shock—because it was so *exactly* how and when he had imagined it. With a party, making her way to the Grandstand. There must have been ten or twelve of them. She stood out, in audacious relief (did not she always?). He could barely distinguish the others—except: but he might have guessed. Of course *he* was there too—the ubiquitous Alan Dunbar.

He said to Cyril, "There—just there . . ." It was a matter now only of retracing a few steps, walking at a slightly different angle, and then . . .

It all happened quickly, too quickly almost. As if he had been thrown onto the stage and his lines not known. There was a man amongst the party: tall, gangling, with a dark greasy forelock and nervous mannerisms. John recognized him as a schoolfellow. Todhunter. Bertram Todhunter.

Bertram saw him at once. "I did not know you were a racing fellow,

Rawson . . ." Better still, his mother was there too. She had a voice which boomed (John remembered it in conversation with the headmaster: "Dear Reverend, I trust you to bring out the *best* in Bertram . . ."). Now she said, "But I remember you, Mr. Rawson. And Mr. Pullan, is it? I remember, Mr. Rawson, you were kind to Bertie once . . ."

It was too good to be true—and probably it was not. Certainly he could not recall any good deeds. He had not dared to look closely at Catriona—he had the impression only of a lilac bonnet with a small rose. She appeared genuinely surprised to see him. Could it be that she had received no message? (Or worse, not listened to any?). His spirits, like a weather-vane . . .

Mrs. Dunbar was of the party also. She looked ill at ease, the feathers of her bonnet drooping. He wondered if perhaps she had been forced to come south by railroad? They were all to meet again for luncheon. Yes, Mr. Rawson and Mr. Pullan must *certainly* join them. "I absolutely insist," shouted Mrs. Todhunter.

He was unable to concentrate on the first race. For the second he put a half guinea either way on a horse called Catherine the Great—and cursed himself for sentimentality when it limped home ninth. He had with him a list of tips, mostly for the afternoon races and for tomorrow's. He thought perhaps that he might offer some advice to Alan. Would that not impress her?

"How pleasant," Catriona said easily, dark-fringed eyes opening wide. He thought she meant their "chance" meeting. "How pleasant it is here. I have often thought, have I not—" looking around: "Alan dear, you are not attending—"

"I have a concern—" he said.

She burst out laughing at that: "When the favourite romped home—the Earl of what's-his-name's—I knew then." She turned to John, "I knew how it would be. He was so *certain*. And for such a large sum of money!"

Alan said sulkily, "It's your ignorance, Pussy, that you make so much of bad forecasts. One good tip and all will be wiped out." He said in a more friendly tone, "I shall have a good season. You will see—"

"I'm surprised," Catriona said, "I'm surprised, Mr. Rawson, that he can tear himself away—that he can be all summer in western Scotland."

John said to Alan, in a voice which he knew to be too solemn: "Perhaps I can give you some help—for this afternoon?"

"Och, my dear fellow, I think hardly—"

Catriona: "Oh, but do tell us, tell *me*, Mr. Rawson." She was being unbelievably demure today.

"I was only—I wished to say that I had a good tip, that perhaps Churchill's Folly in the three o'clock. I shall put something myself."

"Then put it, put it," Alan said. "I'll make my own mistakes. And you can keep your tips. Sell them elsewhere—"

His manner was very rough. I have done nothing to merit this, John thought. But then a wonderful thing happened: Catriona said in that soft speaking voice (how could they be the same vocal cords which had murdered Mozart in Drummond Place?), "Alan, you *bear*. Apologise at once to poor Mr. Rawson. Make friends. I *insist*."

Churchill's Folly was first—and at what splendid odds! But the money meant nothing. It was his triumph: he wore it like a warm coat. Meeting with Alan and Catriona again, he felt that he had somehow won more than an argument. Alan said to him, in friendly enough tones, "My cousin will tell you that *she* took your advice—and now has a pretty penny or two to show for her outing."

"Yes, thank you," she said. "Thank you, Mr. Rawson."

Mrs. Todhunter had come up to where he stood with Cyril. "You are both invited to a little supper," she boomed. "I give them always during the Races. Promise me you will come—Bertie will be more than delighted. My suppers are *quite* the thing, you know . . ."

He could not believe in his continued good fortune. On arrival he heard that Alan was indisposed and not well enough to come downstairs. And then during supper, he found he had been seated next to Catriona. He was even able to talk to her with ease. It was as if the run of good luck which had begun with his winning on the nags was his now for as long as he wished.

He supposed that she was interested—she professed to be—when he spoke of Downham, and the order of his days, and how it would be when he took over the practice. She sparkled—he could not imagine that she would yawn behind his back. And yet, it *was* too good to be true so that he was almost afraid. The cure for that was drink. He drank usually very little, and had no stomach for it, but this evening he took extra.

He wasn't drunk. No question of that. But he was emboldened, full of confidence. He felt certain that he would be successful with her—if only he could find the occasion . . . He tried to imagine slipping his momentous request in amongst the veal custards, the tipsy cake, the devilled pigeon—and not being overheard. All those foods warred in him as he tried to think how he might manage.

He turned to her suddenly: "Miss Dunbar," he said in a low voice, "I have something particular to ask you . . ."

"And that is, Mr. Rawson?"

He said with the urgency of the desperate, "I must see you alone—"

"Mama would have somewhat to say about that! Even now she is looking in my direction. I hope it is nothing *serious* you wish to see me about?" And she laughed.

"You must be the judge of that," he said.

There was a little terrace at the back of the house which could be approached through one of the drawing-rooms. It was a fine night and very warm for April. It would not seem so very odd that they should walk out a moment together.

Her mood did not seem very serious: it was that which alarmed him. He could feel inside himself, through the warmth of drink and the general flush of good fortune, a cold nugget of reality . . .

"Well, Mr. Rawson? And?"

There was nothing for it but to plunge straight in. Here they were, the words he had so carefully rehearsed: but it did not sound like his voice. He cursed the drink which had made him bold but would surely trip his tongue.

". . . If I have not completely taken you by surprise—if from what I have told you of my prospects, the circumstances that is . . . whether it would be in order for me to speak to your father . . . if I were to pay a visit to Edinburgh for the purpose . . . if bearing all this in mind" (Shall I *never* get to the point? he thought), "you would consider . . . would do me the honour of—to consent to be—" (Should he say "Mrs. Rawson"?)—"my—wife?"

He had managed. There was a long silence. Then she said very evenly, gaily, and quite, quite coolly, "Mr. Rawson, of course it is an honour that you should ask. And I am very sensible of that honour. But, you know, I am not free—"

He had not thought of that. He had thought of everything but that. "You have already—" he began.

"I am not *engaged!*" she said, emphasising the word. "I did not mean that." Then she laughed. "Mama always says, a girl is either engaged or not, and there are no 'ifs' about it—"

"Your affections, then—*they* are engaged?"

"Och, what did I ever say about my affections? It is only that it is probable—and I tell you this in confidence, of course—indeed it is almost certain that I shall soon *become* engaged . . ."

His voice came out huffily. He did not feel huffy, only sad. "To whom? Who will be so fortunate?"

"Oh, you would not know him at all," she said, her manner quite airy, offhand, "he is from Cromarty."

"If I had *known*—"

"How could you have known, Mr. Rawson? In any case, I think proposals are delightful—" She said it light-heartedly, as if she wanted him to join in the laugh, to see the fun of it all.

"I was not teasing," he said in hurt tones.

"And I never said that you were—" She spoke a little more tartly now. He noticed that it was not as warm outside as he had thought, and that she was drawing her shawl tight about her.

"Shall we go in again?" he asked.

"But not at all. I shall just go a little way into the garden. And you may come too if you wish." She paused first, to fasten her shawl. She said suddenly: "I don't think you would offer—would ask for my hand, if you knew what I was like—"

"I *do* know." He was protesting almost. "I have spent some time in your company—in Edinburgh. And I have heard from Robbie, from Kirsty—nothing but the highest praise."

"Mr. Rawson, I would make a bad doctor's wife—"

"But I do not intend to *be* a bad doctor . . ."

She laughed, happily, at his poor joke. And then a moment later, not waiting for his arm, moved forward and down the steps to the garden.

She tripped almost at once, before he could stop her—twisting and then sliding to the ground in a swirl of tarlatan and tulle.

He reached her in a moment. He leaned over her, knelt beside her.

"My knee," she said, "it is my *knee*, I think." She sounded angry with pain.

He would have to take her indoors. He had to lift her up, feel the shape of her body. Had to feel the soft skin of her arm where the shawl did not reach, through the fine tulle. He would like to have put his hand on her heart.

Make the most of it, his own heart said. You will never touch her again.

TWELVE

Sarah never knew where the rumours first started. And what did it matter? Evil thoughts, evil words . . . What distressed her the most was that anyone should have believed them to be *true*.

Matilda Paley had tried to protect her from them. She realised that afterwards. The chemist's wife, interrupted in mid-sentence, some fierce looks and a tap with her fan for Mrs. Cookson, the saddler's wife; some long and awkward silences during a whist supper. But somewhere, half-way through the summer, so that she should not hear it from anyone else, Matilda had told her.

"Dirty, nasty tongues, my dear," and she patted Sarah's hand. Her head nodded solemnly. "I thought now my little Sarah will have to know. They say," she lowered her voice to a whisper, although they were alone in the room and the house almost empty, "they *say* that the little girl, little Kate—the false witness that goes around is that she is—" again Sarah's hand was patted, "something to do with Mr. Rawson . . ."

Sarah said bluntly: "You mean—*Sam's* child? But how—whatever? What are they *about*?"

"Ah, well," and Matilda sighed, "invention is easy, my dear. Where there's a *will*. I thought only that you should know what they are saying . . ." She turned her head away. "John's going off, it was made an occasion they said, to smuggle in the child—"

"A famished half-dead bairn like that? I never—"

"Ill-treated by the natural mother, my dear. And rescued by you and yours . . . for those that *wish* to believe, there is never any difficulty. It did not take long to make all the particulars fit, once they had their story."

"Sam—he's not heard any of this?"

"My dear, I'm sure not. If he were sometimes in the Black Swan—

yes, perhaps. But he does not drink. And"—she looked at Sarah gravely, her nodding curls for the moment still—"*we* shall not tell him, shall we?"

But the thought of it, the horrible thought of what was being said, tainted the summer months for her. Although Matilda had assured her it would all die down ("just because there *is* no truth in it—and also because of what *I* have said to anyone at all who will listen." There had even been a reference in one of Mr. Cuthbert's sermons, which Sarah felt might have been prompted by Matilda), but she could not help thinking it was all something to do with Hannah. That there was malice still abroad; that she had not done right about that affair.

And yet, she thought, I had believed all forgiven—if not forgotten. And all the fund of good will in Kate's first weeks, where had that gone? Wicked lies, spreading like forest fires, burning everything in their wake. She was angry too, perhaps most of all, for John (God forbid they should rumour next that it was *his* child . . .), for had he not risked so much for her sake, and then later for Kate's sake?

Also, he was not happy at the moment. It did not need even a mother's eye to see that. She supposed it to be an affair of the heart, although he hadn't confided in her—at all. One day he would marry, of course (he had even said, "When I'm settled in with Whitelaw's practice, I'd like really to be wed . . ."), but she need not face that yet. There had been someone obviously. In Edinburgh? But—*I will not worry*, she thought.

And yet, with children, one had always to be worrying. Ann, with Frank Helliwell—*that* would be all right. Eliza she did not imagine marrying at all (although lately she had heard that Tom at the smithy opposite had been praising her in the Black Swan. And that wouldn't be a very suitable match), while Ned . . . There was no story there, she was sure. He might well marry late. As for Walter—I *ought* to love him, she thought yet again: but remembering the increasingly pudgy face, the sly eyes (where does he get it from, *who?*), the surreptitious pinching of Kate, who never cried or complained, she wondered how she was to do so. To think that he nearly killed me . . . I am an unnatural mother, she thought.

The rumours *had* ceased, just as Matilda had said—disappearing towards the end of the summer almost as suddenly as they had appeared. By early September, Matilda reported that a mere mention of it by someone new to the town—and to the rumour—had brought only laughter and scorn at their credulity ("*That* were a likely tale . . . Sam Rawson—nivver . . .").

If it had been the Squire, she thought now, well, that would have made sense. Fond as she was of him, she had to admit that up until the last seven or eight years, tales of his goings-on abounded. First heard of from Mrs. Mumford—and how many times since?—they stretched over some forty years. Probably, almost certainly, he had more by-blows than he knew of, scattered through the dale—and beyond. But that anyone should think that of *Sam*, even the once. She had never told him of the rumour and would not. It remained to wound, now after the deed; but it seemed to her sometimes, in calmer moments, that the idea was almost *funny*.

When I think back, now, to our courting days . . .

She had been so proud, cocky even (but only inside herself. No one knew. No one must know about her and Sam). To have been chosen by Mr. Rawson . . .

This, a matter for pride, even though she'd been assured that with all that education—after going to *school*—she might do this, that, marry this man, that man. But she had known always the reality. Had seen it from other girls at the school, those who went back to comfortable, well-off homes. *Her* short holidays with the Paleys: in her own mind she was already a governess, knowing just how it would be. Often Matilda warned her, told her cautionary tales. It would be a hard life. And where would be the men to marry?

So whenever the future frightened her, which was quite often, she would think not of the Squire's ever-kindly and strictly paternal interest (whatever others might say of him, never, *never* had she seen a hint of anything), but rather of Mr. Rawson's friendliness. *His* interest. Right from the early days at Mrs. Mumford's, when he had invited her to see the rope-works, and on from the time of the rescue, when he'd arrived so providentially, he had been someone to look up to. Above her, perhaps—or perhaps not—but not like the Squire and all the gentry. Not impossible. Not at all impossible.

Meeting him accidentally, a little on purpose, again and again even before she'd left the Paleys and gone to school. And then later, the shyly arranged meetings by the Kissing Gate (timing it by the church clock. She was always the first there: that ominous pause before it struck the hour, when she'd think, I have it wrong, I have it wrong . . .), the ribbons she tied to the rails, the prayer he said out loud always when, after walking solemnly about the graves, they parted to go home again.

How to escape Matilda's prying—that had been the spice. She had wanted always to know where Sarah had been, where she was going next, whom she had seen . . . She had not enough to do with her days, and her emotions. She must talk, talk, talk—and Sarah was there, a more or less willing listener. But that time, no gossip had reached Matilda.

Sarah had told her mam about it, though. Except that Mam was ill, very ill, and living in someone else's house, Sarah would have spent the holidays there (and would not have met with Sam . . .). But Mam had been so happy about it: long before Sarah had, she had seemed to see the way it was going. She hadn't been frightened for Sarah, never said, "Take care, love," or hinted that she might be led astray (And I knew *nothing*, Sarah thought now). She had just been pleased. "He'll take care of you—I'll not worry . . ." For Mam had been worried, lying there in the bed, swollen. She had grown enormous. Each time Sarah saw her, she was larger, more bloated than before. She had always been big, but now she seemed to Sarah to swell before her very eyes. Through the mass of wobbling fat she could just make out the Mam she knew and loved.

Sam never kissed her, or touched her at all. She had been used to affection. Memories of her da, sitting on his knee, kissing him, being kissed. Mam wrapping her in a tight hug (but those days were past). The Squire even had kissed her once—and that had been like a blessing. But Sam, although he looked at her a lot, so that you could almost call it staring, he touched her only on the hand in greeting or farewell.

But still, it had been a secret courting—of sorts. She thought: I loved the excitement, the danger, the naughtiness. And he was so much older. A Rawson—thinking well of me . . . Then all the excitement, suddenly coming to a head. She had said only something like: "Ten more weeks, and I'll be left school." And he had said: "Well then, we'll get wed. I'll be over to Hawes and see about it." (Not "can we, shall we, what do you say?" Just the fact, the bare statement.) The next day he had been to see Mam. Sarah had not protested at all, and there had been Mam, so happy.

There had never seemed to her really to be any alternative. That same afternoon, coming out of a shop in Downham she had bumped into Charles Ingham. Although he was now as much as eleven or twelve, he had stared at her with the same arrogance as that day at the Abbey. The same dislike. But she had been above it. Soon she was going to be married. She would have the pleasure of bowing graciously to Mrs. Mumford (Oh, those pleasures . . .). But above all she was going to have at last, and for ever, a *family*. She had made her decision. She would not be a governess. She would be a Rawson. What did proud Charles Ingham know of any of it—when all that was left was you and your dying mam (and might God put her out of her misery soon), and a memory of Da?

It had been right to do it. She had been right. *I was right*. He never asked me if I loved him. And did it matter? Does it matter? I know what love is. What I feel for (almost) all the children—even for little Kate. But especially John. Oh, God forgive me, *especially* John.

THIRTEEN

Ned, about to steal a free afternoon to go and visit Becky, came across the market square in the early September sun. A drove of geese, on their way to some fair, could be seen coming up the road from the valley. There must have been nearly a hundred of them: they waddled haphazardly, gabbling loudly—the despair no doubt of the tired men driving them. Their speed could not have been above half a mile an hour, he knew; and with their webs (they would have walked through sand and tar at the blacksmith's first, to toughen them) always in danger of splitting.

But watching them made him laugh and, suddenly light-hearted, he wanted to share them with Kate. He began hurrying on to fetch her—then remembered that she was out for the day. If it had not been for work, he could have been with her. All this month and August too, he had felt against work: pacing the rope walk had seemed to him the pacing of a caged animal, or some prisoner's exercise stretch. I *should not* think like that, he told himself. For it was natural and right that he should work by the sweat of his brow. "In the sweat of thy face shalt thou eat bread till thou return unto the ground; for out of it wast thou taken: for dust thou art and unto dust thou shall return . . ."

Those words gave him always a thrill of fear—certainly he must one day return to the earth. And was it not that which drew him so often to the Kissing Gate, to the churchyard? One moment quick, the next dead —it might be next week, tomorrow, *today*. "For you know not at what hour the Son of man cometh . . ."

The weather for days, even weeks, had been hot: I love September, he thought. The heather, a purple carpet, covering the higher moors, the colour of it altering everything—making autumn all right, taking away some of its sadness. Up there the lambs were weaned, and there were bilberries to be had. The bracken already tinged with gold.

Out of his work clothes now, and setting out. He had his flute with him. Not just for Becky but so that he could play it out in the open, annoying no one but the grazing sheep (and he never took their companionable bleating as any opinion on his playing). Soon he would be high, high up, with the feeling of freedom that he wanted, so that he could breathe from right deep down: his head, his nose magically free of the rope fibres.

And safe too—if he could be anywhere—from Charles Ingham. Even when out shooting, it was not this way Charles came. He had been remarkably free of him anyway for months now, so that he had begun to think that Charles was perhaps losing interest in taunting him.

He came hard by the beck, running a little low in the dry weather. There were some sheepfolds, washfolds, there, where a few months ago the washings had taken place. Then they had dammed the beck and dubbed the sheep, to rid them of the sticky grease and tar salve.

He had now perhaps only half a mile to go. He began in his freedom to sing. A little further on a heathcock, starting up from the heather with its odd sneezing sound, whirred into flight, its long neck out, the sun catching its blue-black plumage. And at the same time he heard his name called.

She was lying back, in a clearing, just a little ahead of him. A basket, a few herbs in it, lay beside her. She had taken her bonnet off. The toes of her boots were turned inwards.

"Nanny, Miss Haygarth—" He felt ill at ease. He was not pleased to see her.

But she caught him, followed him with her eyes.

"Don't ye say good day, then?"

"Of course." He cleared his throat.

"I didn't hear nowt—"

He hesitated. "I was—surprised. I'd not expected to see you this way."

"You don't own t'moor, do ye?"

"No." He cursed himself for his hesitant replies. She went on belligerently, "It's free, eh? I've as much right—there was Haygarths Downham way afore any Rawsons come."

"I never said not. You walk where you please—"

She was sitting up now, propped on one elbow. She tossed her head. "That little smally bairn—t'one ye had wi'ye. T'Irish. Where's *she*?"

"She's well enough, thank you." He *would* not be provoked.

"Ye're up this way for t'old one, aren't ye? Becky?" She was still staring at him. He nodded and she said, "Ye could awhile mebbe—sit down like, here."

He didn't want to. He very much didn't want to. But it seemed impossible somehow just to walk on. Instead he went on standing there awkwardly.

"Well," he began, feeling that he must say something, "well, you're home again—did you lose your place?" He had not heard that she was back. He had heard nothing of her, had not wanted to.

"Me antie—Dad's sister that was looking for them all—she went sudden. They fetched me back. I've to stay home now—till young Martha's able to manage an' all." She watched him all the time she was speaking.

"Martha?"

"Aye. Me sister, she's thirteen but she's no idea like. And Tabby that's twelve—she's all mischief. A right handful."

"Your father—he'll not marry again?"

"If I've owt to do wi' it, he'll not. I'll not have any elmother. They're bad. Allus bad. Didn't you learn fairy tales?"

He did not know what to say. He thought that he was lucky that he had both parents. Her presence—that always made him feel uncomfortable, as if he were mocked (and those strange feelings too, as though she wove some kind of spell . . .). He must think better of her. She had had already a hard life . . .

"I'm sorry. I am—about your auntie. You must be sad."

"I'm not sad. I didn't reckon much to her." She sat right up, alert, brushing something off her boot, an insect perhaps. "I didn't bother grieving. I were at that Festival, that Tea Feast, two week past—"

He knew about the Tea Festivals: day long, night long events, and with never a breath of alcohol. The Temperance Societies had organised them for five or six years now—but he'd scarcely noticed the big one in Downham, or the even larger one in Leyburn. Father approved, and John and Mr. Whitelaw, who'd to deal with problems of drink, said they were a great notion . . .

"And t'markee," she was saying, "t'big tent like . . . Ye weren't at t'dancing night time?"

"No. I—"

"Eh, we danced! There while morning we were—half-three I were at home. Many folk came that likes to drink—it were for t'dancing. All manner of step there was. We'd that dance just t'lads do—'stot' they call it." She'd grown excited, standing up now, shaking her head, brushing her skirts. "And Wensleydale Gallop, they'd that. I love a dance, I do. And we'd reels, square eight, that like. Then last thing we'd t'Whishin—" She paused, looked at him. "Ye ken that?" She frowned.

He shook his head. He liked to dance well enough, did it well enough, but he didn't know local ones, country ones.

"Cushion dance—wi' all that kissin'. Ye must ken. When it's all but done, and we've each a lad, then couples go round. They've to join up. This manner—" She linked her arm through his and pulling him forward, skipped along. Ned followed reluctantly, taken by surprise.

"'Arm in arm, round and round,'" she sang, in a little squeaky voice, "'Arm in arm, round and round, Me that loves a bonny lass, Will kiss her on the ground . . .'" She went fast, so fast that when she stopped without warning, he almost fell against her, almost tumbled to the ground, pulling her too—righting himself, panting, only with difficulty.

"Eh," she said, "eh," sitting back down again. "Warm, it's warm." Then picking up her bonnet, fanning herself with it and looking at him sideways: "Do ye have owt to drink? I could go to t'beck, only for . . . Have ye owt wi' ye?"

He hesitated. He had his bottle, sticking from his coat pocket. She must have seen it, his flute too. "Yes. If you don't mind I've drunk from it." His heart hammered now, he supposed it to be the heat. He should have taken off his coat. Wherever he looked her eyes seemed to be following, her tip-tilted nose too, so that he could see her in a sense even when his gaze moved right away.

"Just a sup then," she said, but without making a move. "If ye please." He uncorked the leather stopper, handed her the bottle. She threw her head back, gulping a great draught: he watched her mouth, couldn't take his eyes off it. He could see her neck, bare, white, the swallowing movements.

"You *were* thirsty," he said, admiringly almost.

"Here—tak it back, then," she said, but without moving. Then as he leaned forward to accept it from her she threw her free arm suddenly, tightly, round his neck. He was thrown off balance. He fell heavily, against her, on top of her, the bottle falling to the ground. And oh the warm softness of her, as horrified he sank and sank and without struggling, without a show even of resistance, lay quite still.

Only a few seconds. He felt her small hands, he knew they would be small, had noticed how small they were that day in the graveyard when she'd mocked him—little pointed piercing hands clasping, fondling his ears. His face was buried almost in her neck—she pulled it up and towards her, her little tongue flashing out and pushing between his lips— his mouth which hung open ready with surprise, with wonder. The blood which had rushed to his face now seeming to burst from him, so furiously did it drum. The rest of him burning too, and now that dangerous rising, pressing against his breeches—it felt like some arc, it rose like a bow. He could not beat it down, the arrow ready to be shot.

"Ye coat, off wi' ye coat," she said. "Have it off—"

Obediently he shed it. And then she was pulling at his shirt, pulling it out from the breeches, thrusting her hands up under, running all over his chest like a little mouse. And still to his horror he grew and grew . . .

"Here, wait—" Then pulling her hands out as suddenly as she'd put them in, she pushed—rolling him over, away from her. Then with a quick movement she pulled at her skirts, thrusting them right up in one gesture, so that they were almost over her head. Under them there was nothing. Nothing but flesh. White thighs—and the dark mound, dense fur. The furry shock of it.

She had spread her legs wide. He found himself shaking, a fearful tremble, the trembling of someone trapped. He was caught more securely than when ever he'd been laid across her: now he could not move himself at all—could not move even his gaze.

She had moved her skirts, arranged them bunched up, so that her head could be seen.

"I reckon ye ken what I showed you, eh? Ye seen one afore—"

Because he hadn't, because he was afraid, he wanted to say "Of course." But he couldn't speak at all, was tied in the tongue now too.

"Get away! Go on wi' ye—staring like that! Ye'll ken what's to do, won't you? Eh?" She paused a moment in her mocking. "I might catch cold there, mightn't I then, if—" She grabbed at his hand before he could move back, pushing, thrusting it into the crevice that he knew was there. His eyes were shut now. "Feel that," she said, "go on, put your finger up—see me smile, make a lass happy. Ye like it, I can tell, ye like it—faces talk—" She chattered on, and then as his finger which independent of him would hardly stop now but moved on exploring, searching at the entrance of what he knew, he *knew* must be an endless unbelievable dark and wet cavern, she pushed him away, saying:

"It's t'other goes in, t'other—let's see him, let's see how he's growed—"

He knew, of course he knew. He thought anyway that it would burst from him, that a wild caged animal, it would escape, burst the bonds of its cloth prison and rush, fly to its true home. He was nearly sobbing with eagerness. But she aided him in, her voice suddenly very low now, gentle, it was like a mother and child—soothing, a lullaby: "There he goes, like that he goes . . ."

It was easy, oh but it was easy, all of it, the cavern not big as he had imagined but made to fit so that he had slipped in as far now as ever he could go—so that he was there, inside, he had reached the kingdom—he rocked, he thrust, he grew, all of him grew, he was six foot tall, never Ned the least of the Rawsons, never . . . but—oh God, oh God no no, what am I doing, this is heaven, she cannot be, oh this person lying in wait to give me this—even when alone I was wicked and swore never never to be again—it was never like this, never like this, never . . .

"That were summat like, eh, Ned?" Receding, not at once. She whispered in his ear then, too soon almost, it was too soon to hear it: "I were good, I were good to ye—" When he didn't answer at once, she said, "You've no cause to worry, if ye was worriting, I can tak care of missen—ye reckoned that no doubt?" Her voice had a little sharp edge now, like her teeth, her little sharp teeth which had dug just now into his shoulders, which he only realised now he had felt . . .

"Weren't I well teached?" she said, sitting up. "I ken, don't I, how to be good to you?" She was arranging her skirts, primly almost. What if someone should come by—what if someone *had* come by? His blood lately so hot ran cold now. *What if?*

"It were t'first one, he learned me, t'first gentleman. That place I had afore they fetched me home. It weren't ever my doing I lost that place. Nay. Knowing, *he* was—and used to being wi' lasses. Very used he were." She smiled to herself, ran her tongue over her lips. "Wanting a good time, always wanting a good time. I were good to him summer nights—he learned me then. Said I'd be safe, I'd never to worrit—"

Ned had wanted to ask, shaking still, suddenly very very tired—how did she know now, how did she know she hadn't to worry? The beasts of the field . . . if they behaved that way, things happened, there were consequences. But she had said—and she said it again now—that it would be all right.

A little later, she said, "This lady come—he was to marry her, t'young gentleman was to marry her. He'd no time for me then, not even 'Good day, Nanny.' Finished wi' me, he had. I'd enough. I told on him then—I told his dad." She paused, reached for her bonnet. "That were how as I went wrong—did it wrong like. His dad, he listened right enow—only he was for doing t'same wi' me hissen. But I said, I said not. He'd an awful stink off him, and *old* . . . I said not. And so I lost it then, t'place. There weren't no one as'd believe what *I'd* to say, that he were just vexed I'd not have him—"

She sighed, lying back again. He could hear the steady click of a grasshopper not far away. A small blue butterfly flitted near them over the bracken.

"That's men then, that's what like they are. All manner on 'em. *All* t'same."

"I'm not," he said sadly. Even as he said it he knew it, profoundly, to be true.

FOURTEEN

December 1847. Usually at this time of year the ladies of Edinburgh are occupied with the balls and gatherings soon to be held in the Assembly Rooms. What will be worn? Who will capture whom? Indeed, already social events abound. Jenny Lind, the "Swedish Nightingale," has just sung in the Music Hall, and the week before Christmas there is to be a big Sale of Ladies' Work (in aid of Relief for the Destitute Highlanders). Among those listed as consenting to receive work is a Mrs. Dunbar of 42 Blacket Place.

But in fact only one subject is being discussed, both by the men in their clubs and the ladies in their drawing rooms—the arrest for fraud of James Dunbar, husband of that same lady who is even now receiving work at her home. And what an amount of handiwork she is receiving! A quite astonishing number of contributions—since for each caller the visit is spiced with the possibility of some first-hand titbit.

Those who have come to gloat, however, will be disappointed—unless it pleases them to hear that the lady of the house is prostrate, which indeed she is. Instead they are being received by the daughter, who although shaken is in possession, remarkably so, of herself. Visitors are more than impressed with her cool and dignified manner. Indeed some go away saying: "The brazen lassie . . ." She has even dared to sing twice at soirées—an execrable rendering of "The Last Rose of Summer" and another of "The Harp that Once . . ." However, when she sees callers now she is accompanied either by her Aunt Charlotte or, more often, by her childhood companion and confidante, Kirsty Buchanan. Where before they would sit in Catriona's room gossiping, now she and Kirsty sit in the upstairs drawing-room defiantly At Home.

And how long has this been going on? Although it seems to Catriona to have been all her life—and to Mrs. Dunbar more than that: this life and beyond, beyond—it has happened all very suddenly. Mrs. Dunbar would have done better to distrust not so much the railways, not so much even the Great Western Highlands Company—but rather her husband. For one day he was James Dunbar, a respected Edinburgh citizen, and the next, a prisoner charged with fraud of a quite astonishing magnitude.

Like so many frauds, his was based on an idea of the greatest simplicity. Luck too played a part. The Registrar of the Great Western Highlands Company when it was first formed in 1843 was a man quite ignorant of book-keeping and even more so of details of share registration. He had been taken on only as compensation for displacement from a Railway Company which had "fallen." James Dunbar knew this. He knew too, or rather recognised the chief clerk of the new company, a plausible rogue called Robert Wilkie. Ten years earlier he had dismissed him from his own employ, for sharp practice and light fingers.

Wilkie had not seemed embarrassed at meeting his former employer: on the contrary, rather pleased. And James Dunbar, to whom an idea had come, not slowly but at once, as if revealed by God, knew that he had found someone who, provided the cut was good enough, would be an able accomplice. It was on his recommendation, a short while after the resignation of the inexperienced Registrar, that Wilkie was promoted to that post.

Their method for making money was simply to declare dividends paid on a sum very much greater than the actual stock registered by the company. Wilkie was well able to take care of the manipulation of funds in the share registration department. Indeed, he became a very busy man, creating fictitious stock to any amount chosen by James Dunbar, and a little later converting it to hard cash through brokers (and there were many eager to be brokers in Edinburgh just then). What could be simpler than inventing names and forging signatures, since the forms to do so were ready to hand? What could be more pleasant and profitable? And since at that time no one could conceive of a company being systematically robbed through its share registration department, who would suspect anything? No checks or counter-checks were used. And if James Dunbar seemed suddenly to be wealthier than ever, had he not always had a reputation as a canny speculator? (Also, was it not *impressive*, the moral and financial support he has been giving to Robert Wilkie—known by some to have had difficulties in his past life but now helped into a position of trust?)

Gradually, but only very gradually, discrepancies are noted and remarked upon. It appears that to December 1844 dividends were paid on a stock larger by 80,000 than that registered. But neither Wilkie, richer by one quarter, nor James Dunbar, richer by three quarters, are too worried—since it is to James Dunbar that any discrepancies will be reported. And this is indeed what happens. A first tentative report by the chief book-keeper in the accountants department is sent to the chief clerk in the Secretary's office, who refers the alleged discrepancy back to that man of probity, the accountant, James Dunbar. He will indeed look into it, he says. "Even now," he tells them, "the Registrar is pursuing an inquiry . . ."

Taking his time, Wilkie produces a statement, together with one from James Dunbar, showing that dividends *have* been overpaid on stock. These are passed by the secretary to the chairman of the company, who allows himself to be satisfied by Dunbar's assurance that a thorough investigation is under way. These assurances are repeated at regular intervals as the inquiry proceeds with mind-boggling slowness through into 1846. There is always someone to blame for the delays in producing a proper explanation—but no one to distrust. Least of all James Dunbar.

And so on into 1847. A year of crisis in the money market and depression in many industries. James Dunbar in the late spring began to further his plans for moving to France after the marriage of his daughter (he will be happy in France, for has not Scotland ties with her stronger than any with England?), an event he is certain will take place by the winter at the latest.

But then in September the newspapers revealed suddenly a fraud of almost exactly the same type, in England. An arrest and a trial pending. The sheer effrontery of the fraud took everyone's breath away. People had not thought it possible. But over the next few weeks a revelation of the English criminal's methods alerted other companies. The Great Western Highlands Company, fearful that in the light of this, their shareholders might become suspicious of unexplained discrepancies, pressed the inquiry more urgently. It *must* be brought to a conclusion, and at the shortest possible notice.

In the numbing folly of panic, James Dunbar thought of leaving for France immediately, taking his wife and daughter with him, and writing explanatory and self-justifying letters to his sons. Both Mrs. Dunbar and Catriona, preoccupied with plans for the wedding (Catriona worried because Alan, leaving for a visit to America at the beginning of October, would not be able to attend), scarcely noticed his white-faced irritability—he pleaded pressure of business.

The hounds drew nearer to their quarry. The result of the inquiry, hotly pursued and now no longer in his hands, was a matter only of days. On Friday he decided that he would tell his family on the Saturday, and that they would flee on the Monday. He spent the next two days not telling them—confined to his room, ostensibly with a sick headache. (He who was never ill.)

On Monday he finally plucked up courage. But it was too late. His declaration preceded his arrest by only two hours. Mrs. Dunbar could believe in neither; the shock prostrated her completely and she took to her room, relying on Catriona to present a brave face to the outside world. Bail had been refused and visits to the prisoner not allowed. They sent in clothes and food but without knowing if they reached him.

Certainly if ever friends were needed it was now. In the Buchanans they had them. To Catriona it seemed that she had never valued Kirsty enough. The foolishly smiling face she was so often impatient with was pursed up now, firm, angry in her defence. Robbie was gallant. Catriona thought: I hardly deserve such friends.

She was all at once humble and strangely defiant (*she* had not done wrong). It was only at night, when she would wake with a start from her first sleep, that the thoughts flooded her mind. Everything would seem unbelievable yet at the same time only too real. Her father—while never lovable or even really loving—had been at the least someone to admire. Of her mother she expected little, but he—he had been gruff, firm, irascible, definite, *somebody*. He had been there and now was not. She had no Alan—already left. No Jamie, no Ewart.

The days dragged. So much had happened so suddenly, so much *would* happen, that this time of waiting seemed to spin out endlessly. And after the trial, after the certain sentence (and she had no illusions about that), what would happen to them then, to her and Mama?

She was to have been married. *Was* to have been. Papa had hurried her on—soon she would have escaped Mama. And the little asked of her: to please an almost middle-aged man who thought the world of her. Of course there would have to be children—preferably sons. And although all to do with that was not necessarily pleasant (from hints she had heard), it would admit her to the secret circle of women who murmured incomprehensibles to each other, made veiled references or hushed their conversation when she came into the room. A lively curiosity would be fulfilled. So far, all had been well: his occasional courteous embraces, his almost reverent caress of her lips had not been bad at all, in fact quite pleasant. She had thought, I could put up with those quite well—and any small advances on them which may be necessary.

Yes, she was to have been married. And *there* was more ammunition for wagging tongues, for a little while only after the arrest it was all off completely.

It happened, she thought, in the worst possible way. Both their letters, written after the arrest, had crossed. She and Kirsty had composed hers together. It had had much dignity, and she consoled herself with that now.

"I could not allow myself," she had written, "to bring on your family all the disgrace consequent on . . ." And remembering how he was to have given her social standing while she was to have brought him the dowry that would save him and his family from genteel poverty: "How sensible I am of all you were prepared to give me and would I know *still* be prepared to give—for is not your family motto 'Loyaltie Above All' . . ." And so on in that vein.

Some of the phrases were quite grand. Mama had not read it—she was not fit to, nor would she have approved. Robbie read and approved. But sadly, within two hours of dispatching it, *his* arrived. It was not so grandly phrased, and was not strictly speaking a breaking-off of the engagement ("He's too canny," Kirsty had commented indignantly). It suggested instead a lengthy postponement. "I could not bring myself to remove you from a home where you are so sorely needed. A mother must always come first. And while she needs you—and that will be I suspect for a very long time—there can be no question of our marrying. As Mother has suggested . . ."

She was not surprised when his second letter came, accepting graciously her "sacrifice." The episode was over. Her pride, not her heart, had been involved. But still she did not like the empty space. And she had reckoned without the outrage of her mother. In her darkened room, windows shut, bed-curtains drawn for much of the day, Mrs. Dunbar received the news—kept back from her as long as possible.

"My life all in ruins, Catriona, och who would ever have thought it—there is *nowhere* at all now I can go in the whole of Edinburgh, nowhere at all—what can I say to folk? How *could* you end your engagement, Catriona—" As she became more excited her speech would grow more Scots. Frequently she would have to stop for her brow to be dabbed soothingly.

"I'm sure now he would have married you in the end—I know all men are the same, it was all fine when my wee lass had a fine dowry—Catriona, how could you do this to me? Didn't you make a bonny couple all said and done if we're not too fussy about age—och he was a fine looking man for nearly forty and he'd been good to his mother, had he not—and that's what *you'll* have to be . . . It's all your father's doing that I married in good faith—och Catriona, if you hadn't written that foolish bit of a letter . . . he'd have come round, Catriona, it was only his way of saying, wait a wee while till I've come to terms with it. But now you've burned all your boats, *all* of them, Catriona . . ."

Kirsty was her greatest support, followed closely by Aunt Charlotte. Both of them were good with Mama, while Mrs. Buchanan sat with her almost daily. What would I do without them? Catriona thought. Her impassioned letter of misery and shock written at once to Alan would be only half way on its voyage. His reply would be a further six weeks at least. By then the trial, in some ways the worst of it, would be over. But after? The years yawned before her.

"Poor poor you," Kirsty said for the twenty-ninth time, "poor poor all of you . . ." But I can hold my head up, Catriona thought. Let the prissy ladies say what they will (and I've heard them when they don't hush their remarks quickly enough), let the ladies of the New Town chatter on—I, Catriona Dunbar, have done no wrong . . .

"Catriona, come and talk to me," Mama said, one cold dank darkening afternoon (but *all* days seemed cold and dank—where were the alpine, piercing blue skies of early winter, where the bracing chill?). "Come and talk to me. Och, tell me *it isn't true*, Catriona . . ."

She tried to ignore all this. "Will I get you another drink, a fresh pillow?" Then when the wailing continued: "Should you like to sit up a little? Let me lift you. I could read—"

"I always *said* about railways, did I not, Catriona—you'll surely mind that I did, always. I said, the Iron Horse—och the iron has entered into my poor soul, it's changed the whole face of Britain—I was happy to be jolted in a *horse*-drawn carriage, Catriona—I'm sure now there's something said in the Bible—the very sight of the railroads, Catriona. *Ill-looked* things . . ."

The room, frowsty smelling, was poorly lit. Of the two lamps one had just gone out. She would have liked to open the windows and curtains out onto Blacket Place: better the damp five o'clock chill than this fusty warmth.

"And I don't have my sons to help me, I'm quite alone, you don't know how long the nights have been and the days I don't know one from the other, Catriona—my only prayer is that the Lord will send for me soon, certainly I've suffered enough, those wagging heads and tongues—I shan't go out and face them, you shan't make me—Catriona, *do something!* What's the use to ask you when you're only fit to make a worse pother of things? If we could just have Alan, has anyone written to Alan, did you write to Alan—he must come back at once, whatever should those Americans want with him? . . ." Her breath smelled sour as she clutched at Catriona, the hair protruding from her cap smelled too; her hands were flaccid even as they were grasping.

There was a knock at the door. "Catriona, you'll save me, won't you, your own mama—you'll never let them point a finger at me, will you, *will you?*"

When the door opened it was the servant, Betty. She said, "Did I do right, miss, to bring them up?" She was staggering under the weight of two large flowering plants. In the poor light their glossy leaves looked waxed almost; from their pink blooms a sweet scent. Catriona gazed at them puzzled. She raised her eyebrows in query.

"They came, a laddie brought them, from Mrs. Carstairs' shop in George Street—"

"But is there no message?"

They had been placed on a table. "Oh," wailed Mrs. Dunbar, "somebody cares. I have support, I have friends—"

"Just your name, Miss Catriona—Miss Dunbar they said. Not a thing else."

Her mother said, "Find out, my love, who has sent them to me, what friend a poor sick ageing woman has in this world? Will you find out now?"

It was evening, nearly three hours since dinner. The nine o'clock tea tray had been and gone. Catriona sat in the little downstairs room. Kirsty and Mrs. Buchanan had left an hour ago, and she had read to Mama and settled her for the night. For herself she did not feel like reading, nor going up early to bed, nor doing needlework. She leafed wearily through a large drawing-room book lying on a table. Finden's *Beauties of the Poet Moore:* from its gilt-edged pages impossibly lovely portraits of Moore's female characters smiled up at her and failed to gain her attention.

The bell rang outside. She heard Betty's voice and then a man's, very low. She did not recognise it. Possibilities rushed through her mind. A nephew of Mr. Wilkie's who had called once and been thoroughly unpleasant? Yet another lawyer—someone from the judiciary?

"A Mr. Rawson to see you please, miss—do I do it right?"

He stood in the doorway. He was still in his outdoor cloak. There was frost clinging to it, and to his hat which he held in his hand. Betty hovered, ready to take it from him. He spoke abruptly.

"I'm staying, stopping at the Clarendon. I ought—I realise it would— that I ought to wait till morning—" He hesitated but still did not move. His accent which she had forgotten sounded strange to her.

"Not at all." She was embarrassed. She was not sure even that she would have recognised him—she had not thought of him, except occasionally, since Richmond. He stood taller than she remembered.

She signalled Betty away. "Your cloak, Mr. Rawson," she said. "You are still dressed for outdoors."

"Of course . . ." but still he did not move.

Puzzled: "Did Robbie—" she began.

"I had his letter four days ago. It was not possible for me to leave my work—quite immediately. Only, perhaps I should have suggested myself first? I—"

She shook her head. "Och, not at all." His face was flushed with the cold. His eyes a very clear blue. She had never noticed them before. "You must be at once by the fire, Mr. Rawson. And tea. Will I ring for some tea?"

But he continued to stand there, neither in nor out of the room, for several seconds. Then:

"I am come," he said slowly. "As you see. I am come, to take care of you—Catriona."

FIFTEEN

7th December 1847

Dear Journal,

Who would have thought, a year ago, such a terrible truly *awefull* Christmas time could happen? Yet here I am, with poor Papa's trial only a few weeks away—and *not unhappy!* (Or only for him—and for Mama, who I am sad to say is not managing *at all.*) Why am I not unhappy, dear Journal? Because I have found, at last, yes I have truly found my—it is HE, yes HIM, my Corsair! And oh, dear Journal, I knew it in a blinding flash, just as I always (forgive me, *Kirsty* and I) always thought we would. Dear Journal, I must not think of Kirsty just this moment, it is too sad. But I have done *nothing wrong.*

This is what happened, dear Journal. There I was, night time, sitting quite alone, worn out by Mama's ravings, and feeling *so* glum, so *without hope.* Those beautiful plants left behind in Mama's room, what were they, I thought, but a peace offering from the Honble Iain—wanting to show a proper concern and be praised for it now that he is absolutely safe? (What a fairweather friend, dear Journal, *he* has proved to be!)

But *no!* Who was it so ready then to take on our disgrace—who *sees* no disgrace, but counts it only a privilege to be allowed to take care of me—asking so humbly if there was any hope, if I remembered what he had asked in the spring, if now that I was free there was any possibility at all? And his first words, after the early awkwardness when, dear Journal, he just *stood* there—"I am come," he said, "to take care of you, Catriona" (not Miss Dunbar, but *Catriona.* I never thought my name would give me such a shock).

But what could I say, dear Journal? Because looking up I saw only my Corsair, my HERO! So straight, so tall, so true (how could I have been so blind—how could I so nearly have missed—my heart flutters with the very notion), those broad shoulders carrying all the weight of my troubles. Strong curly hair to ruffle my fingers through when he has borne me away in his arms through the storm, through the dark valley. And those eyes—how was it I never looked into those *eyes*?

Oh, Journal, I am so happy! So very very happy—

Catriona Dunbar scripsit.

P.S. Catriona *Rawson* to-be! Oh Journal, we are *to be married!*

SIXTEEN

. . . And behold, there met him a woman with the attire of an harlot, and subtil of heart . . . She caught him, and kissed him, and with an impudent face said unto him, . . . Come, let us take our fill of love until the morning . . . With her much fair speech she causeth him to yield, with the flattering of her lips she forced him. He goeth after her straightway as an ox goeth to the slaughter . . . as a bird hasteth to the snare, and knoweth not that it is for his life.

Proverbs 7:10–23

For Ned, a whole year of loving Kate had passed. Eighteen forty-seven, the year of the miracle which had been her resurrection, her flowering. Now she was completely a child. Little monkey, little skinny hairy animal—become a seven-year-old girl now. And if not quite his, not completely his own—then if *wishing* could make it so . . . Father, brother, uncle, protector, he would be all of those.

His little cockyolly bird. Every evening when he came in dusty from work, it was *she* greeted him, *her* joyful face, little thin arms clasping his neck so tight. Now she could run to meet him. O red-haired miracle! God be praised, for it was God they had called upon that evening of John's return when, wrapped in a blanket, in a cloak, she had come into their lives. He wanted only, every day, to say thank you.

"O sing unto the Lord a new song; for he hath done marvellous things . . . Praise him with the sound of the trumpet . . . Praise him with stringed instruments and organs. Praise him upon the loud cymbals . . ." And upon the flute: this year he was to play in church with the musicians and choir for the Christmas service. The Reverend Cuthbert had called on Mother and asked especially if Ned would consider it. Praise and joy: Kate would be there—she could be trusted now not to point him out with noisy delight—he would play for *her*.

He had tried to forget completely about the Nanny episode. Fortunately he had not seen her—or only once and then, bending down and pretending something had stuck to his boot sole, he had escaped immediately into a shop. But since in the New Year her sister would be old enough to look after the family and Nanny able to take another place, he need not be afraid for long. He trembled still, though—he didn't want to examine how he felt, did not want to think about her even. Since their meeting, he had not been wicked, not once. I have put all that behind me, he thought. And it had not been so very difficult. He had had only to pray *at once*, before temptation took hold ("O Lord, cleanse thou me from my secret faults lest they get the dominion over me—so shall I be undefiled and innocent from the great offence . . .").

It was Becky worried him, as always in the winter. On his last visit she'd seemed withdrawn and melancholy—he had put it down to the weather, which although crisp and dry, now had been damp and chill. It seemed to slow her. Nothing, though, slowed down her dog, who wanted to be out in all weathers. "Whining to go, Cap is, long afore sun's up . . ." Sheath round her waist, she was crouched over her knitting. He'd brought her a small ham, for his Christmas gift, in case he should not be able to come up again: "And you've to take care, Becky, Cap isn't the one that eats it . . ."

Only three weeks to Christmas. He came back from work and sang on the walk home. He didn't mind who heard or stared (and Tom and two other fellows coming out of the Black Swan did give him a very odd look). He had it in mind to teach Kate a carol this very evening.

As he entered the house, Eliza was coming downstairs. She seemed about to speak to him—he thought it might be news about John, gone on an unexpected journey north: an Edinburgh friend in some kind of trouble. But she must have thought better of it, for she scuttled past him as if suddenly in a hurry. In the hall a door opened and Father came out.

"Ned."

"Yes. Yes, Father."

"In here. As soon as you are washed."

But what was this? What? He combed, brushed his hair down slick, fearful of he had no idea what. This was the manner of God the Father . . . He tried to think: his returns on the yarn, his keeping of the books —he was two days behind. Confusion and muddle in the Christmas period. Some plough lines which had not been ready for collection. But he felt only nameless dread. He hated the memory of being hauled over the coals. Schooldays ("Edwin, what's this account I have from Mr. Tate—learning may not seem important to you, but good money shan't ever if I can help it be wasted. By the sweat of our brows, son . . .").

There were other people in the room. It seemed to him suddenly very dark, even though the oil lamps were all lit. Mr. Haygarth was standing. He was to the right of the fireplace, his head a little bowed, his hat clutched tightly to his chest. At first Ned didn't notice Nanny. She was on a footstool beside the horsehair sofa, sitting hunched up. It *was* her. Indeed it could be no one else. And Father: he stood exactly in front of the fireplace.

"Well, eh? Well, Ned—"

"Yes, Father. No, Father . . ."

"Well, eh, here's a fine state of affairs. Here's a pretty kettle of fish, eh?"

I am so small—he had never, for so many years now, been so small. He came scarcely to the height of the chair back, his legs were not muscle, skin, bone, but mere soft things full of waste yarn, remnants from the works floor.

"Well?"

Silence. Mr. Haygarth looked up then, but not at Ned, everywhere but at Ned—eyes once frank slid and missed his.

"*Well?*" Father stood foursquare, his toes turned out.

Oh, but what am I to say? The dreadful certainty, coming to him so quickly. It could not be the truth.

"I'm waiting, Ned, for some *explanation.*"

There seemed too many syllables to that last word. Some ex-plan-a-tion. He could not speak, he knew he could not speak. The silence, perhaps one, two minutes old, was like to last forever. He couldn't open his mouth, even to say that he couldn't speak . . .

"Well, if you've nowt to say, son—then Haygarth here, *he* has. Eh, Haygarth?" He turned, suddenly fierce, "Let's have it, then. Tell the lad."

And all the while Nanny had not moved. Once only, her black-booted foot twitched.

Father said, as if to himself, impatiently, "Now *he'll* not speak either—"

Mr. Haygarth cleared his throat.

"She's in trouble—like I said—like I've told your father, Mr. Edwin. Like I told you, sir. The lass is in trouble—"

"And whose doing is that?" Father asked. "Speak up, man."

"She's got no mother, sir." He mumbled into his chest. "I lost me—"

Father said angrily, "Will no one speak up clear? Tell Mr. Edwin what you told me, please. What's all this about *mothers*—there's been wickedness, hasn't there, eh?"

Mr. Haygarth said, "She's in trouble, sir—sorry, Mr. Edwin I mean, she's in trouble. Nigh on, nigh on—" He faltered. From her stool, Nanny said in a loud clear voice, "Three. More'n three."

"More'n three month gone. And she says like, Mr. Edwin, she told me like, it's your doing . . ." His voice faded away.

Father said, sharply now, "And you're quite certain? Oughtn't we maybe have Anne's—your daughter's, word for it?"

But Nanny had gone silent again, her head on her knees.

"She's—she's too upset like to speak, say owt. She lost her mother ye see, sir. Gone with a fever. And then me sister—"

"I know," Father said impatiently, "I know. I mind very well about Mrs. Haygarth. And your sister. God has been very hard. But His ways are strange and past understanding. Remember the book of Job—suffering, it can may be a sign of God's special caring. Have you read the book of Job? Do you read your Bible, Haygarth?"

"Aye, sir. Nay, sir—there's little time, sir."

"There's always time for the word of God, Haygarth. Remember—'many are the afflictions of the righteous, but the Lord delivereth him out of them all . . .'"

For a brief moment Ned felt, hoped, that he had been forgotten. But:

"The Word of God, Haygarth—would that my son had heeded it." He turned to Ned. "There's truth in this then, eh?"

He thought if he said, "I have sinned," that would be best. Just to say that, and having said it, to bow his head, keep it bowed, to accept the blows which would fall.

"I—" he began.

"Well?"

"Yes," he said. "Yes." He looked at Mr. Haygarth, not at Father. "Yes—I went with her."

Father said to Mr. Haygarth, "She's seen the surgeon?"

"She's—there's little need of doctors, sir, women know, sir. Me sister, sir, that was visiting. Nanny's not been keeping food down, sir, not a bite. I've seen it come up, sir. And there's the other sign—"

"Yes, right, that'll do, Haygarth." Father was rubbing his hands together. His gaze avoided Ned's. "You've no need to concern yourself. Right will be done. My son—maybe he's said little—he was never a lad that spoke up—but he's admitted his sin. And I've no doubt he'll pay the price like a man. Right will be done, Haygarth." He gazed before him. "'And if a man entice a maid that is not betrothed, and lie with

her, he shall surely endow her to be his wife.' Exodus twenty-two . . ."
He turned: "You're chapel, aren't you, Haygarth? And your wife and
Anne—Nanny, that is—they're church? Eh? Chapel or church it makes
no odd, it's all God's word. And the Lord has told us, didn't He—'what
a man sows, so shall he reap . . .' "

Mr. Haygarth mumbled, "I'm sure I'm, we're very grateful, sir, to
know she'll be seen right—"

"When did you say—when do they say the bairn—my *grandchild* is
likely?"

Nanny, who had sat up a moment before, stared boldly now at Father. He must have taken it for fear and respect, since he smiled at her
kindly.

"June, sir—they think early June like."

"Then there's not time to lose." He smiled bitterly: "There'll have to
be some swift courting, if we're not to surprise the townfolk. Those
who gossip . . . Let anyone cast a stone, Haygarth—she's not the first
nor the last lass to fall. And I like to think, Haygarth, that had it been
Samuel Rawson, he'd have faced up to his sin and its consequences . . ." He turned suddenly to Ned. "And you, son. There's to be
a courtship. And mind it's seen . . ."

Ned nodded miserably. He did not dare to look around in case his
gaze should meet Nanny's. Father was still speaking to Mr. Haygarth.

"There'll be no hiding, though—what's passed between them." He
shook his head. "A six-month child." Then he turned to Ned: "You'd
best speak to Mr. Cuthbert. The banns, the spurrings, they'll have to be
put in quick . . ."

Ned stood absolutely still, looking at the picture above Father's head.
It was of a soldier saying goodbye to a girl—clasping her to him. He had
used once to make stories up about it. He could hear his heart thumping, but slowly, slowly, turning over in his chest.

"And now," Father said, "we shall all pray." He knelt down. From
habit, Ned followed him immediately. He saw Mr. Haygarth, glancing
uneasily first at Nanny, bend his knees awkwardly. Nanny was the last
to touch the ground. Father, his eyes shut, raised his voice, " 'Have
mercy upon me, O God, according to thy loving kindness. Wash me
thoroughly from mine iniquity, and cleanse me from my sin. For I acknowledge my transgressions: and my sin is ever before me. Behold I
was shapen in iniquity; and in sin did my mother conceive me. Purge
me with hyssop and I shall be clean: wash me, and I shall be whiter
than snow. Make me to hear joy and gladness; that the bones which
thou hast broken may rejoice . . .' "

SEVENTEEN

Sarah thought: last Christmas—as if that wasn't eventful enough. What with Hannah and the babe, and Ireland, and Kate . . . She did not want, particularly did not want, to remember too much about Hannah. For a week before the anniversary of finding the small body, she had had recurrent nightmares, sometimes twice and even three times a night. Mostly Hannah and Ireland and the Kissing Gate (occasionally Arthur Greaves too—she reminded herself that Sam must do something about him, *soon* . . .). Stories that John had told her of his Irish experiences became now real in her dreams. The wailing she heard always: it started almost as soon as she fell asleep (often she knew that she was dreaming and would cry out: "I want to *wake* . . ."), but the gaunt figures, spectres really, which crowded at the Kissing Gate, starving children clutched to them, had the face always of Hannah—sometimes Arthur, as he had been that day he swung on the gate—but mostly reproachful, desperate, yet still sullen Hannah . . .

"She'll swing," Ned told her, in the dreams. Coming into family prayers, white-faced—interrupting Sam, coming up and touching her on the shoulder: "She'll *swing*, you know . . ."

As if, she thought, I haven't enough already. Ned. *And John.* (But that I'll think about later—I cannot face that now . . .) Ned. What folly there. What a *fool* . . .

That had been her first reaction to the news. When Sam had told her (for Ned would not speak to her that evening, but had gone straight to his room, without a word—even for his Kate), she had said at once: "The fool." Then again and again: "The fool, the fool . . ." She could hardly bear to listen to Sam's remarks about "right" and "righteousness" and "scandal" and "fornication"—she had said instead in angry tones: "It'll have to be stopped . . ."

But Sam, as so often, scarcely listened. When his mind was made up

(and how harsh he had been with Hannah), when the matter concerned religion, then he was as a pillar, unmoving. And deaf too. Deaf
to all entreaties.

"I'll get money," she said. "If we've not enough, I'll find it. Squire
now—he'd lend. He must be used enough to such tales . . ."

Sam lifted his hand. She should have taken the warning. But she had
persisted.

"I've not seen the lass—yet. But if Ned's concerned then it'll not
have been him done the—" she sought for the word, "the talking, Sam
—and whatever else . . . He's a good lad. He'll have been 'ticed—"

Sam's hand, crashing down on the table, so that poor Muzzy asleep
on one of the chairs had shot out of the room as if from a gun . . .

"'My lips shall not speak wickedness, nor my tongue utter deceit . . .' There's been evil done—and the price, it's to be paid—and
that's all about it. So we'll have no more talk of buying off, eh? I'll make
as if I've not heard it. Inghams—they may do as they please, but a Rawson . . . The lad's learned his lesson and he must make now of his
wedded life what he can. She seems a bonny enough lass—and speaks up
for herself. What with being a father in the summer—I don't doubt but
it'll make a man of him yet . . ."

But all that had been before John, and his news. It is too much, she
thought, when rushing straight from the coach, scarcely setting down
his luggage, he had taken her aside to tell her . . .

"You never said, son." She repeated it twice. "You never said,
son . . ." The shock, it was too much. What did she know even of this
Miss Dunbar? Miss Buchanan, Kirsty, a little—he had said a little, and
she had feared. But this . . . She scarcely recognised the name. And it
had been she caused the disappointment in April.

"I'm all at sea," she said. "You've taken me aback. And what's all
this about rescue?"

But then when she'd heard, when more calmly he'd told her the
whole story—she hadn't liked it at all. Prison. Fraud. Prison . . .

"We're only just out of all that, son. Hannah—that business. And
now to be tied up with it again." She could not describe the sick feeling
it gave her, just the word "prison." Visiting Hannah. The pity. The
remorse.

"Come now," he had said. "It's Edinburgh, Mother. And far away.
Nothing to do with Downham at all."

"Folk will say something—"

"They'll say nothing. They will know nothing . . ."

In the end, she had believed him. It wasn't, after all, as if that was the most important part of it all. The worst, surely the very worst, was that now she was to lose him. As she had always feared, as she had always *known* . . .

And grand, how grand this Miss Dunbar sounded. Almost quality. John could not have meant it, but it seemed to her that every second remark was about some luxury or smart appurtenance that the Dunbars had now sacrificed—which she, Sarah, had never had or known . . . All John could think about, it seemed, was Miss Dunbar's generosity in agreeing to marry him (*she* is the privileged one, *she* should be the one to feel humble—that such a fine lad should want to give his whole life to her . . .). It is too much, Sarah said to herself again and again. It is too much. When for about the twentieth time John told her of his Catriona's beauty (and it seemed that never, never in Scotland or Yorkshire or indeed the whole world had there been looks to match hers . . .), she had said somewhat sharply, and much more sharply than she intended, "Well enough, son. But bonny is as bonny does . . . I'll wait till I've met her—and then I'll speak my mind—eh?"

That wedding, however, wasn't to be till April or May. Ned's was soon, very soon—too soon. A home must be found, the ceremony arranged: this, that, the other. And all the while Ned struck almost dumb. It was *she* to do all the work (Sam, it seemed, found it enough to speak the Word of God—the practical aspects of it all, they were for the Marthas of this world. And that is me, Sarah thought).

There was Old Jacob Rawson to be told, and it was she of course to do it. She had told him as little as possible, made a great story of their courting through the summer . . .

"Aye," he shouted once or twice, "aye—I thought as there were summat up."

It was only a few steps then to hinting that Squire Ingham would be wanting to help (better not mention John yet—that could come after Christmas. And he could do it, and do it well, for himself . . .). Just a word or two about a visit to the Abbey and how the Squire had always had in mind to help the first lad to wed . . .

"Oh well, aye," he muttered, clapping his hand on his thigh, sending cake crumbs scattering, "if t'lad's to be wed, they'll want a place—the two on 'em. They'll not want to be sharing at Hillside, like poor folk that . . ." He turned fierce, fire-reddened eyes on her: "A few pound on a cottage like—I might manage that. Brass for a cottage. Aye. And let 'em get theirsen a mile or two out—have Rawsons take ower one o' t'villages mebbe Leyburn way . . ." He chuckled to himself. "We'll have Rawsons all ower Wensleydale yet. If they could do it now wi'out t'lasses—that'd be best . . ." He shouted suddenly, "Get Minnie. Where's t'lazy lass? Eh? Nowt to do but idle . . ."

"Ye can go now," he said to Sarah. "I'll send word."

A cottage was found, without much trouble, at Little Grinling: a mile or two from Downham, on the Abbey not the Leyburn side. Ned would have to ride into the rope-works. It had been empty several weeks through the death of the tenants, and was the property of Squire Ingham. Sarah had been to see him, and a straight sale had been arranged at a modest price. She *thought* that Ned was pleased, or rather that he was relieved that the problem was solved . . .

And it was a pretty enough place, even if in poor condition—the tenants had been very old, and repairs had been postponed at their request. It stood just back from the village green in Little Grinling, with its own enclosed garden and best of all, Sarah thought, a mountain ghyll running alongside right through their grounds, rippling and gurgling from under the bridge which led into the village. The cottage itself, although small, was stoutly built, mostly in the seventeenth century. Parts of it, however, dated back to the fifteenth century, when with its stone quoins it had probably first been put up. Its main feature was a two-light window from that date, which had perpendicular tracery and reached up the two storeys of the cottage at the east end.

At least, she told herself, at least they start with every chance. And who knows (although meeting Nanny the day before viewing the cottage, she had not, really, liked her *at all* . . .), who knows that in the end, forced match though it is, it may not work out all right?

She tried at that year's end, and the new one's beginning, to count her blessings. 1847. It had seen the flowering of little Kate (my redemption, she thought). And she must not remember how jealous, how *difficult* Walter was . . . Kate prospered, and grew tall and healthy and would now without doubt live. What a contrast to last Christmas . . . This March would see her birthday: it would be on the 17th, St. Patrick's Day—and she would be eight they had decided.

And Sam had promised that in the New Year, he would take on Arthur Greaves as apprentice at the works. There was room for him now. She would have fulfilled her promise to Hannah.

Taken by and large, it was going to be *all right*. Catriona Dunbar. I will not think of her just now. And perhaps anyway, perhaps she *is* as lovely, and as sweet, and as gentle and as quite, quite perfect—maybe she *is* all that John says?

EIGHTEEN

Here's a happy new year! but with reason
I beg you'll permit me to say—
Wish me *many* returns of the *season*
But as *few* as you please of the day.

> BYRON, "On My Wedding Day"

Choose not alone a proper mate
But proper time to marry.

> COWPER, "Pairing Time Anticipated"

Charles Ingham was with his wife and two of the children. They were speaking with some people in the market square and Ned thought at first that he had not been seen. But Charles, raising his hand, beckoned to him—the royal command. Then eyes narrowed, he took Ned by the arm, leading him away a little from the others.

"My dear fellow—what's this we've been hearing in church—two Sundays now . . ."

"Yes," Ned said. "Yes. I'm to be married." He added sourly, "Natural enough, isn't it—being wed?"

"Ah indeed, my dear fellow, what more natural?" He paused. "*Very* natural. The beasts of the field." He had his hand on Ned's arm, was pressing it, "Come—we're men together. Tell me, Ned, has there not been perhaps a certain—*haste*, eh?"

"Haste or leisure," Ned said angrily, "it comes to the same. And none of it your concern."

"Aren't we just a little . . . I really believe I've struck home. And that's not easy for Charles Ingham. Now tell me, your friend Becky, what does *she* think of all this?"

"And that'll not be your concern either—"

"Really, Ned—and not even 'sir' when you speak. Mrs. Ingham will be watching. Mrs. Ingham *is* watching." His voice altered. "Your infernal impudence, your rough manner with me, Ned. I could take a horse whip to you. You know that—"

"Let me be—"

"Eh now, Ned. I asked only, what would *Becky* say to all this?" He tightened his grip. His breath smelled of brandy as his face, already unpleasantly close, came closer. "Old enough to be your mother, isn't she? I expect *you* think that. But that don't mean she hasn't feelings— Who's to know she hasn't thought—'Well, what a fine lad, if I only had the—had the—had the . . .'" His voice trailed away. "You have a lovely skin, Ned. Good that, to the touch . . . She'll get a great shock there, I warrant, when she hears."

"Let me be," Ned said again. He heard his voice grown ugly, thick.

Charles said: "I think you will never learn that I mean well, Ned." He removed his hand and, lifting it, clapped him suddenly on the back. "I shall raise my voice now, Ned. Dissemble . . ." An arm went round Ned's shoulder.

"No holding back on that order, then, dear fellow. Excitement about the forthcoming event distracting you, eh? An order's an order for all that. A dozen halters, then—by Wednesday?"

Kate. Oh, *Kate*. That was the worst loss. A life without Kate. Soon they would not even be in the same house. And then, who would care enough about her? *Who would care as much as he?* In his blackest moments, he thought, I cannot live without her. He had imagined she needed him (and she did, she did). But it is I, he said to himself now, it is I who need Kate . . .

Everything was new for her. She who had been born a second time, her first childhood forgotten. And this new one all contained in a few months so that she had been two three four five six, all in one summer. With what wonders yet to come? And it was to have been I, he thought bitterly, I to show her it all. To *share* it all. He remembered again that spring day in the churchyard when he had carried her in through the Kissing Gate, and hiding behind a tombstone, she had played with flowers—and Nanny had come in through the kirk gate to tend her mother's grave. . . .

When he had heard about the cottage he had known then for certain that he was to be separated from Kate. Little Grinling was two miles almost from Downham. He would have to ride into the rope-works. Now, unless he arranged to go to his old home for dinnertime, he would only see Kate on Sundays.

There could be no arguing about the cottage—about anything in fact. He had never had a choice, never made a decision—looking back, he saw only that he had accepted—everything. Accepted for Nanny too. She was consulted in nothing. In some ways that gave him a feeling of satisfaction, although he knew it to be wrong, to think like that. But if he had no say in the whole matter, why should she?

Sunday, that had once been his special day, for Kate—he now had to spend paying court to Nanny. They must be *seen* to be keeping company. In the morning in church, from their separate seats, they heard their banns read. The spurrings. In the afternoon he had to visit her house and stay for a meal with her family.

An aunt was living there now, staying until Martha, the elder of the sisters, could take over the house. She was pale and timid, the aunt, and she treated Ned with surprised respect and a little awe—even dusting his chair before he sat in it. Nanny's father was awkward with him. And no wonder, Ned thought. The memory of that terrible interview, hanging over them, seemed to freeze them both.

And Nanny herself? How should he behave with her? She did not seem at the moment at all the confident, impudent, *pert* girl he'd known. This he put down to her physical state. Her family remarked on it too.

"Nanny's a quiet one these days," her aunt said. And her father: "T'lass don't chatter as she used . . ." But then suddenly, her mood would lighten, and she would make as if to snuggle up to him, speak boldly, tease him. The old Nanny. And while he hated it with part of him, he would also feel pity for her. Great pity. Because it was his doing. That she was the way she was—it was *his* doing.

I must tell Becky. When he moved to Little Grinling he would be nearer to her by quite some distance. *I shall have to tell her,* he thought, that I am to be a married man. (But not why: he wouldn't tell her it wasn't wanted, that it was only so that Nanny should not have a chance bairn.) But he had put off visiting her, and put it off so that—something he had never done before—he hadn't even visited her at Christmas. Now the wedding was less than a week away.

He was to be married on Saturday. On the Monday he didn't go back to work after dinner, inventing some excuse so feeble he'd forgotten it half an hour later, then stopping only to steal a potted trout from the larder, to add to his Christmas gifts for her, he set out. Bitterly cold. Snow in the air, in the dark stinging of the wind and the hush which came always before it fell. Perhaps it would even fall while he was there? Fall in a great blanket, burying him and Becky for a month. A week. *Six days* even. Then he would not be able to come to church on Saturday . . . He would not have to marry Nanny.

"I'm to be wed," he announced, almost as soon as she let him in—shuffling towards him with roughly bound feet ("It's t'cold, they've swelled up—starved they are . . ."). She made him sit down while she poked at the half-alive fire. He shivered.

"Spirits—d'ye want a sup? It's *ye* look starved, Mister Ned." With bandaged foot she kicked at Cap, who had stepped in front of the fire. He gave a token growl, and slunk behind the old table.

"I'm to be wed."

"I heard—"

"Who from—who's been this way?"

"None—I said, I *heard*. You've no call to shout like that." She wasn't looking at him. "Ned," she said, "Ned, what you done?"

"There's nothing for it but for me to be wed. I'm telling you—bringing you the news before it's to happen." In his guilt he knew he sounded angry: "I'd meant to be up the while. For Christmas. I've your gifts here—"

"T'wedding—it weren't your notion?"

He hesitated, then shook his head.

"Aye," she said, "aye—and I'll say it, I don't hold wi' folk wedding. Ye'll ken that." She sounded distressed. "Becky don't hold wi' it—even when I were a lass. All that—what they do . . . You'd better live alone as do that—" She was mumbling to herself. "Afore I come up here," she said. "When they tell me—when Becky heard summat bad . . ."

Ned said, after a moment: "Well, if *all* were of that mind, there'd not be many left in Downham. Or in the world for that matter—"

"And what's wrong wi' *that*, eh? There's some should go tomorrow—*could* go, and there'd be no mourning."

"Becky," he said reproachfully, "where's all your hate come from?" He was frightened that carelessly he might let slip the name "Ingham." He added quickly, "And when God loves you—"

"*Where's the signs o' that?*" She spat angrily, shaking her head: "Muck—allus muck in me throat."

"I've a home," he told her, "*we've* a home—it's nearer to you, Becky. Maybe I'll be up more often." He was shivering still. The fire, although she'd stoked it up with fresh peats from the straw skep standing alongside, had come up only a little.

"Aye. Well enow . . ." She nodded to herself. Then with a change of mood, chuckling suddenly: "If ye've bairns come, the two on you—

don't go fetching 'em up here, Ned. Cap'll have 'em." Anything less like a baby-eating dog than the mock-ferocious Cap, at present licking the tails of Ned's coat, was hard to imagine. "Hares, coneys," she said proudly, "foxes, bairns—it's all one and t'same to that one . . ."

"You talk about him as if he was your bairn—"

He thought she might be angry. But she appeared not to have heard. Lifting Cap up, he fondled his ears.

"You're a good lad," she said into the silence, "and Becky wishes you well." Her voice sounded choked. "Fool," she said. "Gert fool that ye are. Hoppling yissen wi' a wife. Fondhead," she added angrily. "*Muttonhead . . .*"

His wedding day. It might have been springtime: confident blue of the sky, a thrush in song, hedge-sparrows in the birch copse in the churchyard—lured out falsely, for it was not a happy day. *I will be good*, he said through his misery, his feeling of doom. (Was this what life on this earth was to be? Only heaven to look forward to?)

Martha and Tabby Haygarth were the bridesmaids. And Kate. That had been Mother's idea. There had never been a question of Ann and Eliza: they were to walk behind John's bride in Edinburgh. Money could not be spent needlessly on dresses which must be replaced in April or May. For his and Nanny's marriage anything would do. The dressmaker had been called in hastily and not very successfully. Neither Martha, who was rather lanky, nor Tabby, who was smaller and rounder, looked well. It seemed as if the same dress had been made for both and fitted neither. Nor did the colour suit.

But Kate—that was another matter. Small, frail, she was transformed. In apple green, her thin arms (sticklike still) could be glimpsed through the transparent fabric. Her wreath of white flowers wove into the gentle flaming of her hair. He had known they were to dress her up, but that had not prepared him for this heart-turning beauty. It was *she*, not Nanny, who was the shock when (although he knew he shouldn't) he turned in church and saw the small procession walking up. His eyes, glancing away from the veiled Nanny, rested long, too long, on Kate. He would for the length of the ceremony have before him this reminder of his loss. Of what he had forfeited. *Oh, my little one, my cockyolly bird . . .*

Nanny was pale. He had never seen her so pale. She trembled when he put the ring on her finger. There came off her a smell of fear, as from some animals. He recognised it through his gloom. His own fear too. His voice shook as he said the words (fateful, for all time):

"I, Edwin Josiah, take thee, Anne Susan, to my wedded wife . . . for

better for worse, for richer for poorer, in sickness and in health, to love
and to cherish, *till death do us part . . .*"

Even here in the midst of life it was necessary to speak of death. And
it was the life in her belly, as she stood beside him, which was the cause
of his death here and now. His death in life.

" 'O well is thee . . . Thy wife shall be as the fruitful vine . . . Thy
children like the olive branches: round about thy table. Lo, thus shall
the man be blessed: that feareth the Lord . . .' "

The voice of the Reverend Cuthbert, from all the Sundays of his
childhood. A university voice, smooth and as from a mind far away,
reading now from the scriptures (he and Nanny had not been thought
worth a sermon).

" '. . . Hear also what Saint Peter . . . saith unto them that are married; ye husbands, dwell with your wives according to knowledge; giving
unto the wife, as unto the weaker vessel . . . Now likewise, ye wives
. . . submit yourselves unto your own husbands . . . For the husband is
the head of the wife . . .' "

Coming out of the church door: if only he could have escaped.
Stolen away, unseen, down the elm-tree-lined path to the kirk gate. Out
onto the road. Over the hills, and far away . . .

But they had of course to go out by the Kissing Gate: the snow of a
few days ago melted now, so that the beck cascaded through its narrow
opening, rushing over the stones, past the dank ivy-coated wall, on its
way to the Down. The light was already going as the procession made
its way slowly down the path. Rooks cawed raucously in the elms behind them.

And it was there at the Kissing Gate, with people watching, that he
had to lean towards Nanny, and kiss her. When he had done it he felt
a great surge of pity—for himself, or for her? She looked so frail. So
unlike the seducer. It seemed she timidly awaited some blow—from
fate, or from man? Nature, God, had played enough tricks on her.

And, he thought, reluctantly taking her hand, on him too.

Their cottage was only partly ready. There had not been enough
time. The new window in the little room at the back was only half-
fitted. To keep out the January cold from the rest of the cottage they
must keep the room firmly shut. They were not to have a living-in servant, but a fire had been lit for them downstairs and in the larger bedroom on the east side—the room where the floor ended abruptly, allowing the medieval window to reach up clear from the kitchen below
(Nanny had wanted it covered in, the floor made flush—but he liked

both the danger and the beauty . . . and when the bairn came, could they not make a little railing?).

The bed was a gift from his family. It gleamed at him with its solid brass. Its chintz curtains were badly and hastily hung.

The cottage felt damp and unlived in. They shivered before the fire. He felt only pity for her—none for himself. Nervously she went twice outside to the privy and came back, her uncovered head damp, her body shaking. They had neither of them eaten or drunk much at the short wedding feast. Now, although food had been left for them, she wanted nothing.

He thought, I shall have to do tonight, soon, what I did in the summer. He could not imagine that it would be as it was then, that this new subdued person would change suddenly between the sheets. It would be all for him to do. Tired but tense, he felt a sudden desire, gone almost as soon as it came, to take her. Had she not been the first, the only? Surely their coming together again would mean something, would subtly but certainly alter everything? He thought now, I cannot wait.

It seemed an age. She said, "I think I'll mebbe—like, go up."

"Shall I carry the light? Those stairs—I could put a light up there first. And the pan, the warming pan—that's in?"

"Aye." She nodded. Then: "Nay—I'll tak light. Don't rush me, eh, Ned. It'll tak a while afore I'd want ye up there . . ." Her voice trailed away.

When he came up she was already lying down. She was on her side, a hump under the coverlet, tousled hair escaping from her nightcap. He made himself ready swiftly. When he climbed in she did not move, and he put out a hand. He touched her on the shoulder, but she pulled away.

"Leave off, will ye, Ned. I'm daul'd oot."

"I'm tired too," he said. "I reckon people are always tired on their weddings—" He thought then that if he truly pitied her fears and fatigue, he would leave her to sleep. Only, something had risen in him: not just the physical stirring—that would die down, must die down (and if it really would not, then he would have to go away, out of the room, go downstairs perhaps and be wicked). It was something else. He *must* have her.

"Come on, love. Just a kiss, then." She turned and he fastened his mouth on hers. The smell of fear could still be tasted, but now somehow it drew him. He felt a great power, because he had made her afraid. (She who had triumphed so, laughed so—in August had she not, in the end, laughed at him?) While he kissed her he pulled her over towards him. He ran his hands down her body. But there, where he had thought to go, he felt thick encumbrance, his hands hindered by wedges of fabric. His touch lingered, in puzzlement. Had she on still her drawers? She who had worn nothing, nothing at all that time?

"What's this?" he began, not knowing how to ask.

"I've said—I'm daul'd oot. Let me be, Ned."

"I'll not take long," he said, almost angrily, but pleadingly too. He hated the note in his voice; the fact that he must have her . . .

How to ask? "Nanny—what's all this—down there?"

"Nowt. I just . . . It's nowt—"

He tried to think: "Are you—is it maybe you're afraid—for the bairn? That it'll be harmed if we do . . ."

"Aye," she said, turning right away from him, "that's it. And I'm daul'd oot too, like I said. Eh, *Ned*—"

"I'm not afraid," he said. "What's to fear? If it's to go, it'll go. And I never heard anything about *you* being pleased to be carrying, either. Anyway—they don't go that easy. I know that. Someone would have said."

But he felt less and less justified. And as he did so he became all the more angry, righteous, determined. He pushed his hand in roughly— before she could stop him—pulling at the cloth. Then as he drew it out, he gasped with horror.

"Is it—are you—*what's this, then?* Are you losing it *now?*" He tried to think of all he knew. A woman bleeding. It meant—

Afterwards, for years afterwards, he was to wonder why she hadn't taken up his question, latched quickly onto his misunderstanding; why she hadn't taken that chance to save herself. Themselves. It was almost, he thought later, as if she had wanted in the end to hurt and hurt and hurt, to exact the greatest punishment of all . . .

"Well, speak then—" He felt the hard part of him go soft, collapsing in protest, in its not being needed. Desire was dying, but something else was arising to take its place. "If you're not losing the bairn, then— *what?*"

"I've me bad time, that's all. That's all about it. Ye can wait, can't you, while it ends?" She pulled the sheet over her head.

He said, shouting almost with pain: "What's this, then—about *bad times?* Women don't . . . That's how they know there's a bairn, isn't it? *Isn't it?* No bad times—"

She didn't answer. The sheet still covered her. He drew it back, pull-ing her up to a sitting position. "Nanny, talk to me. *Tell me.*"

She had begun to sob, pushing her finger to and fro across her nose, shaking her head. "There were nowt. There's no more to say about it—there weren't never one. No bairn. So . . ."

Oh my God, my God, help me. "What are we doing, then? What's this all about? What's this wedding for? What's it *for?*"

"I wanted you—that's why. I wanted to be wed. Us—to be wed."

He choked. He could not speak.

"It were nowt but a small fib—just a little small one. What's that, if we—"

"*How, then?* You've to tell me. Tell me how you deceived us all—"

She had stopped crying. "It were easy. Nowt to it at all. It's me as does t'washing—no folk about to see. And sick, throwing up, all that. Folk saw that right enow—but I've a finger to go down throat, haven't I?" She was brightening up almost, as she told her tale: "And I'd reckoned mebbe as I should be stouter—but me antie, she said as there's some as lose flesh. No one thought to ask further like . . ." She paused, then turning to him, looking at his face, she said, "We're wed, aren't we?"

"Yes," he said sadly. "We're wed."

They were together. Until death do us part . . .

Those words, they were terrible. He burst out suddenly, "We're wed, yes, and no going back. You knew that. Evil one. Wicked girl. Don't you know right from wrong, and that everything's done in the sight of the Lord, that you may have sucked me in, fairly sucked me in, but you've not deceived God—"

"Give ower—carrying on like Mr. Cuthbert. And worse. Like your dad. Like that. Give ower—"

"You *knew.* And God is not mocked . . ." He had got out of bed and was standing in his nightshirt, shivering now with rage and cold. "Give over yourself. I'll go downstairs. Anywhere. Anywhere away from this—from what I've, from what we've done. God isn't mocked, I warn you, *God isn't mocked.*" He began to cry. Desolation overwhelmed. His anger washing over him. "And mind, mind yourself. I'll make you rue, Nanny Haygarth. I'll give you a bairn. I'll give you a bairn if it kills you—" Then: "My God, my God," he sobbed to himself, going out of the room; without a candle, stumbling down the stone stairs. "My God, my God.

" 'I said, I will take heed to my ways: that I offend not in my tongue . . . my heart was hot within me . . . and at the last I spake with my tongue . . . Lord, thou hast been our refuge . . . for a thousand years in thy sight are but as yesterday . . . as soon as thou scatterest them, they are even as a sleep . . .

"'I am the resurrection and the life, saith the Lord. He that believeth in me, though he were dead, yet shall he live . . .

"'And now, Lord, what is my hope?'"

NINETEEN

Dear Journal,

There are but seven weeks to go, which is *forty-nine* days only. Forty-eight nights *alone* and then—I shall be with him for ever and ever (and ever!).

Not a word from the Honble Iain, although he has been told everything. *I care not at all.* We have heard nothing in the way of sympathy even after Papa's *terrible sentence.* I still cannot believe *that* is real, dear Journal. Of course it is the people who are left behind who are punished too. For Mama, I know it is quite the same as if he were dead. If she had not Aunt Charlotte to console her, and to take us into her home (her dear little house in Ann Street—I never thought we should live there, and in such circumstances!), then I dread to imagine what would happen. I try not to think of Papa. It is best. We know now who are our true friends. The Buchanans *most certainly!* (Dear Kirsty has been so happy for me too, these last few months—she is so *good.* I shall never be good.) I don't imagine I shall *ever* feel secure about *anything* again—except John of course!

Dear Journal, perhaps I should write in you more regularly? Certainly I *have the time.* There is little social life for us nowadays, the days are very long. Forty-nine of them will not pass in the twinkling of an eye. No one is very eager to call and quiz or stare at us now. We are quite forgotten.

What do I do with my time, dear Journal? I read. Witness, I have been reading Mr. Thackeray's *Vanity Fair,* which may be only a novel but which has been reviewed in the highest circles. I did not care for it at all. Amelia, the heroine, is too impossibly wishy washy (I do not think Lord Byron would find her at all attractive) and as for Becky, she amused me at first, but then I became shocked by her hardness and I was not at all amused by her wrongdoings—when she *could* have had the love of a good man. I think I enjoyed rather more a story, very new from the library, which is also by a man—*Wuthering Heights*. It is not very well thought of but was *very much* to my liking (Mama: "Is that another of your Gothic tales, Catriona?"—*and* I was caught reading it on the Sabbath!), especially the heroine, Cathy, who although she is often very naughty and haughty and sometimes even wicked, is capable of *real and true love*. The person she loves, Heathcliff, is very well executed and quite the most interesting hero I have come across for a long while. (He is cast in the mould of Lord Byron's heroes, so how could I *not* be attracted?!)

But I had nearly forgot! Since I last wrote in you, dear Journal, *I have been to Downham*—and met His family!! It was all of it quite an ordeal, and proves that I *truly* love him. Dear Journal (I *must* write this), sometimes when he stands with his back to me, looking out of a window perhaps or preparing to mount his horse and I can see the wideness of his back, even his muscles moving under the tight coat, I feel this quite *frightening* need and desire as if I am compelled to reach out and touch him, and when I lie awake in bed with my pillow the only object to hug, I think how I would, how I *will* hug him when we are together for ever, and can sleep so quietly—truly man and wife!

I asked him one day for a lock of his hair—from where it curls so beautifully low down on his neck, then later Kirsty cut from mine and we braided them together (I felt wanting in heart afterwards, dear Journal, that I had not thought Kirsty might mind that it was not *her* hair to be blended with his—). There was enough for two braids, that he and I might have one each as a dear memento. It is hard to distinguish each from the other—both hairs are so dark! (Now see, braided together, we are *quite* one!)

He has the darkest head of hair in his family. That is quite certain. His two sisters are a dull dark brown—they too are a dull dark brown! But perhaps they improve on acquaintance and were a little shy. Eliza *glares* rather at one and says little or nothing. Ann I think has the *sweeter*, more gentle nature.

But perhaps now I had better say quite frankly, dear Journal, about the Rawson family, that I am very thankful I am not marrying *them!* First there is the old man, Jacob Rawson. I was obliged to go and see him. Words do not describe what he was like, and quite how he treated me—I am not accustomed to be spoken of in the third person *while I am present*. Let that be sufficient! And then—John's father. A more upright and religious man you cannot imagine. He seemed amused, even surprised, that I should wish to marry his son and come and live in Downham (which is a *very pleasant* place, dear Journal—and has a most *romantic* gate leading from the churchyard to Downham Abbey where the Inghams live, called the *Kissing* Gate. There are a lot of *serious* superstitions attached to it, dear Journal, which I will write about later—John has told me all about them! He and I of course walked through it and pledged our troth *yet again!*). About our marriage Mr. Rawson said only that he was sure Mrs. Rawson was very pleased—but *if*, however, the manner in which *she* behaved constitutes his idea of being pleased, then I do not rate his intelligence very high! She was not (is not?) *at all* pleased with me. We were at once on the wrong foot. She hinted that I had set my cap at John from his first arriving in Edinburgh—when, dear Journal, I had not even *met* him! and this was such a *travesty* of the truth that I had at once to deny it—a little too loudly I fear, since she then suggested that I "did not think him good enough." Dear Journal, *what was I to say?* I realise, of course, that it is *I* who am not thought good enough, with a father in gaol—but *she will see!* There could not be a better wife for John than I shall be—as I *mean* to be! He will soon forget that he was ever Mother's darling—

Mrs. Rawson would like to know, she said, how I am to settle to life in Downham after the excitements of Edinburgh?! (Dear Journal, at least she was *tactful* and made *no mention at all* of Papa and all the terrible events—although *others* were not so careful. I am thankful to her for that.) However, I wonder, does she picture Edinburgh?! She thinks I perhaps would not find myself suited to be a country practitioner's wife. *Little* she knows what love can do!

But if John is the apple of her eye, his brother Ned is *not*. You do not have to be very clever to see that. (Walter I did not meet at all—he being away at school.) And yet Ned is *married!* I was amazed when I heard. No one had thought to tell me before I arrived. I met him, Ned, only when he came for a meal, bringing his new wife, of course. And what *am I to think of her?* I ask you, dear Journal—she was the greatest surprise of all! Plainly she thought she had married into the nobs— which I suppose in a manner of speaking she has. She is a bootmaker's daughter, I believe. (Quite *why* he married her is a mystery to me!)

She was not tactful with me. I think her behaviour should be called underbred if the truth be told. At table an aunt who was visiting asked some question which related to the trouble at home (and I have *some* pride, it is impossible not to *feel* such disgrace) and I replied, "We had some misfortune. Most of our goods, our worldly goods, were taken. I lost my harp—and of course the piano—" Nanny interrupted then and said boldly, "You mean you had *t'bums* in?" Everyone looked horrified except her—and *perhaps* her husband. *I* of course took it quite naturally —she speaks only as she has been accustomed. "Yes," I said, "yes, we had the bailiffs in, Nanny—"

I am not sure whether Ned and I shall get along. At first I thought not. Then towards the end of the meal, I thought, perhaps yes. He is in some ways rather strange, but he has a very gentle manner and it appears he is very kind. He is especially devoted to the little Irish girl they have adopted (who John, my John, rescued with such courage and at such a risk!). She, Kate, is a dear—her hair is quite the most beautiful shade I have ever seen and her eyes green and she herself so delicate and quiet and refined. I could scarcely take my eyes off her. She is to them all like a new little sister. When Ned arrived she ran to him at once—then he sat her on his knee afterwards and let her pull the laces from his boots and make fancy knots with them (Nanny did not think it very funny!).

Well, dear Journal, that is nearly all. Kirsty comes here tomorrow about her bridesmaid's dress. There is no hope that *Alan* will be back for The Day. He does not sail until the second half of April and all the pleadings in my letters I know will not make him leave the Yankees one day earlier.

Farewell, my dear cousin. You are *very dear* to me. But I need you no longer. (Who do I need now, having *John?*) Come quickly, month of April! The only thing about a new life is that it should begin *immediately*, a girl should not have to wait and pine and to worry what may become of her beloved before he sails into the safe harbour of her arms (Am I not about to be a poet? who would have thought it? But I have read so much, so *much!* And it has *all come true*—). I shall not write again, dear Journal—not until after *29 April 1848*.

> Catriona *Dunbar* (for the last time!)
> 5 Ann Street, Edinburgh.

P.S. Yes I will write it out! (*Dear* Lord Byron—)

> Oh! my lonely—lonely—lonely—Pillow!
> Where is my lover? Where is my lover?
> Is it his barque, which my dreary dreams discover?
> Far—far away! and alone along the billow? . . .
> Oh! thou, my sad and solitary pillow!
> Send me kind dreams to keep my heart from breaking,
> In return for the tears I shed upon thee waking . . .
> Oh! my lone bosom!—Oh! my lonely Pillow!

TWENTY

On the 29th ult. at Edinburgh, by the Reverend Paul Brignall M.A., Mr. John RAWSON, surgeon of Downham, Yorkshire, to Catriona, only daughter of Mr. James DUNBAR, late of 42 Blacket Place, Edinburgh.

There's a woman like a dewdrop, she's so purer than the purest . . .
And I who—(ah, for words of flame!) adore her . . .
I may enter at her portal soon . . .
And by noontide as by midnight make her mine . . .

BROWNING, "Earl Mertoun's Song"

All that unrest, all over Europe. John wondered if it was that affecting him, even though he was a surgeon in a small Yorkshire town and far away from it all. War and rumours of war. Crowned heads toppling. Summer, 1848—and back in April, just before his wedding, the fears—fortunately come to nothing—from the monster demonstration of the Chartists down in London. Mob rule in Europe. But England was safe—as yet. He felt a certain pride in this. Yet he could not rid himself of the smell of unrest, of upheaval and change.

And what greater change than the one *he* had but recently undergone? A married man now, and in the New Year, to be a father. As he rode towards the Abbey, on the last of his morning calls, wiping his brow frequently in the sticky heat, he thought: I have fathered a man child. He was certain of it: the old wives' tale (and he wanted to believe this one) that great nausea, especially if carried past the third month, meant a son. With Catriona it was very violent, prostrating her for most of the day. In the evening she would lie on the sofa, toying only with the delicacies he brought to tempt her—often not touching them. As she herself was scarcely to be touched.

That did not surprise him. When he thought about it, it did not surprise him at all, though he preferred for most of the time not to look back, not to remember too closely. These last few months—they had not been happy . . .

The happiest time was at Christmas, when I could not believe my good fortune, bringing my happiness home from Edinburgh, to the sound of the rails, sitting in the train, remembering, remembering. Nothing could have marred it. Not even the sad business of Ned—the first news on my homecoming.

The happy, happy waiting until her visit in February. A visit which went so well: she had wanted only to please, had been full of ideas for his happiness, for *their* happiness. She had liked, even been enthusiastic about, their small house, saying "We shall do this and this and this." He had to remind her that it was only for a year or two, until Mr. Whitelaw retired—and to point out the fine great house that would then be theirs. She had *seemed* too, to get on very well with everyone. Although about Mother he was not quite certain.

Best of all, though, had been those precious moments alone. Now, when they might have as many as they wished, all seemed wrong—but then, how they had fought for them! And when at last alone: hotly into his arms, clasped tight. (She had written, "that I might be in your arms for ever . . .") And their locks of hair, braided together, had not they been a shy symbol of that other kind of union?

I gazed so long on that hair. And on the wedding day, could it, could *she*, have looked more unattainably beautiful? It was as if her defiance, her courage throughout the terrible events, the trial, the disgrace, the poverty, had brought her in the end this serene triumphant beauty.

So what went wrong? For it *was* all wrong. And it was not, for he must be honest, just the sickness. Before that: the night of the wedding, the honeymoon . . . I don't want really to remember.

The happiest time was at Christmas . . .

Our first night, the night of the wedding, which was to have been quite perfect. Earlier there had been Edinburgh in April: leafy, alive, with its high thin air, promising perhaps a summer which would never come, but warm in the spring sunlight. Then, such coldness. Cold all the way down to York, although there were hot bottles in the railway carriage. Cold in their hotel room—for they would not go onto Scarborough where the honeymoon was to be spent until the morrow. He had complained, and the management had promised that of course a fire would be lit. They had dined downstairs then—and what a poor meal: greasy chops, sour wine, a pudding which would have pasted together the bricks of a house. All this eaten in a draughty dining-room— it was too late to go elsewhere. And while they ate, a fire was not being lit.

She had gone up first. He had thought, I will see all that hair by firelight. (Later—he would see the *other hair*. The firelight, dying perhaps by then, would reveal that dark growth which would be most particularly his . . .) He had allowed her, impatient as he was, a full three quarters of an hour. He had even in the taproom struck up a conversation with a traveller, leaving tomorrow for Edinburgh. But unable to concentrate, he had answered perfunctorily queries about lodgings there, saying in the end: "I was married today. You must forgive my distraction, *ab*straction—" And the man had not laughed, but said at once, respectfully, "Then you have better, more important matters on your mind . . ."

She was sitting by the window when he went up, hunched against the cold. The fire had not even been laid. He said angrily, "I shall see to this at once."

"And have the Boots or some other come up and take a look at me— and you? Och now—"

"Come away from the window," he said then.

She didn't move. "Catriona, love—"

"Undress yourself! And *then* see how cold it is."

The dressing room was a little box only in which clothes could be hung but a person might not stand. He undressed hurriedly in the room, flinging his clothes down carelessly on the not-too-clean floor, taking up the nightshirt laid out for him, pulling it quickly over his head. Then he crossed over to the window. In the draught the candle flame trembled. He put out his hand to her. She was shaking a little, and for a moment clutched at him.

She began, "I thought you see—I thought that—" But he was never to learn what. She buried her face in his arm, against the cuff of his nightshirt. The ribbons of her cap trailed against his hand. "I worship you," she said with sudden urgency, pulling at him. Her clutch was that of a drowning person. Maiden's fears? But he would be gentle. In all the great haste he had felt earlier, and would feel again soon—he would be gentle. Only—this was not how he had pictured it at all: he had thought of everything—except this glassy cold.

The bed was the highest he had ever seen. Catriona knocked her knee painfully as she climbed up. She lay on her back then, staring in front of her. He reached out and drew her to him, feeling through the soft material the cool chilled flesh beneath. In spite of the cold, he was stiffening, growing—unbelievable the speed, the eagerness, almost as if it were separate from him, another person ("The honourable member for Cockshire"—why, *now*, remember a low joke?), pushing, pushing at his nightshirt.

She lay quite still. He wanted her only to say again, "I worship you—" Anything. Any wild promise. Any sign of life at all. He cursed again the cold cheerlessness of the room. His hands feeling her through the thin muslin must be icy. He said weakly, "I have to apologise, do forgive me, these cold hands—"

But all of him was not cold: the heat which burned, ready to go, to thrust where he knew it would be warm. A woman's secret place. A place he had known before only by direct invitation (and paid for in money), known too with such ease. Ellie's body: "Come in" had said the voice always as he stood at the door—now he had to make his own way in. And if he were to break the door down? What of that? His urgency grew as with his fingers, his hands, he continued to stroke. I am being patient and gentle, and we shall both be warm . . .

Perhaps he should offer merely to lie with her tonight? But that had become impossible—a rush of desire, putting an end to his patient caressing, drove him so that indeed it was another person—my member, the member, he thought again—who hastened now to batter down the door. (And worse, worse still, he thought later—in the absence of that spoken or unspoken "Come in" he had not even knocked. But had crashed through, breaking every barrier . . .)

And no gossamer barrier this, but real—he felt her wild clutching and it was not worship now but drowning again. His own desperate clawing —his worst fear realised, that he could not stop. Around the downy entrance, and then to thrust rudely, angrily, determined, his hand helping, savagely it seemed. Helping that other person to enter the house. He heard a cry, a moan—a memory (Ellie who had cried out with pleasure, often from his first touch). Then, ah triumph! Triumph. But even as he emptied, as he gave to her what he had scarcely dared to imagine giving —he felt not the exultation of the conqueror but only remorse, horror, self-loathing. My God, he thought, my God.

His body quietened. The mournful peace now of the battlefield. All the time in the world now to contemplate what he had done—and above all, how he had done it . . .

It had been the longest night of his life. Even creeping home back to Lothian Street after a visit to Ellie, he had invariably slept easily, heavily, until he was called. But that night, after an unexpected hour of sodden sleep, he had woken sharply and completely—surprised to feel her beside him. Her, the beloved ("I worship you," she had said. His heart, his flesh grew cold with the memory). She lay still. Her breathing —he could not tell if she slept. He cleared his throat.

She moved her head uneasily, whimpered a little. He said anxiously, unhappily, "Are you—do you have *pain?*"

She said in a small, slightly pathetic voice: "I have the toothache—"

He felt at once the most tremendous relief. Only the toothache. An ache such as that—it could be remedied at once. He said, "Shall I get you—do you have anything? Laudanum?"

"I have nothing," she said. "One does not expect pain—on these occasions."

"I think, I *hope* that I have—" But searching for a lucifer, hastily lighting the candle and looking through his bag, he discovered only the camphorated variety. He said, "It may not be strong enough." He gave her a double dose, then was afraid that she might sleep too heavily. And in truth within a very short time she was in a deep snoring slumber. He lay awake till they were called.

The Scarborough disaster, he christened their honeymoon visit afterwards. He could not have foreseen any of it. Beginning as it did with her querulous manner, when, still half-doped, she left the hotel with him. On the train she spoke hardly at all, nodding off frequently, her head lolling (and oh how enchanting she looked in green silk—dark hair beneath the brown bonnet, with its bright feathers and ribbons . . .). Then a few miles from Scarborough, coming quite wide awake, she began suddenly to make great objection to the price of the fare.

They were travelling first class. She asked to see her ticket. Ten shillings she said was *too much.* The journey was surely only some forty miles. On lines in *Scotland* it was seven shillings only for such a distance.

But then the train had drawn up at the station (and such a handsome one too—new, stone-built in the Grecian style). Scarborough, a fine Yorkshire watering place. And the sun shining once more. Spring returned . . . A hackney then to Princess Terrace. He had chosen their boarding house from a Register of Apartments at Liberty—confirming his choice with some patients who knew Scarborough well.

This time there was a fire in the room—of sorts. But it needed frequent coaxing and tended to billow forth yellow smoke. The sea-coal had an odd smell, forever afterwards associated with that holiday. But worst of all was the bed. Not aired at all, it was damply chilling so that their night clothes were within minutes wringing and they themselves freezing. The room was clean—but, as Catriona remarked, what bedbug would choose such chill when warm rooms might be had almost anywhere else in Scarborough?

Her toothache returned. He obtained some laudanum, and she slept early and heavily each night. When he looked at the tooth, at all her teeth, he could see nothing. But she would not visit a dentist. At home would do. After four or five days she said that the pain had gone, but declared that with all that sea air about she could not but fall asleep *immediately*. And this she seemed to do—yawning from when they first sat down to eat in the evening.

The weather was bad, cold—it was early May only but he had arrogantly taken it for granted that the sun would shine on them even here in the North. Worse still, had thought that it would not matter. Over several days it either rained or the wind blew so strongly that only a short outing was advisable. Catriona bought headed letter and note paper with views of Scarborough, and wrote to Kirsty. And to Alan (the hated Alan, who was very soon expected back in Scotland). She took out a subscription to Theakston's Library, then grumbled that she had read all the new books in from London. She sat crossly with Geraldine Jewsbury: "I know exactly already the turn of the plot . . ." He himself could settle only to reading newspapers and journals, devouring them as if his life depended on them. Yorkshire *Gazette, Yorkshireman,* Leeds *Mercury,* Leeds *Intelligencer* . . . Flapping the pages over while steady rain trickled down the window panes.

On the few fine days they made some excursions. Carnelian Bay— where Catriona was fortunate and found moss-agates and jaspers for her pebble collection. Scalby Mill, Falsgrave, even one day a picnic in the Tea Gardens. But although the bathing machines were out ready for the season, with their tops brightly painted in different coloured stripes so that one might know if they were John Walshaw's, or Morrison and Richardson's . . . of bathing itself there was no question. They shivered on the sands, and on the cliffs.

One day as they watched the waves rise and fall, frothing onto the sand, Catriona shuddered, drawing her red shawl tighter about her. She made some impatient remark. The view from here was much overpraised, what was there especial about the North Sea? (In *Wester Ross* now—the Atlantic . . .)

"But I love it," he said (Should he not have said, he thought later, "I love *you* . . ."). "I love it." Only the most wooden words would come into his mind: "One cannot describe—it is so terrible—majestic. And it is as if too, it were somehow part of me, and I of it." He offered her this very personal thought. "I feel it, in my bones."

She said, "All *I* feel in my bones is the cold. The extreme cold. *Thank you,* John . . ."

That night he had tried again, slowly, so gently. And it had not been too difficult. He tried to remember what he had learned from Ellie, but because Ellie had behaved so differently (and had she not, in fact, been a whore?), he could do nothing, could think of nothing to do but the bare act. The words he thought afterwards of saying—"I worship you" —choked him. He did not speak at all. Her beauty, and this body he held: they were two things apart. He could not hope to make them one.

Three days home, their small house barely settled into, and she had begun to be sick. At first he had thought it a chill caught on the holiday. Then he wondered if perhaps she suffered from monthly prostration—some girls had great sickness and pain. But when he asked, tactfully, she said quickly in an offhand tone that the time for that had past a good fifteen days ago. Feeling foolish, he knew then for certain what he had done.

Sick all day now, languid, she had become unrecognisable, only lately improving a little in the evenings. It had not helped their relationship. He was waiting, he realised now, for their real life to begin. They were in some limbo. They were—literally—in a halfway house: once or twice she had suggested that after all this was over, after they had moved into Linden House, everything would be better. She had used those very words: "Everything will be better . . ." Not she, or he, but *everything.* (And by then, God willing, he would have a son . . .)

He urged his horse round suddenly, realising he had come to the Abbey turning. As he rode past the Kissing Gate, he thought, why not bury a charm bag? And wish that she be safely delivered of a man child . . . (Had not Mother confessed to doing that not only before his own birth, but again when he had journeyed to Ireland?) A moment later, going through the Abbey arch, he was horrified that even for a few seconds, he should have been tempted to any action so superstitious (No wonder that the Reverend Cuthbert had needed only a few months ago, to preach on the subject yet again . . .).

Clattering into the yard and dismounting, he tethered his horse to one of the iron wall hooks. He went then to the front door. Although Mr. Whitelaw had said that he always went to the side, the Squire on John's first visit as a surgeon had said, reproaching him almost: "Any son of Sarah Rawson's—straight in and up the front stairs."

It was Georgiana Ingham's mother whom he had been asked to see. A Mrs. Featherstone. She came at least twice a year, and usually chose to be ill. He had already seen her yesterday and thought the trouble exaggerated. Now, taking her pulse, he asked: "Did the sago and wine help?"

But since he came in she seemed to have been preparing a speech, working her lips silently. Now he had tapped the cask.

". . . Worry about my dear daughter, you never saw such a worrier as I am, it quite ruins my appetite—and as for my sleep, even with your draught I never closed an eye all night—my late husband said always 'if you had not something to worry you, my dear, you would surely invent it'—and that is because I am always so much thinking of others that I *cannot* put aside my worries—and all of them I do assure you on behalf of others—for myself I have none because at fifty-six the greater part is over is it not—and then you see I—"

"Your bowels," he began.

"You must ask my maid these matters, you have interrupted the flow of my thought—it is a fault with you young—not to be thinking enough of others—*you* will not be kept awake with worrying—" She paused only long enough to draw in breath, "I must admit to pain in my side, the *left* side, and very high up . . ."

He got away with difficulty. As he came out, a servant was waiting on the landing for him. "The mistress, sir, she says to come and see her, sir."

He had been going to the housekeeper's room, to recover calm. He would be given a drink: tea, cocoa, ale. It was one of the good moments to which Mr. Whitelaw had introduced him.

"She says please, sir, will you go to the nurseries to look at Master Richard and please, sir, you mun go afore you see her, you mun see her in t'drawing-room, sir."

Gabbled and garbled, the meaning of the message was clear: he would have to postpone refreshment. He knew the nurseries, and was popular there. He made his way up. Richard Ingham was sitting on a chair by the window, his head bowed. He was a slight boy with his mother's reddish gold hair—his ringlets had been cut off recently, making his face look smaller, more peaky. He was trembling a little. Neither of the two little girls were in the room.

"Well, Richard," he said, "here is your friend the surgeon come to see you. What is the matter?"

There was no answer. The little nursemaid looked haunted. She said, "He's—he's burned like. His leg. Got in t'way of poker."

He said to the boy, "A fine thing—let us see now. What was the poker doing, Richard—that it should come at you?"

"If it's never an accident," the nurse burst out, "you ask him, sir—

he's allus in trouble, he came up—he'd been in trouble downstairs, shouldn't ought to play wi' fire."

Richard began, "I—" He paused, then said again: "I—"

"Yes, Richard." John said it gently. "Yes?"

"I d-d-d-," but he could not get the word out. "I d-d-d-."

"How old are you now, Richard?"

But he could not get that out either. The nurse said, "Eight year, sir."

"All right, Richard. Now—show me." He made to examine the burn. "I know your papa, don't I, and your mama and grandpapa—and Julia and Henrietta? You know me—and Dr. Whitelaw?"

Richard nodded dumbly. His trousers were narrow—John had difficulty turning them up. When he looked at the burn it had begun to blister already. Richard still did not speak. The nurse had her hands clasped tightly, digging her nails into the flesh.

"He's been careless like, he mun take care, tell him, sir, he mun take care and not go down where fire's not tended—"

Richard shook his head vigorously, showing for the first time signs of animation—trying to deny what she said, but more tongue-tied than ever.

"Yes, Richard?" But when still there was no answer he concluded that the shock of the burn had made him for the moment quite speechless.

How would this one do at school? he wondered idly. Eton in perhaps four years' time. And from what he had heard, much much rougher than Richmond . . .

Georgiana Ingham awaited him in the drawing-room, with its windows looking out on to the sweep of drive and the park beyond. In front of the fireplace, as a screen, stuffed humming birds in a glass case.

He saw that a tray with wine and glasses had been placed near her. She said, after the usual greetings, "You have visited upstairs?"

"Mrs. Featherstone? I would think the matter is not serious—"

"No, no," she interrupted, "my son. I speak of my son—"

"Well, I—" he began. She seemed to him very agitated. And beautiful. Certainly very elegant. Beside this pallor of breeding, the image of Catriona's dark loveliness seemed to him almost crude.

"You have seen him—what do you think?" She cut in, her voice precise.

He explained. It was a simple burn, unpleasant, but clean—he had dressed it and what mattered now was to exclude all air. He had impressed that on the nursemaid. And she herself would doubtless be up to see that all was well . . .

"Mr. Rawson," she said suddenly, "you have had more training than just an apprenticeship? You have been in Edinburgh—"

"It was six months under John Goodsir. Anatomy principally. But also other matters. And I attended lectures of general interest."

"Is it possible, then, that you have any acquaintance with—" she hesitated, "disorders of—the mind?"

"If you mean Mrs. Featherstone—" he began.

She interrupted him sharply: "No, no. There is nothing there but foolishness—I am long acquainted with it. No—I am speaking of my husband, Mr. Rawson."

Silence. John said, "I don't . . . what exactly is wrong?" He swallowed hard.

"Cruelty," she said. "Cruelty without cause or reason. Without provocation I should say—unless to irritate him is provocation enough. Richard's burn was his work, Mr. Rawson."

Her lip trembled, and there came over him at once a great need to protect her, to help. Was it not for this that he had become a doctor? He said, without thinking further, "What can I do? Tell me what I can do—"

"Nothing," she said, recovering herself. "Of course you can do nothing. *Shall* do nothing. Imagine—if one were to report something which no one witnessed except Richard! Although that little nurse suspects something—since it is not the first time. Nor likely to be the last, I fear."

"Then I shall speak to your father-in-law, to the Squire."

"You will not. I forbid it absolutely. The Squire has many faults, Mr. Rawson—which I shall not mention here—but he is entitled to what *little* pride he has left in his son. He feels that he has failed with him— this he has told me himself. And it is not to be tolerated, when his health is not of the best, that he should be alarmed where he can do nothing."

"But had you no idea of—this, when you married Mr. Ingham? That there might be such traits? Although *I* had not heard—"

She threw up her hands in surprise. "Mr. Rawson, *you* know what is the upbringing of a girl in my station. I did not imagine, never having witnessed it, that such behaviour occurred."

"And the other occasions?"

"Once it was a cut lip. I made some sort of protest, but he refused to answer me. Mr. Ingham has this way—it was as if I had not spoken. Another time it was a severe whipping. Very severe. More than any childish misbehaviour could warrant. It was—not a pretty sight." She looked down at her hands. "It is almost a conspiracy, Mr. Rawson, that the world outside should not know. The nursemaid perhaps—she had the dressing of him afterwards. But she is afraid . . ."

He said, "My studies did not really include anything that might help. Although very interesting work is at present being done in Edinburgh, on diseases, disorders of the mind—I was not any part of it. I could of course write to my professor. Make some inquiries—"

"Perhaps later. If you would, Mr. Rawson." She looked up at him. "It is difficult for me—a woman alone. My mother is hardly to be depended on for counsel." She smiled. "Rather it is I who must help her . . . I am alone a great deal, Mr. Rawson. My husband needs little company. And little—" she checked herself. "He does not need *me* very much. I have given him of course a fine son, who favours me—a mistake perhaps. But he has no patience with nor love for him. And he is exasperated beyond bounds by that stammer. He mocks it, Mr. Rawson. I do not know now whether the stammer provoked the cruelty—or the cruelty the stammer. It goes too far back. But today he deliberately burnt Richard. Provoked perhaps by an innocent remark. Or, more likely, no remark . . ."

There was silence for a few moments. He thought that perhaps she was more to be liked than he had imagined.

"He has never struck *me*," she said. Then turning her head, arching her neck a little, she said in quite altered tones: "It is enough that I have told you all this, Mr. Rawson. In the meantime, I have an offer to make to you. To your *family*." She was watching his face. "It concerns the little Irish girl you have adopted. I would like her to join my children in the schoolroom. Richard is I think of an age with her—Julia, a little younger. Henrietta is still in the nursery. Their governess, Miss Hooper, is excellent. I think your—stepsister? I am not sure what I must call her—I fancy that she will fit in very well. And it will be admirable for Julia and Richard. Does the idea please you, Mr. Rawson?"

He was taken aback. He wondered how he could be certain that this was not just some whim—that tomorrow she might deny all knowledge of it? He had come across such people . . .

"It will be the wish of my father-in-law, I am certain. My husband's opinion you need not concern yourself with." She smiled up at him, mistress of herself, of the situation. "And now—shall we take some wine?"

All through the meal, Catriona was in high spirits. She even ate well: taking two helpings of currant tart, covering them with cream. He did not ask if she felt better. Her usual response was suppressed irritation and he did not want to break this mood—rather to enjoy it. She chattered, almost the old Catriona, while he listened. Or half-listened . . .

She had heard from Alan. He had brought her back from America a quite new kind of overshoe for dirty weather, "galoshes," which would be quite a novelty in Downham. She talked on and on of him. John shut his ears, thinking only that he had married *her* and not the cousin. He had hoped to be done with this Alan. But "Alan says this, Alan says that . . ." It was not to be endured. He tried not to hear, and instead planned what he would do with his evening.

He thought that he would write to *The Lancet* about a case, patients of his, a family who had eaten mutton from a diseased sheep—there had been several unusual features. And he would write out too, possibly, some notes and ideas on the subject of Charles Ingham. Robbie would know to whom he should refer . . .

She did not go upstairs at once as was usual now, but stayed down sewing by the oil lamp. He stopped to admire: she had begun already some fine embroidery for the babe. She said, "I mean to do so much—a little of this every day. Alan says . . ." He touched her gently on the shoulder, not waiting to hear what Alan might have said, and went through into the small poky room at the back which he used as a study —in Linden House he would have a large one—there he sat down and, arranging his papers, took up a pen and dipped it in ink.

It was then it began. The piano first. She had never played well, although always with gusto. But gusto was ill advised when the aim was not true. Tonight: first a cascade of wrong notes—then a slight pause and—the same wrong notes, at the same speed. Five minutes passed; then ten. He had still only the heading at the top of the page.

He thought that perhaps he should start instead with the letter to *The Lancet*. He took a fresh sheet of paper.

". . . acute stomach pains within three hours of eating the diseased meat . . . violent purging, followed by a stupor bearing a marked similarity to that induced by *opium* . . . the expression when aroused was wild and the behaviour uncontrolled . . ."

It was then the singing began. Once he had found it endearing, the manner in which she exposed the company to those excruciating sounds —and with such confidence. Since her marriage she had not sung at all, although he had suggested singing with her. (Certainly she had not played the harp which with such loving thought he had replaced, as a wedding gift. *That* sound at least was pleasing.)

"Begone dull care! I prithee be gone from me . . ." First there had been a preliminary run of something in Italian, piercing in its discords.

When she was done, she started again. He thought: I cannot bear this. He had intended to wait it out, as he would wait the passing of a tooth-ache (for *that* there was at least a laudanum pill).

"Begone, begone!"

Begone! he thought angrily. My thoughts *are* gone. The lovely crystal clear ideas which, succinctly expressed, were to begin his career: make of him something more than the surgeon-apothecary at Downham. He rose, pushing aside his papers.

"I am trying to think," he announced, in the doorway.

She turned at once; she had not noticed his entry. She said, her hands held over the keys still: "Och, and who's to stop you?"

"I said, 'I am *trying* to think—'"

"Perhaps once is not enough," she said airily. "Try again. If at first you don't succeed, try, try—"

He cut in coldly. He was to regret it. But the disappointment of the evening, his plans—and then her body sitting there so prettily erect (and why should he think of the word "erect"?), a body which would not be his tonight, or the next, or—when?

"Your singing," he said. "It is that which makes it impossible. Perhaps I should quote to you the late Mr. Coleridge, 'Swans sing before they die—'twere no bad thing, Should certain persons die before they sing . . .'"

With a violent flourish she slammed shut the book open on the piano, banged down the piano lid and stood up very straight, tossing her ringlets. She spoke without pausing.

"It is a great pity you are so wanting in soul and lack all that's needed to appreciate any kind of music, indeed with all your disgusting pills and potions you can do no better than make cheap jibes about the imperfections of my voice, we cannot *all* be the fine *exécutants* that the Rawsons are and apart from the flute of your brother—your mother certainly if *she* has a singing voice we have yet to hear it, she is too busy I think singing your praises—you are so fine, are you not? My hero, my fine *hero*—" She had brought herself almost to tears. "I did not know that you carried with you always the surgeon's scalpel—that you might use it on your wife. Hero!"

She flounced out. The room, a moment ago filled with her angry presence, was empty. He went back to his study. He sat there awhile in the silence and the peace. But no words came. No thoughts either.

He came into the room once more. It looked now as if no one had been there. He felt almost that he had lost her. And for what?

"Catriona!" he called from the bottom of the stairs. Despairingly. And then again, "*Catriona . . .*"

TWENTY-ONE

I slept, and dreamed that life was Beauty
I woke, and found that life was Duty.

Ellen Sturgis HOOPER,
The Dial, 1840

I did not know it would be like this, Catriona thought. She had never imagined such sheer physical discomfort. Indeed she had not really imagined her condition (described always in a lowered voice as "delicate") at all. And Mama's letters did not help:

". . . I'm sure I don't know how you are going to survive it, Catriona . . . Jennie Hawick's daughter that had just been brought to bed of a fine little lass and then was gone within the week of a fever . . . I suffered from just such nausea and debility as yours throughout my *whole times* (and for upwards of a month after too!). And speaking of time, Catriona, *at no time* are you to consider travelling up here on those infernal railways. Papa is not at all well, and although Alan has visited him he does not seem to know anyone, the prison governor says it cannot be long . . . It is *all* the fault of . . ."

Her weakness, her discomfort, took up the entire foreground of her life. How could she not have known all this? She and Kirsty: so many years of talk and they had never discussed it. Or only in terms so vague —such as "that time" (just as they described what happened to them each month as "being so-so"). How often had they not discussed their *deaths?* But the making of a new life, and its arrival in the world. Never.

Why should she feel so heavy-limbed, as if *all* of her carried the child? Every morning she dragged herself from bed to sofa and back again. To go in a carriage only increased the nausea. The days seemed long. John, although no longer in the winter doing his rounds before breakfast, was out for much of the time. Often she did not see him till evening. When he asked what she had been doing and she told him "resting," he would say "good," and pass on to another subject. He did not seem anxious about her. She could not have borne it if he had been. At the end of the summer the baby had moved, and the nausea had lifted a little: she felt sick now only three quarters of the time.

She had certain duties of course, since she had a home to run. John's mother too had made it clear that had she been fit she would have been expected not only to pay calls, but to visit the poor—to go "poor peopling," and to take certain families under her wing: as did Eliza and Ann. She had not made friends of Eliza and Ann. Eliza she felt disapproved of her, while Ann seemed frightened.

Her mother-in-law she avoided where she could, pleading indisposition. But on Sundays, at the family gathering, toying with the plentiful food, she would feel Sarah's eyes upon her. When she looked up—and I *will* be bold, she thought—then the gaze would be on someone else. Ann's Frank perhaps (they were to wed in the spring), shy, and being drawn out by Sarah. Or Nanny, being dealt with roundly (it takes one servant to recognise another, Catriona thought tartly). And all the while the dour Samuel would be watching his wife: one word to every ten of hers.

But as to taking poor families under her wing—she, Catriona, had been taken under Matilda Paley's, ever since Sarah had told her of the coming child. How she dreaded those visits: seeing through the window the antiquated bonnet, woolly curls peeping out. And then the voice, which sounded plaintive even when it was not, and the smell: faded lavender mixed with a musty body odour, sending through Catriona fresh waves of nausea. "Since you are not able to go abroad, Catriona dear, I am come to tell you *everything* that is happening in Downham . . ."

One morning, after a fit of yawning and feeling "all-overish" (as Alan had used to call it—only *that* was after brandy), she set out on foot with no purpose whatsoever, to walk around Downham. After Edinburgh, it seemed to her a mean place, although she supposed that some might call it picturesque. Its shape enclosed, imprisoned her. It had not in any way fulfilled its promise, made to her last spring—or was it she who had changed, become disenchanted?

My hero, she thought bitterly, coming up to Linden House, where they were to live—*my hero*. She walked around for a full hour, and met no one she knew. (She dared Fate to allow her to run into Matilda

Paley.) She was wearing the galoshes from Alan. She wore them with pride, defiance almost. All the way from America!

She found herself now not far from the rope-works, about to go down the alley. She had been inside them only once, before she was married—when Samuel Rawson had taken her in. She wandered now into the yard on impulse, picking her way carefully. Already her skirts were fringed with mud, with grease, with indescribables.

The noise inside seemed at first deafening. From where she stood, just in the entrance, she could see Ned. He was walking up and down, occasionally blowing his lips out or frowning. He moved with a steady purposeful rhythm. She recognised the smell of the ropes, the yarns, but on her previous visit she had seen no work being done. Energetically turning the wheel which provided the power for the rope-walk were two boys—one small, fresh-faced; the other dark, with heavy features and one shoulder markedly higher than the other.

Ned, turning to walk back, saw her. On his face, surprise, mixed with pleasure. Puzzlement.

"Mrs. John . . ."

"Catriona—surely you know me as Catriona?"

"You're welcome anyway." He smiled, then looked round anxiously. "There's not a seat good enough for your cloak. All this dust—"

She noticed that he sneezed a lot. "Och," she said, "look at my skirts anyway." She sat down on the chair he had provided. "Don't stop working—for me."

"It's no matter," he said. "We began early—there's been a lot done." Then he said in a friendly voice to the two boys, sitting waiting now by the idle wheel: "To the back with you." He told Catriona, "They brew cocoa through there, it's good on a cold day—they'll have that and still want their dinner." The boys went through, one like a little mouse scuttling, the other following more slowly, his high shoulder making him lope, wolflike.

"That's Arthur Greaves," Ned said. "Hannah's young brother. The servant who— "

"Yes, yes," she said. "Of course." Then he said, "You'll take a drink yourself, Catriona?"

Water, she wanted only water. In the dry ropey air she felt her throat parched. He was back in a moment with a mug. Then bringing a chair over, he turned it the other way and straddled it, his arms over the back, chin resting.

She said, "You must show me everything—about the ropes. In Wester Ross, where I had used to spend my summers, we had no jute.

They would pound up fibre from bog fir roots, for the boats. And the thatch on the cottages, it was held with heather ropes . . ."

From the back could be heard banging, then raucous shouts. Then two swear words, very loud. Ned blushed. "I'll speak to them. It's Greaves—" He made as if to get up.

"No," she said hastily, "don't trouble yourself." And she said in explanation, "I have not led quite such a sheltered life. In Edinburgh they watched over me but they could not keep *all* sounds from my ears. And my cousin"—she smiled then, affectionate memory of Alan warming her—"he took me out and about, and where he should not." She reached again for the cup, drinking from it thirstily. "There was one evening I mind when we were walking together and just as we came up to the Grassmarket, we saw a crowd gathered in the doorway of a shop. And what must Alan do but stop and see what the matter was. It appeared that a man had come there asking for whisky—and had no sooner asked than he began to put off his clothes, and *would not desist!* His choice of words too—that could be heard from outside the shop . . ."

"And brother John—what does he think?"

"Of what?"

"Of that tale. Of the gentleman who put off his clothes—"

"Oh," she said, laughing, surprised (and he was laughing still), "I would never tell *him* such a thing. He—" But she could not think what. She said quickly, "They all say you play the flute. I never heard you. I intended—"

"It's nothing. I'm not so good as I should be."

She said, "At home in Scotland when I did my so-called deep studies —that Mama so disapproved of—there was something, some words in Aristotle I think it was. That flute playing was not very moral, since it was too exciting . . ."

He answered matter of factly, "Yes, it does excite me, very much."

She said, eagerly now (when had she last bothered to have an idea, a want?): "Next Sunday at the house—no, better in *our* home—you could call, and we could play together. I have music could be adapted, and the flute and harp sound well. I play the harp not badly."

"I'd heard that—"

She said: "Well, then—it would give me pleasure."

"And me." From the back—more shouting.

"I'm keeping you from your work," she said. As she gathered her cloak about her, his quick eyes darted over her body and then away again. He said, "My wife, Nanny, she is—also with child."

It seemed odd to her that he should have used those words. She would have expected, "Nanny's to have a bairn," or even, "We are waiting on a bairn too." But he had spoken in the manner almost of the Bible. "She is with child . . ."

She watched Nanny that Sunday, expecting to see tell-tale signs that she too suffered. But there was nothing. Nanny ate heartily. Indeed Catriona had never seen anyone with such little heed for her digestion. Boiled pudding heavy with currants, two helpings, after a heaped platter of meat, vegetables, pastry crust, potatoes. And she told who ever would listen, proudly, that before leaving she'd had already oatcakes and pork fat.

"And I'd two haverbreads, wi' crappins, afore I come out . . ."

Ned called round about two weeks later, on a Thursday evening. He had arranged it, he said, with John. She was upstairs resting when he came. She did not sleep well now. The child would not let her. Those first few feeble knocks on the wall of the womb had long since changed to a steady drumming of heels.

She told Ned, "I shall wait to eat till John comes. He should not be late. And you—your tea? You will eat with us?"

"Yes. Nanny is with her sisters," he said. "She stops the night there."

They went together then through the contents of the music stool. He found much to delight him. "This, and *this*. I reckon we'd wake the birds with this one . . ." She felt a great calm in his company, a deep sense of being *at home*. Ned—so unlike John: colouring, build, manner (and surely, character?). Yet, when she had not been looking perhaps, some easy link had been forged.

"Kate," he said now, "I wish Kate was more musical. She ought to have that" (not "I wish Nanny" but "I wish Kate . . ." Almost, Catriona thought, as if Kate were *his* child, almost as if he thought more of her than Nanny . . .). "She ought to have that. If I lived still at home I'd teach her. Miss Hooper, at the Abbey, she plays them rhymes, but she has no *love* for music."

Catriona said then, "Perhaps she will make a friend of me, and *I* will show her—"

"Ah, yes," he said. "Yes, she must make a friend of you," busying himself with the sheets of music.

They had played some Mozart together when he asked: What about some Scottish airs? She found that his ear was acute. She had only to play with one finger, or sing the tune a little in her bad voice, and he had it. "Lord Saltoun," "The Black Bear," "Peggy's Love," "Who'll Be King but Charlie?"

John, coming in, unnoticed, took them by surprise. He must have had to listen to several bars of "My Love He Lies in Allantown Gaol." She thought at first, from his face, that he was angry, but realised then that he was only very tired. It had been a wet, cold day—he had not stopped to take off his outer clothing before coming into the room. Mud had splashed his cuffs, the front of his coat, his boots.

"Ah, Ned," he said wearily, acknowledging his presence. Then: "I must get myself out of this all, I am in a sorry state. A borrowed mount who cast a shoe, and I don't know what other delays." He looked at them both: "I am glad to see you play the brother's part, Ned." Straightening up, shivering perhaps as he came in from the cold: "Catriona and I," he said it sadly, "we do not always sing well together . . ."

She woke with a start in the night. She was used to this: the child disturbing her with its kicks. Except—it could not be. The child lay still: it was as if almost its very stillness had in some way jerked her awake.

Cold, she was so cold. She moved against the stretched-out body of John for warmth. She did then what she had never done, and could never think in daylight of doing—lifted his heavy-with-sleep hand and laid it where the child lay.

After a few moments he stirred and muttered. "Burke him, Burke him!" His head tossed on the pillow: "Tammie's at it again—a pot of strong beer, smoke nigger-head, *get* him . . ." Dreaming of an Edinburgh monkey. It alarmed her. His inner world alarmed her. She touched his shoulder firmly.

Her mind full of it: "The child," she said, "it doesn't stir."

"What?" he said, starting up, "what?"

"It doesn't stir—the child."

"I hear nothing." He shook himself, turned over, and was at once asleep again.

But the child did not move all the next day or the next. By nightfall of the Sunday she had panicked. Whom should she ask? Perhaps it was quite usual. After all did not some persons, grown persons, lie for a long time still, without wanting or needing to move?

That night she slept heavily—not waking even when John was summoned out (banging at the door, small stones at the window). The beginning of an epidemic of fever in the dank, misty November weather. Ned was laid up, John told her, as he looked in for a quick meal. She didn't know when he came up to bed. When she woke in the morning he had gone again. She could not believe she had slept so long. She felt her belly anxiously. But the baby too slept.

During the next day she thought suddenly: I have the answer. The small cave inside her, where the baby grew, there was no longer space left for him to move and kick. He had grown to fill it all.

Ten days later—and always feeling now sleepy, heavy (and John so busy he scarcely spoke to her), she said to him idly, "Well, it's quite a rest for me. The child having no room to move—"

"What—*no room?*" He frowned. She explained to him. "But—" he began, then taking hold of her hand, asked anxiously, "Catriona, when did you last—" After she had told him everything, very haltingly, he looked suddenly very grave. Holding her arm still, he peered closely at her face. Then he told her that she must see Mr. Mortimer at Leyburn. "As soon as possible. You are his case after all, and I should not wish the responsibility . . ."

She wondered then if she should say that as she was washing, she had noticed (as John would not have—he did not touch her now) that her breasts which over the months had swollen, pushing against their binder, seemed now to be shrinking. Yes, *they are shrinking*, she thought now, a wave of sick panic coming over her.

Old and kind and experienced, Mr. Mortimer was gentleness itself. He told her what *he* thought to be the truth. "There's no way to be certain, my dear. But it's likely, likely enough . . . You will have to be brave."

She did not feel brave. Certainly she was not brave enough to talk about it with John. He was very kind and gentle now.

They had ceased saying "when the child is born." They did not discuss it at all. She had been told to rest (but had she not been doing that before?). Lying on her bed, the curtains drawn against the feeble winter light, she was attacked—with oh, such suddenness—by a great longing to be home. Home. Edinburgh. Even Mama . . . especially Aunt Charlotte. And Alan. Her nostrils suddenly unexpectedly filled with the smell of the gun room in Wester Ross, and his dear presence. Jessie. Uncle Alexander. From childhood—*when I was happy* . . .

She lived somehow through the rest of that dark month, into the next—through all the preparations for Christmas. Holly, ivy, ilex, yew.

Eight months into her pregnancy, on Christmas Eve, while carol singers outside their door sang, "It came upon the midnight clear," she was delivered of a dead child, a seven-pound boy with a fuzz of silky dark hair.

TWENTY-TWO

Ned had been making Kate a doll's house for her birthday on March 17th. It was a secret of course, but it seemed to Sarah when he came to Hillside on Sundays, with Nanny, that it was all he could do not to tell Kate, or at the very least to hint: "If my little cockyolly bird can just wait till March—then she'll *really* have something to play with. And no, little one, no—I'm not telling . . ."

Sarah, on a visit to Little Grinling, was allowed to see it when it was three parts finished. It had six rooms, and attics as well. Each room was to be completely furnished down to the last detail. He had been working on it since September: nothing was too much trouble. Miniature pewter utensils lined the dresser in the kitchen. The main bedroom had a velvet day bed, and a four-poster with satin drapes; there were real rugs on the floors—skins mostly. Tiny loaves of bread stood by the ovens. A newspaper lay on the kitchen table, near the miniature rocking chair . . . Brocade covered the chairs in the drawing-room. What he could not do himself he had persuaded others to help with.

"It's grand," she told him. "You've done well, son." She felt shy always of praising him, had never felt easy with him. It was not like John. Nor did Ned seem to expect or need praise for it. "There's not a minute I've spent on it," he said, "that I've not enjoyed . . ."

Which was more than could be said for Nanny. It was plain that she had not helped at all—she would not have been one of those whose nimble fingers had hemmed doll-size curtains (Eliza and Ann, sworn to secrecy, had been eager to help). In fact, she was obviously bored with the whole enterprise. Already she was enormous: Sarah wondered sometimes if there might not be a mistake with the child's dates. And she was not a good housekeeper. The cottage bore no signs of a loving, caring hand. God knows, Sarah thought, what she feeds him on . . .

Catriona at least (although she was away at the moment, up in

Scotland with her mother) had some idea of how a home should be run —except that she did it all, as she did everything now, in the most lifeless manner possible. Her despondency—John's patience must often be sorely tried.

And yet, Sarah thought, and yet—I can't help but be sorry for the lass. For all the airs she puts on, and for all her grand manner, it was still a heavy blow she had. When I think back to how *I* was: those days when I'd lost my first, when I didn't know and couldn't believe I'd ever rear a child. And the bad days after Walter, when for no reason at all, I didn't want to live. I must be patient with the lass, she thought. When she's back from Edinburgh, I'll maybe try harder . . .

Walter boarded in Richmond with his aunt (Old Jacob's daughter), just as John and Ned had done. Sarah had missed John always—Ned too, sometimes—and had counted the days whenever the holidays drew near. But with Walter: she was ashamed—for she counted instead the days until he should leave Downham again. These last holidays, the Christmas of 1848, he had been particularly difficult. Argumentative all the time, sullen, continually offended—and telling everyone who would listen that he was the unwanted member of the family (he *makes* himself just that, Sarah thought). And so jealous still of Kate. Nothing dangerous—but unpleasant, so that she must always be watching and worrying.

It was an unpleasant shock to her then, when just the week before Kate's birthday, Walter (and a letter from his headmaster) arrived by the evening coach from Richmond.

Walter didn't speak, but handed over the letter. Mr. Tate, the headmaster, had written to them both, in forthright fashion: "Your son is a thief." It appeared that Walter had been taking money from his fellows at school (a sneak-thief too, since he had joined in the hue and cry when first a crown and then a florin and then a bag of sixpenny pieces had gone missing . . .). Finally he had been caught in the act, pocketing a sovereign. He was no longer wanted at the school.

Looking first sullen and then cocky, when faced with the letter he had said only, jauntily: "And what of it, then—what if I did?" Sam had thrashed him, that evening, and then again the next day. He had refused too to speak to him. Or to discuss it with Sarah. When not at the rope-works, he sat with his Bible, not looking up.

Sarah thought that she would never manage the disgrace. That folk should know, here in Downham, that she had a foul-fingered son . . . And how to keep the news from Matilda? The very next Thursday: some cock and bull story about ill health: "He was never a strong lad—

and now the school says they'll not be responsible. He's to be where he can be watched for a while . . ." (And that is true enough, she thought.) "We've thought maybe an outdoor life . . ."

"My dear, he always was pasty," Matilda agreed. "And in an aunt's care—it's not at all the same as a *mother*. If I might?" she added, holding out her glass. "This cold March wind—Madeira is so *warming* . . ."

Two days after that, Sam announced that Walter must begin work, the very next Monday, in the family business. He must learn the ropes —literally. He would go every day and do what Ned said. He would be, to begin with at any rate, lowlier even than Arthur Greaves. And there was to be no argument.

"If I thought anything to the army," Sam said, "I'd let him go for a soldier. But I've a mind anyway to see how he shapes when there's hard work to be done. Any brass that comes his way now—it'll be earned. 'He that maketh haste to be rich shall not be innocent . . .' Proverbs."

But it seemed that troubles never came singly. Just when Sarah had been worrying that the Old Squire might hear, somehow, of Walter's disgrace, and the truth of it all—she learned that in the middle of the night that week, he had suffered an apoplectic stroke.

She went up as soon as possible to the Abbey to see him. She was allowed to his bedside, but he did not know her, or anybody. Over the next few weeks, he regained very gradually a limited use of his faculties. When the finer weather came he was able to sit a little in the garden, staring towards the moors—or he would sit in the library, looking at nothing. His attempts at speech were pitiable.

He would never be Squire again, except in name. To Sarah it seemed unbearably sad. On her visits there she found Charles's arrogant behaviour, his unthinking dismissal of his father, intolerable. And it was he, now, who would think himself Squire . . .

It was when she was distressed already about this (and still, about Walter . . .), that little Bertha, the maid, came to her one day when she sat teaching Kate her stitches.

". . . There you see, you've to keep it smooth always with your left, and then the thimble like this . . . Yes, Bertha?"

"I thought as I'd best say—there's t'lad come from Tofts—he says it's . . ." She swallowed hard. "He says as they're more'n vexed wi' that Arthur Greaves. He's—he's—"

"Yes, well, what—you've not to stand on one leg, Bertha."

Bertha changed legs quickly and balancing on the other, went on: "They're vexed on account of how he's fetched all t'feathers off two o' their duck—pulled 'em out, he did. When—when they was—when they was living. Plucked alive, they said. And then drownded—he'd put stones on 'em like—and when they'd no feathers . . ."

It seemed to Sarah suddenly all too much. Wanton cruelty—when already, everywhere about, there was enough suffering that could not be helped. She found herself weeping, sitting there—the tears running down her face—as she had not wept for Walter's disgrace, or the poor helpless Squire. Somewhere too, somehow, she feared, Hannah came into it.

After a moment, moving nearer to her, little Kate reached out shyly and placed her small hand over Sarah's.

TWENTY-THREE

Old Jacob's birthday. He would be seventy-five in July. Usually the day passed unnoticed, but this year he announced that he expected a celebration, to be held in his house, in the best and largest (and never used) room. He would consent to move his chair in there. At least, that was the first arrangement. Within two days he had announced that there was no question of him—or his chair—moving in anywhere. Celebration there must be, but he would stay in his room, and selected people might come and see *him,* one by one—coming and going at his behest.

Aunt Minnie was driven nearly frantic. Order after order was countermanded—only to be repeated a day or two later. He'd never heard, he would say, of any change of plan.

"I'll say how it's to be—ye've just to do it. Nowt else. *Whose brass is it, then?*" he grumbled, altering the guest list for the fourth time. In the end it was Sarah took over: telling him firmly that if there was to be a party, then it must be a surprise for him . . . how could he enjoy it, if he was worn out with all the preparations? Surprisingly, he ceded like a lamb, announcing only to the window—it was a very hot day, and he had actually moved his chair from the fire: "These Paddies—they need humouring. I'll let her . . ." He had tired himself out with his rages, his whims. Now, suddenly handing over to Sarah a large sum of money, he wanted nothing more to do with it. He, who never left the house, announced that he would be out all that day—they would be surprised, the guests, to find no host.

All through that spring, early summer, it seemed to Ned that Nanny's sisters were always there, always at the cottage. Martha and Tabby. Martha had not been very aptly named since she was less of a homemaker even than Nanny. She managed the Haygarth household in a flurry of broken pottery, burnt dishes, yellowed washing, and mildewed sheets. Tabby, on the other hand, combined fair-haired fragility with the pert vivacity and knowingness of her eldest sister. In her Ned would find himself seeing—against his will almost—the Nanny of perhaps five years ago.

Every night when he came back from work they would be there. They came in with the carter in the morning, and back in the evening. Mercifully Ned did not have to see them at midday since he ate always in Downham with Mother—had done from when he first moved to Little Grinling. He was glad that he did so, for Nanny's cooking was perfunctory and the helpings, large but unappetising, seldom set his juices running.

The other juices—they did not flow either. He did not want Nanny, could not imagine ever having done so. And she—so pleased, so triumphant was she with her burden that she had no patience with, no time for that side of life. It was as if the tremendous appetite she'd shown that first and for him fatal time, had been deflected. It was needed for food, for feeding up, fattening both the bearer and the borne. What a plump child he would have!

A farmer he scarcely knew nudged him in the Black Swan. He joked coarsely: "It'll not be silk, t'bairn's cord, eh lad? Fastened wi' rope, more like—eh?" But Nanny was proud. She was about to become *somebody*. "And I'm to make that owd Jacob a great-grandad," she would tell people—and Ned would wince, feeling at the same time a stab of sick tenderness for Catriona, with her loss.

He was not needed. He was a lodger only, in his own home, his presence barely tolerated, scarcely noticed. The three of them would look up from their giggling as he came in, or stop deliberately in mid-sentence, ostentatiously finishing behind cupped hands. Those heavy late June days, Nanny would move her enormous bulk, saying resentfully almost as she crossed to the range, "Aye, well—I reckon you'll want summat to eat . . ." And there keeping hot would be some glutinous mess of meat, potatoes, oatmeal, leftovers. Who knew what? As if she'd a dog to feed. They would have eaten earlier. Nanny would tell him, "I can't wait, when t'hunger comes on me . . ."

He was not needed. And the juices, which didn't flow for her, they were not needed either. They flowed for no one, not even himself. As the months had worn on he had thought, cagily, shyly, *when was I last wicked?* Perhaps his prayers had been answered? ("From fornication and *all other deadly sin* . . . Good Lord deliver us.")

Certainly in the first months of his marriage, apart from a little half-hearted coupling, he had not done very much about the child, which in his anger that first night he'd vowed to give her. And Nanny, settling in to her new pride as a married woman, a Rawson, had not questioned any of this. Until the autumn—when she had suddenly roused him several times over a few weeks. Half-remembering the hot days of September the year before, he had yielded. He saw himself as yielding, as being seduced. But he had never recaptured that first fierce excitement and joy. Only, afterwards, the sick disgust.

Early in October she announced to him with triumph that what she should have seen—she had not. So she *must* be having a child. *Must* be, since she wanted to eat coal. She bared black-streaked teeth at him. She'd that very morning, she said, chewed through a piece the size of an egg.

"What of it?" he asked. What proof was that?

But she insisted. She had it, she told him, from a girl she'd shared a room with in her first place. This girl had been caught twice so she ought to know. The sign *never failed.*

Ned said bitterly, "You surprise me you'd not thought of chewing the odd lump or two Christmas time. In the case there were those not convinced—"

But since that wedding night she hadn't been easily shamed. Now she replied only, "It weren't needed, were it?"

Part of him was pleased, proud even, about the child. He had not been able to resist, even through his sadness for Catriona, a sneaking triumph over his brother. These slight feelings of pride, of achievement, had sustained, even given him moments of warmth, through the winter months. But when spring came and she had grown so large, he realised he could not wait till the babe should leave her. He wanted it to be born *soon* so that it might have a separate existence. Not be in Nanny.

He missed Kate too. That was still the worst. He had so wanted to be there to see her grow from child to girl, from girl to woman—always with the loving, caring help of the brother-uncle. "Nunky Ned" she called him now (and how he had marvelled that first time! Although, why should a tongue which must once have wrapped itself in agile fashion round the outlandish Erse, trip now over easier sounds?). Certainly she spoke very prettily. And more prettily than ever since going daily to the Abbey.

And that was another sadness. For her, that she should go there, he was glad—but for himself? Now when he ate at midday with his family, she wasn't there. He saw her only on Sundays. Sunday, the Lord's Day, *Kate's Day.* It was then she would put her hand in his and on tiptoe, whisper into his ear the week's happenings. He would play the flute for her too, often making up tunes to fit the rhymes she learned. And the doll's house, he must always play with that, and listen to the latest imaginings. Eliza was sewing fresh bed curtains for the front bed-room . . .

Sometimes he wondered why he did not invite her to stay with them. Just a day or two, now and then. But he could not bear the thought of her being even so short a time with Nanny. It might, *would* corrupt her in some manner. He thought, I will ask her instead perhaps when the baby is in need of companionship, later. Seeing Kate's presence as being the very best for it. With her there, it could not but grow in beauty and strength.

And now, this Sunday:

> "Charley Wag, Charley Wag,
> Ate the pudding and left the bag . . ."

"I learned that this week, Nunky Ned—can you make a song of it, please? *Please*—"

"He's so fond with her, is Ned," Mother said. And then to him: "The sooner your own comes, son . . ."

But the time for his own child came, and went. Seeing Nanny so enormous, bloated almost, the pert features lost in fat, the ankles swol-len, he felt not sympathy and concern but only irritation. What kind of bairn could it be that wanted to stay with her? How could it *not* want out? Yet June turned into July and still nothing happened.

Grandfather's birthday: and most of July gone. The weather was sultry, close. Making his way to the house that Saturday, Ned could feel thunder in the air, the smell of a storm brewing.

He had not wanted to come to the gathering. It was not that he was worried to leave Nanny—she had her sisters, and Mrs. Leeson who was to attend her, lived near. For him, it was the merry-making mood which was absent.

Mother had done everything excellently. He wanted to praise her but was shy to do so. It was quite a spread: cold meats, jellies, blancmanges, cream puddings, iced confections, cakes studded with fruit and heavy with rum, parkins. Walter had already settled in to eating when he ar-rived.

Matilda Paley was the first guest to spot him. He tried unsuccessfully to avoid her. She held his wrist tight and bent towards him. Her breath smelled. She bleated at him: "We're waiting—your mother and I—every day for *good news*."

He mumbled something (was not he too, worried?), and then thankfully glimpsed Catriona. He had seen very little of her since that first flowering of friendship in November. After Christmas she had been a month or more confined to her room and then was no sooner up than she received news of her father's death. Ned had called to offer his sympathy, and she had told him then that she did not truly realise it, that for her her father had been already dead. Then in February she had gone on a long visit to Scotland . . . Now she awaited a child again at Christmas and as before, had not been well or in good spirits. At the Sunday family gathering she was often absent.

Today though, she put out her hands in welcome. "It is good to see you—"

"I'd hoped always you'd call in one day at the works. To see how Walter's shaping maybe?"

"Ah that," she said, "that sorry business." She moved her head, "I know fine about family disgrace. This one at least has not been—very public." They both looked over to where Walter sat in the corner, a plate piled high with pastries beside him, eating steadily and listening, or rather not listening, to Ann's husband, Frank.

"But you, Catriona—you move soon to Linden House?"

"September. When Mr. Whitelaw goes at last to his dear house in Filey." She shuddered. "To think that he is Scotch and might retire to Scotland—and he chooses the Yorkshire coast."

"I expect he'll like it well enough—"

"I had forgot," she said. "You are obliged to think well of Yorkshire! Well, I need not . . ." Then she added, "I have of course meant to come and visit the works. But I have been—not in the best of health. I find this weather so trying. And it must try your wife."

"She doesn't fret, it doesn't fash her, it's just the waiting. She's having such a *wait*."

She nodded in sympathy. At that moment Kate came up behind him, and pulled at his coat. "Nunky Ned, Nunky Ned." He had turned already before she said it again. "I love you," she said, on tiptoe. He bent down and they bumped noses. For a second he had almost lost his balance.

"Kate, Kate—" he said, righting himself. Then:

> "The girl in the lane that couldn't speak plain
> Cried, Gobble, gobble, gobble!
> The man on the hill that couldn't stand still
> Went hobble, hobble, hobble!"

"Again!" she pleaded. "Again!"

"Did I never say it you before, my cockyolly bird?"

She shook her head, looking from him to Catriona and back. Her dress was sprigged muslin, with a cap to match. The mouth that had kissed him was red-stained.

"I learned, I learned to use the globe. I said to Miss Hoo—Hooper, let's look at the places they send the rope stuff from, let's look—but she didn't know!" Her voice rose in triumph. She repeated gleefully, "She *didn't know*—"

Catriona said, "But the poor lady, Kate, she can't know everything."

"But *Richard* knew. Richard said we should look for Liverpool and Manila and . . . and . . ."

Ned thought, I should be at my ease, here, with those I love. But in spite of the great heat in the room, he felt a sudden wave of extreme cold. As he shivered there passed through his mind the smell, the chill of the graveyard. The Kissing Gate garlanded for the death of a maiden—surely Death balked once, waited now only a second chance? O my Kate, take care, he breathed.

"I will look for more strawberries, did you have strawberries yet, Nunky?"

"But your mouth is already so red," said Catriona, "and you ask for more. Will I not wipe it for you? And your cheeks?"

"Red mouth, red hair, red Kate," said Ned affectionately, taking hold of her warm hand, pulling her to him.

Now it was his turn with Old Jacob. The room was unbearably hot: the fire lit, and his chair in front of it.

Grandfather said, "I'd a mind to come and see you all. But there's nowt worse than too many folk." He grumbled to himself, "Are there none from t'Abbey? Is it our food not good enow then, eh?"

He scarcely seemed to notice Ned. "Mebbe they're too grand . . . When a man's got to seventy-five—there's all my years gone and five past—I've not wasted my time, I've not let women or lasses get t'better o'me. I know what I'm about. Daftness never builds owt worth leaving up—and there'll be summat to leave right enow." He chuckled. "Brass for *some*," he shouted. Snuff spilt down his sleeve. "None here from t'Abbey, eh? There's nowt about folk like that to make 'em set theirsen above others. If it's come by being born, we've nowt to do wi' that . . . And I hear tell now Sam's Ned, he's to be a *father*. Nowt but a scrap of flesh he is, skin and bone—"

Ned said, "Can I go now, Grandfather?"

"Aye. Who's that? Aye, get you gone. And fetch me in that Walter . . ."

John said, "No doubt you're worried about Nanny? Eh? I shall be over tomorrow." He stood by the fireplace, a drink in his hand. Ned had waited for him, but he had arrived when the party was almost over.

"It'll be four weeks, Tuesday."

"I know—it's the waiting is hard. And especially for her." He paused. "Whitelaw had one last year, eleven months. And near on *twelve* pounds when it came."

"I don't reckon we've a giant like that—"

"I might send to Leyburn," John said, "if there's nothing by the morrow. At any rate, tell her I'll be over."

When he arrived back at the cottage the sisters had already left, gone with the carter an hour before. He was annoyed with himself because he had waited on—he had not wanted her left alone. And the coming storm oppressed him. All the way back he had feared that it would break and that he would be forced to shelter.

The first rumblings of thunder came as he led his mare into the stable. She did not want to settle and moved restlessly in her stall. Outside the river in the darkening evening smelled sinister. It flowed sluggishly, the grass, the plants at its edge an eerie shade of green.

Nanny was crouched over the unlit fire. She said irritably: "There's your tea left laid."

He saw it: unappetising cold remains of brawn, a stale loaf, withered raw onion. Tabby and Martha's used plates still there.

"I want nothing. There was quite a banquet—you know Mother." He said: "I didn't want you left alone."

"I can mind missen." When he didn't speak but began to clear away, she said angrily, "Let alone. That's woman's work—"

"It'll not get done else. And—you should be in your bed."

She said, "I'll go when I please." She was white in the face with two hectic spots of colour high on her cheeks.

"You're all right, then?"

"Don't I look it?" She turned her head away.

He shrugged his shoulders. There was an uneasy silence. She leaned forward, hugging herself, then letting out a long drawn sigh.

"What is it?"

"Nowt."

The thunder claps were more frequent now. He waited for the sound of the rain breaking through—it would refresh, cleanse. He felt he could hardly breathe.

"And who were there? I were fashed not going. I'd thought to see an Ingham or two."

He thought she was maybe mocking him. "They didn't come. And any road, we'd never ask them."

"Why not?"

"You ask silly ones—why ever should we? They've better to do—"

She said hotly, "You defend them, like as you'd been paid. I thought you'd no good word for Mr. Charles? But mebbe sin your fine Kate's been larning her books wi' 'em, it's a different tale—"

"She's not my fine Kate—she's *all* of ours, our family's. And what of your Martha, your Tabby, that I've to see every day?"

They were sparring again (this night, last night—every night now). Like two children, he thought bitterly.

"I might have reckoned, a mean word like that, from you—"

"Don't you need to go to bed?" He could feel the thunder in his skull.

"Your Becky, then—I can say that, I reckon. *Your* Becky. There'll be no one else'll claim her."

"She's got family."

"Has she, then? They don't own her much in t'town. I never heard tell of her but she were up in that place. I heard too as how you was daft about her—"

"That's a lie," he said, the loaf of bread clutched in his hand. "I said she's my friend—"

"Aye, yourn. Yourn—" She wrinkled up her nose. "You don't know t'half on it, do ye?"

"And what if I don't?" (I will not have anything to do with this, he thought.)

"It's known," she said. "It's known to some."

"What's known?" The storm seemed in abeyance, but not inside him. Half of him wanting to escape, up to bed, to bury his head beneath the sheets. "*What's known?*"

"I shouldn't tell . . ."

"You can tell me—" (He would not, *must* not persist.)

"Mebbe I'll not—"

She parried, they parried. He became desperate to know.

She said, "It's to do with t'Old Squire." She leaned forward again. Beneath her skirt he saw the swollen ankles. "Martha's friend Charity, her mam, she were friend to Becky's mam—t'darkie's daughter. Meg they called her."

"Well?" There was silence. "You'll eat me up," he said.

"You'll eat yoursen up. It killed t'cat, didn't it?"

He was silent then. She can't have liked that because soon without prompting she took up her story again.

"Meg were up at t'Abbey. Old Squire's dad took her on. Skivvy she were, like me. And no more'n fourteen year. Eeh," she paused, bending further over, "it's a stitch, I've a stitch from t'sitting." She waited a moment and then: "T'Old Squire, him that's poorly now, he were just a lad then. And—" she paused again. "It's known how he were, even them days. Always after t'lasses. And it's certain sure as *he had to do wi' Meg.* There were a bairn—so they'd to wed her. He were paid like, Joseph Marsett were. And nowt said. Meg, she'd not t'look of a darkie —and Joseph he'd nowt to complain on—money were good. Only, Charity said as twenty, thirty year ago—there were *folk told Becky.* And it were along of all that—hearing she were Squire's by-blow—that she run off. They reckon she'd enow wi' a darkie granddad—and it crazed her, hearing tell of t'other."

She turned to him. Her eyes lost in the puffy face were lively, excited. "And so your Becky—I mean your fine Mr. Charles, it's a part-sister he has up there on t'moor." She paused. "She'll be more *Mr. Charles's* Becky than yourn."

"Indeed," he said coldly. He hadn't wanted to hear. He didn't want any more burdens. Charles without doubt did not know. Could not know. And yet as if by instinct seemed attracted almost, drawn to hate this person linked to him by a chain whose existence would horrify him . . . Certainly he, Ned, believed the tale. Sadly, it had the ring of truth, and was anyway beyond Nanny's inventiveness.

"You'd best to your bed," he said. "It's late—and if we're to have the storm." He paused and then said more kindly, "Perhaps the bairn'll come tomorrow."

"Mebbe," she said.

When in the end he came upstairs, the false beginning of the storm over, the air still thundery, thick, she was lying on her back, knees drawn up.

"I told a fib," she said.

"Are you all right?"

"I told a fib. It's started then—"

"What? When?" Standing in the doorway. "I'll go for—"

She cut in: "There's nowt. It's only little signs. I've pains, but not— It were a while back, nobbut a little minute after Martha and Tabby were left."

"I'd as soon go," he said. "I'll fetch Mrs. Leeson."

"You'll not," she said firmly. "Asides—I've had these sort afore. You'll mind that. Three week sin."

He gave in then, because he was tired, and he was tired of her. After a few moments she said, "And any road, they're away now, the pains. There's nowt—"

He was hard and fast asleep, within minutes. The thunder woke him. Great claps just behind the cottage. Rumbling. The sky about to come down. A flash of lightning illumined the room. It was then Nanny moaned.

"What's up?" he said in sudden panic. "Is it bad, are they bad?"

"They're bad, they're bad—" She threw herself suddenly across the bed, pulling with clenched fingers at his nightshirt.

"You ought to have woke me—"

The thunder came again. She clutched at him ferociously.

"The woman that's to wait on you—Mrs. Leeson, I'll go for her," he said. Then soothingly, "Storms, you don't mind storms, Nanny."

"Ned—you'll not leave me? Ned—"

He crossed over to the window, pulling himself away. "Let me dress, then," he said. When he looked out, lightning flashed across the village green, crackling over the water of the beck. Any moment now, the rain.

He felt helpless. "Do I get water, boil up water? Is there water drawn?"

"There's no hurry, then," she said between clenched teeth. A spasm overtook her. "Waves," she said, "them waves—they'll *drown* me . . ." Then a moment later: "Ned—*Ned!*"

Twice he made for the door, only to be brought back by her screaming.

"I *shall* go—Nanny, leave off. Mrs. Leeson—"

But she clutched at him. "If ye go, I'll—" Her clutch was of one drowning. "If ye move from here, I'll die. T'window. I'll cast missen down. I *will*, Ned . . ."

She sobbed now between the spasms. They were clustered together now, with barely time to rest between. He had not known it would be like this. He had seen animals—but that had been effort only. A triumphant distress, passing. He had no yardstick to know if what he saw now was *right*.

And he could not escape her. The bones of his hand, they were cramped, he was bruised so strong was her grasp. What chance had he to summon help? Outside the storm still raged. More thunder. Lightning. The cottage seemed to rock on its centuries-old foundations. The air was charged.

"I'm badly," she hissed. "I'm that badly, *I'll die*—"

"No, you'll not." He tried to make his voice contradict the panic he felt. *I must get help.*

But this person holding him wasn't Nanny. It was a small frightened animal. And the high-pitched shrieks coming sharply from her were its cries. But when he said yet again, "I'm off for help, I *must*—" her screams became altered, a voice which terrified him.

"I'll cast missen down—*don't go, Ned* . . ."

He had never known a night so long. The thunder and lightning had given way to hail. Great stones the size of bird's eggs battering the windows.

"The bairn, it'll surely come," he kept telling her. "Surely." But she didn't hear him. Only when he tried to prise his hand from hers did she seem to notice.

She called on her mother. "Mam, Mam—" He knew that if he didn't care, he still pitied. He thought he would do anything, anything to remove this pain . . .

"Can't I just get water?" he said, thinking, planning how he'd steal quickly out while the kettle boiled, would knock up their neighbour, Jack Harper.

Her great bulk heaved with each spasm. So much pain, so much travail—surely it must mean a child soon?

"It'll tear me," she shrieked, "Mam, they're tearing me—*take me*, Mam!" He thought she must be delirious. And always when he thought she could grasp no tighter, her nails would claw deeper and she would crush his hand with a new unbelievable strength.

He prayed. " 'The Lord is my shepherd: therefore can I lack nothing. He shall feed me in a green pasture: and lead me forth beside the waters of comfort . . . Yea though I walk through the valley of the shadow of death I will fear no evil: for thou art with me; thy rod and thy staff comfort me . . .' "

The first light of dawn. He heard sounds beneath the window, someone from the farm maybe. For a second, Nanny relaxed her grasp. He was at once across the room, flinging wide open the window, calling down.

It was Pearson, the cowhand. "I want help!" He shouted his instructions. He said, "It's life and death, life and death, you've to get—"

"Don't fash yoursen, Mr. Rawson, don't fash yoursen, sir . . ."

Help came swiftly. First Mrs. Leeson and then a little later, John. Then Martha and Tabby brought by the carter. White-faced, they were of little help. They clung together downstairs, and would not speak.

John's face was grave. Ned wanted to ask him, "What is wrong?" But he could only wait till John said: "There should have been a bairn a while since. But sometimes, if they're not lying right, there's trouble with the journey out. We're doing—everything. You'll know that . . ."

And still the same sounds from upstairs. He thought that no one could go on so long. He wanted, half of him wanted, to go back up to her. But they had forbidden him. It was not a man's place—he would only be in the way.

The day wore on. The air, after the storm, seemed no fresher than yesterday. He could not eat or drink but only sat with his head in his hands.

John came downstairs about four in the afternoon. "It's a girl," he said, but he was not smiling. He said to Ned: "Come outside a moment—away from the sisters." In the small garden, looking out to where the beck rushed through from the bridge: "She's gone. Nanny's gone." He said it bluntly. Then, "I'm sorry, Ned."

But *why? What had happened?* Where? *What had they done to her?*

"There was all this trouble with the babe, Ned. And then when it, the bairn, was out, it was then she'd a stroke. The brain, you know—sudden blood to the brain. The great effort, and all the difficulties. And the size she was . . ."

Ned was silent.

"These things happen. We could not have foreseen . . . Many a lass goes to her Maker, Ned, for some little thing gone wrong. So much *can* go wrong. To have a bairn, it may be natural, but not if—"

"The *pain*," Ned said.

"Oh, quite natural," John said, almost relieved, matter of factly, "quite natural. A little drawn out perhaps, because it didn't come out easily. But quite natural."

The baby was tiny. She looked more like an old, old woman, wizened, a waxy colour. He could not believe in her, so wrapped round was she, so unreal.

And it was as well he didn't believe in her, didn't think of her as his, since she lasted only till seven that evening. He had not even begun to face the problem of her living. She weighed less than five pounds. That great mound he had thought a prize fighter had been—only this.

For the night he went back to Downham, to his parents' house. John took him—he told Ned that he would have asked him to sleep with them, but that it might distress Catriona. Mother was kind to him, in a bustling manner.

"I'll give you a bairn, if it kills you."

"Thou knowest, Lord, the secrets of our hearts . . ."

"We brought nothing into this world and it is certain we can carry nothing out. The Lord gave, and the Lord hath taken away . . ."

"I'll give you a bairn, if it kills you . . ."

TWENTY-FOUR

1st January 1850

Dear Journal,

A shining new volume, for a bright and wonderful happy, happy New Year! I have not written in you for *so long!* My sadness has been such. Eighteen forty-nine was a year I do not wish to remember (and 1848 no better, God knows!), but now, even in spite of Mama coming to stay next week—if the weather allows—I still feel able to write happily. So I must be happy! (Mama is by the way *much better* since Papa died. The sad truth is that I think *it is good* that he did—) Dear Journal, I am indeed fortunate, I am so blessed—dear Journal, *I have not deserved my happiness.*

Where, though, to begin?! Perhaps, if I don't tire (and I shall not be able to write more than a few pages at one time, I fear, since I am not yet very strong), I should begin with my visit to Scotland. That is, in February of last year. I shall omit the terrible six weeks at the beginning of 1849 when I had no child, no health, and was of a sadness such as poor *Ned* is in yet. I went first to Edinburgh—Aunt Charlotte was not at all well, she has grown far too stout and was confined to her room all the time, which caused me even greater unhappiness and worry— although her spirits were good, and she would have cheered me had anyone been able (dear Journal, she is now *quite well again*). Mama grumbled the whole of my stay, and was as fractious as ever. What makes it so difficult is that she will go *nowhere* by rail and begins nervous posturings at the very notion, yet she continues to speak of it on the slightest pretext—and collects still all accounts of *accidents*, which of course are to be had for the searching only (on this matter of railway travel she is *quite* unhinged—when I first came, she would keep looking at me, saying what a wonder it was that I should have arrived safely!).

But still, dear Journal, there I was in Edinburgh, and of course as unhappy and low and despondent as when I left home, since I brought my despondency with me. (I have discovered that low spirits belong not so much to a place as to the person and are carried carapace-like— but that is enough of Catriona's wisdom!)

Kirsty was of course gone. I have not told you yet, dear Journal, that Kirsty is *now married* and that she awaits a child at midsummer (I am to be godmother!). She was wed just a year ago so that I was naturally not able to attend. I visited her in Glasgow—she is the wife of a fine consultant physician who is at the least thirty-five years of age and whom she met through Robbie. (Robbie also works in Glasgow and will be very famous before long, I am sure—Kirsty's husband spoke *very* highly of him!) Sadly, dear Journal, I could not make the most of see-ing her. She was quite unable to raise me from my melancholy. I am *ashamed* now to recollect how little I rejoiced in her happiness.

My easiest moments on that Edinburgh visit were those I spent with my dearest *dearest* cousin Alan. It was he who saved me—by visiting al-most *every day*. With him, *while he was there*, I could feel for fleeting moments that I was back again in the old days, that I was in the happy land before Papa's trial, before my marriage and the pain and loss of the stillbirth (that dreadful *dreadful* emptiness. There are no words to describe what it is like to have had *death within you*). We did not speak of it, or only a little. He told me—his manner is often a little *rough* but I do not mind—that he knew nothing of these matters (that is, of childbirth), "only how to bring it about" he said, which I thought was rather *coarse*, except that with him it doesn't *seem* so. He is just Alan! And then he added, "I know also how *not* to bring it about and that is *indeed* useful" (I was not quite sure of his meaning? I think had I been less grieving I would have asked).

We spoke much of Papa. I was surprised at how understanding he was—I think that in truth he had a great deal of affection for him and also *gratitude*. He said that I must think always of the *happy days* when I was proud of Papa and that even though what he did was very wicked, it was also very *clever* (which I had not thought of), and that in truth he had done it for the *good of the family*, that we might *all* be rich.

And so we spent much time together, Alan and I, and I shall *always be grateful* to him. However, dear Journal, there *was* one occurrence, to do with him, which I should like earnestly to forget. To this end I shall write it down, since this journal is *quite private* and once it is written it will perhaps quite leave my mind (although if I am *quite* honest, *half* of me would be quite sad to forget it!).

What happened was this—I had decided one evening to retire very early. I went usually by half past nine at the latest, but that night I was already gone up by eight o'clock and was in my night attire and my hair undressed and quite a fright generally, when little Meggie the new maid came up to say that Mr. Alan had called and what was she to say, and I said at once but of course I must see him. I thought, dear Journal, *why not*, and I put on my new cap with the mauve ribbons and was sat in a chair with my new cashmere dressing gown about me when he knocked. And of course it was all right. We sat talking, on and on, he in a very cheerful mood (I think perhaps he had been drinking a little?). We sat opposite each other and he told me, as so often he does, tales of the Edinburgh that he frequents and *I* do not see! He amused me very much with his tale of the corpse at the Infirmary, whose owner had drunk so much good Scotch whisky that it was—*in August*—twenty days without mortifying!! "We are like to say pickled—" When I laughed at this, he said I must be in the steady way of recovery. I told him that it was thanks to him if I were, and that when I had arrived I had been quite *down in the chops*—which is an expression *he* uses!

And so we went on. Then he brought out his watch. He had not realized we had talked so long—he said, "Goodnight then—a kiss, Pussy?" And I put out my cheek, dear Journal, as ever—and of course as ever, without thinking threw my arms about him (my *cousin* after all). But his arms were suddenly very tight and he felt around then for my mouth and kissed me—(I *will* write it) very long and *very hard* on the lips. He tasted of cigars and of drink and also of Alan. I could feel his body too all the time—I remembered that *afterwards*—he touched me too in what I shall call "other places." It was not perhaps so *very* long, but I thought that I might faint, so strange did I feel—I cannot describe it, dear Journal, since I had not felt that way before (and have not felt *since!*), but it seemed to me at the time *quite right*, if a little alarming—yet perhaps not right, or why should I write of it in this odd manner? Dear Journal, I was in the *strangest* of moods for three days afterwards—

He went very suddenly after that—and he did not mention it the next time. Nor shall *I* ever mention it to him (unless it is to say that it must *never happen again*).

But enough of all that, since it is not *really* so important! What I must write of is that on my return (and how wretched I felt to come back to the Yorkshire cold, which is *not* the same as the Edinburgh cold!) something which *should* have occurred—*did not!* And since the month before I had seen it only for the first time again since my tragedy, I suspected at once (and with what terror and despondency, dear

Journal!) that I was again to have a child. And then—this you will not believe, dear Journal—in my fear and upset the quite absurd and fanciful notion came to me, that it was a *result* of what Alan and I did together! Such absurdity, and in a *married* woman too! But still there is no end I sometimes think to the odd thoughts that one may have, and quite without soliciting them—

As soon as I had realised, dear Journal, that it was indeed true and that I *was* to have another child, I became very angry, and not least *with myself*. Why had I not said to John—which was the truth: "I am not yet well enough, I have not *recovered my strength*." Is he not a *doctor?* But it had seemed to me then, that it did not matter what was done to my body (it *is* an outrage—but men do not see it like that—) so that I could not really think sensibly of the consequences. It would after all be over so quickly. It was only to wait till *it was over*, and then to *sleep*. Sleep was my greatest friend in those days—unhappy as I was, I who had never bothered to waste time in sleep, now found in it my greatest solace.

My feelings were very confused, dear Journal. I thought, I do not love John—and I thought also, I must cease to blame him for that, since he came *to save me* and that must *never be* forgotten. But I cannot hope ever to feel again as I felt *that evening in Edinburgh*, when he came in out of the night. I did not think *then*, I had quite forgot how little we had had to say to each other, on the few occasions we had met. I was so certain that he was THE ONE, that just to be with him was entertainment enough—I was going to be *so good* and to love Downham and all the Rawson family too, if at all possible! But all that was when *I thought I loved him*. How different, after I had realised that *feelings are not facts* and that they can pass as if they had *never been.* It was then I suppose that I changed from girl to woman—and a foolish woman perhaps. But what is very important is that I truly felt about the child I must bear, that John would be a worthy father, a *good* father (just as he is a *good* son to his mother).

But that, dear Journal, was the *only* right thing about the coming child. I had once again, so that I felt I could not bear it, that everpresent *nausea*. Nothing would raise my spirits—or still my terrible forboding. *That* had begun immediately, and was made worse by Ned's tragic loss (and although he will not receive any comfort from *any* person—I am ashamed that I *did not offer*). I cannot describe, dear Journal, my certainty of disaster—and that I should have to *live through it*.

Then there was all the upheaval of the move to Linden House—I had complained that the other was too small, but this place seemed to me a mausoleum and I could not at first accustom myself. Meal times, with the apprentices present, were a form of torture. I could not eat meat—mutton especially I could not touch. But eggs, in spite of the nausea, I wanted eggs continually, in any form. "A yellow bairn," they said, "it'll be a yellow bairn." I felt too a compulsion to *walk*. However faint I felt, I must needs walk about and about. I did not care if I endangered the child—I cannot believe that now, but I *did not care!*

And then suddenly, dear Journal, Christmas was upon us and all the preparations for it—and also for the babe, and still I did not care at all. I cared nothing until half past four on December 20th. Then came a sign—the first that I had been led to expect but some ten days early, and then a little later some pain—but not terrible—only terrible because of my unhappiness. At six o'clock I was able to eat two coddled eggs. And then at only eight o'clock after a surprising and *very* eventful ten minutes, I was delivered of a live child!

Dear Journal, you cannot imagine the happiness I felt that evening— and *feel now*. Here are the details! She is small—they said about six and a half pounds only—but *quite perfect*, and of an unbelievable beauty. She is very dark and has already black locks and such large eyes and a mouth like—yes, it *is* like a rosebud!! And she is always hungry but healthily so and scarcely ever cries or complains. John is *delighted* and does not mind at all that we do not have a son (*how could he?*). She is to be christened *Ann*, after John's grandmother and sister, *Charlotte* after my dear aunt, and lastly *Christine*, after Kirsty!

And so, dear Journal, *that* is my surprise! And that is why I am so happy—and why I know now at last what it is to *love*. This, truly, is LOVE—

> Catriona Rawson scripsit!
> Linden House,
> Downham, Yorkshire.

TWENTY-FIVE

"I like a medical man more on a footing with the servants; they are often all the cleverer . . ."

> Lady Chettam in *Middlemarch*,
> by George ELIOT

An April morning in 1853. The last of John's visits was to the Abbey. His patient: Charles Ingham's sister, one Mrs. Ballantine. She had been widowed earlier that year and had been staying at the Abbey since. Although he knew her by sight he had spoken to her only the once, when Kate had had a birthday party in the schoolroom a year ago now. Georgiana Ingham and Mrs. Ballantine—there on a visit—had come in to admire. He too had called by.

But it had not been Kate the brightest star at that gathering. One star had eclipsed her quite: his daughter, Tarley (Kate had not minded. She never sought attention. Nor could she love Tarley more . . .) Catriona had brought her—no leaving this to others, so that both she and the nurse came. *His* daughter: black-haired, blue-eyed, with a habit already of speaking earnestly, her head on one side. Even her (rare) tantrums were delightful. Reprimanded, picked up in his arms, small fists beating on his chest. Tarley. And all must call her that: from when she had first mispronounced "Charlotte," she had been nothing else.

Georgiana Ingham had declared herself enchanted. Also Mrs. Ballantine. She told Catriona, "Mr. Ballantine is from Scotland of course." Catriona made much always of Tarley's Dunbar and Fraser origins. From the cradle she had sung to her (that voice more than ever like a corncrake—but angel Tarley did not mind). Any sort of Scottish air, the words bastardised to fit. Songs of protest, of the Young Pretender. "Tarley is my darling, my darling," or "Who wadna fight for Tarley?"

That party had been only two months before the Old Squire's death. He had not so much died as slipped away. From his stroke in 1849 onwards, he was visiting only, as it were. He did not seem to be living any more at the Abbey. Coming to meals, but sitting silently, nodding like a mandarin, fed like a babe, frustrated by his inability to utter anything other than meaningless sounds. Charles had not been good with him, had treated him as if he were dead already—which for practical purposes was true, since Charles must manage the estate. But when John, after a routine visit, would comment on his father's condition, or suggest how his suffering might be lightened, Charles would shrug his shoulders: "Brain's quite dead, my dear fellow. Can't get a sensible word out of him. A confounded nuisance, these Acts of God. And you surgeons, you flap about helplessly. Ease him out, I say. Ease him out, there's a good fellow . . ."

There had been a small legacy for Mother. In his Will the Squire had said: "No words or deeds can ever express the gratitude felt . . . the Ingham family will always be in debt to Sarah Donnelly-Rawson . . ." Looking at Charles that day, John had thought yet again: it was not for the best. The second son, George, had been universally popular. Had he been the heir he would not have become a Hussar—and would not have been killed in the Ashanti campaign. All would have been better arranged.

As the Abbey came into sight: *I shall have a son—this time*, he thought. The autumn would see him a father again. And three miscarriages on from Tarley (who *should* have been a boy—except, who could have wanted her anyone other than Tarley?), he would, must have, a son.

Yet—he trembled. For although the saying here went, reassuringly: "Aye, well, there's more lambs go than ewes . . ." it was not always so. Nearly two years now since his own sister, Ann, had gone, only four days after the birth of her second child. A fever, and no stopping it, no understanding why. Frank left desolate, with two small sons. But worst of all—and let it not be as it had with Nanny: both ewe *and* lamb . . .

No doubt too but that Ned was not yet over it. Living alone in the cottage out at Little Grinling, refusing when Mother offered to send Eliza to housekeep for him. Four years a widower and almost dead himself—a man who sat like a ghost at the Sunday family gathering. Surprisingly Catriona was not yet out of patience with him—she who was so easily out of patience with so many (and not least the new apprentice at Linden House: Leathley, from Bradford, and blushing head-over-heels in love with her . . .), even she could not draw him out.

Let it not be like that, he prayed.

Mrs. Ballantine had her maid with her, a late middle-aged wizened little woman, who spoke with an accent, a burr, he did not recognise.

"Missus was a throwing up all night, sir, nothing but water, sir—all of three hand basins . . ." She rushed over, producing one to show. He glanced at the colourless mucus. Said: "Thank you."

Propped up with several pillows, Mrs. Ballantine nodded at him weakly. "You will be all right," he said, to inspire confidence. Her heart beat feebly. He felt her abdomen, lax, soft, enormous. "Does this hurt? This? This?" He increased the pressure.

"No." Her voice was weak. She had been losing weight, she told him, but had thought it due to distress from her widowhood. She could not understand that her abdomen should increase in size.

He prescribed an enema, and prepared to go home—and think. On his way out, the housekeeper told him, "Mrs. Ingham is badly too, and in her room."

"Am I asked to visit?"

"No, sir. She asked only that I tell you." She pressed him to stay for wine, cake. Once he had used to like to do this, but now:

"I must be early at home," he said, "to see my daughter before she is put down for her rest."

Back home, he asked: "Where's my Tarley?"

"Gone to sharpen her teeth for dinner—"

He went to look for her. Lifting her up and down, swinging her from side to side, throwing her in the air:

> "Tarley, Tarley, stole the barley
> Out of the baker's shop.
> The baker came out and gave her a clout
> Which made poor Tarley *hop* . . ."

It was a bad week medically. He had several deaths and at the Abbey, Mrs. Ballantine was no better. Her abdomen was more swollen than ever, and here and there he could feel a hardness. He was not happy about the diagnosis.

Georgiana Ingham kept to her room still. He had begun obscurely to worry about her, asking her maid always how she was.

"She's nobbut a chill, sir."

Perhaps I *should* be sent for, he thought. He felt that medical mismanagement dogged him. Both of them will die on me, he thought, in a sudden glimpse.

He saw Charles come in from a day's hunting: fine end of season weather. John told him, "I need a second opinion."

"By all means, my dear fellow."

"Your sister—"

"My sister—yes, indeed. And my wife taken to her bed also. A plague on both of them, I say. But arrange it of course. Arrange it and let me know. Luncheon, dinner?"

"I thought perhaps Mr. Eastwood, at Leeds—"

"Arrange it, then, dear fellow, arrange it . . ."

At home, Tarley, who had been listening in on some conversations, told him: "*Moppet's* very sick." She handed him her doll, showing him, under the velvet overskirts, lace-trimmed drawers. "Papa take *all* off . . ."

He returned to the Abbey early the next morning. If not too much engaged, Mr. Eastwood was to come the following day. The size now of Mrs. Ballantine's abdomen frankly terrified him. Looking helplessly at the great swelling, which seemed to be growing before his eyes, he was reminded of nothing less than a whale. With difficulty, he continued to try and reassure her.

As he came out of her room, a servant was waiting: "The Mistress, sir, please sir you're to see her afore you go, sir."

He had washed his hands already. Going now into Mrs. Ingham's room, carrying his bag, he felt like a lackey—but for no good reason. His feelings towards her were warm: she had been kind to Kate, her generosity more than a whim, and on the few occasions they had met since the interview following Richard's burn (and he had done nothing about that, about her queries—in the end it must have sorted itself), she had been very gracious, intimating always that she owed him gratitude.

She was not in bed, but sitting in a cane chair not far from the window. Her maid was busying herself at the washstand. The room was light and airy, and refreshing after the foetid closed smell of the other sick room. Daffodils and narcissi stood in vases around the room, and a bunch of early violets on the table beside her. In her lap was a partly uncut novel and a paper knife.

For a few minutes they exchanged pleasantries, then:

"You asked to see me?" he said, his manner awkward.

"But of course, Mr. Rawson. I am requesting, you see, a *medical* visit." She smiled, then languidly, lifting her hand: "You may go, Taylor," she said to the maid. "Taylor, dismissed. You *need not stay—*"

"Yes, ma'am, no, ma'am—" She scuttled away.

"These girls, they are so . . . Too much intellect would of course be an impediment, do you not agree, Mr. Rawson?"

He said stiffly, regretting it immediately, "My *mother*—was such a one."

She said with a very composed smile, "Of *course*. And of course also, the Rawsons are in no way lacking in intelligence . . ."

He was certain that he was being laughed at. But, "I am forgiven?" she asked lightly. And then at once: "About my sister-in-law, Mr. Rawson? I can make no sense from Mr. Ingham. And she, she is too feeble. I fear we may yet be in mourning . . . What exactly—"

"Frankly, I cannot give a diagnosis."

"Oh, but surely—it is what you are *for*, is it not?"

"No. I—often a medical man cannot. Or, why should there be consultants? And we have sent for—your husband has agreed—Mr. Eastwood from Leeds will be here tomorrow."

"Ah, very well," she said, as if bored with the subject. There was silence. He said, in an awkward attempt at humour, "And *your* case—you wish for a diagnosis?"

"Indeed I do," she said laughing. "Indeed I do." She laughed immoderately, could not seem to stop. He thought it nervous. His question had not been such a joke.

"Sit down, Mr. Rawson, pray. Please, do be seated."

He was about then to ask her questions on her health when she said suddenly, "I confided in you once, Mr. Rawson, several years ago. About my son, and my husband—" She paused.

He said, "You must forgive me. I had some troubles at home. When I heard no more, I thought all well, and did nothing further."

"It was not necessary, Mr. Rawson. I told him that very evening that were it to happen again, I would leave. And take the children with me. Money would be no problem, my family would gladly support me. But the scandal, had he tried to claim—I would have raised the matter in the highest quarters. He understood, Mr. Rawson, both what I said and what I left unsaid. That is why you have heard no more. Why *Downham* has heard nothing . . ."

"And Richard, how is he?"

"School is good for him. Rough but good. I was frankly surprised. He is fortunate perhaps, in the masters, the boys—Eton is said to be much improved. At any rate, he has not complained."

"But he stammers still?"

"Yes, he stammers. Before strangers of course, and in his father's presence always. It is useless for him to attempt even to finish a sentence. My husband lashes him then with his tongue—he is not a patient man, as you will know, Mr. Rawson. Fortunately for Richard, he addresses him seldom . . ."

John began to feel more at ease. Forgetting for the moment the worry about Mrs. Ballantine. Then:

"I would like the door locked," she said. "Taylor, and others, they often burst in so precipitously, scarcely waiting for an answer. And I should not like my—symptoms overheard . . ."

When he came back and was sat down again, she said, "My symptoms."

"Of course—" He waited.

She toyed with the paper knife on her lap. Her hands were very small and delicate. The light velvet wrap she wore was trimmed heavily with lace about the wrists and neck. "My symptoms. I shall try my best to describe them," she said. "It is a weakness, a *bone* weakness, you know—as if my bones were not there. I am unable to describe it better—"

"No—but that is very helpful."

"I have had it for some little while now. And when I was a young girl, the year before I was married. This same feeling. I was married very young, Mr. Rawson. Only just turned seventeen." She paused. "This—weariness, it is accompanied also by a very restless energy, which will come on suddenly for several hours at a time. I feel—my mind—I cannot settle to anything. And then of a sudden my heart will begin to race. It races so that it quite alarms me, Mr. Rawson. I become very flushed. You would not think of course—to see me so pale . . ."

He did not know. She had not the appearance of a sick person. Her symptoms were all of a nervous nature. He began by asking her a few simple questions: he would proceed in routine fashion.

"Your pulse, then, please. I shall take your pulse." He drew out his watch. Took the small floppy white hand, his fingers over her wrist.

She said, "Your hand is remarkably *warm*—"

A pulse rate of sixty. And even too. Nothing abnormal there. He said gallantly, "I hope that is the truth, and that you are not being polite. I have not always warm hands—"

"A good omen, then, perhaps?" Her voice was neat, precise. She thrust her hand out, "Take it, Mr. Rawson. My pulse—again. You will perhaps find it different—" When he did not take it at once: "Hold me," she said, "hold it, I beg you . . ."

As, flushed now, he concentrated on his watch, he could feel her gaze on him.

"No, quite normal, I assure you. I do assure you—"

"Mr. Rawson—*do not let my hand go* . . ."

In his professional voice, he said, "I shall have to ask a further few questions." Her hand lay loosely in his grasp. He thought desperately.

"Your catamenia, the periods—they are regular?" It was as if he could concern himself suddenly only with that part of her. "And sleep," he said, "I must ask you whether you *sleep—*"

"Mr. Rawson," she urged, in a lower voice, quiet, but it throbbed almost, "Mr. Rawson, John—please. *Please . . .*" Her grasp tightened— then letting go suddenly she took his hand in both of hers, began to trace patterns on it, stroking, stroking.

He felt an unbelievable stiffening, of the whole of him. It was consequent upon another stiffening—he became not merely embarrassed but frightened. Rigid with terror. Rigid with desire. Helpless, awkward, every sort of hazard of the medical profession—everything he had ever heard, running through his head.

"Feel my heart," she said. "You will see then—how it races. My complaint, you know. That it races. Feel it . . ."

He was cold, stiff. I will not move, he thought, trying again to detach his hand.

"Such nonsense—John!" With both her hands she pressed his against her bosom. He was so awkwardly positioned that he thought he might fall. Perhaps he should kneel? Oh, good Lord God, *let me out of this . . .*

But where he could feel the warmth, the softness through the velvet, her heart beat steadily. It was his own that fluttered, seemed to miss, knocked suddenly. Like a woman, he thought disgustedly. I am afraid, he told himself. To be rough, to be firm now, might be *lèse majesté.* Besides, *he did not want to . . .* He had been brought now to one knee. But he felt no ridiculousness, only fear—and a stirring of something remembered. Ellie; his mother, the feel when she had clasped him against her, when he had been small: "It will be *all right*, son—" The softness Catriona had promised and had occasionally given (that now for the safety of the child-to-be he did not dare to take—this bairn *must* run to term . . .).

He said in a choked voice: "We are to—my wife and I—she is in a delicate condition . . ."

"Indeed," she said robustly. "Well, *I* am not. And you, I trust, are not?"

He had to smile. He went down then on both knees. He was completely ridiculous.

She said: "Hold me." He leaned forward—this damnable awkwardness, and the haste—why such haste? Once begun he would be unable to halt. Mouth, hands, and that part of him already so eager, so ready—against his will even, ready to take . . . No, this could not be him. This could not be *her.*

The canopy bed was enormous—the silk curtains were drawn about them. He moved quickly in a dark surprising world. It was like nothing before—because it had been none of his doing. This was not the good-natured warmth of Ellie, but rather, a cool fragrance. He was guided, not knowing where he might go and where he might not, setting out on a journey. Where was care now, where common sense?

Her skin smelled of the flowers that stood by the bed, and was so cool to the touch—it was he so hot, so burning. That long ago rogue thought: I want to help you—and here was help so delicious, a task so delightful. Forget, forget you are John Rawson, surgeon-apothecary of Downham, that she is Georgiana Ingham . . .

Oh, but he had arrived. This was the end of the journey. He was spent: but surprisingly, surprisingly he had given pleasure—those small hands he had thought so delicate: little pointed nails, little sharp cries. So far from the good-humoured squeals of Ellie, the giggling, the nuzzling.

He was spent. Spent—and ashamed. So ashamed. She said, as she arranged herself in the bed, sitting up, pillows all about her: "There must be a reason for the—disarray. The unmade bed. It would not look well . . . I had not thought. Another time . . ."

But there must never be another time.

"My life is very difficult," she told him. He felt himself shaking still, unsteady on his legs (it could not be just the act of love, *that* could not account for this dry-mouthed insecurity), uncertain now of where he had placed his cravat, his collar, his boots . . .

"My life is very difficult." The cool little voice, gentle now. She was about to confide in him. She said: "I can tell you—I can surely confide in *you*, my medical practitioner. The truth is that I have very little social life, and most of that wearisome. My husband does not attract a very interesting circle. Over the years there have been several opportunities for—consolation. But of course any sort of *affaire* in the French manner, *any* kind of liaison outside, would be for me extremely difficult. My husband is of an exclusive disposition. And his jealousy would be all the greater because it concerns something which, as you must surely realise, he does not greatly want. The occasions for—what I have just enjoyed, are few. And I do not lead a London life. Even then, I would need to be circumspect."

My profession, he thought, my standing, my honour. All my loyalties —my family, wife—everything will tumble. And all *for* a tumble . . . He smiled grimly at the word-play.

"I shall die here of weariness—unless I am rescued. Charles wants nothing from me. Neither my conversation nor my accomplishments.

Nothing but that I produce an heir—which I have done. *And* the two
girls besides . . . Also I should tell you, since you are my doctor, and
since too it concerns you—that it is certain—I have consulted in York
and also in London—I cannot bear another child. Not ought not—but
cannot . . ."

Her voice went on: "Mr. Ingham has really no need of a wife—if you
understand me? His interests are in the hunting field, not the bed.
When I married, Mr. Rawson, I knew nothing of men, nor indeed of
life. But I have chosen my lot . . . I must needs make of it what I can.
But you and I—yes, I say you and I, John—I think that we can perhaps
help each other? I think you do not always want to be a country surgeon—that you have ambition and would welcome possibilities of ad-
vancement? I can promise nothing—I tell you that at once. But—" she
paused, "what do you say—John?"

He hesitated. Catriona, he thought. Catriona. And then, *what have I
done?*

"Come, come, Mr. Rawson—I am not asking for your *heart*. Only for
a share in something with which you have been more than generously
endowed—No, do not colour. It is as much a gift as a fine pair of legs.
And much more to the purpose . . . I think you understand what I say
—what I ask?"

"I could not," he said. He heard his voice, rough, blunt.

"You could, Mr. Rawson. You will—" He turned to look at her. He
thought that she was angry, but saw instead that she was crying. The
tears, little jewels in her eyes. Damnable pity, fuelled by fresh desire,
overcame all else.

"Yes," he said. "Yes."

"You may unlock the door, then—the consultation is over. I shall not
expect another visit until my sister-in-law is better. Or not, as the case
may be. My complaint is one for which regular treatment will be
needed. I shall count on you to provide it . . ."

Mr. Eastwood conducted his examination. He was a very tall, very
thin man with an eagle face. As he spoke, at the end of each sentence
he pushed both lips out. He talked to John as they came together down
the wide stairs.

". . . The abdomen fluctuates. Preternaturally distended—I should
say it contains a great deal of fluid. Ten to eleven pints. A mechanical
obstruction of the bowels, Rawson? No pain, but as we agreed the *exhaustion* presents great danger . . ."

Going on into the library where they were to continue the discussion,

John felt only the sick excitement of indecision. I shall tell her, he said
to himself for the twentieth time. What she asks is not only wrong, it is
also impossible. More than that: it is unthinkable. (And yet—was he
not thinking, already, of doing it again?)

". . . some paralysis of the stomach would account probably for the
cessation of vomiting . . . I remember a case, a good lady some fifteen
years ago—upon post-mortem the small intestine was found to have
contracted to an unbelievably small size—and was completely pushed
down into the cavity of the pelvis. Very interesting, Rawson. Very interesting . . ."

John dined at the Abbey that evening together with Mr. Eastwood.
Also there were Mrs. Ballantine's daughter and son-in-law who had
come north that afternoon: to the news that she was delirious.

It was not a merry gathering. Charles sat in his father's place at the
head of the table: that alone made John sad. Last time he had dined
there—again out of courtesy because Mr. Eastwood visited—the Squire
had been alive, and very much in possession of his faculties.

The remembered Abbey dining-room which when he was a child
Mother had described to him with such awe. "And then the Squire
showed me . . ." Now the gargoyles in the grottolike fireplace seemed
to stare at him. He avoided Georgiana Ingham's eyes. Over on the west
wall, Vanessen's rustic party made merry in the Abbey grounds
amongst the rocks and the chalets—Switzerland come to Downham . . .

Mr. Eastwood commented, as he had last time, on "a truly remarkable work of art . . ."

"Hardly worth the upkeep," Charles told him off-handedly. "Fellow
only spent eight weeks on it. It's forever to be touched up. Can't see
why it's thought so deuced remarkable . . ." He wanted really to talk
about his new mare. He sang her praises, monopolising the conversation. He turned to Mr. Eastwood, "And for the swellings, they bled
her of nearly two pints—half the can full. What's your say about that
eh? Is that good medicine?"

Georgiana said, "Charles—Mr. Eastwood will not be at all interested
of your mare. He is not a *cow doctor*."

Mr. Eastwood, however, took it in good part. The visitors looked embarrassed. Charles paid little attention, changing the subject almost at
once, and turning to John.

"Rawson—your brother, is he not yet over the loss of his wife? I
scarcely see him—and less often get a word out of him . . ."

He was at home quite late. He passed Catriona's door—she slept alone now—and thought to knock. But she was with child; she would need her sleep.

On the way to his room he heard crying from the nursery. He turned and went up there. A light shone under the door. Inside, by the cot, the nursemaid was comforting Tarley.

"I nearly thought to wake the missus, sir. There's no stopping her—I reckon as she's *dreamed*, sir."

But now Tarley had seen him. He was no sooner by the cot than her arms went out for him. As he picked her up, small hot hands clutched at his hair. She pressed her damp flushed cheeks against his cold one. Between sobs: "Moppet's *deaded*," she told him.

He reached out with his free hand for the doll: showed it to her. "Look, *there's* Moppet!"

But she would not be comforted. He could not bear her despair. Limp in his hand, the doll stared waxenly, lifelessly back at him. Tarley, reaching out for her, cried again, "Quite deaded. Even *Katie* can't make better." She caught her breath.

"There, there," he said, stroking her, calming her. "There, there. Tarley is my darling, my darling . . ."

TWENTY-SIX

Who e'er Thou art that passest by
And on this Tombstone casts an Eye
Tho' in Youth's Bloom of Life thou be
Cropt in such Bloom lately were Wee,
And as in Dust wee here do lye
Remember thy mortality.

Here lies the Body of Anne Susan Rawson, Wife of Edwin Rawson of Downham, who departed this Life July 15, 1849, in the twentieth year of her Age, And also the Body of her Daughter.

Ned stood always in the same place, at the foot of the grave, where the inscription might be easily read. The stone had lost its shining newness now. The flowers lying near it were fresh. May was a month of flowers.

He should have been visiting Grandfather—it was for that he had taken time off work. Yet he had not gone. Three o'clock of an afternoon and nothing better to do than stand at this grave, and lament. It was the fourth summer since her death. He did not feel love (when ever had he done so?) nor even loss—unless it was his peace of mind he mourned. Only wickedness, guilt. Some days it would grow and grow in him so that suddenly he would feel an overwhelming need just to stand here. In silence.

"You are grown very strange, Ned . . ." Mother had spoken to him severely only a month or so back—when it had been Easter and a time for joy. But the worst was always July. He could not bear it when midsummer was over—and the long month of memory began.

The rooks cawed in the elms, young ones amongst them, with their characteristic cry. The wind blowing in the long grass. Voices. Were they not voices?

"I'll give you a bairn if it kills you . . ."

He was so far away in his thoughts that he scarcely heard the clang of the Kissing Gate. He saw them coming then: the funeral procession. Why had he not noticed the freshly dug Ingham grave? Mourners from the Abbey, the coffin of Charles's sister, moving slowly now past the slightly waving yew. And he, he hid in the shade to the right of the church porch. His heart beating as if he had been discovered in a crime. His body pressed hard against the stone wall.

" 'Man that is born of woman hath but a short time to live, and is full of misery. He cometh up, and is cut down, like a flower; he fleeth as it were a shadow, and never continueth in one stay.' " The voice of the Reverend Cuthbert. He could not escape the familiar words.

" 'In the midst of life we are in death . . .' "

He waited there awhile. He was not seen. He did not see Charles either. Soon they would be come into the church. They would read the Order for the Burial of the Dead. He might innocently attend if he wished. Certainly he had every right to be here, in this graveyard, lamenting his dead wife . . .

" '*I am the resurrection and the life, saith the Lord: he that believeth in me, though he were dead, yet shall he live . . .*' "

He did not want her back—except that he might be more innocent of the manner of her going. And that was not repentance . . . In the midst of life we are in death. *I* should be buried, he thought, not this daughter of the Inghams.

Why had they not tolled the bell? A blackbird singing in the hazel bush not two feet away from him. Death—the victory of death was complete in him.

And still memory played its tricks:

> Arm in arm, round and round
> Me that loves a bonny lass
> Will kiss her on the ground . . .

Charles had tight hold of his arm. "My dear fellow—" Friendly clasp, pressure of Charles's fingers on his upper arm. "My dear fellow, I never see you—"

Why had he come? Why go to the Abbey? But John had said, "You never visit Kate in the schoolroom. You should fetch her home." John, every day at the Abbey last week—and even dining there—attending to

Charles's sister: dead now and buried two days. "Mrs. Ingham remarks, why do you not come for Kate, see how she gets on?"

He had gone to the back entrance of the Abbey. He was not for the front door. In through the passageway, past the board hung with mugs on hooks, the cask of beer for people on business. He sat for a while on a wooden bench: a servant had been sent to know if it would be all right. He wished he had not come.

A footman then to take him up. But coming through into the hall, who should he meet but Charles?

"My dear fellow . . ." And then: "In here. A brandy?"

He did not want to drink with Charles. Or to be with him at all. Charles had already been drinking . . .

"Who was that taking you up, eh Ned? Higgins, Webster? Can't tell one confounded servant from t'other. Those whose station in life it is to be catch-farts . . . You and I, eh Ned, we're appointed higher? *Speak up, Ned*, there's a good fellow—I rule here. Squire now. And you—*you* rule Rawson's ropes. How's that, eh? Or you don't—no, you've a *father* still. I have no father . . ."

Ned thought, I must escape.

"You'll take a brandy, eh? No need to ring for that catch-fart—" He sat down heavily on the huge leather chair that had been his father's, pulling Ned down with him.

Charles's knees into his buttocks, hateful. A hand went round his waist.

"Let me be—" He jerked himself free, struggling, standing upright. His legs might not hold him. They trembled as he leaned against a card table. It was laid out and his elbow moving suddenly scattered the cards.

Charles was sitting back. He was laughing.

"Get me a drink, will you—there's a good fellow."

Am I your servant? He would not. He would escape. But even as he went for the door, Charles, sliding forward, thrust out a leg, tripping him up. He fell heavily.

As he climbed up painfully, Charles barred his way. He had spread his arms out. He swayed slightly. "Ned, Ned—I never see you. Don't come to call, you know, at the works. What to do when a fellow's not wanted, eh?" Leaning forward, he pushed Ned down roughly into a smaller chair—opposite to where he had been. Then he sat down again.

"You won't move? Be a good fellow—just awhile. I'll tell you *a story*. How'd you like that, eh? A bedtime story . . ." He hiccuped: "Tell you a story now—there's this crowd in Paris—in France, you know. They're before an hotel, to watch a balloon go up—did you ever see a balloon

go up, eh Ned? Then out on the balcony a fellow steps out. You take
me, eh? And of a sudden, this fellow throws down banknotes to the
crowd—handfuls of gold—money, brass, shit, my dear fellow . . ."

His nose hurt from the fall, but its throbbing seemed far away. He
would wait a few moments and then try again to escape. Charles,
sprawled once more in the chair, watched him all the while. Occasionally his eyes would narrow. He hiccuped frequently.

"And they all rush to pick it up—gold, banknotes, *shit*—but this
fellow has a pistol. Fires on 'em, fires into the crowd. Wounds some.
There are moves to arrest him—he must be arrested, eh Ned? We can't
have fellows shooting into a crowd, eh? But *then*, what does he do? He
casts himself to the ground, and *there he dies* . . .

"You don't like my tale, eh? But it's a fine tale, Ned—and got
honestly. Committed to memory, you know—" He hiccuped, "This
brandy, Froggy brandy, plays old Bogy with the guts . . ." He searched
round: "Where was I? That's it, Ned—why's he die, eh? German fellow, brewer, strong beer—Krauss, Kraut . . . I don't recall . . ." Then
as Ned with a sudden movement jumped from his chair: "No, you
don't, old fellow—eh now, come back, come back over here, near
Charles . . ." He was crouched forward, his hand in Ned's, pulling and
twisting it.

"He *had meant it all the while* . . . Ned, listen, then—They found a
gold box in his pocket, and on the lid the good fellow's name and *already engraved*—'Died 14 July 1852'—That's a good tale. You think
me funky, eh, you think me tightly screwed, won't pour me another,
eh? not another drink? Ned, here—come here, closer, Ned . . ."

His breath was hot, the brandy seeming to come from his skin.
Waves of nausea hit Ned. "Can I tell a fellow something? Leave Becky
alone, eh? I say—Black—Dirty, you don't want to meddle with dirt, eh
—that's a good fellow! I don't fancy that part you know—Black, our
plantations, all that sort of thing. Plenty of money without. Plenty . . ."

But then as Ned tried to free his hand, struggling, Charles stood upright suddenly, pulling Ned to him. They were locked in an embrace.
No escape. Ned's hands pinned to his sides. Charles's strength, made
worse by drink. He kissed Ned passionately on the mouth. His wet lips
sliding about their target, then his tongue forcing, boring its way in.

Release for a moment, as the heavy head fell on his shoulder: muttering, mumbling into his collar: "Ned—Ned, you're pretty, love a fellow,
eh Ned? *Love* a fellow . . ."

He could not remember getting away. He thought that he might
have pushed Charles back into the chair. Dishevelled, distraught, he

found himself in a corridor just off the hall. He leaned against the wall, trembling.

He would not wait to go up to the schoolroom. He was not a sight for Kate to see. Nor indeed anyone. His head was spinning: as if he had been twirled and twirled in some nightmare blind man's buff.

> Arm in arm, round and round
> Round and round, round and round . . .
> Me that loves a bonny lass
> Will kiss her on the ground . . .

TWENTY-SEVEN

Linden House,
Downham.

12th December 1853

My dearest Alan,

I am writing this and not waiting for your Christmas letter, because I know that I shall most probably receive nothing from you! How *can* you be like this when you are my very own dear cousin and my last *real* link with my homeland? For even after more than five years, I have not become even a *little* Yorkshire—I think that means that probably I never shall! I must tell you too that I am endeavouring to make a true Scots lass of Tarley—I sing to her many a Scottish ballad (she herself has the sweetest of little voices, quite unlike her mother!) and I read to her also tales of Robert the Bruce and many others. I have told her too *about her cousin!*

All this is leading to what I must ask you—this summer we shall certainly come to Scotland (John will remain in Downham). We shall, I think, be in Edinburgh only the shortest of times, to see Mama and Aunt Charlotte, so that they may admire how Tarley has grown. But here is why I hesitate—I know how many times you have said it, that you do not like children at all, *but* if I should come up to Wester Ross, and bring Tarley—what do you say? *I can promise you* there will be little trouble with her. Indeed, I think, Alan, you *cannot but love her.*

I would have thought to bring her nurse with us but I shall naturally need to leave her with Baby. No doubt it would be quite easy for you to engage some sturdy Highland girl who will do all the hard work of looking after a child (in Edinburgh I shall manage for myself—imagine that!). Then I shall be quite free to be with you—and oh it will be like old times, I want just such a summer as we were *used to have!* I want it too for Tarley so that she can know just how it is in Wester Ross (the Yorkshire moors are *not to be compared*), she will only be four years younger than I when *I* first saw it! And do you remember, dearest Alan, that the first thing you ever showed me was more than *one hundred* gulls' eggs you had taken from the island that afternoon—I thought you *so* wonderful. And then Uncle Alexander came and sat with us and said there were to be strawberries and cream for our five o'clock dinner—but it was only early June, yet *so hot,* not like cold Edinburgh. And then there was Uncle Alexander's snuff in the big leather box he kept in his waistcoat—it made me sneeze so. Yellow Irish Blackguard I *think* they called it. *Not* very fitting! How *happy* it all was, dearest Alan—now he has gone, alas, and only Jessie of the servants is left, but you, *you* will show Tarley everything—she is not too young to learn to love *your* Scotland.

Baby is not doing well. We are very concerned. She is such a pathetic little scrap and so plain to look at even without her unhappy mark. And to think that she was to have been the *son* John wanted! (Although he has been most resigned and Christian about it all. He is altogether an easier person now in *some ways,* and sometimes I am almost persuaded that we are well matched.) I too should have liked a son. I say, dearest Alan, *"should have* liked"—in the past, since I think all that is over now. I had so many misfortunes before this last child and so many before that, that I imagine he has thought we should write "finis." Of course one *does not discuss* these matters and I would with no one else but you (or perhaps Kirsty, *dear* Kirsty, I shall hope to try and see *her* in the summer!), I feel that I may tell you anything, dearest Alan (but *please,* dear cousin, do not abuse again *ever* our special relationship—I am certain you know *what and when* I speak of! I had vowed *never* to mention this—and shall not do so again).

Well, the news is—but perhaps you already know it, *if* you have visited Mama, which you should, and which I doubt! that Ewart comes home from India soon. Perhaps this spring. And that Jamie is *making money* in Canada. His work is still to do with wood, but now it is *with the railroads!* Is not this an odd turn of Fate? (Mama is quite appalled.)

Please write *soon,* even if not for Christmas, to say that we shall *both* be welcome! I am excited already, and so is Tarley. The more so when I have told her of the long and arduous journey, and all the sights to be seen and at the end the best sight of all—*you,* dear cousin!

I end now, because even as I write this, here is come Tarley herself! She says—"Mama, where is my prize, *when* is my prize?" (She means

Surprise—for I have for her the *loveliest* Christmas gift. Also—she wants so much a puppy, but *that* must be for the spring!)

Farewell, dearest cousin, and for Hogmanay the greatest happiness and good cheer!

Your loving Pussy.

TWENTY-EIGHT

Sarah said to Kate, "Have you made nothing for your Uncle Ned? I thought he was to have a cake specially baked for him . . ."

But Kate didn't answer. She was sorting a pile of linen for Sarah, and had her back towards her.

"Didn't you hear me, lass? Ned's Christmas gift. There's not long to go. Had you something else in mind for him, then—eh?"

She saw then that Kate's shoulders heaved. That still thin body—but a girl now, no longer a child—the little spiky shoulder blades poking from the woollen stuff of her dress. Her head was bowed.

Tears, Sarah thought. Why? Perhaps she had outgrown her strength . . . In three months she would be fourteen (or what they had calculated as fourteen . . .), and in the last year or so she had grown in height unusually quickly. Often lately she had seemed easily upset, pale, black smudges beneath her eyes. On occasions in the summer she had seemed withdrawn, moody almost. But she was not someone who cried —unless for a reason. Even as a child she had been stoical almost, unlike say, Ann—who had cried copiously, easily, sometimes at the hint even of a sharp word.

But going up to Kate's room two nights ago, Sarah had heard, from inside, the sounds of stifled sobbing. Instead of knocking or of going in, she had turned away. It will be some girlish upset, she had thought. I'll not interfere. Only now—*this* . . . Even as she asked Kate: "What is it, lass? What's the trouble now—eh?" she began to have her suspicions. The idea came to her suddenly: who it was to do with. Who was most likely in this household to be the cause of trouble.

Kate didn't answer at first. Then turning, but still trying to hide her tear-stained face, she said, "I'm just—perhaps I'm weary. I don't always sleep well, you see."

"That's a fine thing," Sarah said. "A lass of thirteen nearly fourteen, that can't sleep. It should be head-touch-the-pillow—and remember nothing. When I'd to work for Mrs. Mumford, there were times I couldn't even mind *getting* into the bed, let alone settling . . ."

Kate nodded and smiled. But the smile was too brave.

"You've not told me, love. What is it, then? We've the care of you here—and I'm bound to say . . . well, you've not been yourself for a little while—have you now?"

"No." Kate hesitated. "But it's nothing. Nothing that won't mend . . ." Her voice was so grown up, so sparing of Sarah's feelings—it seemed incongruous, coming from the body of someone so young. It twists my heart, Sarah thought.

She spoke more harshly than she meant. "Tell us now. You've to *tell us*." She put her hands on Kate's shoulders. Kate did not move. "Is it—does it concern anyone else?"

Kate hesitated. Then: "Yes."

"Someone here in the house, lass?"

"I . . . well . . ." She bit her lip. "Yes," she said again, but in a very small voice.

"And is it—Walter, then?"

Again the hesitation, then a faint: "Yes."

I might have known it, Sarah thought. I might have known it. W-a-l-t-e-r spells trouble. My own son. And jealous of this one from the start.

"Kate—you've to tell me now. Was it saying—or doing?" (Pray God that he has only *said* evil things . . .)

"He—it's what he's been doing. Since the summer. I—" She burst suddenly into tears—tears which Sarah could not stem. She held Kate in her arms, comforting her. I must not care, she thought, whether she is a Donnelly or not. She was sent to me. She is my *own child* now.

When the crying had stopped sufficiently she said, as forthrightly as possible—for only in that way, she thought, will I ever get the truth: "Did he touch you—where he shouldn't?"

"Yes—I mean, no . . . *Yes*."

"Aye. Right. Well—where? Just show me quickly, where? Point . . ."

Kate was quite still for a moment, then very shyly she pointed at her breasts.

"And was he rough? Did you tell him to give over?"

"Yes—"

"But he wouldn't. Is that it?"

"No—I mean, yes, he wouldn't . . ."

"And where did he do—this?"

Kate looked puzzled. She looked too as if she were about to cry again. "I—I told you *where* . . ."

"I meant what place, lass? Where in the house—"

"Upstairs," she said. "In my room. In the summer. But last night again—and once the week before, and—" she broke off. Now she was crying in earnest again. She said to Sarah, weeping as if her heart would break, "I'm so ashamed. I'm so *ashamed . . .*"

And I am so angry, Sarah thought. She told Sam at once. Almost as soon as he came home that evening. "Walter must go," she said. "As soon as we're done with Christmas, he must go."

As she might have known, Sam was in complete agreement. He would have had him out that very night. She said to him, "And I can't help thinking—we've been fortunate. What it might have led to . . . With the little one afraid to say, and then matters getting worse and worse—and then, who knows?" She shuddered as she said it: "We might have had the worst . . ."

Sam had not wanted, however, to talk about it. He wanted action taken, and the matter closed. "Let not these things . . ."

"I'll have Ned say summat to him—at work, after work mebbe. Tell him we've other plans for him. That his sins, they've not gone unnoticed—"

"No one tells Ned," she interrupted angrily. "Ned *must not be told.*" She thought Sam must be crazed. "He'd kill his brother . . . If you've never noticed how he dotes on that lass. If he thought any brother of his had so much as laid a finger . . . It'd be Cain and Abel all over again."

Sam had conceded, in the end. He had given the task instead to John. Then he and Sarah had seen Walter together later. A sullen Walter—to whom they never mentioned the *real* cause of the interview.

He didn't like ropes anyway, he told them. He'd wanted out for a long while now. "I'd like to farm . . ." He looked at his mother slyly: "Find me a place, then. Somewhere they eat well, and the work's all right, and there's prospects." He paused: "I'd a great-grandfather farmed this way, Wensleydale—didn't I?"

"He's a saucy tongue on him," Sam said later. "I'd have done well to leather him—with nowt said . . ."

Walter was lucky. Through one of his patients, John found an opening for him on a farm in East Burton. There were four sons in the family, but one was about to leave. And there was more than enough work . . . Sarah could not wait for him to go. (*My own son*, she thought again.)

Seeing Kate alone, she said: "You'll not tell Ned—about that matter?

About Walter—" (As if she would, Sarah thought, when she could hardly speak of it to me . . . But she wanted to be certain.)

"Promise me, then, little lass—that he'll never hear word of it. *Ever.*"

Sarah told Ned later that week: "Kate misses you—she doesn't see enough of you." Hoping that talking like that she might persuade him: for he had used always to come to Hillside on Sundays, but now sometimes two or even three weeks might pass without his doing so.

Of course I have John come to see me, often, she thought. And I have Eliza at home with me. Eliza is my right hand. Right hand too, to a great many people. She and Jane Helliwell—who had been Ann's sister-in-law (dear, dead Ann), they were both full of good works. Jane: a pleasant, gentle girl . . .

Four years though, she thought, looking at Ned—and not yet over Nanny's death . . . It would not do. His grief was not natural. It worries me . . . Although if I'm to worry, she told herself now, I'd be best really to fret about John's new bairn. *There's* a sadness.

John and Catriona's daughter, and her namesake. Baby Sarah had been born with a large port-wine stain, suffusing the lower part of her neck on one side. John had tried to console them all, telling Sarah that often these marks faded, that they did not grow with the person . . .

Sarah had thought at first that it must be Catriona's family. "We never had markings before," she told John. "It'll come from her . . ." Sitting now opposite Ned, taking up her sewing, Sarah felt a sudden overwhelming pity for the poor little scrap. *My namesake.* She said something to Ned—and felt that he understood.

"It'll be difficult for her," he said. "If she's to shine beside Tarley. Poor small bairn . . ."

Adjusting her spectacles, she threaded her needle carefully, and then as it flew in and out of the stitches, she looked up for a moment. She saw that Ned sat opposite still, but quite motionless. He looked so pale, so lonely, so completely without hope, that she heard herself say suddenly:

"Son, don't take it amiss—but I've thought—you know, you should marry again. Think on it at least. It's no life for a man, alone out there, not even a beastie to keep you company." She went on talking, but without looking at him, her head bent over her sewing. "I know it's difficult. There's not maybe the chances to meet—but there's ones about, you know. What of Frank's sister, that's almost family now? What of her? She's a bonny girl, is Jane. And you could do worse . . . You ought to think, son—maybe getting wed again . . ."

"I've done with all that," he said. His voice was angry. "Let me be. Let me be, won't you."

TWENTY-NINE

Christmas-time 1853. And the best thing, Catriona thought, was to be the new outfit for Tarley. It was to be all in Dunbar tartan—she had sent especially to Scotland: and Moppet was to have exactly, but *exactly* the same, down to the last detail. Mrs. Oldfield, needlewoman, of Downham would make all but the underlinen and the embroidery. This Catriona would do herself. Ned's father-in-law, Haygarth, would make leather boots for both of them, to complete the outfit. Moppet, who had died already three times this year, would be enchanted (and would now perhaps be allowed to live?).

Carrying out the plan was all part of Catriona's happiness that December: a happiness which surprised her, weakened still as she was after the baby in early November. A happiness *in spite of* the baby, and its birthmark. Rather, she would look some days at Tarley, wondering only how she could have been allowed such perfection (and it is not just I who think it, she reminded herself triumphantly). She did not deserve her. For carrying Tarley, she had wished her away.

Often she would look at her, and marvel. *I* never looked so well (even Mama had said just that. "You were a pretty enough child—but *this*, Catriona!"). Already there were two miniatures of her, and a fine drawing she had done herself. And then too, the daguerreotype taken last year when a photographer had visited Downham. Tarley in velvet and lace and standing on a chair, her hand round Catriona's neck (her own gesture too—not the photographer's).

December days, and Catriona sat and sewed. She was not yet very strong and had to rest a great deal. The fine lawn fabric, wrapped in tissue paper, rested on her lap. Her mother-in-law said, not unkindly but off-handedly, as if stating a fact: "*Another* outfit for Tarley? You must think you are dressing a doll—" But, Catriona thought, that is what I *am* doing. A walking, talking doll. Childhood had never been like this, was but the rehearsal for this. When I played at caring for my dolls, when I sewed for them, it was only so that I might be the more skilful now . . .

Baby Sarah was not doing well. Catriona had not been able to continue feeding her. She wondered how much was to do with the feeble half-hearted sucking—after Tarley's vigour—and how much to do with the vivid stain which it seemed the wrappings were for ever unwinding to reveal. "Port wine" they called the mark. She could not bear the sight of it. And yet John did not seem to mind so much. "Poor little scrap," he would say, about this ailing, sickly, whining baby, that was to have been his son.

So little Sarah was now to have a feeding bottle—the latest variety, and the nursemaid was to fill it with sweetened cow's milk and barley water. Catriona had made enquiries about a wet nurse—or rather John had—but they had not been successful. She had felt anyway that two lusty youths as apprentices (and one of them, Leathley, blushingly, embarrassingly besotted with her so that meal times were a torment) were enough to have around the house, large as it was. She did not want to add to the company some strange woman.

So a bottle it was. But still little Sarah did not do well. Tarley said to the nurse when she saw her being washed: "Why does God not make Baby pretty?" Then: "Pretty like Katie?" she said a moment later. For she worshipped Kate, seeing her as a mixture of mother and big sister, and sending shafts of jealousy through Catriona, who would then despise herself for thinking: ah, Kate, cuckoo in the nest (for was not that all she was, at bottom?). Kate was Tarley's friend and confidante. Often she would have something to tell *only* Kate. "My Katie." And it was Kate who had at once realised, without being told, that baby Sarah would require extra love. And had given it. Now it was she most certainly who had awoken, easily enough, just those same instincts in Tarley. I am ashamed, Catriona thought.

The weather just before Christmas was cold, cold. Snow was more than likely. Catriona, sewing love into the stitches, thought that in a white world Tarley would look more enchanting than ever. The needle flew in and out. John asked, "How does it go?" and smiled indulgently. "By the by," he said, "Mrs. Ingham has asked that we bring Tarley up to the schoolroom. The young ones wish to see her again."

"Kate has talked, of course?"

"Yes."

"How is her health—Mrs. Ingham's health, that is?"

He paused. He said, in the stiff way she so deplored (in the deep voice she had once so loved), "I think it is hardly in order for me to say."

"Oh, for heaven's sake! I did not ask for medical details. I asked only *generally*—since you are so often there. I am quite out of patience with you."

He was silent. He had with him a copy of *The Lancet*, and returned to reading it. She could not imagine a more boring occupation. Often he would make notes from it into his leather-bound book, and had at least three times written a letter to it which the magazine had not published. When a few moments later he left the room and the pages lay open, she went over and glanced idly. The article, by a Dr. Tyler Smith, was entitled "Transmission of Secondary Syphilis." And whatever was that? She imagined it something to do with breathing (and, she thought, a tongue twister into the bargain . . .).

Back at her sewing, she remembered happily that her brother Ewart might soon be back from India. Although if the Czar of Russia, "the Autocrat" as the newspapers called him, did not behave a little better, then there might be a war. Regiments would be drafted . .

Four days to Christmas. The great prickly branches of holly came in a cart and Tarley and her nurse went to see. It was so cold as to make one draw one's breath sharply. The sky darkening as for snow. Catriona watched Tarley go, standing at the window. Saw her come back too, the apple cheeks bright with cold. She looked at her, and love melted the frost and icicles on the little velvet coat. She forgot in a moment her worry, her nagging conscience, that little Sarah had refused to eat, had taken nothing that day—that something *must* be done. Here is come Tarley . . .

She felt weak with love. And it was only beginning. She glimpsed suddenly, like some treasure cave opening up: Tarley at her books, on horseback and riding to the meet, playing with the puppy she so much wanted. Tarley grown tall, Tarley Kate's age, Tarley a woman and her *friend* . . . The richness overwhelmed her, the years of joy stretching ahead.

"Mama, please next year I'll *ride* in the prickly cart, did you see Jack Frost was on Mr. Denman's whiskers, he's been writing on *all* our windows but most on mine, isn't that so, nurse, isn't it, Mama?"

"Tarley, draw breath! Darling, draw breath—"

But just to take in breath outside—painful, it was too cold. The little nursemaid said, "Too cold for us like," and looking at the darkening snow-filled sky, "We're in for a hap-up, if summat don't strangely alter—"

That meant a white Christmas then. Like our childhood, Catriona thought. The Christmases of childhood were always white, in the days of the stage-coaches, before railroads and time bills and companies and frauds . . . Only once had Tarley asked, remarking that Matthew and Thomas Helliwell, although they had no Mama, had two Grampies. It had been enough then to say that her, Catriona's, father had gone to God. One day perhaps it might be necessary to say more . . .

Christmas was perfection that year. She would have thought it the happiest Christmas ever if it had not been for the worry over baby Sarah. On the day itself of course, too much was eaten. Such a groaning of the tables: goose and stuffings, hams, puddings, sweetmeats, jellies, pastries, exotic fruits. And then all the lovingly made confections from grateful patients of John's: the wines, the cordials, the blue cheeses, the plum cakes.

Tarley certainly ate too much—more even than on her birthday a week earlier. And on the morning after Christmas woke very early and was sick. Very, very sick. She said to Catriona, nodding her head wisely, "I ate too much, Mama. I do, I did. Baby Sarah isn't so foolish—"

But Baby had hardly been feeding at all, and what she took would not stay down. It had become necessary to think again of looking for a wet nurse, John said. "If there is not to be a risk of it ending badly." But first they must let the cold spell pass. Nothing could be done or arranged in this weather. Already the thermometer had dropped lower than within living memory.

By midday, Tarley was not only vomiting but had also diarrhoea. Her head ached. Soon, the whole of her ached. She told Catriona, "One long twiddly pain, my legs—my *tummy*." She tossed and turned. Outside the snow came down steadily, blanketing the windows, weighing down the trees.

The road through to Leyburn was blocked. Nurse complained to Catriona, "Miss Sarah, she *won't* take her feed, ma'am." Catriona tried then, holding the thick-glassed bottle awkwardly, without hope that any skill of hers could equal the nurse's. Certainly she had not the nurse's patience. Some food was taken with disgust, and promptly returned.

Then the little nursemaid rushed in, distracted, saying that Tarley had now vomited again twice, and that she was crying.

"It's t'pain, ma'am, inside and her *side*, she says."

Of course there must be a fever. As soon as Catriona hurried back to the room, before she touched her even, she could see from the flushed moist face that the child was fevered. John, out on visits since before midday, had not reappeared. One of the apprentices was still at home with his family for the holiday. The other, Leathley, was in the surgery making up pills. She brought him upstairs. He surprised her by the change in him: his air of quiet authority, as if some mantle had fallen on him and he was suddenly by necessity made into the doctor he was learning to be. Embarrassment, blushing calf-love, all for the moment gone.

But even with his new-found authority he could tell her only that indeed Tarley had a high fever—one hundred and three or more. He sounded her chest. "Oh, Mama, Mama . . ." She seemed to be trying to sleep, occasionally giving a half-hearted cough. It hurt her side, she said. Then when Leathley had done examining her, there was another paroxysm of vomiting. He owned himself puzzled. There was no scarlatina about . . . But if it *was* that, then time would show. And Mr. Rawson would soon be here . . .

Her breathing was easy, rapid, as if in a hurry. A hurry to be better, Catriona thought. Her face flushed to a high colour.

And still the snow fell. Catriona could not bear this white world she had thought so wonderful only a day or two ago. When at last John returned—he had been at the Abbey, he said (and she could see the thick flakes on his clothes as he shook snow from his cloak). "I had imagined it might be necessary to *stay* there. I saw myself unable to get through Downham. You cannot imagine the conditions. If 1854 is to begin in this manner . . ."

She could not wait for him to shed his cloak. She pulled at him, "Tarley has such a fever. At once, come and see at once, dear. Leathley has been and he says—"

He said angrily, formally, "You *must* not consult Leathley. He is endeavouring, they are both endeavouring to learn—"

She said impatiently, "But this is *serious*."

"I don't doubt. So are many cases that I see. Panic is no help . . ."

"*At once*," she pleaded, pulling at him again.

But he seemed driven to obstinacy by her very urgency (this same man who had once hung on her every word). Yet in the end he paid attention to her anxiety, her fretting, panicky as it was. As they went upstairs to the nurseries, "And the little one," he asked, "does she eat?"

Catriona said impatiently, "Och, not too well. But nurse will take care of that—"

When he saw Tarley, he too was concerned, as she had known he would be. "Papa, Papa . . ." but she scarcely opened her eyes, clutching at him with hot hands—reddened, even the little fingernails blood-filled. "Tummy, tummy," she cried, tossing her head. And then was as violently sick again.

"I would get Wilson if I could. If the Leyburn road were even half-way passable."

"But *you* should know what is wrong!" she cried (and was to cry again and again the next day, and the next). "You *must*—you are a *doctor!*"

He said calmly, but she could see, annoyed and agitated inside, "Indeed I am a doctor. But my own child—I want to hear what Wilson has to say."

"But what is it, then, what is *wrong* with her?"

He spoke bluntly. "It is too early."

"But what it could be, what it *might* be—"

"Do you think there is really *anything* I have not thought of?—Scarlatina is possible, meningitis, pneumonia . . . or some simple fever and stomach upset, acute now but subsiding soon. All these are possible. The last, the more probable." He said, more gently, "Do you wonder now why I don't want Leathley given this responsibility and frightened before his time? Why I should like a second opinion . . ."

She did not bother again with the baby who, she heard, both took and kept a feed at eight o'clock. She herself could not bear to so much as leave Tarley's room. She ate in there—what little she could eat. "It does not help," John told her. "Nurse is there, within earshot, beside her in a second."

"I shall sleep there," she said, the next day, when after a restless night listening for cries she had come in about six to find Tarley no better.

John, looking anxiously out at the blinding white landscape said (but only to give her confidence, she thought): "The fever—it'll burn itself out . . ."

Tarley's presents, barely played with, stood about the room, brought in from the day nursery. The Dunbar tartan, dress, cloak, the bonnet with its fur trimmings, the new boots, the lovingly embroidered underlinen. Moppet, already dressed up to match, sprawled on a little wicker chair. Catriona brought her over yet again, but Tarley, hot-handed, pushed her away. The dark curls were lank, thin, the features drawn, pinched almost.

Catriona sat by the bed. She talked to her, told her stories, recited verses. Whom did she reassure?

"Mama is here, Tarley. Tarley—*you will be all right.*

> "And I'll have none o' your nesty beef
> nor I'll have none o' your barley
> but I'll have some o' your *very* best flour
> to make a white cake for my Tarley . . .

"And when you are better, we shall dance 'O Who'll Be Queen but Tarley?'" Again and again she would bring Moppet over, as if Tarley's refusal, or acceptance, were some kind of omen. She had begun to think in omens, in charms, in warding off the evil eye. Terrible fears lay always waiting to rush to the surface. If, the great *if*, Tarley were *not* to get better?

She could scarcely drag herself away to go through to the other room where baby Sarah, again refusing her food, lay pinched and white. Catching a glimpse of the birthmark, she turned away, shamed by dislike. The nursemaid told her: "Me mam, she reared twelve and some on t'bottle—she said make t'mix thicker and it'll be longer down."

"Yes, make it thicker," Catriona said. "Do that." She had not dressed her hair, had put on clothes only hurriedly.

"This is a foolish extreme," John said. But he was unable to hide his worry. Today, Sunday, they should all have gathered together at the family home as usual. John trudged through still-deepening snow to excuse himself. The few visits he could make and which reached him took all his available time. Ned in Little Grinling would be completely cut off.

"Mama, Mama," shrieked Tarley, then gave a sudden stifled cry. But as soon as Catriona came, she did not know her. She cried then for "Papa." Delirium. All throughout that day her temperature rose and rose. She had to be sponged constantly. John said then: "This is pneumonia."

"But what happens? What will happen to her—will she—"

Some words, not to say them was to ward off the worst.

"We shall have to wait. One waits," he said, tight-lipped.

John had sent for his mother. She came that evening. Her sturdy robust manner should have been a help, but Catriona could think only that she wanted to be left with her panic—as if somehow by excess of fear and concern she could hurry on the illness, complete the journey to the crisis.

"And my namesake?" Sarah asked, almost at once, within moments of her arrival.

Catriona explained. Sarah sat then with the baby, attempting herself to feed it. She was angry, critical of Catriona.

"As soon as this trouble is over, as soon as Tarley is on the mend and the weather lets up—then we must have a wet nurse . . ." But when Catriona told her about the nursemaid's mother and the twelve children—some on the bottle—she said heartily: "Indeed so—and she's buried as many. Catriona, you're very innocent, and—" but she didn't finish the sentence. Instead she looked at her: "I think you're a caring mother."

Of course I am a caring mother, Cationa thought. But about Tarley, what could she be but frantic? A whole day of laboured breathing, of useless and probably painful linseed poultices. Some beef tea taken, but not wanted. And the pneumonia crisis no nearer.

Tarley clung, tossing, to whoever was at the bedside. She didn't recognise her grandmother. That night was terrible. Sarah, going home, said she would return in the morning. Brandy administered was rejected. There was a constant changing of flannel nightgowns. Catriona had lost count of time. She talked to a Tarley grown deaf, although she muttered and called incessantly.

She talked to her of treats to come. "Soon better," she kept saying, "and then in this fine winter weather you may *skate*. And wear your new muff and the tartan cloak and dress—it is Dunbar you see, and Moppet she too is Dunbar . . ."

Tarley, tossing, foetid breath, thickened lips sore and bright red as if stained with carmine, eyes dark-rimmed and fevered and seeming to see nothing.

"Mama, Mama, Papa—puppy," she murmured suddenly. "Puppy . . ."

"But yes, dear one, yes." She leaned over, the too anxious mother, longing only for the time when she would be able to keep her rash promise. "A little dog, of course, just as soon as you are well. What sort of a dog, Tarley? Tell Mama, what colour puppy? Should you like it black and white, with one ear up and one down? Just such a one as we saw on the journey to . . ." her voice meandered on, as if to stop talking would be to allow Tarley to slip beyond reach.

But Tarley as though not hearing, went on: "Puppy, puppy," and then, "Papa, Papa—"

"Mama is here, Mama is with you, Tarley."

"Papa, puppy . . ." again.

Sarah was back in the room now. There was still no chance to get through to Leyburn—no let-up in the snow, banked several feet outside. "I shall stay the night," Sarah said. She was very grave. At intervals she would disappear to help with the baby. "There's concern there also," she said, her eyes boring through Catriona's as if reading them.

> "Tarley Warley had a cow
> Black and white about the brow,
> Open the gate and let her through,
> Tarley Warley's little cow . . ."

Now here was Kate, the other side of the bed. Kate who was already at thirteen almost a little mother.

Kate, help me, Catriona wanted to cry. Kate had been brought over but must now be taken home—it was surely too distressing? John said that she might go and sit with Baby. But she came back in to Tarley, and then disarmed them all by bursting into tears.

Terror overtook Catriona. As the day wore on into the dark dull hours of the afternoon—the grey sky, still surely snow-filled, the early lighting of the lamps, the gloom of the sick-room—she felt a terror grip her, that she knew what others did not, what John for all his learning and his more justifiable fears did not: that all was lost.

Steam filled the room, uselessly. The breathing was impossible now, rasping.

"Tarley," she said again and again, "*Tarley*, get better for Mama, for Papa—" Then, in despair, "Get better for *Baby*. Baby needs Tarley—" She could not bear what she saw.

She shrieked, "*Live*, Tarley, *live!*" Sarah, restraining her. But she was too strong—she *would* breathe life into Tarley. Now she had her in her arms, her mouth on Tarley's mouth . . .

John took hold of her. She was gripped, pulled back. Still she struggled. Then she began to shriek and cry, uselessly, unrestrainedly, in a shaming, hopeless fashion, as if no one else was there.

He said, his voice deep, dull, breaking, "She's gone, quite gone—"

Laudanum, sleeping draughts, chloral. The fevered dream where, by her breathing, by her willing, she brought back the dead to life—where, half awake, she dreamed that she tried to get from her bed to rush to the bedside of the dead child.

Of what use to learn that that night, as Tarley lay lifeless and growing cold, it had been the coldest night of the century? For Catriona, it was the coldest of her life—such cold, she thought, as enters the bones and never really leaves them.

And care must be shown to the baby, concern. Little Sarah still lived, but perilously. Why, Catriona thought—urgent in her blasphemous wicked thoughts (I *will* be so wicked)—why could *that* one not have slipped away?

The letter came from Alan four days later. A cheery Hogmanay one, telling of London in the snow, with even the omnibuses stopped.

". . . quite an uncommon thing, Mr. Dickens would perhaps recognise it. But London is quite unprepared, unlike us northerners! They (softly!) do not know how to deal with it. Pussy—it is a cab and *pair* now, hansoms become tandems, if you can imagine such a novelty. (Perhaps St. Petersburg is like this—except that I believe them to be well equipped for such contingencies.) Snow is four feet high in the streets—and yet it would have needed only the fire engines to hose a little. No clearing has been done—and one must of course watch for avalanches from people's roofs if one does not mind oneself—

"Well, dear Pussy-coz, until the summer! Tell Tarley please that although I detest children, she is not one (a riddle—what is she, then?) and will be welcomed with my most *especial* manner. And if she has not already that puppy, why then we shall see what we can do!

"Now you cannot say I never write—How does Baby do? I have seen your mama twice lately. *What* patience is needed there! If you had seen me, and heard me, you would indeed have been amazed by,

"Your devoted cousin and liege lord
Alan"

THIRTY

Georgiana Ingham was sitting in the warm room, a fire roaring, freshly stacked. John welcomed it after the sharp air outside. Although it was April now, there had been a heavy white mist earlier in the day. Its chill lingered on. As he had come past the Kissing Gate he had been unable not to think of the snowdrops still in the churchyard, that Tarley would have loved.

From the start, this visit to the Abbey—to Georgiana—did not seem to go right. From the moment he walked in he was ill at ease. But at first she did not speak about either herself or him. Only about Charles.

"I suppose—pray take a seat, do not stand there so awkwardly—I suppose that I cannot ask you to speak to my husband, on a certain matter? You will no doubt say something troublesome about a medical code, or medical manners, or whatever the nonsense is—"

"I have said nothing." But it would have been better if he had kept quiet. She did not like to be interrupted.

"*Or whatever the nonsense is* . . . I wish you to speak to him about drink. I consider that he drinks to excess."

He was interrupting again, he could not stop it. "Has he been rough, cruel to Richard?"

"No, it is not that. Nor is it anything he might do or say to me when he has been too free with the brandy—*you* know that I am not molested. Indeed—and this you *may* not realise since it is perhaps so horrible—what he *does* wish for is, I am certain, perverted. He wants only the unnatural. I need not say more. But nor can I stand by and see him so frequently the worse for brandy. It is not seemly, it is not becoming. It is an embarrassment for me. Kindly speak to him. Today, if possible."

He felt weak at once with cowardice. This was something he could not even imagine doing. But she did not seem to require assent immediately. She was busying herself for the moment with one of her coral bracelets, caught up with some of her ribbons . . .

All the way here, he had been thinking: I would like an end to this affair, to have done with it painlessly—for it to be *as if it had never happened*. How could he have got himself into such a fix? Almost a whole year now. Novelty had long ago ceased. Worse still, it had become habit.

Discovery: the least of his worries. Only once had there been any scare—when he had thought the door locked and it had not been. But they were dressed at the time, and talking after . . . He had been horrified later to realise how much he had almost hoped for discovery— just so that the whole business might be over. To think, he remembered now, that he had once paid Ellie—and been her friend. *This* was not friendship—this was mistress (how little he could escape puns . . .) and servant. Nor had she after all done anything for him, for his career and prospects. And what had she meant to do? A word in the right ear—but what ear, and what word?

He was not certain anyway what, if any, his ambitions were nowadays. He did not want to leave Downham. The days of real possibilities, when he could have altered his future entirely, had been Edinburgh. Had he not waited once outside his professor's house in George Square, hoping that John Goodsir might come out (a man so absorbed in his thoughts that he scarcely lifted his head as he walked) and once addressed, speak to him directly? What comments, what observations had he not rehearsed? ("Sir, if as you say your study of Nautilus has led you to adopt a logarithmic spiral as a teleological chart in nature's designs, then how do you see this law at work in the increase of organic bodies?" And this man with the huge hands, the deep thoughtful eyes, would say . . . But there his imagination deserted him always . . .)

I was obsessed, was I not, he thought now, with Catriona? Walking, albeit hopelessly, too much in the environs of Blacket Place. But had there not been chances *since* to follow ideas through? Those letters to *The Lancet*, those case histories from whose bare facts I had thought once to advance new theories—where have they gone?

I want the energy, he thought. Epidemics, bad weather, my everyday care of the people of Downham, that is sufficient to drain me. And it was not as if his home had been a haven of peace. If not quite a battlefield, it had at least lately been a house of sorrow.

Tarley's life, snuffed out. Wantonly, it seemed to him. Wantonly. As the small flower-wreathed coffin had been carried through the Kissing Gate, he had tried to bow to God's Will. But deep inside him it had been impossible, unimaginable. As had been the death itself. But he had voiced out loud his resignation, pressed it on Catriona—since if he could not manage, he the head of the house, then how could it be hoped that she—?

She was not managing. Heavy-eyed each morning from the night's sleeping draught, she was often not fit to speak to before he went on his rounds. Looking in later he would find her "resting," and since he ate his meals at odd times, often several days would pass without their exchanging more than a few quickly spoken words. About little Sarah perhaps: now doing well, and almost unrecognisable, so bonny had she become. Although Catriona did not think so: "She has a look of your mother already. It was as well we named her . . ."

Little Sarah's improvement dated from within a few weeks of Tarley's death. Only two days after, their worries had been raised to a fearful pitch when, bottle in hand, the nurse had cried hysterically, "She's taken nowt—this bairn'll go. There's a mark on her. *She'll go . . .*" Then Mother had taken the matter into her own hands. A wet nurse was found: one who did not even have to leave her own baby, since (sadly) she had lost it only two days earlier. The milk, still coming in regularly, was at the ready. She had lost children before but had five still living. Pink-cheeked and plump, she had spoken resignedly of her lot: "It's t'way o'things . . ." Now with the help of an unmarried sister she was prepared to leave her brood and live at Linden House for as long as she was needed. Annie Mather. Our saviour, he thought. For within an hour of her arrival, their worries had been lifted: Sarah, milky-mouthed, could be seen sleeping, calmly, peacefully—contentedly . . .

"It is true, of course," said Georgiana now, "that Mr. Ingham is not so rough with his son as once. But then he has not the same occasion—now that Richard is so much at school."

"And you say that he is happy there?"

"Not *un*happy. Which surprises me. Although I understand they have reformed the place utterly. They even have cubicles, one to a boy. And he has been lucky too in his—what do they call it? *fagging*. That he must do it for someone pleasant—"

"It is not the Eton of his father's day?"

"If it had been I would have had him educated at home. No boy should have to suffer as Mr. Ingham did. Imagine—*fifty* boys sleeping where now there are only fifteen. Some without beds at all. Filth, rats, unmentionables—night-soil everywhere. Nowhere to wash. And then the door locked every night until morning—to allow torture, roasting, scorching, branding (and perhaps *that* is where he learned his tricks . . .), drink, behaviour of a—disgusting nature. Even once, I believe, *murder*. That was Long Chamber at Eton." She added: "It is only in *drink*, I may tell you, that I have heard any of this. The sooner he curbs this weakness for the bottle . . . For that is what it is, a weakness. *And I will not have it.*"

John said, cursing himself for his hesitancy, "I do not think, really, that this is a matter about which I could say anything. I—" Trembling at the thought, he tried to imagine himself with Charles, putting "a friendly word in your ear, if I may . . ." No, it was not possible.

"But it is a small matter—five minutes of your time. You are very short of time?"

"No—but I would rather not. I *cannot*, I am afraid."

"Cannot—or *will not?*"

He would have to give in. He could at least promise. He might even (dare he?) *pretend* that he had spoken . . . "If it is possible, then, if I see the opportunity, I will consider raising the matter—"

"Pray do not *put yourself out*. I notice that for the simplest request, difficulties are brought up. We will have no more of that subject. I leave it now with you. Although it is—which I forbore to point out to you—part of your duty as his doctor. But *you* would not see that . . ."

Foolishly, meaning nothing, he took out his watch. Glanced at it quickly, put it back.

"You are in haste? You would rather be somewhere else?"

"No, of course—"

"I am sorry certainly," she said acidly, "I am sorry if I keep you?"

"But no. That is—" He sat on the edge of his chair.

Then: "Are you not going to ask me about my *health?*" she said. "You are a—surgeon still, are you not?"

"Indeed—" He spoke awkwardly. "How have you been? And is there anything that I . . ." His voice trailed away. What was he saying? What was this but an invitation to an invitation?

"How foolish you are," she exclaimed, biting her lip, "how foolish! Are you—no longer interested? Come here, come closer. Is there nothing you would like to do, nothing you have—done before?"

He sat there woodenly. He could not think what had come over him. "What—" he began foolishly.

"Don't!" she said sharply, "you **don't** address me in that manner. 'What' indeed! Where is your respect?" But when a moment later he fumbled again for words, she laughed, flirtatiously.

"Come then," she said gaily. "To it. To it—"

He could not, he absolutely could not move. It was as if his body, rebelling, spoke for his spirit.

"To it! I said. *John*—what is the matter? Do *I* have to—is it for me to—John, please," her voice was more irritable now, only half-laughing. "It is for me to say No!" She put out both hands. "Quick. Now. I assure you no one can, no one *will* enter—"

Oh, these word-plays. Today, hardly a move, hardly a thought that did not carry one. But she had not perceived this last . . .

"Enter, John—" she spoke only a little playfully now.

"I cannot."

"What do you mean, cannot? Surely you are not telling me you are incapable—"

"I can't—that is, what you require, what we have been used to doing . . ."

"*Cannot*, John?"

But it had come over him in a great wave. The room filled with their joint presences. His wife and daughter. Tarley, before whom he would never (and in heaven, was not all known to those who sat with Christ?). Catriona, the mourning mother. If she were to discover . . .

"I will not. It is not 'I cannot,' but 'I will not'—"

"Ah!" she exclaimed angrily. "Now we have it. *Will not*. You must be very sure of yourself that you can say yea or nay to *me*—" Tears of rage had sprung to her eyes. "You humiliate me, Rawson. You humiliate me!"

But it was he who was the one humiliated. He said with stiff politeness, "Nothing was—nothing could have been further from my mind. It is just . . . Mrs. Ingham"—he said her name with formality—"madam, I am very sensible of honours, of kindnesses—in the past. But for the future, I have my post, I have my family to consider. I—"

"Country doctor. Nobody," she jeered. "No doubt you saw yourself rising under my patronage. Up in the world. Up. Some dizzy heights."

"Never."

She recognised the truth perhaps. And that she had gone too far. He, certainly, had gone too far . . .

"Indeed," she said, "indeed. It has gone on *quite long enough*. I refer of course to this ridiculous, undignified encounter. Please go, as soon as possible. Do not trouble to return. It will not be necessary, I assure you. You will arrange for me to have further supplies of laudanum, antimony wine, sarsaparilla . . ." She ran off the names.

"And now—go."

THIRTY-ONE

Little Sarah did not need her. About this at least, Catriona thought, she could be happy—if she had had it in her to be happy about anything. Mrs. Mather was so good, so strong. Catriona did not resent her presence in the house, even found a curious comfort in just sitting with her. "You don't mind me, I trust?" she would ask, and Mrs. Mather, one generous breast already exposed would say: "Never, ma'am. Nay, Baby likes it, likes to see her mam—don't ye now, Babbit?"

But Baby would be otherwise occupied than in looking at her mother, and Catriona would sit—just the watching being a kind of wound: inflicting the pain on herself, imagining somehow that if she only sat this out, this agony of seeing the child she didn't want, then in the end something would change.

"We give you enough to eat, Mrs. Mather, you are sure there is sufficient?"

"Aye, ma'am, thank you, ma'am." As Sarah guzzled: "I told my bairns, this is a good meat house. Those lads, ma'am, that are larnin' to be doctors—they'll eat well, I reckon."

"They're young," Catriona said. "They work hard."

"Happen then, you too, ma'am, you—I says it respectful like"—she spoke so naturally it was not possible to take offence—"happen you'll mebbe get one yoursen. One that's hearty—" She blushed. "Get a lad, I mean," she said, changing breasts.

Never, Catriona thought, never. Wanting to say: I could not endure the carrying, and then the bearing . . . But above all, *I could not endure the losing.* She thought, I shall continue to sleep alone. And with one exception, that resolution had been possible, had not been put to the test.

She slept alone because it was necessary, she told herself—*assured* herself. Exhausted as she was always by nightfall, yet nervously strung up so that she needed always a sleeping draught, by the time John finished work and came to bed she would be at last asleep and not to be disturbed. Then in the middle of the night she would wake, and she would need to light a candle and perhaps read for a while or, as she did often, prowl the corridors of the silent house.

Once only, John had come in. She had been asleep then. He had been strange, beside himself almost. She would have thought, had she not known better, that he was freshly in love with her again—so strongly did he call on her name, and cling to her, touching all of her: ". . . that you are still here, that you are still with me, my darling love . . ."

But it had all been in the cause of *that*—yet again. The words of love, those words of love had been only to guard against, forestall any objections she might have. And I was deceived! For nearly two weeks after, until the catamenia and the welcome flow of blood, she had lived in *dread*. How could she face again the nausea, the swelling, the vertigo? And for what? A child lost, or kept long enough to love deeply—and *then* lost. Or, one which she could scarcely love at all . . .

But by the others, little Sarah was loved. John seemed to do so, very much. Her grandmother loved her stoutly, loudly. So did her Aunt Eliza and Uncle Ned—and Kate. And of course Annie Mather, letting down for her in abundance the milk nature had intended for her own.

I could never do that, Catriona thought. Never. She tried to imagine such generosity. And failed. She is a *good* woman, she thought, tears springing.

One day in March, the crocuses just out among the gravestones, she had met Ned walking in the churchyard. She had been seeing little of him: she had not felt well enough to attend the family meal on Sundays. (And he, she thought often, was only a ghost of his former self . . .)

He was over now by Nanny's grave. He crossed at once to Tarley's stone. Catriona had with her a flowering plant and some branches of pussy willow—she had gathered them from a hedgerow that morning. Rounded, furry.

He said, "She'll like those."

"They are the first," she had said, "Tarley liked always the first of anything—Easter eggs, the prickly brought in at Christmas—she made a little ceremony of anything in so far as she was able. As much as she understood—she had only four years after all . . ."

"Yes."

If it had been anyone else, she would have expected them to say something more—or better still, to go and leave her in peace. But with Ned, the silence that followed, it did not seem to matter.

"Tarley's at rest," she had said to him suddenly, looking around her. "I know she's at rest, and yet—"

He did not try to fill in the words for her as another might have done, but merely remained standing there, silent, the headstone between them. "In loving memory of Charlotte . . . 'The Lord hath given and the Lord hath taken away . . .'"

They stood thus for a long while. A chill breeze that had plagued her on the walk here was replaced now by a weak but steady sun. Warmth crept up over the stones. Her pain was not any the less, but very gradually a strange sort of peace descended on her. Covering her like some warm cloak.

"I'll walk with you," she said, a little later. "If you return to Downham. I came on foot—though I should not."

He nodded assent, smiled. "I've to be back at the works." They walked together towards the Kissing Gate. Nettles were springing up on the bare ground before. There were clumps of snowdrops still, just beside the Gate.

He opened it for her. "I'm here too often, maybe, Catriona," he said. "She's—been gone five years, all but. It is just that—"

He did not finish his sentence. In her turn, she paid him a compliment, and did not fill in his words for him.

But the peace, it had not lasted. So much sorrow, so much anxiety. Aunt Charlotte died at the end of April: by the time Catriona heard of the gravity of the illness it was too late to travel. She had not wanted to go up for a funeral, nor did she want to see Mama, who would now be in a distressed state and even more difficult, since she would have to leave Ann Street. Her letter in January after Tarley's death had been all about her own woes—together with a few snippets of news about Kirsty. (*Kirsty's* husband was doing very well for himself, and had a post of great importance at Glasgow Royal Infirmary. What news of John?)

And the war with Russia—what anxiety that brought. No Ewart, home in Scotland, visiting Yorkshire. Instead, all the cares and concerns of a brother in Bulgaria. Although his regiment was in pleasant surroundings, with enough to eat and game to shoot, there was still the worry of cholera. What chance would they have, all herded together as they must be in a camp? And then, if they should go into battle—how to hope that Ewart would live? Why should he be singled out for survival? There were all these thoughts (and more) for the long watches of the night.

Alan. She had written to him only the once, in January. She had told him that she would not be coming to Wester Ross. And this in spite of John's protests, his argument that such a visit could only do her good. That it might even be described as a specific. But she knew that the painful memories would have travelled with her; and that once there, the might-have-been would stalk her over the hills, along the white sea-shore. Tarley would be everywhere—because nowhere.

Alan had written back, a dear letter of sympathy, and chiding her for not coming. "But—another time. It is postponed only . . . And if I go to London in the spring, Pussy, why then I shall make Linden House a so-pleasant stage on the journey . . ." But here it was June, and he had not been. Now he would be going to Wester Ross.

There were warm, even hot summer days (sun-baked stone, elm trees in full leaf, the young rooks calling), when she was cold all the time: living in that frozen country of the mind, with its chill of dead bodies. She had made herself face the truth that Tarley's body had grown not only stiff but *cold;* that she had no longer known her mother. Of what use, she thought now, that Tarley had gone to her heavenly Father, since it must surely be her mother that she cried for? Was it not Papists who believed they had a Mother in heaven, that Jesus' mother was there for them to run to? *Who would be mother to Tarley?*

Big Sarah, as she thought of her sometimes now—although, God knew, she was small enough in stature—big Sarah forcing her to sit and sew with her. Other than a little mending, she had done nothing since the underlinen for Tarley's Dunbar outfit . . . She did not want to do any now. And above all she did not want to sit here, in Sarah's house, with Sarah (and listen no doubt to John's praises. I can praise him for myself, she thought, *should I wish to do so*).

And what was this fault-finding? No delicate hints this time, but straight criticism.

"You think nothing of John. I'm forced to speak my mind. There are some who wouldn't—but I do it for the best."

"Of course. *Naturally* . . ."

"It is no manner of reprimand, Catriona. I only speak as I find—and we'd maybe just leave it at that. It's said."

"And has John been complaining, then? Has he some quarrel with me, that I *know nothing of?* I am only his wife after all and cannot expect to be in his confidence—"

"That'll do well enough, Catriona!" She bent her head over her sewing. "Angry words—they do nothing for those who give them, nor those who *get*. I've meant everything only for the best . . ."

She said little more then—other than to exchange small gossip, commonplace observations—until late in the afternoon. Then she said suddenly, "I know it's been difficult for you, lass. But—when you've a son of your own, you'll care for his happiness. And that others should concern themselves with it—those that *ought* to. That's all."

"And now—if you will pass the candle, I shall just set about waxing this thread . . ."

"Your mother was here, and reproached me. This afternoon."

"Well, yes," he said tiredly. "She worries I think, about the child. That you don't care enough . . ."

"Oh, it is that, is it? I thought otherwise. And what am I meant to do for the child, pray? We have a nurse, do we not—and Mrs. Mather. I concern myself with Mrs. Mather. I have been there already this evening."

"Then there is no more to be said—"

"I'm sure I don't know whatever you mean—if there is anything I should do, and do not, then it is because I am not well. Because I am too tired."

"You cannot be forever tired," he observed, in a weary tone himself. "You need a change of scene perhaps. It is possible I could arrange for a locum, and then we could go for a few days to the sea. Say to Filey?"

"Och, I thank you—the prospect is delightful. I would not. I would not."

"I am out of patience with you," he said suddenly, angrily. "No one has suffered before you, I think. That is the impression we are to have. But I see—things, everyday in my work. People who are in far worse case. Yet you—"

"*You* were not feeling. It was nothing to you—in January. At the time, yes, because a doctor should always save his patient and must feel bad if he does not. But *otherwise* . . ."

"I felt nothing? *I* had no feelings?" His voice was astonished, pained. "You think no doubt because I've to be about my work all day, and am not able to sit on a sofa weeping by the hour—that I don't *feel*? There's no word but *daft* for all that. And bad. Yes, I dare to say *bad*—and that you're a bad mother—"

"*Stop!*" she cried. She ran over to him, and would have rained blows down on his head, laying about her with her fists—but she felt instead, suddenly, only a great weariness. "You cannot be forever tired," he had said.

But I can, I can.

Home, she wanted to go home. And I don't mean Edinburgh, she thought. I mean Wester Ross. Only there. Wester Ross, and Alan.

The smell of the sea, the white-sanded shores of the Atlantic with its warm breezes, its crashing surf—never that unkind, harsh chill North Sea. And the resinous scent of the bog-fir splinters when they are thrown on the fire—great flames leaping up. The smell of peat charcoal. Even the smell at night of burning horn, acrid, from the tinker encampments in the hills.

The long, low thatched house. The welcome from the servants, and especially comfortable Jessie, who had always been there. The horse-drawn sledges we were used to be driven in before the roads were built. Wild swans on the wing, rising over the loch. And sunset—there are no such sunsets in England. And then at evening the croak of a ptarmigan, flying down from the hilltops at evening to feed on the heather below.

Then, oh yes, oh yes, her mouth watered (when had she last been hungry?). The black cherries, the great bowls of black cherries. Bees' nests in the moss at the foot of the heather. How often we found those: and the taste of the bee-bread and the wild honey. The island where the crowberries grow, where we may go together by boat. The *taste* of the crowberries . . .

Only there, and only with Alan, can I be healed.

Why ever had she refused to go, pleaded fatigue? Why had she elected to stay here where all was so dreadful, when she might be *there?*

The longing that had come over her was so strong, so overwhelming in its intensity, that she thought, I would kill, I would *murder* to get there. It was as if she were full not of sorrow, but of some deep anger. That I might be there, now, *this moment* . . . Weary as she was, the difficult journey (and how Mama had loathed it), even with all its discomforts, would not worry her.

And, *I could pack and go now.* Who would stop her, who could? All that next day she thought only of how she might arrange it. Of how, in the morning, when John had gone off on his before-breakfast rounds, she would take the Courier Coach from the market square. Who would think anything, seeing the surgeon's wife? She might be going to Harrogate to shop, or to Leeds. Her trunk: that could be sent on to Edinburgh, since she would have to be first there.

She woke very early next morning, and was ready too soon, far too soon. Surprising John by being dressed already before six, she told him, "I shall go and shop in Harrogate . . ."

But he said only that that was good, but that she must not tire herself. If the day should become hot . . . "And you will see," he said, "what benefit you will have by exerting yourself just a little . . ."

It came over her then that she could not bear to be with him for another moment. The violence of her anger towards him amazed and terrified her. When he had left and there was still half an hour to go, she went into his room. He had left behind on the bedside table his pocket case of drugs. She opened it idly. Inside, all the small japanned tins, neatly inscribed: "Suppos. Morph Gr: ½, Pil. Plumb et opii: Gr: 1, Pulv. Tart. Ant. . . ."

How she hated it all. How she *hated* that life. Pulling out each tin, opening it roughly, she emptied onto the thin cotton rug, pill after pill, powder after powder. Pil Cannab. Ind., Pil Colocynth, Pil Opii.—all, all, until they lay a small vulnerable heap at her feet. Then she trod them in hard, rubbing with the pointed toe of her boot, again and again. In haste, such haste to be gone—to be done with this life.

She wrote on a piece of his paper, using his quill, and his seal for the envelope:

"*Do not write to me*. I shall write to you. As you said, I need to go away, and that I should have a change of scene. I do not know when I shall return—you may tell what stories you wish (you may also *think* of me what you wish). Baby will not miss me. She is well cared for.

"I have gone first to Edinburgh. From there I shall go to Wester Ross. I shall write and tell you what is to be done about my belongings.

"*Do not write to me . . .*"

THIRTY-TWO

The dog Cap lay curled up in the corner on his rags, whimpering occasionally. He did not come out to see Ned. Did not even bark when he arrived.

"He's badly," Becky said. "I thought as mebbe he'd been in a fight wi' a fox. I seed one about. He'll try any, will Cap." She said it as proudly as ever.

"Will he eat?"

"He'll tak nowt." She threw him an end of oatcake over. It lay untouched.

"Summer sickness," Ned said. "It'll pass." He tried not to think how Becky would be when Cap died. Yet the dog could not last forever, and was over eight already.

Becky said, "I reckon it were t'sun as fetched you up here. Eh—the way it's been. I thought as it'd nivver fair up . . ."

He had thought so too, lately. Day after day riding to work in driving rain, buffeted by winds, or shivering in a drizzle. The river Down had risen to its highest mark under the bridge, and when he had been yesterday to collect Kate, the waterfall by the Kissing Gate rushed and tumbled through its opening. At home too, the beck beneath his window raced frothily all night.

He had been nervous yesterday, going to the Abbey. Of late, except for times when he knew for certain that Charles would not be there, he had scarcely dared to go for Kate. Over sixteen months now since Charles—but he did not want to remember.

"From fornication and all other deadly sin . . . Good Lord Deliver us." *And all other deadly sin* . . . did it not mean just those very things? He would look at his body sometimes, and shudder that Charles should have desired him (*As I desired Nanny*). He thought often, I cannot bear the shame of it all.

Home again after that terrible time, he had torn off his clothes, had washed all of him and especially his mouth. He remembered now the frantic washing of his mouth. His fear that Kate should even see him before that was done—that he should, unwashed, *speak* to her with that mouth . . .

Yesterday he had taken a risk but it had been all right. No Charles. And Kate so happy to see him. Her hand in his, as if she were still the little child he had used to lift on the front of his horse, and sing to at night. Saying now, easily, "Miss Hooper remarked that the 'gust' has quite gone out of Au-gust. And it has, hasn't it?"

"I thought as it'd nivver fair up . . ."

"Well, it has, Becky. And here I am, come to see you." He put down his bag. "Some things for you." He took out potted meats, some cordial, a few brightly coloured sweets. He had meant to bring some clothing. He was aware, felt bad, that he did not nowadays take such care with his gifts. "And the newspaper," he said, "if I haven't left it at work. I was to read to you—"

"I'd sooner talk—and that's the truth on't." Her voice was croaky today. She cleared her throat: "That news—I reckon nowt to a' that. Muttonheads, all on 'em." Cap shivered, and whimpered a little in his corner. "Mind yissen, me own lad," she said roughly, running her hands over the dog's face, caressing him.

Ned gave her some family news—he had taken lately to telling her more of what went on in the family, rather than news of the outside world. "Catriona—she's not been well, and has gone up to visit in Scotland. Kate can speak some French very prettily. And she sings—"

"Yer music," Becky said suddenly, "ye nivver mak it now. T'flute. There are days I reckon I'd as soon hear 'at as yer talk—eh?" She turned to him, as if she'd meant it in half-jest.

"I lost the joy of it," he said. "When . . . *Next time*, I'll bring it next time."

A loud thump on the door. Ned jumped for fright. But Cap, who would at any other time have given furious voice, scarcely stirred. Becky, starting, said warily: "*What's that?*" But before Ned had crossed to the door, another thump. Then two more.

"Easy there—" Through the narrow gap ajar he could see just a cloak, or something dark. But then as he pulled the door wide open he saw, standing there—dear God but it could not be—Charles Ingham.

He had been drinking. No doubt about it. Even as he pushed past Ned, stumbling a little in the unaccustomed dimness, his gait, the smell off him . . .

Why Charles? *Why here?*

Becky was in one of the corners already, huddled, a broken chair in front of her like a gate. "Nay—*what?* Becky sees no folk, Ned—"

Ned said, and at once wished he hadn't: "It's Mr. Ingham, Becky . . ."

"*Squire* Ingham," Charles said languidly, slurring his words. He swayed a little, peering round him, his riding whip hanging loosely in his hand.

Becky called out, her voice far too loud for the small space, "None on you are wanted here. None on you. Or yourn—"

"Who's that now?" Charles asked in an affected manner. "Is there someone else, some other human—a human being in this hovel? Someone besides Rawson. Ned, dear fellow, how are you?"

He put an arm round Ned's shoulder. Ned was unable to move. He thought, this cannot be really happening. And then he thought, but this is what I have always feared—that somehow Charles would find me out. That in his low-down persecuting manner he would follow me up to the one place which is quite my own. Where I *take care of Becky*—

He said to Charles now, "You heard. She doesn't want you here. It's her home—" Then as Charles tightened his grip: "Leave me be—"

Charles, smelling of drink, wanting to embrace him. And then horror of horrors, his lips brushing Ned's neck . . .

"*None on you*—or yourn!" called Becky. "It's Becky's home. *Becky's home—*"

Charles, releasing Ned, taking notice of her properly for the first time: "Indeed," he said, "and I have always fancied to see it. I've asked this good fellow—often—'show me what Rebecca's home is like, eh?' Haven't I now, Ned? Haven't I? Be a good fellow—*answer*." He rocked on his heels. "Answer Charles, eh? Always said I'd pay a call. Then Mrs. Ingham—you know, that lady now, married to Squire Ingham— she said where I might find you. We talk, you see, Mrs. Ingham and I— sometimes have conversation. Pretty she is, thinks she's very pretty. But Ned here—he's prettier . . . Woah there—" Nearly losing his balance, he righted himself. "Damnation take it, you don't offer a fellow a seat —where's a seat, eh?"

"Go home," Ned said. He was standing just out of Charles's reach now. Charles did not move. Just stood there, swaying occasionally.

"Tell you something," he said, "*this* for Rebecca now—story in the newspaper, you know. Good this . . . They exhibit in Valencia—*Spain*, you know—a child of fourteen months and—wait, is this not *rich?*—this child is *half-black* and *half-white* . . ." He hiccuped. "And that's not all, they say it's covered in the most extraordinary marks—"

"You can stop this," Ned said. "Stop now. And get out—"

". . . The *legs* I understand—a fraction odd—and the arms—one is natural and the other *like a monkey*—"

"Why such a story *now*? *Can't you be off*?"

"But my dear fellow—she—"

"*Get out!*"

At once Charles's hand came down, heavily, before Ned could avoid him. With his thumb he pressed and kneaded the flesh above Ned's wrist. He had a cut, Ned noticed, half-healed, on the pouch between thumb and forefinger. Ned thought suddenly that he would like a fine dagger so that he might plunge deep into the cut—he felt consumed with hatred, thinking of twisting and probing, the wound growing deeper. He trembled: what I might do, had I a knife . . .

"Surly devil—speak to me, eh? Think you can say what you will . . . *Get out* indeed—I tell you, Charles Ingham gets out *when he wishes*—" Ned's arm was roughly twisted. "You don't want to fight me, eh Ned— a weak legs like you. It wouldn't do. You've no more chance than a cat in hell without claws . . ." His words were all slurred together. "Good mind to take a whip to you. Speaking to a fellow like that. Take my boot, eh? Eh, Ned? My surly son, I can silence *him* soon enough— young May moon. He grows worse—has effrontery to be happy at school. Hear that, eh? I learned to beat there. And be beaten—fellow there, beaten to death, you know. But Father, dear old Squire—doesn't get to hear of these things . . . Too busy wenching. Or was. W*as*. Wenching all his life, till God struck him. Filthy waste of time that, filthy. But you—*you* wouldn't agree, Ned, eh?"

"She wants you to go," Ned said. With enormous effort he had calmed himself. His voice was controlled. "If you'd just leave now. I'll take you out." When Charles did not leave go of him, he said, "Please, now." Placatingly: "It's *her* house—"

"And her—" Charles looked around in dazed fashion. "And her— dog." He said, "If you call that bag of bones a *dog*—"

"He's badly," said Ned, stung, "or he'd have you—"

"Nonsense—you're speaking nonsense," his voice so thick and breathy, "all love Charles. Sick or well, love Charles, there's not a dog but's my friend." Releasing Ned, he swayed over to where Cap lay.

"Come on, old fellow, give me the time of day. It's Squire Ingham. Come on there, come on now—*to attention!*" Cap gave a half-hearted snarl. "What's this, sir? What's this, eh? Not recognise your betters— come *on* old fellow. *Come on there*—" His voice had grown menacing, angry. "*Come on* . . ." He put his hand down. Surprisingly, Cap didn't snap but only lifted his head tiredly, sniffed at Charles's hand, then nuzzled against it. Drooling a little, he licked it thoroughly, first the front, then the back.

"See," Charles said triumphantly, "I think you see what I mean now . . ."

He moved away then and walked towards Ned, who was standing guard over Becky. She crouched still in the corner. Ned said, "Get out and leave us. Just go—"

Charles's hand came out again, gripping Ned's arm firmly. Ned said again, more sharply, sensing Becky's distress: "I've told you, leave us be. *Leave us be.* Coming calling here . . . Coming calling at the works, and now *here.* I don't need visits from you—" And then the pent-up anger of years: "Why can't you *let me be?* There's terrible things, things I won't mention—you've been wicked to me—and I don't need you, want you in my life. We've nothing, we've no friendship, we're different worlds. What's a squire to do with me that dirties my hands at the ropes—"

Charles, thrusting his face at him, "You know *well*—Ned old fellow, eh? Your mother, eh, don't I owe *her* something—long time ago that— there's your brother too, eh, been known to dine at the Abbey . . . He's sent for often enough, God knows—women's complaints . . . You know well there's Rawsons in and out the Abbey, in and out, eh?" He hiccuped. "*She's* a Rawson, isn't she, eh—the one who shares the schoolroom. Little Irish slut—"

"*What did you say?*"

"Steady old fellow, push a fellow like that and he might fall—"

"*What did you say?*" Ned's hand going out at an angle, striking Charles sharply against the cheekbone.

And Charles reeling back with shock. But for seconds only—then anger, sobriety almost, coming over him. "God. Damn you, you *dare* strike me! Stand back there—you *dare*—" and as suddenly as Ned had struck him, he lashed out with his whip. "Dog, Ned, you dog—take that. That. And that. You'd strike an Ingham, would you? Eh, *would you?*"

Unable to defend himself as the leather stung him again and again, Ned heard himself sob. Cries he would have done anything to conceal, escaping him.

But then, his head bowed, he felt suddenly the impact of Becky's body—smelled her—as she came between them, pushing, pulling at Charles's legs.

Charles, thwarted, jerking out with his knee, knocking her over.

"Interfering bag, *rag bag.* Bag of stinking rags. Eh, ask yourself, *would you be up here* if you hadn't stank out the town below? Filthy stock. Black blood, *tainted* blood—"

By now she was lying, half-kneeling where she'd fallen. Ned, recovering himself, had moved forward. He put an arm about her, to lift her.

"It's *you*," he said to Charles in a shaking voice (what did it matter what he said now?). "It's you—the stench of your wickedness, your evil ways. It's you who *stink—*"

"Mind," Charles said, "Mind. I warn you—"

Becky was muttering, head down. Charles held the whip still coiled. Ned thought, Let him dare to strike Becky . . .

"Mind. Be warned. Or, I *use this*." There was silence. Then in a wheedling voice, his tone changing suddenly, "Ned, come nearer. Ned, there's a good fellow . . ."

(As if I'm a difficult dog. As if he has only to coax me . . .)

"There's a good fellow. Come on. Nearer. I shan't hurt." He hiccuped loudly. "Ned, dear fellow, you can't want *her* stench on you. Can't want her arms. Ned, I shall be sick—" He came nearer.

Ned's skin, his whole body, smarted where the lash had been. Nausea too. When he wanted to speak, acid rose in his throat, blocking it.

Then Becky called out suddenly, her voice clear, shocking: "*Brother!*"

Charles, surprised perhaps to hear her speak, stopped only to say arrogantly, "He's no relation of yours. Don't gull me with that. You're *trash*. You'd be a *Rawson*, would you? Trash—when you're trash through and through—"

"Ye ken nowt—*nowt* . . ." She spoke disgustedly. Then when Charles didn't answer, "Brother—" she said again.

Ned said, "Becky, let be. He'll go, he'll be away. There's things best not said . . ."

"*Brother*—ye didn't ken as that's so, eh? Nay, ye don't ken . . . *Inghams*. Becky doesn't do wi' Inghams . . ." She shot out an arm and pulled at Charles's leg. "It's you now, *you* I call brother—"

"*What?*" Charles's voice, explosive, urgent. Suddenly sober. "*What?*"

She shambled away, without speaking, leaving both of them. Going over to Cap and pulling straw over his rags.

"Out with your damned lie. *Explain* your damned lie—"

"It's no lie," Ned said. His voice was absolutely calm. It surprised him—its authority.

Charles just stood. Unbelieving. Willing desperately, it seemed, that these should be just the ravings of an ageing, crazed woman.

"You're mad—"

"She's not," Ned said. But he was trembling now. "It's the truth . . ."

He heard again the pert little voice of Nanny, in the hot July evening, before the storm—before her death (". . . and it's certain sure as how he'd to do wi' Meg . . . and it were along of a'that—hearing she were Squire's by-blow—that she run off . . .") "It's known," he said. "There are folk know—"

"Explain yourself," Charles said, "she's mad—*explain yourself*—"

But then when Ned, trembling still, gave his account, told all he knew—Becky silent all the while—Charles stood. Drooping mouth, vacant expression. Listening, listening. With horror.

He did not suggest it was a lie. And it had the *sound* of truth. Ned, telling it, thought that. He said to Charles, "There's many know. Only they'd never tell—"

Then Becky spoke up suddenly, shaking her fist at Charles: "Ye hear, I want none on you. None of yourn. Becky's nowt to you." She said angrily, sobbing now, "What'd I want wi' ye all? Ye'd liefer Becky'd been a lad, eh? If I'd been a bonny lass even—but Becky weren't *bonny* . . . I want *none* on you—not Ned—*none on you*—"

"God, my God," said Charles. He spat violently. Then lurching towards the door he opened it fully, stumbling outside. He could be heard vomiting. Ned, looking out, saw the heaving of his shoulders.

Becky was shaking, muttering to herself. Ned thought, I don't know to whom to turn, *I don't know what to do.* As he drew nearer to Becky, she said, head averted, "Be off wi' ye—"

Charles, sick and sick again, had become helpless. The smell of alcohol, of vomit off him, was overwhelming. He collapsed against Ned. "Sorry, old fellow. Can't—" He put out his hand, felt for the wall, moving along the floor away from Ned. Then fumbling with his flies, he stood swaying. An unending stream poured from him against the inner wall. Afterwards he could not fasten the buttons. A moment later he fell to his knees.

Ned said, "I'll take him back. I'll get rid of him." When Becky didn't answer, but only stared at him, he said, "Are you all right? Becky, are you all right?" She still didn't answer. The dog behind her whimpered. Ned said, "Hush you then, hush you—"

He had to help Charles onto his cob. He thought he would never manage. Could not believe in the strength needed to set the flopping body astride. He led him down from the moor, stopping every few yards to right him. Then Charles would say, sleepily, as if drugged, "Good of you, dear fellow . . ." Each time: "Good of you, dear fellow . . ." And by the morning, Ned thought, he will remember nothing. All that he has learned—blotted out . . .

By the time they reached the Abbey, the light had almost gone. He led Charles as far as the front door, pulled the bell, and when a footman answered: "Your master—" he said.

Then he began the journey home. Twilight was coming on fast. He thought, Should I find my way back to Becky's perhaps—see that she is all right?

He was to wish he had done. She must have come down the moor that same night, or at the least very early in the morning. It was the verger, going through the Kissing Gate, who looked over at the river and saw her body, trapped just under Downham Bridge.

An omen. A curse—Ned, shivering, felt it like a curse. He mourned yet again for someone he had helped but had not helped enough. He had not been able to enter her mind.

And, he had not been there when he was needed. He had not been back to see after her. But almost—he had almost gone up on the moor again. Only he had been so exhausted . . . Turning back from the Abbey, after delivering Charles, he had felt scarcely able to walk: certainly he had wanted neither to think nor to talk—only to sleep. And he had slept at once, heavily, as if he had taken laudanum.

Then the next morning: the news of her suicide. After Charles and he had left, everything must have become suddenly too much for her. The precarious balance of her mind . . . He remembered how once they had thrown stones at her, and how her face had been then. The terror. And I vowed, he thought, I vowed that I would protect her, care for her . . . And yet, while he slept, in the watches of the night, she had made one of her rare excursions—putting an end to the whole sad business of her life: and doing it as near as she could to the Abbey . . .

God help me, he thought, that I did not go back, that I did not try to comfort her. God help *her*.

That afternoon after work he went up to her house to see to the dog. But the place was empty. The rags and straw lay as they had been left. He tidied up a little. Then he went outside, walking about in the bracken, calling the dog's name.

"Cap, Cap—" The sheep looked at him with mild curiosity. A rabbit, white-scutted, bolted in the late August evening.

He thought: Maybe he can live off the land—if his fever's burnt out. Charles's vomit glistened beside the door. He stood for a moment looking out over the heather and the moorland turf. Then, shivering, he made his way down the moor.

THIRTY-THREE

It was long and difficult, the journey she was to have made with Tarley (the great Western Highlands Company had not in the end brought the railway up . . .). As far as Aberdeen there was the train, but after that it was the steamboat to Inverness, and then lastly, the uncomfortable mail carts. Although now at least there were proper roads, built when Western Scotland had had a potato famine as in Ireland (but with this difference, that the roads unlike the Irish ones all led somewhere . . .), so that it was now possible to avoid completely pack horses and sledges.

Still, in spite of this, it was a great journey. And she had her luggage to worry about: she had not been able to wait long enough in Edinburgh for it to be sent up—so she must wait and worry about that . . .

Alan. He met her some fifteen miles from the house, so that they might do the last part of the journey together. She had not even been certain that he had the message about her arrival, since there had been scarcely time for a reply. But now the sight of him, the dear *familiar* face, made all the worry, all the discomfort worthwhile. She could even forget, for a little, that all the way there she had been thinking, "If Tarley, if Tarley . . ."

It was so light in the evenings that although they came to the house at six, she might expect hours yet before the real darkness came down. The first sight of the house: long, low, heather-thatched and *just as she remembered* . . . And then Jessie—who was all the servant that was needed now. Jessie had grown very old and very deaf. But Alan said that she cooked as well as ever—perhaps better because she had not the youth and strength to run too much about the house distracting herself with other errands.

He had not kissed her in greeting but just as they were about to go into the house: "Kiss, Pussy?" he said. She had been a little afraid then —perhaps it was a memory of the time in Edinburgh. And certainly, as his arms came about her, she felt suddenly an icy chill. *Not what she had expected at all.* It was to have been so warm, their greeting. But this cold, it was diffused over her whole body, in no one place but running to her very fingertips so that she was afraid to touch him, afraid of that icy cold which she felt now always lay in wait for her. A return to that frozen country of the mind, with its dead chill . . .

The first meal was special. It had always been special: the first meal after arrival. Although it was not the time of year for venison, there was smoked deer's tongue, and then fish Alan had caught. The taste of really fresh oatmeal, the remembered flavour of the little potatoes, the sauce which had some herb she could recollect but not recognise.

When they came to eat the pudding, Alan said, "This is for you—" He did not eat it, having only some goat's cheese. The pudding was very creamy, almost like a drink—soft and creamy and sour at the same time. It had in it heather honey and wine too, he said. He was sure she had had it before, but she could not remember, could not recognise it at all.

Jessie smiled at her when she went into the kitchen to thank her—she smiled too while she waited on them at table, and whenever Catriona passed her in the corridors—a friendly innocent smile. She had always been there, it seemed (even twenty years ago, when first seen, she must have been over fifty . . .), she belonged to the house and to the family. But her gaze did not say, "Where is your mother? Where are Jamie and Ewart? Where is *everyone else?*" It seemed only to say that any arrangement Alan might make would be right—and natural. He was the laird.

She was not sure whether to get into bed or not. She didn't know what it was she had thought—that Alan would say something, that he would come up the stairs with her? But she had begun to shiver, as if she remembered the cold of that night in York—so she climbed into the bed. It was the same small four-poster, not very high, that she had first sat up in, proud and almost grown up, aged twelve—or was it thirteen? So many years and years ago.

When she had climbed in she lay very still. Nothing was happening as she had imagined it. Her candle—should she snuff it? Through the heavy curtains which she had pulled a little apart, a thin ribbon of moonlight crossed the floor. Outside an owl hooted. And again.

"Well," he said, coming and sitting on the end of the bed, placing his candlestick on the table at the foot, "well, Pussy?"

She did not answer. She had half sat up, leaning against two of the pillows. She had not her nightcap on.

"Jessie's been gone awhile. Asleep. If you stand down in the corridor there, you can hear her. She ever was a snorer—remember? But now . . ."

He smiled at the memory. She smiled. He ran his hands then suddenly without warning over her face, her hair. His hands smelled of— she did not know what—a memory . . . Up and down her shoulders, glancing over her breasts, and then pressing the thick material against her nipples as he passed. "Oh," she said in a small voice. Then pushing back her hair, hand leaning hard against her forehead, he kissed her wetly, fully on the lips—the forbidden stolen kiss that she remembered, that had given birth to all this. And then his tongue was in there too. A stranger. Now she must faint or else—she kissed back then with a sort of desperation. Soon, soon, willingly, she would drown.

And so it was. But such a time it took to drown. And such a pleasure it was. Such lingering hardness and softness so that she did not think at all what she was doing—only that it was *Alan*. Oh my bonny, bonny Alan . . . Probing fingers searching out what she had never known to be there. And again, hot breath in her ear, breath moving her hair, "Catriona, *Pussy* . . . for years I've wanted . . ." And what was this? Any blush that she might ever have had, any shame that she might ever have felt, it was as nothing, the palest of glows beside this fire. And where did it burn the greatest, where did the flames burn highest? She had not thought that *there* anything happened but pain, or its dull brother, discomfort. But now, ah now, the burning would kill her, if hands brushing by, probing, forgetting and returning—if the real part of him, if what she had never seen of Alan were not to come into—but this was as never before, ever again. "Oh Alan, oh and oh," she cried as he thrust, but she knew he could not hear. "Ah stop," she cried, "ah stop," fearing only that he might, knowing that he would not. Then, "Sh—Alan, ah love, oh *love* . . ."

After such fever, no weakness, only warm peace. The brow that grew cooler, the bodies which lay alongside, so still. In all the years of knowing him, all the years of sleeping beneath the same thatched roof . . .

They had lain together before—outside, on the seashore, in the heather—but not like this, not like this. She had not known Alan. It was indeed this, to *know*, which the Bible meant. And I never understood.

His mouth tasted a little of the cigars he smoked, but his hair smelled of woodsmoke. She touched his hand.

"A happy Pussy?"

"Yes."

He said with easy arrogance, "Och, I knew I could make you happy." Then, after a moment: "What a waste—that I teach you and you go away. No, wait, rather what a waste, how much I learned once and have wasted on—them . . ."

"Them?"

"Aye, them. Well," he said, "from whom else would I have learned myself, unless from—them?" He paused, and then: "But of all the women, ever . . ."

"Yes?" Then when he did not speak, "Did I make you happy?" she asked.

"I am not used to hear you so humble, Catriona . . . But the answer, aye—it is so."

She began in a small voice, "The other women—"

"Och, the other women. We've not to speak of them at all, Pussy. It's you in the bed, is it not? It's *you* with me now—"

Indeed, indeed it was. He had mistaken her interest for jealousy. I am not jealous, she thought with wonderment, with surprise perhaps that he should have thought so. He has after all always loved me. It is just that only now he shows it. What I feel, she thought, is curiosity.

"What are they like?"

"Who?"

"The women?"

"What women?"

"*The* women, silly billy. Your women—*those* sort of women," she said, in desperation.

"Good. Bad. Some indifferent . . ."

"You don't take my question seriously. I shall not ask it again." She said it in her coldest voice, knowing him well enough to guess that it would provoke at once the answer she wanted. It was the riposte of childhood, of girlhood.

"I shall not ask it again," she repeated.

He said lazily, "The London lasses better than the Edinburgh perhaps. *Perhaps.* There are more go there to try their fortune—"

"But if you must pay—" She tried to imagine this world which must certainly exist, which indeed was such a normal part, it seemed, of so many men's lives—and yet was *mentioned not at all.* She explained haltingly some of her puzzlement. Her ignorance he must surely take for granted: how could she know anything (since it was never spoken of) of the world of fallen women, of the Magdalens? (Was it not called sometimes an *under*world?)

"Depending on your taste—some like it plain and some—fancy . . . there are all sorts to be had in London. And—a man may be a long time with one person, one woman. But you knew that—that I have mistresses? Except of course just now. I have no one the day." When she didn't speak, he went on in the darkness: "You see, from one—one thing is learned, one trick. And from another—another, and so on . . . For such women, naturally you need better money. But all of them, all sorts, are grouped together as 'unfortunates.' That is the way of it. It *is* unfortunate, but—"

"That is the name for them—"

"Aye. Some are prostitutes *prononcées*—"

"But how do they come to this? Do they ever tell you—do you know?"

"The good life. Since for some it *can* be the good life. Those who are more expensive. And the best for *them* is if they can acquire a protector. Pussy—surely you have read *novels*? You know what I speak of—"

"Yes. About that, a little. But the others—"

"Well, you must imagine," he said, "how it can be good if you have begun without a bite or a sup or any fine feathers—and then as a result of your *generosity* you are to be seen at Almack's, or Gunter's suppers, or the Opera . . . Casinos, theatres, and you bejewelled and on the arm of some member of the aristocracy, or a rich man in wool, a cotton king —whatever. Such women—some very famous members may have been through their portals—" He paused. "That is of course word play, a punning for which I apologise . . ."

"I had not seen it . . . But," she persisted, "they are not born, these girls, knowing all they ought, all they need. Are they then servant girls who have been seduced, or—"

"Some, yes. But as many, not. You must realise that for the great majority, it is just a means of eking out a precarious living. Better than starvation, or want. And they have always the pox too—the clap, I should say—to consider . . ."

"What is that?"

But he had had enough. When she said, joyfully almost: "Now, *I* am surely a Magdalen. An unfortunate—"

"What nonsense you do talk. And how ridiculous you make yourself. And when it is time for sleep too . . . My dear Catriona," he said it wearily, "you are a Magdalen neither in *esse* nor in *posse*. Let us leave it at that . . ."

In a few moments he was fast asleep. She was afraid to move him, and slept hardly at all.

Possibly she did not need much sleep. Over the next nights it seemed to her that probably she did not. There were other ways now to kill time . . . The days too, they were not long enough even with the high northern light, for all they would do. Since she must go shooting with Alan—and his muzzle-loader, the black powder smoking: carcasses of grouse, ptarmigan, partridge, black game. They took with them always Alan's setter: of the Gordon Castle strain, bred specially for him, and able to go after jack snipe, knowing the sedgy pools where they were to be found. And then in the evenings: Alan smoking furiously against the midges—the only thing here not perfection (had they not driven a bonnie Prince Charlie in hiding almost crazy?). The long days out, with perhaps only barley scone to eat. Then home again—and those meals. Now it was the raspberries, the famous raspberries, which were in season. She did not think about leaving, or going anywhere else, or that any other life existed.

"We shall stay, then—we may—as long as you wish . . ."

How ought she to be with Jessie? It had been hard at first to feel natural with her—however naturally Jessie might behave. For was it not the same Jessie from childhood, who had brought her up cooling drinks when she had a fever, or hot ones when she was chilled, who had fussed over her inside? . . .

But the truth was that this was a Jessie now whose sight was not good enough to see what was going on, and above all whose hearing was not good enough. For, Catriona admitted to herself, blushing, there was certainly something to hear . . .

"We have taken a great risk," he said, sometime during the second, enchanted day.

She had not thought of it—so stupid had she been. *What if*—? She would not be able to pass a child off as John's. Or at least, not to John . . .

She had said to him, "*Do not write to me*—" She imagined his telling all who asked some tale about her ill-health, her weakness. But she had not left under a cloud—except in his regard. I shall throw myself on Alan's mercy, she had said to herself then, not being quite sure what that should mean.

So far it had meant this—happiness never before suspected. And that such happiness should come from her body, from Alan's, that was the greatest surprise. When she had thought before of lying in a lover's arms, had it not been really—if she were truthful—something of the *spirit*, deeply of the spirit? Could this here, now, be of her deepest self?

But of course it was. Such a growing up, becoming now a growing together. We should have married, she thought, cousins or not, we should have married. It was a solution, an idea so simple and obvious that it must never have occurred to him. Nor to me, she thought: it never so much as flashed through my mind, because it would have been as if to marry a brother . . .

She said it one day, after they had been over to the island, "Perhaps we should have *married* . . ."

He had stopped her tongue up with his then, and when he had done, "*That* is the sort of marriage we need . . ."

"It was only an idea—in jest."

He said, "And an idea let it remain—"

But about the other—there was not to worry. That small practical matter—he had explained that he of course could wear something which would prevent the seed, his seed, from reaching what he called her "germ cell"—but that it would be for him thick and dulling and that *she* would not be so happy. He explained that she must use a small sponge, which she would insert and attach with thin string so that it could be easily removed.

She asked, "Do *they* do this?"

As the days went by she asked such questions more and more frequently, often because he seemed to like it, was not shocked—was even amused. "What do they do, these women? Do they do this? Do you do to them *this* and this, and *that*?"

(Could she be that same person who *had not wanted to live*? Who had left her small child to others, and who now *seldom thought of Tarley at all*?)

"The answer is simple enough," he said once, to some query. "*Good* women do not enjoy themselves in this fashion. Men must usually travel a little, or at least spend a little gold, to be with those who do."

"But I am—"

"Not a good woman . . ."

She had not thought of it like that. Although she *knew* herself to be wicked (because she had left John and Sarah), she was Alan's dearest cousin.

He added, "And as such you are my dearest dearest coz. Come to bed—"

When she tasted him that night for the first time, it was the flavour of the salty sea, but it was too that sweet-sour milk and honey and wine: the love potion of that first supper a full long fifteen days ago.

THIRTY-FOUR

Marthwaite, their name was, the family Walter had gone to—to learn to be a farmer, some eight or nine months ago now. And it was the old man, old Mr. Marthwaite, who came up to Number Three, Hillside, early one evening that October. He asked to see Sam—but Sarah insisted that she too should be present.

"I'm the lad's mother," she said firmly, as the gaitered farmer was led into the icy cold room. Prayers had been over only for some ten minutes. Although there had been sunshine during the day, in the evening it had turned very cold, with an autumn chill. The room felt damp.

"Let's have it," Sam said, almost as soon as they had closed the door behind them. Kate had been left reading out loud, to an audience now of just Eliza, who was sewing her way through a dozen layettes for paupers to be finished by the New Year.

"If the lad's not pulling his weight—not doing a day's work for the money, then you've to tell us. No beating about . . . If the lad needs a lammacing"—Sam picked up his Bible, as if to give weight to his words—"you can depend on Sam Rawson to give it . . ."

But more, much more than a sound thrashing was needed, in fact demanded, by Mr. Marthwaite. Sarah thought, listening to the sorry tale: where does all this trouble *come from?* Is it Donnellys, or Rawsons—or who?

There had been three sons at home on the farm (the fourth had left just after Walter arrived), and no daughters. Sarah had thought at the time: we've chosen well. There'll be no trouble there. But last Easter the family had taken in a girl cousin, from a small village just outside Settle. She'd been orphaned and was already known to them quite well before. Jess, the second son, had liked her always and after a few months—with everyone's approval, he'd announced that they were betrothed.

Walter, on his rare, reluctant visits to Downham, had never mentioned any girl living at the farm. And I am not surprised, Sarah thought now. Not when I hear what I do . . .

The wedding was to have been at the end of October. *Was to have been* . . . His brothers, Mr. Marthwaite said frankly, his brothers had teased Jess for arranging to wed without proof. "An' I were t'same—I'd liefer see a bairn safe into t'world afore they goes to kirk. And a lad at that. It's best. But Jess—there's to be nowt o' that, he says to us. Nowt o' that . . ."

Unfortunately, what Jess had not availed himself of, it seemed that Walter had. And the girl was indeed about to wed with proof—of Walter's virility.

It is too much, Sarah thought. Let's be done with him. Let the lad go as far away as possible. It appeared too that he was not at all repentant —although he had already left the farm and was boarding at an inn in Wensley. "It were all I could do," Mr. Marthwaite was saying, "all I could do to halt Jess—that he didn't raddle yer lad wi'in an inch o' his life . . ." He shook his head sadly. "An' now—what's to be done?"

If it was a question of *money* . . . But it seemed all of it more complicated than that. There was Walter to be sent for and spoken to— decisions to be made, the law to be laid down. Sam was all for leathering him soundly before any talking was done at all.

"You'll not make a Ned of me," Walter told them, looking obstinate as well as sullen—and anything but sorry. "I'm not throwing my life away, tying myself up with trash—just for making a mistake the once. Or the twice maybe . . . Anyway, she can't cook—she makes pastry you could crack your teeth on—"

Sarah said, "You should have thought of that before you—" but she couldn't think of a word for what he'd done, any word that was all right—"before you went with her," she finished lamely. "The mischief's done now."

Cornered, Walter had turned pathetic suddenly. He didn't want, couldn't, *wouldn't* marry the girl . . . He cried, begged, said his life would be ruined. Sam, who had left it too late now to thrash him, was non-plussed. Sarah was disgusted.

"And the Inghams," Walter was sobbing, "*they* can father where they will, and folk say 'how grand,' or 'what a wencher' . . . They *do*. But when it's one of the Rawson lads, then it's a different tale. *Get me out of this* . . ."

They did, of course. Sarah thought that she had known all along they would. Money talks, she said to herself—and without even asking Old Jacob, I have some. Of my own. Squire Ingham's legacy to her: his last expression of gratitude for the risk she had taken so naturally, so willingly, all those years ago. She had no special plans for the money. It was good to have it, and that seemed to her pleasure enough for the time being. But now: it was used to arrange matters with the Marthwaites—and to buy Walter a passage to Australia on the next convenient ship sailing from Liverpool, together with money to see him settled.

"He can populate Australia with chance-bairns, for all I care," she told a shocked Ned. "I shan't hear about it—or it's to be hoped I won't . . ."

But that matter settled, it seemed to her that all her other worries came upon her. The niggling worry always about Ned and his sadness; the present worry about John, and the absence of Catriona. (At least she had not to concern herself about her namesake, who prospered still with Mrs. Mather . . .). When, if ever, could they expect Catriona back? John would say nothing, or so little that she could glean no real information. She thought that perhaps *he* did not really know . . . Nearly thirty years married, she thought, five children—and not one of them happily married (unless I am to count my poor dead Ann . . .).

The night before Hallowe'en she dreamed about the old Squire. She seemed to be a child again, and he a middle-aged man as he had been then. He held her hand as they walked from the Abbey to the Kissing Gate.

"You know why it's not a true kissing-gate, eh?" he asked. He lifted her up so that she almost cleared the top of it.

"I can fly," she told him. "If you let me go I'll *fly* over the kisting-gate . . ."

But setting her down again on the road, he said only: "*Kisting*-gate it may be—but everyone that's christened *and* wed, they pass twice through the Gate, eh? So there's more brides and bairns go by than kists. Many, many more. So remember that, Sarah Donnelly, eh? Kisses, not kists . . ."

On Hallowe'en morning, very early, and feeling very foolish, she set out for the Kissing Gate. It was the effect of the dream perhaps—or it was because of the good fortune she had had last time she was so superstitious, but she had decided that—provided she met no one thereabouts —she would try to bring some good luck to the Rawsons.

Two charm bags, buried before seven in the morning. One of them had some ribbon from a little jacket she was to give baby Sarah, the other had a few strands of Ned's hair from when he was two or three years . . .

She prayed too, as she buried them. It's always best, she thought, to bring God in as well. That He may not feel offended.

"Dear Kissing Gate," she said, "dear God the Father—please bring Catriona back to her bairn, and to my son. Ned too," she said. "See if You cannot make him once again at least a little happy . . ."

THIRTY-FIVE

John was sent for to the Abbey. It was November now and the weather cold. The road was hard beneath the horse's hooves. Last night, a hoar frost, and this morning the bare trees by the Kissing Gate—and the Gate itself—were covered with rime.

Driving out there, he smarted with wounded pride and worry: about Catriona. The last letter he had had—if it could be called a letter, since it was no more than a scrawled note—had said only, would he forward by whatever he thought the fastest means, her galoshes and the sketch-book and drawing materials from the second drawer of her bureau? And she had received safely (thank you) the trunk of clothes sent to Edinburgh in July and then forwarded. He had been surprised she should still be in Wester Ross in October, but beyond remarking that the weather was very beautiful, very mild: "just such as we are used to have here. Yorkshire, what I saw of it, cannot be compared . . ." she mentioned nothing, giving not so much as a hint of when she might, even if she would, return. He felt a fool whenever he was asked, and that alone aroused his anger.

He was angry too about the child. She *should* have worried about her. Little Sarah, still happily on the breast, was now growing normally and would be weaned in the New Year. Mrs. Mather was a good woman, a good nurse, plentiful, bountiful, patient (Catriona need not, only *should* have worried . . .), and deserved only that her own child should have lived. Now after nearly ten months he had become quite used to her presence, felt towards her a steady sort of gratitude which surprised him by its depth. (He must never think of what might have been—how very nearly *two* small coffins had been carried through the Kissing Gate.)

Most evenings before he had his tea, he would visit her in the nursery to admire little Sarah's progress. Mrs. Mather called herself "Mattie," and Sarah "Babbit." She spoke to her all the time Sarah sucked, or sang to her. He was certain of this since twice when he had been in there she had quite unselfconsciously attended to Sarah: opening her dress quite naturally when the child, who could stand sturdily and almost walk, pulled imperiously at her clothing. "Mattie has summat for Babbit," she would say, "Babbit want a sup, eh?" He fancied sadly that Sarah's first words would be, not "Mama" but "Mattie" . . .

He had had of course to say something of Catriona to Mrs. Mather. He explained: "Mrs. Rawson—she is still in poor health. She may yet have to go abroad" (What country shall I invent? A warm climate. Egypt, say? Something so impossible that *all* will be forced to believe . . .). And Mrs. Mather would say understandingly that, no doubt of it, going back where she'd been born—your own country, always best in times of trouble.

Mother of course knew all, or almost all. She had said, "It's not for me to come between man and wife, son" (and he thought that probably she had not meant to—but that she could not resist some little righteousness now. She had warned him in the past—words which he now interpreted as warnings . . .), "but if my counsel's needed, I'd say then—you've to be more firm with her when she's back . . ." And Ned —Ned had guessed something of the truth. "She'll have had to go away," he'd said in a calm voice of acceptance. "It'll have been the loss unhinged her."

But the rest of the family? Luckily he had not had to explain anything to Grandfather, whom no one had told. At the Abbey, Kate had no doubt said something acceptable in the schoolroom.

Not that it concerned them at the Abbey. It was Charles who had sent for him today and he was not likely to ask. Otherwise he was rarely there. When he saw Georgiana in church he felt only shame and remorse. On the very few occasions when they had been forced to acknowledge each other, she had done so with ostentatious and icy politeness—somehow increasing his shame, her very coldness freezing his misery. His only comfort being that certainly *she* was not the cause of Catriona's departure. However great had been his wrongdoing, Catriona had not known of it.

He found Charles sitting in a chair in his bedroom, a plaid rug round his shoulders, over a dressing gown. A glass of brandy and water and a decanter were beside him. His manservant was carrying through his hunting boots. His yellow labrador bitch, ageing round the muzzle now, was whining at the door. She came in with John.

Charles said affably enough, "There you are—come in, dear fellow," and then to the manservant, "Get that bitch out—"

"*Out!*" he yelled at the dog who, tail between legs, slunk out. "No patience," he said to John. "Can't stand the beast near me. Can't stand anyone. I feel so damnable, never felt so damnable, be a good fellow and sort me out . . . Marsh!" he shouted at his manservant. "What the deuce with those boots, meant to go out today—Rawson, I should have been out, dear fellow. If I weren't so damnable. Meet's at Leyburn, should have been at the Abbey, no, damned thing—meet's at *Leyburn*, I'll swear. Can't get it right, anything right. Take a seat, Rawson, take a seat . . ."

John said, when he could, "What's been the trouble now?" A foolish question, since this excitable, irritable man was plainly very sick, and equally plainly most unlikely to give a proper history. Take his pulse, he thought. Talk calmly, gently. Forget our relative positions (and above all, forget that I have had carnal knowledge of his wife . . .).

"The lot, the damned lot. Can't sleep, and bloody restless, have to keep talking, dear fellow, have to keep talking. Can't sit quiet, you know. Can't sit quiet. Nights, they're damnable. Can't do with nights. And this—" he moved his position stiffly. All the time his knees had been shaking, up and down, up and down, jerking. "This *damn* pain. Pain in my damned shoulder. Don't care to move this shoulder. Have to move it, you know, can't sit still all the while. It's worst nights. Confounded state of affairs, can't swallow—there's a good fellow, make that all right. Hurts *damnably* when I swallow—"

"How long, then? When did all this start?" He thought perhaps he might have to ask Marsh too for a history. His master was fast becoming incoherent.

"Sort me out, would you. Not all these damned questions. Haven't been right for a week—five days. God knows. Just fatigue at the start." He shook his head. "Not feeling myself, not Charles Ingham, you know. No damned appetite. A day's hunting and I felt better—damned state of affairs, I told Marsh, better go today. Feel better then. This shoulder, my shoulder. One day could manage only hot wine, water. No appetite. No appetite since. Then this pain. Damned *pain* started. Can't eat—can't swallow, dear fellow. Brandy and water. That's about it . . ."

He did indeed look ill. He swallowed with difficulty. John looked in his throat. He was puzzled. This, together with the other symptoms— he did not know. A list of possibilities ran through his mind at breakneck speed. He was alarmed.

"It's difficult—I can't say . . . At this stage. Possibly—what we should do, I think—"

"Get me out of this discomfort, would you. There's a good fellow, get on with it. Tell me what it's about, eh? What I have, eh? Tell me. *Say what the hell it is—*"

"I think—"

"Is there no decent surgeon around here? Get Wilson from Leyburn —he's good, they say he's a good fellow."

"I would prefer really to wait. We could see—could try first, say, antimony . . ."

"Get him, I said. No, wait, there's a fellow. Eh, damnable pain. Get someone from *York*—that's it, fellow from Leeds, get him, eh? Eastgate is it, Westwood—damn the fellow's name . . ."

John thought, if it is to be all over again like Charles's sister, and the beginning of the affaire. If I am asked to dine as a courtesy—I shall not.

But because he was gravely concerned about Charles's condition, he decided to send at once for a second opinion. A message went to Mr. Eastwood. In the meantime, Mr. Wilson came over from Leyburn that evening. But like John, he felt that to decide what precisely was wrong was as yet too difficult. Palliative measures and patience were his recommendations. Charles took them a little, but only a little better, from his lips.

"We don't want old Whitelaw," he said, in the midst of some other tirade, "there's a good fellow—don't bring old Whitelaw. Did for my mother they said. Thin blood, she had—and then he takes off. Confounded surgeons . . . *Who's that here, eh?*"

He had planned to see Charles as his first visit of the morning, but he was still dressing when a servant sent from the Abbey came with an urgent message. "He's very badly, sir, and Marsh says to come at once, sir . . ."

"Your mistress?"

"T'mistress she's in London, sir, she went yesterday was a week—"

"Tell them that I come *immediately*."

Charles was pacing the room so fast that he must surely be fevered. He did not stop even when John came in. Did not like it when John put a hand on his arm. His condition had visibly worsened—although his manner was slightly less irritable.

"If you could rest a moment, sit quiet—" John said.

"Can't stop, dear fellow, got to keep walking."

"A moment, while I examine you. Ask a few questions—"

"Must keep moving, God help me, must keep moving. So dry, thick, can't swallow, you see. Damnable thirst, damnable thirst . . ."

As Charles passed by him, John held up the glass of brandy and water for him to sip. Charles shuddered, almost with horror—but half grabbing at the glass, he held it sideways to his mouth. Then as if it were poison, he threw it to the ground. He was shaking all over, convulsed almost.

"Sit, you must a moment. We must look at you . . ." Knocking at the back of John's mind, wanting full entry, was a notion he found so horrible that it must be, *could* be, only the wildest of medical fancies. *He must be wrong.*

Charles had sat down now, but still compulsively twitching. Brandy dribbled from his chin onto his front. John signalled to Marsh, who came over with a towel wrung out in water. Charles screamed as he approached, a croaking, hoarse scream:

"GET THAT AWAY, TAKE THE DAMNED WATER AWAY!"

"Calm down while we take a look at you, *please*." He had to force the mouth open and even then, so spasm-ridden was the jaw that he thought, indeed feared, that it might clamp down on him. There was a thick viscid secretion about the mouth. It formed a sticky web. The voice, still hoarse, had thickened.

John said to Marsh, "Your mistress—she must be sent for at once."

He went home only to arrange for Leathley to do the more urgent visits. He would go back then to be with Charles. Wondering and praying, he asked himself how long it would be before Mr. Eastwood might arrive. His first message had not stressed the urgency—a day or two might pass. Dear God—*a day or two* . . .

He wrote again now, stressing the haste, saying what possibilities he had thought of, and then—the worst one of all (which in his own mind he had decided already was a certainty). Back at the Abbey, he found Charles a little quieter. He and Marsh succeeded in getting him into bed. There he was able to examine him. He found a mass on the colon —the bowels had not been opened. No urine, he learned, had been passed for a considerable time. Twice during the examination he saw, from the raised nightshirt, evidence of sexual excitement. He did not flatter himself that it was on his account (although as far as proclivities went, he might suspect—certainly from hints Georgiana had let slip . . .), but saw it as one of the symptoms.

Catching Charles in a lucid moment, he asked him: "Were you bitten lately by a dog? *Try now to remember*—any altercation with a dog? Even a fox, could you have been involved with a fox, say?"

Charles was jerking his head on the pillow. He spoke through the web, at intervals trying to spit out some, but becoming only the stickier.

"No dog that isn't my friend, dear fellow. Haven't seen anything but good dogs. They all love Charles—there's not a dog but's my friend. My yellow lady, she's all right. Hounds, they're sound. Lurcher. Terriers— *all* good dogs."

In the afternoon he slept for a while after some laudanum. To administer it had been very difficult. John had brought with him *The Lancet,* and also some notebooks. He sat near the bedside with these. At intervals he took out his watch—how long before Mr. Eastwood might arrive?

The yellow labrador had insinuated her way in and slept now by the foot of the bed. In her dreams she twitched and then whimpered several times. Charles, waking suddenly, sat up. He called out, his mouth full.

"Shoot that dog, eh, shoot him—come here, there's a good fellow, come here, good girl, good dog, eh? *Shoot that dog!*" He began to throw himself about, wildly. It took all Marsh's and John's strength to hold him. "Rag bag, bag of bones, brother to a bag of bones, how d'ye like that, eh? Filth—father is filth, father to a bag of bones, a witch, filth—I have a son, there's a good fellow, get my son, eh? First sign of damnable cheek, beat 'em. That's right. Best thing, roast them, eh? Brand 'em—no damned impudence, infernal that is—Good thing, school. No, *damnable.* Eton damnable, brand 'em. Long Chamber, all boys sleep Long Chamber. Rats there, better shoot rats. Rats eat crap, eh? Too many rats Long Chamber, kill 'em, put 'em in a sock *smash* 'em now, *smash* 'em against the bed . . . Drink, no drink, no *water,* lock us in at night, lock us in Long Chamber—get rats. Beat sense into me, will you, eh? No, you don't now—Dodds, Benson—my God *help me*—filthy, your hands off me, *scorch* me would you—My God, they're branding me, God damn you, hands off—water, that'll scald, cruel, *cruel,* God help me, *God help me*—no one hurts an Ingham like that— damn you, the *pain*—I'll brand you Richard, brand you my boy, best learn soon, teach 'em, eh—Dodds, no you don't, *my God help me . . .*"

When, when would Eastwood come?

Charles lay for the moment quiet. In a lucid interval of short duration, he seemed to recognise Mr. Eastwood standing by the bed.

"Well," he said through thickened lips, "good to see you, my dear fellow. Fortunate I'm not a dog, eh? They'd have shot me long ago . . . Great nuisance, tell Mrs. Ingham, been a great nuisance . . ."

Within moments they were holding him down again. Mr. Eastwood, he of the eagle face, pushing out his lips as he spoke, took John downstairs for a few moments' talk in private.

"Yes," he said. "No doubt at all. Yes. Hydrophobia it is. Indeed were he a dog he would have been more fortunate and seen an end to it—"

"But how? How rabies? He recalls no bite. Although his memory at this stage naturally—"

"We are asking a lot of memory, you know—we could be going back two months. *Six* months even—cases have been known. On average, well, it will not have been *more* than two months. It *can* have been two weeks . . . Thank God anyway we see so little of it—and thank God *you* have never seen it before." He paused, and then continued gravely, "And how has he contracted it, you ask, if not a bite? We shall not have the occasion, I fear, to ask him any further questions . . . But a bite, a bite is not necessary, you know. No, no, I am afraid it is not. A lick will do, a mere lick—when it is on mouth or nose, membranes say— or where, for instance, the skin is broken. A cut, however small, is sufficient. We know that much about the mode of entry. And—the prognosis, about that we know the worst. Hopeless. Quite hopeless." He nodded sadly. "And a fine man. What do you say, forty? Not old. There's a son, sons?"

"One son. He is away at school."

"Mm. Sad business. Messy business. I had hoped never to see another case. Endemic—but we must stamp it out. *Shall* stamp it out . . . Now, this matter of the Russkies, the war, Rawson. Alma, Sebastopol, all that. It goes badly, eh?"

John said, "My—brother-in-law, Mrs. Rawson's brother—we have never met, but he is in the campaign—"

"Indeed, indeed, a sad business. And your wife, how does she do?"

Charles, waking, was screaming again. Now he wanted only death.

"Shoot this dog," he cried, "shoot this damned dog, *shoot Charles, eh?*" he wheedled thickly, whining, paroxysms seizing him, clutching furiously at John, his grasp unnaturally strong. "Shoot him, shoot Charles, eh, put him out of his misery, eh, there's a good fellow, FOR GOD'S SAKE SHOOT ME . . ."

And I would—I would if I could, thought John, alone with the horror. I would if I could.

And then towards evening, about half past four, when the light had gone and lamps had been brought in: as Charles lay quiet and exhausted, two or three teaspoons of broth dribbling from his mouth, his hand went out for some bread on the table beside him, and his jaws, snapping in their paroxysm, seemed indeed like a dog's. Afterwards, he was quiet again. He lay like that until about ten in the evening. Occasionally he would try feebly to spit. He did not speak again before he died.

John thought, At least I shall be able to say to Georgiana (and during such an exchange, their embarrassments surely would be forgotten?) that the death itself had been peaceful. Exhaustion, all horrors spent (and he would not describe, even mention those . . .). At the last, breathing tranquilly.

THIRTY-SIX

Put your head, darling, darling,
Your darling black head my heart above;
Oh, mouth of honey with the thyme for fragrance,
Who with heart in his breast could deny you love?

IRISH, Anonymous, sixteenth–seventeenth century,
translated by Sir S. Ferguson

It was uncommonly cold that April, even for Edinburgh. To Catriona
it seemed unbearable—although springlike weather and signs of the
summer to come would have been no better: would have seemed a
mockery, with its reminders of past happiness.

She had been already three months back in the capital. Mrs. Dunbar
shared a home now with her sister, Catriona's Aunt Isobel. Their house
was new, built in the Georgian style only a few years previously. It was
in Clarendon Crescent, over the Dean Bridge, and not far from Princes
Street. Inside they had as much space as they had ever had at Blacket
Place, together with very fine views: from the back they could look
right across Edinburgh New Town and over the Firth of Forth—even
beyond the water to the Kingdom of Fife . . .

She looked at the views often, since she was not out and about a
great deal. She saw that they were beautiful, grey skies notwithstanding
—but they served only to increase her sadness.

All is sadness, she thought. Not least had been Ewart's death. Although it was some months ago now, the news had come through only
slowly. He had not been killed in battle but had died of Varna fever—
named after the place he had been at in Bulgaria. His regiment had
been moved into the Crimea, where he contracted the illness. He had
died in the Barrack Hospital at Scutari. She had heard at first very little

about the circumstances of his death—then gradually, and mainly through the newspapers, she had learned more and more. Often, before Mrs. Dunbar should see it, she would cut out or accidentally damage any references in *The Scotsman* . . . Then against her better judgment, she read a book giving first-hand accounts of conditions in the Crimea. I must face it, she thought. It may not be wise to distress myself, but I *must* know . . .

She learned that when regiments such as Ewart's crossed the Bosphorus into Russia, the four-and-a-half-day voyage took often as many as fourteen days—with insufficient water and only salt rations to eat . . . It was described how when they at length came off the boat they were many of them nothing but spectres. Stripped and washed, they were "no better than the Irish of ten years ago." *He* should know, the writer had said, since he had been in Ireland then also. (And so too was my John, Catriona thought. When he rescued and brought back from the dead our beloved little Kate. But I think there can have been no one there in Russia to do that for Ewart . . .)

She did not receive letters from Downham, nor did she expect to. She did not write them, either—just as she never wrote now in her Journal. She could not bear even to re-read her old ones. (Glancing through once, she had thought: I do not like that person. Had even thought: I do not *know* that person . . .) So that she was very surprised to receive one morning a long letter from, of all people, Ned. He was not a person she imagined spending much time with correspondence.

He wrote very simply, telling her all the news. Downham was the same as ever. The Reverend Cuthbert had preached another sermon against the superstitions of the Kissing Gate. The railway was coming to Leyburn. Charles Ingham had died—"but perhaps you have heard that already?" (How could I? she thought. I hear nothing. And if it was November, then I was in Wester Ross still and far removed from any newspaper . . .)

"Baby Sarah is grown nicely," Ned wrote, "and you would be proud of her. She can say 'Katie' very loud and clear and many other words too. Kate is with her very often . . . And that is all I shall say for now, dear Catriona. We await always news that your health is better and that you may be well enough to come home again. You should know that you have a friend always in, Your loving brother, Ned."

How could I go back? she thought. *How could I?* I have become a person who cannot look at the past—and yet who has no future. She thought that she might, at some time, write a reply to Ned, although she was not at all sure what she would say. He is the only person there, she thought, whom I should not mind knowing the truth. But she would not tell him. She could not write it down—even for herself . . .

And yet, strangely enough, only perhaps a week or so later, one cold dark afternoon, she found herself with her Journal open in her hand. She was alone in her bedroom. Her aunt was out and her mother, who was not well, was resting. Looking now at the blank page, she was filled suddenly with courage. Sitting down, she took up her pen, dipped it in the ink, and began—quickly, quickly before she should change her mind . . .

> Edinburgh,
> April 1855.

Alan has left me.
There is no other way to write this—And I cannot really think either, what it was that I hoped for. Had he not *always* said that he was not for marriage (and imagine the scandal of a divorce, *if* we could obtain one!). He has rejected me absolutely and completely. I cannot think of any way at all in which it could ever again become *as it was*. I had thought always, quite without realising it, that whatever might happen between us there would still lie true and shining all the happiness of the last twenty years. That we had only to go back if the present should end—and so foolish was I that I did not think it *would* ever end.

But what we had done—we could not go back, we *could* not. That is I think what happened in the Garden of Eden—or rather I feel that somehow I *understand* what happened there. I have not been able to accept that childhood is gone for *ever*—and he with it. Whether I see him ever again or not—it is gone. This is something of death yet again, that while someone lives they should be as if they were dead—and the worst is that nothing, but nothing will ever bring back *how it was*.

It was my importuning. And *his* temper—which I had never really seen before in *my* regard—and his restlessness, which I knew so well but *did not think* applied to me. He had never wanted to talk of our future (and I know now—that he did not think we had one. But for that I was too blind. And too *proud?*). I might have divined from the manner in which he steered every time the talk in quite the other direction. And when he began to say often, and more and *more* often: "When you go back, when you are in Downham again . . ." and I would tell him, "*Never*, I shall *never* go back—" and once he laughed and said, "Pussy, where *shall* you go, then?" (And I *had not realised* either, that my pet name, that I loved so much from him, that it has also a *low* meaning.

That it is not only from Cat—Catriona, but that it is something very coarse too, so that I cannot but think now that he had that always in mind, and that the word has been on his lips on so many *other* occasions, in the roughest of talk—) I told him that time that I wished to stay with *him*. He affected at once great surprise and said casually, "You would not want to be with me when I am here, there, and I don't know where else—travelling, and in rough places . . ."

It was then that we fought. Oh, how we fought, as never before (we had never been used to fight *at all*) and it was *with words only*. I wanted to be like a wild cat, I could have been, I had the claws—but I was tame Catriona, I was house-tabby. I spat and hissed only and used my tongue—I think to too much effect, since it all ended in his *great anger*—and finis to everything.

"You are like all the rest of them," he declared. "The rest of *what?*" I asked. "Women," he said. "Oh, painted ladies, I suppose you mean?" I said (and that was about the tone, the grand tone of all of it!), and he replied, "Oh no, all women—all are the same. And it is because of this that we, that men become sated and must needs move on." And if he did not take care, he said, it would end always in clinging—"As *it does now*," he said.

All that day and some of that night there were very ugly words spoken, so ugly as I do not wish to remember, and by the morning of the next day there was no going back at all—there was no way to *kiss and make up*. And he would not have wanted to. *He would not have wanted to.* "I could do," he said, "if I never saw you again—" (Yes, those were his very words . . .) But I will not weep any more—I am tired of staining pages of books and papers and even prayerbooks (A truly brave person, even a woman, does not cry). *It is over*. He is gone. He will return some day, soon or late, but only as an acquaintance—I shall not want to do with him, nor he with me. He had always this bad side of him that others did not like—and now I must remember only that. Dear Journal—it is *this* to have the heart broken. Not to *lose* someone you love, but to see that you *should not* have loved.

It is not great the life here. I want the energy I suppose, to do anything worthwhile. I had hoped perhaps to see Kirsty—she has had news of me, I hear. And *she* was nearly to live in Edinburgh again, since Mr. Mackenzie, a surgeon lately here, has died in the Crimea—like poor Ewart a victim of the fever—and there was question of Kirsty's husband taking his place in the Extra Mural School here. Bu it is not to be.

I spend time reading, but not poetry. I would not. It would remind me of John, and *those days*. I read instead novels, a great many. I am three times a week at Inglis' library in Hanover Street—it is one of the few reasons for which I go out. I am reading just now a new Geraldine Jewsbury. This is called *Constance Herbert*. The heroine who learns that her heredity is tainted with insanity renounces her lover on the eve of marriage—it is very dramatic and will absorb me for the space of a day or two.

Nothing is said to anyone exactly of *why* I am here. I am not thought to have disgraced myself, although Mama is sometimes odd in her remarks as if she had guessed, or would rather not guess, what has come about. I am supposed still to be recovering—though she does not think I am doing very well in that regard. Only last week she threatened to *write to John* about me. And then another time it will be, "You cannot live there again, in Yorkshire, Catriona. You are not *strong* enough. I will not hear of their wanting you back . . ." What is in her mind too is that the Honble Iain has been widowed, and she can now say to me—and *does*, "If you had but played your cards right, Catriona—" She even said once, but below her breath, "If John should have some accident . . ."

The truth is that some days I have come to feel that life is not real at all. Where once it was *too* real—now it is not there at all. It is at once all a dream, a nightmare—I would like to *wake* and find everything fresh. A new world. If that were to happen then I would want to wipe the slate clean—to have a *second chance*. Then perhaps I would behave as I think I would have done had things, everything, been better. I would have:

> Loved John,
> Been a good mother to Sarah,
> Behaved well in Downham—

But all that is might-have-been. I *have* had some kind of happiness, such as I never dreamt of—but it was of a sort that should not come again. I think perhaps *goodness* and happiness are not such frequent companions. We are not often blessed that the two shall come together —more usually it is Duty *or* . . . I think I should have known that, since it was certainly taught to me. Now *I know it indeed*. Some people are wanting in spirit—but I think I have always had too much. Now, it is broken. *I* am broken . . .

That is all. I have written it, and now cannot write any more. May God help me—and all those I have hurt . . .

All the rest of that afternoon it grew darker and darker outside, and colder. In the evening there was sleet. Catriona sat in the upstairs drawing-room, alone. Mrs. Dunbar was already asleep, and Aunt Isobel went up always immediately after the tea tray was removed. But she did not feel that what she needed this evening was a companion . . . She might, she supposed, play the piano for a little? Or the harp . . . Certainly I shall not sing, she thought. She crossed over to the window.

I am too restless to go to bed. She took up *Constance Herbert*, and finding her place, read a few pages. But then she thought, I don't want to know what happens. What do I care about her inheritance of insanity, what do I care whether or no she is united with her beloved?

The outside bell rang. Its sound made her for some reason cold. As she sat there she shivered a little. I wonder? Aunt Isobel had few visitors so late. It will be some nuisance, she thought.

When he opened the door for himself and came in, she could only sit quite, quite still. She felt the colour come slowly to her face. She was flushed, with fear perhaps but also with a kind of fierce joy. *It could not be.*

"What—how—why should you? I am not—"

"Your mother. I had heard from her . . ."

He continued to stand there, as he had stood once before. He had on still his great coat. Sleet-snow on the shoulders, on his hat. He cleared his throat. Then:

"I am come," he said, "to take care of you—Catriona."

THIRTY-SEVEN

Now is Christ risen from the dead, and become the first fruits of them that slept. For since by man came death, by man came also the resurrection of the dead . . .

The blackbird, it was a fledgling only, had been savaged by a cat. There was blood about its head, and one wing torn and quite limp, and blood too from other smaller wounds. It lay twitching and trembling in Richard's hands. Kate stood beside him. Ned asked, "How did you come upon it?"

"We f-found it in a c-corner of the churchyard."

"Not far from the birch copse," Kate said, "where there may be a nest. I think it had only just escaped a cat—we saw one run between the tombstones there." She put out a hand to touch the bird. "I can feel its heart—"

"Will it live, do you reckon?"

Richard nodded wisely. "I have reared s-several. One or two, they have even preferred to stay."

"You had become mother," Kate said. But she did not laugh. Often he would expect from her voice, even her expression, that she would laugh—but there she was. Gentle. Serious.

She told him, "I was to come home from my lessons and Richard, whom school has set free till Easter—he was to bring me back. And we thought to come through the Kissing Gate and bring flowers for our graves. So you see what good fortune that we should be just passing. For Blackie, I mean—"

Richard said, "I was s-s-surprised at Miss Hooper, that you should have your lessons on Good Friday. You should have l-let me s-speak."

"Oh, she would have paid little attention to your pleas—she is not very impressed by you, she has had the teaching of you once. Besides, we must have the Collect of the day by heart and the Epistle too. 'In burnt offerings and sacrifices for sin thou hast had no pleasure then said I lo I come in the volume of the book it is written of me to do thy will O God above when he said sacrifice and burnt offerings for sin thou wouldst not . . .'" She let out her breath. "Is that not well got, Uncle Ned?"

Ned said, placing his hands in his pockets, "And I—I'd come to fetch you back too . . ."

"But you have been so often of late! You were used to be working at this time—"

"I can please myself, mayn't I, my cockyolly bird? Greaves—he can be left now. And the new apprentices, they want the life to be mischievous."

Richard, head bent over the bird, said: "If only I c-carried some b-brandy—"

"That is the first thing we must give it," Kate said. "Brandy in warm milk. When you are back at the house. You should go up with him to the housekeeper—to Mrs. Williams' room—"

"S-see," he said to Ned, "how well she knows her way about."

"And so I ought! I am more there than you, am I not?"

Richard nodded, and smiled. He too, Ned thought, is gentle, and serious. (But he is nothing to do with Charles. He cannot be. There is nothing. Nothing.) He had grown to look very well. Although he was not tall he gave at first that impression. Favouring his mother, his hair was a pale gold, and he had the Old Squire's eyes. His head now was beside Kate's as together they bent over the bird. His hands clasping the bird had nails bitten to the quick.

Well, but here they stood, the three of them in this graveyard. Downham kirkgarth. Becky did not lie here. Because she had taken her own life she might not lie in hallowed ground. Charles slept now, with his ancestors. God is vengeful, Ned thought. Vengeance is mine, saith the Lord. Charles's illness, the rabies, it had been surely from Cap. A dog did not need to have been furious—he had been told that. Sometimes they were only quiet and ailing: as Cap. (But I did not know any of this, he thought, when I found his stiff, half-eaten corpse, less than a week later, amongst the bracken not more than half a mile from her home.)

"We are such good friends," Kate said to Ned, "Richard and I. And only were *very* occasionally vexed with each other in the schoolroom."

"But I was away l-latterly so much. The G-Greek from Mr. Cuthbert—"

"Oh, if you must learn Latin and Greek," she said fondly. Then: "Give me Blackie a moment, that I may hold him."

He passed the bird to her with enormous care, his hands resting over it a little, until it should be accustomed to Kate's hands. They were very white, her hands, the veins standing out blue.

"Do you feel now, how his heart races? Uncle Ned, *you* feel it—"

Her hands were blue-veined. Milky white. And the veins ran up surely to the thin white skin of her upper arm, there on the inside. In his mind he touched her.

She had become so beautiful, his cockyolly bird. *And she can only grow more beautiful.* He trembled, but with joy, to think of the beauty that lay ahead.

It had not been wrong to be dead for all these years since a seed might lie in the earth, in the dark, and still live. He said inside himself, weakly triumphant, I believe.

The three of them stood for a few moments just outside the Kissing Gate. Above in the elms the young rooks called noisily. The leaves were not yet out on the sycamore. Across the road the first daisies flecked the grass white. Richard, who had hold of the bird again, separated from them. He would take it back to the Abbey, care for it, and Kate would come and see it tomorrow.

She and Ned began the walk back. At once, she took hold of his hand.

"Darling Uncle Ned, *darling* Uncle Ned. For Easter you shall have—what? *What* shall you have?"

"Now is Christ risen from the dead, and become the first fruits of them that slept . . ."

I am the resurrection and the life, saith the Lord: he that believeth in me, though he were dead, yet shall he live . . .

PART TWO

1877–1886

ONE

"'I'm a toff, I'm *immensikoff*,'" sang Will Rawson, on a cold afternoon of January 1877. He danced at the same time: long legs, red hair. At not quite twelve he was nearly as tall as Ned, his father, taller already than his mother, Kate. He would outstrip easily both parents. "'I'm a toff . . .'"

"Sing it now—*all* over again," said his sister, Flo. "Please, Will . . ."

Kate, watching her children, thought: all that sisterly pride. Flo, at seven, must be surely Will's greatest admirer. Although his brother, Patrick, ran her a close second . . . *His* admiration, even if only that of a three year old, was perhaps different—and special. A source of wonder to me too, Kate thought now, since it is not even tinged with envy. Even though he cannot walk, and will never be able to dance himself . . .

They were all four at Linden House, on a visit to Catriona. Kate, nearly thirty-seven years old (and over twelve of them married to Ned . . .), *completely* a Rawson now. That she should have grown up in their father's home, delighted her children. "You never changed your name at all!"

She sat with them now, in the morning-room which looked out onto the market square, round the big table. Flo was colouring in, and Will was entertaining . . . They had come over from Little Grinling, where they lived still in the cottage from Ned's first marriage. Now it was a happy home . . . The visit was to see Catriona about the arrangements for her son Paul's twenty-first party. His birthday was on Old Christmas Eve, January 5. (And what surprise and joy, Kate recalled. His birth: nine months almost to the day after Catriona's return from Scotland. I remember so well now the rejoicing. A son for John at last. And my fifteen-year-old self, drinking infant Paul's health in champagne . . .)

Patrick said, apropos of nothing, his useless legs swinging from the chair: "Cousin Sarah has a funny mark, a funny mark—but I love her . . ."

"Where's Cousin Paul *anyway?*" asked Flo.

"I think he's out walking," Kate said. "His mother thinks so. He is not to have much to do with the party."

"He can't have known *we* were coming," Flo said. With her straight black hair, her white skin, her high creased forehead, she looked anxious, as if the colouring-in were a life and death matter. It was her usual expression. And yet, Kate thought, she hopes always somehow that by her very concern, her efforts—she can bring about anything. Although Flo was little mother to Patrick, she had not at first been able to believe, about the legs. ("If he *tries* to walk only! When I try and try, *I* can do things . . .") Just as at first *I* could not believe, Kate thought. When what had seemed to be a perfect child—and I had lost two between him and Flo—when the legs were seen to be helpless, hopeless: when it was explained to me that never . . . I was not bitter—except perhaps a little, for him. But I could not help thinking—of words said to me years ago, by Georgiana Ingham. I am not so foolish now—but in those first days, when I had just learned, I wondered if they were not true . . .

"I want to see Uncle John *and* Aunt Cat—"

"Uncle John was away and on a train journey," said Kate, "and is very tired. He stays in, so that you will certainly see him . . ."

"Cousin Paul—he *must* come back before we go." She laid her crayon down, and wiped her fingers on her pinny. "Willy Willy Wilkin—give us 'Hoplight Loo'—*please* . . . Mama, doesn't Cousin Paul *want* a party? I wish *I* might come to it . . ."

"Well, you may not and that is that," said Kate, but gently. "It is for grown people only."

"Aunt Cat might want me to help *cook* . . ."

At home, Flo's cooking was ambitious and frequent. Kate, remembering how Sarah-Mother had allowed *her* in the kitchen (as she had not Ann and Eliza), even though it was inconvenient and often annoyed Mrs. Cowley, who cooked by the day for them—said yes, always. But today, in Catriona's house, "I think not, darling. Perhaps with the flowers . . ."

She wondered when Catriona would come. She had been resting when they came, with a headache, and they had seen her only for a few moments. They hoped to make the final arrangements for the caterers, and the lights, and flares. And to check the guest list. Whatever, they would stay only till the daylight went and then would go back early with Ned. He was now at the works, but would come to collect them.

The rope-works were the same as Kate had always remembered them —the same size, the same amount of business. And Ned seemed content enough there (although, she often thought, it is a wonder when he must work daily with that unpleasant Arthur Greaves, with his unreliable temper and odd ways . . .). Although they lived still at the cottage in Little Grinling, it had been somewhat enlarged. And the stephouse outside had been made into a bedroom for Will. He went next autumn to school in Richmond and would board there with his cousins just as Ned and John had done. And Walter (we have not heard for *years* from him. And I am so uncharitable, I do not mind. I do not think Sarah-Mother minded—it was not *he* she mentioned on her deathbed . . .).

"Why does Grampie not come to the party? *He* is grown up—"

Ah, but that was difficult to explain. Sam went nowhere, did nothing, talked to no one—the children saw him only once a week when he had been especially spruced up for the occasion. For the remaining six days —he drank. It had started only after Sarah-Mother's death. Immediately after. He had never drunk alcohol before, either publicly or privately. But what began with whisky for a cold, turned in his sorrow to whisky with everything. Surprisingly he had survived already some fifteen years of this life. Eliza looked after him at Hillside with the help of Jane Helliwell. They gave him just a little each day, enough to keep him from delirium. Occasionally, he would find the stores. And then . . .

"My next number is 'Hoplight Loo,' ladies and gentlemen—and *then* I shall sit down and read quietly and you can cry 'encore' all you wish. When I am very famous you'll be glad you saw the beginnings. That you knew of Will Rawson . . .

> " 'Oh, I'm a handsome nigger as ever you
>   did see,
>   Teeth as white as ivory, and skin like
>   ebony.
>   My hair is crisp and curly, my heart is
>   firm and true,
>   But I think I'll throw myself away and
>   marry lovely Loo.
>   Then *Hop light Loo* and shew your pretty feet . . .' "

As he sang and danced (and it was the nigger minstrel Mackney he copied—an act once seen by Will: never forgotten), Kate wondered yet again—where did his gifts come from? Ned had music—but he was not a comic, did not dance. She thought of unknown Irish forebears (And Sarah-Mother too: the da she spoke of—who had danced the best of all the haymakers. Might not he be reborn?).

Will had finished, to applause. He sat down as promised, picked up an illustrated magazine, and was at once absorbed. His gift for concentration. That is Ned, she thought. (So much that is good is Ned. And it is a good marriage too, she told herself. Ned and I, it is a *good* marriage . . . In this world we must not look for what we have not, but for what we have . . .)

"Now say, Mama, what sort of people *come* to the party? Do the Inghams come?"

"Well—yes. Just the eldest boy. Francis. Not the girls—they are too young. Paul wanted Francis. They have done some lessons together I think once with the Reverend Staveley at the vicarage. Paul was behind with his studies . . ."

But Flo had gone over to the window, lifting the net curtain. She said: "There are two persons just coming to the front door. They are not *patients*, I think. They don't look at all indisposed. Just very grave —Now they go up the step . . ."

The outside bell clanged. Flo came back to sit down. She said, "Patrick, I will *teach* you . . . Say after me:

> " 'Willy, Willy Wilkin
> Kissed the maids a-milking, Fa, la, la!
> And with his merry daffing,
> He set them all a-laughing, Ha, ha, ha!' "

He had three lines by heart, and was inventing one of his own, when the door of the room was opened roughly, hurriedly.

"Aunt Cat—" began Flo.

Catriona was white-faced. Hand on the door-knob, rattling it as she spoke:

"Kate—something very grave. At once, if you would—*please* . . ."

"They had with them a warrant, and powers of arrest, they said. And that was that. They have taken him away already, Kate . . ."

"But did you not—had you *no* discussion with John?"

"Oh, only a little. The very smallest I assure you. I am only the wife who must face all of it, everything—the disgrace . . . No, they were here only—what? less than fifteen minutes. He went with them at once.

It seems he may have even to spend tonight in the cells. *Kate* . . . It is not to be borne."

Kate was thinking: solicitors, bail, Ned . . . "Of course we send round for Ned, at once. Eliza, if she can leave Father . . ."

"*He* must not know," Catriona said. "That at least I am composed enough to realise. It will drive him further—could unseat him completely. *His* son, a common criminal, and not merely charged, but charged with—" her voice broke, "with—indecent assault . . ."

Kate was still trying to take it all in. Such was Catriona's indignation and distress that she had been able to make out only a small part of the whole.

"Oh, I shall tell you all," Catriona said. "All. All that I heard. It is terrible, *terrible* . . . Och, I mean I am used, *should* be used to disgrace —but *this* . . ."

"Catriona—calmly, darling. Shall I get you first a drink? Or your salts, your smelling salts, where are they?"

"No—no. I can—I shall tell you . . . It is—it concerns the railway journey he made yesterday. He had, you know, to change trains at York —for Leyburn—and was back here quite late. I thought nothing but that he was very tired this morning—he did his rounds early, then wished to rest this afternoon. We sent Wright out on a visit for him . . . *But* it appears—" She put her hand to her forehead, where a band of white hair grew in with the black. She was still a fine-looking woman. "I am sorry—I shall compose myself . . .

"It appears that on the journey to York he shared a carriage with a young lady—or *woman* I should say." Her voice was indignant. "There were no other occupants . . . When the train had been some time in York station—and he had already left for Leyburn—it is then she alleges (*alleges only*—I tell myself that) that he . . . that an assault was made on her person . . . that it was of a certain nature . . . Kate—you understand?"

"Yes—yes. But for this . . . they believe her? She is at once *believed*?"

"But yes. If she *says* so and is distressed and dishevelled. A pitiable state, they said. Very shocked. She had described him, you see, as a doctor, and that he practised in Downham . . . I do not know or care what details she gave. But they were enough. From that—they have been able this morning to decide everything, and arrange warrants. They will charge him formally at the police station . . ."

She had calmed a little for the moment. "Och, it will be proved all right that it is nothing—the wrong man—all that, as soon as we are in court. *Before* surely. But now . . . I do not know what to think, to do

. . . My agitation is such—" Her voice rose. "It is Papa all over again. My father. Disgrace. Prison. Courtrooms. Bankruptcy—"

"I do not think it will come to that," Kate said gently.

"What can you know that have never had a family disgrace? What? It is railroads again, railroads, railroads. They are to be our family's undoing . . . I was not understanding enough of Mama and how *she* felt —now it is I, I am to be punished . . . The Great Western Highlands Company—but that at least was *fraud* only . . . There was some daring, some courage, some resourcefulness . . . But this—"

Kate said, as cheerfully as possible, keeping her voice calm: "Well, if he has not done it . . ."

"We do not know. I was not allowed to speak with him—to speak alone, that is. I learned only the facts—the alleged facts on which they rest their case. The two men that came—they were detectives. Oh, but no, it is all so sordid—"

She looked around suddenly: "And where is Sarah? Do you know where Sarah is? Out—out, I might suppose. Just when she is needed . . . I have not been fortunate, Kate, in a daughter. I cannot think how she contrives to aggravate me always. Of course *she is not here*. And then at other times, she is too much so . . . Although I must say, for one who expects back soon a fiancé that she has not seen for *four* years, she shows remarkably little excitement. It is not natural. *She* is not natural. I cannot think why she cannot be like everyone else. She is—"

"Catriona—" Kate said in gentle reproof.

"And Paul's party, my son's party," continued Catriona. "What is to be done? The news—it will be noised around Downham—it will not take long. And Sarah's Edwy . . . *he* will hear. As soon as he arrives he will hear and then what? And at Durnford Castle where Paul has this friend—Mallison, Malyon, I forget—who brings a party over on the fifth—the news will be there."

"It will take time," Kate said. "It would be at once . . ."

". . . the girl who is behind all this—they gave her some name such as Newton, Newly—it is said she is a Roman Catholic. If that is so, she will not hesitate to *tell lies* . . ."

"Catriona," Kate said. "Talking—it will not help us. Let us send for Ned . . ."

"What is it?" asked Flo. "What was it?"

Will scarcely looked up from his magazine.

"We must leave soon," Kate said. "We must go without Papa. He is needed here . . ."

"But listen to this," said Will. " 'The bridge over the River Tay when completed will be nearly *two miles* long, with thirteen high girders of more than two hundred feet each in length, each span weighing a hundred and ninety tons and using more than *eighteen thousand rivets*. The Tay Bridge—' "

"Hush," Kate said. "That is enough, Will. Aunt Cat will not wish to hear just now about railroads . . ."

Sarah thought: As soon as I am back I will try to make Papa speak to me again. She had not been very successful the day before, although he had talked with her a little when he would speak to no one else. That, she thought, is some sort of achievement.

He had been released on bail of £500, and was now home again but refusing to discuss the case at all. And nor would I, Sarah thought. It sounded to her—but she did not know what. Altogether, she had not decided what to think. Her first reaction had been—*but he cannot have done it*. Then she had thought, more robustly: these things happen . . . The trouble was—they happened to other people, and were done by—other people. They did not happen at home . . .

She had always had an easy relationship with him—one of her earliest happiest memories was of days spent sitting behind him in the gig while he went on his visits. Sarah Rawson, the surgeon's daughter—to be invited in for a bite or a sup, or given some small treat to take home . . .

Yesterday, he had not wanted to talk about it at all. A defeated, bearded figure, just back from the police station. She had said after a while—and she had been alone with him: "All right—I don't care what you are supposed to have done or not done to a Miss Catholic Catchpole or Slapstick or whatever—I believe in you. As far as I am concerned, the whole affair don't matter at all—and is all a nonsense."

She spoke indignantly without being sure what she was saying—it was more the spirit of it. But in the end, after a long silence he had said only, rather stiffly: "I must face the consequences—one must face the consequences of one's actions, whatever they may be . . ."

"The actions, or the consequences?" she had asked rather saucily. He had ignored that and said after a moment: "Justice is all we can hope for—any of us. We should be content with that." Later he had told her, "You should not—a girl even of your age should not really be thinking of and discussing such matters. It is not possible for you to understand —certain things . . ."

"Oh, cheer up," she had cried, "come to the party—you will *have* to come to the party—be cheered up there . . ."

He had relapsed then into silence. Which she thought hardly surprising—it would take courage for him to appear among all the guests. The news was travelling already round Downham, and in a day or two's time . . .

She reined in her mare a little. The horse was always frisky and ready for the home road once they left the bridge at Little Grinling.

She looked her best in a riding habit (and it was not just that here was an outfit which hid completely her birthmark . . .). In fact, that really is how I became engaged, she thought. That I looked fetching for once.

She had met Edward on the hunting field—at a time when she was riding to hounds at least once a week in the season. He had crossed her first—quite dangerously, and they had had words. Perhaps he liked her spirit—she was not sure (he had not seemed to like it later)—but whatever, her reactions or looks or both had aroused his admiration, and the next time out he had given her a lead, showing her all the best places. And the next time, and the next time. He was a Hussar, and was gazetted to India three months after they met. She realised now that she had not really known him at all. Certainly no better than she knew his (autocratic) mother, his rather spiteful sister, Maud, his great friend Major Lawson-Pollard—"Polly"—and other members of his circle. She had picked up a few of their mannerisms, but for the rest . . . The tour of duty in India was to be four years, and because she could not think honestly of what else to do with her life, she had found herself thinking: Well, yes, I suppose that I might. And she had been able to say "yes" but without going to the trouble of marrying him—yet. But the four years which had seemed an indefinite postponement were over, almost. He would be here within a week of the party, coming straight up north when his ship docked.

She kept his photograph, in uniform, on the table in her bedroom. Sometimes she looked at it. Lately she had in fact looked at it more often—hoping that by doing so she might be able to resurrect at least a few of the emotions she had felt (and they had not been very strong) in the days when they had ridden together, danced together . . .

But the engagement had, if nothing else, pleased Mama. And that was no mean feat. Paul was able to please her just by *being*—whereas I, Sarah thought, made my greatest mistake in being born to her at all. Or perhaps—and this is a very bitter thought—by not dying *instead of Tarley*. I should not know that—but from remarks let slip: it has not been difficult to guess . . . If I had not been loved by Kate, I think I would know very little about mother-love.

Indeed when I was small, I was often confused—and because Mama was away in the very early days and then ill or busy with Paul, I said

"Kate" more often than "Mama"—even though she *was* my mother
. . . (Almost my first proper conscious memory. Kate holding my nose
between her finger and thumb, and then "chopping" it off with the
other hand, while she sang: "'Marjorie Mutton-pie and Johnny Bopeep, They met together in Gracechurch Street'—that's in *London*,
Sarah!—'In and out, in and out, over the way, Oh, said Johnny, it's
chop-nose day . . .'").

By rights, she thought, I shouldn't love Paul at all. Or even like him.
I should be truly *jealous*. When I think what he has had (and not even
wanted all of it). Latin and Greek, a *real* school, and now university, at
Oxford. And all that under the terms of great-grandfather's will. (*He*
was an odd enough character—the little I was old enough to see of
him . . .) All that money left to Paul, which he would inherit the day
of the party (and I have not one penny I may *call my own* . . .). Then
the command that he must be sent away not to Richmond School but
to a grander one. Old Jacob had chosen Marlborough because he
thought it *sounded* well—according to Papa—and because it was a quite
new foundation and would admit a doctor's son. Paul had seemed to
like it well enough, although not too much—his happiest times seemed
to be spent walking in the Savernake Forest.

Darlingus stupidibus. That was what she called him. Even now. A
childhood joke which had stuck. Dating from the days when, full of
envy at his learning Latin, she had cried indignantly: "I know it too!"
Big sister: eleven to his eight—"I know it too . . ." Devouring his lessons, learning all he learned. To show her cleverness she had put "us"
or "a" on the ends of words (she was his "sistera"). The ending "ibus"
had delighted her and, unable to find where it went, she had placed it
whenever and wherever the fancy took her . . .

If only I had been *allowed* to use my brain. But it is not wanted at
all. (She blushed when she remembered her excitement after reading
some five or six years ago, of a woman's college in Cambridge. And I
thought, I *dared* to suggest, that I might enquire into it, see if I would
be suitable . . . Papa had disapproved, Mama was disgusted. Finis . . .)
And my schooling: how poor that was. Anything at all I found interesting—"You will not need *that* . . ." And everything, but everything,
sacrificed on the altar of Accomplishments (at the end of the day, I
sing, paint, and play atrociously).

She had come almost without noticing to the bow bridge. Only the
Abbey road to pass by, and she would be in Downham. The Abbey
looked picturesque, etched almost, in the January afternoon. I like the
building better than its inhabitants . . . Although she had, she supposed, no quarrel with the son. And the girls were too young. And Mrs.

Ingham, Frances Ingham, was a gentle and placid enough person—kind but a little uninteresting. Georgiana Ingham—she could not take to. She imagined her to be like her son. And Richard Ingham she had always disliked. "I do not like thee, Dr. Fell . . ."

It was something to do perhaps with Kate—that she did not think him courteous enough with her. His manner was always so cold (although to her, Sarah, when she met him—he was pleasant enough). Perhaps it was something to do with the time when, collecting birds' eggs for Paul—she had met him, up on the moor, and been told off roundly for stealing.

"They are only birds' eggs!"

"They are only the p-pride and hope of their p-parents. And I think it is too late now if you should put them b-back . . ."

Such nonsense. She smarted at the memory. The river, as she crossed it, was shadowy, darkening already in the winter light. She thought of her grandmother who had *risked her life* for an Ingham.

At home, she had a daguerreotype of that Sarah—her namesake. Usually it was in a drawer, but just this last week she had had it out, beside Edwy. I am very like her, she thought often. She had been told so, too. As to looks it was quite true. Character: she was not certain. But she *felt* like her often—for what that was worth . . .

"Ah well," she said cheerfully, the other side of the bridge now, passing the Kissing Gate, "Sarah Rawson 1820, perhaps you can tell Sarah Rawson 1877—should she marry Edwy?"

TWO

Disgrace or no disgrace, worry or no worry, the party must happen. First, all the preparations for it, and then—the day itself. And here it was. But as far as Paul was concerned it could have been cancelled and no harm done. He had not looked forward to it at all, even before the upset about Father.

Linden House, at the cost of much time and trouble, had been transformed for the evening. He had not had to do anything—had not been allowed to. The drawing-room had become a ballroom: later, about half past nine, the Leyburn Quadrille Band would play in there. The dining-room had been made into a drawing-room. Two rooms were laid out for supper. There were flowers and plants in every possible place—even Flo had been allowed a hand in decorating. The Inghams had sent a profusion of camellias and other flowers from the Abbey hothouses. (It was as well, he thought, that Francis Ingham had been invited.)

Now, sounds of the piano came to him where he had taken refuge, in the room leading off his father's surgery. If he could have put in his place at the party some stuffed monkey who would go through all the right paces—but the monkey would have to please Kate, who had done so much towards everything and who *must* not be disappointed . . . So, ten minutes in here only, a quiet smoke, and he would return.

Sarah found him there. She said: "You're a fine birthday boy—even Papa's braver. He is in there talking to the Tofts. Any number of his patients have come up to him—"

"What do they say?"

"Oh, what you might expect. Only better perhaps. How they've always thought well of him, and how it don't matter *what* he's done. Some of them—it is downright embarrassing. It is as if they cannot keep off the subject."

"Can you?"

She looked thoughtful. He liked her looks best when thoughts could be seen working over her face. She said, "We must live with it till the Assizes, till April. At least he has bail . . ."

"I never thought he would not—"

"Oh but yes"—she reached over and, taking his cigar, puffed it twice —"is this what you smoke at Oxford? Yes, it is refused if someone might flee the country, or is dangerous—"

Laughing, he retrieved his cigar. "You will smell of it still when Edward returns, and then what will he say?"

She said: "I want you to look happy—and you do not . . ." But it seemed to him that it was *she* who did not look happy. Possibly she had had words with Mother at some time during the day—but it looked to go deeper than that. He might ask her. But when he thought about it, he could not. Even in the name of their old friendship, which should have made it easy.

"It is the worry about Papa," she said. "Happiness is not really the order of the day . . ."

Her dress was a sickly colour, two shades of green in satin and silk, and not well cut. Although part of the front was open and quite low, it had been built up round the neck with tulle. Because of the mark. ("Well, it's the mark of Cain," she had said gaily once in childhood after one of their—rare—fights. But he remembered too how she had said, after accidentally in some game he had knocked her just under the chin: "You must *never* hit me there . . ." He hadn't asked why, but aged six, he had known. If he hit her there, she would bleed. Might even bleed to death. The blood, vivid, massed, lay waiting just beneath the skin . . . Only, over the years it had, just as Kate had told her it would, grown paler. Nor had it grown with her . . .)

"I don't think there is any chance now that Mama will come down— she said nothing to you?"

He shook his head. "No matter. Since Kate will manage it all—"

"She has not arrived yet."

"But it is all done—in order . . . she had the arranging of everything, so that now it may be left—and I am able to skulk in here . . ."

"You may not! We go back immediately . . . She was in a terrible mood—"

"Kate? Kate in a mood?"

"Darlingus stupidibus, no—Mama. Her headache was beginning. I think she knew she would not be able to come, and wanted to come *too much* . . ."

"That could be." He got up reluctantly, flicking ash from his waistcoat. "The first quadrille with me, darling?"

"Who else?" She took his arm as they walked back. "We have been much too long away—there will be trouble . . ." The piano sounded very near now. They were almost at the dining-drawing-room. She asked: "When do you expect your Oxford friend from the Castle, and *his* party?"

"Stephen? Ah, not till ten. At least ten . . . They must dine first."

In fact, odd and affected in behaviour as he found Stephen Malyon ("I shall bring a *party*—all sorts, a regular lucky dip, dear fellow. Such as my dear mama only could organise. She has not revealed all to me yet—but it could be, who knows? Ethiopians, Jews, even Roman Catholics. Sons of her friends, you know, *daughters* even of her friends . . . Can you bear that?"), he thought that his presence would make the evening less of an ordeal.

It was mostly older people in the room, sitting out. He would have to walk about and be congratulated. And to see Father too, looking pale but otherwise composed, that embarrassed him—although it should not . . .

A voice said, "I should have greeted you. I do apologise. I thought for a moment you didn't know me—it's Francis Ingham. From the Abbey." But said so easily, so humbly, that it did not seem at all reproachful. Paul thought, I was dreaming again. It was he after all who had wanted Francis (Sarah, who quite unreasonably disliked him, had not . . .). They got on well, and had shared Greek coaching on several occasions with the Reverend Staveley, here in Downham. Francis was much younger, but reputed to be very brilliant. He would go up to Cambridge next autumn.

"Shall you join in the charades later? I think games have been planned . . ."

"I think not. Rather not—" He blushed. Paul was about to tease him, persuade him, when from the corner of his eye, he saw *her* arrive.

Kate. Aunt Kate. His Kate . . .

"I love you, Aunt Kate" (I am three years old, four, five, six . . .). "I *love* you." Said so many times over so many years that you the listener may make now of the word "love" what you will. I know, Paul thought, what I mean by it now . . .

"Aunt Kate, you are so beautiful, why are you so beautiful?" She was beautiful but sad. He had been certain she was sad.

There was never a time when I did not love her, only a time when I did not know it . . .

She is my secret.

Nearly fifteen years ago and a summer expedition to Hawes, where

Grandma had lived, and then across the Buttertubs Pass and up to
Muker. It was to have been quite an outing. His parents—Father taking
a rare day off—Kate, cousin Robert Helliwell, Sarah . . . But it had
gone wrong from the start. First Sarah had a cold with some fever, and
said that anyway she didn't want to go. Then Mother had had either
one of her headaches, or Sarah's illness, but whichever, on the morning
she too could not go. Paul had insisted loudly that *he* must. And since
the fourteen-year-old Robert was enormously keen too, and Father
more than willing, they had set out—with Kate as mother.

He remembered little of the journey in the pony-carriage except that
they had climbed up and up. And that it had been hot, very hot. So hot
that they should have realised. But the storm warnings did not come
till too late. Of the middle of the day he had only blurred, happy memories. Kate, uncovering a jug, pouring amber-coloured liquid into a glass
for him. Thirst. Kate throwing her dregs out onto the heather: "For the
hobs . . ."

It must have been sometime in the late afternoon—and when they
were already not as far on as they should have been—that they realised
what was happening to the weather. They were very high up, crossing
the Buttertubs Pass, when the sky grew lowering. The Pass itself, with
far below its vast "Buttertub" potholes, grave of innumerable sheep,
was difficult enough. But with a sky about to open, and little light . . .
Father had begun to rue the whole expedition, and because Kate had
seemed frightened Paul had felt frightened too. They were still some
way from the village of Muker, but Father hoped to make the "Farmers
Arms" there.

And then, down had come the rain, and the hail too. To be safe on
the Pass they must keep to the centre of the narrow rough track—but it
was becoming more and more difficult to see. Paul was crying by now.
All of them were cold, wet, frightened. And then perhaps just half a
mile or so outside Muker—and they could have gone no further—they
came upon a small inn. Lights shone from it. It had seemed like Paradise. Father, shepherding them in, had said: "We are luckier than the
Holy Family, I think." And then, when he had spoken to the publican:
"There is no going back tonight. The storm only just begins. At home
—they must worry, I am afraid, until they see us back."

The frightened pony had been stabled. Then the publican's wife had
fed them all, wrapped in blankets: bread, soup, brandy. He had had
brandy in his milk. Sleep, they would have to sleep the night there, and
the publican was sorry he had only two possible rooms, both of them
very small. So Father and Robert had taken one, and Kate would sleep
with Paul in the other. He had been put to bed very early—as soon as

the bed had been warmed. Kate would come up when she had talked a little downstairs—she had made friends already with the publican's wife.

He had been asleep when she came up. He thought the storm must have quietened, but when she opened the door, he became aware of the howling of the wind.

There were no shutters and only the thinnest of curtains in the room. She had a light with her which she placed by the bed. He didn't move because he thought she would be more pleased with him if he slept.

"Paul?"

He didn't answer. She blew out the candle then, but it was still quite light. The storm was getting up very fast. In a fury the rain lashed the tiny window. She was undressing—he shut his eyes again and when he opened them, there she stood. She must have been lent a nightgown by the publican's fat wife: she had looked lost in billowing white. Then she had taken the pins from her hair. It had fallen slowly, slowly, down. In his memories now, it fell always more and more and more slowly. In the flashes of lightning it had shone red, like fire.

It was the thunder which came after that frightened him, and he cried for her. "Darling, what is it? It's woken you," she had said at once. "You are not to be afraid—" and she was with him in a moment —folding him in her arms, catching him up in all that stiff soap-smelling white.

Perhaps she had been going to fasten back her hair, perhaps she had nothing to tie it with, but she climbed in then at once, up into the high bed (he had had to jump). He clung still to her, while the world outside tried to come to an end. Thunder, lightning, hail—while he had slept safe in Kate's arms . . .

"My dear fellow—a thousand, no, *twenty-one* thousand apologies . . . How late we are. And the dear old Leyburn Quadrillosity already fiddling away . . . Dinner was *incroyable* and never, never ending and *then* there was the '51 Cockburn, a port *who* can resist . . ."

They had just been about to play games before supper and had given up hope of the Castle party. Now here: extravagantly dressed Stephen Malyon—the doeskin of his evening trousers dyed a newly fashionable dark blue, silk monogrammed buttons on his coat with its lightly padded American shoulders—and with him far more persons than Paul had expected ("They often look rather *bold*, some of the girls who stay at the Castle," Mother had said). Hopeless to remember names. Probably by morning they would not remember his.

". . . And such a *clatter* we have made, as it might be a troop of

Hussars . . . some I see have escaped already and are Lancing (I am a waltzing man myself . . .). We have here—Miss Kingsman . . . Mr. Millbrook . . . *Miss* Millbrook, Mr. Welling, Miss Childs, Captain Tandy of the North Yorkshire Militia . . . We have one absence only —Miss Straunge-Lacey, indisposed, alas. She was brought to Yorkshire by her brother—known to me in Town. Now, where does he skulk? Nicholas, dear fellow, over here . . . Rawson, I present Mr. Straunge-Lacey. Written 'Straunge' but pronounced 'strange'—*pronouncedly* strange I may say. All of them . . . Doubtless the jest is of Norman origin . . . Foxton Hall is their home, in Lancashire under the sign of the Red Rose. And Roman Catholic too . . . But did I not *warn* you?"

Stephen's victim did not seem to mind very much. He was a little older than himself, Paul reckoned, perhaps twenty-two or -three. Very tall, he made storklike Stephen appear awkward. But except for his eyes, an attractive brown, almost sherry-coloured, he was not particularly good-looking. He appeared distracted too, his eyes over-lively, darting about the room. He rose and fell on his toes. When Paul apologised for Stephen ("Mr. Malyon I'm afraid doesn't respect anyone—or anything . . ."), he appeared not to hear. Stephen said in an aside: "He has sampled the Cockburn to some effect, I fear. Another thousand apologies . . ."

The Lancers had come to an end. He saw that Sarah had been dancing with one of the Castle party. They came back to where he stood with Stephen.

"And now we are to have *charades,* I believe . . . How I *love* to act. Dear lady, dear Miss Rawson, I have volunteered for the principal roles. But first I have an errand to perform—you will excuse me? Rawson, dear fellow, I look so forward to the cutting of the cake. And your speech . . . Shall they hand you coffers full of your grandfather's gold?" He tapped Nicholas Straunge-Lacey lightly on the shoulder before moving on: "*Dear* Romanist . . . 'I mean to have a Baldacchino, Ah but tell me what you mean O . . .'"

There was a small sitting-room used by the apprentices for preparing and making their notes. A large chest had been carried in there, full of old clothes, hats, scarves, bonnets, parasols, boots, and props generally. It had been part of Sarah and Paul's childhood (and was now a source of joy to Flo and, more especially, Will . . .). This evening it was to be used for charades—although it was rumoured that the party from the Castle had brought also some props of their own.

Sarah, who did not really care for any party games, including charades—perhaps most particularly charades—had been delighted when

Stephen ("Rather Ridiculous Stephen," as she called him to herself) had said: "*You* are not to perform, dear lady, but to watch . . ."
Pleased with the order, she did not question it. Why bother?

Now she sat in the front row of the audience, firmly placed there by
Stephen. She had a Miss Millbrook, who was not acting, to talk with.
Further back she saw Aunt Eliza and Kate sitting together. Kate had
been dancing earlier with Papa (and how brave he is, Sarah thought.
No one from the Castle had hinted anything, not even Stephen—which
meant, wonder of wonders, they possibly did not know . . .). Aunt
Eliza, for once free of Grandpa, looked restless and out of place, as if
she wished to be back. Sarah saw Kate lean over and whisper to her reassuringly.

Dressing up was going on for the second charade. While they waited,
Francis Ingham brought the Reverend Staveley over to her. They exchanged nothings. She would have liked to say something brilliant if
only to impress an Ingham (I may detest, but they shall not think
themselves my superiors. Only she could not imagine Francis thinking
himself superior to anyone . . .). She liked Mr. Staveley: the little they
had seen of each other they had got on well. In his late thirties possibly,
and vicar now of Downham, he was a gentle person—bearded, with a
square face, and sometimes, she thought, too serious manner. His complexion was fresh, but his nose too big perhaps for good looks. She
knew that he coached Francis in extra classics and had been no mean
scholar himself.

He said now: "Your brother is not about, Miss Rawson—he does not
perform?"

No. *Where was Paul now?* She looked around and could not see him.
The party with a part-invisible host . . . She said as much to Mr.
Staveley.

Miss Millbrook asked: "Mr. Rawson is not a party man?"

"He doesn't care for charades—as a performer. That is why I would
have thought him in the audience . . ."

But he was not. As a child, though, given all the important roles,
he'd played them—perhaps because Mama had insisted: he was not naturally centre of the stage. (What torment they had been, those charades. Surely that was why *she* did not care for them now? Mama,
showing some of her rare animation: "Paul shall be my wife," she
would say, suddenly topsily-turvily enthusiastic. "I shall be Bonnie
Prince Charlie and he shall be Flora Macdonald"—or it might be characters from Walter Scott . . . But Sarah was always, as an afterthought,
the maid or the seamstress or the farmhand . . . She had burst out
once: "Well, Grandma Rawson was a servant anyway, so why not me?

why not?" And: "Precisely, just so," had said Mama, "you will make a
very good servant girl and shall have that part today. You play it to the
manner born . . .")

The second charade was about to begin. The first she had guessed
quite wrong—Miss Millbrook not at all. She had thought because in the
first part they had spoken much of "kissing in the springtime" . . . and
in the second had bemoaned the way someone walked: "His *gait*, my
dear, really, he looks as if he is being roasted on a spit . . ." (this—
Stephen), that in the last they would have shown "Kissing Gate . . ."
But it had been all the while: "cuckoo-spit."

Now they came on, dressed soberly as if for church (perhaps it *was*
"Kissing Gate" this time?). They carried prayer books. All the women
were men and vice versa. Stephen was recognisable if not by his height,
by his voice. A very fat lady, veiled and padded out, led the procession.
They grumbled. ". . . And it was so cold, my dear," came Stephen's
voice, "I was forced to keep my little hands in my muff, all through
the sermon . . ." The next speaker, she *thought* Mr. Welling, acting
very woodenly and reciting with a haste that showed he feared to forget: "Why-we-are-nearly-at-the-kissing-gate-see-here-is-as-usual-some-
lovers'-token-I-think-John-loves-Mary-look-at-this-scrap-of-dimity . . ."

There was a long wait before the second scene: of weary travellers,
trudging over the snow-covered moors. Drama of a heavy-humoured
sort. "There is an inn, *at last*. Have they room for us? . . ." "No room
at the inn?" A rosy-faced Stephen in a maid's cap, blobs of red on his
cheeks, replied: "No room for the likes o'you . . ." "What is this, and
what is a bonny lass like you doing working in an *inn?*" And she:
"You're nobbut a half wit. I'm your long lost sister . . ." "Blanche!"
"Brother . . ."

They ended with a tea-party. Sarah did not think it worth the wait.
And she had not guessed. Miss Millbrook thought it "churchmouse,"
and swore the travellers had feared a mouse at the inn. The plates at
the tea-party were quite full, which reminded Sarah that it was, thank
God, almost suppertime. ("I think I prefer *tableaux vivants*," whispered Miss Millbrook. "Were you at the Cole-Douglases last week?") A
tall and very padded lady with an enormous black hat complained bitterly of toothache: he-she wore a large bandage on the lower part of the
face, and sat with head bowed.

"And *Flora*, what would you like?" squeaked Stephen. "You have
eaten nothing. Could you fancy, say, a *muffin?*" The fat woman shook
her head. "With *her* teeth, it will have to be a very soft muffin,"
Stephen said, and leaning across, ripped the bandage off, knocking the
hat sideways at the same time.

It was Edward! Sarah's Edward! Immense white teeth beneath the little moustache, tight-curling hair, red face. "The word is *muffin*," he announced, to applause. And then was away from the teacups and standing in front of Sarah.

In a few moments there was a crowd round her. Miss Millbrook said, "Oh, *that* was the trick Mr. Malyon planned . . ."

But Sarah was not pleased at all. She felt shocked, and deceived. Edward had always had this childish side—but after more than four years' absence, to return in this manner! . . .

Now Aunt Eliza and Kate had come over. "Why, Sarah, but look— what a surprise for you, darling . . ." What a surprise indeed. Stephen, dressed still as a woman, joined them to be praised, congratulated.

Edward had hold of both her hands. His smile was confident, and as she remembered. His voice perhaps different. "Have I not *surprised* you? It was Malyon's idea. Maud was not allowed to come, she would have given all away . . . We docked several days early and I thought to surprise you anyway—I was in Yorkshire by this morning and about to call on you when I met our friend—and we hatched this little surprise . . ." Then: "Let me look—have you changed at all? Your letters— you did not half keep a fellow waiting for letters . . . Well, say *something*. An audience waits on you, and I am only here for five months, you know . . ."

She was polite because there were people there, and also, she did not know *what* to say. She tried to smile warmly, but she felt her mouth stiffen. She was faint too as if she had had a shock. She thought with horror: he is a complete stranger. I *cannot* have promised to marry him . . .

"How happy you must be," said someone.

"Yes, yes," she said. "After all it is *four* years . . ." Then, after a little, breaking away, she said: "Edwy, I must find Paul. I must find Paul and tell him the soldier is home from the wars . . ."

He had made his escape as soon as he heard the charades were about to begin. He thought: I can snatch another half hour of peace, then I will return for the last parts of it, and sit with Kate . . . The cake and the speech he could not avoid. (And, Sarah must grant, he *had* danced twice just now, a waltz and a quadrille, before he escaped. One with Sarah, one with Kate. He felt that rather more had been expected of him . . .)

He'd been only ten minutes or so in the room off the surgery, feet up, smoking again quietly, when he thought he heard a knock. "Yes?" Then: "Come in—" But there was nothing more. He lay back again, feeling cold. The room had had a fire earlier in the day but now there were only warm embers. Oxford in the *summer*, he thought suddenly, and longed to be there. Last Mayday, going off by himself, riding all the way to Wychwood Forest. Thirty-six miles in all, and nearly lost in the forest but *not worried*. As it grew darker he had heard nightingales. The trunks of the beeches had gleamed in the half-light. How I love trees. Kate is a beech . . .

He thought then that he heard a groan—then, against the door, more of a thud than a knock. Jumping up from the sofa, he made straight for the corridor, went at once to the door. Outside was a small passageway off the main corridor, leading to the surgery and dispensing rooms. In what little light there was he saw a crouching figure, in white. His boot, knocking against a fallen glass, scrunched it underfoot. Groans, and the figure heaved.

"What's this—what's up?" But the sounds—and the smell were unmistakable. Afraid of walking in the vomit: "I'll get a light—" He was back in a moment, and saw then the extent of the mess. All round the kneeling figure whose head was bowed, his chest still heaving.

"Oh, God, God . . ." He spoke through a mouthful of vomit. Paul put a hand on his shoulders. Between spasms the man turned, and as he lifted his head a little, Paul saw his face. Ashen white, the cheeks tear-stained, eyes screwed up. One of the party from the Castle. For a second or two he didn't have the name . . .

"Look out there—lean *right* forward . . . You're Malyon's party, aren't you?"

"Ah, God . . . Ugh . . . for the *greater* glory of God . . . Ugh, ah . . . No more . . . good boy—"

Paul contemplated the mess. My party. My coming of age. Oh, my God. At least the drunk—for drunk he must be—had shown some presence of mind, for hanging over the chair in the passageway, safely out of range of the vomit, was his black evening coat and tie. He was flailing his arms now. Paul was afraid he would fall forward into his own mess.

"Keep still there, sit back on your heels and I'll get you up—wait . . ." He fetched quickly two towels from the surgery and wrapping them over the man's shoulders, with difficulty he raised him up. He was like a dead weight—but mercifully seemed to have finished being sick. His voice was tearful.

"Never had drink before—that's trouble, thought was joke, eh? Don't tell R.O., can't hold it . . . lost it all . . . had fever, should be, should be . . . bed fever . . ."

Paul said, "We're going to my room to clean you up—take some of

your damned weight, if you can . . . Try. Make the effort . . ." They
were going up the narrow stairs which led up the back from the surgery
to the upstairs living quarters. Halfway up there was another incident.
". . . Stop, got to stop . . . ugh . . . Whoops, Barnaby . . ."

Just as they reached his room, Paul thought he heard his name
called, but although he stopped to listen he did not hear it again. He
could do not to be found now . . . He felt tired at the thought of explanations, embarrassments. Little noise reached them from below: just
the piano and a light babble of voices—the band would not be playing
again until suppertime. The charades, he judged, would be safely under
way.

"You're Straunge-Lacey—aren't you?" he said, the name coming to
him suddenly, "from Lancashire, isn't it?" They were inside the bedroom now. He pushed him into the wicker chair. "Finished? Want a
bowl?"

"N. F. Straunge-Lacey . . . must go Herr Baumgarten German class
. . . special, got to go to Jesuits' Feldkirch . . . Matric first . . . don't
like study long time ago . . . tell Father Purbrick . . . tell the R.O. . . .
bloody cold in study rooms . . . going to *pray* now . . ."

"Look, I'm going to clean you up. Pray later, eh? Plenty of time for
prayer when you're back at the Castle—"

In his room the cover was off the bed, the bed already turned down,
his nightshirt laid out. The fire burned steadily. It looked very inviting.

"Won't pray now . . . think want to piss, yes, want to piss . . ."

When Paul had fetched him a pot, helped him, then with cold water
and a cloth, cleaned up his face and hands. He tried then to unbutton
his shirt.

"No, *other* buttons . . . want to piss . . . better get down there, at a
party, you know . . . Malyon's friends . . ."

"I'm Malyon's friend—and it's my bloody party. You don't want to
piss again either. You just did." As he flopped again, arms hanging over
the side of the chair, Paul said, exasperated, "Look, if you want to go
downstairs again—*you have to let me help you* . . ."

"Yes . . . thanks . . . feeling rotten, mustn't sleep, don't go *bed* . . ."

The last thing I want, Paul thought, is this Straunge-Lacey asleep in
my bed. The sooner he could be got down . . . "I'm putting one of my
shirts on you—wait there—now help a *little* . . . there we go. A bit
broad in the chest for you . . . but all right . . . I'm just going for your
coat." Hurrying down for it, he met no one. "Sit up a bit, would you?
Now—rinse your mouth . . ."

"Look—don't know you . . . going to be a good boy, though . . . Nick
they call me . . . feel beastly ill, shouldn't like Rose see me . . . Rose

prays for me, all that sort of thing . . . Love God, love Our Lady . . ."

Paul had hoped the cold sponging and wiping would have sobered him up, but he seemed as incoherent as ever. Oddly enough, although he had not thought him handsome at all when first glimpsed earlier in the evening, looking at him now—being *forced* to look at him in fact— he saw him as that now: in spite of the red rimmed eyes, faintly puffy, and the face drained of colour. Although the features were irregular the mouth was well shaped, and the eyes—when they could focus—were as much to be remarked on. And had he not noticed them earlier?

"Think all right now . . . No—got to *sit* little bit . . . won't forget, been good friend . . . fool touch drink when can't hold . . . next time say *nolo* . . ."

A knock on the door. And then before he could answer, Sarah's head coming round.

"There—*found!*" Then: "But—what ever? Darlingus stupidibus, what *are* you doing?"

"You can just help me," he said. "This is my birthday treat . . ." He explained to her quickly. As he spoke, Nicholas was smiling at Sarah, at them both—looking happier, but scarcely more sober.

Together they got him downstairs, each of them taking one arm. He planned to hand him over to Stephen. (Even if Rawson wine-cup had completed the damage, it was Cockburn '51 the main culprit . . .) He did not feel much like supper, or a cake cutting and speechifying. He was about to say this, when Sarah remarked casually: "By the way, Edwy's returned—early. He turned up tonight as a surprise." She did not look at all happy.

"And by the way too, I don't think he knows about Papa yet . . ."

Kate could see, in Eliza's manner, the beginnings of worry about her father. Kate had promised that she would take her back to Hillside as soon as the cake was cut, but she looked restless already—distracted only for a while by the charades. She had always been earnest, had never smiled often—her sense of duty, Kate thought, had always been so strong—but now after years (more than fifteen now) of anxiously watching over Sam, she had forgotten it seemed how to play at all.

She had coarsened in looks as she grew older, the dark hair winged with white, a faint moustache, her features more pointed. She spoke now often with vehemence, as if every point were of great importance: rarely looking at the person to whom she was speaking. Jane was much gentler. Pale and now much plumper, she was concerned always for Eliza. Eliza's worries were her worries. Now this Christmas and New Year, she was away with the Helliwell family, and Eliza must be alone.

But for the party, Bessie Arkwright, the chemist's wife—who often helped out—would sit with him.

She said to Eliza: "I shall take you in ten minutes' time—it's only a short walk but I would not want you alone. For me it is different—and besides, I should like to see him—"

"At this hour," Eliza said. "He'd best be asleep . . ."

As they went to make their farewells, Kate saw Edward, alone.

"Where is your affianced one? Where is she? She was with you but a minute ago . . ."

He smiled. She had forgotten the large, very large white teeth showing now beneath the confident moustache.

". . . And what a surprise you have given her? I did not know you had such mischief in you—that you were such a tease—" But she had said the wrong thing perhaps, for he replied huffily: "Did I not act well, then?" He looked irritated. "And now, I have lost her already." He added: "She will have to be brought to heel . . ."

The conversation dried up. Kate excused herself: she was to take Miss Rawson back. He did not offer to escort her. That marriage is not made in heaven, she thought. It will be a disaster . . .

Eliza's face was twitching with the anxiety to be gone. As they came through the hall, Kate saw Francis Ingham in earnest conversation with one of the party from the Castle. He had his hand raised to make a point. Although so like his mother in looks, he at that moment resembled more his father. She thought again—what a fine boy he is: feeling suddenly a wave of tenderness for him almost as if he were her own.

Outside it was bitterly cold. The market square almost deserted, except for a few persons standing near Linden House (there had been quite a crowd earlier, to see the flares), waiting idly to watch guests departing. Leaning against the railings, at the end nearest to the Black Swan, Arthur Greaves stood, slack-jawed. He mumbled something. She supposed it to be "Good night." She gave a little nod of acknowledgment (I must never *show* my dislike, she thought).

"Good evening then, Mrs. Rawson—eh?" His shoulder in the moonlight looked exaggeratedly raised: "Good night to you . . ."

It was not like him to be so polite. She said: "Good night to you, Greaves."

Eliza pulled at her arm. Kate said, "I wonder he's not cold standing there—" But Eliza was impatient to arrive back.

"Please God, Father's sleeping . . ."

They heard the sounds before they had opened the door. At once Bessie Arkwright came hurrying through the hall. She clutched at Eliza, the other hand on Kate.

"If you'd not come. I were just about to send . . ."

"*Where is he?*" Eliza asked, clutching at her.

"In the kitchen—I shut door. I couldn't abide hearing . . ."

"Let me go to him, Mrs. Arkwright." In a moment Eliza had left them—hurried through, untying her bonnet as she went. Bessie Arkwright clung to Kate.

"I'll not be left with him again—there were nowt to do. After yon Greaves were here—it were all I could . . . He were in a right dander, was Mr. Rawson . . . calling, banging about—and he'd drink hidden . . ."

The voice came, loud, Eliza's low notes beneath: " 'The fathers shall not be put to death for the children, neither shall the children be put to death for the fathers: every man shall be put to death for his own sin . . .' "

"But why—*what was Greaves doing here?*"

"Mrs. Rawson—I'd never have let him in, late as it were too . . . but I thought it were rope talk. He said he'd to see him right away—and Mr. Rawson were just there, awake and not abed yet . . ."

Kate said patiently (how could anyone be so foolish?): "But Mr. Rawson has so little to do with the works now—"

"He'll fancy he does . . ."

"Maybe he speaks sometimes as if he did, but my husband—he has all the concern now . . ."

"Miss Rawson—she's never to ask me again. I'll not mind him more . . ."

"Just tell me what *happened*, Mrs. Arkwright."

A little mollified, but righteous too, she said: "I let him in, and the first matter . . . the old man were sitting quiet and he says, Greaves says, 'That'll be fine news about your lad, eh?' and Mr. Rawson asks, 'What's that, what's that?' Then Greaves, he says, 'Well,' he says, 'you ken what's to do—that t'doctor like to be up before his betters—and all along o'what he done to a lass . . .' And then Mrs. Rawson, when the old man says fuddled like, 'What's all that, *what's all that?*' then Greaves, he tells all . . . words he used, I'll not dirty my mouth . . . but he's there saying it all ower and ower, while's he's certain the old man has it . . . And *then*, when he'd left—I'd this. You can hear. There were no stopping him . . ."

"I'm sorry," Kate said. "I'm sorry you've had the upset. Miss Rawson will want to apologise—"

" '. . . for whosoever shall commit any of these abominations, even the souls that commit them shall be cut off from among their people . . .' "

The kitchen was in disorder. Half a dozen plates and mugs lay broken on the flagstones. An almost empty bottle, on its side on the table, neck over the edge, dripping. Sam, in shirt sleeves, gaunt, his eyes bloodshot, paced to and fro, shouting. He kicked the broken pottery as he went. When Eliza came near, he pushed her. Then, very suddenly, he collapsed in a chair before the table, legs sprawled out.

Kate said to Eliza: "It is Greaves's fault—I am appalled. I shall speak to Ned. He *must* not be allowed to interfere in our lives . . ."

Eliza said only, as she and Kate tried now to lift Sam: "I always thought him a clarty customer . . . I've no call now to think otherwise."

" '. . . for whatsoever man he be that hath a blemish he shall not approach; a blind man or a lame . . . or crookbackt . . . and ye shall be holy unto me; for I the Lord am holy . . . defile himself, he shall not defile himself, defile himself . . .' "

"Oh, dear God," said Kate.

Eliza said, "I shall put him to bed—he is violent only in his words. Once we have him lying quiet . . ." She wanted Kate to go back at once to the party. She could manage well, she said. She was used to it.

But Kate would hear none of that. Of course she would stay. It took a long time—and there was Bessie Arkwright too, to placate and see off the premises—and because of it she was late back at the party. So late that there were groups of people coming out, going home. A carriage was coming up the hill behind her as she turned into the square.

As she was passing the Black Swan, it drew up alongside her. A voice called: "Mrs. Rawson—"

Because she knew it, she did not turn at once—because of the shock. Richard Ingham had opened the door, and was stepping out now. She did not want to look. But he said, very stiffly and politely: "M-Mrs. Rawson, you walk alone?"

I have to see him in church, every Sunday, she thought. That is enough. She said, her voice unsteady: "I have been seeing to Mr. Rawson—Samuel Rawson. I go immediately into Linden House."

"It is that I am on the way b-back to D-Downham and thought to c-collect my son . . ."

She thought then that she might say: "He is a fine boy . . ." She wanted to say it, but she had begun to tremble—and in seconds the chance had passed. Now he was saying, "If I m-may escort you in?" his voice stiff, impersonal. The accompaniment to a common courtesy. And yet, he touched her. Fingers on elbow. Taking her arm. Face, voice, impersonal. And yet, he touched her. Once again, after more than fifteen years—his touch. Richard and she, joined together.

THREE

I measure every Grief I meet
With narrow, probing, Eyes—
I wonder if It weighs like Mine—
Or has an Easier size.

I wonder if They bore it long—
Or did it just begin—
I could not tell the Date of Mine—
It feels so old a pain—

EMILY DICKINSON

Richard, Richard, always Richard.

When did it all begin? Once upon a time, she thought, I loved to
remember the beginning. That day by the Kissing Gate, in the churchyard. The barn owl in the sycamore tree. Ned, the blackbird, the flowers
on Tarley's grave. Watching the water rush and froth down, the height
of two men. Standing and looking towards the gates of the Abbey, the
ruins, the mellow stone of the house beyond. And Richard and I—sharing a thought. That was all. And it was never the same again. I went
home that day with Ned, darling Uncle Ned. But I knew. That day by
the Kissing Gate, *I knew.*

When did it all begin? Farther, much much farther back. With
Sarah-Mother's voice: "You've to take lessons at the Abbey. It's Mrs.
Ingham says. Eliza, she'll look out your pinafores. We'd best . . ."

John, Uncle John, took me. And how afraid I was. Those peering
faces. I knew that I was something remarkable—I had been told so
often. And that I was fortunate too; saved by the merest of chances.

Saved to be taken trembling with fear up to the Abbey and into the schoolroom.

For the first few moments it seemed that they stared and stared at me. Henrietta was only two or three and had been brought in by the nurse for a fairy story. But Richard, who was my age, and Julia, they both gazed at me, wondering. Miss Hooper with the tightly curling hair, who came from Mrs. Burrows' governess agency (she told me that later. I thought at first that she had always been there, grown in the stones of the Abbey), she looked at me too.

The whole of that first morning Richard did not speak—and nor did I. Miss Hooper was quite despairing. Julia, nearly two years younger, spoke without cease. Richard in fact would not answer even when spoken to—I at least was excused because I had been allowed my first morning just to sit "and see what it is they do"—then when at last he tried to say something, he could not. The words would not form. When I was asked that evening, when Father said, "And how do you like the other children?" all I could think to say was, "He cannot make his words—" And then I laughed nervously, and Eliza said, "Oh, Kate, we must not—he cannot help such things. It is only something a little wrong with him, such as he cannot alter . . ." (It had been kind of her not to say, "And once *you*, Kate, you could only speak gibberish.")

He didn't talk to me for three whole days, and then when we were drinking our milk in the garden—it was a fine summer morning, Julia was making a necklace seated on Miss Hooper's knee—Richard, frowning, spoke to me suddenly. He began in a rush, "I have, I have s-s-some—" But he did not finish the sentence. Standing behind Miss Hooper, he pulled at my arm then and making a sign of secrecy, he beckoned me to follow him. We went round to the left, out of sight, to the stables and outhouses.

Up a ladder—and I did not fear, I followed him without fear—and into a small loft. Below us the horses stamped and snorted. Grooming one of them was a boy of maybe fifteen. When he saw us, he called out a greeting at once to Richard. And then a moment later, followed us up. Dick Newell—he shared a name with Richard, but he had been always Dick, it was he in charge of this place: Richard's Infirmary.

Dick took me at once for granted, did not even look at me curiously. He said only, "Mind ye feet now, miss—" It was dusty up there and probably dirty. A fledgling starling waddled towards me, beak open—then flapped his wings.

In the nursery and in the schoolroom there were animals: a squirrel, fiery red, bushy tailed, interrupting our lessons with his antics; a cageful of white mice that we fed with oats and peas through the bars. But up here in his Infirmary every animal was maimed or ill. It was his secret, Richard's secret . . .

There was a three-legged rabbit in a wooden hutch, nose twitching through the bars. A young tawny owl, huge headed, feathers ruffled. And what else? It seemed to me in the poor light that the whole place was a scuffle and a flutter.

I was afraid then, but Dick said easily: "He's lazy, that stare," touching the bird's head with his finger; it gave a harsh call. "He's after summat to eat—and he'll not bother wi' larning. Don't want to fly off—do ye, eh?"

I put out my hand and stroked it timidly. It was young, its body still brownish coloured. It called again, a creaking sound. Then Richard spoke to it. He didn't stutter. He said, "Fat *and* lazy, aren't you, Johnny Bopeep?"

Dick said then, "We'd a throssel, Maytime—hadn't we, Master Richard? Flied off, he did." He turned to me, "It's all t'young Master's, this is. But I've t'care of it—else I fed and watered there'd be nowt . . ." Then he began to ask Richard some questions, mainly about the baby owl. Richard answered him in a voice of quiet authority. He seemed to me then much older than his eight years, much older than I. And I had thought him, in the schoolroom, such a babe.

But it was when Dick mentioned Mr. Ingham, when he said to me laughing: "I'm surprised t'Master he's heard nowt—happen if *he* finds 'em . . . Happen he'll be better not told." It was then that Richard began to tremble. He changed at once. Dick didn't notice, but I did: Richard's hand gathering up hay for the rabbit, shaking, jerking. *I knew nothing then.* Nothing of the burn, the beatings . . .

Down the ladder again. "You'll be missed," Dick said. Back in the stable, he bent right down low and signed me to climb up, piggyback.

"Up wi' ye, miss, little miss," he said to me, and we rode as fast as could be round towards the corner of the garden, Richard running alongside and Dick calling out:

> "Matthew Mark Luke and John
> Hold me horse till I leap on
> Hold it fast and hold it sure
> Till I get ower t'misty moor . . ."

I didn't tell them at home. But Dick's aunt, she took in the washing for Mrs. Tofts and she said to me, "Our Dickon—he says he seen you, Miss Kate . . ."

Richard, Richard, Richard. I did not like Mrs. Ingham, Georgiana Ingham. No, that is not true. I liked almost everyone then and even when I was afraid, I did not *dislike*. And she was kind always, frighteningly elegant, with her little firm voice and her air of being somewhere else, belonging somewhere else—always on her way to or from. Julia and later Hetty running to her, pulling at her skirts. Richard standing hang dog—and then she would say, "And have you spoken today?" and she would ask Miss Hooper, "Has he spoken today?" But that was only at the beginning. He became less timid, he did gain confidence. And she cared for him, about him. Certainly she sought to protect him from his father—that frightening figure. Though *why* he frightened me I am not certain since he virtually ignored me, except once to swing me over his shoulder (alarming enough in all conscience . . .). Only once did he quiz Richard in my presence, and then I had thought claps of thunder would break—but he must have grown bored since he struck his own thighs, and not Richard's—and then walked away suddenly.

But *she*, really she was kind to me. "Little Irish girl," she would say often as if I were not a Rawson. When she brought in sweets, fruits for the others, there was something always for me. And exactly the same. She did not make a difference.

And that is why, perhaps, I was underneath deceived.

We were rivals in the schoolroom, Richard and I. Often I knew better. It was not that he could not answer because of his impediment, it was that he did not know. I would surprise myself sometimes by what I knew. History, geography, the tales of Shakespeare. Ned talked to me, there was so much I knew because he talked to me—he answered questions I hadn't asked, before I knew I was ignorant.

We were rivals—even now and then a spat. But we were friends. We strove for Miss Hooper's attention, to be first with her. Less was expected of Julia. Hetty was not yet part of the schoolroom. And he and I had the Infirmary.

In January we shared ownership of a fox cub that Dick had found in a hedge—the only one of the litter alive. He said their birth must have been on account of the hot summer and gentle autumn, and that the hunt had surely had their mother. I thought often that Miss Hooper knew our secret.

Richard never stammered when he sang, so we stood often with her round the piano. In those early days we sang, "The cat sat asleep by the side of the fire," and "My father gave me an acre of land, Sing green bush . . ."

Two years passed. He went to learn Latin and Greek with the Reverend Cuthbert ("He goes hunting," he said to me. "When I have the l-l-living and m-may choose, then it shall be s-someone who does not"). He was to go away to school, to Eton as his father had done.

Richard aged twelve, Tarley visiting the schoolroom, Catriona bringing her. Then Richard nearly thirteen and home for Christmas, coming into the schoolroom and saying to Miss Hooper, "Miss Hooper, may I watch awhile?" And I who am not a showing-off person, I showed off to him that day, that I knew French so well. There were few animals in the Infirmary and no birds—Dick had the care of it entirely while he was away. We went out together to look.

He told me that it was not perfect at school. They had scarcely enough to eat and must needs spend all their money at a shop called Joe Brown's, where they bought buns and lemonade and brandysnaps. And there were older bullies who put salt in their dinner beer; and a rough way of life which he would not speak directly of. He did not mention his stutter except to say, "I am m-mocked of course." But there was also one master at least who was kind to him, and showed him how he might use the library as a haven. So that although he was not quite happy it was for him better than home—since he had not there the fear of his father.

Hetty, six now, sang with us round the piano. And Richard too, a child again at Christmas.

> "Sing sing what shall I sing?
> The cat's ran away with the pudding string,
> Do do what shall I do?
> The cat has bitten it quite in two . . ."

Walter pawed me. Walter coming up behind me, that next summer, the fat pinching fingers on my waist. I cannot move—it is the stuff of my nightmares. Because Walter could not be escaped. He was there, in my little back upstairs room with the sky-blue curtains, in the summer evenings before it was quite dark. The creaking floorboard on the landing outside—and I had no key, and did not know how to ask for a bolt.

I did not speak, I was too ashamed always to speak, too afraid to protest. I did not know why he did it. "Dirty Irish," he would say, prodding me, squeezing my breasts—that I hardly knew I had—squashing the nipple. "Dirty Irish, aren't you?"

I said nothing, to anyone. Until, until Sarah-Mother forced it out of me, and I broke down weeping noisily, weeping and weeping.

The shame, there had been such shame with it. And then Richard— when I saw him I felt unclean, as if by looking at me he would know what had happened. That Walter, spitting on his hands first, had dug far, far up—twisting, turning, his jagged fingernails tearing, so that when later that summer I bled for the first time I thought it was *that*. Up and up and up, while I thought that the shame would kill me. *That* I could never tell Sarah-Mother. "You like it, eh?" he said. "*Tell the truth now*, you like it?" And then he set to again.

But he went, he was sent away; and I was safe.

I told Richard I had been ill. I said, "I have been ill while you were away." And what else was it but an illness? I did not die of it.

And all the while the end was there, waiting in the beginning.

The last time of innocence—it was in the graveyard. We found a savaged blackbird. And Ned came. I went home with Ned.

Why were we walking out? I think that Richard had asked that he might bring me home, for had not Miss Hooper set me some task? He was free but I had still to learn the Collect for the day; tasks must never be left undone. Then we gathered some daffodils from the garden, a few early primrose, a little bunch of violets, for Tarley's grave—and Mr. Ingham's. I had not said anything much to him about his father before, except that I was sorry. But then as we were in the garden together, something was said—was it about his return home for the funeral? And then suddenly he told me all, as we were gathering the flowers. My head bent so that I scarcely saw his face but heard only his voice—which had grown exceedingly deep, overnight it seemed to me who had not seen him since Christmas. He told me of the burns, the thrashings; it was not a long story but I had not heard it at all. I knew nothing of any of it—only that he had been afraid, that his father had been rough, fierce with him.

He said then, "You can s-s-see that it can only be better, school . . ."

We came up to the Kissing Gate (as a smaller child how passionately I'd wanted to swing on it, and Ned had said sternly, as if there'd been truth in it, "Them as swings on t'gate, swings on t'gibbet . . ." and yet little boys in defiance or ignorance, *they* swung on it). Then just as he would have gone up the steps to open it, we both turned at the same moment.

We were facing the Abbey. From where we stood we could hear behind us the crash of the force onto the mossy stones below. Nesting rooks cawed in the churchyard elms. Ahead we could see the Abbey gates, standing open, the ruined arches, ivy covered, and beyond the house itself, serene, mellow.

All his, I thought suddenly, *all his*.

And as if—what terror this, what joy—as if I had *spoken*.

"All mine," he said sadly.

He turned back. I spoke hastily, to hide my feelings.

"Would you rather not?"

"It was perhaps the m-manner of getting it—"

He had his hand then on the Gate. It creaked as he pushed it. I noticed on one of the lower bars a scrap of dimity tied. We went through.
The spiky flowers on the sycamore tree were just opening. On the bank
on our right, on the unkempt ground, there were nettle shoots, wild
daffodils. As we walked along the winding path, I thought: how good
that he should have all that—the Abbey, the land around, all that
beauty and grace—but not that it should have come this way, with such
suffering. I thought about *all* the suffering—Aunt Catriona that had
lost Tarley and become so ill that she must leave us, Uncle Ned still
sad, Richard who had lost a father—and what matter that he had not
loved him? He would not have wished on him the death he died. It was
very terrible, Ned said . . .

And then—it was after we had visited the graves—we came upon the
blackie. And Richard had bent down at once, the bird enclosed in his
hands. All else was forgotten. And then suddenly, seeing his head lowered, the tenderness in his face for the wounded bird, I thought that he
too was wounded and that I might yet heal him. It was as if I were suddenly no longer a child. *I knew then that I loved him.*

Then just as suddenly the moment was gone. Only seconds later and
dearest Uncle Ned was with us, and I was talking fast, fast—a child
again, leaving at once the country I had only glimpsed.

"Darling Uncle Ned," I cried, "darling Uncle Ned!" And the blackbird, the fledgling, it did not live the night.

I was seventeen and a half when I went to school in France, and
nearly nineteen when I returned. It was Mrs. Ingham's idea that I
should go, but Sarah-Mother paid for it with her money from the
Squire—the same money which sent Walter away. I was to be a governess. First to the twelve-year-old Hetty, then when I was no longer
needed there I would have the highest recommendations for a post elsewhere.

Miss Hooper wanted to live again with her mother, who was in increasingly poor health. Mrs. Ingham said, "Sound and pretty French,
good needlework, I shall expect you to pass both on to Henrietta . . ."
And my French *was* good, and the needlework I loved—fine drawn
thread embroidery, *point de Venise, araignée.* I even had lessons in
lace-making (Sarah-Mother was envious almost, a little tart some of her
remarks—just a suspicion: "*I'd* never those advantages . . .").

It was a shock when I saw Richard again. "Why *Kate!*" (He never stuttered over my name, never.) "Why Kate, how you have changed . . ." He too. It was not appearance, nor voice—though it was deeper still—but an openness, a confidence almost as if he *knew* now that he owned the Abbey. (But she had the power still, *she* was regent.) He was not to go to the University, although there had been talk of it: he had won two or more prizes.

Fifteen months away and yes, I had missed him, but only as I had missed everybody, *everything* to do with Downham. Ah God, I was homesick. "*Irlandaise, la petite irlandaise,*" they called me, because of my story. But I had become Yorkshire. I was Rawson. All through that grey autumn and winter in Bordeaux, the dusty spring and summer, I longed for home and fancied it never bad weather in Downham. The sun dappling the trunks of the beech trees (as if there were not beeches in France), doves in the Abbey dove-cot, the rustlings of the housemartins who nested in the eaves above my little room, new lambs feeding in the churchyard, the sighing on windy days of the trees by the Kissing Gate.

Above all I longed for Ned. When I wept at night I thought, dreamed even, that he came to comfort me. I thought again that I was small and sat on his saddle—I was his cockyolly bird. In my mind I played with the doll's house. I played with it from room to room— drawing the velvet curtains, making the tiny four-poster, sweeping with the miniature broom. I imagined and remembered the placing of every ornament, every piece of furniture. Signs all of Ned's love. I was a child again.

They invited me that first evening to dine at the Abbey. It was Julia's pressing, I think—Richard may have urged it too, but it was Julia and I who were then the easy friends. Companions in the schoolroom— Richard away for most of the year—we had become each other's confidante. When I left for Bordeaux she had said she would write to me, and had not. Now she said: "I have so much to tell you, so much . . ." Her life had changed while I had been away. Next year in the spring she was to go to London for the season. She had grown very tall, too tall her mother said, and very slender, with her father's colouring but her mother's features: in these she resembled Richard. It was the eyes were different—he had his grandfather's, the Squire's, very deep-seated, of a particular shade of blue (it was Sarah-Mother told me of them—by the time I knew the Squire they were faded, as if the colour had been washed away).

Hetty was allowed downstairs since I was to teach her. She had changed in the year, grown heavy and awkward, no longer a little child.

Throughout the meal, eyes narrowed, thick-browed, she looked at me with suspicion.

Mrs. Ingham was very gracious. In that strange room with its grotto-like fireplace, opposite me, a panorama blending Switzerland and the moors above Downham, we talked of my adventures, of Julia's plans. I told them of how Sarah had grown, and that little Paul could recite already his alphabet.

But I shook that evening. I *shook*. As if I had had some great shock and could not understand. I was not for one moment at my ease.

I did not look at Richard. I could hardly speak to him. And he, he knew nothing. We neither of us knew. What, after all, was there to know?

They were difficult those first months. The teaching went well enough, but I could not like Hetty—perhaps because I realised that she did not like me. I had not cared for her too much in the schoolroom before. Perhaps she was like her father—she had been quarrelsome, wilful, and sulked often; now she was petulant, difficult to deal with, sly even. During the actual lessons, she would behave quite well but at other times her dislike was quite apparent.

But I seemed to please Mrs. Ingham. Ours was a strange relationship. I caught her looking at me often. Then she would suddenly praise my work—as if that had been the thought in her head. A little before they left for London, she hinted that I would perhaps be needed for Hetty only till Christmas, or Easter at the latest. "You will want to be away . . ."

Julia, full of excitement and anticipation, made a great fuss of me. I must be shown everything—ball dresses, day dresses, silk, satin, velvet, a flurry of rich lace in the undersleeves, parasols, gloves, a fan opening into a water-colour of the Abbey. Hetty became jealous, but when I tried to include her, she repulsed me, going off in a sulk. "Leave her," Julia would say. "She is only a *child*. It is enough that you have the care of her in the schoolroom."

Richard was busy, or so it seemed to me. I saw little of him. When we met outside or were together in the same room, it was easy, and became easier. I thought that for him, I was probably almost family—but where was the *real* easiness we had been used to?

In hiding only. During late April there was a sudden spell of unusually cold weather. Ned became ill with his chest, sufficiently badly to be away from his work (and causing Sarah-Mother to say yet again, why could he not leave Little Grinling and come where she and Eliza could care for him?). I was worried—always concerned for Ned.

I came out of the Abbey one afternoon, cloaked against the piercing wind, to begin the walk home. There had been sleet earlier in the day and now, as I turned into the main road, a shower of hailstones came at me. I had my head down and did not notice Richard, until he spoke my name.

He was beside me with the gig, its leather hood up. He was just back from Leyburn, he said. "I shall take you the rest of the way home."

We spoke little, then as we came up into the market square he said to me, "Kate, you are worried—" and I said only: "Uncle Ned is ill. That is all."

But with that he turned the gig round at once. He said, "Then we s-shall go and see him—that he is all right."

And we did that. I think all the way to Little Grinling we talked without stop, and all the way back too. Ned, amazed, delighted, *happy* to see us, was found not to be so bad after all. "Nothing that won't mend," he said. And his spirits were good—I had thought to find him very low.

We sat with him for an hour perhaps—I was very late home. Afterwards I was to think that as we sat there he gave us in some way his blessing. Richard felt that too. It was as if in his presence that afternoon, we had both discovered something—the lost years, perhaps—and were never to be the same again.

After that it became quite the natural, quite the accepted thing that if he was there, Richard should give me a lift home. Soon, Julia and her mother left for London. Gradually, gradually it became natural too that I should stay longer and longer at the Abbey, that on the lift home I did not go directly. At home it was only necessary to say when at six, seven, eight in the evening he brought me back, that I had been helping with this, with that. Sarah-Mother did not mind. She was happy, I think, that I was back at the Abbey. I felt guilt only that I was often too late to help Eliza and Jane Helliwell with visits to the sick.

And so the enchanted days began. Warm weather, sun: all around the bridge, the Kissing Gate, the trees were in full leaf; aniseed-scented sweet cicely grew by the river-side. I would awake very early, before the light, and hear already the garden full of thrushes. The martins were building again under my eaves. At the Abbey the gardeners swept the apple blossom into baskets, but the trees tossed by the May winds shed as much again. In the meadow alongside, the buttercups were out.

We were together. And I could only wonder afterwards that no one noticed me—so bright of eye (always bright of eye. I caught myself in the glass, dazzled, dazzling). Hetty had begun to spy, even then. She said to me one day, "Why do you go home so late?" But when I gave her some easy answer, she seemed to forget about the matter. I thought it an idle question. In her lessons she had become much sweeter, unnaturally good sometimes.

So when did the real part begin, the *real* loving? At first the happiness was only that we were together, and able to be so. We spoke often of the time we had missed. And, we were always touching. It was not very much at first, the touching—hands held, or fingers tracing my features, clasping of waists, my bonnet off and my hair pulled down, kisses in my hair. Kisses, more and more kisses, of greater urgency. Then love —we used the word "love." "I love you, Kate," and I would say, "I love you, Richard." I felt as the spring turned into summer that a fever grew in me. More, more, more.

So that when we came to find each other's bodies, it was no surprise. And I would not have thought it one. It was as if by being with him all those years, knowledge had grown secretly. Touching, we only rediscovered.

But we could not be alone often enough, long enough: outside I was afraid always of discovery—imagining people concealed in the immature heather, thinking the lightest rustling in the bracken to be a footstep . . . It was not safe. And for that we must journey so far; no sooner up on the moors it seemed than the gold half-hunter must be drawn from his waistcoat—I would take it out with trembling hands, to find only minutes left, that should have been hours.

Yet we did not fear the servants. Dick Newell, head groom now and father of three, he was the only one who I thought noticed. But he was our friend, unspoken. For the rest, it was none of their business what the young Squire did (just as it had not been their business what past squires did . . .).

A day of rain, the first for two, three weeks, and Hetty safe with Mrs. Wilkinson, the housekeeper—a great maker of jams and jellies and candied petals, sent down frequently for us to taste. Hetty was allowed to help. That afternoon, we walked along the corridor from the schoolroom. Where were we going—hands swinging, longing to touch? I have no memory. But then turning the corner, coming to a door at the far end of the passage, Richard, unlocking it, said—his voice tight: "In here, in here."

It was the Old Squire's room—or rather, had been: now it was kept locked up, unused. I had been in there perhaps once as a child, to see him. He had been ill and had not known me. He had sat up fretfully in the great bed and I had wanted to leave. I remembered the painted wall: the same painter as in the dining-room had been at work, and the Abbey ruins and the house, with the church and the Kissing Gate only inches away, had stared at me as I waited to go. But unlike the other work, it had not been retouched. It looked now like a memory. The room seemed crammed with furniture. Porcelain candelabra stood on a huge table beneath the window. Beside the bed on a small chest was a bronze of a gun dog—one of his surely—pointing. There was an air of faded grandeur about the whole room.

Richard had the key from downstairs. "It is mine," he said. "You forget I am master—I am s-squire, and have all these keys." And we laughed. Why had we not thought before? At once in there, and he lifted me onto the bed.

"Ah, my darling . . . ah, *Kate*. Kate, I *love* you . . ."

We lay on the bed together. It seemed to me anything he might do, anything he might ask—it would be all right.

"L-let me." Such unbuttoning, such unlacing, that my breasts might be found. And then so gentle, so gentle. Where was my shame now— the terror I had felt when years ago Walter had crushed and twisted, with his "Dirty Irish, dirty Irish . . ." My chemise was unbuttoned, my hair was down, it fell over my face.

We were the first people to have loved. "Darling, darling, I love your hair—"

"I shall never have it up again, it will be there for you always, always." My hair lying over my breasts now and Richard parting it like curtains—and then our mouths exploring, exploring. Somewhere in the distance the church clock striking.

Five. "And I said I would not be late home. Aunt Catriona—I had promised, for Paul . . ."

"Then I shall t-t-take you there. At once."

Such a hurry, a flurry, the lacing up again, the buttoning.

Then kisses, yet more kisses. "Tomorrow, tomorrow." And I say: "You are not used to stammer with me, you had stopped all that, why do you stammer with me today? I shall kiss it away, every time you stammer—I shall kiss it . . ."

Days, weeks—I am not certain. They seemed to be ours, and endless. We were not afraid. We did not fear Mrs. Wilkinson even. She had the house keys, it was true, but why visit there in the afternoon? And Richard left his key always in the lock . . . When we went, we left always by the back stairs. Hetty thought usually that I had gone much earlier. It was easy to creep out by the stable entrance and be home in a roundabout way within half an hour. Our secret. Richard's room, at the head of the main stairs, always likely to be visited by servants, the centre of the traffic—and next door to Hetty: it would never have done.

"Grandfather," he said, "grandfather—was famous for women—"

"And you—are *you* to be?"

"I am to be famous for loving Kate. I shall be famous for loving Kate Rawson. No—Kate Ingham, Katharine *Ingham* . . ."

I said it after him without thinking, laughing. We giggled. We were as we had been years ago in the schoolroom.

Sometimes he knelt by the bed, and then he would bury his head in my skirts, his hand on my breast. He was near, so near where Walter had been. One day I wept. I began and could not stop.

"Love, what is it? *What is it?*"

His head, pressing in *there*. The memory was terrible.

"I cannot—Walter, what he did—I *cannot* . . ."

"But you can tell me—"

I told him so haltingly. He listened very gravely. I could hardly speak for the shame of it. I told him everything. I knew that he was angry—I had seldom seen him angry, and I said quickly, the tears still wet on my face: "But Walter is gone now. It is six years, at the least."

He said, "You will let me m-make it all right. I shall make it all right." Then: "My love, my little love."

They were the same hands which had held the savaged bird. It was I who was to have healed Richard, it was I who was to have healed his wounds. But it was he who healed me.

"Was it this, was it here?"

I have a fever, I thought. Flushed with fear, I *have a fever*. His hand lay on my thigh. Such undressing again, such unlacing and discarding of skirts. He parted my thighs. It is his hand, I thought, Richard's. I must remember, it is *Richard*. And all the while the memories came tumbling from head to crotch. I had not thought I remembered so well. I searched for distraction, I thought of the bird, and of how we had walked through the Kissing Gate—of the waterfall rushing down onto the mossy stones.

"Shall I—Kate?"

I caught my breath, and sobbed. His other hand held mine.

"Then I shall stop. You are not to be made afraid."

The traveller going only a little way into the strange country.

"Yes, yes, anything—yes."

"Shall I—shall I?"

The secret evil that had been Walter . . . All gone, all gone. This was the most loving search.

"Oh, but *yes*—" My happiness, I could not believe in my happiness.

"I love you, Kate."

Soon, too soon, Julia and her mother would be back. And not long after that Hetty would probably be excused lessons for a while, and I would not be required. Certainly his mother would have liked Richard to come also to London—or rather she would have liked him to be of the temperament that would have enjoyed it. But he was not—it was from her side of the family that all that stemmed. He was happy, happiest of all, in the country. That he was manifestly unlike both his father and his grandfather seemed to leave her sufficiently relieved.

Two days before they were to return, he gave me a lift home. We had in the back two of his dogs, a yellow spaniel called Perry and a very young terrier. We were both sad, and why not? But we had not spoken —by unconscious agreement perhaps—of what we would do, how it should all be. The afternoon before, lying there, one of us had said— what matter which?

"Shall we always be together?"

And the other had said, "Always. How ever not?"

Today, just as we came to the Kissing Gate, he drew up. In the meadow on our left the kingcups were out, but it had been very hot, very dry for over a week—already the grass was beginning to have a parched brown look. The river ran low, exposing the lichen-covered stone of the bridge.

An oxen-drawn waggon was crossing slowly, in rhythm with the hot afternoon, but otherwise there was no one about. Stepping down, then holding out his hand for me, he said—explaining himself, but suddenly nervous:

"Darling, d-darling Kate. We—"

"Yes?" I had jumped down. We stood before the Gate.

"Darling—I did not jest when I said 'Katharine Ingham.' *I did not jest.*"

But what had I thought? A practical person—yet I had not thought anything more than, *I love.* And it had been enough.

"Stand there," he said, "the other side of the G-Gate. If someone should pass—let them see, let them see . . . And now s-say, 'I, Katharine Rawson.'"

"I, Katharine Rawson . . ."

"'. . . pledge my troth to Richard Ingham—that we shall always be one and never twain that only d-death or ill will can part us . . .'"

"I, Katharine Rawson . . ."

"I, Richard Ingham . . ."

"I love you," he said, again and again.

Then we were both the other side of the Gate. We stood back, under the oak tree. Its leaves were tinged with russet. There, almost hidden from the road, we kissed to seal our pledge.

Then as we drove off again, the terrier yapping restlessly in the back, "Well," and he was blushing suddenly, "well, I have not *said*, Kate—I had thought we did not need the words—there are eighteen months only, and then I may do as I wish. I am you know m-master here, but not quite as I would wish. For a little, we shall d-do best to manage as we can . . ." Then he said in a rush: "But I expect we shall not wait—Kate, darling."

"She will not like it," I said. "Your mother will not like it. I am . . . a Rawson is not an Ingham—"

"But a Rawson may *become* an Ingham." He sounded very determined. "And *that* is what I shall do . . ."

The next day we exchanged locks of hair. His, I bound in my bracelet —where I had already little Sarah's and the first dark curls of Paul.

Julia was back. And so happy. London had been wonderful, wonderful. The praise she had had, the flirtations. Excitement hung in the air. Her speech was spattered with words I had never heard. Anything she had found satisfying was "filling at the price," or more often "fillupey." "Oh, but it was *fillupey*, Kate!" Her mother complained of it, but almost with pride. "Fizzing" was the highest praise—for days everything fizzed . . . Dark eyes alight, it was to me that she told it all. Hetty, glaring, hung behind.

She had a suitor—someone of whom Mrs. Ingham approved. It was certain he would follow her up to Yorkshire. He would be here for the shooting in August . . . "And oh, Kate, I am a little in love, you know, just a *little*—and when Mr. Whyatt comes his sister will be invited too and we shall be quite a party . . . I have made *so many* friends—"

Two days later Mrs. Ingham told me that Hetty had a little cousin coming to stay for one month, and that I should be free for at least that time. Hetty would be away for a little after. She said, "They cannot but be glad to have you home for a short while . . ."

I thought at first when I no longer came to the Abbey that I could not endure it. I scarcely listened to, did not hear what Sarah-Mother said. But the first week, one of storms and summer gales, passed somehow. Richard was to tell his mother at Christmas. Even if—and I did not have much hope that would be so—*even if* she were not deeply angry, telling her would alter our lives, make us public. "When she knows," he said, "she will watch us, they will watch us always. We shall *never* be able to steal away."

Just how it would be arranged at Christmas I did not know. But I had trust—and after that, only one year and *no one could stop us.*

I was distracted those days, could scarcely carry out the most ordinary duties: the sewing, the visits, the readings expected of me. And twice a day, without arousing suspicion, I had to walk out by the Kissing Gate.

Julia and her mother were often out, sometimes for the whole day. We had arranged that if it were free for me to come up to the Abbey, Richard should knot a plait of hazel on the bottom bar of the Gate. To the left for morning, to the right for afternoon. And if he were seen near his barn owls' sycamore tree, plaiting wood, who was to think anything? Once even, we met each other by chance there—engaging in fevered, hurried conversation, staying there too long. "I think I shall tell her," he said. "This is nonsense." For any real emergency we arranged then, we should leave a note, as cryptic as possible, in the trunk of that same sycamore.

Ah, that joyful day when, coming by early in the morning, I saw on the right the little plait of hazel. Oh, dear God, it was all I could do not to run. Hurrying home at once, praying: frightened there might be something, anything that would keep me there.

"I must go to the Abbey," I said to Sarah-Mother.

"But you had—"

"They asked—I met . . . Hetty is to be alone, with her cousin, and we are to go out together. It is a special request."

Acting unlike myself. It was not like me, this life of deceit. And the visit I had been meant to do, with Aunt Eliza—an old woman, the saddler's widow, blind and dying of a growth—I could not believe that I lied for this. But it was not just for myself: I could not bear to think that he might sit alone, waiting and waiting, while our chance passed. I thought little of wickedness then, had not thought even that what we *did* might be wicked. It was our secret—and so different was it from Walter, that it could not be *this* that people spoke of as shameful. It could not be.

At the Abbey I saw Hetty first.

"I have come to work on the embroideries. Take no heed of me—"

"Where shall you do them?" She looked at me curiously.

"I am not certain yet."

"Julia and Mama are gone out. Isabella and I, we should have gone also, but Isabella has a bad knee. We shall *read* together."

"Tell her I am sorry . . ."

"But Richard is about."

"Well," I said, as easily as possible, leaving her and beginning to climb the stairs, "then I expect I shall see him . . ."

The corridor was empty as we walked down it. Once inside, Richard, talking all the while, locked the door carefully and placed the key on the table. I too talked all the while.

Then we were on the bed.

"Ah, Kate, I love you, I love you." It had been so long.

"You made it all right," I said. I did not speak of the waiting, but of the touching—my gratitude: "You made it all right."

"And again—shall I again?"

Oh, but yes. Yes. I had no shame, could not remember now that with him I had ever had any.

"Your hair, I love your *hair* . . ." The kisses rained. The urgency. So urgent. Then stammering a little, afraid that I might be afraid, he asked if he could—if I wished to see *him?*

But why not, why not? Only, I had shown him so much—his hands were so at home on my, in my flesh—inside me: I was shy then, and eyes closed I let him guide my hand to where he was warm and hard beneath the cloth.

Then trousers off, under-trousers off—he offered himself to my hands. And trembling, for I thought it ugly and was afraid: "Ah, but it is beautiful," I said, and immediately it became so.

We lay for a while quite still. He grew even then beneath my hand. I was at peace: I thought again, anything he might do, anything *we* might do—it would be all right. *It will be all right.*

Then, "A little," he said, his hand on my thighs, "only a l-little . . . A love kiss, you see."

The lips he was to kiss were so wet, they opened for him where first his warm hand had been. "Only a love kiss," he said. Oh, but he throbbed at the entrance, resting there. Kissing. The sweet smell of him.

Then coming into my awareness, at the back of my mind—a rattling, a shaking. A clicking sound. It was I who heard the first, I who cried, "Oh, dear God—" Then, hand over mouth, pulling away, but even as I moved, knowing what would happen.

The door flung open now. Georgiana Ingham, standing there. She had on still her large round straw hat. Hanging at her waist, a steel chatelaine—and all its keys.

"Katharine! *Richard!*"

He had got off the bed and stood trembling before her anger. She looked to me like some avenging witch.

"I l-l-l-," he began. "I l-love—" Then bursting into tears.

"Love, love, love—what a story! Great heavens . . . Arrange yourselves at once—*both* of you—"

But we could not at first move. Her furious voice continued: "It is thanks only to Henrietta that I have had *any* suspicions, I am of such an innocent and trusting nature—see now how that *trust is abused*. I would not have thought, I *would not have thought*. And cheap, you make yourselves cheap. That is a disgusting sight, an undignified sight—" She screamed at me: "Dress yourself, cheapskate. *Get out of my house—*"

Richard said, "I am m-m-." He tried again. "I am the—"

"*I* am mistress, Richard, *I* am mistress. And if it is the word '*master*' that you are stuttering your way to, let me tell you that you are *not yet* master. You are nothing but a stupid witling, a young Maymoon—" Then: "*Get dressed!*" she shouted at me. "Your hair—"

Shaking, my knees near to collapse, with stiff fingers I tried to lift up, fasten back my hair. Half-dressed, I knew I was a ridiculous spectacle: my discarded hoops lay across a chair, my skirts over the bed end. But Richard, I shook for Richard. I could not bear that he should stand undressed before her scorn.

"And you, sir—you who are worse than unbuttoned. That your own mother should have to see—" Her voice rose again to a scream: "You are your grandfather's—indeed, yes. And he, unbuttoned"—she moved about the room agitatedly, kicking against a wicker chair—"in his dotage, in those last days, unbuttoned as *so often he had been in his youth*—you hear that, sir? Richard Ingham—who begins already to go the same way. It is not enough that you had a foul-mouthed brute for a father, but you must also needs take a leaf from your grandfather's book—who was always in search of some trollop—that could not keep his hands off a pretty servant—"

I could hear that Richard tried to speak, that the sentences would not form. He had his arm round me. I buried my head on his shoulder. We trembled together.

"She is cheap indeed. Let her weep, *let her!*" She was beside herself, "And now tell me—have you left your mark?" Then, "Tell me—" she pulled at my hand, "*has he?*"

"No—" I screamed back at her. Not knowing what she meant: "No, no!"

"*Please God* you tell the truth. Richard will tell me the truth, I *shall* have the truth. And you—but *you*, I never wish to see you again. *Out of my house!*"

She watched us dress. My humiliation was complete—because of his. Then, unable to endure the blinding, scalding tears, the matted hair in my mouth—and she screamed at us still—I rushed past her to the door.

I was still not fully dressed, my boots scarcely fastened, my hair everywhere.

Richard began to follow me, I felt his arm catch mine. But I shook him off.

"Not now, my love, not now. *Leave me, please.*"

I scarcely knew where I was going. I stumbled down the corridor. I did not care whom I met. The door of Julia's room was open, and empty. I took cold water from the jug and bathed my eyes. After a few moments a servant came in. She looked at me in surprise.

"It is—all right," I could scarcely remember her name, "it is all right, Susan. I have not been feeling well. I lay down in Miss Julia's room—lct my hair free. I think I may have a fever . . ." My voice trailed away.

"Ye mun tak care, miss—"

Indeed I thought when I returned home that I might have a fever. I told the family so—going at once up to bed.

I lay awake all night. In the distance somewhere a tawny owl hooted, again and again. Tossing on my pillow in the airless darkness, I lived over and over that afternoon—from the moment when the door had been flung open in fury. But of our love, of what we had done, of what was to become of us both, I did not dare to think.

He came to the house. I was with Aunt Eliza and Jane Helliwell. Although I had not slept I had no fever and beyond remarking that I looked tired no one had noticed anything. And Sarah-Mother was confined herself to her room with a chill.

His visit caused great surprise, and a little awe. Aunt Eliza's expression was dour, but reverent.

"Why here is Mr. *Ingham!*" And at once Bertha, the maid, was sent for wine, tea, cake. We were about to go out to visit a woman whose husband had died two days before, and had on already our outdoor clothes.

He said politely, "But you were about to l-leave?" I could see that he was distraught beneath the outer calm. He could not have slept either. Yet we did not dare to look at each other.

"It is nothing," Aunt Eliza said. "The delay, it'll not worry us."

In an atmosphere of great unease, or so it seemed to me, we made polite conversation. Richard gave no reason for his visit but that did not seem to worry Eliza and after about fifteen minutes she said that she and Miss Helliwell had best leave. "Kate may follow or not as she pleases." We were to be alone, without it seeming to be of concern to anyone.

We were afraid even to touch, sitting opposite ends of the room.

"Kate, darling, I have been—I did not know what . . . She has made such a sad b-business of it all. And m-means mischief. I could not, have not said yet—it was a folly to try and speak to her while she—I was afraid, darling, I was afraid . . ."

I too had been afraid. The ghost of her scorn stood in the room still, in the air about us. But gripping the chair arm tightly between finger and thumb, he said with an almost unknown petulance I had not seen since the early days of the schoolroom: "But I am master. *I* am."

Yes, yes, of course, yes. I was bruised, though. I could not explain how I was bruised. I felt black, blue, my skin thin, my hair too heavy for my head.

"You say nothing. You don't speak—"

But I could not answer.

"You are ill—darling?"

I shook my head. Violence had been done. And my own foreboding, I could not explain that. My sense of something terrible to come.

We sat awhile in silence. Then he burst out again, "In the night—I made the resolution. She cannot . . . I shall tell her it is so, and must be. That when I am twenty-one—that she may live elsewhere, but that I shall l-live with whom I please as *my wife. You* shall be Mrs. Ingham . . ."

But still I could not answer. It was too much, I felt too much love.

And then only a moment later, I saw coming up the path, Aunt Catriona with little Sarah. She held Paul by the hand, and her head was inclined towards him, saying something gently. Sarah had seen me seated by the window. She made little patterns with her fingers.

It was only minutes before we were all sat together. Paul was trying to sip his mother's wine. The children had come to see their grandmother, but since she was not well—then they would not stay long. And little Sarah would have it that I came back with them to see the story she had written, and illustrated with scraps. She was at ease with Richard, speaking out of turn, staring at him, earning a rebuke from Catriona. Paul clung to his mother's skirts. He did not like strangers.

Richard. And all the while I wanted to be alone with him, to be able to speak to him, for yesterday never to have been.

I did not know what to do when I got a summons from Mrs. Ingham. A servant from the Abbey brought it to the house. She requested that I come up immediately.

"It is about some arrangements only," I told Sarah-Mother. "They have people to stay soon—a suitor for Julia. It will be to do with that."

I was seen in the library. A room I thought of as friendly. But Georgiana Ingham's manner was not friendly. She said at once: "Well—and have you come to your senses, Miss Rawson?"

"I had not left them," I began boldly. I would be courageous. "Nothing has changed. Richard has spoken—" I hesitated.

"Indeed, Richard has spoken. *No*"—her voice sharpened—"do not look about you. Both he and Julia are from the house today. *Indeed* Richard has spoken. Such childish tantrums—we have had as if he were a small child again. Exactly so. As if my wisdom, a woman of the world, as if all that went for nothing. We have had 'I will this and I will that.' And all stuttered. It is a sad business."

When I said nothing, she repeated: "It is a sad business, *is it not,* Miss Rawson?"

But she had frightened me now.

"I don't know. I had thought—perhaps—I—"

"Now it is *you* to stutter, I suppose." Her voice cut. "And what do *you* suppose? You suppose that you may after all marry him—you suppose *that?*"

"Yes," I said simply, finding once again my courage. I had only to be brave until this was over. Just a little while . . . Her words could hurt, but they could not harm.

"You think perhaps that I object, that what I have to say—it is on account of—" she paused, "of lowly birth. You think that *that* is all?"

"Yes, I had thought that. From your remarks, I had thought that." My words came from a dry mouth. I thought that I must be brave and ask her exactly what it was she wanted of me. Why I should not immediately leave. Had I not been told never to come to the Abbey again?

"Since Richard has spoken—" I began. But at once she interrupted me. Her words flowed.

"You have nothing, nothing. It is a family of such vulgarity—I think you *cannot* know the derisive scorn, the mirth with which Jacob Rawson's pretensions are greeted! That is, when people bother, when they can *spare the time* to discuss it. It is pathetic, Katharine, it is pathetic—how I have pitied your family. Their chase, with money, after what cannot be bought. And *it cannot be bought*—do not deceive yourself. Old Jacob's every move has been to make himself further a laughing stock—I cannot think that in Downham the Rawsons are held in very high regard. And as for your sister-in-law—"

I said hotly, "I am proud to be a Rawson. I am proud—"

"Do not interrupt me, you dare to interrupt me! Ah, but yes"—she pointed her finger at me—"proud to be a Rawson indeed . . . Perhaps in your pride and your hot *Irish* temper you say just that. But—Katharine, *you are not a Rawson.*"

My tears of anger stung: "What is that to you—since you have despised enough already the Rawsons? It was Sarah-Mother, it was Ned whom . . ." My arms, held rigid by my side, in my mind's eye flailed wildly. With an immense stick I set about Georgiana Ingham.

"I say it with meaning, Katharine. For a purpose. You are not a Rawson, you are not, it is not *known* that you are of your adopted mother's family. Even that is not known. Who or what you are—that is not known, Katharine."

Pushed down, down—to somewhere deep below; dark waters engulfed me.

She said sharply: "You know your origins?"

"Yes." I added warmly, "I remember. I remember that I must have had a mother who loved me. And a father."

"You remember, yes. And what you don't remember—they tell you. I think that is true?"

"Yes."

"But not everything—not *everything*?"

"I don't understand—"

"That you are *foul*," she burst out suddenly. "That you are foul inside—that you were riddled with it. Disease, *unmentionable* disease. That you were nursed back to life—but that you may not, *should not* ever give birth to life. That you are—tainted. It is too disgusting to speak of—"

"Then *who has spoken?*"

She ignored me. "And it is you *dare* to wish to marry my son. To make bad blood run through the pure stream. Featherstone. Ingham. I have—"

"*It is not true.*"

"Not true when your own brother told me? Ah yes, a medical man has secrets. There are matters he may not say, may not divulge. But he was someone who—*at that time*, not only my doctor but also—I was his confidante. There were problems. I must listen, and solve them. So it was *he* who told me *that*—and that I may not tell. It is not spoken of, he said. I said, is she to marry then? I shall intervene, he said, it is no matter. But I, Katharine, I was to say nothing. I was never to speak of it. *Then*—it did not concern me!"

"*It is not true—*"

"Do not keep repeating 'it is not true.'"

But I had begun to believe. Even as she spoke I knew that I had always known it to be true. Walter had taunted me. "Dirty Irish." Her voice went on, "And it does not concern them, *they* are not concerned. *They* will wish you to marry, never fear. But I, *I* am concerned—"

I said, "I must speak to Richard."

"He is just now with his solicitor in Leyburn—more nonsense to do with what he wishes for you. We have had a *great deal* of his plans. But Katharine, do not think to speak to him of this. Do not tell him of any such matters. Foolish, he is foolish, reckless, he will defy everything, he will pay no attention—for the moment *he is not himself*."

I thought that I would run from the room, I thought that I would rush from the Abbey and hurry, hurry along the road to Leyburn. That I would meet him coming back and I would say . . .

But as I moved, she put out a hand as if to stop me. Her voice changed to a wheedling tone.

"Kate, you could not do this to him. I think you could not—I implore you, do not tell him. Pray, *do not tell him*."

"Let me alone," I said roughly. Blood had rushed to my head. I felt stirring in my hands the same energies as when I had wanted to set about her. I was afraid then to move.

It was as if she read my mind, for changing her manner again, she said coldly, as if she had already won: "I ask no promises of you. I think only that you will know where your duty lies. Your adopted family will at least have instilled Christian principles in you—a clear sense of right and wrong. You will know what you should do. It is your chance to be a woman of honour . . . But if not"—she lowered her voice—"if not, I shall make for the Rawsons such an unpleasant place that Downham will not hold them. I have the means. I am not without influence. You understand me?"

I remained silent. At least I would not say to her "Yes."

"I trust you, Katharine . . ."

I left the note in the sycamore tree. I said, "Meet me at the Kissing Gate tomorrow Thursday at four o'clock. It is better you should not try to see me before this—"

The clock was striking four when I saw him come. I think I had hoped, for a little, that he would not find the note. I had gone already through into the graveyard—I had brought flowers for Tarley. I had thought that there might be other people about, that I might have to make some excuse—that it might be necessary to express surprise.

But no—it was quiet everywhere. I heard the Gate open and shut, his steps up the path.

I came down towards him. For ten minutes or more standing by Tarley's grave I had been turning myself into stone. In the close summer heat, the sun appearing only fitfully, I had made myself a body of stone. And stone cold too. My face, my hands held before me—all stone cold.

"My love—" he said at once, his voice loud. Hurrying at the sight of me. He reached for my hand. I averted my head.

"Love—love, what is it? Do you cry?"

I could hear the frantic note in his voice. My hands were clasped tight—he could not have prised them apart. My head was still turned right away. I feared already that emotion would choke my voice.

I said, "It is all a mistake." And then repeated it. I had the words by rote: "It is all a mistake. I don't care for you at all."

"B-b-but Kate—*what is this?*"

"I don't care for you." I repeated it dully. My head still resolutely turned away. When I felt him touch my cheek, his hand on my shoulder, I pushed it away angrily.

"You do not seem to understand—I don't care for you. I do not love you, I *never* loved you. It is all a mistake. I have been foolish and mad . . ."

"N-never, you are never to say that. Kate, indeed you *must* be m-mad, darling. This nonsense. I cannot understand—"

"Then you must try," I said coldly.

But it was of no avail. My simple words—they were not believed. And I could not look at him.

Then he put his arms suddenly about me. In terror and longing I burst out: "Let me alone! It *cannot* be you are so dull of mind—that you cannot simply understand that *if* I loved, *if* I cared—I care nothing now. I want nothing to do with you . . ." I shook my head. The whole of me shook: "You disgust me. You disgust me with your pawing and your—to have seen—" the words tumbled over themselves in my terror that I would not be able to finish them. "And not just that, that you are so ridiculous. B-b-b . . . like a baby. That you cannot even speak properly . . ." Turned and twisted I used his mother's words, his mother's weapons. "I am sick, sick of you. And ask you only to go—"

The ice descending again. Now a shaking, trembling cold. He had only to touch me now—another touch, the slightest touch, and I would be undone. I said, "And now, *will you please go.* At once. Leave me in peace—"

I did not see him go. He said nothing more then. I heard the sound of his steps, the rustle of some branches. And then the Kissing Gate opening. Creaking. Shutting.

After a while, I walked very slowly back to Tarley's grave. There were sheep in the churchyard today. A lamb nearly weaned, ambled after its mother, as she cropped the grass between the tombstones.

I sat for a little on the grave. I looked at Tarley's flowers, wilting already in the sticky heat. The language of flowers: I thought through all my pain that I should have brought for *him* today, had I been able, briar roses. "I wound to heal . . ."

I need not fear now that he would come after me. I read once again Tarley's inscription. She would have been nine, almost ten. I wondered at that moment why I should have been brought back from the dead. Why, why? Tarley, the fortunate one. I thought even that. The quick and the dead. Tarley died. I am dead too, I thought. From now on, I am dead.

FOUR

Rain pattered on the courtroom roof. So heavy it might be hail. Just what one might have expected, Paul thought. Ten in the morning and it had been raining since first light. Miserable weather for a miserable day.

From where he sat in the gallery, above and slightly to the rear of the dock, he could see Father, standing now while the jury were sworn in. Paul looked at each of these in turn. In his mind he said fiercely: "He did not do it . . . *Kindly do not believe what you hear . . .*" Repeating it for each one of them. Except, he thought, they will have read about it: this is York, the Spring Assizes, and they are local people. Perhaps they have already decided . . .

Only he and Aunt Eliza were present. Mother had never intended to come and was in any case far from well. Sarah, who would have done, had been persuaded by Edwy to stay away—not without difficulty (Edwy had in fact taken the news quite well—hearing about it the day after the party. Possibly he saw himself as noble in some way . . .).

The Clerk of the Court: "Gentlemen, the prisoner John Frederick Rawson is indicted . . ."

At least the heavy rain had deterred some of the sightseers. Although when they had arrived, it seemed to him that half the population of York were seeking entry to the courtroom. A dripping, noisy crowd. Aunt Eliza, jostled, became even more grim-faced. And what was more, while they had been waiting in an anteroom, she had seen HER. Paul, who had been reading a book on Matabele Land (anything to distance himself), head down, had not noticed. But Aunt Eliza swore that it was the girl. "We shall see . . ." Breathing heavily, snorting almost, she had commented: "And as bold a piece as ever invented a fairy tale—which is all it is. No decency about her *at all* . . ."

Here was Mr. Sergeant Balfour, for the Prosecution: "Gentlemen of

the Jury, it is my duty to state to you the circumstances . . ." Dear
God, he thought, we are to have the whole story once more—and then
again, when *she* comes. We shall have to have it from her lips. Even if
some of it, a little of it, is true—then it is she has led him on. Invited
him. I know there are such women. And she is one.

". . . a case which has excited unusual interest, and one which as we
all know has been canvassed and discussed in newspapers and homes
throughout Yorkshire . . . it is one on which some persons might be inclined already to form an opinion . . ."

That at least is fair, he thought. In justice they should be reminded
of that. But as for the rest: he did not want really to hear of Miss
Nugent's distressed state on the platform of York station at eight thirty-
five of a January evening. ". . . and the words of the prisoner when
seen the next day—'I do not know what it is I have done. I cannot now
recall.' And this, gentlemen, only some fifteen hours after the event. I
put it to you that . . ."

He felt that people in the courtroom were looking at him as well as
at Father. He felt that they said, "There's the son. That's his *son*, you
know . . ." He was ill at ease, restless. And in one week, less, he must
be back at Oxford. A fellow, damnably stupid, who had chosen the
wrong subject (but no one at Marlborough had so much as suggested
even reading for a class in Natural Science Schools), who had left it too
late to change—who had involved himself in arguments about religion
until the small hours, had flirted with Anglo-Catholicism—and was now
in two months' time likely to be plucked—without a feather to fly
with . . .

But here now was a witness for the prosecution: the main one. A fat,
freckled woman in black bombazine.

". . . I am the wife of George Barnes, a messenger, of 14 Queen
Street, Scarborough. I had to change trains at York on the night of
the second January . . . a young girl . . . I see her come running up
the platform. The train had been stood already more than five minutes.
She hadn't her bonnet on and her hair was all about her. She was crying and calling. I was the first to her. 'Where is he?' she said. I said,
'Who's that, love?' She said, 'The doctor, the doctor—' I thought she
was maybe poorly so I said, 'We'll get a doctor to you . . .' There were
other folk about by then. I told her not to fash herself and that we'd
take care of her—but she became very agitated then. 'The gentleman
was a doctor,' she kept saying, 'where is he?' . . . I noticed then she had
a swelling on her lower lip . . . another lady who was fetching the stationmaster . . . I carry smelling salts as often as not but was quite without . . . She said then—'You *must* run after him—the gentleman, the

doctor who was in my carriage'—she'd grown very distressed—'I think he has not finished his journey—if you hurry, you will catch him . . .' And then she added, 'You will find that he is—' must I say the word? I would rather . . ."

"The witness must report the conversation exactly as heard . . ."

"I am sorry, sir. And then she said—'You will find that he is—unbuttoned . . .' She said this twice: 'You will find him unbuttoned . . .' And then she said—'Help me, help me, I have seen something I should not. He has tried to—' I would rather not . . . if I must, then . . . She said, 'He has tried to—in a certain place . . .' I am not sure I recollect now exactly how it was said . . . 'I have had a shock,' she said over and over . . . I should say that the front of her dress, it was torn at the bodice and all of it very disarranged . . . she had no coat . . . we took her then to the stationmaster—I think the constable was—"

The story seemed to have gone on forever. He did not want to look at Father, or watch him at all. *May this soon be over* . . .

Mr. Sergeant Holberton, Father's counsel, said only, "I have no questions to ask the witness . . ."

The time had come for *her* to appear. Now she was being called. The coughing in the court renewed. Sergeant Holberton was rustling his papers. Father spoke briefly with Mr. Bewley, his solicitor, over the front of the dock. A feeling of excitement. Paul thought: when she comes in, I shall not even *look*. Nor when she gives evidence. Let her notice I do not even *look* . . .

But he did. It would have been impossible, he told himself, not to. She was dressed very simply in black, except for her bonnet, which was cherry-coloured velvet shaped like a mob cap, over fair hair only just visible. He thought her features nondescript and forgot them immediately. (*If* Father touched her at all—I cannot think what he was about. Except that they say often it is these mouselike ones that provoke . . .)

Mabel Emily Nugent. "She *looks* a Mabel," said Aunt Eliza in one of her stage whispers. "*Mabel*—*Jeze*bel rather. I know her sort . . ."

"Tell us now, in your own words . . ." He thought that he would not look at her while she spoke. In fact he would not look at her again, if he could help it. He grew more and more distressed for Father. (And Aunt Eliza was no better. He saw that she worried now about Grandfather—she did not often leave him for a whole day, although he would have Miss Helliwell, and Kate too was coming over . . .)

To show his indifference to it all, he ostentatiously took a letter from his pocket. It had arrived last night, but would bear reading again. Absorbed in it, he need not hear what she said—in her cool little voice. Certainly she did not *seem* upset.

The letter was longer than he had remembered. It was written in a bold hand. The capital letter at the beginning had been illuminated, in red and gold.

Foxton Hall,
Foxton,
Lancashire

April 1877

Paul Rawson Esq., Sir:

"Wine is a mocker, strong drink is raging—and whosoever is deceived thereby is not wise . . ." Proverbs 20.

You must have been wondering how any gentleman—and alas, I was born to that estate—could be such an unconscionable time making his apologies (and returning your shirt, which our housekeeper will do under separate cover—). The truth is, and you may perhaps have guessed this, that *I do not remember anything* of my delightful evening at your home. That is not strictly true (I am not famous for truth—be warned!), since I recall *very mistily* certain kindnesses—but nothing about their author. I have a plan to remedy this. More of that later.

It is my very real feeling of shame which has dried up my pen these last two months (Bless me Father for I have sinned it is *three* months . . .) so that you must have wondered *a.* whether you would ever see your shirt again (and it is one of great charm—), and *b.* what sort of guests Malyon has for a house-party? The short answer to *b.* is that when in Town, he is quite omnivorous. A Straunge-Lacey does not stick in his maw at all, especially if a charming younger sister is part of the bargain.

Seriously, I have done such penance as you cannot imagine. It shall never happen again. I am such a person can be drunk just with the excitement of living (sometimes—at other times I dare not think how I am to *fill* three score years and ten). "Good wine is a good familiar creature, if it be well used . . ." *I never have before*—or rather I should say, I never had—except for some beer at school. And now sadly I can recall nothing of the famous Cockburn '51 (which *omnes praeter me* both enjoyed *and* digested). Malyon I am sorry to say, having acted the part of the Tempter, is not repentant at all—

He tells me that you come down from Oxford this year. I envy you a little. I am Roman Catholic and so—I lead in some ways I am afraid rather a restricted life. I was some time in Feldkirch in Austria—the Jesuits have a school there (I was first at Stonyhurst, not far from here)

—but that is not University. Both my mother and the R.O. (do you use that splendid term for fatherhood? The Relieving Officer—because *he pays one's debts* . . .) they think the family circle to be sufficient. It is large enough in all conscience—cousins from here to eternity and too, living near us—other Catholic families. I am second child of seven (mystical number) and second son. *"L'éspoir est ma force"* is our motto —and we go back unnecessarily far. Norman I believe. We have been here *much* too long.

In short I live a life of moderate ease and mental sloth in idyllic surroundings. Would it amuse you to reform me? Quite seriously—why not come here some day, and see all for yourself? I invite you—

Write anytime, and a carriage will meet the train.

I remain,

Yours constantly and repentantly,
Nicholas Straunge-Lacey.

He left the letter lying open on his knee. It seemed to have come from another world. Three months—had almost forgot the incident, buried in his mind with the party which he had not much enjoyed. In between, the Lent Term at Oxford had been and gone. The Straunge-Lacey shirt—somewhat disgusting: he thought he must have destroyed it . . .

". . . Mr. Balfour, you may not ask the witness leading questions . . ."

She had some relation with her, a woman in her thirties with a high colour, and a righteous expression. Paul saw that she watched Miss Nugent anxiously. She need not fear, he thought: *that* one is very self-possessed. He gazed around him, anywhere but at the box. He began to play his childhood, boyhood game of turning everyone into trees . . . Kate was a beech, had always been one—like the beautiful beeches fringing the Abbey lawn. Sarah, a blackthorn—lovely blossom, lovely fruit, but prickly . . . The jurors. He amused himself: a crab-apple, a weeping spruce, an Italian cypress, a laburnum, a hornbeam, a yellow poplar . . . And her, what of *her?* An aspen. *Populus tremula* . . . All that trembling in the wind, from a tree—not too tall—really so sturdy, so well able to look after itself.

"I object . . ." Sergeant Balfour said.

Father's counsel, Sergeant Holberton, cross-examining now: "I am quite proper—"

The judge (a purple-leaved plum . . .): "Mr. Holberton, if you have a part you must have the whole of the conversation."

Father had his head in his hands. Paul bowed his. I shall let it all wash over me. That self-assured little voice . . .

". . . Why should I not? I had a ticket of the first class . . ."

". . . Is it your custom to choose, select a carriage in which there is only a gentleman?"

"Objection."

"Objection sustained."

". . . I do not have a custom, I am not accustomed to travelling— alone."

"You had not travelled alone before?"

"Never."

"But you selected a carriage . . . may I put it this way, there are carriages, are there not, which are for Ladies Only?"

"I had not the choice—"

"What is this? No choice—"

"My brother accompanied me. We could not get a cab. When I came onto the platform there were perhaps only two or at the most three minutes before the train must leave. It—that carriage, was the nearest to us . . ."

". . . Miss Nugent, I must ask you, your behaviour when once settled in the carriage—"

"Objection!"

"I will try again. Let us see . . . You are settled in the carriage, Miss Nugent. The train is in motion. What did you do then?"

"Do? As anyone . . . I sat . . . I think—I imagine that I began to read within a few minutes of the train's leaving."

"A book of a *romantic* nature?"

The Judge: "Mr. Holberton, where is this leading? I am being very patient but—"

"If your lordship would be patient a little longer . . . I am coming to my point."

"Thank you, Mr. Holberton . . ."

". . . I am not now able to recollect the book's title. It would have been from Mudie's, and suitable for a journey. Possibly—I do not recall —something of Miss Broughton's . . ."

". . . something of Miss Broughton's? Thank you, Miss Nugent. A book then, of a somewhat sensational nature—telling of young girls compromised, of lurid adventures—"

"M'lud, I *object*—"

"Mr. Holberton, if you would confine yourself to the matter in hand —leaving the higher flights of literary criticism to those more competent, and perhaps more objective . . . Thank you."

". . . Miss Nugent, did you speak to the accused?"

"No."

"Did the accused then speak to you?"

"Yes. After we had been travelling perhaps some twenty minutes, half an hour . . . Yes."

"And what did the accused say?"

"He asked me, if I recollect rightly, where I was travelling. If I was going as far as York. And I said—I said then that I should of course have to, since I did not think the train stopped again before then—"

"You knew then that for the remainder of your journey you would have to stay where you were? He too?"

"Yes—"

"Mr. Holberton, *where is this leading?*"

". . . and what was said next?"

". . . that in fact I was going as far as Harrogate. He said that he too must change at York for Leyburn."

"Miss Nugent, did the accused tell you he was a doctor—a surgeon?"

"Yes."

"I see. *Thank you.* Now, could we have some more of the conversation—if it is within your recall?"

"I said then only—something to the effect, that I had thought I might miss the train—and that it was necessary perhaps to be one of the royal family or at least titled, for the train to wait. That it was not personal like country conveyances. Then he said that he supposed I was not titled—"

"You took him to be jesting?"

"Of course—"

"And the nature of your conversation after that?"

"The weather. This and that. Something I think about my brother, gazetted to India . . ."

Paul thought, I hate you. This story that we have heard not once, or twice, but it seems already a score of times. Although Mr. Holberton is *for* Father, I too would like to know where it is we are heading. We have witnesses yet, two addresses, a summing up—all this before it can be over . . .

But when, suddenly, it happened—it came all at once. Mr. Holberton was cross-examining still.

". . . and yet, the train had been standing seven minutes—some witnesses say ten—in York station . . . the accused could have been apprehended almost immediately, for the alleged offence. Is that not so?"

"Yes—"

"Why, if you were so distressed, did you not leave the carriage immediately, and seek help?"

"I—it was a question of—"

"We have heard earlier, have we not, of how you wished to *jump* from the window? Why then were you not at once onto the platform? If not in pursuit—then to seek help . . ."

Her voice, still firm, still assured, hardly hesitated at all. "Because I—because it is not true at all. Any of it."

"What is not true?"

"My story. It is none of it true. He did nothing. It is a fabrication—"

"Miss Nugent. Do I understand you to say that *there is no case?*"

The murmuring, the muttering—hissing even. Voices raised, heads turned . . .

"Order!"

The rain beat down still on the courtroom roof. Her voice wavered only a little. ". . . It was I—disarranged my clothing. The rest . . . my hair . . . my bonnet. The time that I was alone in the carriage . . . it was the last of the train . . . had been the first carriage when I arrived late for the journey . . . I wish to say . . ."

This case need never have been brought, Paul thought with anger. Father, Mother, all of us—we need never have suffered. Father especially . . .

There was a sensation still in court. Beside him, Aunt Eliza was making a snorting noise. He was afraid that she might leave the gallery—and make a personal attack. Thank God that she had not her umbrella with her . . .

". . . and these are your final words—that the whole charge, that everything you have said previously"—it was Sergeant Holberton, not her, who appeared flustered—"that we . . . that there was no truth in any of this?"

"No. None at all . . ."

"Miss Nugent, do you know what the nature of an oath is?"

"Yes—"

"Do you know what contempt of court is?"

"I— Yes."

He would have thought Father would have at least looked at him, or raised his head—or given some sign. But perhaps it was the shock: the shock of relief. But he had his head bowed still, his shoulders hunched.

"Is it possible that as a Roman Catholic you should not feel yourself bound? . . . a matter perhaps for your own Church . . . that you should have wasted the court's time in this manner, to say *nothing* of all the unnecessary and long-lasting suffering caused to an innocent man—a man whose whole livelihood depends on the trust and good will of his patients . . . the matter to be reported to the Director of Public Prosecutions who will decide what proceedings—if any—will be taken against you . . . mockery of the whole concept of justice . . ."

Except that her lip trembled, she showed little reaction to the telling off by the judge. I waste my time looking at her at all, Paul thought. May she be punished . . .

She had stepped down now. The atmosphere in the room was still tense and a little excited. Silence had to be requested several times. But thank God, thank God—it was all but over. Witnesses as to character, not needed now.

". . . and it remains only for me to tell you that you are a free man, and to wish you Godspeed. *The prisoner is discharged—*"

Aunt Eliza, collecting her umbrella from the room where it had been drying:

"The Jezebel, Paul, the *Jezebel* . . . And I said no less. There goes a bad girl, I said, did I not? To think . . . Mother would have turned in her grave. *Her* John . . . She wouldn't have stood by today and let the lass get away with it. *Jezebel* . . . And the way she stared at *you*, Paul, who had your head in a book. Bold. Bold."

As she picked up the umbrella, she was muttering to herself (she had not lived all these years with Grandfather for nothing): " 'And she painted her face . . . and looked out at a window . . . so they threw her down and some of her blood was sprinkled on the wall and on the horses, and he trod her under foot . . . and the carcase of Jezebel shall be as dung upon the face of the field . . . so that they shall not say, This is Jezebel . . .' "

FIVE

In everything that women attempt, they should show their consciousness of dependence. There is something so unpleasant in female self-sufficiency, that it not infrequently prejudices instead of persuading.

Their sex should ever teach them to be subordinate; and they should remember that, by them, influence is to be obtained, not by assumption, but by a delicate appeal to affection or principle. Women, in this respect, are something like children: the more they show their need of support, the more engaging they are.

MRS. JOAN SANDFORD, *Woman in her Social and Domestic Character*

In her dream she stood the far side of the Kissing Gate. Edward was outside, at the bottom of the steps, looking up. But it was her hands that clutched at the iron bars.

"Let me in," he said, but politely. It was his distant, rather mocking manner. She thought, in the dream: He is not really serious.

She clutched at the gate. She was almost shaking it. She said to him, "Don't come any further. I forbid it."

"You talk nonsense—"

"I forbid it." Her dream-voice was raised. Behind her the wind was blowing, lifting the canopied leaves. It seemed to be growing dark. He must have noticed that, for he said, "I have only come to take you home."

"Which home?"

He was endlessly patient, if mocking.

"Your home. Dr. Rawson's. Linden House. You are the surgeon's daughter. Sarah, *please*."

He came towards her. Panic assailed her as his face drew near.

"Don't dare open that gate—"

"But Sarah . . . Sarah, I am Edward, your fiancé." Those teeth—the mouth, the lips drawing back from the enormous, confident white teeth. The hair . . .

Her only safety lay in staying resolutely where she was. Her fingers clenched round the bars.

He said, "It is not for you to decide, you know. *You* have no say. It is for all, that place where you stand—it is for all."

"No," she cried, shaking her head, turning it away so that she did not have to see him.

"I have *authority*—" She saw his arm raised, then his hand near the latch of the Gate.

"No," she screamed, bringing down her own hand like a hammer, beating with clenched fist against the bars. Indeed he might not come in. And the more so, she thought, since she could not get out. *I cannot get out* . . .

"No! God, my God. No! No! Shan't . . ."

She woke, her gown bathed in sweat. Her arms, fists clenched, were outside the bedclothes. Her whole body ached. For a few moments she felt certain that her dream had truly happened, so amazing was its reality. She stared at the familiar ribboned wallpaper in an effort to convince herself.

There were sounds of life in the house. She saw that it was nearly seven. The servants were about. She heard her father's voice: he was coming round the turning by the stair. His tread was heavy, deliberate. She imagined that perhaps it should be lighter: that he should be lighter of heart. Had he not been vindicated? Perhaps for him the smirch, the upset, remained. Something stuck. And had he not said to her, "I am guilty," or words of that sort, as if all of it had had on him the effect of —as if it had made him feel that he had done *some* wrong. He feels, she thought, he *feels* that he has brought disgrace on us all. That he is indeed guilty of that.

In spite of waking quite early she was late down. But when she came into the dining-room, although the apprentices had left, Mama was sitting there still.

She frowned as Sarah came in—looked over at the grandfather clock. "What kind of time is this—to come down? The bell—"

"I never heard it." She thought: I had meant at first to apologise.

Mama raised her eyebrows. "What were you doing? You have not been riding?"

"Like this? No, of course. I have been reading—" (this eternal catechism, that I must be answerable for my every action).

Mama looked away from Sarah, fingering a letter beside her plate, turning the envelope over. "Your days are not very ordered. And they are very selfish. Reading is well enough—but since it is recreation perhaps you could indulge in it *after* work is done."

The letter was from Paul. She could see that. To change the subject and to avoid further conflict, she asked: "Does Paul have any news?"

"Possibly. He does not tell me of it, though. Here there is nothing but some religious matters—and references to persons of whom I have never heard. His examinations, of course, are not far off—he speaks of those. He hopes not to be—plucked, is that the word?"

Sarah watched her as she spoke. She saw her suddenly as having aged. Great bands of iron grey in the black hair: they showed below her ribboned breakfast cap. Her face had become heavy, her lips if pushed only a little more forward would be sulky. The expression was one of discontent? Of disappointment? She seemed to sag, as if all of her were dragged down by defeat. Sarah felt that she had only just noticed—that it had been since the trial, as if that had been the final dead weight that had dragged her down, down, down.

Once she must have been young, she thought. And then: of course her life has already been altered once before by a criminal trial. My grandfather. *What* a family we are (and then some other hushed-up business—a servant, the one who had murdered her child . . .). But at my age, Sarah thought, at my age, she was already a mother, *twice* a mother. And mistress of a house.

"Your trousseau," Mama said, interrupting her thoughts, "you do not sew very much of it. The wedding will have to be much more seriously thought about. Edward's mother has not—" Then as if forgetting what she had been about to say: "When do you see Edward?"

"He comes tomorrow."

"You see, his leave will soon be over and—"

The door burst open and Florence came running in. Kate just behind, carrying little Patrick, rebuked her, but gently: "You are too hasty. Aunt Catriona will be frightened."

Florence put her arms at once about her aunt.

"Aunt Cat, Aunt Cat—miaow for me . . . *Please*."

"Kate—my dear! Flo, darling, of course I will. A kiss for Patrick, then . . ."

The room was full of them, happy. Sarah kissed, and kissing.

"We are very early—we shall stay only a few moments . . . We heard, you know, that Will loves the school—he does not even mind that he sleeps away."

Kate was so beautiful. Sarah thought: She will always be beautiful. Even early in the day like this, hastily dressed perhaps, with Patrick pulling at her chignon, stroking her hat, even her face.

Florence said, "And I am to go to Richmond, to see him, to see Will, *aren't* I, Mama?"

"We shall call on Ned," Kate said to Catriona. "Patrick likes to see all the ropes—"

Catriona said, "And to receive a black look from Greaves—shall he like that? That is one of the unexpected gifts of any such visit."

"Ah, him," Kate said. She played with Patrick's fingers.

"Ned is too kind. Greaves should go. You know my views—John's views."

"Ned does what Mother would have wished," Kate said. She spoke gently still but very firmly. Sarah thought, Mama should mind her own affairs.

Patrick said twice, "Cake, cake . . ." and Kate said: "Flo has baked some moggies for Grandpa and Aunt Eliza—" She said to her daughter, "It will depend, you see, whether Grandpa is well enough—he is old and often some days is too old to see people. You understand?"

Then she turned to Sarah: "Sarah dear, you are very quiet. What shall you do today?"

Edwy stood in the drawing-room.

"You," Sarah exclaimed. It was as if, horribly, he had come because of the dream.

"Is that all the greeting I get?" He laughed. He sounded a little nervous. His teeth flashed white. "It is almost as bad as—at the party."

"Ah well," she said matter of factly, "at least you have not come hidden in a pie, with blackbirds or the suchlike—or disguised as a washerwoman."

"You would like it better if I did? No—say. Tell me now."

As he watched her: I don't care, she thought. Come how you like. She realised for the first time that it did not matter, none of it mattered —whether he came early or late, as himself or disguised, it did not matter. I don't care.

"Is it the surprise, then? Because I said tomorrow, and am come today?"

"Well, hardly, Edwy. I would not—"

"Then look pleased, dear, look pleased." Taking out his watch, he checked it against the clock. "You are three minutes slow here, I see." Then: "Our plans for today," he announced, smiling at her. "We are to ride out to the Falls, if the weather permits. I came over here on Dodger—you and I shall ride to the house together now. So—if you will dress up fetchingly in your riding habit—"

"That is an order, of course—not a request?"

"Of course."

"Shall *Maud* be there?"

"Ah, do I detect a—little . . . are you and my sister not the *best of friends?*"

"There is no love at all lost between us. You know that . . ."

"We are very frank today, are we not? I shall be equally so. *She* is very frank about you. She says that you are very clever: 'I am sure she is very sharp, your affiancéd,' she says, 'but she has no style—' "

"So I am to have *style* now? I could not care at all. *She*, of course, is pretty and piquante. Am I to aspire to *that?*"

"What is all this nonsense, Sarah? It seems to be quite the fashion for girls to be bold nowadays in their manner of speaking. It was *not* so when I left England. My mama has remarked on it particularly."

She would, Sarah thought. She knew that she was behaving badly, but she said only: "Edwy, I have always been bold in my manner."

"Ah—please, get ready to go out—*do*. Prepare yourself. Tell your mama." As she made a move to go, he added: "Poor Polly has just been posted as a defaulter at York—the evils of gambling, when there is not the wherewithal. He is at the house today, and in *very* low spirits. It will take all of Maud's charm to raise them. Pray do not *undo* any of her work . . ."

The rain streamed unremittingly down the windows. It had held off only until they arrived at Edwy's home. Now, half an hour after luncheon, they were still waiting for it to clear. The expedition to the Falls grew less and less likely. Maud, all blond curls, frizzed fringe, and sharp tongue (it is *she*, Sarah thought, who is the sharp one), was flirting with her Major. She seemed as pleased to have him in the same room with her as to be on an outing with him. Cissy had joined them while they waited, although she was not to go with them. She looked at Sarah worshippingly. Rather than sit on one of the chairs, she sat at Sarah's feet. Sarah had not seen any of them since the trial and dreaded some reference to it—knowing that she would find some barb even where none was.

Maud said now, looking out the window, "You are *always* bad, brother dearest, at prophesying weather—"

"Better," said Edward, "better than the Galloping Major there. He arranged once a whole day's outing in May—and the result was *snow* . . ."

Sarah thought suddenly, irrelevantly: this is not the life for me. It had become as difficult to pass the time here as when at home. Worse, since she was trapped in a large room with people who, it seemed, could only find something to say to each other when engaged on some joint venture. The planned expedition, with its dramatic scenery, would have been just that . . .

"The horses were very restless when I last looked," Edward said. "Thunder in the air?"

"Here's a little filly who's restless, eh?" said the Major, turning to Maud. "Champing at the bit, is she?"

Indeed Maud was the most restless and irritable of them, taking little bites out of everyone's peace of mind, disrupting the atmosphere whenever it was about to settle—afraid perhaps that a speck of peaceful dust might settle anywhere. When now Edward said, with an air of great finality, "I say—Polly put the kettle on, and we'll all have tea . . ." she looked over apologetically at her Major: "Polly, Edwy always *would* wear a catch phrase to death. It takes him so long to learn them, you see." And then to her brother: "Dearest, to say *that* catch phrase was already *vieux jeu* when you left for the Indies. Just because we have a Polly here does not extend its life . . ."

Sarah leapt then to his defence, but only half-heartedly, and only— she admitted this to herself—to spite Maud. The afternoon wore on. At intervals one of them would go to the window and declare that it was just about to clear.

"If we are not gone by three, *since* we are not gone by three, it is hardly worth the effort. Even for a much smaller expedition—"

They had exhausted albums. Sarah would have liked, whatever the weather, to set off somewhere. "What does it matter?" she heard herself say petulantly. "It is only rain." She felt a passionate longing to be *out*.

Then Maud had the idea of telling fortunes. Sarah received this idea with a sinking heart, knowing it would be dreary. She guessed that it was suggested particularly to defy Edwy's mother, who disapproved— she could remember her saying in her forthright manner: "No—it is only an excuse, my dear, for holding young men's hands . . ."

"Sarah, you may try your skills with Cissy."

"But Maud—"

"We must all sit very quiet. It is so important—tedious but *very* important, that we should sit absolutely quiet with the hand held in one's

own. Dear Polly understands and will allow it—won't you? Eyes closed
at the first. Edwy—since you have no partner you shall just sit and
gawp."

Cissy was pale and withdrawn: the hand Sarah held was so limp and
chill that, trying to keep her eyes closed, she kept feeling it slip from
her grasp. And she could remember so little of the lines of palmistry
that she feared it would all have to be an exercise in pure imagination.

The clock struck the half hour. Soon they might ring for tea. She
opened her eyes stealthily, and saw Maud's hand being stroked and patted by the Major—on his face an expression of foolish bliss. She saw
then that Edward was watching *her*. His look was quizzical and half-
amused, a little superior. She closed her eyes again quickly. He fancies
he owns me, she thought indignantly.

"Now, all open your eyes. Polly, you too, and we shall begin. Sarah
dearest, let us see first what you predict for little Cissy."

Cissy had coloured faintly. She looked sacrificial.

"Well, are you ready, Cissy?"

"Yes—Miss Rawson."

"Please, call me *Sarah*—"

"Yes—Sarah."

"Well—" (Well what? Travel, she thought desperately, perhaps
Cissy might travel out one winter if they were in Egypt.) "I see you in
a hot country . . ."

"*Marriage*," said Maud. "Everyone is interested in that. You are not
very skilled," she said.

"I did not know that I was supposed to be . . . Four children," she
said, "all beautiful. A rich husband, excellent health—a little trouble
here, about the middle line. A want in spirit, a tiredness. You or someone near to you is involved in some adventure . . ."

Eventually it was over. Cissy thanked her adoringly.

"Why am I left out?" Edwy asked plaintively.

"Oh Edwy, you have had so *many* turns—so many other times. And
Cissy is only a child. Now—for you, Polly."

The Major beamed. His moustaches seemed to turn up further.

"Oh, but what is this—naughty, *naughty*." Maud slapped his hand
playfully. "Not one love affair but three, four, *five* and at least two
marriages. And what is here?" She frowned: "You will go across the
water—no, it is not a cold country. You will meet some adversary—it is
not human. Tiger, boar, *lion*? Then—fame, recognition, some sort of"—
she crinkled her eyes up—"is this a decoration? Red ribbon, cross made
of Sebastopol gun metal. How exciting—or wait, yes, or it could be a
title. Major the Rt Honble *Sir* Lawson-Pollard. Oh, Polly dear—"

Edward said obstinately, "I should have a turn. It don't seem fair—"

"Ask Sarah, then."

"But she is—"

"I would not," interrupted Sarah. "I find it all ridiculous. You have made up what you please . . ."

Maud said, "You spoil everything. All our pleasure. You are such a *superior* person. And I do not mean it in the best sense."

The Major looked embarrassed. Edward said: "Here old girl—look, Maud, Sarah is almost family, you know."

"And that is why I may speak frankly. Ring for the tea, Cissy."

Edward said placatingly, "Polly put the kettle on, we'll all . . ." His voice faded.

They rode back together, she and Edward. The rain had stopped a little while before. Although the road was muddy, even plashy, the air was soft and fresh. The early evening sky was a watery blue, as if sunshine might break through at any moment.

Tea-time had gone well enough. Edward's mother had joined them and then it had been suggested they should all go to the drawing-room. Soon after that the Reverend Staveley had called. Perhaps because he was a gentle person or perhaps because the vein of irritability had worn itself out, the atmosphere became easier. And that in spite of Edward's mother.

But still she was glad, glad to be out, to be on the road going back to Downham. And it was, was it not, when they were on horseback together, that she liked Edward best—after all, had they not first met on the hunting field? If he admired her at all, it was as a horsewoman. Sarah, flying over a hedge. She looked well in a riding habit—the evil mark not alas quite hidden but certainly, for the moment, forgotten . . .

"I hope you were not too put out by Maud," he called from a little behind her.

She had been dreaming. "What is that?" she asked, reining in her mare. Then: "I expect it is because I lack style," she said carelessly.

He came up alongside. "It is just her foolish mood. She don't mean it . . ." He was for him very serious. "It will be different when we are married. I think you will find then that she is quite altered towards you. Everything will be different." He seemed anxious to keep her sweet. She felt only that she could not be bothered. All this business of Maud . . .

As they came up to the bridge: "Let us go the long way back," he said. "By the Abbey." A dog cart could be seen coming in the opposite direction—as it approached she saw that in it were Richard Ingham and his son Francis. Just before she and Edward came over the bridge, they turned the corner towards the Abbey. But they must have noticed the two of them, for almost at once they drew up.

They had evidently been fishing. There was tackle on the bench beside them, oilskins. Sarah's little bay mare was restless, backing, rearing, champing, head tossing. The chestnut in the dog cart rattled harness as if in sympathy.

Edwy said, when they had all exchanged greetings, "How brave that you made a day of it—we are only just out now, having waited all afternoon for the weather to clear."

Francis had flushed at the sight of Sarah. Richard said, "We have not done much—it is the idea of fishing rather than the act. And besides, it is early in the s-season." He smiled at Francis. "Also I have to confess that we spend most of the time just in conversation. It is g-g-good when a father and son have not the time to say all they wish . . ."

Sarah thought yet again, I do dislike him. Smarting once more from the memory of his reprimanding her—those birds' eggs of nearly fifteen years ago—she wanted to say: "I am surprised you should go fishing at all—that you should consider it moral."

Edward and Richard were talking on. She heard Edwy say: "I think Egypt, sir. We are not certain yet—the posting. I must be in London at least till the autumn."

Now Richard had turned to her: "And your father—he is well?" Then when she had answered him as politely as she was able: "Tell him we would like him to d-dine with us—very soon. When he has an evening to spare. I shall send word round." He added, "N-not work. Pleasure. For the p-p-pleasure of his company . . ."

And then they were gone. Sarah thought: he is just making an ostentatious show of being charitable to Papa. But Papa was acquitted. It is not needed. She said to Edward, "I am tired of that man's—of that family's *charity* towards the Rawsons. It is all nonsense. It is all a continuing thank-you for that rescue. My grandmother—she would have done well to leave the boy. By all accounts he wasn't worth saving."

"That is strong," Edward said, "that is strong, by Jove. Sarah, there is no need—"

She knew that once again she was behaving badly. She said, to ease the situation, "Well, I like his horse, if not him. That grey he rides out often."

The dog cart had clip-clopped away through the Abbey gates. They were just coming up themselves to the Kissing Gate. Suddenly it was as if she were inside last night's dream. The flavour filled her mouth, her nostrils.

"We stop here," she said, reining in her bay with difficulty.

"A visit to family bones?"

"I can't go on," she said.

"Sarah, dear Sarah. We can turn about. It is only five, ten minutes' ride at the most, and we are at your home—"

How like him to misunderstand, she thought. Then: but I am being unjust.

"The engagement—our engagement," she said. "I was referring to that."

"Ah, *that*. Well—but it is not long. We must wait only till September . . ."

Only till September, she thought. And then for the rest of my life.

The rest of my life. Rain glistened still on the Kissing Gate. Drops fell from the iron.

She spoke with difficulty. "I don't wish to—what I mean is, Edwy— quite simply, I would like to end our engagement."

"Sarah—" His mouth opened. She saw the teeth again. She thought irrationally, the dream possessing her once more, I must stay *this* side of the Kissing Gate. "Sarah—but what *is* this? And why here? Why now? Did Maud, or Mother—was it something this afternoon?"

She said firmly, "No, Edwy, nothing. Except that I don't wish to go on. That I release you. That I *don't wish to marry you.*" She had surprised even herself. Until she had spoken a few minutes ago, she had not known of her real feelings. Now she felt only the most enormous haste to be through with the matter. To be quite, quite free of him.

"I shall pay no attention," he said. "I did not hear you—that is all to it."

"Why cannot you take me seriously?" she said, anger growing in her. She dismounted and stood holding, stroking her mare. "I suppose you cannot imagine," she said sarcastically, "that someone somewhere, might actually not think it the most wonderful thing to be your wife—"

"If *that* is to be the manner of talking. If that is how we are to converse . . ." Now she had made *him* angry. There would be no stopping him now. He said, "Well, then—let me tell you that of course it is at an end. Perhaps *you* had not thought that it is not every man—perhaps not *any other man* who would have asked for the hand of a person so set up with herself, so—" He had remained mounted, and spoke to her as from a great height: "It is not just my sister who finds you difficult. Others thought it a great feat of bravery that I should have taken on such an opinionated chatterbox—what sort of an army wife would you make? You think you do me a favour. It is *I* who have done the favour. And—to have taken no note of that—mark." He hesitated over this. His anger seemed to grow and grow. In the distance, coming over the bridge, was a waggon with two or three people.

"Lower your voice," she said.

"I am not shouting. I was not impassioned. After all I have done—to have offered a secure life and my *name*, a not inconsiderable one, to someone so unfortunately marked . . ."

"That is not just," she said. She murmured it: "That is not just. I have not done anything to deserve that."

Suddenly, letting go of her mare, she stepped up and opened the Kissing Gate, almost immediately closing it again, roughly. She was not sure why—the pleasure perhaps of clanging it shut? of being free outside it.

The waggon was passing the end of the road. She busied herself with the mare's bridle.

"What do you do?"

"Oh fudge. It is no concern of yours . . ." She mounted again and then, turning the mare round: "I shall ride for a while, up on the moor. While the light is good."

He would not follow. She felt safe in that. But the need to ride off, to go away by herself, was overwhelming. She could feel in her head a great throbbing as of enormous energy crying for release, fighting for it. It was not words unspoken—for she had nothing more to say. It was only—it was *good*. On the lower moor, where it was grass, she would canter, gallop even . . .

Halfway there she remembered the ring, and other gifts. She would parcel them up. The relief, it was so great that it was *almost* happiness, made her light-headed. Her mare was light, she was light. Riding, riding, they were as light as air.

SIX

"But I have no idea," Paul told Kate, "I am without direction altogether. A fellow *should*, I know, be going somewhere . . . At least that
is how it seems to me. Only—I do not have to make my way. Great-
grandfather and the money, and all that—well, see how different, how
difficult it is for me—"

"It is not difficult at all, dearest. Only in your mind is it so. You have
been sitting too many weeks at home—you will not decide anything
there."

"Before, I had the University. I did not see beyond. *Dear* Aunt
Kate—"

He took up her time. He had always taken up her time. On how
many occasions, sitting in the big room of the cottage, had he not asked
her what to do?

"Why, Paul—you who might go anywhere! You could see the whole
world. And you have scarcely travelled, you know . . ."

He said (because nothing she suggested would be any good: he
wanted only to ask, not to be answered. Wanted just to be with her),
"Well, I would not want to go alone. And Sarah—"

"Sarah is not at all happy at the moment."

"Mother is still very angry with her over Edward. And finds her
something to do at every moment of the day. Not that *I* am in very
great favour since Oxford—since I was plucked, left without a feather to
fly with, as they say. The money is thought to have been wasted. I
spent too much time in religious argument."

"Well, you must talk, and what better time to do it than there,
where you have companions . . . And what of your friends? Why do
you not see them?"

"One is to be married, and thinks only of that. It is very sudden. I

shall attend the wedding, I daresay. Another goes to Jamaica. Another
—I really cannot recollect . . ."

"And the one from the Castle? The one with the rather odd
manner?"

"I hardly see him now."

It had begun to rain outside. For August it was unusually cold. They
sat round the fire. Will was out. Patrick, in his chair, had fallen heavily
asleep, cheeks flushed. Flo, her expression very intense, was threading a
card for her mother. She said: "Come and live with us, Cousin Paul."

And why not? My early self, Paul thought, that always wanted to be
here. All those times of sitting in the high-backed chair, watching Aunt
Kate. Telling her things—aged six, aged sixteen: "Let me tell you what
happened. I got into hot water, but really . . ." And she was on his
side, always. But when it was something he could not tell—perhaps
something hot and shameful—it was then he would play the trick. He
had this way of telling her in his mind, at night. He would lie there in
the stillness: remembering, feeling almost the time when he had seen
her in the candlelight, her hair falling down, down all about her, before
she undressed, before she climbed into the high bed beside him. And he
would think then that she was there with him again—in the bed always.
But it was so innocent, he knew he did not do wrong. Then he would
tell her, quickly, so as to have it over, whatever was the latest, most
dreadful shameful secret. *He would tell her*, and it would be all right.
The next time he saw her, it was always all right . . .

Flo said again, "Come and live with us, Cousin Paul."

"But it is such a small home, darling," he said. "Where should I
sleep?"

"In the stilt house, the stephouse. When, if we have ever a nurse to
live, she shall sleep there. *Will* will sleep there soon. *Please*, Cousin
Paul—"

He shook her off, laughing.

"Where shall I go, then?" he said matter-of-factly. "France? Italy?
Ah, dear Aunt Kate—*you* come with me."

"But of course," she said calmly. "Anywhere you please. Anywhere
but Bordeaux."

"Constantinople? Trebizond?" he pressed her, teased her. It was so
easy, to speak lightly—he knew that he spoke as a lover, and that she
did not know it: and that was half the happiness, half the pain.

Flo said, "I don't know Treb—Treb—what? Patrick doesn't either. So
you *may* not—"

Her mother hushed her. And it was in the middle of this exchange—

almost, he reflected later, as if Kate had thought for him—that he had the idea.

"I know," he said. "I have just thought. I know where I shall go . . ."

A few days before, thumbing idly through an illustrated magazine, he had come upon two drawings of Foxton Hall, accompanied by a short descriptive article. "The Elizabethan home of the Straunge-Lacey family . . ." Particularly stressed by the writer, however, was the *arboretum*. It had been planted in the grounds some sixty years ago now, and contained trees of more than usual interest. "Were it open to the public," the writer had said, "its paths would be crowded with lovers of the rare and beautiful in trees . . ."

At the time he had thought little more of it, other than to smile to himself in recognition . . . But then, talking to Kate, he had remembered suddenly the letter from Nicholas Straunge-Lacey—four months ago now. The casual invitation (". . . why not come here some day, and see all for yourself? Write anytime, and a carriage will meet the train . . ."). And he had thought: Why not? It will pass the time.

He wrote to Foxton the next day, and if there was any surprise, Nicholas' letter in reply did not show it. He sounded genuinely delighted.

"All the family is at home," he wrote, "save the son and heir—but we are unusually without visitors and I shall *rejoice* in the presence of one who is not: (1) a schoolfellow, (2) a cousin, (3) a priest, (4) in the pay of the R.O.; perhaps I should add (5) nor a female . . . I *had* thought of going to Europe but shall stay here and experience the unexpected pleasure of your visit. If you are seriously interested in natural history, then you will be *delighted* with the arboretum here. Did I speak of it? At other times there is shooting, and tennis, and even the *démodé* croquet. Toxophily was rampant once, but now seems all but dead (Cupid has perhaps gone into hiding?). Simple pleasures such as walking, hill-climbing—these await you. Our fells rival your moors . . ."

And then he had written: "P.S. Deep in shame, I have to confess I *would not recognise you*, I cannot remember . . . ('Fill ev'ry glass, for wine inspires us, and fires us'—with what? Never again. 'Looketh not upon the wine when it is red'—I had not theretofore, and *have* not thereafter . . .)"

Lancashire was first perceived through a blurred train window. Early on in the journey it had begun to rain: at the station it was still coming down, not heavily but steadily. There was no Nicholas. When he heard his name called out and found a coachman only, he felt almost slighted, unreasonably offended. He thought, I should not have come, I am not wanted. He was given apologies but no explanation, and was too awkward to ask for one.

The journey to Foxton Hall was to take an hour or more. On the way the rain stopped, and moments later the sun burst out, altering everything. The roof of the victoria remained up, but he could look out on a landscape of an unearthly rain-washed green: at great waterfalls, at birchwoods, at hillsides covered in fern. They drove through a small village, and then a little way outside it, a large Tudor house came into sight. He thought afterwards that he would never forget that first view, taking him by surprise—black timbers, whitened plasterwork, the long winding drive, the ornamental gardens, the lawn with its great trees, the small lake glimpsed on the left, and behind it all, trees, trees, blending, merging into the tree-covered hillside.

Stepping out into the courtyard he forgot for a moment his fear, his discomfort. Ten minutes inside the house and it had returned. He was to take a late tea with Mrs. Straunge-Lacey in her sitting-room.

When he had imagined her it had been, irrationally, as somehow fitting her name: that she would be lacy in some way. And the description fitted. He would in any case have known she was Nicholas' mother: she had the same tall graceful build, the same almost too long face and narrow forehead—hers, though, was heavily etched across—the same arched eyebrows. Strands of a chestnut brown like his could be glimpsed together with the grey hair under her lacy cap. She wore lace wherever possible, it seemed: on the fichu front of her elaborate tea-gown, and again on its elbow sleeves, which were edged with great creamy lace ruffles.

"You do excuse us, Mr. Rawson, that my son did not meet you? The illness is not at all serious—he complained of a weakness yesterday and today there is a raised temperature and some fever. A little later, the two of us shall go and look at him. You forgive us?"

No, but of course it was all right. He had not expected. Yes, he *had* expected, but . . .

"Milk, Mr. Rawson? I hope China tea will be refreshing after the journey—"

He wondered why he should have been afflicted suddenly with such a clumsy tongue, especially since she seemed to be doing everything at all possible to put him at his ease. After all the generalities, there were the little questions—but she did most of the talking.

"Your father is a medical man, I understand? *Such* a lot of good these people do in the world—*can* do in this world. My great-uncle was a much-loved consultant, you know, at Guy's Hospital. Not a Catholic, of course. I am a *convert*, you see, Mr. Rawson. Our Lord was very good to me—within weeks of meeting Mr. Straunge-Lacey, I found the True Faith. My family naturally were not pleased. There was a certain amount of suffering—gladly borne . . . You have brothers, sisters, Mr. Rawson?"

"Ah, a small family," she said in answer. "How—*homely*."

He had not mentioned Tarley. Tarley was not real. But in a few moments he found himself, indiscreetly he thought afterwards, confiding about Sarah and the broken engagement.

"How *wise*—" she said, over the teacups. Half of him wanted to laugh at her and the other to sit back and enjoy the luxury of someone such as this giving him her full attention; indeed seeming to like him.

"God's ways are very strange, but He knows best . . ."

Paul ate the thin bread and butter, and occasionally looked about him, when her intense gaze permitted it. The room was long and low: in one corner he saw a small alcove with a statue of Christ, showing outside his robes a brightly painted heart.

"The Sacred Heart watches over me, Mr. Rawson. My visitors are used to it. Some are even comforted . . ." The chair beside the statue was covered with a lacy shawl and what looked like two prayer books lay on it.

Then, when he was wondering if perhaps he should not go—and what he should do when he went—she rose and, taking his arm, led him over to the window.

"Nicholas has not told you anything about anyone?" She pointed out across the lawn, far below them, for it was an upstairs room. "Look," she said, "there are some of the family."

Two boys were bent over adjusting a croquet hoop, "Hubert is there, with Benoit. They are fourteen and fifteen, and go to school at Stonyhurst." There was a young girl with them, leaning on her croquet mallet, watching. Again, the same chestnut brown hair, this time heavily curled.

"That is little Elfrida. She is thirteen and at Princethorpe—the Benedictine convent, you know. I hope—the ground looks *very wet* for croquet. I would have thought . . . The older ones are mad for tennis now. They plead for an ash court. I am told croquet is quite *passé*, but it does not *seem* so. And I am sure that you, Mr. Rawson, will be urged to play *both*."

Her hand lay lightly on the sill. Below him the figures, which had been as if in a painting, began to move. There was the faint thud of a mallet. Someone called out. An older girl, walking slowly and carrying a small black book, passed just beneath the window.

"Rose. Ah yes, Rose. My eldest daughter, Mr. Rawson. I had hoped she would go with them today. But there—she would not. Hermione, our second girl, *she* went with the shoot. Just for the luncheon, that is. Hermione is seventeen and came out this year."

She was standing, still, at the window. "Rose comes from the chapel, I think. Our chapel, you know, Mr. Rawson, is disguised as stables. It was thought prudent in the seventeenth century when it was added on. I have married, you see, into a family who have suffered a *great deal* for the Faith. Not only at one time financially (you have heard of the Recusancy fines, Mr. Rawson, for non-attendance at church in the days of the Reformation, and after?) but also in person. One Christopher Straunge-Lacey was martyred in 1584—*I* think that he should be canonised, or at the least beatified. But he has not yet even the title of Venerable . . ." Her voice sounded far away, as if she were speaking to herself. Then she turned to him suddenly.

"Mr. Rawson, my daughter Rose wishes to enter a convent. I tell you this, in case you should find her at all odd in her manner. Some do so. But she has, I think, a *naturally* retiring disposition. She wished to enter immediately on leaving school but has been persuaded to wait till she is twenty-one—these are our wishes, and she respects them. The truth is, Mr. Rawson, that neither I nor Mr. Straunge-Lacey," she looked away from him again, "I—we cannot *really* wish this for her. I find it hard to explain since you must think surely, *sincerely religious* as I am, I could not wish anything better for her. But although I hope and pray, daily, that one of the boys *will* become a priest, I *cannot* feel the same about Rose becoming a nun. Her father shares my sentiments—even more strongly. It is the shut off, final quality of the life . . . In my case perhaps it is that I have not the Catholic *heritage*—but"—and she shuddered—"I am reminded of—burial, death." She drew herself up, then turned to him, her eyes glittering: "You understand, Mr. Rawson?"

"Yes." (Why should she confide in him thus? Why had he confided, even so little, in her?)

As she moved away now from the window—ready to dismiss him perhaps—he expected her thin hands suddenly to bless him.

"By the way, Mr. Rawson, I hope you don't *smoke*? Mr. Straunge-Lacey does not permit it at all . . ."

It was too much. All of it. He might have guessed that it would be too much.

They sat at the dinner table: the younger ones were down too, Elfrida in white muslin. He had been asked by Mrs. Straunge-Lacey if he would take Rose in to dinner, and he now sat awkwardly beside her.

While waiting to go down together they had made stiff conversation. She seemed to him very self-possessed, looking like none of the rest of the family (until she had turned towards him suddenly and he saw in her Nicholas' eyes—taking him aback completely, so little had he expected to see them in anyone else). Thinking she would be somewhat dowdy, he'd been surprised to find her simply but well dressed in cream-coloured silk, showing off her dark colouring, with ribbons to match in her hair and a heavy silver cross around her neck.

He was the only person not family, except for an elderly Jesuit, grey haired and bespectacled, who lived there as chaplain. Augustus Straunge-Lacey presided at the table, alarming Paul with his great jutting forehead and heavy jaw. He looked as if anger smouldered beneath, waiting to erupt at any moment. Hermione Straunge-Lacey (she who had not come to his party in January) had some of the same heaviness in her face, the squareness of jaw. Yet he could see that, vivacious, a trifle loud, and certainly the most immediately noticeable of them all, she would be generally found attractive. Sitting opposite to him she was dressed fashionably in pale blue satin, cut rather low, and amethyst velvet, with long ivory ear-rings and, it seemed to him, too great an amount of jewelled butterflies in her hair.

He did not like her. She said, but he did not believe her, how sorry she was that she had not been able to come over to Downham.

"It was the lightest of indispositions, but I did not think it wise . . . also I was not quite out, although I had been allowed to join the house party . . . I suffered I think from change of air."

"And now it is your brother who is ill," he said.

"*His* is not from change of air. He has been all the summer here. He is dull and goes nowhere—"

Elfrida interrupted from further down the table: "You *cannot* call Nick dull—"

Hermione ignored her. "Have you seen my brother yet, Mr. Rawson?"

"He was asleep," Paul said. Together with Mrs. Straunge-Lacey he had stood in the doorway of the bedroom. Nicholas, the bedclothes half thrust off, his pillows tumbled, had lain in a heavy fevered sleep, his skin flushed. He had been snoring slightly. "The *poor* dear," she had said.

Hermione said now, "And how tedious it must be for you, that you have come all this way—to see him. Nick has always something, if it is not a fever then"—she threw back her head—"oh, no matter. It is fortunate he is not the heir. Everard, there is nothing wrong ever with *Everard*."

"Ever Everard," chanted Hubert, looking up from his soup.

Beside him, Benoit chimed in, "Everard the *Ever Ready*—"

Their mother looked at them witheringly, but it was Augustus Straunge-Lacey who, silencing the whole table and thrusting his head forward from his very slightly humped shoulders, delivered them a short deep-voiced homily.

". . . and to speak when spoken to. You understand, sir? And *you*, sir?" Then slowly and methodically he resumed drinking his soup.

Mrs. Straunge-Lacey said in a bright voice, "Everard is in Switzerland. In the *Alps*. With three friends. He has been before and is a most enthusiastic climber . . ."

It seemed to Paul for the next quarter of an hour or so that he was bombarded with questions. It was as if they all suddenly took notice of him.

"Do *you* climb, Mr. Rawson?"

"Do you travel?"

"Have you visited—"

"Do you like—"

"Shall you—"

Except for Augustus Straunge-Lacey, and the Jesuit—one Father Bromhead—the only persons who did not seem to fire at him were two elderly people. One, a thin and large-eyed woman who trembled most of the while but spoke hardly at all, was addressed as "Aunt Winefride." The other, a small wizened man who looked as if he had been smoked or pickled or both, was a second cousin, he gathered—but called by everyone "Uncle Kenelm."

It was when the table had been cleared for the dessert that Hermione said: "Well, what shall we *do* tomorrow?" She sounded almost angry. "Should we drive over to the Thistletons, and suggest a *picnic*? Or—"

"Remember, my dear," her mother said, "that tomorrow is a *fast* day for some—the fifteenth is a feast day, Mr. Rawson, the *Assumption*—I think you are old enough to keep the spirit, Hermione . . ."

"My dear fellow," Nick said. He was lying back on piled-up pillows. "My dear fellow." He pushed the bedclothes restlessly. "You know I'm most awfully sorry about this—you should have come to see me immediately. I sent word."

Paul said, "You were asleep. It's good to sleep. I wouldn't have disturbed you."

He rubbed his nose. "Have you been horribly bored? Did my family bore you?"

"On the contrary—"

"Well, tell me then, what did you think—" His eyes were bright, fevered. "Sit here, come over here, there's a fellow and sit on the bed. No, here. Now tell me what you thought of Hermione? Is she not a stunning girl, did you feel any of her bite, her tongue, she can sting—if you are not on the alert, then she may quite put you in your place." He talked fast, breathlessly. Paul was not certain—for had he ever seen him in a normal state?—whether it was the fever or his usual manner. "The boys were there, I expect, the Brothers Grim—no, that is not just, for they are very jolly. And they are only schoolboys after all . . . Then the R.O.—what did you think of *him?* Did he speak to you *at all?* And my mama—you were closeted together for hours. Sybil is her name, you know. The wise woman . . . What did she say, by the way? Ah, and Elfrida—did you not *love* her?"

He wanted to know so much. It did not seem necessary to tell him anything, really. Paul found himself saying, "Charming, amusing, kind, very kind, pretty . . ." He felt ill at ease and that it had been a mistake to come. He was overwhelmed by them all (and yet, if he had been told then, if someone said now "You must return at once to Yorkshire," he thought: I would plead to be able to remain. To see more . . .).

"And Rose, my sister *Rose?*"

"I think I barely spoke to her, but—"

"Ah, there you have it! She scarcely says a word. She is so still, everything about her is so quiet. Her thoughts are quiet, you know. And deep. She is the holy one, you know. Did you realise that—that she was so holy?"

Paul said, "It is no surprise. It is an explanation rather."

"Rather! Exactly—but you have no idea how holy. It is no use for any of them—the R.O., Mama, Hermione, anyone, to make plans for her. She has her mind made up." He pushed at his hair. "I count on her, you know, to get me into heaven. I rely absolutely on her prayers. Miss Mouse, I used to call her. I stopped that only what—two, three years ago. Miss Mouse, Queen of the Rosebuds, *ora pro nobis.*"

Paul sat awkwardly on the end of the bed. He said, "I shouldn't stay with you. You should rest."

"The sooner I'm better and can be up and with you. What did you plan for tomorrow? Shall you join the shooting or are you for something quieter? Just as soon as I can arrange everything . . ."

"You mentioned an arboretum—"

"Our magnificent tree-garden. Grandfather's Folly. Of course, of course. And I shall escort you. There is a book, you know, in which all the tree names are set down and their sites and origin and so on. We shall look at that." He changed the subject yet again. "And the R.O.—I expect you *disliked* Father?"

"No. I—" He had begun to feel that in this catechism lay mines, traps, that he would be sent dizzy spinning into some dungeon of disgrace. The feverish chattering continued.

"His word is quite absolutely law—I didn't ask you if you smoked? That is quite quite forbidden, even for guests—he can smell it, you know, even if he should pass the bedroom door. And the maids sneak, I swear it." Then: "You are not sorry I invited you here? You will like it, be happy? We shall be happy together, I know. I must calm down—the light, it hurts my eyes. I have the most terrible ache in my head. I could wish that—what a nuisance it all is. Look, Rawson, would you—read, just for a while. Just to calm a fellow down."

"But yes. Read what? What would you like?"

"That pile on the table. You will see some poetry. There on the top, where there is a marker. Something of Mr. Swinburne's." Paul read:

> ". . . I shall go my ways, tread out my measure,
> Fill the days of my daily breath
> With fugitive things not good to treasure,
> Do as the world doth, say as it saith;
> But if we had loved each other— O sweet,
> Had you felt, lying under the palms of your feet,
> The heart of my heart, beating harder with pleasure.
> To feel you tread it to dust and death—"

Nick lay absolutely still. Paul, looking up, thought he had gone to sleep. His own eyes were heavy. He closed the book—it snapped shut. He had forgotten the marker and began to fiddle, looking for where he had been.

"I think I might go to sleep now," Nick said. "Your voice—I must thank you. I don't sleep with this fever. In the day, but last night not at all."

Paul rose. He thought that when he was in his room, he would smoke. He imagined with pleasure the smoke curling upwards, calming him, leading *him* towards sleep. When he remembered that he might not, he thought that instead he would kneel in front of the fire, drag on the cigarette there, and let the telltale smoke rise up the chimney . . .

"Come here a moment, Rawson." He had sat up. He flung open his arms, wide. Fever-bright eyes stared from the flushed face. "Here a moment. You may kiss me goodnight. Give me a good-night kiss. So that I may sleep." He caught hold of Paul's arm. Then drew him against him. The heat of the fever came off his whole body, from the skin, from the damp nightshirt. His hot cheek: dry lips rested on Paul's cheek.

"Thank you. And now I shall certainly sleep—Paul. May I call you that?" His voice was slower now. "I am of course known as *Nick*. You may call me Nick . . ."

He woke to pouring summer rain; the gutter outside his window was overflowing already. Looking out, watching the rivulets rush down the leaded panes, he saw beyond the lawn and the belt of trees, a forest of damp green. The faint flush of heather on the distant fells was darkened: the light from the rain lent the massed trees an almost eerie aspect. He wanted to explore, at once.

Sybil Straunge-Lacey was already at breakfast when he came down, and almost finished. She was eating a square of toast which she first weighed carefully in a pair of small gold scales set on the table before her.

"Today is the Vigil of the Assumption," she said in explanation— although he had not asked, "You will excuse those of us who *fast* . . . By the way, Father Bromhead is saying a later Mass at half past ten if you should wish to attend . . . It is such a *dear* feast day, the Assumption, and although it is not a dogma—that is, the Church does not *require* us to believe—I of course do."

"Believe what?" he asked politely, looking uncomfortably at the large helping of kidneys and scrambled eggs he had just taken.

"That Our Lady, Christ's Mother—that her *body* was taken up into Heaven. *Assumed* . . ."

It seemed to him reasonable—but he could not see why a fuss should be made about it one way or another.

He thought he would say that, and other things, to Nick. But when he went to his room, a maid was just carrying out a tray. Nick said, "Look, I'm very sleepy. Can you amuse yourself? Will you promise to come back and see me?"

There was no wind outside, it was a still, gentle rain, unending, it might have been raining from the beginning of time. He did not tell anyone that he was going out. Sybil Straunge-Lacey thought that he was with Nick. It seemed to him that it might be the best time to visit the arboretum, when he could be certain to be on his own. He wanted also time to think.

He felt alarmed, threatened, almost suffocated by them all. Wanted Nick to be up and about with him: wanted him to remain in bed, an invalid, leaving him, Paul, as free of him as possible. I do not know what I want, he thought. He was appalled too that in spite of what he saw as the essential ludicrousness of Sybil Straunge-Lacey—she *must* not be taken seriously—he should feel an attraction, a hunger almost for her certainties.

At first as he made towards the arboretum, he was followed by a plump, elderly spitz dog he had noticed about the house yesterday and that appeared now apparently from nowhere. He trotted at Paul's heels, occasionally stopping to bark, pointed muzzle lifted upwards. The arboretum was to the left, beyond the yew hedge which hid the kitchen gardens. Once in it he saw that it was larger even than it appeared.

He had entered by a greenway flanked with weather-worn statues. Dryads perhaps? Avenues of dripping trees seemed to lead off everywhere. Rain trickled relentlessly from his hat. The wide grassed bays were spongy under foot. Walking down an avenue of limes and elms, he thought that he might easily become lost, and found himself constantly retracing his steps to be certain. The house came into view again, and then was lost.

He was amongst oaks and ashes which from their age he supposed to be originals. And suddenly he was back at his old sport of seeing people as trees (he had not done so since Father's trial, when he had made *that* girl into an aspen). Nick is an ash tree, he thought, looking at one now with its upward pointing branches, its high domed crown, graceful, yet strong. Then, seeing the fruit hanging thickly, a wet shiny deep green, colour suddenly rushed to his face. The ash, which could not make up its mind—that was sometimes all male and sometimes female; that was sometimes, often enough, male with female branches.

The dog, still with him, shook its wet coat. If he became lost, the dog would know its way back. He wandered down a close, dripping avenue of crab apples and cherries, the edges grassed with lilacs. Coming out into a silver birch walk, he saw already that it was midday. The house was in view now. He stood still amongst the pale birch trunks, with their wet shiny black diamonds—and longed for Kate.

When he came back into the house, it was to be met by Rose and Elfrida. Elfrida, spindly legs glimpsed where skirt and boot did not quite meet, said: "Oh, you are a sight!"

Rose said, "There is no need for that," but smiling. Then to him: "I am sorry, Mr. Rawson."

Elfrida persisted, "He is dripping. Actually dripping—"

"The trees are dripping, you see," he said foolishly.

Elfrida took hold of his hand, "Come with us at once, Mr. Rawson. We must hang you up to dry."

They took him to the housekeeper's room. Mrs. Thompson was very fat with a round, pleasantly wrinkled face. She sat in the warm room, an apron over her bombazine. To Paul she seemed more like their nurse.

"That's right," she said, "get yourselves into trouble and come to Tommy for help." Her tone was affectionately grumbling. Paul she treated as if he were one of the family, hanging up his wet clothing and scolding him at the same time, pushing him towards the fire.

Rose said, "The doctor is calling about Nicholas. We don't think it too serious."

"Well, I prayed for him—if old Tommy's prayers are any good. I daresay God likes them well enough."

"He likes them very much," Elfrida said. "So much that Nick has already said he feels much better—or rather that he feels that *soon* he will feel better . . ." Paul watched her nose wrinkle. It was dusted with freckles.

Rose said, "Mr. Rawson, where is poor Fritz-dog? He was with you. And was *so* wet . . ."

Niggling at the back of his mind was a worry, which had come to him suddenly in the warm room. He wondered if they knew of the court case, Father's trial, the scandal.

Oddly enough it was Nick who broached the subject, that afternoon, asking: "What became of that dreadful business—you hinted in a letter?" But when he had told him, "Nothing will have been seen here," he said. "The R.O. would not remember a name anyway. And he cuts out from the newspaper, before the ladies should see it, anything with the faintest whiff of impropriety. If *The Times* offend thee, pluck out its pages . . ." His eyes narrowed suddenly. "Of course, although your father was vindicated and all that, I should not have liked the girls to see it—especially Rose." He sipped from a drink by his bedside. He asked suddenly, "Are you angry—with the girl in the case?"

"I was. Now it seems all past. I was made angry again when I learned that *she* is not to be prosecuted. That is not right. My father will never be the same again. He is a wounded man. He behaved from the first, you know, almost as if he had no chance. As if he were guilty."

"Perhaps he was—"

"Well, scarcely. After her admission."

"I'm sorry, I'm sorry, dear fellow. Dear Paul. I make these idle remarks—I search *excitement*, you see." Then he changed the subject quickly: "What is it to be this afternoon? Will someone not play billiards with you? There is a room off the hall. Or battledore, shuttlecock —that you may do indoors. Elfrida would enjoy that. Do you do archery? Tomorrow if the weather clears—Rose is very talented, when she can be persuaded to compete. Hermione was quite jealous at one time. Now she has other interests."

"They are not very alike," Paul said, "the two of them."

"Not at all alike. The Wise Woman is afraid for both of them. I am certain of that."

"But why afraid?"

"She is afraid that neither will marry. Rose, for excess of holiness. Hermione, through complete lack of seriousness—she is like me in that regard . . ."

He dreamed that night that he and Kate were walking together. They were going to the churchyard; he supported her arm; it was about to rain, the sky dark and lowering. He knew they must hurry. "To be safe, darling," he said, "we must reach the Kissing Gate." In the dream he half pushed, half dragged her along; she went where he wished, she needed him so much. In terror they reached the Gate just in time as the heavens opened. Quick, quick, he must get her past, through the Gate, and into safety. The narrowness of their escape made him tremble with relief. He woke to shame.

The weather changed that day, the sun beating down fiercely as if in celebration of the Assumption. Dragged there by a laughing Elfrida, he went to Mass in the stables-chapel. Nick teased him about it later. That evening and the evenings after, he went there too for family prayers at half past nine. They recited the Litany of Jesus and a decade of the rosary together with an examination of conscience.

In some strange way, he felt himself to have grown completely at home. And yet he was the stranger, the odd man out. They were so fiercely, so self-satisfyingly Catholic. He was pitied—although never in words. Coming from a background in which those who were born Romanists—or worse still, had Poped—were regarded as beings apart, here it was he who stood alone. Of course some of this feeling could be caused by the family itself: its history (its *proud* history), the outer trappings of wealth and position and the self-confidence these bred, all went in some part towards explaining everything.

Except, what explained Nick? And what, worse still, explained his own feelings towards him? So that no sooner had he left his bedside, his curious glancing conversation, than he wanted to return. And yet all the time he sat there, he would be thinking: this is not for me, I am not at ease.

But it was the whole family, they had ensnared him. Perhaps in the end, by charm. He was enchanted. *Enchanté,* the French said. I have been enchanted, he thought.

Twice in the next week, Sybil Straunge-Lacey asked him to take tea again in her sitting-room. She wanted to know, she said, "how dear Nicholas is progressing." And then she talked to him, confided in him, as on the first day: so that odd, ridiculous even, as she was, she ensnared him further, he knew, by drawing him into the family.

Everard. About Everard, she worried, *they* worried, that he was in no hurry to marry. It was so important when a family was old, and especially so when it was an old Catholic one, that the next generation should be assured. When he mentioned that there were three other sons, she said gently, that perhaps he did not understand about the first born of a family. She worried again about Rose. About Nick: "He is often restless. He was happiest after his Austrian stay—after Stonyhurst he was more than a year at the Jesuits' place there, at Feldkirch. I think that suited him. It is not easy, Mr. Rawson, to be a younger son . . ." She worried about her husband's health, about Benoit—the Jesuits complained of his unruly manners in class—about Hermione . . .

Certainly Hermione was not on good terms just then with her parents. And continuous fault was found with her. She had the appearance of one ready to pack her bags at the first excuse. He overheard her being reprimanded about her dress, that it was too low-cut—and her answer: that it was not to be endured. "I am no longer in the schoolroom. Soon, very soon, I shall dress as I please . . ."

One afternoon Paul was in the billiard room with Elfrida, who was at the piano—or meant to be—her little fox terrier, Imp, curled at her feet. He had been telling her about his home, about Downham, about the Kissing Gate. She was fascinated by all the customs, the superstitions, the beliefs.

"I would be afraid," she said. "In case there was a *ghost* in the Gate."

"You are meant to be practising the piano—"

"*Silly* old piano." She ran her fingers, then the back of her hand, up the keyboard, in one long trill. "Tell me more about your family."

He was telling her the story of the finding of Kate, when Hermione came in. She strolled about, then picking up a billiard cue angrily sent two balls cannoning.

"If they were all starving," Elfrida said, "then why did no one *do* anything?"

"Some people did. My father did—"

"They are all Catholics, the Irish, aren't they?"

Hermione said in languid tones, looking very like her father although the sentiment sounded like her mother: "*Irish* Catholics—it is not quite the same thing. They have never had to suffer for the Faith—"

Paul said, turning round, "Is not, was not *that* suffering?"

"But"—she opened her eyes wide—"that was not for the Faith. That was mismanagement of the crops. It is foolish to rely on a potato, is it not, when it has been seen to spoil so easily?"

Elfrida said, "Listen to me, Mr. Rawson—down, Imp, down! Listen to me play this right through, and *no* wrong notes . . ."

Nick was well again. Over a week of the visit had passed while he had been in bed. Often he would seem better during the day, sitting by the window in his room, only to have a return of the fever in the evening. Paul, in between a few days' shooting and many games of tennis— he and Elfrida, perhaps, against Hubert and Rose, or Benoit and a haughty Hermione—spent much time sitting with him. They read and talked: of everything. Their hopes and ambitions, their likes and dislikes, their—very different—schooldays. He was surprised to find himself talking, quite easily, of matters he would have found difficult to discuss with any but a few people. But of Kate and his love, he never spoke. He would have trusted no one with that.

Nick would mock. Lying back in the cane chair at the window, long legs outstretched, he would mock everything, everybody, and not least himself. Saying: "Paul, I don't like these tea-parties with the Wise Woman. Our Lady, I call her sometimes—Our Lady of Foxton Hall, pray for us sinners. She prays a great deal you will have noticed? If you think it a shrine in her sitting-room, then you should see her bedroom— a pre-dieu and no less than *four* graven images. To say nothing of the pictures . . ." And then just as suddenly his mood would change: "I am serious now, you believe me? I am serious when I say this. Paul, I wished—I could ask you for friendship. Indeed I do, I do ask you for friendship. You will be my friend?"

The second afternoon after Nick's full recovery they went for a walk in the arboretum. Nick had with him the book with all the placings of the trees and the dates of their planting.

"People come sometimes especially to see it. Grandfather's Folly—his *pride*, of course . . . He planted it after the Great French War—he'd lost an arm at Waterloo and his nerves were all over the place. It was too, a garden for his bride. Augustus, he was. And she was Rose, another Rose."

They had come out of the avenue of Red Oaks and were in the Conifers Walk. Nick had the book open.

"This is difficult—these here must be Spanish Firs, sometimes called

Hedgehog? And now farther on, Swiss Stone, is it? Bhutan Pine, yes. Douglas Firs—even *I* know these. And here he has sent to Japan, for this Tiger-tail Spruce . . ."

To Paul, they were all beautiful. He would have liked to spend longer with each. But Nick grew impatient. In between the naming of trees, he would quote unexpectedly perhaps three lines of a poem, as if to show that his mind was elsewhere. Then he would return.

They had been now down the Cherry Walk. It led to where there was a yellow catalpa, in flower.

"He has had this brought from China, I see. In—1849." He snapped the book to suddenly, putting it back in its case. "Enough.

> "I shall go my ways, tread out my measure,
>   Fill the days of my daily breath
>   With fugitive things not good to treasure—"

Then, turning to Paul: "And if—if I should ask for more?" Pause. "If I should ask you for more than friendship? Ah, my God—if I should ask for love?"

Yellowish, brown-tinged blossom of the catalpa, dark green of the leaves. The sunlight straining through. Paul, taken aback: "I don't—know."

An arm went round his shoulder. Nick was taller than he. He drew Paul's head onto his shoulder. His voice was full of suppressed tears. "If I say—ah, dear God—if I say that I never asked anyone before, if I say I never, nothing in my life, that I never felt like this before."

They stood there. Paul still could not answer him, could not speak at all. The first drops of rain went unnoticed. Then patter, thickening, all round them. Scurry, flurry of a willow-warbler. Nick: "Look, damn this rain. Damn this climate, always wet. And this time of year. August, always the worst. Run for it—" Then, "Follow me—darling." Rushing on, running ahead, forcing open the door of a summerhouse. The air inside was dry, dusty. There were books lying on a table, some bamboo chairs on their sides.

Nick pulled him through the doorway. He was laughing. "The house on the edge of the forest. See, you're wet—we both got wet. Here, come here—"

Paul fell clumsily into his arms, was wrapped in them, pinned against the wall. Nick still laughing. Saying between kisses, "Now say you never, you *never*—not in your schooldays. Nothing like this. Just tell me—"

Paul, pushing his head away, thought: this is not happening to me. And then again: I do not know *what* I feel.

The rain was slashing against the window. There was a curious smell, dry, bitter—the old books perhaps, the dusty bamboo. He felt then suddenly, fear, and a little joy.

"Paul, could you love me? Will you give me your heart? I don't ask for any more, you know. Just to kiss, just to hold—

> "But if we had loved each other— O sweet,
> Had you felt, lying under the palms of your feet,
> The heart of my heart, beating harder with pleasure
> To feel you tread it to dust and death . . ."

He was never at his ease with Augustus Straunge-Lacey. Although he had been at Foxton nearly a month now, and would leave in three days' time, he was not really certain that he had been noticed by the father at all. Few words had been addressed to him and once, when out shooting, he could have sworn that he wasn't recognised as a guest—or only after some puzzlement.

Augustus seemed a heavy, brooding figure who, shoulders hunched, stalked the grounds looking as if he would like to catch someone out, almost as though he had a great reservoir of anger which *must* be used up. At other times, perhaps exhausted by unused emotions, he could be seen sleeping heavily in the library. Between him and Sybil Straunge-Lacey, Paul had never heard anything but the most mundane exchanges ("Remind me to speak to X, would you, my dear?" or "I trust you conveyed my greetings to Y?"). Only as they knelt together at family prayers did he see any link between them. And yet they must have discussed, occasionally, the seven offspring—must even, once upon a time, have begot them . . .

These were the parents of Nick. He marvelled at this. He marvelled too that he should love Kate still, so much. That nothing at all should have changed . . . And yet everything had: because, he thought, I love Nick too. Against my will, against my reason, I love him. But he did not fear that more would come of it. Since that rainy day in the arboretum, Nick had been only his teasing, his mocking self. It was as if, certain of securing the heart he asked for, he now might rest. And wait.

Hubert said, "All angels are happy, some Straunge-Laceys are not happy, therefore some Straunge-Laceys are not angels."

"No," said both Nick and Father Bromhead from different sides of the dinner table. Everyone but Augustus Straunge-Lacey was present.

Paul, crumbling his bread, saw Rose smile quietly. She looked over at him suddenly, and smiled with him. That she should have Nick's eyes so exactly and be so different amazed him.

"Well, disprove it," said Hubert.

Hermione said, "Oh, these syllogisms as you call them, they weary me so. Sillyisms, I call them . . ."

"That will do, dear," said her mother. "If it amuses the boys."

"My turn," said Benoit. "Mine will be better. And here it is: Some Protestants are ugly, no Straunge-Laceys are Protestants, therefore no Straunge-Laceys are ugly . . ."

"Benoit," said Rose, "you have been very rude. When Mr. Rawson is of that religion and is present."

"I did not say *all*, but *some*—I'm sorry, Mr. Rawson, I'm *sorry*—now, disprove it, somebody."

"It is self-evidently false," said Nick.

"Simply," said Father Bromhead, "ugly is in the conclusion but not in the major premiss. It is an illicit major."

"How amusing," said Hermione. "An illicit major. It sounds like an army man guilty of irregularity."

Aunt Winefride trembled. Sybil Straunge-Lacey said: "Hermione—I have already had to speak to you."

". . . *Reductio per impossible*," Father Bromhead was saying, "of all methods *reductio per contra* is the clumsiest . . . what we had said earlier about the principle of the first figure . . ."

"Well, I never," said Uncle Kenelm, as if to himself, "Well, I never."

Sybil Straunge-Lacey said brightly, "I had wanted to say, we must all pray for fine weather on Friday. For Rose's birthday. And Mr. Rawson's last day. Just now it is *so* uncertain. Father has in his Breviary—have you not, Father?—a special service for sending away the devils of bad weather. Perhaps we could have that? It would be enough if the storm clouds were to be removed just a little way away. Four or five miles would do . . ."

Nick said, "Perhaps someone *there* has a birthday?"

"He is such a spoilsport," said Elfrida. "Are you not, Nick?"

Hubert said, "Bags I wield the censer and sprinkle the holy water—"

"This is absolute superstition," said Hermione. "It is not religion at all." She turned to Paul on her left: "What do you think, Mr. Rawson, do you not agree that it is superstition?"

"Yes."

Nick said carelessly, "Paul—but what of the superstitions of that place you live—Downham, and the Kissing Gate—what of all that?"

"That is different," Paul said. "I would not—" But then he could not remember what it was he would not. Feeling Hermione's gaze on him, he lapsed into red-faced silence.

And on Friday the devils were not exorcised. They were not willing to move the four or five miles prayed for but remained persistently at Foxton. It rained heavily all day, and the birthday picnic planned had to be cancelled. Instead there were party games indoors for the half dozen guests and in the evening some dancing.

The next day Paul left. Elfrida asked that she might come in the carriage to the station with Paul and Nick. She brought Imp on her knee. Nick complained that the terrier was shedding hairs.

Elfrida said, "You will visit us again, Mr. Rawson, won't you, *please* —and please become a Catholic. Usually our family marries Catholics from other Catholic families—Mama says that is best. But I should like to marry you. If you will wait five years or so . . ."

She giggled and pushed up her freckled nose so that her forehead was wrinkled. When Nick told her not to tease, she said, "Oh, but I am *serious.*"

He found himself unable to look at Nick when the time came for farewells. His last sight as the train steamed out of the station was of an excited Elfrida, Imp in her arms, holding up one of his paws and waving it for him.

SEVEN

They say that "Time assuages"—
Time never did assuage—
An actual suffering strengthens
As sinews do, with age—

Time is a Test of Trouble—
But not a Remedy—
If such it prove, it prove too
There was no Malady—

EMILY DICKINSON

Will, face blackened with burnt cork, was performing one of his turns for an audience of his sister Flo, brother Patrick, and two small girls from the farm across the way. It was his farewell. Tomorrow he was due to go to Richmond for the new school year.

Inspired by a visit to the Christy Minstrels that summer, he cracked his fingers, danced with his knees up to his nose, sang, "Who dat knockin' at de door?"

Kate was of the audience too. Watching her son with love, she thought of his plans, his threats, to run away and join a troupe. One day that summer after a minor family tiff he had shouted at Ned that he would "go tomorrow, and never return to school, never, never!" But Ned, knowing of course that it was not meant (yet), had said only: "If that's what you want, you'd best go, then . . ." A deflated twelve-year-old Will. But she reminded herself ruefully, for his turns grew better with each year, that in the end he would go.

He seemed today with his exuberance to fill the entire ground floor of the cottage. Of course it was too small—how many times had they not said that? But she could not imagine leaving it. Nor could Ned, ever. "I was first sad in it," he would say, "and then happy—more happy than any man's a right to be in this world. I'd not want to move from that . . ." And she would think too: here in this building is so much of the history of Ned and me. It was here one evening that we first crossed a line, altered our relationship in a way I would never have thought possible—indeed had not thought of at all.

The little girls were begging Will for another. "Again, Will, again." Red hair, incongruous black face. When finally he had ended, she said to him: "And you saw your father at the works? You've arranged the journey tomorrow?"

"Yes." Then he added, "I lost my temper."

"Will—not again. With *whom?*"

"It was on account of this fellow. There's some strange man wandering round Downham begging. He was at Grampie's and at Aunt Cat's and then at the works. He says he knows Uncle Walter—in America. He says they fought together in the war—for the Yankees he said, I think. He came in while I was there—just a ragged-looking fellow. He hadn't really anything to *say.* Dad gave him money and he left. I didn't believe the story anyway—"

"Good for you," Kate said.

"But *Greaves* has to interfere then, and he comes over and he says, to Dad: 'You're a daft fool, givin' to *his* like—he'll be up to no good, I reckon. Like as not he'll be around and murder you in your beds . . .'"

"Will—you'll frighten the little ones—"

"But it was only what he *said.* And he said it with such relish too. And the fellow looked harmless enough—just simple. Then Greaves said, 'And any road I mind that Walter, he were nobbut a half-nowt—' And I was so angry, because he *is* a relation and Greaves has no business—so I took up stance for a fight, and Dad stopped me and . . ."

Kate sighed. She wanted to smile at his absurd loyalty. She sighed inside too. Would *I* defend Walter?

She thought of him hardly at all these days. When he had first gone to Australia, it had seemed (which it was) the other side of the world, and as a consequence, not *real.* That had been far away in 1854. And yet, only some five years later, had not *she* herself thought, seriously thought, of going to the Antipodes—after losing Richard? Reading that advertisement and thinking: that could be me. Going far, far away. As far away as possible . . .

She had seen it in the Yorkshire *Gazette:*

Swan River, Western Australia, to sail the 10th April 1860,

the regular trader Palestine Al 427 tons. W. Johnson, Commander; lying in the London Docks. Has superior accommodation for passengers. For freight or passage apply to Felgate and Co., 12 Clements Lane, Lombard Street. *Free passages are granted to single women* . . .

For days it haunted her, and at the last she tore it out of the newspaper and secreted it in a drawer. Certainly for a while she had taken it seriously enough. In those dread dry days of loss after the affair of Richard. How far can I get away from my love, how far can I distance my heart? She had for a little while really and truly imagined that within herself lay the strength not only to make the break from England, to go to the other side of the world, but even there to make a new life: that there she would *forget*. Above all, she would be removed forever from the terrible temptation to rush over to the Abbey, or to write the letter that would reveal all—to tell Richard the truth and let him make of it what he would.

But, she would think then, he would marry me, *of course he would marry me*. He would defy everybody, everything, ruin his life—children would come. Then with horror she would think of the misshapen, disease-ridden offspring she might foist on the Ingham family—and the Rawson—what shame she would bring to names respected in the dale and beyond. Ah, no . . .

She did not leave England. She survived that spring, as she had survived the terrible autumn and winter of loss, as she would doubtless survive the summer to come. And the next, and the next. Death and oblivion did not come for the asking. Ah, help me, God. In a strange way she had felt anger against John, resentment—seeing him, she would ask herself: Why did you bring me back? Was it for *this?* She could speak of her suffering to no one. Why did I not die? why may I not die now? But in reality, she smiled when she should smile, went about all her everyday duties: helping, visiting, reading to the sick. She deceived even Sarah-Mother—no mean feat—so that she remarked only, "You look peaky, Kate. We must ask John for blue pills, or sarsaparilla." And then had said nothing more but kept tactfully quiet when Kate, with a sudden flare of temper, had replied: "I don't need medicine—the last thing I need is *medicine* . . ."

The idea of emigration grew paler, less of a possibility, not because the pain was any lighter but because she knew she had not the courage, was not a pioneer. It was in people or it was not. She thought, I have left one land already and grown up in another, made myself a citizen of it—I cannot do that again.

And then had come that dreadful day in late July, her loss already a
year old, when John, coming over to the house, said (little Sarah following behind him, for she often rode in the gig with him now): "The
young Squire—they say he's to wed." Then he had turned to Kate:
"You'll have heard something of it?"

Sarah-Mother, almost as if sensing something, said: "She's not much
there these days, son. She's grown beyond them. That was young
days . . ."

John laughed. "Kate, I think you are no longer in touch." He said to
his mother: "I had it from Mrs. Wilkinson, the housekeeper. She of
the excellent jams—today she pressed on me some delicious-looking
blackcurrant. She says it is not public knowledge yet but will be tomorrow. The lady arrives this evening. Evidently it should have been Julia
—if you understand me. It was *her* beau." He laughed again, "I am
confusing even myself. Richard does not marry another man—he is to
marry the *sister* of Julia's beau. A Miss Frances Whyatt, I believe. And
the dowager"—he said the name with faint distaste—"is reputed to be
very pleased."

Sarah-Mother said, "It's always good to hear of a wedding—"

"And I've no doubt this is a good one," said John. "And good that
he should marry and beget an heir, and perhaps a second son for good
measure—then all concerned may breathe in peace."

Kate wondered how it was possible to swoon upright, not to fall, not
to black out completely. The pain was one of recognition. It has happened.

Voices went on round her. She was not noticed, thank God she was
not noticed. She felt inside her that had Ned been there, he would have
noticed. For days, weeks now, months even, she had avoided him, his
gaze, being alone with him. Once he had remarked, with concern, that
surely something ailed her, and she had said then, "Oh, it is only some
debility, summer sickness—I have physic for it . . ."

Just as John was leaving, standing for a moment at the door with
him, she saw the back of the Ingham carriage going down the hill towards Leyburn. As soon as the meal was over, she sat herself in the
front room, by the window, ostensibly tatting. The wait seemed inter-
minable. Then after two or three false alarms, she saw at last the coach
come into view.

It was all over in a moment. Nothing to see—glimpse of a feathered
hat, but otherwise nothing—no one. Richard, surely there, was well hidden. It was enough, though, to know that SHE was inside. The horses'
hooves could still be heard, sounding fainter in the distance. Now the
carriage would be turning, now they would be on the road to the

Abbey, and now—for what could stop them? they would be driving past the Kissing Gate . . .

Ah dear God, help me to wish them well. May I learn only to care that he may be happy. Pray God—and this the hardest prayer of all— that *he does not love me still*, that there is not for him now, nor ever will be, the slightest pain.

The wedding was to be in late September. What haste of Georgiana Ingham, Kate thought—for she was certain that it was her work— perhaps she is afraid that he may yet change his mind, that everything is to be done again.

She wondered later why she had not tried then to get a place as a governess. The family might well have approved. But she had felt that she was held together at that time by too frail a thread. She could never have found in herself the strength, the energy, to take action. There was all the arranging, the strangeness of some unknown persons' home, the tales she had heard of great unhappiness.

But the problem was solved for her, in part at least. A few weeks before the wedding, Sarah-Mother was asked if she could possibly spare Kate for the next three or four months, possibly six? Frank Helliwell's youngest brother, Timothy, had a wife, Mia, who was expecting a child at Christmas. She had been advised to lie up—two babies had been lost already—but was finding now that the time hung on her hands. Could Kate come as companion?

The work was a godsend. Indeed she saw it as literally sent by God. God's answer to her cry for mercy, for the strength to go on.

"When you are married," Mia said, hands folded proudly over the swelling plainly visible beneath the simple house gown, "when you are married and have little ones . . ." She spoke more and more often of the joys of being a married woman: the position, the satisfactions, being needed, running one's own household and so on. And although hers was not yet arrived, of the joys of raising a family.

"When *you* are married, Kate," she said, yet again.

Kate said, "I shall never marry. I have thought—"

"What, *never marry?* But my dear—and you are so fetching—I don't know what your family is about. It surprises me that with your looks you have reached twenty and are not yet spoken for. Whatever next? Not to marry! Do you dislike men, then? You have not gone unnoticed *here*, I can tell you . . ."

She realised the truth of that within the next few days. She had been already nearly two months when the second Helliwell son, Edgar, came to live with them for several weeks while changing his job from one in

Harrogate to one in York. He had visited three or four times earlier, and she had liked him well enough then, feeling quite warmly towards him for the resemblance he bore to little Matthew Helliwell, Ann and Frank's son. But now, like a frightened pony, she shied off. As with Ned but for different reasons, she avoided any possible occasion that they might be alone together even for a moment. But his eyes followed her about, and in company he went out of his way to pay her attention.

In the end it was Mia, very near her time now, who was the spokeswoman. "Edgar wonders—his affections are very much engaged—I am to find out if there is any hope?"

Kate shook her head. "I could not. I cannot—"

"No, do not be hasty," interrupted Mia. "I do urge you. He is the soundest of men. We should all be delighted, and your family, the Rawsons, they too. It would be the happiest of endings . . ."

And she had been in a way tempted, dear God, yes. She liked him well enough, and that together with respect and admiration—it would perhaps have been sufficient. But to ask for, to say: no children. Ah that. If he had said to her, "The only thing I must tell you, that I do not wish for children. I am determined to be without issue." If—and what likelihood that?—if, then I could have done it, she thought, I could have married him.

But she told Mia, twice, "No, I cannot. Never."

"This is nonsense, Kate. Listen to me . . ."

She liked Mia enough to confide in her, something at least. Why not —half the truth? "I loved someone else. Am not over that—"

"All the more reason then!" Mia cried.

"I cannot. While there is still hope, I cannot," she lied.

"Oh well, if you hope still. If there is *hope still*, then all is understood. I must tell him that although not spoken for elsewhere, you are not quite heart-whole as a biscuit—to use the old phrase. May I say that?"

She wished she had not told Mia even so little, for although she did not say anything more to Kate that day, it was not long before she was pressing her hand and saying: "You will not tell me who he is?" Her head on one side, coy. "Not even—his initials?"

I shall never, Kate thought. Never. Never. It sounded to her, with its other meaning, the saddest word she knew. Never. Never Richard.

"You will not tell me who he is? No, I see that you will not. A secret beau . . ."

Two days before Christmas Mia had her baby: a fine eight-pound boy. Kate was to stay for the lying-in period, but when the month was up

she would not really be needed. She could not bear the idea of returning home. Without saying anything to the Helliwells, she composed an
advertisement and took it into York.

A well-educated Young Lady desires an engagement as
Companion Governess. Has resided two years in France and is
accustomed to travel. Address K.R., c/o Messrs. Nicholson,
Booksellers, The Shambles, York.

After three weeks there were only a handful of answers, and none of
them would do. One, reading easily between the lines, she could see
wanted more a servant. Another, she was to be companion to an old
gentleman: he had recently lost a very young wife. Another, she was to
go to Madeira. In spite of her fine "and is accustomed to travel," she did
not feel that she could . . .

She appealed to Mia, confessing what she had done. Mia said immediately, "Oh, you naughty dear little thing. We shall arrange something
at once—" which she did, finding Kate within four days a post as companion to an elderly lady, friend of a friend of her mother. Mrs. Mabel
Precious, living on the Yorkshire coast, at Filey.

It was like an anodyne. The days passed: the remainder of the winter, spring, through into a radiant summer. Her duties were very light,
nor did she have to think very much. And she was asked nothing about
herself. Mrs. Precious was not really very interested. She was kind, if it
did not put her out—but as she was of a happy temperament and for
the most part comfortable, plump, in good health, fond of her food and
able to digest it, she had sufficient time left to show interest in Kate's
welfare. She had said at the beginning: "You are peaky, my dear, and
could do with the sea air."

A small fishing village originally and latterly a seaside town, Filey
seemed to Kate perfect, with its Georgian houses, its wooded park, the
steep winding road down to the sea. And then the sea itself, the North
Sea, with the brightly coloured flat-bottomed cobles of the fishing fleet,
their brown sails, their high prows.

She was to be fattened up, by order of Mrs. Precious. And to this end
she was fed a nourishing local fish soup—of crab, mussels, cod, haddock,
scallops, served with cream and fresh parsley, and her appetite (and
that of Mrs. Precious) titillated with a concoction of crab and egg and
sherry, served in the shell. On warm afternoons she and Mrs. Precious
drove in an open brougham down the front, picnicking on the long
sweep of beach if the tide was right: setting up the coaching table with
a white cloth and a large tea: plum bread, almond tarts, curd tarts, fruit

cake . . . Well fed and sunning herself, Mrs. Precious would be mellow and easy. Kate might walk by herself, past the donkeys and the squealing children and out onto Filey Brigg: a natural pier, a mile-long strip of shelving rock stretching out into the North Sea and said to be an unfinished work of the Devil.

It was a gentle life and although still very unhappy, she would find that for long periods of time she did not think at all, but moved in a kind of semi-pleasant dream.

Alas, that it could not last. Several times during that summer the old lady was visited by her grandson, a personable young ensign in his mid-twenties. He could not keep his eyes off Kate, and in spite of her lowly position—after all, she was only paid companion—such a high opinion had Mrs. Precious formed of her that she began to hint that her grandson's suit would not be discouraged. "He has made already several very unsuitable entanglements—I cannot think of better than for him to settle down. The end to our worries . . ." He was amenable, wanted only encouragement. She would speak to her daughter, his mother. Soon.

"No," lied Kate, "I am not free. At home—someone—we must wait, you see, till his prospects are better. I had not told you . . ."

Three days later Mrs. Precious died suddenly, very peacefully, in her sleep after an afternoon spent on the seashore. A few days, the funeral wake—and she was no longer needed. The eyes of the ensign followed her at the family gathering. She had only to grant the smallest encouragement, but she could feel only a cold gooseflesh, a horror of being forced into any sort of decision. Her manner was, for her, brusque to the point of rudeness. It was meant as discouragement and received as that.

Her post no longer existed. There was talk of other work, of being a governess in another part of the family. It would perhaps have been the answer. But she felt after the undemanding affection of the old lady, the ease, the solace, a great sense of loss. She was suddenly very, very homesick, longing passionately for sight and sound of Downham. Soon it would be autumn; the chestnuts, guardians of the church, turning. Up on the moors with their great stretches of purple, bracken already tinged with gold was being brought down for fodder. The church clock, with its too-long pause—I miss even that, she thought.

She travelled back by train from York to Leyburn, arriving in the late afternoon. It was a day of festivities: bunting and decorations in the market square. The Kissing Gate was garlanded with flowers and leaves, marguerites, chrysanthemums.

No one had thought to tell her. The birth three months earlier of Francis Charles Whyatt Featherstone Ingham. And today the christening celebrations. The next Sunday she watched from her seat in church the whole family come in: at their head, Georgiana—triumph not just in her little smile but in her whole walk as she made her way proudly up to the steps of the box pew.

Oh, dear God, teach me not to hate.

"John is very concerned about Mother," Ned told her, within days of her arrival. "I'd—we'd thought of asking could you come home. He doesn't think she'll make the spring."

Indeed her colour was very bad and she was breathless on exertion, but bustled about nearly as much as ever. Eliza never left her side. But Sam, well, vigorous, hardly looking a man in his sixties, refused to fuss about her. He behaved almost as if blind and deaf to the obvious signs. When Sarah-Mother said that she was "only a little tired," he agreed with her: only making her promise to rest perhaps more often. "It is just a trial sent by the Lord," he said. "There's maybe been too much visiting the sick—'Blessed is he that considereth the poor: the Lord will deliver him in time of trouble . . .'"

It was just this attitude which made it so much worse for him when the inevitable happened. A severe cold spell in early February and every symptom rapidly worsening. She was in bed only one week. Every possible relation gathered round. Eliza sat immovable on one side of the bed —a small one had been moved downstairs to the front room—but it seemed to be Kate that she wanted. She spoke of her "da," and said: "If I could just mind the songs he sang me—how did it go, then?" and "You're a Donnelly, certain sure," she would say, clutching at Kate's hand. "But Yorkshire by adoption—you know that, eh—where you belong?"

She wanted to talk about Walter. Once she even asked for him. John, so that she would know they were doing their best, wrote to the last address they had, and this seemed to reassure her. But it was already more than six years old, and even were the letter to reach him and he to set out immediately—there was not the time. She was weakening now, not daily but hourly.

Sam meanwhile was victim of a heavy cold, and had to stay in bed himself. Kate brought him up hot milk which Eliza had laced with whisky. "He's not a drinking man," she told Kate, "but a drop'll help him." Although they did not actually keep the truth of his wife's illness from him, he seemed unable still to realise it. As that last week wore on, tossing in his bed with a low fever, he would ask how she was doing, and then murmur in answer only: "The Lord will provide . . ."

Two days before she died, she had put a hand out to Ned, suddenly.

He was at her bedside, seated just near her pillow. She pulled at the cloth of his jacket. "You're good, son." Earlier in the day her mind had been wandering but she seemed now quite lucid. "Hannah," she said. "You mind Hannah, Ned? All that business." She spoke with difficulty but her voice was clear: "If I'd only *helped*. If only—but God was good." She turned her head as if searching. "Kate. He sent *you*, Kate. God wasn't angry after all. Only . . . But I didn't help Hannah. Another woman, that hadn't my good fortune—and I couldn't reach out a hand . . ."

"Hush, Mother," Ned told her. "Hush. Don't fret yourself with the long ago."

"Arthur," she said suddenly, raising her voice. "They call the little one Arthur. Her brother. She gave him to me. In my care, you know. Before they . . . before they hanged her . . ."

Ned had taken her hand in his and was stroking it. Kate saw that there were tears in his eyes. Sarah-Mother was silent for a few moments, then she went on.

"Ned—you're a good lad. A good lad. That Arthur, he's been no good . . . they said, feathers off a duck, and the duck still alive . . . I kept my word to Hannah, I kept it, didn't I? He's to have work, with us. You'll keep him, son—keep him at the works, whatever. So that he's always taken care of. You'll do that? You'll do it?"

"Yes, Mother," Ned was saying. "Yes. Yes."

"I'd rest better with promises made, and kept. I can trust you? You'll not forget . . ."

"No, Mother. No."

"Promise me, then. Say it so I can hear." Her voice had become fretful and anxious. "There'll be no need to call on God—just give *me* your word. Tell me, son, that you promise . . ."

"I promise," Ned said. "Greaves will be taken care of, as long as I live. I *promise*. And now"—he laid her hand back on the counterpane—"rest—and don't fret anymore . . ."

The next day a large hamper of food and wine came for Sarah-Mother from the Abbey. A card was with it, written by Frances Ingham —but beneath the conventional expression of sympathy, Richard had added: ". . . in the spirit of my grandfather, and in memory of a never to be discharged debt . . ." (But that is true, Kate thought—*he* would not be here had it not been for her courage.) His handwriting, that she had known from the schoolroom . . . When Eliza was downstairs, feeling like a thief, she stole the card from the hamper, slipping it into her bodice while Sarah-Mother slept.

An hour later, waking, Sarah-Mother said to Kate a curious thing.

Clutching at her hand, her lips very blue now: "Are there folk about?" and when Kate said: "No, not this moment—" she asked, "Sam, is he about?" Kate shook her head. Then Sarah-Mother said: "You didn't take Walter to heart, eh? That—that thing Walter did . . . the way he was with you . . . we mustn't tell *Ned*, you know. You'll not tell Ned?" She turned her gaze right on Kate, her eyes wide open. Suddenly very lucid: "Ned will—" then she corrected herself. "You'll take care of Ned?" She was pressing Kate's hand gently, but as if her touch could speak. "He's been done by badly. A good woman—" She was wandering again. She murmured into the pillow, "A good woman . . ."

"Yes," Kate said, "yes. Of course I will."

Sarah smiled to herself, "He's making you a house for your dolls, and it's to have—he said, it's to have . . ." The words drifted away, but the smile remained.

She came round only once more to talk to John. When Sam came in, she did not recognise him. Told at three o'clock the next morning that she was sinking, he rushed from his room still in his nightshirt, his feet bare, spurning the arm Eliza offered him. He was too late by perhaps half a minute.

Kate thought she would never forget how he behaved then. Grey hair damp with fever, eyes darkened, he stood for a few seconds at the foot of the bed as if struck. Then he seemed suddenly to realise that he had now truly lost her. Grabbing the bed rail, shaking it, he had given a great shout. And then with his head thrown back as if groaning to the sky, he called out: " 'Man dieth and wasteth away, yea, man giveth up the ghost, and where is he? As the waters fail from the sea and the flood decayeth and drieth up, so *man lieth down and riseth not*, till the heavens be no more, they shall not awake, nor be raised out of their sleep . . .' "

For Kate, and Eliza too, it was the beginning of a nightmare. Within a few days of his wife's death Sam had begun to drink—not as heavily as later, but noticeably. Charitably, everyone supposed it to be something which would pass as he came to terms with his loss. He who had never drunk wine or spirits in the ordinary way, who had had to be coaxed into drinking a toast at family celebrations, over the next few months was more and more often to be found in his cups. Again and again in the middle of the night, she and Eliza would be woken by the sound of him stumbling round the house, candle held aloft, shouting the word of God. Sometimes, before they could reach him, the dull heavy thud of his body falling.

The rest of the family helped as much as they could. John intervened and tried to reason with him, but was told—with every relevant biblical quotation—to go elsewhere. Ned fared even worse: he was a "whitened sepulchre" . . . On Sundays, when for the sake of the old days they gathered together still, then she and Eliza brought—forced—a washed and tidied Sam to the dinner table. A man who scarcely spoke, who had been quietly drinking all the week. He did not go any longer to the rope-works. They were Ned's now, the sullen Greaves his second in command.

Catriona became a friend. She came round often to see what she could do to help, and when she thought it seemly, brought young Sarah and Paul with her; although she did not like to do this often in case they should see or hear something to upset them. Kate had always found Catriona easy, even though she knew others had not. Now she was more than ever grateful for her support. The ten years between their ages narrowed to nothing. But she did not tell Catriona her secrets. And as the months and years passed she could imagine less and less confiding in anyone.

This is to be my life, she thought. Although gradually, as Sam, no longer wandering about at night, settled down to a pattern of drinking with which they would have to live, she realised that Eliza most probably would be able to manage on her own—the more so as her friend Jane Helliwell wished to live at the Rawson house with her. Who is there to care now, she thought, whether I marry? It will not arise again . . .

Already it was the summer of 1864. Ned, leaving work early one Saturday of sunshine, taking little Sarah and Paul up on to the moors with their tea. Kate was asked to come with them. Early in the afternoon just as they were to set out, Paul had made a scene—something about his clothes—and Catriona had forbid him to come. Sarah had wanted to ride, had insisted. At eleven she was now very sure of her mind. Ned rode his chestnut, and Kate who was never happy on horseback, sat on Eliza's old pony—so gentle and slow that she thought it might have been a quicker journey on foot.

It was a cloudless day, and hot. Larks hung high in the sky. They rode round the edge of a barley field; thick with thistles in flower, it had a purple tint, forerunner of the purple soon to come up on the moors. For most of the way, Sarah rode on ahead. They climbed up and up and then, as they came to a stone cross and a path stretching two ways, Ned called to Sarah: "No, there—lass, you'll be best to the left."

But Sarah said stubbornly, "I shall go right, Uncle Ned. I like that way—"

A solitary sheep, bleating, alarmed, scuttled away from them. They rode on behind Sarah, but Kate could see that Ned was not pleased. He said: "I should have been firmer. The other way—the view is better."

"Maybe she wants to follow the beck," Kate said.

"There's water the other way too . . ."

A broken-down stone barn, a cow house perhaps, Kate thought, came into view. It was only partly roofed. Stones from it lay all about on the grass and the heather beyond. Sarah leapt down from her pony, and then as Kate and Ned came nearer, called out: "This was someone's home. I played house here one day."

Ned said, his voice sharp, "What were you doing up here?"

"I came with Matthew—Matthew Helliwell, and my other cousin. Last year. And no one knew."

Drawing up to where she held her pony, Ned said: "Well, I've no mind to stop here. And it's no place for a game, either."

Kate said, "Gee up, Sarah. Do as Uncle Ned says—"

But Sarah had already run off into the house. Ned followed, Kate a little after. She saw that he was very agitated.

"I shall stay here," said Sarah, from the open doorway, the stones leaning crazily above. "I always have my own way when I'm with you and Aunt Kate. Don't I, Aunt Kate, don't I?"

"Indeed you do," said Kate grimly.

Ned said, "I'd reckon maybe it's not safe—I'd thought it quite down now—"

"You know it, Uncle Ned?" Sarah said. She looked at him. "Did you play here? Was it your play house?" She added, "You know, a witch might come out."

Ned said, "Come away. I said—No."

"And I say yes . . ."

"Sarah," Kate protested. "Sarah." Dismounting, she reached out towards her, but Sarah evaded her grasp and it was then, turning, that Kate saw Ned's face.

He was crying. His head half away from her so that she might not see. At once she remounted, and said in her loudest voice: "I shall go the other way. You may follow or not as you please."

Very soon Sarah was coaxing her pony ahead of them, her tantrum quite forgotten—which was her nature, Kate thought. She herself was alongside of Ned now.

"Ah Ned, you were pained—"

"It's nothing. Don't mind me. Take no heed," he said. She could see that the tears, unattended to, ran down one cheek. She did not know what to think. He talked so little of himself: it was always care for the other person. His past. Of Nanny, she had only a faint memory: she had not liked her but that did not mean anything—then. Nanny had been there for a while—and then she had not. She remembered that she herself had grieved for Ned. She remembered that he had said, "I lost my bairn. A little lass. But look—I still have you. My cockyolly bird . . ."

Always the older people had kept, in their own way, she thought, the real truth of happenings from her. An old woman had lived on the moors—and died. Sarah-Mother had said, for the news had somehow reached the schoolroom and Kate had asked something: "Yes, that was Ned's friend Becky. He was good to her. He's a good lad, at bottom . . ." But Kate had not asked more. Now she wanted suddenly to know everything. For a very long time now I have been old enough, she thought, to know it all. In my grief, I have been selfish.

They had brought some tea with them, and a rug fastened on the back of Kate's pony. They settled not far from the beck. Bogmyrtle grew by the water's edge; there was some heather, not yet out, but mostly brownish coarse grass and bent. A slight breeze stirred it.

Eliza had made some parkin. It was very heavy and without enough ginger, the coarse oatmeal clinging to the teeth. There was spiced tea to drink. Sarah wanted to put out fragments of parkin for the hobs or fairies. Ned said they would not come out till the sun went down. She chose then to go away and hide it in all manner of unlikely places: "So that they will be smelling and searching for half the night . . ."

Thin ribbons of cloud streaked the sky. Kate said gently when they were alone, seeing him give a great shiver: "You're not cold?" He had still his jacket on. She had unbuttoned hers, taken off her hat.

"Someone walked over my grave, I don't doubt."

"It's the dead you're thinking of," she said.

"Becky—that used to live there—in that place. I was thinking on her. I wouldn't—there's no one would get me in there now . . ."

She said suddenly: "Ned, would you tell me—some of it?"

He did not insult her by making difficulties or questioning her meaning. He said only, "If you really care to hear—"

Sarah was coming into sight, riding habit tucked up, waving empty hands.

"I couldn't 'tice any. They're not about, the hobs—"

"Oh I do, Ned," Kate said. "I do."

So she found herself three days later at his cottage—the most natural thing in the world. How many times had she not been as a child? Old Susan Ruddock, who cooked and cleaned for him, made a six o'clock meal and said she'd be away. It was unusually damp and cold, weather they had not reckoned for. They sat by the fire: the wood, not quite dry, crackled.

She leaned forward and took his hand in hers; his were cold.

"Dear Ned, you were going to tell me. Tell me all your life. As if—" she hesitated, she had only just thought of it: "as if you met me for the first time."

"That wouldn't do." He smiled then. "I'd say little."

"Just tell me then. *All that happened.*"

"The Inghams—" he began, and her heart, it plummeted. How to escape—it came back always to *them!* But she must not, would not think of herself. She continued to hold his hands: it was as if neither of them were willing to notice, neither willing to let go . . .

"The Inghams—it was first on account of the old Squire—when he was young. And that story of the darkie—"

But no one had told her. She knew nothing. It was possible to know nothing. There had been little gossip at home, only a little in the schoolroom. Sarah-Mother had always discouraged it. "Let the past bury the past . . ."

"The Inghams," he said again. And then the whole story: Becky's death, Charles Ingham's death, all that had gone before. She could not remember later how they had come onto his marriage. Perhaps she had asked something, as: "What did Nanny think of Becky?" or "Did Nanny ever go there with you?"—something which had showed she wanted to know all about that too.

He said then, "I can't tell that tale, not all of that one. Some, yes." She saw that he was unhappy. "I did wrong and was punished. That's most about it."

But when he began to tell her of the night before Nanny's death, he began to cry then as if he had waited till this very evening, fifteen years later, to weep over it, to mourn.

"Why, Ned," she said. "But it is all over now, dear. It is long ago."

She had hold still of his hands. And it was then that it happened, that a weeping Ned, overcome by emotion, a Ned she did not recognise, was suddenly covering her hands with kisses, the tears running onto them. Then turning over her hands, and then he was forward and down on his knees, was cradling her head in his hands. He pulled at her hair—it tumbled down, first one side and then slowly the other.

"Oh, my little love, all my life—I would never touch—oh, my little love." His lips were all over her face, and yet she knew his kisses, how many times had Ned not kissed her?

"All I *ever loved,*" he was saying, "see the veins there, on your hands, your throat, my little cockyolly bird, if you had but *known* how I loved you . . ."

Because it was Ned, because of that, she knew then that he might have done anything he wished. She would not have stopped him. It was at once frightening and reassuring. This is only Ned—but then, *this is Ned, Uncle Ned, what is happening?*

She was alarmed. Even while he touched, caressed her face, her hair, kissed her neck, it was fiercely, almost despairingly, as a man drowning. Now he clung to her. But she felt for him such pity, such gratitude— she would do anything, almost anything, to repay those years of caring.

Freeing her hands, she pushed him away gently. Tears welled up in her eyes.

"Ned, ah Ned." He had sat back now on the floor. She saw that he trembled still. As she pinned her hair up roughly, she reached for her shawl and said: "Let us walk by the bridge before the light goes altogether." John, who had some visits that side of Downham, was to come for her. "We could watch the river—and we would not miss John like that."

He did not speak as they went out, walking the short distance past the village green on their left, over to the bridge and the main road. The air was much warmer: although still damp it was more like a summer's night. In the fading light, the water of the beck could be seen gathering speed on its way towards the cottage; the brown stones glimmered black.

Nor did he touch her as they leant over the bridge. Ordinarily he might have put an arm about her shoulders. She felt as far away from him as ever, in the whole of her life, since she had first known him to be there. An icy strangeness. It was she who shivered, standing by the water. *He will ask me to marry him,* she thought. A notion so possible yet impossible, so terrifying in its implications. It could not be. I who am unclean. Harbourer of disease.

"Ned, dear," she began, grit in her voice, "Ned."

Then rounding the bend, the lamps of John's gig, the spanking trot of the black mare.

"Hallo there—holloa!" The rattle of harness. The gig drawing up. "Ned, old fellow—you would let Kate take cold?"

EIGHT

There's none less free than who
Does nothing and has nothing else to do,
Being free only for what is not to his mind,
And nothing is to his mind . . .

EDWARD THOMAS, *Liberty*

O weary days—oh evenings that seem never to end—for how many years have I watched that drawing-room clock and thought it would never reach the ten! and for twenty, thirty years more to do this!

FLORENCE NIGHTINGALE (age thirty-one)

Eighteen seventy-seven. Only two months left now—to peter out, thought Sarah. And then inexorably, 1878. She thought, I cannot see the point of 1878. It mocks me. Her life would not change (although *she* might if others had their way: "Sarah, cannot you be more gentle/kind/enthusiastic/pious/thoughtful/respectful/disciplined/caring/polite?" and so on and so on through the whole catalogue of virtues). Mama would not change. The only difference seemed to be that Catriona did not now expect Sarah to marry.

Yesterday, Sarah remembered, she had said: "It is hardly worth my while, Sarah, it is hardly worth my while, all the efforts to find and then encourage a match—someone suitable—since without doubt you will only have done with him within weeks of the bells ringing. The one thing I had looked forward to was a married daughter—I can imagine making a *friend* of a married daughter. You have certainly disappointed me in that regard. Now *Tarley—*"

Tarley, Tarley, Tarley. Sometimes Sarah, hating the name, the very

sound and all that it stood for, in a vain endeavour to love the memory
at least of a sister she had never known, would think of her as Charlotte. Charlotte Rawson. Except that *she* would by now surely be a
married woman. She would have married well. She would have been
beautiful. It was impossible that the Tarley of the miniatures, of the daguerreotype, would not have fulfilled her promise. Beautiful. And with
all that warmth of affection too. It was that, so often, that Mama
lamented. She would say, "Tarley was always so affectionate—Tarley
said this, did that . . ." And Sarah would think: yes, maybe Tarley was
loving, clung to you, kissed you. Yes. *But when ever did you put your
arms around me?* If I could summon up even one memory of your affection, of a time when you kissed me other than in the course of duty,
when you called me by an affectionate name . . . *As Kate did.* If I was
ever in trouble, to whom did I run but Kate? All through childhood:
the birthday surprise, the first treat after a long childhood illness—Kate.
And even when she was newly married and had her own children (and
I was an awkward girl, ugly duckling, most unattractive to you), even
then she had time for me . . .

But at least there was, just now, one good thing. Paul's happiness. Although now he was away staying in London, with his friend Nicholas,
he had been since his return from Lancashire in September a changed
person. She tried to conjure up a memory of Nicholas, glimpsed at the
party, but could not (so much had been blotted out by the surprise return of Edward . . .). Paul spoke incessantly of Nick's family—the
'Strangers' she had christened them, after their oddly pronounced
name. The only disquieting element was the interest he was showing in
their religion. He had not actually discussed it with her, had said only:
"It attracts me, I cannot tell you how much it attracts—" and she had
said then only: "That is not what religion is about . . ." (She had expected him then to question her, pursue the argument. She did not
know what she would have answered.)

Since coming back he had made a great study of trees, and also
flowers and insects: filling notebooks and sitting up late with drawings
and pressed specimens—so that Mama had remarked acidly, as if chal-
lenging him: "You did not show such industry at the university, I
think." And Papa had said tiredly: "You could have been, who knows,
a doctor, a scientist—had you shown the interest."

Mama would have liked him to do more painting of what he drew,
and less scientific study. She hinted yet again that in her youth she had
not been untalented. Indeed about the house in dark corners were pale
water-colourings of the place in which she had spent her youthful summers: Wester Ross, in the Western Highlands of Scotland. Once Sarah

had asked, "Have we no relations there?" and had had her head bitten off. Paul said, "There is a cousin or the suchlike but I am told he is un-pleasantness itself. Crusty Scotch laird. You may forget all that . . ." Although what visits she had made to Scotland had been amusing: She and Paul had been twice for Hogmanay to Paul's godmother, whom they called Aunt Kirsty. She had four boys and four girls and a husband who was a consultant at Dundee Infirmary.

She thought: If I could see Papa as happy as Paul. It seemed that he would never be himself again. She wondered sometimes that he did not take the squalid train incident further, insist on a prosecution, on his rights . . . But probably the law did not work like that. She did not know. Certainly it seemed that although he had got his good name back—somehow when returned to him, it was not as he had left it.

She would see him often staring—perhaps at a blank patch on the wall—staring without purpose; then he would as suddenly stop, and blinking rapidly, shake his head as if to clear it. He went more slowly about his work. The almost hearty return in the evening she remem-bered, the boots clattering, going through to change, the "By God, I am *hungry*—" All that was gone now. And she did not think really that Mama helped. Although she did not often allude directly to the court case, she would refer to it obliquely in a way which did little to restore his pride. As one day last week.

". . . and where is the interest you had once in finding causes for—hayfever was it? All your gifts seem to have deserted you. Except of course for a talent for getting yourself into hot water—becoming the victim of an hysterical female. A doctor should know better. Nearly *thirty* years of dealing with such persons, and then unable to recognise one when she crosses your path . . ."

He had silenced her then with a look. She liked that about Papa, that he still seemed able after everything occasionally to do that. But some days, in a frenzy almost, Mama would throw out remark after remark, as if hoping they would bounce back at her, when they hit only with a dull thud.

Yesterday had been like that. "In Edinburgh," Mama was saying, knife and fork suspended over her roast mutton, "in Edinburgh there was never that small-mindedness—"

"Remember," Papa began, "that I was there. The Scotch are not—"

"I beg to tell you," she went on, ignoring him, "their law is the finest, *and* I may add, their medicine. I mind that you were not reluc-tant to come and pick the brains of the best Scotch surgeons. The pity is—all that education—that you should now be a country surgeon—"

Sarah said, "But that is—"

"Please not to interrupt. It is nothing at all to do with you. You cannot possibly . . . the *arrogance* of supposing that you have any idea of what is being discussed, that you have anything to contribute. An undeveloped mind—"

She cried, stung: "Whose fault is that?"

"Not mine, I assure you—not ours. No one stops you, I can assure you, from developing qualities of mind and heart so that when others speak of what is closest to them, that you know not to interfere—higher education is not required for that. It is a lesson can be, must be learned, and at a much younger age—"

"Catriona," Papa had said, "most if not all of that—it is unnecessary. And beneath you."

"Who are *you*, I may ask, to tell me what I may and may not say to my daughter? It is I have had the bringing up of her—it is the mother is it not, who is with her continually? And it is I, thanks to the rough way in which she has cast aside Edward, it is I shall have her in the home for all the years to come . . ."

"Enough, Catriona."

"And don't," she went on, under her breath, "don't imagine that . . ."

Sarah had stopped listening. She had not fought her back, thinking: What is the use? She looked at her now and thought: May I never be so bitter. She thought too that once Mama must have been young—and full of hope.

Where is my hope? she thought.

For a long time now, she had found herself again and again holding her breath. She would notice it suddenly—that she had not been breathing normally: as if, she thought, she had suspended life for those moments. It had become a habit. When she realised, she would let the breath out despairingly in a great sigh. Sometimes for a while after she would feel she could not get enough air and, hungry, thirsty for it, she would take great gulps. Then for a while, if not peace, a sort of strength.

Three days after the conversation at the supper table—when Paul had been away over a week—she woke sharply from a bad dream. The worst was that she could not remember it. The flavour was with her still, but she knew only that she had been trapped somewhere, yet again, that she was being chased (but by whom, what?), that she could not escape, that *she could not breathe.* It was with relief almost that waking, she greedily took in air. And more air. And more. I cannot have enough air, she thought. It was as if she were banking it against some terrible famine.

She sat up the better to take in more—and yet more. She could not stop. She heard herself gasping, crying almost. Her lips tingled with it. Her finger-tips. I shall be free. I shall escape . . . Her mouth now, thick, numb. Her fingers too—she could not feel them. And the breathing, it would not stop. It was not her doing it now; not her at all. She drummed her fingers that she might feel them, drummed them hard on the bedside table. Suddenly one hand, then the other—the thumb went into spasm. Then the whole hand: it was the shape of a duck's beak in the wall-shadow game. She called out between pain and fear, breathing faster and deeper, "Help, help . . ." Such numb lips. Then her whole body arched back like a bow. She cried out again: "Ah, help, *help* . . ."

It was Peggy the maid who found her. Coming in to bring hot water —and rushing to Sarah's bedside.

"Miss Sarah, ma'am, what is it, Miss Sarah—*are you badly?*" And then screaming herself.

But soon there was Papa to see her, and calm her down, and Mama in dressing robe, repeating, "Stop it now, stop it now, Sarah . . ."

Mr. Wilson came over from Leyburn at midday. She was examined very thoroughly and asked, gently, innumerable questions. She felt for the first time since it happened, safe. It was a reassuring voice from childhood. And such exhaustion too—let them do with her what they wished . . . As she lay there, unbelievably weak, sentences floated through the half-open door. (Was she thought to be deaf too?)

". . . primarily rest, John, my dear fellow. Primarily rest. Overstraining of the nervous system—too much stimulation. All that sort of thing. Lovers' tiff set it off, eh? No? Crossed in love? Not a bit of that, eh? Nervous, you know. Essential not to exercise the intellectual functions. *Rest* . . . Dover's Powders ten grains every three or four hours—as you think fit yourself. Carbonate of iron, eh? If they don't agree, of course, ammoniate of copper. *Your* judgment what you would do. *No tea*, be strict about that. Cocoa, yes, very nourishing, make with water. Above all, no stimulation—brain to *rest* . . ."

Now he was standing at the foot of her bed.

"Well, my little lady—you're a fine lass, eh? Too much reading, too much riding—too much everything. Bed rest for a week at least, and then the sofa, three hours every day. And bed by nine o'clock. One day a week of complete rest. *And no books*, eh?"

She lay on the sofa covered by a rug, even though a large fire was kept lit all day. The medicine at first, when she was in bed, had made her very sleepy but as the dose was lessened she felt more lively. Holding her nose, she drank the cocoa she had always loathed. Under the rug she concealed a copy of Browning. *The Ring and the Book* was read—her eyes on the page, her ears to the door. Early in bed, saved from the long tedious evening downstairs, she read more than ever. For the round of social calls, she professed herself too weak. All in all, though not much of a life, it was better. Only, where does it lead? she asked herself.

Paul came back. He glowed with happiness. Both Mama and Papa cautioned him: his tales of London, they would excite her. He must promise not to speak of it more than once a day and then only for fifteen minutes . . . Oh, but I am hungry for it, she thought.

His third day back, he went out for a long walk. It was a late November day of reds and golds—a day to forget winter and remember autumn—the sky suddenly clear blue through till the early afternoon. She would like to have gone with him, but she was allowed only the gentlest of exercise. He was forbidden to take her out driving lest his talk over-excite her. Seeing him set off just after midday: Where is my hope? she thought yet again.

Hope came that afternoon, half an hour after tea. Paul, rushing in to where she lay on the sofa, bounding across the room: "Is there anyone about?"

Her book fell from beneath the rug. "No—Papa is doing visits. Mama plays whist till five—"

"I've had an idea." He sat at the end of the sofa. His eyes shone. Even to see him, healthy, glowing from outdoor exercise, made her feel tired. She had been all day dispirited.

"What have you done to deserve that?" she asked gaily. She feigned a bantering mood, "And what shall you do with it, now you have it?"

"No, listen, darling. I have had an idea. *Such* an idea. It's about the future. Best of all I would love you to *guess*—"

She clasped her hands together, closed her eyes. "You—are going to paint portraits? You—are going on a natural history expedition to Africa. You . . ."

"No, but darling, it's about *you*." He prised her fingers apart. "Listen —I've been feeling so happy, it came to me, you see—I was walking back just now, over the bridge near the Abbey and I looked across towards the Kissing Gate—the leaves are quite off the sycamore—and the sun just as it was setting shone through the trees behind—and I thought suddenly: Well, I could make *her* happy too. That is what I want to do, you see—" He spread her fingers out on the rug, "Now, Silly Sally, what would you like to do best in all the world?"

She was at once struck dumb. In all the world? Anything, everything

—her mind raced, as she tried to remember. "Did I say—travel? To be an intrepid traveller perhaps—did I say that?"

"Yes, yes," he said impatiently, "if you want to travel, of course we'll go. We'll go. But no—something you wanted to do, somewhere *special* you wanted to go—" He paused. Then before she could think again, he said in a rush: "Why not—why don't you go to University? Like you wanted—" For a moment he hesitated, as if the old unsure Paul. "You did want?"

She could feel her breathing growing faster, deeper. "Did I say that?"

"Why, darling, you know—"

But she was only trying to gain time. For very shock she was trying to gain time.

He said, "I feel the most terrible egoist, that I should never have thought of it. It came to me, you see, with the sun through the trees, behind the Kissing Gate—*that* is what I can do for her. *Do you want to go?*" he almost shouted.

Because it was all too much, she said again, dubiously, "I don't know . . ." So many barriers put up, she couldn't believe that a few words between tea and supper on a Wednesday could topple them.

"Because *if you want to, then I will pay*—and to the devil with any of them who say you mayn't!" He flung his arms about her. "I am so happy," and then again: "to the devil with *anyone* who says . . ."

He had left her soon after that. "We mustn't make you too excited. Before anything else, you must get well and *strong . . .*"

"No one shall say anything," he said next day. "It is my money. And I am of age. I may do as I wish with it. While you—you are *twenty-four.*"

"But treated as eighteen. Or less . . ."

At first they did not tell anybody (except Kate—she told Kate at once. "The greatest secret." While Kate said, "And are you *happy?* I so much want you to be . . ."). They spoke about it together, sitting in a huddle. It was almost back to childhood. The excitement.

She said, "But I cannot just go there, to Cambridge. I know nothing. I have forgotten what I did know. My fancy decoration of culture, of general knowledge, it will not go for much amongst serious people. Paul, we must keep calm. I shall have to study first. I have not one word of Latin—"

"But *remember*, darlingus stupidibus? All that. *Cara sistera—*"

"Newnham or Girton or whatever, they will want more than *that.*"

"Of course, of course. And *I* am not one to talk. We shall find out all that, all we need. And as to *which* university—we could draw lots, I suppose."

"Yes, yes," she said. "Let us draw lots . . ."

She did not sleep that night, just as she had not slept the night before. She could not imagine that she would ever need to sleep again. The fevered happiness—and the only fear, that someone might notice. Whenever sleep beckoned, even ever so slightly, then fingers pressing on her excited head would jerk her back to wide awake. It would not matter what anyone said, since no one could stop her. *They could not.*

I am going to escape. In her mind's eye, the Kissing Gate flapped wildly open in the wind—setting her free.

Darlingus stupidibus. Thank you.

NINE

Dic mihi quod feci? Nisi non sapienter amavi.
(Tell me what I have done, except to love unwisely?)

OVID, *Heroides* 2:27

Foxton Hall
3rd December 1877

My dear Paul,

"L'espoir est ma force" . . . your friend Nicholas Straunge-Lacey greets you. I have not been very long about answering you, have I? Are you not impressed? (I shall give, later on, my *considered* comment on all *your* news.)

The metropolis last month—what a fine visit that was! And how I relished my brief escape from the *longueurs* of life in damp Lancashire. I love London in the early winter, fogs and all.

Here, of course, has been great excitement—ten days now since the WEDDING, and Hermione really and truly married to her non-Catholic. Although I must say, Catholic Protestant Hottentot or whatnot, her Adolphus, her "Dolly" is (but tell it not in Gath) rather a *foolish* fellow—making me glad that *I* was not marrying him. But she is naturally as delighted with him as ever—and the fuss about religion in the end died down, as I *predicted it would*. There was a great flurry of Jesuits and some tears (not mine), then all was resolved, and an amicable settlement reached. Truth to tell, there is not a little rejoicing that the "difficult" one is to settle down.

And now—what is all this about your thoughts of Poping (perhaps you should think also of becoming a Jacobite, there is not a little of all that here, you know, if you but scratch the surface—my allegiance, *if questioned*, would be there), and are you really serious? If so, then welcome—but you may not like all the company you must keep (a certain sitting-room with its statues and its pieties is as Catholic as the stables-chapel you so like—and you may not distinguish between the two, so there!). By the way, I write what I wish since I know *you will not leave this letter lying about*.

Revenons à les noces—the sun shone, believe it or not (it has been hidden since), there were even photographs taken outdoors. Father Bromhead presided at the attenuated ceremony (no Nuptial Mass for these two—and instead of incense, just a faint odour of second-best), while as for the Wise Woman she was at her most unctuous—and more Catholic than the Pope. There was not a blessing from Him, by the way, but Cardinal Manning was gracious enough to—I forget what. Really you cannot imagine what it was all like, with the good brothers Grim so clean and tidy (and so delighted to be removed even two days from school—ditto Elfrida, who looked as if butter would not melt etc.). As for Everard, he was I think just a little peeved to be of such little importance. (He will probably pass his honeymoon on a glacier—perhaps he has found even now an Ice Maiden who is willing. Seriously, the R.O. would rather he did not climb so, with such dedication, since the risks are somewhat, and he is the heir—) They would of course like *him* to be married as soon as possible, so that lots of little Straunge-Laceys may come quickly into the world and assure the continuation of the line—and the greater spreading of the True Faith. I don't think Hermione will do much to help in that way, since I think Dolly will make certain that they are little man babies (you know the ruling? that only the girls need be brought up in the Faith, and that the boys may take the husband's religion), all good subjects of the Queen. I know that the Wise Woman prays already that she will have only girls—

For myself I do not think that such an arrangement, compromise, is at all right, and that the Catholic Church should be firmer in this matter. And apropos all this—how I love rules and hedges and barriers and firm declarations—how else are we to enjoy and delight in the vaulting over them, the destruction of the barricades and all the rest of it—and then, *to come safely Home at the end*, thanks to the prayers of loved ones! The prayers rising up from the pure in heart, and body—no, *I do not mock*. You will learn that I am *never more serious* than when I hold up to ridicule—

And now for Rose—"Queen Rose of the rosebud garden of girls" (Mr. Tennyson at his *better*—not his best). She looked very well indeed, since she was persuaded, being a bridesmaid, to pay some attention to her toilette. She was very richly clad—grosgrain silk I think the newspapers said—and her beauty was in fact remarked upon (I have to say that *I* had not thought of her as beautiful, the beauty being in her soul).

Hermione looked—quite remarkable. At one point, for a very short time only, she was just a little uncertain-looking, a little shy. A little winter violet. But already by the wedding breakfast—the wine partaken of—she was herself again, except that she leaned on Dolly's arm and made a fine pretence of being about to be the Little Wife and other such unlikely nonsense, since it is certain that she has worn the breeches from the beginning, and will continue to do so. (Ah, how she used to relieve the tedium of my days—with her anger and her moods—what shall I do without her?)

They are both in their honeymoon now, at Nice. They return just before Christmas but will spend it with Dolly's family, who will have a big house-party in Norfolk.

Well, that is the lot of us. Ah no, you say, but where is the Devil in all this, where is old Nick? Ah now the truth of it was that Nick was well behaved throughout and sweetbreathed and sweet smelling and sweet spoken and sweet tempered. So GOOD that you would not have known him—and all were aghast in wonderment at who was this splendid angel youth. It was Lucifer *before* the Fall of course.

Now this next part is *not* jest. We are to be a small party at Christmas, I think only family and perhaps a cousin or two, and it would please me *very much* if you would perhaps consent to pass it (and the New Year!) with us? Come on December 22nd if you can. Say YES! An early reply will please,

> Yours faithfully, and constantly,
> Nicholas Straunge-Lacey.

P.S. What shall I say, that you will understand? Perhaps—"Beauty and length of days, And night, and sleep in the night—" What do you think?

"*Eighteen* hours, to cross the Monch-Joch. We had been detained a week, you see, by bad weather. We slept the night in the new hut on the side of the glacier, but we did not get away till five in the morning . . . one of the party fell in a crevasse but climbed out—the snow was very soft . . . Coming down, we drove our alpenstocks in and plunged our arms in the snow up to our armpits and then stepped forward— twice I was held up by the rope . . . We asked the guide if there was any danger—the porter was weeping and wringing his hands, thinking he might never see his family again . . . fragments from the glacier . . .

at the bottom a bergschrund which might have engulfed a hamlet. And the snowstorm turning to rain . . ."

So this was Everard. Paul felt he had been listening to him all his life: when he became lord over all he would be far worse than his father, since he would be pompous but without the true feeling of authority, the presence which Paul could not help granting Augustus Straunge-Lacey.

And yet they were all listening politely—except perhaps Nick, who looked as if about to split his sides. Paul could see his mouth quivering with suppressed laughter. "But I have heard it all before," he complained after, "and it was no better then." Aunt Winefride's eyes popped. Uncle Kenelm said occasionally, "My word, my word." Rose listened with a grave dignity which Paul found touching. (Nick said, "Perhaps her confessor has said—you know, a penance for her sins.") There was also a rather owl-eyed girl cousin: she looked as if she were perhaps listening to someone else. To Hubert and Benoit he seemed to be some kind of hero: they hung on his every word.

He was arranging now with heavy elaborateness—to represent this and that—his cutlery, a salt cellar, a pepperpot, a wine glass . . .

"Next year I would like to go to the Zermatt district, I have plans to traverse the Lysjoch, which although not difficult, can be very dangerous —and even impossible in bad weather . . . of course the Val Mastalone now, in the Italian Alps . . ."

The arboretum was a silvery world of frozen branches, iced-over glassy puddles, bird-deserted leafless trees. Paul thought it more beautiful than ever. Frost-tipped, the conifers stood out against the sky.

"We have already twelve degrees," Nick said. "Pray that we get real ice. If it holds, there can be a party. A St. Stephen's Day party . . . Last year Hubert and Benoit spoke of one at school. Quite superior according to them. Quite wild. They smoked, you know. Of course that is the way with them, the Fathers—it is all licence or all constraint and never the middle way. It was they I think bred in me that very love of rules, and the breaking of them. Look, cigars and matches, can you imagine— given to us by the priests—and then at home, *we may not smoke*. It is fortunate that I do not care to. I have seen the R.O., by the way, pick up a letter and *sniff* it to discover whether the writer has offended. What nonsense it all is . . ."

He thought it nonsense, too, about Sarah. He told Paul that privately he thought him mad. Had it not been for Sarah's transparent happiness, Paul would have felt about it all that he had made a miserable mistake. But once she had realised, and accepted his offer, then it had been as if he had snatched her from the jaws of death. Relief, great happiness. By the time he left, plans had been laid, letters written, arrangements made. (His idea): she was to study Greek and Latin twice a week with the clergyman, Mr. Staveley, beginning at once in January. She had told everyone of her plans, announced to everyone: "*it will be so.*" Both his parents had registered disapproval. The same arguments were trotted out. And behold, here now was *Nick* saying: "I have never met her—but you will ruin her life, you know. Women are not constituted, *designed,* to live in this manner. It is all against nature. You have only to look about you—you have only to *listen.* And if she has still hopes of being married—has she? Well, you may forget those—"

"I think of her happiness," said Paul.

"What is happiness?" asked Nick, turning at once to something else; as one who did not want an answer.

Alone in his room, with its big double bed and hangings, Paul smoked again up the chimney. Tomorrow was Christmas Eve and he was surprised to be homesick. He supposed that some of it was to do with the upset over his coming here. Mother especially had been very displeased. It was all at such short notice: "And I am to be left with Sarah, who disregards the doctor's orders and is likely to make herself ill with foolish excitement." (She even dragged in Grandfather: "And that poor crazed man who will be expecting to see you . . .") "You were but just now in London. Really I cannot understand you these last few months . . ."

Some of it was that, but some of it was also, he thought, because of his damned uncertainty over religion. He knew that his feelings about religion were mixed up with Nick (but whatever would get done, he thought, if first everything must be pure?). And Kate: he reminded himself that Kate must really, deep down, belong to the old religion. She would surely have been baptised in it—which meant, if he had learnt aright, that she belonged forever. So that, were he to change, would it not in a way forge yet another precious link with her?

Nick was so much part of his life now. Excepting his deep love for Kate, how dull seemed all that had gone before. He would not have believed it. The stay in London with all its excitements (and the news of Hermione's sudden engagement) had passed in a rush of happiness. Nick had never repeated again the episode of the summerhouse. It was as if it had all been the remnants of his fever—now, assured of Paul's love, he wanted nothing but the most chaste of embraces. And words, words.

The day after his arrival at Foxton he had had tea with Sybil. He had been summoned to her room. Only ten minutes in and she had said, "But it is *wonderful,* my dear, that you are thinking, seriously thinking, of becoming One of Us." Her hand rested on his. "Father Bromhead—"

He had shied away then like a nervous horse. The one person with whom he did not want, would *never* want to discuss it. Other than Nick, only oddly enough with Rose could he imagine doing so in that family.

He attacked Nick later: "It is *you* who have told her. That's damnable—"

Nick said innocently, "But you had not *said* that it was in confidence . . ."

The owl-eyed cousin was called Alice, and when actually spoken to was found to be very pleasant. She was an orphan: her father had been killed before she was born, in India, during the Mutiny. Her mother had been made ill by it all and had died when Alice was only four. She had been sent to a convent called Poles, where she had been moderately happy. The holidays had been spent with relatives. "Rose has been my greatest friend. She has been like a sister to me." Paul wondered—the outsider watching—whether the Straunge-Laceys intended her for Everard. If so, he was paying her little attention. He paid *everyone* little attention. With his father's heavy brow, shoulders already stooping, he would sit waiting for an opportunity to take the stage. For several moments he would address his audience, then lapse back into the waiting state. Poor Alice, Paul thought, if that is to be her destiny.

A hamper sent by the Straunge-Laceys to those boys at Stonyhurst who could not go home for Christmas. It had been a family custom for some years now. A goose, two turkeys, several chickens and hams, six bottles of sherry and port, and two of raspberry vinegar.

Presents among the family were given after Midnight Mass. All gathered together in the enormous Tudor drawing-room with its richly carved ceiling, its panelled oak walls with their worked medallions of earlier Straunge-Laceys. Inscribed above the fireplace, as on the back of the great oak chair in the hall: *"L'espoir est ma force"* (Hope is my strength).

Paul had brought with him what he thought would be sufficient gifts: mainly sweetmeats, cakes, Yorkshire specialities. In his turn he was embarrassed by the amount of and the thought that had gone into the gifts he received that night. Nick had given him no less than five books—mostly poetry, but one containing woodcuts of flora; Rose, a water-colour of the arboretum, seen from the lake. Elfrida gave him a brightly coloured scarf knitted by herself. She told him engagingly: "I *was* making it for a cousin, but when I heard you were coming . . ."

They must rejoice. The snow lay thick still, but not too thick for access. And the ice on the small lake was firm, quite firm enough for a St. Stephen's Day party. It was to begin in the afternoon and go on into the night. In the morning they made preparations and practised their skating, especially dancing. Rose surprised Paul by her grace, Elfrida by her clumsiness. Alice would not venture on the ice at all. Paul could not persuade her and wondered if Everard, who spent the morning shut up with his father, would.

A small enclosure was built on the ice with a log fire burning. Those who could only slide had to be kept separate from the skaters for their own safety, so that a length of rope was laid along the ice to mark the boundary. The sky darkened soon after luncheon, heavy with unfallen snow. By the time the first guests arrived it was falling softly. When it stopped, servants and men from the estate came and swept it away. Later in the intervals of skating they came and removed the skate-cuttings.

From about three o'clock onwards guests were arriving all the time, usually in quite large groups. There must have been more than thirty, some very brightly, even outrageously, dressed. There was a party from a house about a mile away. Paul had seen most of them at Mass, at Foxton. The son of the house was called Reginald. Paul remembered Hermione making scathing remarks about him ("I believe his mama actually thinks there is *hope* there—the very idea! And too, as if I could ever settle down only one mile from home . . ."). Whizzing past Paul on the outside, he all but knocked him down not once but twice. "Dreadfully sorry—and I don't know you, do I?" Then the second time: "Look—I don't know you, do I?"

"Yes, you do," said Paul, "you knocked me over about a quarter past four."

"Did I now? Dreadfully sorry . . ."

But at that moment all attention was diverted by Nick, one of the most skilful and graceful of the skaters, who was attempting to jump over a chair placed upside down on the ice. He succeeded and bowed to the roar of applause. Then repeated the trick, only to fall heavily. Rubbing his hip bone ruefully, he said to Paul in an aside, "I see you've just been down—all but." Then: "That wretched Reggie wretch—you will see, he'll be drunk as a rolling fart before the party's out . . ."

At first everyone merely skated around before going in for refreshments. The quadrille band was to arrive about six. Chinese lanterns were used after darkness fell: blue, green, crimson lights. "Oh, how pwetty," said Reginald's sister, who was very affected and looked through Paul as she spoke. She had trouble with her r's. "Oh, but we must have ices," she said a little later, "I *adore* ices. And to eat an ice *on* the ice, so deliciously Wussian, don't you think?"

Before the dancing began, Father Bromhead came out and took a stately turn. The lake seemed very crowded now. Everard and Alice were among the dancers. Rose surprised Paul again by her grace, her assurance. Elfrida, laughing, stumbling, had to stop. The glow from exercise, from drink—the never-ending supplies of hot punch—excited Paul. He thought only: how dull if I had stayed in Downham.

Once he collided badly with Rose. It was his fault entirely. "Miss Straunge-Lacey, forgive me—"

Nick, sweeping by, threw an arm about her. Paul said: "I was apologising."

"Rose," Nick said, "she *is* a rose, is she not?" He had still an arm about her. Their two heads were caught suddenly in the coloured lantern light. Both of them so unalike and yet for that moment—their eyes. They were both laughing. "*Please* call me Rose," she said to Paul.

Later after the dancing and when some of the older people had gone in, there were games on the ice. Chairs were brought out for musical chairs. They played hissing and clapping. Behind the lake and the bright lantern light, the arboretum could be glimpsed, shadowy, eerie, unreal. Afterwards Paul and Elfrida and Nick and two others were involved in bear-fighting. Elfrida, who could not skate fast enough to escape, grew very excitable. Imp had come out to join them and stood on the lake edge yapping.

As Paul caught her, "You'll spiflicate me," she cried. He could feel her uncorseted ribs as he tickled her mercilessly. "No, *don't* . . ." And she giggled again.

In the deserted library at two in the morning, he and Nick talked, drinking nothing stronger than China tea. Inevitably, as always now, the conversation seemed to have turned to religion. Paul had remarked casually about Father Bromhead that he found him very pleasant if somewhat dry.

"But mainly he does not fit in with the idea in my mind—in the mind of most people surely: that of the scheming Jesuit. 'Jesuitical' is after all not a *kind* adjective."

"Oh, but he is an admirable man," Nick said. "Only, I do not like him at all. Or any of them for that matter. At Stonyhurst really—it would not do, you know. Feldkirch, where I went after, in Austria, was

a little better. The food was good and the dormitories heated. *But* . . .
Of course I admire them tremendously—if Christ *must* have soldiers
then they are a first-class army. And after all, doesn't it often occur that
a ruler, himself quite meek and mild, has troops of an alarming feroc-
ity?" He downed his tea. "And they counsel women, of course—at that
I believe they are excellent—"

Paul said suddenly, for no good reason, "Then Rose is bound to do
what she is told?"

Nick looked surprised. "In a manner of speaking, yes."

"And that is why she waits till she is twenty-one?"

"Yes, of course. I mean, it is known that what the parents want—
that is God speaking."

"Even if it is something wrong?"

"Wrong-doing? Of course not. If *sin* is involved—"

But the peaceful end of the evening had made Paul calmly argumentative. In his attraction towards this religion it was these very pockets of
strangeness which lured him the most.

"But what of 'the end justifies the means'—and all that?"

"A saying heard too often, and quite misunderstood. But that apart—
look at what happens, say, in battle, when we must kill so that others,
including ourselves, may live."

"And if to save a life," Paul persisted, "you must, say, tell a lie?"

"What is truth, though?" Nick asked carelessly, as if hoping to end
the conversation there. He offered Paul brandy, but when Paul refused,
he poured into their cups the remainder of the tea. He said suddenly:
"It's all very difficult—the whole question. After all, it is—well, by *sin*
that we come into the world."

"But surely not," argued Paul, "if by that you mean—"

"Oh, but yes. The whole language. It is quite plain. It is a great evil
of itself. It was only learned after leaving the Garden. But it must be
done so that the race may go on. And it is to be done for that purpose.
A *necessary* evil . . ." He looked away from Paul. "Do you not find it
disgusting—truly?"

"No, not at all. I—"

"To think that one's mother—that one's *sister* might . . . Hermione,
perhaps that is different, but . . . It is all there, Paul, the Word of God
—the end of marriage is procreation. Only—" he seemed almost to be
talking to himself—"Our Lady, the Virgin Mary—*she* was a virgin. It is
a very important fact, that. One that must not be disputed."

"You seduce me with your certainties," Paul said. "You are so certain
of everything—"

"But how can I not be?" He looked back, open-eyed. "It has all been proved to me, again and again. Ask me anything. Go on—do. To prove it is unimaginably easy." He pushed aside his empty cup. "But to live up to it. That is another matter."

The lake had been tidied. Before they were up, secret armies had swept clean not only the skate-cuttings but the litter of party enjoyment.

"Everyone must skate again," Nick said. "I shall sing on the ice. Rose, bring your fiddle out." But she was tired and would not come out at all. "Elfrida—bring the piano. We have invited several to join us after luncheon."

Two knickerbockered young men appeared whom Paul could not remember from yesterday. Everard, looking very serious, had said he would come out "after I have spoken with Father in the library."

Nick said: "He must always, even in holiday times. These serious talks . . . I am not at all sure what they are about. I think this time it is to do with engaging someone different in charge of the arboretum."

Everard appeared an hour or so after the meal. The light was already going. He wore a fur cap atop his fur-trimmed skating suit. The would-be elegant effect was spoilt by a shabby red muffler. As he skated heavily by, the fringed ends of the muffler flapping, Nick called out something impudent. Everard ignored him and continued towards the far side of the lake, the arboretum side. Paul was watching as, skating round the edge, he stumbled and fell. He fell awkwardly, the back of his head striking against a stone at the water's edge. He lay quite still where he had fallen.

People were over there within seconds. Nick was first and as Paul came up, said: "My God, my God." Then: "Get Father—" Paul did not know whether he meant Augustus or the Jesuit. As he began to skate back across the lake, his legs heavy, shaking, Nick called after him, "Hurry, *hurry*, then!" Struggling to remove his skates, he saw Elfrida.

"I'll go for Mama—" She pulled at his sleeve, "He's bad—say he isn't bad, Mr. Rawson . . ."

Augustus Straunge-Lacey was discovered fast asleep in the library. When Paul put a hand on his shoulder, the touch urgent, he opened his eyes. He woke suddenly and completely, suspicious at first, then the outrage leaving his face quickly. He hastened out as he was, in his carpet slippers, shuffling with little care over the ice.

People seemed to have come from nowhere. There was a crowd round Everard's body. He could not at first be seen.

"For Christ's sake—a doctor. Has no one gone for a *doctor?*"

He had not stirred at all. There was the question of whether he should be moved. After a while and with the utmost care he was brought up to the house and laid in the drawing-room. The red muffler contrasted strangely with the intense white of his face.

Father Bromhead brought him the last Sacraments about seven that evening. The family and Paul were all in attendance. Elfrida explained after, that although Extreme Unction was the Sacrament of the Dying, often it brought people back to life. She explained too that even though Everard had not made the responses, or shown any sign of life, that did not mean he might not have heard—and prayed.

He did not recover consciousness and died just before midnight.

The funeral was to be six days later, on the Thursday. All the next day telegrams were being dispatched, carried over the ice-bound roads. Paul's first thought had been that he must go. Indeed he wanted to leave. But when he said that to Nick, Nick had said in a shocked voice: "You would desert us?" He said it dramatically but as if, strangely, it was truly meant: "You would desert us?"

"You cannot need me. I would be only a hindrance. And I am not the family."

"Not the family—but you are my friend. What sort of friendship is it, then, that you leave us all when we need you?"

"But your parents—"

"They, I am certain, will think it cowardly if you should leave us now. Stay—at least until the funeral. At least until you would have left."

And so he agreed. He supposed that amongst so many anyway, his presence would scarcely be noticed. Over the next few days the great hall-bell rang continually as the carriage, with snow on its roof, brought yet more relatives, yet more friends. Perhaps it was only fifteen or sixteen, but it seemed to him fifty—a hundred.

"Terrible, tragic accident . . ." the words echoed again and again. He lost track of names, faces; was polite to all. No one was curious as to who he was. In small groups the young and middle-aged walked gravely through the icy grounds, or prayed beside the body, laid out in the library. The elderly sat all day by the fire. In reverent tones, happenings and people were discussed. At meal times, salt and pepper were asked for in reverent tones too. All the time there was an undercurrent of subdued pleasure, as if a meeting for any other excuse would have been a delight.

Paul spent much time himself with Elfrida, who seemed the most upset of the brothers and sisters. Hermione, who had come up with

Dolly on the second day, was sick and spent most of the time in bed. Nick he saw little of: he was a great deal with his parents, especially his mother. Augustus was scarcely to be seen at all except at meals and not always then. He appeared shocked. He walked stiffly and as if not seeing those around him, his posture more stooped than ever.

Nick said, "Grandfather died very suddenly, you know. About twelve years ago now. He died in the arboretum. His heart, I think. He was found just slumped down beneath one of the beeches. He loved his trees so . . ."

Rose did not say much, so that he could not tell how much she was affected. She seemed preoccupied, helping her mother with all the arrangements. Once he met her coming in from outside; the cold had lent her a little colour. As she pulled off her gloves, he said, "I am so sorry about—your brother. I had meant to say something earlier." Then as if he had been waiting to say it—and perhaps he had: "I shall pray," he said. "For him—for all of you. That is, if you think God . . . I mean, my Protestant entreaties . . ."

"Of course God will listen," she said gently and in a matter-of-fact tone, but smiling at him as if he had given her great pleasure. (He had expected that she might protest a little or even, as Nick or Elfrida would have done, explain to him the theology behind both of their remarks . . .) "He will be delighted, Everard too." Then: "I am just going to see him—my brother, I mean—before luncheon. Should you like to come too?"

That night he dreamed of the Kissing Gate. He was surprised for in the daytime he had not thought of home at all (and scarcely even of Kate . . .). Snow covered the Gate and the pillars beside it. Arum lilies were fastened to the bars. The churchyard behind was white: a coffin, speckled with melting snow, stood on the path. As he walked up to it, he saw that Francis Ingham was already standing there. "I am the guardian of this gate," he said to Paul, "and you may not come in." But he smiled as he spoke. Then: "I am a guardian angel," he said. Paul said, "But Francis—that is Roman Catholic talk. *Guardian angels* . . ." Francis replied, smiling still: "Yes, that is why you may not come in . . ."

The next morning after breakfast, Sybil Straunge-Lacey took him aside.

"Dear Mr. Rawson—a favour." She put her hand on his. "We *do* want you to stay. You have been such a support. This afternoon we expect two more nephews—young boys over from Stonyhurst. Mrs.

Thompson says it will be simpler to put them in Nicholas' room. Perhaps he may share yours?" Without waiting for an answer, she patted his hand and moved away.

Nick said later, "I hear I am to move in with you." He added carelessly, "No smoking in the fireplace while I am about."

The remainder of the day, Paul spent with Elfrida and two of her girl cousins—and Imp, whom Elfrida carried everywhere now. Most of the afternoon they were in Tommy's, the housekeeper's, room where Alice joined them.

He and Nick went to bed early. It was a still night, and not quite so cold perhaps, the pall-like snow beginning to thaw. The ice on the lake was no longer safe. They talked, lying in the great bed, for a long while. Emotionally he had never felt so close to Nick. He thought, it is no wonder that I love him. Gone was the mocking Nick of before Christmas, the withdrawn Nick of these days of mourning.

He said to Paul: "I think I have been very moody, odd, these last few days. I haven't slept, you know. I am the only one besides the Wise Woman that the R.O. will speak to. He has been weighing me down with terrible future responsibilities." A little later he said: "I think I shall try to sleep now. You have made it possible. Kiss me, would you?" He turned his face towards Paul, like a child's.

Within minutes he was asleep. Paul lay awake, afraid to move lest he wake him. The household was quiet—the only sound outside the barking of one of the gun dogs. Soon after, startling him, there was the shrill cry, over and over again, of a vixen. In the arboretum perhaps? He waited to hear the eerie cry answered and somehow as he waited he slipped into sleep.

He awoke suddenly. Nick's face was buried in his neck. He was crying. Muttering too between sobs. It was impossible to make out what he was saying. He clutched at Paul, clawing him.

"Nick—Nick. What is it?" It must be a nightmare. "Nick—wake up. *What is it?*"

But he did not seem to be asleep. The weeping, he would not, could not stop. "Paul, hold me in your arms. *Hold me.*" The name "Everard" —Paul could just make that out. Not once, but over and over and over again.

"I don't understand. Did you love Everard so much?" He spoke to Nick gently. "I did not know. You *mocked* him so—"

"But that is it. I have been wicked. I shall be punished . . ." He lay still in Paul's arms, and wept. After a while, very gradually, he quietened. Paul thought: perhaps he will sleep now.

It was then, just a little while later, that it happened. He could not make out what time it was: no light escaped the shutters. Afterwards when he remembered it all, he thought only, I should have been able to stop him. I would have stopped him, had I not loved him . . . Such a small step from quiet clasp to embrace, from embracing to kissing. And the violence, the despair of those kisses; of the love-making and the union that followed.

Although even when he was completely honest with himself, he had to say: it was not my doing. Nick had returned, if not to the mocking Nick, to the Nick in command. In everything it was his way.

But "Darling, dear love, darling, I shall be punished . . ." Now here, afterwards, it was back again to the tears, the pleas for reassurance.

"Paul, when I was—before I was—I used to be good. God loved me. I could look at God. At Our Lady—" He buried his face again in Paul's neck. Outside, the dawn was coming up. From the trees below the window, the first chattering of birds: "Our Lady will intercede for me—'Oh Blessed Virgin never was it known that anyone who fled to thy protection implored thy help or sought thy intercession was left unaided . . .' You know that prayer? And then Rose, my Rose, she will intercede. It won't matter what I've done. Tell me, Paul, it doesn't matter what we've done. That Heaven is not closed." His voice was harsh, dry. "Rose. Rosa Mystica. I count on Rose to save me. The prayers of a nun, of a *virgin*. Tell me it is all right, that she will save me . . ."

On and on and on, as if some secret unknowable terror had been released.

"It is all right," Paul told him, "it is all right. Yes, she will save you. Rose will save you."

The coffin, draped with a black pall, stood in the chapel. Yesterday had been the last chance to see Everard. As he lay in the library the throng of relatives and friends paid their last respects. Elfrida had held Paul's hand.

There were candles of unbleached wax on either side of the coffin. Its foot was turned towards the altar. Paul knelt between Elfrida and Alice; Uncle Kenelm and Aunt Winefride were in the same bench. Earlier that morning Sybil had lent him a book that he might follow the service: he could have shared with either of the girls and was surprised that with the twin preoccupations of grief and the funeral arrangements she should have bothered.

But she had wanted perhaps to speak to him. For in handing him the prayerbook she had taken him to one side: "Now my dear, I want just to say—in all our sorrow, what you have done for Nicholas . . . Although you are not *as yet* of the Faith, you have been able to help him.

He is not a strong boy." She laid her hand over his, her face came nearer. "And now he must be one day father of the whole family—"

As she spoke, he felt all the time as if he had been found out. She knows, he thought. She does not know she knows, but she knows—something. (And she knows too that once Nick was deep inside her, was part of her. He became faintly disgusted, even embarrassed at the thought, *as she must be.*)

"It is a very particular responsibility, Mr. Rawson, *Paul*. He must begin to be serious—it was in any case time he began to be so. And *you* will help . . . I have put him especially in the care of Our Lady."

As they had brought the coffin in, Father Cuthbert in black stole and cope had sprinkled it with holy water. Hubert and Benoit were altar boys. The antiphon was "*Si iniquitates* . . ." ("If thou O Lord wilt mark iniquities, Lord, who shall stand it?")

"*Miserere mei Deus*," they had chanted. Now as the Mass for the Dead began, he saw that already Elfrida's face quivered. Nick sat further ahead with his parents. Rose, and a pale Hermione accompanied by Dolly, were near them.

"*Deus qui proprium est* . . . O God, whose property is ever to have mercy and to spare, we humbly beseech Thee on behalf of the soul of Thy servant *Everard Mary* . . . that he be taken up by Thy holy angels and borne to our home in paradise . . ."

"*Dies irae, dies illa . . . Pie Jesu Domine, dona eis requiem.*" Father Bromhead, reciting the Pater Noster as he walked twice round the coffin, sprinkling holy water again, and incense. Hubert and Benoit standing by with lighted candles. And then the burial itself. Another Straunge-Lacey to join the dust of those others going back hundreds of years.

"*Requiescat in pace* . . ." For a few moments, Paul forgot everything else. Then returning once more to the chapel, they recited again the antiphon "*Si iniquitates*." He did not look at Nick.

"If thou O Lord, wilt mark iniquities, O Lord, who shall stand it?"

TEN

I peeped through the window,
I peeped through the door,
I saw pretty Katie
A-dancing on the floor.
I cuddled her and fondled her,
I set her on my knee,
I says, Pretty Katie,
Won't you marry me?

NURSERY RHYME

"I wish you could be rid of Greaves," Kate said. The china bowl before
her was dusty with cloves. She and Flo, sitting together, were pushing
them into oranges, covering the fruit completely, their finger tips brown
with the powder.

Ned said: "A promise is a promise." And then more easily, "But he is
better always in the summer."

"He makes mischief," she said. "At Paul's party last year . . ."

The fire in the cottage leapt high. Outside, snow could be seen on
the sill. Little Patrick, fastened into his swing, went gently to and fro
watching his mother.

Flo asked, "What happened, Mama—what happened?"

"The winter is more than half over, Kate," Ned said. "So . . ."

Ned was too easy, too good, she thought. She had made him happy
and in making him happy had made him too good. Deeply trusting.
Perhaps he had always wanted to be so and it was just that she had allowed it. A serene middle age: that had been her gift to him. Only
sometimes now would he return to less secure days, to memories ragged

at the edges that would cause him to tear at her hungrily as if, deeper and deeper, he would in the end burrow to safety.

"He looks always to see what unpleasantness he may stir," she went on. Although she thought that she should not, in front of the children. "He is worst of all when he smiles—"

Ned said again, as if patiently explaining to a child, "Ah well—that is the way of it. It is his unfortunate appearance."

She said, "I don't speak of his appearance, Ned."

"I'd rather you'd not . . . It's no fault of his, the Lord knows that."

She said obstinately, "I could just wish he did not stare so. When he is bad in the winter—if I so much as go into the works. And the children. They are afraid of his looks. No, not his appearance, his *looks*— the ones he gives them."

Ned said, "His grudge against the Rawsons—deep down—that's the manner it takes. He's a simple soul, and he doesn't forget. And that's all about it."

But Greaves was not always better in the summer months. Years ago, twenty-five perhaps, one June day he had plucked alive two young ducks and then sunk them in the River Down, by the Kissing Gate. Sarah-Mother had wept.

And he had been too in a bad mood that day already more than fifteen years ago now, when she had walked up to the works after a sleepless night in which she had known—known without a shadow of doubt—that Ned wished to marry her. She had been thinking as she walked across the square and then up the turning: he will ask me, and I shall say no. I *must* say no. Someone she had *never thought of marrying*. But he would be owed at least the dignity of an explanation, and that she dreaded . . .

The sight of him the night before, his face in the fading light, watching as John lifted her up into the gig.

"Kate—I see you—we meet on Sunday?" She had thought then, I have till Sunday. But in the watches of that long night she had realised: the sooner she saw him the better. One part of her hoped that he regretted already what he had said and done: that he would want it forgotten. But it did not seem to her likely. I know Ned, she thought.

Oh, but then how, she had asked herself, how, when I have said "No, I cannot"—when I have said that, how can we ever be the same again? She felt in her a double sadness, not only from what she must say to him but also because it was as if she were undoing in some way all that was past. No one—not even Sarah-Mother—had been to her what Ned had . . .

As she had come through the door of the rope-works, Greaves had had his back to her. He was moving some bales of twine. When he turned, he stood almost barring her way, the humped shoulder pushed exaggeratedly high. She thought for the first time: why, he *exaggerates* it—

"Yes?" His voice was surly.

He must not be allowed to be rude, she had thought then. Ned would not like it. Nor Father. But to correct in this manner she hated, had not the stomach for at all. And it frightened her. She closed her eyes a moment. Then in a rush, "Greaves, you should say 'Miss Kate' . . ."

He lifted the shoulder higher still, looked through, beyond her. "Miss Kate," he said as if he were speaking of, rather than to her.

She asked, "Is Mr. Ned, the young master, is he there?"

The new apprentice—a soft-faced boy, very gentle and eager to please, came up to her: "Please Miss, Miss Kate. I—"

Greaves cuffed him so sharply, back of hand swinging, that Kate winced, the sound making her smart. The boy's eyes filled and his head hung, turned away—so, she thought, that she might not see his tears. In sudden compassion and longing she said to herself: *I want a son.* But then, realisation. In the short interval between Greaves's slouching journey through to the back and Ned's appearance, she lived a lifetime of barren years. And such a feeling too of protest, of rebellion—almost hatred for this family who had rescued her when she might have slipped away in peace . . .

"Let us go out a little," Ned said. "A moment while I speak to Greaves—"

She said, "I interrupted you at your work. And I was brought up not to. Mother said."

"But that was always good—when you came in, and oughtn't. That first time when Mother brought you—she and I talking (Ann too, that was meant to be watching . . .). And you made that tangle, hemp in your hair, round your ankles . . ."

"Ned," she said, "Ned, about last night."

They were walking in the direction of the Castle. He had slowed his pace for her. He was very quiet. The road winding uphill: "I thought—" she began, then burst out: "Did you mean it, Ned?"

"Mean? But how not, my little Kate—" He too spoke in a rush. "I worried all night, worried that I'd maybe frightened you, that it'd been the wrong kind of talk. That I'd presumed where I'd no right—" He wasn't looking at her. His head was lowered slightly. He had taken hold of her arm now to guide her. A grinning chimney sweep observed them from near the Castle wall. "I'd thought to write to you—tonight. About —but you'll know maybe what I'd a mind to say—" He hesitated, but only for a moment. "Kate, if—we could be wed?"

The sooner it was done . . . She spoke at once: "Ned—I can't. The truth is—my love, you honour me so much. I cannot think of a compliment greater." She paused, and felt her heart turning heavily, slowly over: "I cannot. And—that is all." She could hear the break in her voice. "And Ned—please dear, you are not to be hurt. It is *I* who cannot—I would, if I could."

She thought at first that he was going to accept, say simply, "If that is how you wish . . ." Thinking, that will be the end of the matter. But for her there was a sudden rush of emotion, remembering all the love she had to give him, and too, worse perhaps, all the love for his children —*their* children. Now it is my turn to weep, she thought. How good that as they walked on up the road now, no one came by.

But he had not been going to accept. He said stubbornly, "You would if you could—Kate, what sort of talk is that, eh?" He took hold of her hand. He said almost angrily, "If you're not of a mind to say yes —then it's no, and have done with it. Don't carry on—"

She had begun to cry. How like women, that they were always weeping. (And yet *he* had cried too—and only yesterday.)

He said, "It cost me a lot, to say what I said. I deserve better in the way of an answer."

Because he had hold of her arm and because the path was clear ahead, she closed her eyes, then said in a rush: "Since I mayn't have children, then it's not right to say yes. You need children—you lost that child and a wife. You deserve better, it's in *that* way you deserve better . . ."

"What's this—mayn't have children? Kate, *what's this?* Did—is it Dr. Wilson? What's it about? And how *in heaven's name do they know?*"

"I can't—" She felt her mouth too big for the words. "There's no way I can say . . ." The shame (she who had been lifted above shame with Richard), the shame of discussing such a matter with Ned, who had known her so well, so long.

"To me, you can—"

She shook her head.

He said: "Is it fair, right, to say such things and then not to . . . How do I know, then, it's not some daft fancy?"

"Don't speak like that," she said. "You were never used to speak to me like that."

"You see me angry," he said.

"Then you mustn't be. Richard—" she began, and then broke off. She felt as if she were being hit. "It's *not* a fancy—"

"Well," he said, "if you won't tell—" This was not the Ned she knew, this angry man. She had seen him, she supposed, stern before: with the apprentices, with Greaves. But with her, never.

Adding to her distress was the certain feeling that she had hurt him. "I don't want to go back home, in the house—not just now," she said.

"I can't have you fretting," he said. They had turned back down the path they had first walked and were not far from Linden House. He said then: "If she's within doors, would you go in to Catriona?" His voice was gentle.

Inside the house, when he had left (and he had said little, only suggesting to Catriona: "Kate's upset—she'd best rest awhile"), she had astonished herself. Tears—they might have been dammed for a lifetime. All the tears gathered since the day she spoke to Richard for the last time.

They happened almost as soon as she began to talk to Catriona. And how little, she thought now in 1878, how little I told her. Paul, who had been with his mother and who stared now at Kate as if she were a new, a different person—her distress puzzling, confusing him—was sent back to the nursery. Sarah was not in evidence.

Trying to remember what she had said then, Kate thought now: I told her only what I must. Ned expected me to confide in her. I wanted to. But I could not tell all. Not even to the woman who, after Sarah-Mother, I had perhaps known best of all. (Better certainly than dear, good Eliza—to whom I could have told *nothing*.)

"But who," Catriona asked almost at once, "*who* has told you this nonsense—for nonsense it must be. Where have you heard it?"

"In the town. It was here—in Downham."

"Gossip. Something overheard. Something misunderstood, Kate. And *I* cannot understand it. Certainly I cannot—"

But Kate could only echo Georgiana's words, as she had heard them ("diseased, unclean, tainted . . .").

"What person, though, Kate—what *person*?"

"I heard it—from someone who—this person had it from one who *must* know."

"I demand then that you tell me." Catriona, holding her by the shoulders, shaking her—who had comforted her, on whose shoulder she had wept only moments ago.

"Let me be!" she cried.

"Is it that you do not wish to marry Ned? Is it that? If it is only that—"

"No—no. Yes—I—you know that Ned is dear to me and—" Still the tears flowed. She had thought that no more could be left.

Now here was Catriona, gentle again, but saying quite firmly that she would speak to John: "And then we shall have it all out . . ."

She had thought first to put a stop to that, to cry halt to the whole shameful business. To say that she would never have wanted to marry Ned and that was that. But then, tiredly, her face still twitching from tears shed and unshed, she had agreed. Catriona might talk to John . . .

She heard nothing of any sort for nearly three days. Sam had a bad summer cold, for which he took too much whisky. She and Eliza found yet another hiding place in which he secreted supplies. When on the third day he seemed to have a fever, Eliza asked John to call in. Kate avoided seeing him. She felt that she could not bear the shame of wondering if he knew; if Catriona had yet spoken to him . . .

That night, without warning, she felt flood back into her the memory of her shame with Walter. The prodding fingers, the pain, the goose-flesh of humiliation. It was as if it had just happened. *As if it were yesterday*, she thought.

Catriona called the next morning. Eliza was out. They sat together in the front room.

"Such an embarrassment," said Catriona, "that I should ask any such thing. John was appalled." She explained to Kate that she had had to wait on a suitable moment to speak to him, and that had not been until last night. "I *cannot always approach him.*"

That Catriona's marriage might not be perfect—that indeed it was probably difficult, Kate had noticed but did not think about very much: registering that she had often seen them disagree over Paul, and that little Sarah had often to go to her too-busy father for love. (And what had been those hints and whispers about their long separation the year before Catriona had carried Paul?) She thought now: I have not been loving and understanding enough of Catriona.

". . . and when I asked John—as delicately as possible—these matters, they are not always easy to speak of, Kate. But his short answer was: *it is all nonsense.*"

The words—they were more shock to her than relief. She could not at first take them in.

"And I must add this, Kate. I am detailed to ask you. It is very important. You must tell me who has *said this to you?*"

The same old question. Of course she would not tell. And forgetting for the moment anyone but Richard, she thought too: of what *use* is this knowledge now? If I had known five years ago . . . And then remembering: but now it will be all right for Ned.

For a while Catriona went on insisting. "It is for your own sake. Such a wicked lie. It cannot be left . . ." She stayed with Kate all that morning. Just after midday, John came too. Once again, Kate felt shame. He insisted, Kate must tell them. *Whom* had she overheard?

"There is always malice about," said Catriona. "And in a plaće such as this. Edinburgh was no better—"

They handed Kate a piece of paper. "Write it down," they said. "The name. Please, Kate."

She had stared for many minutes at the blank page, torn from John's notebook. Then, feeling sudden anger fill her heart, almost absent-mindedly she traced a capital only. "G."

They had thought, at once, that it was Greaves. She could not bear that, could not in justice let that pass.

"It is something of which he is quite *capable*," John said.

That was not at all the same thing, she had insisted. It *had not been Greaves.* Reluctantly they accepted her assurances. She felt that they did not believe her. That Ned would not believe her either.

Catriona kissed her goodbye in the late afternoon. She seemed reluctant to let Kate go, as if this mission had in some way given her purpose. Releasing Kate from her embrace: "Now go and tell Ned," she said. "Tell him you will have him."

And she had done so, of course. And been happy, almost. Certainly happier than she had ever dreamed possible during the last five years. That very next Sunday, watching Georgiana Ingham climb up the steps to the family pew (with Richard—and Frances), she had thought with a feeling almost of relief: she is not worth my hate. She does not deserve anything so real. She is a nothing. I could have betrayed you, Georgiana Ingham, she thought. But I did not, will not. You are not *worth my hate.*

The wedding was on a blustery October day, the wind lifting the leaves from the elms in the churchyard. It was a popular match, every Rawson rejoicing and it seemed half the town too. The Kissing Gate garlanded. And Ned so *happy.*

It is more blessed to give than to receive, she thought, again and again those first peaceful, almost happy months. Early the next summer Will was born, a seven months' child. And it was with his birth that all the memories came back. The *other* memories. ("Can you really remember nothing?" Sarah-Mother had asked. "*Nothing* at all?") Memories from further back, and further away than she would have cared, had ever *dared* to look . . .

ELEVEN

Sarah said: "I have no Greek, you see."

He put his head on one side. "Ah," he said sadly, "she has no Greek . . ."

She liked him at once. The Reverend Staveley. Matthew Staveley. She had of course met him socially many times but she did not think she had ever had more than the lightest of conversations with him. Now, over the next six or seven months she was to visit him three times a week: to become more at home in Latin, and to make acquaintance with Greek.

Paul had arranged it. She had had to do nothing—although she would have quite liked to. She had so much energy now. After Paul's surprise, she had begun to recover almost at once and had felt hardly able to bear the enforced rest until Christmas: without Paul and with Mama still in a slight sulk over Sarah's decision. But now here was the New Year. 1878, bright and shining like a new penny . . .

Some, a great deal in fact, of the study she could do for herself: the History, the Scriptures, and the Arithmetic—that was just to learn again. She was preparing herself for an examination called Cambridge Higher Locals, only some nine years old, which she could sit quite soon after going to Newnham Hall—the younger of the two women's colleges in Cambridge—which had accepted her for the autumn. If that went well, they would see if she might proceed to Tripos and do degree work. Classics, she hoped, would be her subject.

Of course it was always possible that she might find she could not *manage* the Latin and Greek. (Possible, but not probable. If I wish to do it, then I shall do it, she thought.) Papa in fact had suggested just that. "It's not so much your *brain*," he had said, "as coming to it so late. A lad, he'll often have done it before he's time to notice. And when he does, the spadework's over with. Too—there are some just not suited . . ." But that remark had in its turn made Mama angry. She said yet again that *she* had learnt Latin: "Some at least, and without any *difficulty at all* . . ."

The Reverend Staveley did not think that Sarah would have any trouble. The more so when he heard how hard she intended to work. He at once set her a cracking pace.

"And you are really to go to Newnham Hall," he asked that first day. "You are not the slightest afraid?"

But she *was* afraid. "Yes. I am."

"You are accustomed to be from home, though? I think perhaps the men students—to say nothing of the dons—will not be favourably disposed towards you—"

She said stoutly: "I had heard that. But we are all together—the women. I believe there are some thirty or more of us, and that we shall manage very well."

"Bravely spoken."

He had not voiced any opinion about women's education, had not said whether he approved of her aims or not. And she did not wish to ask him.

He was an attractive person—she could think of no other word for him—both as to looks and character. She knew that in Downham he was much loved and respected, far more than the Reverend Cuthbert had been. He was unmarried, although it was said (she thought she had heard it from Edwy's family) that he had been affianced when he had had a living in Somerset, but that the girl had died two weeks before the wedding. It had been soon after that he had come to Downham. She supposed that was why in his early days here he had been spoken of always as rather solemn. She did not find him so now.

The worst thing that could happen to me in the next few months, she thought fatalistically, is that I might fall in love with him. How *difficult* that would make everything. It seemed to her that something like that—some sudden, uncontrollable, unexpected emotion—was the very hazard which might be lying in wait to spoil all her new calm. Her new happiness. Unrequited love. But then, she thought, I have never, I realisc, been *in* love (Edwy was all a mistake). And it is not really necessary—only, because it *is* the unknown, I am a little afraid of it. Just as I am afraid of October and Cambridge.

But she realised very soon that what she had made was a friend. Within two or three weeks she was certain of it. She had expected someone drier. Had expected everything really to be drier: the work, the whole feeling. But the lessons in the book-lined study of the vicar-

age, facing out onto the lower market square—she so absorbed as not to
hear the horse-traffic, the people going by—they were not long enough.
And she and he, they had other tastes in common: discovering early on
a shared passion for Browning. Sometimes after the morning's study
was over, they would indulge it—arguing about an obscure passage,
pointing out an undiscovered delight . . .

Those cold January and February days, she made a good start, "a
firm Greek foundation," while the log fire hissed and spat, and the
stuffed sea birds and moorland birds in their great glass cabinet stared
at her.

Guillemots, tern, grouse, curlew, lark . . . "My father's," he said
once. "They were his pride. I had rather be out amongst the real thing,
but Miss Staveley—my sister, they spell home for her."

Sarah was not sure what to make of his sister. She kept house for him
and seldom went out. She was several years older than he, already well
into her forties, and grown rather stout. Sarah she regarded always with
a sort of reserved surprise, as if to say: "Why are you here? Not of
course that I shall *ask* . . ."

"She was happier really in Somerset. She has not many friends here.
But she is happy for me that *I* am happy—which I am. Yorkshire people are very warm. Even when they are not showing it—"

"Not everyone thinks that."

"But I do. And this is a fine living—in Downham. It was a fortunate
chance, or a divine one perhaps, that had Mr. Ingham and I at the
same school."

Ah, she might have guessed that. Of course the living was in Richard
Ingham's gift. But that they should be friends . . .

"I am not an admirer of Mr. Ingham's," she said primly. Irritated.
(She would like to have said, "And I think that at some time he, or his,
insulted Kate or made her unhappy. And *no one must do that.*")

He continued as if she had not spoken: "He and I had not seen each
other since I think some day when the Prince Consort came to school,
and he and I had the organizing of it all. We met again by chance,
when he was visiting Mrs. Ingham's people. I was at the time thinking
of a change of parish."

She was gathering up her books to go. She said: "I am sorry. I heard
that you had—a bereavement."

"Yes, I took this living because *she* died. It was necessary to leave.
The—memories were painful." He spoke not briskly, but quite firmly:
"That is the past, however. The present is"—he smiled—"that you must
prepare for me, Virgil, the *Aeneid* Book Twelve, the twenty lines beginning: '*hic mentem Aeneae genetrix pulcherrima misit . . .*'"

One morning in the middle of February, she was just leaving the breakfast table to get ready for going to Mr. Staveley, when Paul came downstairs—a sleepy look still about him. There was some mail waiting for him. He looked through it eagerly but perhaps not finding what he wanted, picked up an envelope idly. Then:

"What do you make of this?" he asked. He had coloured. She was surprised to see how he had coloured. In his hand was a Valentine. It was quite large, with real lace round the edges, and hand-painted. The Cupids were quite audacious. Beneath them, in Indian ink, in small firm capitals, the sender had written:

> I love (and he loves me again)
> Yet dare I not tell, Who:
> For if the Nymphs should know
>   my Swain,
> I fear they'd love him too.

"It is by Ben Jonson," she said idly.

He said, "I cannot understand, I had thought perhaps—" He frowned, staring at the envelope: the same neat capitals addressing him at Linden House, Downham. Sarah looked closer.

"It is franked in Portsmouth."

"I know no one in Portsmouth."

"It is a practical joke . . ."

He said carelessly, "You mean no one would care enough to intend it seriously—"

"If it had come from where the Strangers live, I might have thought —what is her name? Elfrida—that it was *she*."

He had coloured again. "It is not from that family at all. And," he added, "it would hardly be the behaviour of those in deepest mourning—"

"I am sorry," she put her hand on his arm. "Darlingus, I'm sorry."

He had picked up the card again: "How it *teases* me," he said.

"But is it not meant to? Is that not one of the purposes of a Valentine? Depend on it—it will be one of your Oxford friends."

"No—I mean to discover. Seriously. Although I shan't give whoever it is the satisfaction of *knowing* I was puzzled." He held the card up to the light, as if that would give some clue.

Sarah said, "Whose heart might you have captured? Think back . . . your party. Before that . . ."

They threw names at each other—some so ridiculous as to set them both laughing. "Half the amusement," he said, "is in wondering who."

"It might have been me," she said. "Had you thought of that?" Then after a moment: "Someone is in great earnest," she said. "No, truly. A card such as that. I sense it. It is only half a jest."

"*Sarah* . . ." He sounded exasperated. But she noticed that when Mama came in, just a few moments later, he hid the card.

"Who will win the Boat Race?"

"You are an Oxford man, Mr. Staveley, and must support your side. *I* know who will win." She had become very much for Cambridge in everything. In spite of Paul.

"And does your brother say nothing to that?"

"Nothing. He was not a rowing man."

"Nor I. Nevertheless, a loyalty is a loyalty." He said teasingly: "It is not a race taken very seriously except by those who row it. I asked only to provoke you. And because you had become too solemn. You need other company than Caesar and Livy."

"But I have the Scriptures," she said with mock gravity, "and Horace. And perhaps Herodotus, soon . . ." She thought that he liked to tease her. For certainly she worked hard—terrified that if she did not the jewel would elude her grasp.

"Remember, then—'nec scire fas est omnia,' as Horace said. Meaning?"

"It is not permitted to us—we are not allowed to know everything—"

He expressed delight. "And the saying itself, you may interpret as you wish . . ." Then he added: "I am not a rowing man but was once a betting man, in a very small way. Shall we? For this race?"

"Our family fortunes," she said, "were founded on a five-shilling stake . . ."

In the event Oxford won, by ten lengths, and the poor box in Downham church was the richer by five shillings. But he did not always counter her studiousness with teasing. One day, when it seemed that she had asked for more tasks than he was prepared to give, she said to him directly: "It don't matter to me how hard I work. Is it then too much for you—that you must correct it all, and have already so many other duties?"

"Perhaps," he said very gently, "the truth is, that I am not wholly in agreement with the venture. That is all."

She stared straight ahead at a beady-eyed puffin in the glass cabinet opposite. "Go on," she said, a little rudely, "pray continue."

"It is only that—it is not my belief women should emulate men in matters of scholarship. Nor that they should have access to wide reading, which may disturb or do harm, obscuring and damaging those qualities which belong only to women . . . I have thought long on this, and have tried to believe otherwise, but—"

She interrupted unkindly, "I suppose that she—your intended, *she* was not clever?"

"No," he said quietly. She had hoped he would be angry, such was her shame at what she had said. "She was not *clever*, as you say. Intelligent, lively, amusing. Yes. But all that is beside the point—I was giving only my opinion, or rather my deep *feeling* that the life of the intellect is not for a woman. That it cannot bring her fulfilment, since it is not that for which she is made."

" 'Man for the field and woman for the hearth,' " she said, " 'Man for the sword and for the needle she'—Mr. Tennyson, 'The Princess,'

> 'Man with the head and woman with the heart
> Man to command and woman to obey
> All else confusion . . .'

"Yes?"

"Yes," he said. He added with a smile: "Which is not to say I do not think Mr. Browning the finer poet . . ."

Easter fell late that year. For several days before, the sun shone. On the Saturday in the churchyard, the people of Downham were decorating their dead—where the graves were upright, watering the earth beneath to soften it, planting daffodils, violets. Laying pussy willow on the flat stones; jugs and vases of flowers. Inside the church the font was decorated with ferns and early primroses. Hothouse flowers from the Abbey were wreathed on the Kissing Gate.

Most of that week Matthew Staveley was very busy. There were several cases of severe illness in the parish, and he had also to read day by day, the Passion Week gospels with the children at the school. Sarah herself had to be away from Downham. Her elder Helliwell cousin was to be married at Easter and she was a bridesmaid. It was her first meeting with Sibby, the bride to be, and they found at once a great deal in common. Not least the same sense of humour. The wedding, held in Harrogate, was a great family occasion, with Grandfather Rawson the only member unable to attend.

So it was not until the Wednesday of that week that she had another lesson. As they went through a lengthy passage in the *Aeneid*—full, for her, of difficulties—she found his manner strange. He was not as gentle as usual, nor as decisive. He seemed preoccupied, even nervous. Twice he took out his watch.

"Do you expect someone? I can leave early—"

"No, no. I have nothing till five o'clock. I must read then to old Cummings, at the Lane Cottages. He breathes now only with difficulty . . ." He had put the watch back. "Now—'Aeneas miratus enim—' Here 'enim' has the function of a strengthening particle—a common usage in Virgil. 'Aeneas marvelled indeed' . . ."

When she was gathering up her books to leave: "Miss Rawson," he said, "would you lunch with my sister and me? We could send word to Linden House that you stay."

He seemed very concerned—she could tell by his voice—that she should accept. She had eaten there once or twice before, when the weather had been very bad in February and early March, and even the short walk home had seemed uninviting. Today they sat, the three of them, eating their way through stewed pigeons and cold mutton and plum tart. Miss Staveley watched Sarah with an (if possible) even more surprised look. The conversation was entirely trivial.

"I received a postcard from Florence," she announced at one point. "The place, not the person," she added, when her brother misunderstood. Then to Sarah: "Do you not think these postcards an excellent invention?" Later she said, over the pudding, "Soon we shall have fresh vegetables from the garden. Our father—himself in the Church, you know, a Canon at the Cathedral—he said always when the spring came, 'Soon we shall have fresh vegetables from the garden.'"

Matthew Staveley hardly spoke at all. When after the meal, Sarah rose to leave, he said: "I have to go up to the church. Perhaps you would care to walk a little—and see the decorations. It would take only a short while."

Outside it was strong sunshine, more like May or June. As they came up to the main gate, she hesitated and drew back—from habit. He noticed at once. He said, more lightly: "You cannot be superstitious like that. And you a modern woman—"

"Oh, but I can," she said. "We are not speaking of reason."

"Well, then—we shall walk round, and through the Kissing Gate."

At that she protested. If she was with him, the clergyman, it was all right anyway. "The very nonsense of it," she told him.

"But that is what you have said already, that it is non-sense . . ." He spoke easily enough, but that exchange over, he became very nervous once more. He opened the Kissing Gate for her—the Abbey flowers must have withered, for they were gone now. They walked slowly up the cool path, the oak tree nearly in leaf. The elms in the churchyard were a brilliant green in the sunlight. Three sheep had wandered in, one with an early lamb which ran from sheep to sheep, nudging and being rejected, until it found its mother.

"When it is fine like this on Easter Day," she said, "then the hay and the harvest will be good. It is a saying."

"Miss Rawson," he said, "we are quite alone here." He cleared his throat. Then speaking quickly and easily as if his nervousness had suddenly left him: "I know that you are in your twenties and of an independent turn of mind, Miss Rawson, so that it is not necessary for me to speak to your parents before I say this. I have been wondering, you see, if in spite of the plans you have been making for your future, you could reconsider—" he paused for a moment—"could *alter* that future and do me the *very* great honour of becoming my wife."

There was a long silence. He stood looking ahead of him, facing now towards the Kissing Gate, and the waterfall. She could see that his nervousness had returned. But she was so taken aback that although she searched for words, she could not speak at all.

"I think," he said slowly, "that I have not done this—expressed this, in perhaps the best manner possible. I—in my one previous experience, she—the lady to whom I addressed myself—she was waiting for just such a request. We both knew that. It was a formality only. But now—I ask without any sure hope. Only—*and this I should have said before anything else*—a very great respect and admiration for you, together with a deep affection"—his voice seemed to break—"such as, I had not expected to feel again . . ."

"I cannot say—I did not think—" she began haltingly, fingering the braid fastenings of her jacket.

"My feelings—have grown slowly," he said. "But the realisation, of their extent, has been very sudden. It has been with me all Passion Week, and these last days. I felt now that I must speak."

"I am glad that you did." The words came from her spontaneously. But she wondered then if she had said too much, for he answered at once:

"Then I may hope?"

"Mr. Staveley—the honour of course, but I have said, I do not know *what to think—*"

"If your worry is that you would wish still to use your mind—in the way that you are using it now, then some, a little of that, would be still possible. In a limited way, of course. Not a university education but—intellectual companionship . . ."

She remembered the dream of the Kissing Gate and Edwy and how she had known the next day exactly what she should do.

". . . 'For a chance to make your little much,'" he said, "'To gain a lover and lose a friend . . .'"

It seemed to her very important that she should put the space of at least a night between herself and any answer. But perhaps he had guessed this, for he went on: "Should you like time to come to a decision? Have I that much hope?"

She spent a sleepless night, almost. A white night, as the French called it. And no dreams at all, even of the shortest. The Kissing Gate was not to be commanded.

Yet she was amazed by the way in which part of her, without hesitation, had almost answered a ready "Yes." Now, with time to think, she could not escape the fact that she was very tempted. True, she did not love him. But then she had not loved Edwy. And anyway, to be "in love" as it was called, if it had not happened to her so far—so late—why should it ever? (And according to some, to many, it was often the worst of foundations for a life-long union . . .)

I need a girl friend, she thought. So that we might talk it through. She would have perhaps asked Paul, but he was staying in Lancashire with the Strangers. And could he have helped? she thought. The next day, sitting at her bedroom table, she wrote out in two columns the points for and against marrying Matthew Staveley. The balance was tipped very nicely in favour of accepting.

And yet. His views were so different. I would end up—the vicar's wife. The first child, and the days of Herodotus together would be doomed. No more *Iliad*. She would, envious, have to watch him coach schoolboys in Tacitus . . . Seldom had she felt such easy natural attraction and friendship, but to lose at one blow all she had striven for, and had *almost* within her reach. *I cannot.*

She was cowardly and wrote to him. She spent several hours that next night searching Browning for an apt quotation, one that might assuage. But could find nothing. She was surprised at the sorrow she felt—for both of them. I would like to have my cake and eat it. I want *everything*, that is my trouble, she thought.

When she had delivered the letter—hurrying away because she saw Richard Ingham's carriage at the door—she walked on in the direction of the Abbey. She stood for a while on the bow bridge, watching the river Down. It was low from the dry weather, and ran clear and brown over the white stones. The alder catkins hung dry by the water's edge. There was no one about. She looked over towards the Kissing Gate, and then the Abbey. On just such a day as this (except that the river had run fast and swollen . . .), nearly sixty years ago now—her grandmother had jumped in, without hesitation. Altering her life, Sarah thought, beyond her imaginings—and with it, ours. If she had not, *I would not be here.*

She often felt like her namesake. Her memory of Sarah-Mother was a child's memory. A child's-eye view. But now, today, she could feel (and strangely, most often when she *walked*) that she was blood of her blood. *She* escaped, that Sarah. Perhaps she went only from one trap to another. But she fought. I feel that if I had known her then, if she knew me now—we would recognise each other.

"But you will teach me still?" she said to Matthew Staveley.

"Of course. It will be as if it had never been . . ." (But no, she thought, that is not possible.) His hand trembled a little as he passed to her her Greek paper.

"Your tense here—incorrect. It should be *aorist*. The action was already completed. 'When he *had* heard this, he gave up hope.' "

TWELVE

My master Bukton: when Christ our King
Was asked, What is truth or soothfastness,
He not a word answered to that asking,
As who sayeth: no man is always true, I guess.

CHAUCER, *L'envoi de Chaucer à Bukton*

More than six months now since he and Nick had become lovers. Paul never thought, and did not want to think, how the affair might end. It was enough to be happy. And he was. Nick and he had been together in London for two weeks in February, and then Paul had spent Easter at Foxton. There the sun had shone on them all, relieving the gloom of the mourning clothes (worn even by the servants), illuminating the shrine made in Everard's memory: his crucifix, his rosary, a black-edged carte de visite showing him as a schoolboy, another in his mountaineering costume (Sybil Straunge-Lacey remarked sadly, "To think how often I commended him to St. Bernard . . ."), and a third, face only, on a mourning card. But the worst of the shock seemed over. And Nick seemed not unhappy. (He had written after the London visit: "Such happiness we have had, have we not? And you have forgotten and forgiven that first time—that I should have panicked, felt remorse. Take no heed that I fear death, and punishment—*Do not we all?*")

There was a new Pope. Pius IX had died. Perhaps the new one would be less of a political figure—Father Bromhead was going to Rome after Easter and hoped to bring back reports. Paul had spoken to him about being received into the Church—although it was not to be yet. There was no hurry. And too, his great wish to belong to the Straunge-Laceys' religion, and his (physically expressed) love for Nick: of course the two could not be reconciled. Yet it seemed to him that Nick, in his complicated torments, straddled the division somehow . . .

In early May, Nick went to Austria for two months, near Feldkirch. He was to stay with friends he had made when at school there. He told Paul that he had toyed with the idea of securing him an invitation also, but the practical difficulties had been too great. Paul, in his turn, wondered why he had never thought of inviting Nick to Downham again. In the autumn—he thought joyfully—*I shall do so.*

It would not be difficult. Mother would not dislike him, since she would not find him threatening as a girl might be (she will not think I am to marry Nick . . .). He thought of how he would show him everything. Drives to Aysgarth Falls, to Bolton Castle, Leyburn Shawl across which Mary Queen of Scots had escaped. The great Autumn Fair in Downham with the fire lit in the market square and the drovers, their plaids wrapped round them sleeping out, the unshod ponies clattering down the cobbles. The Castle, the Abbey, all the lore of the Kissing Gate . . . And yet somehow, it would not. When he tried to "see," to imagine, Nick in Downham, again, nothing happened. It was as if he looked at a blank page.

In early July Sarah went to stay with the elder of their Helliwell cousins, recently married. Sibby Helliwell had had a miscarriage and they had taken a house at Scarborough for a month to help her recovery. Later Sarah would join Paul on Loch Tay, in the Perthshire Highlands, where godmother Kirsty and her family had taken a house. And then—cause for rejoicing—in August he would go to Foxton for three weeks or more.

Sarah was happy, and settled. No, not settled but rather: excited and full of anticipation. In early October she would go to Newnham Hall. The coaching with Matthew Staveley had gone well, and his parents if not pleased were reconciled. He was no longer blamed out loud . . .

While Sarah was in Scarborough he had a letter from Nick. Nick was a fitful correspondent. From Austria he had written only twice. This letter, which was very long, seemed to have been written in a state of some excitement.

". . . And so I am to marry! Imagine me there, on my knees before the Sacred Heart, *promising*. Alone with the Wise Woman, one feels quite helpless. It has ever been so. And the R.O., *that* was no better—'It is your solemn duty. I have wanted to speak out. God cannot intend —a family so ancient—at risk of extinction.' (Ah but, I wanted to say, if not Hubert—and it does seem that he seriously intends to be a J, and the more so since Everard—cannot *Benoit* at least be steered in the direction of licensed fornication?) But they will not trust. The loss of

Everard, I fear, has unhinged them. If one can go, they think—so can two (and why not three, four?).

"Now as to whom I shall marry—well, that has not been really considered as yet. But I am not to be dilatory. Alice, perhaps? She is family, yet distant enough to bring in fresh blood. And it was known she was favoured for Everard (myself I do not think he would have minded one way or the other. At table, he scarcely noticed what he ate).

"If you detect in all this an hysterical note, you are right. I do not wish for any of this. My feelings about women, and virginity—they are the same as ever. It seems to me still too dreadful to break that seal. (And yet—how are we to come into the world? Let others do it, I say. Let others do it, Paul . . .) But I am somehow to surmount all this. Although, since possibly it is only the first time which seems to me the desecration—perhaps a young and willing widow, would that be the answer? It is not that I am adverse to the company of women. Well, not too much. But if we are to speak of love, then there is no question which is the best. (Are not David and Jonathan put before us, a signpost as it were—shown to us from our earliest days?) And also, as to whom I truly love, there is no question either.

"But although no one but you can hold the same place in my heart and my—(I write too freely, it is the emotion of the moment. I would be grateful if you would *destroy this letter*). The truth is that I *must marry* and as a consequence all of which I have just spoken (*all that means anything to me*) must end. We may see each other of course, but everything else—no. Not just because it is sin, great sin, which it is, but because of this (wretched) promise . . . I love you, Paul. (*Marry*, indeed! She extracted her promise under duress. So is it *valid?* I shall ask the Js . . .) Yes, I love you, and shall always remain,

> "Yours faithfully and constantly,
> "Nicholas Straunge-Lacey

> "P.S. 'I shall go my ways, tread out my measure
> Fill the days of my daily breath
> With fugitive things not good to treasure
> Do as the world doth, say as it saith;
> But if we had loved each other . . .'

> "Remember?"

For a few days Paul was shocked and unhappy. Then after a while it seemed to him that it was no more than he had expected. He had not thought such happiness would last. But before: there had been friendship. There would be friendship again. The one loss he could not have borne would have been that of all the Straunge-Laceys. He realised that he had not imagined, even, a time when he might no longer go there. Nick married—it would be all right. (Only that would be lost which should have been lost. He thought too—nothing to hinder him now from becoming a Catholic. It had been *meant*. As soon as he arrived he would speak of it, commit himself absolutely.) I could as well have loved a woman, he thought. It had been chance only. He, she, whoever: there at the right moment. Someone, anyone able to lift him above his impossible love for Kate. The completely unattainable. (And yet once, *I slept with her . . .*)

He seemed that summer to see her with new eyes. If anything, he loved her the more. He suspected that his feelings of resignation about Nick would not last, but while they did she was part of the peace.

She looked so beautiful that July. He went out several times with her and the younger children. He carried Patrick in a sling on his back and they took their tea up on the moors. Will joined them sometimes—but only on condition that when they had all eaten he would be asked to perform. Turn after turn, standing there among the tussocks of grass and the heather—the larks high in the afternoon sky. He had only to see an act once and it, or a version of it at least, was forever in his repertoire. And at the end, always, Flo's favourite: "Champagne Charlie."

If only, Paul thought, I could tell Kate. But he had not been able even in his imaginings to confess to her the Nick story . . . And if he were really to tell her (even half of it, a *quarter* of it), what would he see then in those green, thick-lashed eyes so gravely watching him now, listening? She loves me so much, he thought proudly. In a way that is right and *allowed*, she loves me.

Two days before leaving for Scotland he ran into Stephen in Leyburn. He had not seen him since Oxford last summer. Stephen, it appeared, had been out East ("very hot, very dirty. I shall not repeat the experience . . ."). Over a brandy they exchanged news.

"Ah yes, Nicholas *Straunge*-Lacey. We brought him to your party. I am *quite* out of touch—"

"He thinks of marrying—"

"Does he now? Old Nick, the young devil himself. To *whom*, may I ask?"

"No, just in a general way—"

"Marrying in a *general* way? Gender unspecified? Yes, well, but that should suit old Nick very nicely . . ."

On the way to Dundee, Paul spent a few nights in Edinburgh with a little-known second cousin—a Dunbar—then from Edinburgh he went as usual by ferry boat over the Forth, then travelled for the first time on the new bridge over the river Tay (opened only two months earlier: six years in the building and almost two miles long—a new Wonder of iron and stone). They all went together from Dundee to the house Kirsty's family had taken on the shores of Loch Tay, near Aberfeldy. There, during the whole fortnight, it rained almost without cease. He hoped that at Foxton he would do better. A few days before his departure he telegraphed Nick from Aberfeldy the time of his arrival. He did not return to Dundee, but travelled directly from Perth.

When he arrived, hot and dusty (the sun, unbelievably, had shone the length of northwestern England), Nick was not at the station to meet him. Nor was the Straunge-Lacey carriage. Surprised, and disappointed, he enquired twice of the stationmaster if there was any message for him. There was nothing. He took a four-wheeler.

The journey seemed longer than he had ever known it, then as Foxton Hall came into view in the sunlight, he thought, It will be all right. As it was the first time.

But like the first time, there was no Nick. A manservant (out of mourning now) sent word hurriedly to Sybil Straunge-Lacey. She arrived, looking palely flustered.

"My dear, we thought it was not for another ten days . . . I am chagrined no one should have met you. Some misunderstanding, surely. Nicholas is not here, as you must have realised. He has an Austrian acquaintance staying—someone he has met through Feldkirch friends. They have gone bicycling for the day . . ."

A duty visitor, Paul thought. How tedious for Nick.

"And he is here another week. Did not Nicholas write to you? He assured me—really, I am so sorry . . ."

Once again too he had to take tea in her room. Everything the same, the statue, the rosary, the fine china. And he was drawn out about religion too. (Yes, he *had* made up his mind. And he would speak again with Father Bromhead, and no, he had not yet told his family . . .)

"Only another year," she said, "and we shall lose our Rose—behind bars. A figure of speech, I should say. She will, I think, be visible face to face in the convent parlour, on occasion." She spoke bitterly.

If Nick was not there, Elfrida and the faithful Imp were delighted to see him. "I didn't *know* you were coming today. Nick did not *say* . . ." She told him that Fritz-dog had died just after Paul left at Easter. "We buried him in the arboretum. By a marked oak tree."

Nick and the Austrian had still not returned by dinner. Once again,

Paul took Rose down. Hermione, who had lost a child in January, perhaps after the shock of Everard, was expecting another and did not come downstairs. He heard that she must take care, lying up for most of the day. Rose too seemed delighted that he had come.

Sybil complained of Nick's lateness: "I fear always an accident. Life is such a fragile flame—*we* have seen how easily snuffed out . . ."

They arrived finally about half past nine when all were in the drawing-room. Sybil had hurried into the hall when the bell clanged. Paul followed her.

"Paul—my dear fellow! What *do* you here?" Then: "You didn't receive my telegraph?"

"No—"

"At Dundee. I wired Dundee. And too, I had written there earlier."

"But I came direct from Perth. I was never back in Dundee."

"What a nonsense . . . I had been certain to reach you." He turned then to the slight dark man, standing just behind him. Paul disliked him on sight. He was outfitted in bicycling costume of patrol-jacket and knee breeches, in dark blue, with a round cap above his sun-tanned face. They were introduced: his name was Franz von Hartberg. Paul did not care even for taking his hand.

Apologies were being made. They would wash and change at once. No, they did not need food, thank you.

"Just now we are so fortunate to find an inn which is serving dinner and where also they are happy how we are dressed . . ." The timbre of the voice grated on Paul. He wondered if it did not on Nick.

Seeing him alone for a minute, a little later, he was about to say something, but Nick spoke first (his hand touching Paul's, shocking him with memory. If it needed so little . . .). "Look—it's *so* unfortunate. I had written to you that you come ten days later. Franz stays, you see, at least another week. I had—no choice in the matter."

"I could still leave—"

"Nonsense. Now you are *here*. It is all the most fearful duty. But what can one do? Feldkirch connections . . ."

"But I shall see something of you afterwards. Only—what now of this marrying business?" He asked it lightly: "What of that?"

But Nick was already turning away. "Don't come to my room and talk—there's a friend. All this fresh air. I shall be asleep as never." He called over his shoulder: "Do you bicycle? Arduous but *very* delightful. And quite wins over the tricycle . . ."

Two was company, three . . . It was an embarrassment, Franz's presence. No. It was he, Paul, *he* was the embarrassment. And although in

their (few) private moments together, Nick would indicate to him yet
again what a bore this all was (*"noblesse oblige,* though why it *should* I
cannot think . . ."), his manner in front of Franz was perfect. And true,
Paul was invited on all the outings—they were seldom at home—but
Franz made acceptance impossible. He did not insult him exactly to his
face, but was merrily sarcastic about him.

"The little Protestant boy . . ." he would preface his remarks—when
Nick was present but no one else. "The little Protestant boy who is so
interested of *trees*—of course he has just now the possibility to study
them each day here at this so beautiful Foxton . . ." The platitudes
and the grating voice. Nick would say nothing. "Nicholas is unhappy
that you don't like that he should *bicycle* each day. But the legs grow
strong—so." He bared a calf . . .

Hermione could not stand him. Lying in a hammock in the garden,
she told Paul so. It formed almost a bond between them. She was at
least honest: "I tried to flirt with him the first evening—and saw at
once that I was wasting my time. I had thought Austrians more gallant."

Elfrida did not like him either: Franz tried to make up to her, tick-
ling her hair, chucking her under the chin, praising Imp. "So charming
a little dog—but not then so charming as his mistress—ah, so?" But his
approach did not succeed. She and Paul grumbled about him to
Tommy, but Tommy said only that the Hall had seen many odd folk,
and would see more. "Monkey-face," Elfrida called him. "And the way
he dresses—he is altogether the most *horrid* confloption."

Only Sybil seemed delighted. "Nicholas is quite himself again,
and this Herr von Hartberg is so courteous. The Austrians have such
charm . . ." She was standing by the ornamental pond with Paul: "You
know, my dear, what—Nicholas has promised?"

"Yes."

Once again her hand closed over his—the blessing. "We hope—Alice,
dear little Alice. She is with other relations in Wales now, but returns
to us next month. Can you believe it—on her *father's* side, which is not
our family—there is also a martyr? A nun, you know. In China I think
sometime in the last century." She paused, then lowered her voice: "I
should not tell you this of course, but Nicholas—he has always been my
favourite. I know God does not—that it is not right. God must forgive
me for it. I think He does, because I had a vision once—about Nicholas." Her hand on his tightened. "And now, my dear, you are going to
come up to my room and *pray* with me. I know that you are very,
very near to the Faith now. We shall say together one decade of the
Rosary . . ."

It was a very long week. There were bear fights with Elfrida. For a few days water-pistols were all the rage, until Benoit, intending to shoot Franz from a window, drenched Father Cuthbert instead. Augustus forbade them.

Paul spent much time alone in the arboretum. There he smoked, and sketched. He brought in specimen leaves from the more unusual trees, and pressed and drew them. As he walked about, the sunlight dappling the foliage, he played the old game again: to everyone a tree. Nick was already an ash. Sybil he made a weeping willow, Hermione an acacia, and Rose a Cedar of Lebanon. Elfrida was a larch, Hubert and Benoit hornbeams, Father Cuthbert a Lombardy poplar. And so on. Franz was a goat willow.

Elfrida said to Paul: "You've changed."

"In what way?"

She looked confused: "Last time you were—I don't know. But this time you're puzzled or unhappy or something." She paused. "That horrid Monkey-face. I wish he'd be caught out in something and have to *absquatulate* . . ." Then she added: "Don't he and Nick ask you to go out with them *ever*? It is very bad manners. When you are Nick's friend—"

"Of course I am asked," he said. "But I would rather be with you."

"Truthfully? True as you're a Catholic?"

"Yes—except that I'm *not* a Catholic."

"Oh, but you soon will be—" She pushed back the hair that stole from her bonnet. "Come and chase me in the arboretum—but *no* bear fights. My last ribbons were quite spoilt . . ."

The last day of Franz's stay there was to be a lawn tennis party and tea outside afterwards. It was a warm, hazy afternoon. The fine weather had held. Paul could think only: he goes tomorrow. That morning Nick had said to him, but as one who could not stop: "Nearly over—and have I not been charming? Would not my manner deceive *anyone?*"

There were few outside visitors, perhaps four or five. It was possible for everyone to have a game. The tennis was not to be taken seriously. Elfrida, unhampered by long skirts, did better than the corseted Rose, who even with a looped-up skirt must surely be hampered (Sarah grumbled always). Hubert and Benoit (and sometimes Elfrida) obligingly fetched balls. Sybil sat in a cane chair within the court, which was enclosed and netted at either end. Uncle Kenelm and Aunt Winefride and Father Bromhead sat too round the edge. They talked and scarcely watched the game.

The heat became sticky. Thunderflies appeared. In the last game

Paul, partnered by Rose, played Nick and Franz. And were easily and severely beaten. Afterwards, when Rose was just laughing with him over their trouncing, Franz walked over to them, Nick following just behind him.

"Ah so, what a defeat!" he said. Then turning to Rose, "You are not minding, madam?" She shook her head. When a moment later she went to join her mother, he said, "You see, Mr. Rawson! You have in partner with you this *Röslein rot*, this lady who is so charming—but it is not *equal*, the game. You wish perhaps that *you* are so fortunate to have a pretty boy who plays with you?" He smiled.

Paul stared at him angrily. He is not worth a reply, he thought. Nick had already moved away. When Franz is gone tomorrow, Paul told himself, I shall have it out with Nick. I am not to be treated like this.

He could hardly wait for it to be tomorrow. Dinner was a torment. Hermione, down for the first time, said something which upset her father. It was thought that she was missing Dolly, who would not be joining her till next month. Sybil, wearing one of her lace-trimmed dresses, of moss-green satin, was in a fluttering mood. After the meal Elfrida was persuaded before going up to bed to play a little piano piece, a berceuse, which she did with many wrong notes. Rose then played the violin—he had heard her only twice before. She played as if alone. Franz was at the piano: then she accompanied him, while he sang from Beethoven's song cycle *An die ferne Geliebte*. He sang very well. Paul could have wished he did not. His voice, unlike when he spoke, was light and tender. Nick, sitting head back on one of the sofas, had his eyes shut. Boredom perhaps?

In bed—and he went up early, just after Sybil—Paul settled to sleep, but could not. As on all other nights, it was here that memories crowded in (Nick at Easter: "I asked that I should sleep in here again, with you. I said we had so much to speak of, and that I had been sleeping poorly, with bad dreams"). It all became unbearable and he thought suddenly: I shall have it out with Nick now. It is not because of this afternoon—that does not count. It is all the other neglects and insults, the whole week of humiliation.

He would go and see him now, and alone with him, the easy intimacy of talk, it would be all right. He would not ask for, expect more. But I cannot wait, he thought. We should have spoken earlier. I should have braved him the very first evening . . .

Although he walked carefully, his slippered feet seemed to clatter on the oak corridor. Going up the short staircase to Nick's room, he heard a clock down below strike eleven. He knocked on the door. A few seconds, then Nick's voice, guarded, muffled: "Who's there?"

"Paul. Only Paul."

"Look, Paul, there's a good fellow"—his voice was hurried—"I'm feeling rotten. Too much sun. Could it wait till morning?"

"But surely—yes."

Nick's voice again: "Good night—Paul. God bless you. Good night—"

He turned away. Balked, frustrated in his need to talk—his great need to talk—he was for some reason near to tears. On impulse, he began walking heavily, noisily: till his steps could no longer be heard. Then he turned. There was no one about. Taking off his slippers, he crept cautiously back along the corridor and up the short flight of stairs.

Nick's door again. Standing outside it, he felt that he was someone else. This is not I. I would not behave like this (but I do. I am . . .).

He knew then that he had known. Only a fool would not have known. They spoke German, when they spoke at all. But it was not words that reluctantly, shamedly, he listened for.

Sounds that he could not mistake, and the blood rushed to his face. A great wave of nausea. He trembled, standing there, a ridiculous figure in his bare feet. Self-disgust, self-hate. Were there light, I would be an eye at the keyhole. I would be even *that*.

Perhaps it was only a minute or two—less—but it seemed then, and in his memory later: half a lifetime. Back in his room, he wept.

He came down to breakfast late, after a sleepless night. He hoped that Franz would already have left and Nick be in the carriage with him. But he appeared as Paul was about to sit down. A Nick glowing with good health, well-being. He saw Paul and said at once: "I'm sorry—"

"What—I—"

"I'm sorry," he said, his hand on Paul's wrist. "About last night. What did you want? My head, it ached unbelievably. I wanted only to be alone. I slept at once like one dead—and am *quite* refreshed now." He glanced over at the clock. "Franz is not yet down. We must hurry breakfast—the carriage will be round in half an hour." He paused. Paul was silent. "*Noblesse oblige* still. The latest, you know, is that I must go with him to London . . ." Paul was silent. "Have you eaten?"

"Yes," said Paul shortly, walking straight from the room. There was nothing there on the sideboard he could have faced. He could not eat at all.

He never knew how he got through the rest of that morning. He moved as if dreaming. (Would that I were.) He sat for a while quietly in the chapel, but prayer—or what he thought of as prayer—he could not. Anger and bitterness clouding, confusing everything. He looked at the red lamp, kept alight beside the Sacrament. He could not remember so much as a word of any prayer he had ever known. How could a mind be in such turmoil?

And yet all the time at the centre, something cold, hard. It must come from within him, be his. A fragment of ice. The bleakness, hardness of winter weather.

Everard's death; the night before his funeral. He remembered all that, and much, much more. When the idea came to him later in the morning, as he walked in the arboretum, he could not believe that that, either, should have come from him. *I cannot, will not.* But already it had seized him with a sort of cold passion. *This is what it is to be wicked . . .*

And yet, there was good in it—what he planned. It was not a wholly evil notion. But he must act at once—*now*, before all was confusion again. He passed into an avenue of oaks and ashes, leaving behind him the slender silver birches. Nick: the ash.

I could kill, he thought, hastening to make reality of his idea. Making it so that he could not turn back.

Rose was sitting on a bench near to where the herb garden began. The lavender flowered just by her. He could smell it. She was sewing, something of white cotton. A raffia basket stood at her feet. He saw the small neat stitches as her needle went in and out.

She smiled at him. "Did you see my sister? Hermione, I mean—"

"Yes." On his way he had seen Hermione in her hammock. She was snoring gently. "She sleeps," he said.

Rose laughed. "I had seen her too. But it is *good* that she does—" She brought out some scissors from her basket. "Do you walk in the garden?" she asked, "because the fuchsia just now—"

As if she were not speaking, he began: "Miss Straunge-Lacey, I wished to say—"

"Oh, Rose," she said. "*Rose*, please. It is my wish to be informal. You are one of our family."

He did not hear Elfrida come running up. From behind, her arms were flung round his neck. "I did not see you *all* day—"

Disengaging himself from her embrace: "Run off just now—would you?" He surprised himself by the sharpness of his tone. Trying then, too late, to soften his words. Her face fell.

Rose said then, her hand on her sister's, "You could take in for me the first of these little garments. Tommy expects them—she will make up the parcel." She turned to Paul: "We are making a layette," she said in explanation, "the young sister of the coachman, she is to be confined very soon—and the family have little." She handed over the garment, wrapped in its paper. Elfrida, her lower lip trembling, took it and was gone.

"She is so fond of you," Rose said—not in reproach but as quiet fact: "She looks up to you and admires you tremendously."

"I don't know what for—"

"No," she said. "Often we do not know what it is that others see in us . . ." She put away the needle-book, closed the basket. "Nicholas comes back in two days—is that right?" Paul had sat on the bench beside her. She turned on him—Nick's eyes. The shade, exact. It was only that they danced more gently. "You *are* enjoying your stay?" When he did not answer at once, she said, "I had thought—perhaps—you were not."

He said in a rush: "Some religious turmoil. I wanted—I have not been able to decide. Once," he said, "just after your brother's death, you accepted my prayers. Now—I ask for yours."

"But of course," she said, simply. Sounds came to them from across the lawn. A shout. He looked over. "There go Hubert and Benoit," she said. "Lawn tennis again. Should you not like to join them?"

"Did you not want my company?"

"Indeed. I am delighted." She smiled. "I did not know you wished for mine."

"I wish for *more*—"

Again—the eyes. But this time wide, surprised.

"Miss Straunge-Lacey—Rose. There is something else—" the words spilled out: "I know that you are already—that you are as truly engaged as if you had already a bridegroom. There is no way in which it can be correct for me to say this—*I know I do wrong*" (Oh, God, he thought, *indeed* I do wrong), "but if you should think that ever it would be possible—that there might come a time . . ." He spoke in circles. He could not stop. Words, words, and no turning back. And then—he had said it.

"Certainly I should have spoken first to your father," he finished. "Except that I ask—with so little hope . . ."

She didn't speak for a long time. He saw that she was crying. He said then desperately: "It should be easy for you. Just say that you are already—that you do not feel anything for me and would not—" (But it was he who wished to feel nothing).

"My plans," she said slowly, "my whole direction—is different. I—"

"Say 'No' at once, and we will hear no more of it." He was horrified at what he had done. Wished now to undo it. "Forget that I have spoken. Forgive me only . . ."

And yet as he sat beside her he was drawn in all his turmoil by the peace which surrounded her always. Even when, as now, she wept. An air like the air he breathed walking amongst the trees. (O Cedar of Lebanon.)

She said gravely: "The honour. Do not think me unfeeling. If I do not answer at once, it is not because—there are so many different ways of coming to God, Mr. Rawson—and of bringing others to Him." Her voice faltered. "I must not think that what I want is always—the best. God speaks with many voices. I must always be open to that . . ."

"But of course. I would not—it must come from your deepest heart." He felt still, appalled. *What have I done?*

The sun had gone in suddenly. A dark cloud filled the near sky. Shouts came to them from across the tennis court. Imp, without Elfrida, dashed, yapping, over the lawn.

Rose's empty hands lay folded on her lap. They were small and strong. "I would need time," she said. "And—your prayers, Paul."

The atmosphere in the house those next few days: he imagined they were staring at him, whispering about him. Twice he saw Father Bromhead look long at him. He had made it up with Elfrida ("We were in the midst of a conversation, Rose and I—I had not meant to snap . . ."), the snub forgotten. He wondered if Rose had spoken to her mother. He fancied Sybil's manner altered towards him, Hermione's too. And then again—he did not. His feeling of enormous wickedness persisted.

He was not even certain now what he wished to happen. In some sort of prayer, such a prayer as someone stubborn in their sin might make, he left it to be decided. If yes—then he had not lost the family. And he would have, as near as he might, Nick. He would have his revenge too. An eye for an eye. A virgin for a . . . He had no illusions as to how greatly he would hurt. But if no—then the matter was ended. His hate and his anger: he would have to deal with them otherwise. For much of the time he felt a great calm—as perhaps a murderer might feel, who had done the deed.

After two days Rose wrote him a short note, brought to him in his room. "I have told no one of our conversation—except of course that I have had to take counsel . . ." He imagined then what she might say to her confessor. What advice would she be given?

When on the third day Nick came back, he avoided him, much as he would (a phrase he had just learned) an "occasion of sin." Pleading a headache, he talked to him only so far as was needed for civility.

On the morning of the fourth day, she came to him. He was sitting alone in the library. With that curious grace which came to her so naturally, but which always surprised him, she stood before him and with her hands held out open, said that she would be his wife.

From that moment it seemed—uproar. He could not go back now. And indeed, at once, he was plunged into the world of reality: that he must speak to her father, to Sybil ("She knows now," Rose said, "and is so happy"), to Father Bromhead—there must be assurances that his intention to become a Catholic still held firm. Throughout the house there was excitement. Elfrida was the first.

"Was *that* why you did not want me that day, dearest Mr. Rawson? —*Paul*, my brother now. Soon. Oh, *what a* conflabberation we shall all have . . ."

Then at midday, cake and Madeira in Sybil's room—and the dreaded tête-à-tête. At once she took both his hands, pressing the fingers inside her palms, and then with her head on one side, she said: "I am so happy. I *know* we can trust you with our flower—I had not thought— we had none of us expected . . . It has of course been a matter between her and her confessor, but she knew what were our feelings . . . Mr. Straunge-Lacey, so delighted too. We had dreaded so . . ." She shivered. "I know that often it is God's will, but—we could not. Mr. Rawson, Paul, my dear—God has been very good to us."

"And to me," he said. And then wondered at once what he could have meant.

"I had grown so fond of you," she said. "And about the other, I had prayed so much—you know, God so often answers us in a manner *quite* unexpected . . ."

The interview with Augustus Straunge-Lacey in the library before dinner that evening did not last long. They both, it seemed, wanted it over with as soon as possible. Augustus appeared hurried.

"You don't smoke, do you? Can't approve of a smoker for a son-in-law . . ." Practical matters were soon disposed of. Paul had property, was a man of means. Rose was accustomed to live in the country. Her dowry, the marriage settlement: "We'll come to all that, eh?" Evidently her dowry to the convent would have been substantial. "You'll take great care of her? A worry—daughters. The sons and the estate— enough responsibility, worry, with *them*. And then last year—our great loss . . . She's a fine girl. No beauty, of course. A great worry off our minds—don't like them being shut up. I've told Bromhead so. He sees my point of view . . . Another whisky? She's never looked at a man, you know. Never been interested. Her mother and the Season—a waste of everyone's time . . ."

Hermione. He had amazed her, and she said so. "You must tell me more of it, sometime. Rose has never been the confiding sort." She put her hand on his. "Brother Paul," she said lightly, "or should I say Uncle Paul? If this lying about in a hammock means anything . . ."

There were the congratulations, the polite comments of Hubert and Benoit and Uncle Kenelm and Aunt Winefride. There was a long, searching talk with Father Bromhead. It went well: because I am so wicked, he thought. He had tried in the course of it to say something, even so little as, "I have sinned, I have done wrong . . ." but it was not taken up. "We are all sinners," Father Bromhead had said. The words glib; the meaning perhaps not.

There was much to be done, to be arranged. Little time to think. It was not to be a long engagement. He must write to Sarah, that she might prepare the ground at home. Mother and Father—how would they take it? And Kate—he would deceive Kate. He *could* not confess. She would believe in him and be happy for him.

And then there was Nick. That first day, the day on which Rose accepted him, he did not know how to face him. But Nick made the decision for him. He became ill. That evening he went early to bed, complaining of a headache. Next day he was confined to his room with a summer fever. His parents, the whole family, expressed concern. He had been travelling, exposed to infection. There were fears always of cholera: even now there was some in Blackburn, in Preston . . .

Paul did not visit him in his sick-room. At first he was advised not and then—he could not.

Nor could he, for the remaining days of his visit, walk in the arboretum. Nick, the ash tree. Was it not the Irish, who said of it: "The ash, with its crown in heaven, and its roots in hell"?

THIRTEEN

"Who are you? I am Miss Seppings. I shall tell you about myself. I wait in the doorway here, to make new students feel *at once* at home. Welcome to Newnham Hall. We are quite a family here, you know."

She paused for breath. Sarah, whom the cab had just set down, stared at her bewildered. An overweight girl, with a heavy jaw and a frizzed fringe, she wore a dress of some limp material in a dull green: loosely cut with much drapery and puffed shoulders.

"Miss *Porson*, did you say? Someone must tell Miss Clough that you have arrived—she is the sister of the poet, Arthur Hugh, you know—you will see his picture in her room—and she looks after us like a mother. I have been here two years now and have designs on the History Tripos. I was educated by the Quakers at their school in Sidcot. I am twenty years of age. Your room will be one of those freshly papered and painted—at least I *hope* it is one of those ready, Miss Porson . . ."

A maid came hurrying along the corridor. Her attention was caught. Sarah, with relief, was handed over to her.

The room, when she was shown to it, was smaller than she had imagined but when she opened the window, it smelled outside of the country. In the remaining light she could see that beyond the garden lay only fields. Sheep bleating in the distance.

Inside, the room smelled of fresh paint. The wallpaper was dark and leafy. When she had unpacked, the room looked bare still. She must send home for more to fill it. She had brought no pictures, no cushions. Only a few photographs. Two of Paul, a small painted one of Kate, another of Papa. She had not one of Mama and would not have dared to ask.

And yet, bare or not: It is my room, she thought. I have come to Cambridge at last. I have had a room of my own before—but never before have I had a life of my own . . .

She had been up so very early that morning, to be on her way to London. By afternoon, sick with anticipation (now it is *really* happening . . .), she was sitting in the Cambridge train. A Ladies Only carriage—opposite her a well-dressed woman and her daughter returning from shopping in London: "And then, my dear, I have never seen such a fright. No fashion sense at all, I fancy she wears still a shawl mantle . . ."

Such had been Sarah's nervous state that she had imagined they spoke of her. Looking out of the window at the level countryside, she had felt thin-skinned, vulnerable. Where the bright confidence, the optimism which for nearly a year now had buoyed her up? Even by Kings Cross she had begun to be homesick. At my age, she thought.

". . . the ribbons we were to have found at Whiteleys . . . trimmings of spangles and jet . . . seventy yards of chenille, that would be scarcely enough . . ."

She had left home without the blessings she could have wished for. Paul (to whom after all she *owed* all this) had been hurried, distracted, arranging the visit of his Rose. The Stranger. (And what am I to make of all *that?* she thought. The foolish haste of it. I shall not like her, that is certain.) Most of September when she had been preparing for Cambridge and Newnham Hall, when she had had to get together if not a trousseau, at least an outfit—all had been confusion.

He had not told Kate. When Sarah told her, she had been as surprised as anyone. "And now," Sarah had said to her, angry herself, "we are to suppose he has been all these months, not realising he was in love with her. So *this* has been his secret . . ."

Mama she could not have expected to be pleased. But it had been with Sarah that Catriona had been angry. In her mind she seemed to link both actions: Paul's paying for Sarah, and his becoming engaged. ("If he wishes to waste his money making you even more discontented with your lot, there is no more to be said, except that it is not right to spring on a person another person of whom one knows *nothing*—except that she is a Romanist and he also is to become one . . . och, if your Dunbar grandfather would have heard of such a thing . . .") While Papa, poor Papa, his opinion was not asked. "This is a *great* surprise," John said only. He spoke flatly, slowly, as always now. As if not only the talking but the very effort of thinking was a trial. He worked now, if anything, harder than ever: his patients, who loved him, taken well care of. But for the rest of the time it was as if he were half-dead. Even *she*, with her chatter and her enthusiasms, could not rouse him to life. He had become very elderly, although only a year or two separated him from Uncle Ned—who did not seem to her old at all.

". . . Rainbow beads, or moonlight beads—they would add a delight-ful touch, do you not think?"

She had seen so little of Paul in all the flurry, and today, when she left, he had been gone already two days: to fetch this Rose that she might meet everyone before the wedding (which was to be soon enough—late November . . .). Sarah was to be bridesmaid, so that even more of her precious last days had gone on hasty fittings at the dress-maker's.

And it was not even as if Paul seemed happy. Excited, yes—but his eyes did not meet hers. And they were dark-circled, wary. About it all he had said to her only: "Darling—it was the biggest, most important decision of my life" (And well he might say that, she thought), "I mean to make a great success of it all—" Then he had looked at once as if he must off somewhere else—in body, and in mind.

". . . Oh, it would be best to agree to a tailor-made costume . . . With her, it is the stand-up flounces . . . I think gaugeing *quite* the most delightful . . ."

The two women had got out at Audley End so that she was alone in the carriage when the train arrived. Cambridge station was ugly, the platform very long. Outside there was a row of cabs, and some competi-tion. A girl just ahead of her said to the cabby in confident tones, "Gir-ton College." She saw several men waiting, young and obviously un-dergraduates—one was trying to manage some polo sticks—but no other girls looking lost.

Her luggage was hoisted up. The cab rattled down the Hills Road, left down Lensfield Road and into Trumpington Street. It was then, with the sight of the first colleges in the darkening evening, that she began to believe she was in Cambridge. Along Silver Street then, and over the iron bridge, congested with traffic. Here the backs of several colleges looked onto the river. She saw footbridges reaching away into the twilight.

Turn left, then right. A little way along, and then, drawing up before a pleasant red brick house in the Queen Anne style. She was here. She had arrived.

There was a knock at her door: "Miss Rawson?" A small girl with pointed nose and friendly eyes: "I am Miss Alexander. You must be be-wildered with names. I have brought with me Miss *Hudson*. She is also new, and we shall all three go down to dinner together."

Miss Hudson was small also but pudgy with it. Her eyes seemed lost above the puffed cheeks. Her complexion was pasty. As they made their way down the stairs she looked at Sarah almost continuously, so that

Sarah thought she might stumble. Except that Miss Alexander was talking all the while, she would have asked her (politely), "What do you see that you must stare so?" (It is not my mark, she thought. It *must* not be that.)

At the meal itself she found Miss Hudson seated opposite her, although perhaps because of the food she was not being stared at so closely. Miss Hudson wished to teach, she told Sarah. Her greatest ambition was to have a headship of a school—or best of all, her *own* school. Although her general manner was diffident, as soon as she spoke her voice sounded confident, even a little self-satisfied.

"My interest is mathematics. My dad said, 'Jessie, if they'll teach you how to make four shillings do the work of five, then it's welcome home . . .' Where are you from, Miss Rawson?"

"Downham in Wensleydale. You will not have heard of it—it is a small town in the North Riding of Yorkshire."

"Oh, but I am from Sheffield. So we're both Yorkshirewomen in exile . . ."

Another new student was on Sarah's left. She had been introduced as Miss Graham. She talked most of the time to her neighbour on the left, loudly, throwing her head back and not so much laughing as snorting. She had a lot of wispy fair hair, slightly greasy. Sarah was tired and not hungry. The lump of meat on her plate was charred and looked unappetising. When she cut into it the inside was raw. She pushed it to one side. Miss Alexander, on her right, said: "Oh dear, it is often like that. We are used to it."

"I daresay I shall manage," Sarah said wearily, smiling.

"And you have seen Miss Clough of course, and been a little fussed over? She is very motherly, and will even see to breakfast in bed when you have a cold . . . Tomorrow I expect you will be interviewed about your studies and what lectures you must attend—outside, in Cambridge, as well as here . . ."

Indeed, yes. And already this evening she had been invited to a "cocoa," as they called them, but it would not be until after nine. ("But it is not really etiquette, you know, to refuse—and especially in your first days . . .")

Someone else was speaking of chaperones. They must have chaperones to go into lectures in the town. From all sides voices came at her.

"And what is your subject, Miss Rawson? Were you living at home, Miss Porson? And what did you do before, Miss Rawson? . . ."

In a moment's sudden silence a voice further down the table said: "I travelled, I travelled. Oh, rejoice for me. I left the shores of Albion and what did I see?"

Voices, and more voices. The babble, the cross-talk, the excitements and the phrases and names peppering the chatter. But this is like *school*, Sarah thought, and felt for a minute or two quite alone. To think that I might be in Egypt with Edwy, she told herself. That seemed to her an indescribably worse fate.

Towards the end of the meal she was surprised when her neighbour, Miss Graham, took time off from snorting to turn on her suddenly. Sarah had been explaining, quite simply, something about her past life —she could never afterwards recall exactly what—when Miss Graham, who she did not know had been listening, looked at her coldly for a moment, then burst out rudely: "I must tell you that however you may have managed your life before, this is quite different. I can see already that you have a superior air and think that this will be a place like any other. I am new myself—but I am used to managing, you know, I have already been to one college. You are rather young, I fear, Miss Rawson?"

"I am twenty-four—"

"Just fancy, I would have thought nineteen at the most. There will be no need to grow up here, I assure you." She turned back and applied herself to her boiled pudding as if she had said nothing. Miss Hudson looked terrified. For the rest of the meal she stared again at Sarah as if by so doing she might protect her from another attack. "Oh dear," said Miss Alexander, under her breath, as soon as Miss Graham had finished, "what have we here?"

The "cocoa" was given by Miss Seppings and Miss Alexander together, in Miss Alexander's room. The room was both cluttered and crowded: Sarah met there some more of the new students. There was a Jewish girl, a Miss Meyer, whose father was a doctor in North London so that they had at once some common topic of conversation. After her, she talked to a Miss Woodward, a grave, statuesque girl with heavily coiled ash blond hair who came from Bath. She had to be drawn out, and appeared to think a great deal before she spoke. She knew who some of the others were and pointed out to Sarah a very pretty girl with a tiptilted nose, sitting over in the corner. "A Miss Sorrell, she is American and very, very rich. She has stabled two horses here and I believe intends to hunt."

Although Sarah was not hungry, she ate from a paper bag of small cakes being passed round. Her cocoa was not very hot, perhaps because there were too many people. Miss Alexander said engagingly to the room at large, "It is not the best cocoa, I am afraid—it is stored from last term and has quite taken up the taste of paraffin . . ."

Miss Seppings had changed into a dressing gown of very similar material to the dress she had worn earlier. Miss Woodward remarked to Sarah, with a half-admiring glance, "I am quite taken with this 'aesthetic' dress, but have not as yet had the courage—she looks well enough but it is difficult not to look wan and/or untidy . . . I have shocked my family enough by *this* venture, without altering also my mode of dress. It is all too new . . ."

"You would look well in it," Sarah said, and meant it. For Miss Woodward had the height for it. Miss Seppings did not. "It is I who would look the fright." Talking on, they then discovered that both were hoping to proceed to the Classics Tripos. Miss Woodward said, "I have not yet worked seriously at all and am still quite at sea. I think these Higher Local exams—Groups I think they call them, because the subjects are grouped and one must pass a certain number—Groups may be my downfall, and arithmetic my stumbling block." She told Sarah, "I have an uncle here in Cambridge, my mother's brother—he is a classics man and it is from there I have the *idea*. I fear that it may remain only that . . ."

The purpose of the gathering, or one of the main purposes, was for the new students to be informed about life in Newnham: the rules, how their days should be ordered and so on. Miss Seppings did much of the talking but fortunately allowed Miss Alexander, whose voice was far more attractive, to do the rest. Certain hours, Sarah learnt, the building was kept quiet for study—mainly in the morning and early evening—those who had musical instruments were begged to play them at other times ("You don't want to hear my *banjo?*" Miss Sorrell asked lightheartedly from her corner. Miss Graham looked at her witheringly).

Miss Alexander told them: "Of course we are chaperoned to lectures, but all sorts of concessions have come about recently—women's rights are really triumphing—the Natural Sciences students may go to Christ's College to hear the men's lectures there if Miss Clough goes with them. And now History students may go also into King's, and listen to Mr. Oscar Browning. I was there. Fifty undergraduates and then four of *us*. Quite an achievement for women's rights, do you not think? For that college is the very one where a professor described us as 'forward minxes'—just for wanting to sit our exams. They are the richest college in Cambridge and quite the most famous outside. Mr. Oscar Browning —nothing to do with the poet by the way—is a well-known figure here, sometimes referred to as 'O.B.' "

" 'O.B., oh be obedient!' " said Miss Seppings in her bright voice. She added disarmingly, "That is not my joke . . ."

Miss Sorrell, who it appeared was to do History, pricked up her ears about the lectures. "And are they *really* good?" She laughed most of the time, but now appeared serious. Miss Graham eyed her again with scorn. To Sarah she seemed delightful. When a little earlier Sarah had hesitated over her name, she had said easily, "Sorrell. I guess it sounds kind of like '*sorry.*' Only I ain't, so there . . ." And she had laughed again.

But now at last the party was breaking up. The day which had begun at five in the morning—she had not been able to sleep a moment longer —could really be allowed to finish. Back again in her room, peace and fatigue washed over her. It would be all right—probably.

Before getting into bed, she took from her writing-case a small card and looked at it for a moment or two. It was in Matthew Staveley's hand. Three days ago she had had a farewell luncheon with him following a revision lesson after the summer break: "So that your mind comes to all of it fresh, but not wiped clean . . ." She had promised to write to him. Yesterday he had sent her this card:

"I have translated this for you, from one of the Greek *scolia*. I had meant to give it as a farewell but then had not the courage. It is for your comfort if you should feel strange:

" 'A man should consider a voyage from the land, to see if he would be able and would have the skill; but when he has come upon the deep, he must needs run with the wind there is . . .' "

Those first few days were ones of sunshine. The smell of autumn— the colours too, the reds and russets and green-browns. Sitting in her room (and she might have been in the country: looking out one day and seeing that two cows had strayed into the garden), she found it difficult to believe in winter. It was warm enough to play lawn tennis, which she did with Miss Woodward—warm enough too for Miss Hudson to sit outside and watch them—or rather, watch Sarah. She kept inviting Sarah to her room. "We've not our subjects in common," she would say, "but we've Yorkshire—we've that." (Sarah had discovered since that Miss Graham came from there also, from near York. She hoped that *she* would not be invited.)

Although Miss Hudson had seemed to her quite fat the first evening, over the next few weeks she swelled visibly. Her appetite was insatiable: anything was fuel. "I can't think clearly," she said, "till I'm filled up." At breakfast she would waddle over to the serving table for a second helping of sausages or bacon. Only the rather bony haddock defeated her. Sarah, often still full from unaccustomed cocoa drunk late the night before, could eat little or nothing at that time.

In a sudden fit of homesickness she had written to Kate—but her letter had crossed with a large parcel from Little Grinling. They had been thinking of her. It was mainly food: some pepper cake with pieces of sugared ginger in it, some butter toffee made by Flo, crab apple jelly, and two bottles of port. The wine was because: "I am worried, darling," Kate wrote, "that you may not always feel *strong* enough . . ."

There was a photograph at the end of their first week. On a day so mild it might have been early September. An informal group photograph. No one was hatted. She and Miss Woodward had still their tennis bats in hand. On her other side sat Miss Hudson with three books on her lap and her hands folded over her stomach. When we are all long dead and someone looks at our picture: she will look forever studious, Sarah thought (just as Miss Woodward and I shall forever look sporting . . .). Miss Graham had moved when she should not and appeared very blurred. Miss Sorrell, who had acquired a kitten from somewhere for the occasion, sat happily with it in the front row. The picture was taken by the West door. The sash window was open and a smiling Miss Meyer and another girl leaned out.

The weeks turned into a month—such order to her days, such happiness—and then, only a week or two and she must go to Lancashire for the wedding. It seemed to her that she had been here not four or five weeks but five years. And such excitement in her studies. She had written twice already to Matthew Staveley. Of her delighted discovery of Aristophanes ("He is *funny*—no, please do not croak like a frog when you read this . . ."), of Euripides, and of Livy, and Tacitus ("Full of political lessons for us today, so there! I made that very point last evening at a debate here. Am I not a 'forward minx'? Shall I explain that reference to you in my next letter? . . .").

One afternoon she was asked down to tea in Miss Alexander's room. There were three girls she did not know and Miss Graham. They all discussed the Misses Brontës' novels. In the midst of commenting on the curates in *Shirley,* Miss Graham said suddenly, and in her usual, rather unpleasant manner: "Rawson, Rawson . . . the name teases me. I feel certain I know that name." She returned then to Charlotte Bronte—and a few minutes later had to leave for a five o'clock class. Miss Alexander seemed relieved when she had left—the discussion went on until Sarah saw to her surprise that more than two hours had passed and the dressing bell for dinner had already gone . . .

She joined the choral society, an interest she shared with Miss Sorrell, and rehearsed conscientiously, enthusiastically a motet of Mendelssohn's. She walked into the country, to Grantchester—the "Long Grind" as it was called: a popular walk with the undergraduates. She saw a great many of them crossing the meadows, capped and gowned.

She herself managed to tear her dress going through some brambles. Mending, which they called "working," they did in parties one evening a week with one of them reading aloud. Sarah liked best to do this and was currently reading them *The Mill on the Floss*. For once she was glad of Miss Hudson's now open adoration, since she was able to persuade her (allow her, rather) to sew fresh braid round the bottom of the torn dress, leaving Sarah free to read aloud . . .

It was Miss Woodward she saw the most of. The two of them went shopping in the town. Sarah bought cushions and some material in an orange shade for curtains to go with her wallpaper. Together they varnished each other's bookcases. They found that they had more in common than their subject (and Miss Woodward was having great difficulty with that . . .), for when Sarah was speaking one day of some happening two or three years ago, saying: "But that of course was when I had expected to be married . . ." Miss Woodward had said, "Oh, but I too was once in that condition—and for *three* years! He was a naval man . . ." So Sarah had told of Edwy. It seemed as they spoke to have been much the same story for both of them.

". . . and all the time I was thinking *that* in Downham—you were thinking *that* in Bath . . ."

Miss Woodward had said, "It puts me in mind, my tale, of Miss Austen's *Persuasion*—except in reverse. The marriage was so much urged on me. My intended had already an excellent career and came back even more covered in glory." She added: "Well, I do not think you would have been happy with your Edward, and I know I would not with mine. I might not even have *known* that I was unhappy—and is not that perhaps worse?"

Autumn had brought some grey skies now with fog sometimes in the morning and in the early evening a mist coming up from the river. But the afternoon that she and Miss Woodward went to King's College for vespers was one of the most beautiful yet. As they came into the chapel, the last of the afternoon sun streamed in, golden, illuminating the vaulted roof. It became for her part of the music, the singing. There were not too many people: they were fortunate enough to get stall seats. They sang "O come, O come, Emmanuel." A candle flickered by each of the high-backed oak stalls. She thought that she saw Francis Ingham and then as they turned to go out—was certain. How foolish, she thought. I had forgotten him, that he was here (And yet Matthew Staveley had mentioned it twice—had, she knew, seen something of him before he went). Perhaps I did not want to admit, she thought, that I must share this place with him. And that *is* a wicked thought (the more so, as my quarrel is not really with him).

Strangely enough she saw him again, this time to speak to, only a week later. Miss Woodward had been several times to visit her uncle: now she said to Sarah, "They give a tea-party this Sunday. Some undergraduates will be asked. They would like it if I also bring a friend." Her uncle, a Mr. Vernor, had been a Fellow of Queens', but "after loving for eight, or was it ten years, a Miss Jepson of Taunton, he threw up everything and married her. As you know, or may not, a Fellow of a college must remain single—so that he lost his Fellowship but is now a coach in classics, and is kept not half busy. He has some of the best men come to him."

The house was a large new one in the Madingley Road. Mrs. Vernor had a just-fading loveliness. Her husband plainly adored her, and although he appeared absent-minded much of the time, when present, he fussed over her constantly ("Now, my dearest, you are not going to do that *yourself?*"). The children were all quite small and only the eldest, a girl of about ten, came in to tea. Meta. She had a look of Flo, but none of her manner: Sarah found herself staring at her. Meta perhaps noticed this, for she came up to Sarah and took her hand. "May I stand with you awhile?" A little later she insisted that she show Sarah her doll's house.

"You may make me something to go in it. Do you do Greek? Then you may make me a little Greek book for the papa doll downstairs . . ." For about a quarter of an hour, Sarah had to play with her, and the doll's house. Meta was very excitable and when Sarah suggested they go back, she became quite agitated: "No, no—we must finish this game. You started it, you *promised* . . ."

When at last they were going downstairs again, Meta still holding her hand: "That's my uncle Cecil's room. Uncle Jepson." She pointed to a closed door. "He is my mama's brother, and not quite, not always—" She tapped her forehead, then burst into laughter. Sarah thought she would never stop. But then she said in a conspiratorial whisper, drawing closer, "He has a terrible cough and may not come downstairs—otherwise he would be here. He likes to make friends." She paused, then added in very adult tones: "They say his mind is very *simple* . . ."

Downstairs Meta was reprimanded by her mother for monopolising Sarah. "I think she must have taken a great fancy to you, Miss Rawson. My niece has been looking about for you, though—and I, too." Taking Sarah's arm, she led her across the now-crowded room.

Francis Ingham was standing by a table, alone, contemplating a slice of seed-cake. Sarah was surprised and pleased that he did not recognise her at once. Mrs. Vernor said: "Miss Rawson, I must introduce you—one of Mr. Vernor's ablest students—a King's man . . ."

She saw shyness, hesitancy, struggle with natural courtesy. Her name had been enough to jog his memory.

"Miss Rawson is with our niece at Newnham Hall—" Then: "Ah, but if you already *know* each other . . ." They were left together. Sarah saw that he wore part-mourning: a black crape arm band on his jacket. The conversation moved stiffly. He told her something of his first weeks. He had been rowing: he found it always—although at school he had not been very good, and was not now—perhaps the perfect counterbalance to study. "Better I think than chasing a muddy ball. The rhythm of Catullus and the rhythm of the oars—they marry better. And you?"

"There is a gym—which I do not like. And lawn tennis, of course—or there was on the sunny days last month . . ." She steered the exchange then to Downham, and what news there might be of it. She mentioned Matthew Staveley. Francis said: "He had spoken of you to Father, and to me. I think he has so much enjoyed his coaching of you . . ."

At least, Sarah thought, he does not stutter like his father. Only his hand holding the teacup betrayed his slight nervousness. She did not find it unattractive.

"My grandmother has not been well but is now better. Mrs. Ingham, I mean. And my aunt Julia, Father's sister, stays with us. Her husband died some weeks ago, you see. He had been ill for a long time. Some form of anaemia, I believe. My cousins, two of them, were at school with me, but both are younger than I . . ."

He talked more easily now. Perhaps he too was sometimes a little homesick? After a while, Miss Woodward came over and joined them.

Two days later, Sarah left for the wedding.

FOURTEEN

O thou that lookest sweetly through the window,
maiden in thy face, and yet withal a wedded bride.

PRAXILLA, translated from the Greek by Francis Brooks

The marriage of Mr. Paul James Ewart Rawson with Miss
Rose Elizabeth Muriel Straunge-Lacey, eldest daughter of Mr.
Augustus Mary Straunge-Lacey, of Foxton Hall, was solem-
nised according to the rites of the Roman Catholic Church on
Monday last. The bridegroom was accompanied as best man
by Mr. Cecil Balfour. The Reverend Clement Bromhead S.J.
officiated. None but immediate relatives of both families were
present. Breakfast was at Foxton Hall after which the couple
left for London and then the Italian Lakes, where they pass
the honeymoon.

The bride, given away by her father, was attired in a
princesse dress of white satin trimmed with point d'Alencon,
wreath of orange blossoms and lace veil. Her ornaments were
rubies and pearls, the gift of the bridegroom. The bridesmaids
were Miss Sarah Rawson and Miss Elfrida Straunge-Lacey.
They wore dresses of ivory silk and cashmere, trimmed with
cardinal, and ivory silk caps trimmed with the same colour.
Each wore a locket with the monogram of the bride and
groom, presented by the groom.

"Thank you, thank you, darling Paul, for the locket," Elfrida said, "I
shall wear it in class—Mother Bede does not allow any jewellery but
when I explain about *this* . . ." She hiccuped.

Paul said: "Bridesmaids are not meant to be intoxicated—"

"No, no. It is quite all right, I am only bosky, not obfuscated *at all*. Anyway I can be as much so as I please—I do not leave till Monday. It is you who must not be, since you must stand up and speak and say about Rose—that she is a beautiful flower and—"

"I shall say nothing of the sort." He lifted her hand from his head. "No, go away, Elfrida darling. I have not married you—" He took her hand and squeezed it. Then Rose, who was looking very serious, kissed her, and she ran off.

They were all there at the wedding breakfast except Hermione, who was eight months into her pregnancy now. Dolly had not wanted her to travel. As Paul sat in the place of honour, Rose by his side: *It is done*, he said to himself. *There is no turning back.* Certainly if he had not thought marriage a serious undertaking before, in these busy last few weeks he had realised it. Although it was all tied up with religion, with the act of becoming a Catholic, somehow—he was not sure how—he kept the two separate. He learned about the Four Last Things, the Seven Gifts of the Holy Ghost, Cardinal and Theological Virtues, Indulgences, Latria, Hyperdulia and Dulia, the Communion of Saints, Mortal and Venial Sin, the Seven Sacraments, and the Commandments of the Church. He was a willing pupil, and quick to understand. He found interesting the similarities to his flirtation with High Church Anglicanism, in his Oxford days.

But it was all in the head. He knew that. He *intended* to be good—but that was for the future. Now, in the present, he made haste, such haste, to be *over with the sin*. Then and only then, might the sinner creep into the fold. No sin that could not be forgiven (except Despair and Presumption—but these two, as defined, it was not that. He had not, was not committing *those* . . .). Then and only then, he would be good—every promise made would be honoured. Love, cherish—yes. Everything, anything. And since she seemed to him, more than he would have thought, easily lovable—it would not be difficult.

And it was that lovableness he supposed that had made her, against all his expectations, immediately and completely *friends with Sarah*. He had feared the worst. Seeing Sarah get out of the train—her face, its expression. "*She* is not with you in the carriage?" And then the studied, careful talk all the way to Foxton, of Cambridge and what she had done and would do: that she had met Francis Ingham of all people, quite by chance; that she was to help found a Browning Society; that the food was by and large really rather awful—tending towards heavy puddings, not quite cooked. And then: "Oh Paul, darlingus stupidibus —*why* get married?" She burst out with it, as if she had been saving it up. "And to a *Stranger* too . . ." Then she laughed. They both laughed. (The truth lying in a joke, he thought.) And she had thrown her arms about him: "I shall try to like her," she had said, fighting back tears. He dreaded Sarah's trying. He knew from old that she could not. She either liked, or disliked.

Ah, but then, she *liked*. Very much. He supposed it to be completely Rose's doing. When they arrived she was already waiting in the hall—she had been sitting in the great oaken chair. As the door opened she went straight to Sarah, took both her hands in hers, and said something so ordinary ("You must be cold"?)—so ordinary that he could not remember now what it was. *Then* she had said—quite simply, as if she offered Sarah tea or wine or a seat by the fire: "I must thank you for your brother—that you share him with me so lovingly. I had wanted so to meet you . . ." Then she spoke to Sarah at once about Downham and her visit there. "I brought your dress back with me. We shall try it on this evening—if you are not too tired . . ."

It was then that he realised that she had never *expected* Sarah to dislike her. It had simply not occurred to her. Her early remarks had been not placatory, but natural. She spoke (and did she not always?) from the heart.

Although he should not have been so surprised, he thought, since she had won over already a heart *far more* hardened against her. But as to exactly how she had won Mother's on that first visit to Downham he was never quite sure. She had not said—had not felt the need to, perhaps—anything such as: "Thank you for Paul" (It would have brought her only, most probably, "Thank you for snatching him . . ."). The first two days of the visit had been for him torture. As always when upset, Mother wounded herself the most. Since his change of religion was the easiest to pick on: in an aggressive manner, she quoted *ad nauseam* comments passed by Scots dignitaries—all of them derogatory. He suspected her of inventing them. She looked unhappy. Father's only comment on her behaviour was to say: "She had always a temper. Once it was attractive—and so was she . . ." His tone unexpectedly bitter.

Rose got on well with John, showing a genuine interest and concern in his work. Of Mother's barbed remarks she said merely, "That is of course what we were taught always to expect—it is just that I had not yet been tested—" She seemed more anxious lest he should be distressed. Sometimes it frightened him almost, her calm strength, her pliancy, her refusal to be hurt. On the Sunday of her visit, there was the question of their going to Mass. There was a Mass centre at Leyburn, but the time—it would be a *great* inconvenience just then, Mother said: the brougham was needed, and so on and so on. It *could not* be more awkward. But "Why then, we shall not go," Rose had told her, "and that is all there is to it. And *now*—you had promised me I might see Paul's first childish drawings . . ."

Later she said to Paul, "She has been very beautiful, and would be still if she were not so sad." She added: "Your father is sad too, but hers is the greater. For I think she has done it to herself."

Then after four or five days of this, Mother had had one of her blinding headaches. Usually she lay alone in her room until they passed. Sometimes he would hear her walking up and down, restless, agitated. She said now: "I shall go upstairs. It is all this talk of—rather this *atmosphere* of rosaries and masses and—I don't know. I have incense in my nostrils. Certainly I shall not need your Purgatory, Rose, since I have it here . . ." About half an hour later, taking up a copy of *Middlemarch*, which Paul had been reading aloud in the evenings, Rose had gone upstairs. Paul had been with her. She had knocked on the door and then announced gently, "I have come to read to you . . ."

He wondered after what passage she had read, or what thoughts expressed: indeed, what had occurred during the hour or so she had spent in there. But for the remainder of the visit, peace reigned. The references to religion were as frequent, but they were not barbed. Insults changed to something resembling an affectionate joke.

Kate had liked Rose, too. And Rose had liked Kate. But that he had expected: he felt only sadness that he could not say, "But Kate, I love you still the best." That he could not tell her the whole story.

It was while Rose was there that he had made many of the practical arrangements. His great-grandfather's, Old Jacob's, house was his now. In the terms of the will it was to come to him at the age of twenty-five or when he married—whichever was the sooner. Great-aunt Minnie lived there still, together with a few servants. She was semi-crippled now—as if the legs which had answered Old Jacob's every beck and call were resting at last—and lived on the ground floor only. He would not move her out. Instead he bought a house which conveniently came up for sale at the end of the town nearest to the church and the Abbey. As far as possible, he thought, from Linden House, without leaving Downham. And near, too, the road for Kate's . . .

Rose was delighted with it. Back at Foxton, he showed Sybil Straunge-Lacey a drawing of it and also a photograph. She said to him, rather oddly, "I think this will suit very well. Of course Rose would be at home anywhere. A labourer's cottage . . ." He had said then, "But I am not offering her a labourer's cottage—" and wondered afterwards if this had been some delicate reference to what she might well feel was his inferior social standing.

But her manner with him was always gracious, and he had had on that last visit to submit to no less than three "little confidential talks." With Nick—it had been quite different. He had been there for part of the time at least, and it had seemed to Paul impossible that others should not notice the set face, the sarcastic manner, the walking out of the room when Paul entered . . . Except that it was surprising always how little people saw when their expectations were otherwise. And often too he would even—in mockery apparent to Paul, but seeming to the others affection—throw an arm about Paul's shoulders. "*Dear* fellow . . ." But yet how much he must be punished, Paul thought, when he heard, as he did so frequently now, the remark: "How delightful, what a happy arrangement that it should be a *friend* of yours who marries your sister . . ."

Nick was to have been best man at the wedding. There had been no way to avoid that. But then—and Paul might have guessed this—he had gone to Austria at the end of October, and three days before he was due back had telegraphed that bad weather kept him in the mountains. "Deeply regret, unlikely will clear . . ." They were to find a substitute. Telegrams hummed back and forth. Paul was in Downham. Within twenty-four hours he had arranged for an Oxford friend to stand in. He wrote to Rose, whom he knew would be upset. And he kept his own counsel.

Now here at the wedding breakfast, his glass sparkling with Veuve Clicquot, Rose beside him, the words spoken which could not be unspoken, he felt a certain peace. Perhaps in the end, he had done right? (Without God's blessing, what use to go forward?) For certainly he must go without Nick's blessing. It might be even that he must go with Nick's curse . . .

They took the train to London where they were to stay for five or six days before leaving for Italy. He had planned already how each hour of the morning and evening would be spent, having found out first what she had seen of London, what she would like to see again, and what was her particular taste in theatres and amusements. He found her easy, with a quiet decisive enthusiasm. Yes, please, to the Grosvenor Gallery: "I have heard *so* much about it." No, thank you, to the Tower of London. Yes, yes, yes, to Kew Gardens.

The nights, he had not planned. The first evening at their hotel, sitting with her in the restaurant—*I am married*, he said to himself with sudden disbelief. The feeling of a waking dream persisted. Perhaps it was unnatural fatigue. He drank heavily with the meal, trying to assuage the dry-mouthed light head, aftermath of the wedding breakfast champagne.

He looked for signs of nervousness in her, for a repetition of the slight and attractive hesitation at the altar. (It had been momentary only—her voice was soon back to its low, confident firm tone.) *I am married*, he said again.

When he came upstairs she was already kneeling by the bed, wearing the heavily embroidered and extravagantly ruffled nightgown which had so surprised him when he had seen it laid out before dinner. He realised he had never seen her with hair down before. It was not plaited, even loosely, but tied back. Her eyes, Nick's eyes, were tight shut.

He did not speak, so as not to disturb her. Then she turned to him and said, "We must pray together. Should you like that?" She put her hand on his, and then closed her eyes again. Still dressed, he knelt beside her—as he had knelt, only this morning at Foxton. But he could say nothing. And he dare not think.

Sudden fatigue overwhelmed him when, ready now for bed, he thought to climb in. She was lying still, her head propped up on the pillows. He had expected her to look sacrificial—a lamb led to the slaughter—but when he looked again he saw that she was gazing at him, watching him with quiet interest as he made his last preparations for the night: pocket watch in its stand beside the bed, a final drink of water for his parched throat.

Then he did not get in, but sat on the edge of the bed. He was seized suddenly by reality, the waking dream over. He could hardly move, as it came to him, the enormity of what he had done. And done forever. Nor was that all. He had not thought, really, of what was expected of him. Only that it would punish Nick. Otherwise he had succeeded until now in pushing it to the back of his mind. He had not thought that *he must do it*.

He would not have believed it of anyone else, that a person should be so clouded, so confused. People said of their actions: "I was blind to the consequences . . ." I have been that, he thought. He had known all along what it was that would be done to Rose—but I never thought, somehow, that it is *I* must do it.

He could not pray. He could not feel desire. Nothing. Yet how many times had he not felt desire when he need not, should not? And now I am not thinking of Nick, but of all the girls and women since Kate—*who must not come in this room*—all the other girls and women to whom I have been idly drawn: hot summer days, glimpse of no more than an ankle, a scent perhaps, the brush of a hand. And now he had all this.

For a few mad moments he imagined himself saying: "I know what it is that—married people do. What I might ask of you, what it is habit-

ual to ask. But I shall not. You are free. You will see that I shall ask
nothing of you . . ." The idea seemed at once to free him of some
dreadful burden. And of guilt too. Nick punished, and yet not punished.

But he did not say it. Instead, leaning over, giving her a chaste kiss,
"We are both tired," he said. "I hope that after all the excitement of
today—that you will sleep. You are used to sleep easily?"

She nodded her head, smiled. "I wish," she said, slipping down on
the pillows, "I wish so much that Nick could have been with us today."

He was a restless sleeper that night. It seemed to him that in no position was he comfortable. And there was too much light in the room. Although not enough to see whether she slept or not. She was very still,
but she was a still person: her breathing was steady. He felt some of the
time that her eyes were open, felt even—but he would not turn his head
—that she looked at him.

He dreamed. He was back at school again, walking in the Savernake
Forest near Marlborough. First he was in the open, in a long grass walk,
the turf short, the sun falling on the rich green of bracken and ferns.
Then he was farther in and amongst the great old trees, the oaks
gnarled, the huge tall beeches above him, enclosing him. He thought
that he was awake, and remembered that he had been happy there, but
now was sad. Why am I sad? He met Sarah, walking alone too, and
asked her. She said matter-of-factly: "What can you expect? You have
come in by the wrong gate. You should have used the Kissing Gate . . ."
He answered, "*That* old superstition—" But she gave him a pity-
ing look. "You know nothing. You should ask Francis. He knows. I
have seen him three times at Cambridge . . ."

He woke, got a light, and saw that it was not quite two o'clock. He
had thrown off the bedclothes and felt cold, and alone. He would have
liked to snuggle up towards Rose, to burrow. No question now but that
she was asleep. She lay on her side, turned away from him, breathing
deeply. The bedlinen, pressed close, outlined her body.

For November the weather was very mild, often pleasantly sharp and
dry with a clear blue sky. He enjoyed, and thought that she did, their
days together. On the last afternoon before leaving for Italy, they visited the Grosvenor Gallery. He had been twice before and knew his
way round it well: showing her Watts's *Love and Death* in the West
Gallery, and the Millais, the Richmond, the Alma Tadema. Holman
Hunt's *Afterglow in Egypt*, Whistler's "Nocturnes." The original crimson hangings had been replaced since his first visit by ones of a dull
olive green.

"These," he said to Rose, "these are the 'greeny-yallery' of which Sarah told us—the very colour that some of her fellow students wear in their 'aesthetic' dress—"

She remembered. And liked it too. "Kate would look well," she said, "with her hair. That such a beautiful colour should ever have been unfashionable . . . So much for fashion . . ." She liked too (surprisingly, he thought) the "Nocturnes"—but was polite only about the Leightons. It was in front of the *Nocturne in Black and Gold, the Falling Rocket,* that a moment later they ran into Stephen.

"Rawson—dear fellow! And—?" He took in Rose at a glance. Paul was proud of her appearance on that outing, the blue velvet Rubens hat, simply trimmed with ribbons, the close-fitting sealskin jacket. He knew that before she had not troubled . . . "What have we here?"

But then when all was explained, Stephen continued: "How did I not hear of this? Of course, I *was* two months in *France* this autumn. But *sans blague*—I thought it was *Nick* to marry? No?" He smiled at Rose, "I have had the pleasure only of meeting your younger sister—I did not know what I was missing. Or what Rawson would be gaining." He looked a moment at his gloves, then: "Now dear lady, dear Mrs. Rawson—what have you seen? The Watercolour Gallery? Dicky Doyle's quite delightful fairies . . ."

He was with them a full half hour. "Ah, Passionate Brompton," he murmured every now and then, striking an attitude. Later in the afternoon, when he had left them, Rose said thoughtfully: "How should such a one know about Nick? I had thought it all quite a family affair . . ."

Paul muttered something. "Gossip travels—"

"Anyway, that is my mama's idea—Nick's marrying. Quite her own. *All* her own." She smiled gravely. "You are such a one should be a husband, Paul. But Nick—never . . ."

Arriving in Italy, they spent one day in Milan and then travelled down to Lake Garda. Rose seemed to him happy—or rather, she did not seem to him unhappy. Everything interested her. She had not travelled before. She had brought with her a diary in a locked leather case: she wrote it up often in the afternoons or evenings, sometimes asking him the spelling of a place name.

At night, it was no different from that first time. Except that now he said nothing at all. He had spoken about it once only, the last night in London, when he had said suddenly, surprising himself: "You need not submit. There is no need to submit—" Then his voice had tailed away. He left her to make what she could of the remark. She had frowned, as if puzzled, and then when he said no more, she had spoken easily of something quite other. The thought passed through his mind, that perhaps she *did not know*. Often, he had heard, girls were not told. If then, she expected nothing . . . But strangely, he found this notion unattractive. There is no pleasing me, he thought, burying the problem once more. Thinking: time enough to worry when we are in Italy. When we are home again even . . .

Precipitous cliffs edged one side of this largest and most beautiful of Italian lakes. The mountains rose behind. Under a clear and blue winter sky: grey-green olives, dark cypresses, the rich green of the lemon trees. In the harbour at Gargnano there were cannon balls cemented in the walls, from when twelve years ago the Austrians had shelled Garibaldi's troops. Indeed, the town of Riva and the northern part of the lake were still part of Austria-Hungary. Their hotel on the lake's edge had in it more Austrian visitors than Italian.

Amongst the visitors was a tenor of whom neither of them had heard, but whom they supposed to be famous since his name was spoken in reverent tones not only by the Austrians in the hotel but the Italians also. Heads turned when he came into the dining-room. In one of the hotel drawing-rooms there was a grand piano and in the evenings, sometimes also in the mornings, the tenor would sing informally. To applause and requests he would reply always, "I rehearse only . . ." Certainly he seemed unaware of his audience. A piano in his room for him and his accompanist would have been a more obvious solution (Paul had arranged easily enough a piano for Rose. "Yes, *please*, dear Paul," she had said to his suggestion). However, neither Paul and Rose nor any of the hotel guests wished to question this delightful arrangement. The waiters too made a point of hovering about in the drawing-room. Often the manager would stand in the doorway.

On about the fourth evening, the music chosen seemed to Paul familiar. Because the tenor was "rehearsing," he sang often the same piece twice or even three times. One of the songs haunted Paul with its strange beauty, moving him almost to tears. Partly it was the voice which soared in such unlikely fashion from the tenor's rotund and rather fussy body. But also it was the sense of *déjà vu* . . . (Only, where?) He spoke to Rose.

"Surely, Beethoven. I think they are all from the song cycle An *die ferne Geliebte*—Franz von Hartberg, Nick's friend, he sang from them when he stayed with us. It is there you have heard them?"

Yes, it had been there. And as he sat beside her, and as the songs continued—some familiar, some not—again and again sweat broke out on his forehead. He felt dizzy, feared that he would not be able to get up, thought that already all eyes must be upon him. The blood beat in his head.

When he stood up at the end, "Are you all right?" she asked anxiously: "I saw that you did not look well just now. We are perhaps too long on the steamer this morning. Our visit to Limone . . ." Upstairs she said, "You must be at once to bed, and to sleep."

But he could not. Something had happened to him. He trembled still, said in a low voice, "I am all right. It is only that I love you." He thought over and over again, I must say: I love you.

I love you. The gas lamp in the room was still lit. She had on the same nightgown, freshly laundered now, he had so admired before. He kept saying, "I love you," as if to make it all right, and himself strong and able. He had never thought that he might not be *able.*

What if I cannot? Such a long time about it. Not just the ten days in the past, when he had not—but now. He had not imagined it would take so long. He was embarrassed by the light in the room, by the moisture beaded on her dark forehead. Her eyes were closed. I make her suffer. Perhaps she suffers. He could not think whether he did it right. Outside, beneath their balcony, he heard voices shouting. Italian voices. He had forgotten now which country he was in, where he was. I am in Rose.

But had he not been there days, months, years? I cannot, *must* not be so long about it. "I love you," he said, riding her again and again. Deflowered. Rose deflowered now. He felt a frightened triumph even while he feared failure. Deflowered, demolished, the whole family. The fall of the house of Straunge-Lacey . . . *I will do it.* Again, I will do it.

Suddenly, she cried out. Then she shuddered, a great shudder, her head turning from side to side. He could not stop, to see what it was he might have done. She suffers. A second later, and he too cried out . . .

She said nothing. Then—or ever. But when he asked her, just before turning down the lamps: "I—have I hurt you?" she shook her head. He saw that lying there, she smiled at him: gravely happy.

He slept so heavily that he had to be shaken awake. They were to go that morning to Catullus' Sirmione (had Catullus not written of it: "*Paene insularum, Sirmio, insularumque ocelle*"—Sirmio, little eye of peninsulas and islands? But had he not also written: "*Da mi basia mille, deinde centum, Deinde mille altera*"—Give me a thousand kisses, then a hundred, then a thousand more . . .). As they travelled the narrow road into the town, going in through the ancient gateway, he could think of nothing but the night before. All through the day it was the same. The tenor left the hotel that afternoon: he was to sing in Rome over Christmas. They did not go in the drawing-room after dinner, but walked for a little by the side of the lake. There were stars out, and no wind. The cypresses standing still. The air as of late autumn. They went up early to bed.

He could not speak of—neither of them could speak of the night before. But he was invited once more. He knew he was invited. And all the remaining days. Although he could not speak of it, he lived for the evenings, and those cries of pleasure. In the mornings, sight-seeing, driving, walking. Then in the afternoons: "You must be tired—we should siesta . . ." A little time left then before dinner and then—how soon could they go up? Sometimes, because she was going to play the piano, they went up immediately. He had bought her Schumann's *Nachtstücke*, which she knew already, and she would play these for him.

He had torn the embroidered, ruffled nightgown. She said only: "Hermione gave it to me—it was from her trousseau. She had too much, you know—and has such good taste. I cannot choose clothes . . ." But of *how* he had torn it—he could say nothing. Who could, who would speak of such matters? It seemed to him that if he were to, everything, all his happiness, might as in the fairy tales disappear.

On their last night after a farewell expedition all day into the mountains, tired with fresh air, they had gone straight to sleep. His arms had been about her. He had to be forever touching. In the day when they were with others, he would be thinking, soon I shall be able to touch her again. In the middle of the night, he woke. In his sleep he had turned away from her. The shutters were only partly closed: moonlight filtered in through the opening.

Almost without thinking, he woke her. She did not come to life at once—stirring sleepily. But then soon, very soon, it was as always. Always. "I love you," he said. As he had said the day before, and the day before that. As she had never said.

After a while as they lay together, silent now, he realised that she was crying. He thought that he could see—then he felt, fingers on her face, the tears running down. He was appalled. He could not think what to do. He asked foolishly: "Are you homesick?"

"No." She shook her head, turned away.

"We are soon home. Should you like to go to Foxton?" (Pray God that Nick was not there.) "Christmas in Downham. It can be altered—"

"No, no. I am not. No." She burst out suddenly, "The saints weep when they see heaven. I am only a sinner, but . . . It is—that here we have no abiding city. I had never wished it otherwise. But now, because of you—*with* you, that I love so much—" She laid her hands, hot, dry, onto his. "Those who love God, they weep with joy at a glimpse of Heaven. While I . . . And I . . . Too much happiness . . ."

"Yes, yes," he said, soothing her. "Yes. Yes." All these last few weeks he had been thinking only of his good fortune, of their good fortune. His delight that all should be so well that might have been ill. Now he thought with sudden terror: Is this to be my punishment? That in spite of what I have done (because of what I have done?), I am to be so much loved . . .

FIFTEEN

The spring equinox. For days the wind blew from the north-east, tearing savagely at the new tree buds, at the last remaining beech leaves. It howled round the cottage at Little Grinling, coming down from the moor, weaving into the fabric of Kate's dreams.

In Downham, Sam Rawson had just drunk his way through his day's allowance of whisky—the modicum which kept him from withdrawal and delirium—and made edgy and restless by the mournful sound of the gale, he pushed aside his empty jug and stood up. A hunt under the bed revealed no secret store.

In the front room, Eliza dozed before the fire. She had been up all the previous night with a dying woman: a family she had looked after closely for many years. (Kate had come over and slept, so that Sam should not be alone.) Very much later she woke with a start and realised that it was far into the night. No sound from her father's room. He must have settled without trouble—often he slept in his undergarments, when she would not wake him. Leaving her door as usual wide open, to hear the first shout, she went to bed.

Earlier, Sam, craftily letting himself out at the back door, made his way first to the Black Swan. T'Dirty Duck. Some in there recognised him, of course, but he had a plausible tale to tell.

"'And the Lord said to Elijah . . .'" he began, but could remember no more. "I've to drink," he said, "my grandson's to be wed. Nay—he's *been* wed . . ." He became confused again. The bottle, the only bottle that they gave him, he slipped in the pocket of his old pilot jacket. Then he visited the Malt and Shovel, and the Downham Arms.

The wind had died down a little. The moon shone through racing clouds. He began to walk to Leyburn, then bottle to lips, he turned off and onto the lower moor. Another bottle—he felt fevered, confused. Too hot. He pulled off his coat, tore open his shirt. Then—he could not see very well. He staggered about, clutching the last bottle for fear of losing it. Stumbled, and fell. Getting up he moved forward a little, only to fall again. Rolling over now, landing in a ditch.

There, within minutes, he was asleep. On his back, snoring. An hour later the rain began. It rained all that night, and into the morning. A cowman, going to work, came upon his drowned body. He did not know at first who it could be: reporting to the constable a tramp, or a beggar.

Eliza, half-dressed, distraught, on her way through Downham searching, knocking, asking, met the bearers of the news. Within minutes, John was on the scene. Ned was sent for immediately, and Kate. Kate sat all day with Eliza. Rose and Paul must be told— No, not Rose, for she was expecting a child. Catriona forbade it. No risks must be taken with the first son of the first son of the first son . . . Some lie of an easy death was fabricated instead. And to make sure that she should not be upset by the funeral, Paul was to take her to Foxton for a short stay.

Nearly eighty years after Old Jacob and his timid Annie had first brought their Samuel through the Kissing Gate to be christened, Ned and John bore their father's coffin through to be buried. He would lie beside Sarah-Mother. Big Sarah.

Kate, standing in the damp churchyard, in the biting east wind, remembered that death. And the fevered husband, thunderstruck, who had shouted to the sky:

"'Man dieth and wasteth away, yea, man giveth up the ghost, and where is he? As the waters fail from the sea and the flood decayeth and drieth up, *so man lieth down and riseth not . . .*'"

"*Lag na fola,*" Kate cried out in her dream, the night of the funeral, "*lag na fola . . .*" Her head tossing from side to side. "*Lag na fola—poll an churtha . . .*"

Always the same words. And others too: a great flood of them. Then, as every time in these nightmares, she woke to Ned's arms tight about her. His voice gentle, concerned, reassuring: "You were dreaming—"

"It was the Kissing Gate again," she said into his shoulder. "They moaned and moaned—and it was dark, so dark. Nothing grew. They were so thin, so fragile, Ned, they passed *through* the gate . . ."

"It's the funeral," he said. "It's that brought it on. Father's death. You'd the caring of him so often. All those years. You and Eliza . . ."

But it was not that.

I am always wandering. The sky grows dark. It is a black snow-filled sky. Terrible fleshless birds, birds perhaps that never were. They have wings and beaks but no feathers, no flesh. The sky is full of them. I can hear the whirring of their wings. And then the moaning begins. Closing in on me. When I hear the moaning, I know then *there is no hope.*

It had always worried Ned—her nightmares. For here, she knew, was something he could not suffer for her, share with her. They came from her experiences, not his. Sometimes in their early married days—even before, when perhaps they had been talking very closely, easily—he would ask her shyly if she remembered nothing. "Does it never—have you no mind how it was, in Ireland, before John came?"

"Nothing," she had said truthfully, "nothing." It was as if wiped out. As if when found she had been only a babe-in-arms—her first memories ones of Downham.

Then to make him happy she would tell him of rides on the front of his horse, of daisy chains, of songs and rhymes, of the first wondering sight of the doll's house ("Mine," she had said, "*my* home?"). Of all the joy he had given her. She would strain back even to earlier days. But they were so faint always. A negative—the glass plate smudged and scratched. It was sensation more than sight. Once when listening to Ned playing his flute, she had remembered, as if it had belonged with the sound, that she had sat at the window. There were pillows all round her, but she felt pain. Snow fell outside in great flakes. Smiling faces appearing, disappearing. She had seemed always to be eating: stuffed with food. Voices, all of them piercingly loud. More voices. Afterwards she had been told that she had looked so thin, so transparent—for so long. But she had *felt* it too. She could remember that. Every sound magnified, piercing the thin skin. Walter's raucous voice shouting close by her—she had experienced that as pain.

"And that is all I remember." In those days she could say so truthfully. Later, when she had the nightmares (and the memories), Ned would say: "But the language. You speak the language, you see. It *is* there . . ."

The same language his grandfather—Sarah's father—had spoken. And had Sarah-Mother not asked again and again (in those sad days, after Tarley's death—before Walter), "Do you remember *no* words? Can you say *none* of it now?"

The real memories—the ones that stalked her now in her dreams, her nightmares—they had come strangely enough with her first child. Her lovely red-headed Will.

But not at once. The third day. She had been propped up on pillows in the cottage room, the fire burning brightly, loved and familiar objects all about her. Will, so newborn, so knowing, had fastened hungrily onto her nipple. The milk was already heavy in her breasts: more rushed in in a hard flow and as it did so it was as if some curtain were drawn back.

In came the memories. So sudden, so much, that she cried out. The monthly nurse, watchful during those first dangerous days, rushed to her side.

"It's nothing, nothing. A sudden pain . . ."

Lag na fola: "the hollow of the blood." The place where cows, horses, gave blood—the blood-letter drawing it from their necks. Pints of blood flowing out. Blood: drink, *food.*

Those were the good days. Something to eat. Hollyberries, beechnuts, nettles, dockleaves, the barks of trees even. But then:

Such a deep gut pain, it is past hunger. Tearing at me. That is where life is. I am all belly. And cold, so cold. They say the sun has gone, never to return. I am holding a child's hand, but I cannot see the child. "*An droch thinneas,*" they say. "The bad sickness." We are afraid. I can see people, but they are shadowy. They disappear.

Memory: a bitter taste in her mouth, bitter whether she ate or not. Something scalding hot, a mouth full of grit and then the pain, still hungry. On the ground, pulling, tearing. But it all tasted bitter. Earth, grit. Smell, taste. With the memory came a stench too. It was everywhere, it belonged to night and day, to the whole land. *Poll an churtha:* "The Burial Hole." We do not walk by it. We are afraid.

She knew *a dhaid,* her father, had gone. He was cold. She could not see what he looked like, but he was cold. A baby cried. She could not see the baby either. She saw rags, and heard crying, crying. Then it stopped. No more crying. But there was moaning, wailing, sometimes it was she who wailed. Then silence.

One memory. I try to evade it as if I had invented it. I did not invent it: I resurrected it. It was all the while there lying in wait for me.

She sits by the fire. Turf, peat, dying. *He* kneels. I can remember only a little of him—I could not tell you how he is dressed. He is my brother and speaks with a deep voice. His hair is red like mine. He must work, because only if he works can we eat anything. The baby is dead. A *dhaid* is dead. I stay close to a sister for warmth; we are always holding and touching, we are a litter of puppies.

Only if my brother works can we eat, but to work he must have strength. Only she can give strength. So I see now that he is eating her, so that very soon *she* may eat. He will bring food for all of us. Hair, it is all hair—dark red, black. He sucks as a baby sucks (as *my* baby sucks now . . .). But already, memory goes.

Before the dark curtain is drawn, the days turning into night. Before the silence. Long before I am rescued—he is gone.

Perhaps he fell at the works, perhaps even our mother's milk was not in the end enough—perhaps that too failed? Surely it failed. How not? I chase his memory—but he is gone.

Now, tonight, because of Sam's death—because perhaps of how he died—the horrors which lie in wait always, leap out at me. When first I revealed that I remembered something, they wanted, everyone, to know if my name had been Donnelly.

But strangely, names never come to mind—only endearments, pet names, Christian names perhaps—little else. All the memories, the facts that make us certain we are who we think we are—I have none of those. I have—more painful, truer—images, scents, smells, sensations—horrors.

In my dream tonight, the scores, the hundreds of matchstick arms, held out, supplicating—they form a carpet. In my dream also they moan—how we moan, we starving ones. I am not they. They are so thin that without opening it, they pass through the Kissing Gate.

SIXTEEN

Newnham Hall,
Cambridge
15th May 1879

My dear Rose,

Just lately I have been thinking about you a great deal—and this you must believe, since I have been a poor friend and scarcely written after all my promises! I am ashamed when I realise that this is your *first* letter from me since I returned here to Cambridge last month.

Now before I write you any of my news, I want just to say this, because of your dear letter to me and because of all the pleasant times we have had together. You will not be surprised if I say that I have always wanted, always needed a friend such as you—although I did not deserve one. And the religious differences between us, they are *not to be thought of* and make only an interest. You must never think that because I disagree, I disapprove—the two are so different, and I have told you this, I think, but I repeat it now in writing, to be certain. I think perhaps there are many ways to heaven—I only wish I could be certain I was going there! but as you said, it is the *will to good* that is important. I believe—what do you think? that our friendship is all the stronger for the differences. But I can understand, and I repeat this, that for Paul to have been of a different faith would have been *in your case* impossible.

Also, I want to hear from you soon that you are taking GREAT CARE of your dear self and that you are resting as you should and gaining great reserves of strength for THE EVENT. You cannot think how excited I am at the notion of being an aunt—the novelty has not yet worn off. I am only so happy that I shall be at home in Downham just at the time when you will need me. I had always used to call your family the "Strangers," which now seems more than a little rude (I did not know how much I would love you—so there!), but it does seem all right that I should call it—my niece or nephew—"the (little) stranger . . ."

From that terrible joke you will see at what intellectual level I live—but the greatest of brains must rest! Are you tiring of explaining and apologising for me to your friends and your family acquaintances—that you should have a bluestocking for a sister-in-law? But even though I am thought very odd, and resigned to it, the truth is *I have never been so happy*. Everything is quite perfect—or rather, what is not quite perfect (and you shall soon hear some of my grumbles!) seems only part of it all. Truth to tell I would be afraid were there not bad days (and bad persons—well, not bad, but unpleasant, ill-humoured. I shall come to that!).

Of the students I told you of, all are here still except Miss Meyer. She has gone home, just last week, to nurse her mother—she is the only daughter. She is one we could have ill-spared (unlike another whom I shall mention in a little—). Then there is the delightful Carrie Sorrell, who is from Massachusetts and stays only until next Christmas. She is so easy and friendly (note the "Carrie"—she said she could not be bothered with all the formality when we must all live so closely together. It is quite a matter here, asking permission, "proposing" that we may use Christian names—and usually waits on considerable acquaintance. Carrie insisted the first day this term, when I went down for a sing-song in her rooms—she has a banjo there *and* a magnificent Steinway, all her own, not hired . . .). Of little Jessie Hudson (yes, she had 'propped' me, and it is Sarah, love, Sarah love, all the day), I see all too much—and perhaps you should take that literally, since she must weigh now all of twelve stone! She eats— I have never seen anyone eat so indiscriminately, of anything that might be called food. Her pockets are always full of nibbles in case she should starve between one meal and the next. She is the only person has not noticed the prunes at breakfast are fermenting (they come from the bottom of a barrel, I think, and are desirous of becoming wine . . .).

You must think me very uncharitable—but you know that my tongue is sharp—to speak thus, but there it is. Jessie is really rather a nuisance. I keep thinking what a shocking drear home life she has (a father who thinks *only* of business, and a mother who ridicules her—I should know something of that—together with a horde of brothers and sisters all of whom mock her). And then she has not many friends here. But, oh dear, it is so difficult when I am about to go to bed for an early night, or when I have just set up all my books and the table and am to work for two hours without a break—and then in SHE comes, and sets about telling me all her woes, past and present (*and* eats all my biscuits—so that I must go into the town for more!). I am not at all patient—you will see that I am not for heaven—I can scarcely be civil to her some days. But she is not put off . . .

Also, she is very clever—although she don't *look* it—and hasn't need of working the hours I do, so that I am constantly disturbed and am not to mind at all. Ah me . . . But I *love* my Latin and Greek, and not my arithmetic at all, but that must be done for next month when I sit these wretched exams (and *then* I may proceed to Tripos work—is not that exciting?).

My days are so full. That is why, I fear, I did not write you when I should. This term is soon to become *very* exciting with so much going on. There is to be a fortnight next month known as May Week, named after the Mays—which are races on the river when the boats of each college try to bump the boats of another (with celebrations and parties and balls and dinners to go along with it all—I am *sure* you know of all this. Or Hermione would . . .). Miss Alexander's brother, who is at Clare College, rows, so that we must go and cheer, but we are not to stand on the tow path, but must watch from the meadows. Also, for the festivities and sights I cannot dress *too* smartly since I am still in mourning for Grandfather.

I forgot to say of poor Carrie Sorrell that she was out for the last hunt of the season and was dragged by her stirrup after a fall, but is all right now. She was badly bruised, but so cheerful with it, and all so soon forgotten, that I scarcely thought of it when I wrote of her. How seldom it is that someone is both rich *and* delightful. About Miss Graham, of whom I said I would tell you more—well, she is as unpleasant as ever, and the only person to make direct reference to my birth mark. "Have you spilt something?" she asked me, in her loud manner. "There—on your neck. You are quite stained . . ." I would not mind, though, if that were all, but there is so much. For instance, again in front of others, she said a great deal that was very rude about Downham. "*I* have heard of that town, the whole population I think must be backward, it is quite a byword for foolish superstition—you have a Kissing Gate, have you not? Which is not a kissing-gate at all but something to do with coffins and rites and *fearful* things that may happen. Is it not right that if you swing on the Gate, you will *hang*? And that you must go through it always, and not the main gate—however roundabout. Really Miss Rawson—and we are in the *second* half of the nineteenth century!" (I have caught her tone absolutely. I can hear it again, for she sneers as she speaks—) But the worst, which I must write about, since it upset me so, and I would not like to speak of it to Mama or Papa, was about the second week of term—she came to my room, when I was alone, and she said, with an air of great triumph: "At last! I remember now where I have heard the name *Rawson*. Do you recollect York Assizes two years ago, Miss Rawson, and all the fuss in the newspapers? Your father is a doctor, is he not? And it was he was accused of forcing attentions and worse, on a young lady—am I not correct?" And I replied to her, "Accused only," I said. "And acquitted." "I know nothing of that," she said. "I remember only something sensational, that I should not like in *my* family. Are you not embarrassed?" I told her coldly that I was not. "Well, certainly you have no cause to seem so *superior*," she said . . . I was not aware that I *had* been superior—but then we are all in trouble with her. Even poor Miss Meyer, only three days before she was to leave (and so distressed and disappointed about it)—well, you know that she is Jewish, and Miss Graham said, addressing everyone, but looking very pointedly at her, and apropos the political scene—"That old *Jewish* gentleman who sits on top of all the chaos, which *he* has made—he should be forced to wander for the rest of his days—" Now as to choosing between Mr. Disraeli and Mr. Gladstone, I am not partial either way—but this was not a political remark. Do you not think it sad that some people must look always to see how unpleasant they can be?

Now for happy matters. There is to be a new hall built here—we have grown so large, and so popular! It was always allowed for in Mr. Champney's, the architect's, plan for this place. More and more students wish to come—I have been very fortunate to be able to live inside, and not in rooms in the town—or even over in Crofton Cottages which however comfortable are *not* the same. A Miss Pontifex, who applied to come just after I did, was only *just* fitted in here and has a dreadful top-floor room next the bathroom, through which the bellrope passes—*she* does not need waking!

I am often with Dorothea Woodward, whom I grow to like more and more. We both made a "false" start to our lives. She is "Dodo" to her family and her relatives who live here. I am often with *them*, having been invited already three times this term! On two of the occasions Francis Ingham was there—he is a much-prized (soon to be literally true, I think!) pupil of Mr. Vernor's. Many of the lectures here and the teaching are of such poor quality that the undergraduates must rely on a good coach if they are to do well at all. Mr. Vernor is very able, and Francis very clever—so that altogether I have grown quite to like Francis. When he forgets to be shy he has quite a dry wit. And is it not nice that the University should have *two* people from such a small place as Downham?

I think one reason I am so often at the Vernors' (I am asked again next Sunday!) is that I am for some reason a great favourite with their eldest daughter, Meta. I think I told you something of her? I am a sort of heroine to her, although I have *done* nothing to earn it! Last Saturday when I was there for tea and tennis she put her arm through mine immediately on arrival and would scarcely be separated from me—which was very difficult for tennis! They, the family, do not like to cross her too much since she then has such screaming attacks, quite like a mad thing. I saw one this last time (and all over some nonsense about a tennis bat. It was *not* a pretty sight). And her mother is too soft with her, it is all "poor little Meta, poor little dear . . ." Her reprimands are all token ones (for all my mama's faults, neither I, nor your Paul, were brought up or spoiled in quite that manner—Meta's every whim is pandered to).

As for Mr. Vernor—while all this is going on, where is he? He is such a dear, pleasant man and impossible to dislike, but he hears, he sees— *none* of this. He is in Macedonia or Sparta or Thessaly. So Meta may scream all she will, and Mr. Jepson (Mrs. Vernor's brother, who is not *quite* right), he may moon as much as he pleases. Actually Mr. Jepson is a sad embarrassment. It is most curious to watch him, catch him unawares. *He* watches *me* and looks sometimes as if he might speak, but then does not. It is all very sad and pathetic and harmless. Once he stroked my hair when we were all stood in the garden, but quite without seeming to know he was doing it. Where *his* mind goes (or has gone), I sadly do not know . . . More usually, the exchange is something like this:

Mrs. Vernor (to her brother): Martin dear, should you not perhaps *change* before tea?

Mr. Jepson (looks confused): Who has spoken?

Mrs. V.: *Me*, dear—your sister. (To herself) Oh now, where is Mr. Vernor? He was to have been here *ten* minutes ago . . . [You see, dear Rose, she has married an absent(minded) one, except that *his* mind is absent on great matters!]

Mr. J. (suddenly coming to life, and beginning restlessly to unbutton and button his jacket. He then bursts into tuneless song): "Up in a balloon, up in a balloon, All among the little stars sailing round the moon, Up in a balloon, up in a balloon, It's something awful jolly to be up in a balloon . . ." (Voice, which is rather thin, fades away.)

There—I have written at rather great length about these Vernors, but of course really now I do not see so many people outside Newnham Hall—or at least I am not in many *homes*, so that perhaps it all seems more remarkable. Before I end, I would like to say to you—would you care to ask little Flo that she should make you some garments for the babe? I know she would be shy to offer, but she sews and knits so well, and *so* longs for a cousin. There has not been a new babe in the family since Patrick—and him she cannot do enough for!

Have you been to see Kate? Has Kate been to see you—often? I can promise you that when the Stranger arrives there will not be a more caring person than Kate will be for you. (Did I tell you that the very first person *I can ever remember* is Kate? I think I must have thought she was my mother—)

I have just lately heard, by the way, that Edwy is married! No one at home can have noticed, or thought to tell me. I saw the announcement here, in *The Morning Post*. I see that she is from Leicestershire. *His* family would not have told me—they thought, along with him, that I was a very ill-mannered girl—but she appears very suitable from the sound of it, since she is a daughter of a Brigadier in some Foot Regiment or other. She will be used to the life! How odd it all is when I think that it could have been me—and instead here I am, quite heartwhole. *Quite*, quite free—and intending to remain so . . .

Write to me soon that you have forgiven the long silence (do not all these many pages make up for it?) and also that you are well, and taking very good care of your dear self,

> I am, Your loving sister,
> Sarah Rawson.

SEVENTEEN

They had been given the finest of the guest rooms at Foxton. Hermione, as the first married daughter, had used to have it on her visits. Now it was theirs. (On Paul's long-ago first visit, Elfrida had shown it to him: "That is the *best* bedroom. The carpet is fearfully valuable, they say, and the chairs and things are Hepple-thingummyjig. Isn't it absolutely splendiferous?") The furniture, the drapes in it were all beautiful, but it was the bed which dominated the room. A Hepplewhite four-poster, its elegant fluted columns contrasting oddly—as did in truth the rest of the room—with the heavier Tudor feeling of the house and its furniture. The bed hangings were of pale rose silk.

Rose. Ah, yes. But what a wasted room. Yet how they had delighted in it last winter, and again this spring. Now, sitting for the moment alone in it, he looked about him and saw it as a place of unhappiness. Near the window was a fine Georgian chest upon chest, with a secretaire drawer: he drew this out now and sitting at it, tried to write a letter to Kate, whom in the haste of getting away for Christmas he had not had time to see.

"I am sorry," he wrote, "that we shall be missing Will's impersonations during the Linden House party—give him our love and encouragement (by the way, I thought his Captain Cuff act at the Penny Readings in the summer quite first-class and *very* stylish. Downham at his feet . . . I fear it won't be so long before he seeks a much larger audience—). His 'Fashionable Fred' is even better than his "Champagne Charlie." Very fine. Is it not fascinating what comes out in a family in the way of inherited gifts, and where and when?! You must be proud. Dear Kate, I shall not see you now until well into January. Again, thank you for all your wonderful kindnesses to the *three* of us. Christmas blessings . . ."

They had seemed at first very simple, the Christmas arrangements for that year. He had promised to bring Rose to Foxton alternate years, and this time had thought to take Sarah with them, as well as the baby and its nurse. Sarah was so fond of Rose, had liked Foxton so much on the wedding visit, and as usual was not getting on too well with Mother. They would not be lonely at Linden House as there would be a gathering of Ned and family, and some Helliwells, together with aunts Eliza and Minnie.

Then almost at once the complications had begun. Paul and Sarah (and of course Rose too) were bidden to the twenty-first birthday party of Kirsty's son Calum (the third of five boys and three girls) on December 27 in Dundee. They were invited to stay on for Hogmanay celebrations and festivities and, if they wished, for Paul's birthday too. Paul had accepted gladly for them all. Kirsty had not yet met Rose, and was very eager to ("I am sorry, though, that we shall not see the wee one! Beatrice is a dear name. But I am glad, for your mother's sake, that she is christened also *Charlotte* . . ."). They would travel from Lancashire on the twenty-sixth: a tedious journey, but the welcome and the happy time they would have would be worth it all.

But then Rose had pointed out that the Requiem Mass for Everard on the anniversary of his death would of course be on the Saturday, the twenty-seventh. She said quietly but firmly (and how well he knew now that firmness) that for the Mass she would like to be at Foxton. (He had not commented that Nick felt no such urge to rush across Europe to offer up prayers for his dead brother.) She said to him: "The day has meaning, Paul. I should like to stay. I can follow up and shall miss only the first party . . ." Immediately Sarah had said that she too would stay on, and accompany Rose. They would travel on the Sunday.

The simplest perhaps would have been if *he* had stayed behind too, but in a fit of obstinacy (and remembering that Calum had followed his mother's invitation with an excited one of his own—they had been good comrades on fishing expeditions on Loch Tay), he thought to himself: Why should I?

And also (although he was reluctant to admit this)—to be free for just a day or two of the whole problem, the sad, heavy thing that his marriage had become, he could not but welcome that.

I *should* be happy, he told himself. How often had he not said that, lately? I *would* be happy, he thought, we would be happy, except that: it was not as it had been. And for that he blamed the child.

She had had an unusually long labour. Five days from the first signs. And two of the days in acute distress: with old Dr. Wilson calling every four or five hours, and Mrs. Pullan, the midwife, who had *seemed* calm, beginning to shake her head dubiously. "Weak as she's getting, she'll have nowt to push wi' . . ." And indeed Rose's appearance, when he was allowed to visit her, shocked him. Fortunately, her eyes were closed —he could not have borne to look into them—but her face had a sunken aspect, her skin a grey look. Dr. Wilson told Paul that she was becoming dehydrated. "Soon I shall have to act," he said. "If nature won't . . ."

Kate had sat hour after hour holding Rose's hand. Earlier Sarah had been sent away. "I would not wish her to see me. To know—" Now Rose did not speak at all, but only bruised Kate's hand. He had not been wanted (as, he thought, I am not wanted now). Eventually, Dr. Wilson confirming that she had not the strength left to push the child out, instruments were used. A vigorous eight-pound girl, little the worse for her ordeal: Beatrice Charlotte. She had for a short while some small marks on her head from the forceps but otherwise was perfection.

Rose seemed too weak to care. That he could understand. She opened her eyes to smile at him, at the child, only with the most enormous effort. At first he feared from hour to hour that she might not live (And I have done this, he thought. It is my doing. Yet *she* is punished, it is she who suffers). But later, when her survival seemed assured, she continued—not to care. He could see the painful effort she made to return to this world at all. But when he spoke to Father about it, he said only, "It is to be expected. She has had a close call. A difficult, exhausting birth, it often takes them like this . . ." Both he and Dr. Wilson recommended champagne, which she dutifully drank. It caused her only to weep, for which she apologised weakly, and wept the more.

Alone with her once, he had asked: "Was it—very terrible?" thinking that perhaps in some way, he could be made part of it—even so late in the day. That he should be, not just the cause, but a fellow sufferer. She had not been able to answer him, though, and had looked at him only, silently, with those eyes.

A wet nurse had had to be found for the child. Even there, there had been trouble—with the monthly nurse insisting that feeding bottles had improved beyond recognition, that it was now a "scientific art," and that "at my last post, Baby was a little beauty on Savory and Moore's Food . . ." Mother had come on the scene, and laid down the law. Kate had meanwhile found someone in the town, a Mrs. Hurrell, who was prepared to wean her own baby—a healthy little girl of nearly nine months. Paul had prayed that the milk might suit. His prayer had been answered. They had not to worry any more about Bea.

But Rose . . . Although gradually she recovered enough to be up and about, the weakness persisted. And the more efforts she made, the greater it seemed. Even more worrying than her physical condition was her want of interest in anything at all. It was as if, for her, a dark curtain had come down on everything. And he could not help. He wanted only for all to be as it had been before—in the happy days, in Italy. But the months passed, and the improvement was only slight, if at all. All around him counselled patience. If they were perturbed they did not show it. Every sort of tonic was tried, solely or in combination. Spirits of ammonia, gentian, ipecacuana, columba, Peruvian bark. She took everything given to her, did everything she was told. And after a fashion, she did seem to be a little better. But he could see that it was not right.

Where was the Rose who had shuddered, who had groaned with joy? At first, he had not dared to touch her at all—had not dared to so much as think of it. One day all will be well, he had thought. We shall be as we were. But he was afraid. What if he should give her another child? And then on their wedding anniversary—Bea nearly four months old—a shy overture on his part, and: oh, but it *must go well*. But it had been as if lying with the dead. She had not resisted, it was not that—she had yielded sweetly. But where was their delight gone, the delight that they had shared, and never spoken of? He feared that he hurt her, wondered if perhaps the instruments had damaged her. But he could ask no one. Certainly he could not ask *her*. A week or two later, he tried again—but it was no better. And was he right to run such a risk?

Her patient melancholy, her loss of what looks she had had (her skin so lifeless now, her hair thin and drab, her figure tired), her refusal to quarrel even when provoked—what he saw as her saintliness—irritated him beyond bounds. The angrier he felt with himself, the more angry he felt with her.

And thus it was this Christmas time. All the difficulties with the arrangements, and then she had not been well in the days before so that there had been some question of their leaving. She had scarcely recovered from a very heavy cold, and her face was sore and chapped. All the way to Lancashire he had felt this great urge to fight, to provoke somehow, in any way, a quarrel. Sarah, happy and chattering of Cambridge, was, he knew, concerned for Rose. She talked mainly that Rose should keep her spirits up. Fussed over her too, with foot-warmers and wraps, as he knew *he* should have done.

Earlier this afternoon, when they were unpacked and settled in their room, she had turned on him suddenly Nick's eyes (he had seen Nick's eyes cold, but never like this—without life). It had been in answer to some remark of his. Then she had smiled at him, but so bravely that it was not to be borne. She said: "I see now that I have forgot my *Garden of the Soul*. I forget *everything* . . ."

"You are impossible," he said. "Everyone must be thinking for you all of the time—and *then* it is not done properly—"

"I'm sorry," she said. "I'm so sorry."

He lifted his hand to strike her. And as suddenly dropped it. He was terrified. But he thought she could not have seen. Her head was turned away. She was busy with some small parcels, Christmas packets, which she moved from the drum table to the Hepplewhite chair, and back again. And back again. About unimportant matters she seemed at the moment quite unable to make up her mind . . .

All the family were at the Hall. Hermione and Dolly, and the thirteen-month-old Ivo, the first grandchild, already taking a few hesitant steps. The baby cage had been brought out. Ivo's nurse and Bea's did not seem too friendly: on Paul's first visit to the nurseries, he had smelled rivalry, a clash of temperaments. Fortunately Mrs. Hurrell was of a placid nature, and likely to be the peacemaker between them. (He had felt shy of asking that she should have stout sent up, and extra meat, but feared that Rose might not have thought to remember. And Kate had impressed on him the importance of Mrs. Hurrell's diet. "It is *Bea* you are feeding," she had said with a smile.)

Hermione was expecting another child in March. She seemed well this time, and although urged to rest by Dolly and by Sybil, insisted on much exercise. She had grown more like her father in looks, and also had become rather forceful. She appeared very glad to see Paul. She said to him, "This business of Rose—it is all a little exaggerated. Do they find *nothing* wrong? I was seven months on a couch (or a hammock) with Ivo—she has had no difficulties in the carrying. And it is *six* months since the confinement—surely all is forgotten? I have no patience with it. And scarcely to *play* with the child! I cannot tell you the delight, Paul, that I had with Ivo. Watching him washed, and brought to me all sweet and clean—the little fingers, and toes. It was all quite a novelty. Does she not enjoy *any* of that?"

Elfrida, who had come to the station to meet them, was in a great state of delight and excitement, with two babies to fuss over. She hinted at a shower of hand-made gifts to come, for him and Rose and Sarah *and* Bea. "At school, Mother Jerome said she has never *seen* such sewing . . . So *much* of it, I mean," she added hastily.

Nick was not there. Paul was glad of that. To bring to Foxton a happy Rose (and he had done that twice): yes. But for Nick to see her now . . . He would surely think it my doing (as it is, it is).

"The feast of the Nativity, without Nicholas," said Sybil. "You are both so unlucky again, Rose and Paul. And Miss Rawson, Sarah—you have never met our Nicholas. He was with us for his Feast Day on the sixth. And then, away again to his beloved Austria . . ."

No mention was made of his marrying. Sybil looked away as she said: "Alice—she is not able to be with us either." Hermione told Paul: "Her plans do not go too well there, you know. I heard a very strong rumour that Alice is to marry—someone rather older, I believe. And all done without Mama's help . . ."

Sybil had said to him (tea alone with her, and two decades of the rosary, his second afternoon): "My poor little flower, Paul. She was never robust, you know—as Hermione. I *know* my dear that you are doing all you can, but there is not—you do not think that she is pining for the convent? I imagine myself (and I have prayed about it greatly) that some good tonic is needed. What do they give her? I shall speak to Mr. Straunge-Lacey—I think, Paul, that we might arrange the waters at Harrogate? The chalybeate—*iron* is the thing, you know."

They were at Foxton altogether some ten days before he should leave on the twenty-sixth. He could not wait to be gone, fancying even in Sarah's manner some sort of reproach: that he could not somehow make Rose better. Sarah herself had developed Rose's cold—or it could have been Hubert's or Aunt Winefride's but whoever the donor she was for some days wretched with it—seeming to be all large, damp handkerchiefs. By Christmas Eve, it was drying up, but she coughed incessantly. The weather was bitingly cold, with an icy, tearing wind. Indeed it was bad all over Europe. In Paris, he read, the Seine had frozen over.

He was to leave very early on the morning of the twenty-sixth. Waking up an hour or more before he was called, he lay awake, anxious. He felt suddenly that he did not want to go. He had wanted to so much, but now that it was here . . . (I am become as wavering as *she*, he thought.) Later, when he was packed, he said to her: "You will be all right, you and Sarah? You don't take a maid with you? You are *certain* you wish to come?" If I could just go, he thought, and know she was not to follow, that would be best.

She said gently, "But no. It is *quite* all right. I *wish* to meet your godmother." She added, "I would not have consented, had I not." Then: "I do want truly to please you, Paul . . ."

But for some reason, what she had said, her own words, distressed her, and almost at once he saw her eyes, Nick's eyes, fill with tears. She turned away at once—he knew out of consideration for him (had she not said, "Pay no attention to my tears, *please*. They come from nowhere, mean nothing . . ."), but it aroused in him only unreasoning anger.

A servant was knocking at the door for his luggage to go down. The carriage was on its way round. As the door closed again: "But that is it," he said, "exactly it—you wish to please and cannot. In any way at all. Is it not that you try too hard perhaps? It would please me more, and be easier for you, if you did not bother to try." Then beginning to go out, to follow his luggage down: "Come or not on Sunday. But please, I implore, *do not* bring your tears . . ."

She had not in the end seen him off. He supposed it was almost certainly that she did not wish to be seen crying. It was so early anyway. Sarah, coughing harshly, had already said goodbye last night. Had he seen her he might have sent a message to Rose—something light, easy, to mitigate the harshness of the words he was already regretting.

By leaving so early he was able to spend a few hours in Clarendon Crescent with his Edinburgh cousins. Also staying in the house was another of the Dunbar family: a bald and very stout man he supposed to be in his late fifties. Alan Dunbar. It appeared that he owned the house in the West Highlands, in Wester Ross, where Mother had spent so many of her childhood summers. He did not speak much, except to say that he was not often in Edinburgh now: "except for Hogmanay—" He eyed Paul, and said: "You have a look of your mother . . ." and then lapsed into silence. Another of the cousins said to Paul in an aside: "He was very kisky last night. The drink always shuts him up—the next day . . ."

He took a cab from Clarendon Crescent, down Princes Street to Waverley Station. The journey to Dundee would take only some two and a half hours—thanks to the magnificent bridge over the Firth of Tay. And the weather seemed fair enough, which was good, for the first part of the journey was the worst (and would remain so, until they should build a bridge also over the Firth of Forth—a river only half as wide as the Tay).

The sun was just about to set when he left the train at Granton to board the paddle-steamer *John Stirling*. It was about five miles across and up by ferry to Burntisland. He was glad of the good weather, and wished the same for Sarah and Rose. There was a little wind in the rigging only. And the steady sound of the paddles beating either side.

But soon he began to feel cold. Fortunately, on arrival the Dundee train was waiting for them. He saw the claret- and cream-coloured carriages of the North British Company. It was quite dark outside now: a December evening, and the moon almost full. He stepped into a first-class carriage, banging to the padded door, shutting out the steam and the sulphur fumes. Inside was comfort. Foot-warmers, head-cushions.

He laid his head back. Above him, the ornate brass lamp swung as the train started off.

The Kingdom of Fife: Ladybank, Cupar, Leuchars. Up the vale of Motray Water, and into St. Fort. Soon they would be crossing the bridge. A middle-aged, well-dressed man with a pock-marked face joined him in the carriage at St. Fort. They exchanged the time of day and a few remarks about the weather. The train was taking now the northern bend towards Wormit, and the bridge. Paul, on both his previous crossings, had seen it only by daylight. That had been impressive enough, but now, looking out of the window, nose pressed against the glass, he saw it by moonlight. It was even more beautiful: with its graceful lines stretching away out of sight, the river calm below it, and its scores of tiny lamps strung across seeming to beckon the traveller. In the centre the tall lacy fretwork of the high girders.

"It's a fine piece of work, is it not?" said his companion. He took from his waistcoat a gold Albert and held it to his ear. "An engineering marvel . . ."

Paul agreed. He had a sudden urge to say, almost as if he must make some impression, "My grandfather perpetrated an amazing fraud on the Great Western Highlands Company" (And where were *they* now? Surely long ago amalgamated with the Highland Railway. Mother did not like, ever, to discuss it . . .).

Still holding his watch, the man was studying it now as they turned and entered the bridge.

"Not so fast, I think. We do not go so fast today. I have known them take it—forty miles an hour. I could have sworn the girders wavered . . . I time it now always."

As they entered the high girders the sound of the wheels changed to a roar. The train clattered. For Paul, it was always a thrilling moment. Then, out again, and after a little while, down the incline to Tay Bridge Station.

"Twenty-five," said his companion, putting away the gold Albert. "Very reasonable." Then: "Good night to you," he said as they stepped out at the station.

A few moments later a porter was calling, "Carriage for Mr. Rawson . . ." Then, "Your carriage, sir, Mr. Rawson sir, it's here the noo . . ."

He enjoyed the party more even than he had thought he would. He forgot always how at ease he was with Kirsty and her family (her benevolent, very bald, and much-respected surgeon husband, a pillar of Dundee Infirmary; her eight children . . .). The house was very large and new and well appointed, and accommodated everyone easily. There were many visiting friends and relatives. Paul's room had two big high beds. For the night of the party he had to share it with a cousin of the family.

And Kirsty herself: the small, always smiling face, slightly wrinkled now, beneath the little lace cap, and the grey hair. So happy always, it seemed to him, in contrast to Mother's frequent discontent. He told her of Alan Dunbar, but she said only: "Och, he was never a favourite of mine. He was always fond of the bottle—I would not have thought he would wear well. The poor man . . . ."

Calum, Andrew, Flora, Robbie, Catriona, Ranald, Duncan, Maggie— *and* all their friends and cousins. Music, feasting, dancing. Constantly expressed regrets that Paul had not brought his "new wife," but of course they understood . . . So much to eat, so much to drink. He was amazed at how, without Rose and the downward pull of her sadness (and with drink perhaps to assuage his present guilt, for he *had* behaved badly), how light-hearted he felt.

In fact so well did he eat and drink that the next morning he did not feel healthy at all. The cousin who shared the room was even worse, and would not at first so much as raise his head from the pillow. When Paul made a very late, an almost too late appearance for breakfast, he was much ragged. But by afternoon, having eaten and rested, he felt much better. Since he would not have to meet Rose and Sarah's train until after seven, he decided to take a long walk with three of the boys —to recover his health completely. He knew that he should have tried to attend a Mass in Dundee—but he had slept over far too late.

It was a fine afternoon for their walk: a clear winter day, the air very still. They were quite a way from home already at sunset. The moon was just coming over the horizon when it was suddenly eclipsed. They watched for only a little while, then began to hurry back. Just after four, the rain caught them. It was very heavy, thudding to the ground, soon running in rivulets. As they rushed back through the garden to the safety of the house, he saw trees in the shrubbery bent with the weight of it.

Changing his clothes, taking a hot bath in his room, shivering still, he thought of Sarah and Rose, and the paddle-steamer over the Forth. Outside his window, he could hear that a wind had got up. Reaching for his watch, he saw that with luck they might have escaped it. The ferry journey would perhaps have been over before? But the rain alone —*that* would have been bad enough . . .

By the time he was dressed and downstairs, the force of the squall alarmed him. It would stop for a few moments—only to begin again more fiercely than ever. The downstairs shutters banged and rattled. The wind moaned and howled round the house—every time a little louder. From the back, near the outhouses, they heard breaking glass, the clatter of falling tiles.

He had to leave in the carriage soon, to meet them at Tay Bridge Station. He would go alone. The family would await dinner for them. Everyone expressed concern at the terrible journey they must be having. Kirsty thanked God that they had not to cross the Tay also in a ferry.

When he stepped out of the house, the force of the wind at first took him aback. He clutched at the portico for support. The coachman said worriedly: "We'd best hurry, sir—it'll be a bad drive. It's a *verra* coarse night." He added, "And the train'll no' be late."

Clouds raced across the evening sky, driven by the wind, obscuring the moon. Occasionally they parted—to show fallen tiles, broken chimney pots, glass lying on the road. And always rain lashing against the carriage windows. The journey had already taken longer than it should have done, when they were forced to stop for five or ten minutes because of branches which had fallen across the road. The horses had grown very excited, made restless by battling with the gale. By the time they were on their way again, he had become seriously worried about missing the train's arrival.

But it was impossible, and in any case dangerous, to travel any faster. Over the next ten minutes the pace grew slower and slower. As they approached Union Street Bridge he took out his watch yet again, and saw in the half light that it was nearly half past seven. He had already missed it. Tired and cold, Rose and Sarah would be kept waiting.

At Union Street Bridge, thinking to hurry in by the exit gates, he discovered they were shut. Everything against him. He spoke to a man standing there.

"Ye canna come in this way, sir. There's *glass* doon—" The man was shouting against the wind. "It's fra' the roof, and it's blowin' aboot."

Battling against the wind himself, he went back to speak to the coachman. But he had hardly done so, before he heard a great shout. And then through the darkness, four or five people running. Then more. Two women, pulling their bonnets down, hurried past, brushing him.

He at once left the carriage, walking, then running back towards the gates. He plucked at the sleeve of the man nearest to him. "What is it, what has happened?" All around voices were raised. A woman shouted out: "It's no' in. There's no train—"

"What is it, what has happened?" He turned desperately to another: "*What has happened?*"

The crowd was growing every moment. He was jostled about. Then suddenly, from farther up the street, a high-pitched voice. And then another. He could not make them out at first. It was more like a scream. *"The bridge—it's doon . . ."*

He could not remember afterwards if it was one hour, or three hours, or three minutes later, that he sent the carriage back: telling the shocked coachman, "At once to the house—tell them the bridge is down. And that I'll get news up—when I can—when I know . . ."

He had had to fight his way out of the crowd, now grown enormous. Then to fight his way back in again. People were still appearing from everywhere, from all the streets around. All the gates to the station were closed.

What he wanted to know most was: *had the train left the other side?* Could it possibly be, was there any hope that it was still at St. Fort? Noise, rumours, rippled through the crowd in great waves. In the anxious darkness he shivered with cold and sudden fear and then *hope* . . .

He did not know at what point he ceased to hope. He moved with the jostling crowd as if swept. But no one had any real news. No one had the truth.

He stood there in South Union Street, his heavy ulster wrapped round him. He was shaking all over and seemed to be crying. But it was someone else weeping. The sound of crying was all round him. Growing louder and louder. Wailing. Keening.

But it did not have to be true. Someone, somewhere must know *what had really happened.* The atmosphere in the crowd was restless. It would not take much for anxiety, mourning, to become panic. Pressed against him was a woman who smelled of fish, her wet shawl gathered tightly about her as she elbowed Paul. Suddenly she called out shrilly, her voice above the others: "Where's ma bairn? *Where's ma bairn,* then?"

The rain was easing off now, but not the gale. A carriage passed near the crowd, going on towards the station. A voice said, "There's the Provost's carriage—that's Mr. Brownlee . . ." Then in another great surge of the crowd Paul was pushed forward.

Further towards the centre of the crowd, fighting had broken out. The scene was growing very ugly. More breaking glass. Shouts of anger mingling with the wails. Then from the outside edges, a rumour spread quickly that there was news at the Telegraph Office, in Dock Street. It was the Caledonian Railway's own office. At once a mass of people began to move away.

Paul went with them, working his way steadily to nearly the front.

But when they reached the office, the doors were locked there too. Then for a moment one was opened and the superintendent peered out. Paul, at the head of the crowd, shouted: "*What has happened to the train?*"

The man shook his head in frightened fashion. "We don't know, we don't know. Keep the crowd quiet, sir. You're a gentleman, sir—tell them they've not to worry. When there's news . . ." Agitatedly, he banged the door shut, before Paul or others could force their way in.

For a few moments Paul tried to pacify those around him, and the crowd beyond too. But already the shouting and wailing had begun here. He waved his arms about, tried to call for order.

"Do not panic," he called, "*do not panic—*" in a voice filled with terror. He was not able to be still. Only when he was *doing* something, could he manage the waves of horror, the sick feeling of unreality. *Let me wake up soon. Let it be only one of my nightmares* . . .

Then he was back at the station. There if anywhere there *must* be news. The crowd had grown bigger still. The police had appeared too, and had cordoned off part. The noise was no less.

Again rumours washed through the crowd. Hope again. *Hope.* "It's true, then—there *wasna* a train . . ." A man near to Paul had heard it from a man further back. The train stood still at St. Fort. It had never begun the crossing. The people in it would come round later by Perth. It was *fact.*

But then he heard that there had been an earthquake. It was an *earthquake* had brought the bridge down. A man behind Paul cried out in a loud voice: "It is the Lord's doing—the Lord in his *Wrath* . . ." Someone shook Paul's shoulder: "They shouldna travel the Sabbath. It's a *judgment.*" A woman told him, "They were drunk—that built the bridge. The Lord sees all . . ."

"Three hundred souls gone doon." The cry went up, "There's three hundred souls—*three hundred souls* . . ."

"Where's ma bairn? Where's ma bairn?"

"There's bodies on the shore, there's bodies been washed up . . ."

"*Where's ma bairn?*"

" 'But they also have erred through wine and through strong drink . . . There is no peace saith the Lord unto the wicked . . .' "

"Where's ma bairn?"

" '. . . and ye shall be left few in number, whereas ye were as the stars of heaven for multitude, because thou wouldest not obey the voice of the Lord thy God . . .' "

"*Where's ma bairn?*"

He was outside the station most of the night. At times, roused from his stupor of fear, he would think that he should try to go back to Kirsty's house—that her family, with their friends in high places, would know somebody who would know *something*. Also they might be even now—probably were—out looking for him. And when, and how soon, could he send telegrams? Word came through to the crowd that a ferry-boat had been out to the bridge. The provost, the stationmaster, the harbour master, a doctor, aboard.

Had they rescued anyone? *Was there anyone alive?* But information petered out. Perhaps it was not true. Perhaps no one had been out to the bridge after all . . .

Not long after that incident, Paul moved together with a great many of the crowd to the Esplanade—there, with first light, they would be able to see the bridge at least. Or what remained of it. The police were there too, along the Esplanade. At intervals carriages passed by. Almost at once, Paul found someone who could give an account of the ferry-boat . . . No, he learned, they had found nothing. Nothing but broken stumps. They had had a difficult journey. The tide had been on the ebb and they had had to fight angry waves to reach the bridge at all. There they had listened: if there should be anyone calling from the piers.

"But it was silent, mon, silent as the grave . . ."

Near Paul were two women. One of them, her plump pleasant face creased with anxiety, smiled at him. He burst out, wanting to touch her arm, to clutch her: "My sister. And my wife too. I've lost my sister . . ."

The woman nodded, frowned: "Bairns—had ye bairns?" her voice concerned. The other woman pressed close.

"I've a little girl—"

"A wee lass, ye've a wee lass? Och, the pity o' it—how *big* is she?"

"Five months—"

"The wean's only five months—och . . ."

The second woman pulled at the collar of his ulster, pushing her face near his: "*Ma lass*—she's there. Ma lass and her bairn—*a bonny wee bit lad* . . ." Her voice rose to a scream.

Paul wanted to say, tried to say: "But my child's at home. It's my *sister* was there. My sister and my wife . . ." But the words would not come. Choked in his throat. He was crying now, great heaving sobs. Behind him rose again the keening.

In the early morning the wind died down, and as the darkness changed into dawn, the first light showed them faintly, and then clearer and clearer—the bridge. Unmistakable now. The wonder of iron and stone: broken-backed. Twelve bare stumps stood up out of the water. Paul borrowed field-glasses from a man standing up in his carriage—he would take a lift from him later, try and reach somewhere he could tele-graph from, get a cab back to Kirsty's house.

Through the glasses—and in his frantic despair he half believed that *he*, somehow, might see signs of life—he saw only the now calm waters, frothing gently at the foot of the piers. Handing back the glasses, climb-ing into the carriage, he said in a trembling voice, which he tried to keep calm: "No hope, then. No hope at all."

"I heard tell," said the man, "that it's no more than seventy-five aboard—it was the Sabbath, you see. So many folk—they'll not journey that day . . ."

He should have been glad at once. But three hundred or seventy-five —he could not *feel* the difference when two were Rose and Sarah, Sarah and Rose.

He managed to telegraph both Downham and Foxton. He went back then to Kirsty's house about nine or ten for a wash, a shave, and some food which he could not eat. But it was impossible to stay there. He felt restless, and thought that only at the station, waiting for more news, would he be able to control the trembling of his limbs. Looking at the two high, white-covered beds, he knew that he could not sleep to-night. To lie still, to think . . .

At least he had now the facts. The train had left St. Fort on time, it had entered the bridge and then, as it went through the tunnel-like high girders in the centre, either the weight of the train on the bridge, in a force ten or eleven gale, had had the girders down—or, the snap-ping of the girders and the iron columns which supported them had sent the train hurtling down. Of course there would be, as soon as possi-ble, an enquiry. And of course it mattered exactly *how* the accident had occurred—but either way, all six coaches and seventy-five passengers had plunged one hundred and sixty feet down, in the darkness, into the angry waters.

Calum was with him for some of the time in the afternoon. They went for a little into the Royal Hotel—already filling up with journalists and artists, who had come at the first news of the disaster. Paul hoped that perhaps from them he would learn something—news perhaps of a body, for the divers had now been out twice—but they were too busy themselves milking anyone who would for information. He went instead back to the station—telling Calum that he would return to the house in the evening. But he knew that he would not.

He was easiest in a keening crowd. Others who suffered. Away from the curious. It was only relatives here now. The weather had grown bit-

terly cold again. There was another squall. Hail in a darkening sky.
Night came on, and still they waited. At sunset one body had been
found, by mussel dredgers. It was a middle-aged woman and she was
brought up to the station and laid in the refreshment room. She could
not be identified.

Although the boats would not be searching during the night, Paul
remained in the waiting-room at the station, set aside for relatives. He
sat there numbly, not talking, trying and not managing to drink some
soup brought round by women from the local church. Sitting near him,
rocking to-and-fro, was the woman who had cried out for her daughter
and grandson. He tried to pray in the night, but could not. I have forgotten how to pray . . . He said now only: *Rosa Mystica.* There was no
reality. Nothing was real. Then when he thought of a life without
Sarah—it was not possible.

Early in the morning, he thought that he would go back. There
would be answers perhaps to his telegrams. It was said that the arrival
of the journalists had improved the service. They had insisted on it. If
answers had come, then arrangements would be made, someone would
do something. But what? He tried to think who would come from Foxton, from Downham . . .

He walked from the waiting-room along the platform. A train had
just come in from Perth. He put his head down, pulled at his hat. His
eyes were dry, gritty, from lack of sleep. His face and body ached. Fatigue and nausea washed over him, so that for a moment everything
went black.

Behind him there were steps, running. He thought tiredly, to make
way—when suddenly an arm was thrown about him:

"Darlingus stupidibus—Paul, *darling* . . ."

And then she was in his arms, weeping. He wept too. They stood, for
how long, not moving, clinging each to the other.

They went into the Royal Hotel and sat together for a while. It was
market day and although still very early, the city was crowded with the
curious, the sightseers. Some journalists, routed through Perth, had
come on the same train as Sarah. Paul drank some coffee, but did not
care to eat anything. Sarah would not either.

"My telegram," she said. "I am perhaps here before my telegram.
When I came along the platform and saw you—I could not believe.
What a confusion . . . And I knew all the while what you would
think—"

"Yes, yes." He said again and again: "I thought you had—that I had lost you too." He kept touching her, his hand reaching out, clasping hers.

It was simple, the explanation: why she had not been on the train. She had woken on the Friday with a slight fever and although a little better on the Saturday, she had not been thought fit enough to travel the next day.

"But—Rose," he said. "Rose . . ."

"Rose *insisted* that she come. I said—told her, 'It's a brutish journey.' I said, 'It don't matter—we may wire Paul.' " She was near to tears now as she spoke. "But she *would* go. It was not to disappoint you . . ."

He should have prayed. He should have said thank you at least for Sarah. Should have asked, surely, to be forgiven. But he could not. All the way to Kirsty's in the cab, he trembled. Sarah held him tight. "It is only shock. It is only shock. And sleep," she said, "you have not slept—"

At night time, he said to her, "I cannot sleep alone." He showed her the room with its pair of high beds. She understood at once. "Of course, darling." She told him that she would probably cough all night: "But if that don't matter . . ."

With her there, it wasn't all right—but it was better, much, much better. For the first hour or so they talked: sometimes of the disaster, sometimes just of this and that. In two days' time Dolly was to come up, to help them. The Straunge-Laceys were to offer a £50 reward for the recovery of Rose's body. That morning a Mass had been said, for all the victims. Another tomorrow. Letters were being written to Paul and would be sent as soon as possible . . . He had heard it all before, in the morning, at the station.

He was afraid really to tell her anything. He could not have said any of the real secrets of his heart. And, he told himself, *she would not wish to hear.*

He told her only: "My last words to Rose. They were unkind."

Not long after that, he slept. He awoke for a while in the night. Perhaps because she coughed. But she must have settled again, for she was breathing deeply, steadily. He lay awake in the darkness, eyes closed, listening.

EIGHTEEN

The same day that Kate discovered about Will and Sukey, she also accidentally met Richard—something which very rarely happened (after all,
she took enough care that it should not).

Easter was very early that year, and spring hardly come, when one
bitterly cold March day—the Tuesday before Easter—she went into
Leyburn with Paul. She was very often with Paul now. Since the tragedy at the end of December, he had spent more and more time with
her. No longer the casual calling at the cottage, sitting round the fire or
the kitchen table—but an almost frightening dependence. After Sarah's
return to Cambridge in January, he had seemed to want to be with her
only.

She knew that he had lost all order to his days. Often he merely sat,
head in hands. Sometimes he did not speak at all. Because she was a
practical person, it went through her mind occasionally to say: "You
must *do* something. A person may not sit forever with their grief—when
there is a child to be loved." But she thought also that when he was
ready, he would live again—as Ned had done. Although she had not
been grown, she remembered clearly Ned's grief: he had loved her still,
and shown it—but there had been no joy in it. It had been a very long
while.

So like a wounded animal in hiding, it was best for Paul to sit here
day after day with her and the children, until he should begin to heal.
(Flo could understand but not Patrick. He asked, could Paul not move
now? Paul sat so still. "Is Cousin Paul getting my legs? *Please* say he's
not getting my legs . . ." He read a lot now, quite well, and wanted to
read to Paul.)

Once she had said to him: "You could try talking to me, darling.
You have always spoken to me, have you not?" The terrible thing to her
was that he said nothing. "If you should say anything wild—the wild

things people say in the early days of loss, then with me, it will not matter . . ." She hesitated to suggest Matthew Staveley, whom she knew would be sympathetic and helpful, because of Paul's change of religion; but when she mentioned the Jesuit he had spoken of at Foxton, he said only, "No, thank you." He had been to Foxton, she knew, for a short visit, travelling back with Dolly—but he would say nothing of this. She feared at one time drink, remembering Sam. Feared it so much that she never offered him anything of that sort, even Ned's excellent and very mild home-made beer.

But he showed no interest in drink, or food either. He had lost a great deal of weight. Kate knew that Catriona was worried, but to discuss him with her, she would have felt to be disloyal. Often she thought: I have been mother, where I would rather have allowed Catriona . . . But he would not spend time at Linden House, preferring always to ride over to Little Grinling. John she feared could not offer comfort—he would be taken up completely with work: the busy time of epidemics, winter bronchitis. Catriona had for a while shown great interest in the child, Bea—but when that had not brought Paul back to life, she had seemed to lose heart.

He has some great burden, Kate thought now, some real or imagined concern about Rose's death—or the manner of their life together. She remembered what Ned had told her of Nanny, and how he had felt after her death. Had he not often said that if it had not been for her, Kate, he would not have wanted to go on *at all?*

Now, whatever Paul fancied he had done, or left undone, he must live for the child. (But it is not for me to tell him, she thought. I have just to *be*.) She herself saw a great deal of Bea: a baby with a cloud now of flaxen curls under her bonnet. She was very active and they thought that she would walk early. Flo was enchanted with her and asked continually to be up in the nursery at Paul's house, to see her washed, or to play with her. In the summer Kate had promised that they might take her out for the day. And "Yes, *please*," Flo had said excitedly. "She has a cousin-aunt who *loves* her so." Patrick was prodded: "You are a sort of *uncle*, and will be expected to read to her, *whenever* she asks."

It had been market day in Leyburn when they went in together. Paul had left her, to go to the bank. She had to take some books to the school and to speak with the schoolmaster. On her way back to meet Paul, coming down an alley she made way just before the corner for a woman carrying on her head a wide tray of cakes and buns. The woman passed, to reveal almost at once, just behind—Richard.

She looked at anything but his face: fixed quickly her gaze on his coat buttons. He had on a short frock-coat, high buttoned, with a velvet collar. The alley was narrow—it was too late to ignore him. And they had never come to that. The rare occasions when they had had to address each other: how civil they had been. And so now:

"Ah g-g-good day, Mrs. Rawson . . ."

"Good day, Mr. Ingham."

Not even "Kate," not even "Richard." For a second, she met his eyes. They had not changed. They were in colour if anything brighter. She looked away at once.

A greeting was enough, surely? She could walk on now. But then—in her haste to be past him, for the encounter *to be over*, she moved perhaps too fast, too sharply. The high heel of her boot caught on a gap in the stones—feeling herself falling, she flung out her arms, and in a second was held by him.

Very quickly, as soon as she was safely upright, he let her go. Afterwards she never knew which had been the sooner: her haste to be free of him, or his haste to be rid of her. To be as near as that, she thought, it is not to be borne. (Twenty years, more than twenty years, and it is as yesterday.) She shook. Now it would be *her* stuttering. Her voice trembled.

"I am so sorry—I quite—I had thought myself falling . . ."

"No. No." His voice. He was still too near. Outside the narrow ginnel was the main street—and safety. She did not look, only heard: "You are not harmed?"

"Not at all. I must thank you. Forgive me." She made a move. Then feeling that she had been rude, she said hastily, awkwardly: "Everyone is well at the Abbey?" (Why should I wish to *cry*? she thought. Am I to weep in an alleyway, and wish yet again to explain it all—*to what purpose?*)

"Yes, yes. My s-son returns tomorrow—your niece too, no doubt. Francis reports meeting her . . ." His voice was dry, or so it seemed to her; dismissive. "He is very happy there still. My m-mother is not so well. We shall have to speak to Dr. Rawson. I do not think it s-serious—"

"Ah, *her*," she burst out suddenly, as if someone spoke for her. She was appalled. Years of silence. And what am I saying? "Ah, *her*."

"What do you s-say?"

"*Her*," she repeated, almost as if for a moment she had Georgiana Ingham in her grasp. She trembled.

He spoke coldly, but his expression puzzled. "My m-mother has done nothing to merit that. She is old and not in the b-best of health." His tone grew more icy. "She has d-done nothing to you that you did not already wish d-done yourself . . ." Very deliberately, he stepped to one side for her to pass. A cold fury.

"Indeed, indeed," she said, terrified by her own anger and hurt (where was it hidden? and why *now?*), "from what she has saved me! From *what she has saved me*. I see you—stupid as ever! Stupid . . ."

She could not be away fast enough. The tears had wet the veil of her bonnet. Her ankle ached where she had twisted it.

"Darling," said Paul, "I had thought I lost you." He looked so concerned, as if hidden everywhere nowadays might be loss. "Kate, Aunt Kate, *what is it?*"

"I fell a little, tripped, as I came through the ginnel. The pain—it brought tears to my eyes . . ."

"But you are all right? I have your arm now—we shall go into the Crown at once. Something for you to drink—" His loving care. His face turned tenderly towards her.

What would he think if she told him: I have just lost in one moment what has taken twenty years to build. I am naked again, defenceless. I killed my love once and have been forced to kill again—so nearly was I discovered, so nearly undone. It is not just in dreams that the past is as yesterday and the years forgotten. In real life too. I could not tell Richard what a mother he has. I could not tell him I love him still. Neither truth would help us—and he, he has grown only to hate me now . . . Paul would not believe this if he heard it: that he has an aunt so foolish, and wicked—that she cannot be grateful and content *always*. I who have Ned, she thought, and all my children. He who has lost a wife . . .

"We should not be late," he said, "if we must go together for the desk." He gave a great sigh. He had not touched his drink. Often now he seemed to be holding his breath—then these great sighs. As if he forgot to breathe; and forgetting to breathe, would not need to go on.

It was just before midday when they reached Rawcliffe's, the joiners and cabinetmakers. Because it was market day, furniture was standing out on the road in front of the shop. Mr. Rawcliffe was to make a desk for Patrick, specially designed so that his legs were supported, and also so that he might push it about a little. It had been Will's idea—and he had recommended Rawcliffe's, because he knew the family from the Penny Readings. The desk would be for Patrick's birthday just after Easter.

It was of curled elm, except for the writing surface, and was very roomy, with a secret compartment which Mr. Rawcliffe showed them both now. He said: "There'll have to be one on you only as shows *him*. His dad mebbe. The lad's best to think it his secret . . ."

They arranged then about the desk's delivery, and whether his name should be carved on it. Kate was shaking still. Perhaps that was why she did not hear at once what Mr. Rawcliffe said a few moments later.

He repeated, "T'young one—you'll be expecting Master Will back soon, ma'am?"

"Yes, yes," she said. "I expect him back. Thursday."

"And—he'll mebbe be acting—reading like again this summer?"

"I couldn't stop him," she said with a smile.

"Mrs. Rawson, ma'am," he began, curiously hesitant. He was a gentle-faced man, with a wrinkled, concerned forehead. He said again, "Mrs. Rawson, ma'am—" he looked about him. Another man, his brother perhaps, had come into the shop from the back. "Ben—can you stop here? I've to go through for summat—" He turned back to Kate: "If I could—I've a mind—if I could speak wi' ye alone like, ma'am. If Mr. Rawson'll excuse us—"

He led the way through behind the shop. "You'll not mind we go this way? It's muckier, but quicker like." An apprentice passed them in the yard; he was carrying two drawers from a chest. "Eh there, Charlie," said Mr. Rawcliffe, his tone warm, affectionate. "They're nowt but woodspoilers," he said to Kate, "but good lads."

In the saw-pit as they passed, two men were sawing elm rhythmically. They chanted, "Addle and tak't, addle and tak't . . ."

"All right there, Bob? Aye, Geoffrey?"

She was shown into the house and sat down. Mrs. Rawcliffe appeared in the room for a moment, was introduced, said hastily, "He were wanting a little word wi' ye, ma'am," and was gone. As soon as they were alone again, Mr. Rawcliffe came straight to the point.

"It's—I don't think, ma'am, as they ought to see so much of each other—your lad—and our Susan. Sukey's nobbut a larl small un. Fifteen hardly—Friday was a week. That'll be young for keeping company. And when t'lad's nobbut a young un too. Not seventeen—"

Kate said weakly, "He's not even *fifteen*, Mr. Rawcliffe."

There was a silence. He looked more worried still: "If he told us a fib—I don't ken—I don't think as he *said* rightly. He seemed—when he's acting, playing those—what's that one of Mr. Dickens' he does? them songs. And him starting up on his own like—"

But Kate was quite lost. "What *is* all this? Mr. Rawcliffe—I know nothing of this. If I had—"

"There's nowt wicked, Mrs. Rawson, ma'am. It's only—it were last summer. And Sukey, she'd wanted to say summat to him, after t'readings—she'd thought him that good like. And I'd taken her up there in't first place, to hear it all, so we'd a word wi' 'im together. And I said to him then to come and tak a bite wi' us. And to mebbe do a turn or two again. And he did, ma'am, and that were the start—"

Kate said, "He will go anywhere to do his turns, jump at any invitation. If he has been a nuisance . . . I knew that he had visited you, but not—this."

"T'long and short on it were, they was struck wi' each other. But nowt else as we could see. We'd nivver have left 'em wi' out one on us there like. T'missus she's very strict, but t'lads, they're from home—four on 'em gone to be apprentices except the one he's gone for a soldier. They'd stand for nowt. But ye see, Sukey, she's had all them notes, *letters* like—from your lad . . ."

"Surely not? From school, from Richmond?"

"Aye, ma'am. I'd a word wi' her, least my missus did—we'd found 'em ye see. Hidden." He looked at her face, anxiously. "Nowt bad in 'em. It's not that. It's only like—they're too *serious*. I'm afeard, ye see." His voice broke. "She's only a larl small 'un . . ."

Kate said at once, "You are not to worry any more. Mr. Rawson and I will see to it immediately. As soon as Will is home. Thank you for speaking to me, and for your thoughtfulness." Then, on impulse: "May I see—Sukey?"

"It'll have to stop," Ned said. She was amazed by his reaction, the loudness of his usually low voice. She saw that he was shaking.

"Speak low," she said. "Or go where the little ones can't hear. They're not asleep—"

"It's not right," he said then in a quieter voice.

"But nor is it *wrong*," she said. "There's been nothing bad—unless it's that he's been smuggling out notes. It appears he got someone who comes through to Downham twice a week, to bring them. A man from the carter's family works at the school, or the suchlike. *I* shan't tell on him for that—only scold him. It's something that he does any lessons at all, with all his other interests . . ."

"Kate, it's—" He frowned. Then changing the subject quickly, as if to pull himself together: "How did you find Paul—this morning?"

But a moment or two later he was back at it again. He said, not looking at her (And oh, my darling, she thought, if you knew what else had happened to me this morning . . .): "What's she like, then—this *Sukey?*"

What had she been like? Kate thought: Perhaps because I was still shaken from the Richard encounter, and then by Mr. Rawcliffe's tale, which I thought was going to be *far worse*—I was in too sensitive a mood, too impressionable.

"Lovely," she told Ned. "Lovely."

Here had been this little girl—and she had been not only young but small too—with a mass of butter-yellow hair tied with red ribbons and a face not exactly pretty (the upper lip perhaps too long, the mouth too full) but with a lively beauty of its own. Her complexion was very flushed—emotion or nature, it was hard to tell.

She had been too shy to speak to Kate. Her father told her: "Sukey, you mun say as you're sorry—about, ye ken—"

"I'm sorry," she had said and then burst into tears; Kate had wanted at once to hold her in her arms.

"Don't take on," said her father, "Sukey, don't take on. Where's ye mam? Fetch your mam in now—"

In the end it had all been settled, amicably. Will would be reprimanded, as she had suggested. The visits would not be forbidden, but there were to be less of them. And for a time: no notes. The tone of it all in the end had been "We'll see, we'll see. Time alone'll show . . . better safe than sorry . . ."

It was the effect on Ned. She had not bargained for all this upset— even anger. For he was angry now with Will, far more than the occasion warranted. And yet he got on well with his eldest son, was so proud of him . . .

"*You'd* like anyone," he said to her now. "Such a heart you have." He said it sadly—but angry too.

"Ned—that is not true" (Georgiana Ingham, Georgiana Ingham). She sought around. "I dislike Greaves—"

"You reproach me with *him* again."

"I looked only for an example . . . *Of course* I can dislike—but she, she was a dear girl. I have told you, described—"

"We'll be done with it, then," he said shortly.

But in the middle of the night, head burrowed in her neck: "My Kate, my cockyolly bird . . ." When she knew then, sleepily, that he wanted to talk of it.

"Walter," she heard him say, "it puts me in mind of that. The trouble over Walter . . ."

"How not, love," she told him, "how not? Only Will—he's nothing like Walter. Is he now?" She could still not say the name without a shudder. "And he's not been getting anyone into trouble—has he then, has he now?"

"Not yet . . ." Then he said more despairingly, "It's not that. At least, it's partly that. Only—"

She said, "It's Nanny, isn't it? You're reminded."

His voice was muffled. "Yes." He paused. "Haygarth, cobbler—Rawcliffe, joiner. And then—"

"But love," she said, "it's quite different. Everything, all of it."

"Like father, like son—"

"Oh love, but Ned—you didn't do wrong." She thought again, "Or if you did it was such a little sin—and *her* doing mostly. This is different, quite, *quite* different . . ."

But he would not be comforted.

Will said to her, because it was she who spoke to him the first: "No one shall stop us—"

"Your father will. And you have not to speak to me like that . . ."

He was at once repentant. He flung his long arms round her. His curls brushed her ear. "All right, then. *Please* darling Mother, will *no one* take her away from me, because she is my dearest Sukey and my *friend*—"

"You are much too young," she began.

"Of course I am not too young. *We* know how we feel—do we not? And as soon as ever we can marry . . ."

"Promise me, then," she said, "that you will do what Mr. Rawcliffe asks."

"I was so cross at first I thought I would run off *now*."

"*Will*—"

"And start my own troupe. *That* is what I plan to do. Anyway. And Sukey shall be my leading lady—"

"All right," she said, "all right." She could not help smiling. "But first you must study all your lessons. And do also what Mr. Rawcliffe asked. And then we shall see." She added, "They thought you were *seventeen*, you know—"

"Well, when I *am* seventeen . . . But hallo, hey wait, have you heard this one? It's from Mr. Gilbert's *Pinafore*—I have it from the score, you know. But wait till I see it performed. Mr. Rutland Barrington does it, you know. Sukey will love it . . ."

He registered a very solemn expression and began to sing:

> "Bad language or abuse
> I never, never use,
> Whatever the emergency;
> Though 'Bother it' I may

Occasionally say,
I never use a big, big D—
What, never?
No, never!
What, *never?*
Hardly ever!

"I love you," he said, and was gone.

NINETEEN

What bird so sings, yet so does wail?
Oh, 'tis the ravished nightingale,
Jug, jug, jug, jug, hereu, she cries
And still her woes at midnight rise . . .

"I am to ask you to *promise* to come to tea next Sunday," Dorothea Woodward said. She added, "It is Meta, of course . . . But I was in any case going myself, so—if you would?"

"Of course," said Sarah.

"There will be others—it will not be just family. And Uncle Jepson, he does love it so when visitors come. You are not too embarrassed by him? He has always been quaint and rather sweet. But mainly it was Meta—she plagued me so, that I was there just the *once* without you . . ."

"It is no trouble, I assure you. I like to come. And I cannot always be studying. It is not good—"

"*I* should study more. I quite despair of my stupidity. Uncle cannot be proud of me at all . . . Of course there will be other invites for you, later. More grand. I think a garden party in May Week—if the weather should stay as beautiful. It could be June *now* . . ."

Indeed it felt like it, Sarah thought. Although there were some few days to go, yet the weather all May had been so fine, with so much sunshine, that it seemed to her the weather could not break. In Madingley Woods where she had walked with Dorothea, the bluebells were a thick carpet, the wood sorrel out. Another time they had gone over the fields to Grantchester—in the meadows there the cows were almost knee-deep in buttercups, the speedwell a hazy blue. Above the hedges, the oaks were in full russet-tinged leaf. Lying in bed, she would listen to the birds in the early morning—the garden warbler, doves from the dovecot, in the distance a wood pigeon.

But the best were the nightingales. She had not heard them before and at first did not recognise their song. They did not sing in Yorkshire. But almost every night now she would wake, sometimes for an hour or so, sometimes until dawn—and listen to the nightingales. She thought that she would always remember.

She had not expected to be happy this term, at all. It was too soon. In the Lent Term, in spite of the solace of her Greek and Latin (which she was growing to love more and more), and in spite of friendships, and delightful days skating on frozen Coe Fen, she had never ceased to mourn Rose—and to grieve with Paul. Her sorrow apart, she could not shake from her mind the memory of those dark cold days of horror she had spent with Paul in Dundee.

They had arranged to stay on for at least a week, in the hope that Rose's body would be recovered. And too, Paul had not wanted to return home. But the diving operations in the Tay were not being very successful: although they had found carriages and even the engine, there were no bodies. One only had been washed ashore. People were becoming impatient. At the station the refreshment room had been turned into a mortuary. On the marble-topped counter the flotsam continually being washed up on the shores of the Tay was laid out as it was brought in. Shawls, cloaks, shoes, a box of pearl-handled forks, a hamper of game, muffs, scarves, bonnets . . .

Paul went out twice with the diving boat. She told him that he tortured himself. But he could not rest: at Kirsty's house he was seldom still, counting the time only until he should go back into Dundee, and the station. The crews of two whaling boats had offered to help in the search for bodies. It was their belief that the bodies of the dead did not rise until the eighth day. Sarah, hearing this reported, had seen the hope in Paul's face. That day, the fourth, a body of a woman was found, and lost again. The mussel dredgers, who knew the river bed like farmers know their land, were out searching too.

Dolly had arrived on the Thursday. She had found that difficult. She scarcely knew him: at Foxton she did not suppose she had spoken alone with him more than once at the most. Now she felt that he came between her and Paul. His manner was pleasant enough, but he impressed on them continually how compassionate of him it had been to come up, "considering Hermione's condition. She's deuced shocked, y'know . . ." But Hubert and Benoit were not old enough, and Nick too far away. Paul said enigmatically, "If they had sent him—it would have been unbearable—" She had agreed. A grieving brother—it would not have done.

Gales again, interfering with the diving, with the search. She herself had feared the finding of Rose: of how it might be, for rumour spoke of the whaler's hooks further mutilating the bodies. She and Paul went about together, leaving Dolly at Kirsty's waiting for news. They walked the cobbles, greasy with frost; noticed occasionally that the city had a life of its own, a modern jute industry, shipbuilding yards, an ancient history. It did not seem the same place they had stayed in before with Kirsty.

Paul tortured himself, she thought, by attending the sherriff's enquiry, listening to the divers' accounts of what they had found, and not found. On the eighth day she and he decided that if Rose's body was not recovered within the next three days they would go home. Dolly had left already that morning. In the afternoon one body was found—a man's. The next day, four bodies. Every day there were more objects laid out on the marble counter. On the tenth day, they saw an umbrella, some cuffs, a child's sock, two bonnets, and a large bag of leather and velvet with an ivory clasp.

"Yes," Paul had said to the men in attendance, "yes, I know the bag." The mud had been sponged off it: it looked only damp, the velvet portions bedraggled. Inside: only a lace handkerchief, a pill-box with cough lozenges and a hard leather case.

"Her diary, I think," Paul had said, touching the brass of the lock. His hand was trembling.

They had wrapped the bag up in some pieces of old flannel and brought it home to Yorkshire. He had not told them at Foxton that anything had been found. "It is *her* only they wish to hear about . . ."

But there had been nothing to say, and now with May three quarters gone she no longer expected Rose's body. In the remainder of January some thirty-three had been found, mostly men. Since then, a very few more. Paul she knew was resigned now. But not to Rose's death. At Easter he had seemed a little better but had it not been for Kate, and her caring, she would have felt reluctant to leave him and return to Cambridge.

She had written to Matthew Staveley about him. "If there is anything at all *you* can do to help, please. You will have thought already, I know, but will have felt hesitant. He cannot accept her death (and *why should he?*—now you will tell me off for being rebellious . . .). I do not know anyone to whom I would rather he spoke. If only it were not for the difference in religion . . ."

"How is your brother?" Francis asked. "Do you hear from him recently?"

"Thank you. He improves—a little." The shadow of Paul's grief crossed the sunlit lawn. Yet another warm day and the Vernors had arranged the tea-party in the garden. There were only some half dozen guests from outside. Seeing Francis already sitting in a chair, Sarah had crossed over at once to him. The other visitors were mainly pupils of Mr. Vernor's except for a cousin—or a friend, she was not sure which—a weekend guest from London, introduced as Mr. Ashby. He seemed much opinionated: his pronouncements came at regular intervals, the only voice to be heard in his group which stood and sat at the other side of the lawn. His penetrating notes came across to them now.

"Bernhardt, my dear. *Sarah*, the divine. I was not impressed *at all*. *Une tragédienne du boulevard*—nothing more . . ."

Francis smiled. Sarah asked him: "And your family, they are all well? I seldom see your sisters—"

"Isabella, she does the season, of course. Not without protest—it is my maternal grandmother insists. Although Grandmama Ingham has been giving advice, as is her wont . . . But Cicely and Laura—well, they grumble away in the schoolroom as usual. They do not have a very good governess, I think . . ."

Meta, dressed in white with a shower of blue ribbons, had run across and was sitting now on the grass at Sarah's feet. Francis said, "Meta here reminds me a little of Laura."

"Do I look like a Miss Ingham, is that it, is that it?" Meta put her head on one side. Then she returned to looking up at Sarah. Mr. Jepson had just come out from the house and stood, feet slightly apart, on the fringe of two small groups. Cup and saucer in hand, he swayed very gently to and fro, not seeming to look anywhere in particular.

For Francis, the Tripos exams had just begun. She thought that he looked tired: violet shadows under his eyes, a rougher finish to his skin. She said, "I am fortunate, I have until the Michaelmas term next year —and then it is only Part One I attempt . . . I shall go to the Senate House next month, to hear the lists read—I am sure you do well."

Mrs. Vernor swooped by, and tried to remove a protesting Meta. "But I was *listening* . . ." Sarah said at once that yes, it was all right, Meta was not troubling them. Immediately Meta seized the opportunity to talk.

"Miss Rawson, where's Dodo, and have you seen her *hat?*"

"It is a very jolly new hat," Sarah said. "We bought it together at Ballards. It is a Langtry hat—after the famous beauty. Why do you not go now and look after Dorothea—after Dodo?"

As Meta went—and Sarah feared it would not be for long—Francis said, "And the new building at Newnham, Miss Rawson, what is the news of that?"

"It will have students this October, although they will not be papered and painted quite like us—it is all rather bare still. And there is the public road between us and them, you know, which makes for a rather strange division . . ." She saw that Mr. Jepson stood mooning at her now, although he was a fair distance away. She hoped he would not cross the lawn to her.

"So much that is new," Francis said, "just now. These *trams* . . . Last year when I saw the tram lines laid down ready. You have been on them?"

"For the excitement, yes. Miss Hudson and I have ridden to the station. It was rather like sailing on a calm sea. Very pleasant. But the horses are shockingly overladen—that don't seem right."

"I had noticed. But the horses in the hansoms—the ones on Senate Hill, how do those cabbies manage them? They are shockingly high spirited . . . They are ex-*racehorses*, are they not?"

Meta had returned. She interrupted constantly. "I have brought you more sandwiches, or would you rather have *chocolate* cake?"

"Perhaps Mr. Ingham would like some of the plum cake, Meta?" She turned back to Francis: "Ah now, I think I have to congratulate you on a prize, *again*. You cannot win them all—"

He smiled. He seemed a little embarrassed. "I had not realised the news of that one—I have surprised even myself. Perhaps most of all myself. But it is, all of it, only for a short time. The rest of life . . ." He shrugged his shoulders.

"Is not all prizes?"

He smiled. Finishing her tea, putting down the cup and saucer, she said: "But I think you want to travel this summer? That is what Mr. Vernor said—"

"We go to Italy." Blossom from the quince tree under which they sat had fallen on his knees. He brushed it away. All the edges of the lawn were scattered with fruit blossom. Near them the lilac bush was heavy and fragrant with purple flowers.

"Where in Italy, Mr. Ingham? Do you tour?"

"Father and I are going. We tour, yes." His hand jerked suddenly, slopping tea into his saucer. For a moment he seemed taken aback, then: "We shall be in Florence, of course, and also—" he paused. "And then—no, I am sorry, forgive me, Miss Rawson—how foolish. The capital, the new capital of Italy, its name—I forget—we are there . . ."

"Rome," she said, a little surprised. "You mean Rome."

"Yes, *Rome*. Of course, Rome. We travel in the first instance from England by—by—by—" he paused again. "We go on the water, by—what is it called? I—"

"You go by *sea?*" She was puzzled, but also a little alarmed. He was playing a practical joke perhaps?

"I—I—" He looked for a moment blank, then he laughed nervously. "I am so—so sorry." He stumbled over the word. Sarah, turning, saw that Meta had left them and was walking on the other side of the lawn. Mr. Jepson was with her.

"I am sorry," Francis repeated, "my mind—quite blank. Shimple, shimple words, quite forgot . . ." His voice sounded thick.

She said, "You have not overworked? Your brain perhaps—" She saw that he was trying to shape words.

From the far side of the lawn came Mr. Ashby's voice: ". . . for a definition of the word *deputation*—quite perfect. 'A noun of multitude which signifies many, but not much . . .' Mr. Gladstone's they say. But *I* say, hardly! Too apt, too witty . . ."

In a nervous rush, Sarah said, "Greece, do you not want to go to Greece? Since I have been studying I have thought, how I would *love*—"

"Yesh." His voice had thickened more. Searching for words, he floundered, "Yesh—Mishter, man Downham can't m-member name—shays, he shays . . ."

She leaned forward, seriously frightened now.

"Mr. Ingham—*Francis* . . ." He had put his hand to his head. She saw that he tried to speak still, but could mouth only. His cup and saucer fell to the grass.

"Oh, *help* . . ." But already two people were running towards them. Francis had slumped forward. Mr. Ashby's voice, loud and clear: "Alarums and excursions, what is this? Oh, I *say* . . ." Now Mrs. Vernor stood beside them. Two of Mr. Vernor's pupils had taken hold of Francis and were lifting him. His arms hung limply.

"We must get him at once into the house . . . a doctor," said Mrs. Vernor, "a *doctor* . . . Will someone?"

Mr. Jepson, who had worked his way across and now stood, bewildered, and blocking the way, said: "I will, here's a fellow will go . . ."

"No, Martin dear, I think not. No. One of these boys . . . *Where* is Mr. Vernor?"

Then Meta began to scream. As Francis was carried in, she gave short shrill cries. "Oh, oh, oh . . ." Sarah, crossing over to her, took hold of her arm. "*Stop that.*" Her voice was sharp. "Not now, *please.*"

Francis had been taken inside and laid on a daybed. Sarah was in the room with him. She saw that he was conscious. His eyes looked at hers, puzzled, anxious. His breathing was heavy. But he did not seem able to move, or to speak.

Mrs. Vernor took Sarah aside: "As soon as Dr. Faber is here, should we see about Mr. Ingham's *relatives?* His father, my dear—he has a father? Perhaps the sooner someone is sent for . . . It all appears —rather grave. I would not want to waste time . . ."

Dr. Faber lived only ten minutes away and was soon there. Examining Francis, although he could not give a diagnosis, he told Mrs. Vernor and Sarah, well out of Francis' earshot, that he took a very serious view indeed. "The young man is conscious, but paralysis is almost total—and there are other signs . . . I would like to be reassuring, *but*—" He pulled at his beard. "The family lives near?"

"I think not," said Mrs. Vernor. "Mr. Vernor knows, but cannot be found—"

Sarah said, "He comes from Yorkshire. Mr. Ingham and I live both in the same town. His family is known to me, so that if you would like, I perhaps—"

Mrs. Vernor laid her hand over Sarah's. "My dear, if you would . . ."

Dr. Faber said, "A telegram should be sent at once. If nothing else, the young man *needs* his parents."

The tea-party was by now in confusion. A few guests had left almost immediately, saying that they felt their presence would be only a nuisance. The affected tones of Mr. Ashby, who had not left, could be heard even in the sick-room. Mr. Vernor had been found: he had gone to the top of the house to fetch a book, become absorbed in a quite different one—and forgotten to come down again. A servant had been already despatched to the telegraph office—Sarah having supplied the Ingham address. A note had also been sent to the provost of King's.

Dorothea, looking incongruous in her new hat, seemed much distressed. She kept apologising to Sarah. "But what for?" Sarah asked.

"That it should happen at my family's house . . . I feel that it is something *we* have done . . ."

Mr. Jepson was wandering about aimlessly. Sarah met him twice, humming and singing under his breath. She wondered if he realised fully what was happening. Meta, to keep her out of the way, had been sent upstairs to lie down. After Dr. Faber had left, Mrs. Vernor asked Sarah, would she perhaps go and sit with Meta "just for a little while"?

"Is he going to die?" Meta asked Sarah. She was sitting on the edge of her bed. She had unthreaded a great many of the ribbons from her dress and twisted them round the brass rails of the bed. "Tell me, tell me."

"We do not know, Meta. No one knows. We *hope* all will be well."

"It is very *serious*, though?"

"Very serious."

"Darling Miss Rawson—" She flung her arms about Sarah. "God struck him, didn't he, *God* struck him . . ." Sarah thought she was about to scream again, but instead she began only to sob quietly.

A woman had appeared in the doorway. "I'm the children's nurse, miss. I'll see to Miss Margaret. Now," she said, "now, now, now, Miss Meta . . ."

There was no improvement at all in Francis' condition. It was nearly two hours since he had collapsed. It had not been thought advisable to move him, except to put him to bed upstairs. A nurse had been engaged to attend him and would come in an hour. Another message was sent to Newnham that Sarah and Dorothea would not be back for dinner, but would eat with the Vernors. The family seemed to wish it.

It was not an easy meal, however. Dorothea seemed in a highly nervous state, and on the verge of tears. "It is the atmosphere," she told Sarah in an aside. Mr. Jepson watched both her and Sarah, occasionally tilting his eyes upward, or shaking his head. "Poor little Dodo," he said, in a cheering-up tone, "what ails poor Dodo?"

"Hush, Martin," said his sister in a reproving tone.

But Martin's behaviour was as nothing beside that of Mr. Ashby, who persisted in acting as if nothing untoward had happened at all. The general subdued tone of the conversation gave him an unequalled opportunity for shining brightly and loudly.

". . . and altogether, my dears, it was *quite* an omnium-gatherum— Lord Devon was there, and the Ladies Sherborne and Waterford, and I don't know who else . . . a great deal brighter than at Mrs. Burdett-Coutt's, when Mr. Irving read us *Macbeth*. The *tedium*, my dear. He may have seen a dagger. *We* did not . . ."

They awaited an answering telegram from Downham. Francis' parents they could not expect before morning. Someone had already made enquiries about possible trains.

As Sarah was about to ask the latest news of Francis, before she and Dorothea should leave, there was a shout and a cry. Meta came running down the stairs, her feet bare, her cotton wrap trailing behind her half-fastened.

"Miss Rawson, Miss Rawson! You are not going, *please?* You *promised—*"

"I promised nothing."

"You must come and settle me. I cannot sleep—"

Once again Mrs. Vernor asked—and Sarah agreed. She went upstairs. The nurse came in and gave her opinion, and a warning to Meta. But she did not sound very confident.

"She is afraid of me," Meta said. "That I shall tell stories to Mama.

And that she would have to leave. Read to me, Miss Rawson. Read to me."

Sarah read for a while some George Macdonald. But Meta's calmness did not last long. After a few pages she began to cry loudly. "He will die, I know. He will die, here *in this house.*"

"But Meta, everyone must die somewhere. And some time. You are not to think of it. It don't help to dwell all the while." She shut the book. "And now, if you will let me tuck you up . . ."

"You must not go. I can't *sleep*—"

Sarah got up. "Am I not worried too? Is he not my friend?"

"Don't go. I shall scream—"

"Meta, please . . ." She saw the by now familiar signs of a tantrum: those alarming screaming attacks which the family, it seemed, would do anything to avoid. The last had been about—if she remembered rightly —an iced cake, which she thought one of her younger brothers had stolen.

But now she had begun already to scream—she had taken the fastenings from her hair and pulled it all about her face. Her eyes looked round wildly, like a horse about to bolt. Her screams grew louder.

The nurse came in. "Don't let Miss Rawson go, don't let her," screamed Meta. "*I want Miss Rawson*—"

Then Mrs. Vernor arrived, flustered, a little embarrassed. "Meta dear, Meta . . . Miss Rawson—"

"I'm frightened. Mr. Ingham *frightened* me. Miss Rawson, *don't go!*"

Mrs. Vernor left for a moment and came back with a homeopathic remedy. But Meta would not be calmed even sufficiently to take the drops. She shook her head violently. Then grabbing at Sarah's hand.

"Promise you'll stay, *all the night*—"

"I shall just settle you. Then I must go to my college—"

"*Don't go! Don't go!*"

She was never sure afterwards how long it had taken, but she had in the *end* settled Meta. Only at the price, however, of promising that she would sleep the night at the Vernors. She would have to be downstairs, for Meta's room was very small and would not admit of another bed. It had finally been Mrs. Vernor's pleas rather than Meta's screams which had persuaded her.

"The noise and the upset, for the invalid. I am sure it can be heard. Also, you know, her younger brothers and sisters . . . And frankly, the tantrums frighten me, Miss Rawson . . ."

Dorothea left soon after in a four-wheeler to go back to Newnham. She took with her a letter from Mrs. Vernor, explaining about Sarah.

Resignedly: "All right, Meta," Sarah said. "I stay with you." She added more kindly, as Meta threw her arms about her, "You will know that I am there, and not *too* far away. And in the morning I shall see you—and you will have slept very well . . ."

She was exhausted when she reached her room. On her way downstairs from a last look at Meta, she passed the door of the sick-room. The nurse was just coming out. In answer to Sarah's query, she shook her head. "No change," she said sadly.

Mr. Ashby had taken Mr. Vernor out into the garden a little while before, "for a rendezvous with my Lady Nicotine," he said. She could hear their voices now—or rather, Mr. Ashby's. Mr. Vernor she pictured sitting quietly with his cigar, relieved of the need to speak, and glad of his thoughts of Thessaly . . . His duties as a host performed.

In the hall before she visited Meta, Mr. Jepson had taken her hand suddenly, shaking it very formally and saying: "Wanted to thank you, yes, yes. Kind to all the family. Very, very kind. Nice—" Then giving a nervous laugh, he had wandered off, humming, and singing under his breath: " 'One night I went up in a balloon, On a voyage of discovery to visit the moon . . .' "

She undressed slowly because she was so weary. It was unbelievably warm for only late May, and before getting into bed, she opened the french windows very slightly. It was so still outside that the curtains scarcely moved. Standing there in a borrowed nightgown, she fancied she could smell fragrance from the garden—the honeysuckle perhaps. Whatever, it seemed stronger than the men's cigars, which she could not catch at all. (She wished she could say the same of Mr. Ashby's voice . . .)

It was surely a garden for nightingales. She expected later that she would hear them, for she was not anticipating much sleep. And indeed it seemed to be only when she lay down at last, that the full horror of the afternoon came over her. The shock, the fears for the morrow, the little that she could do—and the distress that awaited the Inghams. It cannot be, it must not be, she thought.

For an hour or so she tossed and turned. Occasionally a few sentences, perhaps extra loud, were carried across and through the doorway.

". . . has a little shake-down in Park Lane, or so he dubs it—*I* should call it a mansion . . . Mr. Haweis at St. James the next Sunday—his method of preaching, quite too sensational—it might be, my dear, a Dominican in Italy. . . . shall not accept the next invitation, it is the *evenings*, one is expected to devote oneself to *petits jeux*, and it is *too* tedious . . ."

She must have drifted into sleep. Waking with a start, she saw the flapping of the curtains—then the windows creaking as a man's figure appeared in the room. In the moonlight, she made out Martin Jepson.

"Ah, ssh—" he said, his finger to his mouth.

She had sat up now, wide awake.

"What are you doing in here?"

"Nothing, little love." He hesitated. "Would you let a fellow speak to you, just for a while?"

She said, keeping her voice very low, "Really—I might have screamed with fright. The shock—" She pulled up the coverlet. "And really, you should not, you know—"

He was standing at the end of the bed now. He looked hangdog: "A fellow is really sorry. Just for a moment, then? Five minutes?"

"Just for a moment."

Silence.

She asked him, "What was it you wanted to say?"

But still he did not speak. She could make out that he was staring at her—just as he always did. To jog him a little, she laughed and said, still in a very low voice: "Well, say something—now you have audience of me."

His voice was rather breathy. "Can a fellow sit there—look—just on the edge of the bed . . ."

"So long as it don't add up to more than five minutes *in toto*," she said easily, humouring him. "Then you must be gone." She thought then of lighting the lamp and trying to make out the time.

He sat down heavily, not at the end of the bed, but in the middle so that he caught one of her knees. He felt soft and large, seeming to take up a lot of the space.

"Angel of mercy—little love, angel of mercy to Meta, eh?" His brow had creased. "Meta's a little frightened one. You are strong. All right, that's right." His voice was breathy still and rather thick, as if his tongue wandered about his mouth. "There's something I want you to do, would you do something for a fellow?"

She thought that really she must persuade him to leave. Otherwise he might talk in this fashion for the better part of the night: sitting there into the dawn, meandering on . . .

He said now: "You see, really you are a *horse*. Leaping over the chasms. Little one, you are so strong—they say, don't they, 'strong as a horse'? And you," he whispered it, "you then are a horse. Sing to me now, sing to a fellow—"

"What is it to be then—a lullaby? Come, Mr. Jepson, horses cannot sing . . ." She spoke in good-humoured desperation. But she was aggravated too. She said, more gently, "Please, enough. We both need sleep.

It has been—this afternoon, these are not everyday occurrences, and Mr. Ingham, our friend, he is very—he is *gravely* ill."

She thought for a moment that she had been successful. But then suddenly, he groaned, very loudly; and then leaning forward, took hold of both her hands, clasping them tight.

"Want you to do something for a fellow. I've got something here—wait a moment." He was tightening, then loosening, then tightening his grip again, hurting her hands. "Wait a moment. Shall just show it you—"

He was much too near her. "No, now you *do* have to go. This was not part of—I allowed only . . . *Please*, Mr. Jepson . . ."

She eased herself backwards, her spine against the brass bed rails. She could feel them press into her flesh. She tried to pull her hands away. Suddenly he let them go. But those few seconds, the seconds in which she was free—lost. She was too late: those same large hands—and they seemed to her now enormous—coming at her. One of them covered her mouth. Too late a scream rose in her throat. She kicked out. Her arms flailed.

"Little love," he said, "little love. So *strong*—"

Oh, but then, how could she ever have thought him soft, gentle, feeble, flabby? Such immense strength, pushing her, pulling her down on the bed. Now he was kneeling on her. The pain . . . His hand still covered her mouth. She could not open it sufficiently to bite. Could scarcely breathe. Any movement at all seemed impossible. The blood beat in her head. She shut her eyes in terror. He had changed position now, falling heavily onto her. The hand over her mouth pressed harder still.

I am going to die, I am to be murdered, this is murder, this is to be murdered . . . His free hand moved over her roughly, prodding, grabbing flesh—then urgently lifting up her nightgown. It seemed to her that any moment now, the other hand, pushing up, would cover her nose. Already she felt she could not breathe. His breathing as heavy, shuddering. Then for a second or two the exploring stopped. She could not feel his hand on her body. *It is over, he will leave me.* Oh, God, *let it end* . . .

But he must have stopped only to unbutton himself, because a moment later—ah, but if she could have *cried out*. Oh, dear God, where was the pain greatest? Her back too, that would break. *She would break.* And all the time as he thrust, he half-spoke, half-sang to himself.

"I ride, I ride—ride a cockhorse to Banbury Cross . . . Over house-top and chimney-pot, tower and spire . . . it's something awful jolly, up in a balloon . . . awful jolly, *I ride, I ride*, up in a balloon . . ." Then he became silent for a little—just the sound of his breathing, his grunting.

And then as suddenly it was all over. His grip on her mouth tightened momentarily—and then he let her go. Now he was climbing off her. She could not move at first. *Now I can scream.* But it was too late. Of course it was too late. And almost at once, she heard the sobbing. Opening her eyes, she saw him beside her—sobbing. Drawing in breath, great gulping sobs. She thought disgustedly: it is for me to cry. But nevertheless she was rendered helpless. She turned her head away a little. She saw that he was still open at the flies—bunched shirt showed white at the opening.

She could not speak at all. Her lips moving stiffly would not let out sound. *I could not scream now I could not save my life I might now be killed soundlessly without protest* . . . Between sobs, he said, "Don't tell on a fellow will you? Little love. I am disgusting, he's a very wicked fellow, God will punish Martin . . . Don't tell on a fellow, there's a little love . . ."

She thought to put out a hand and push him, push him right away. But her hands, even her hands would not go where they were directed. It seemed in ghastly parody of Francis that she could not move, could not speak, might never move again.

A minute or two later he shuffled out—not as he had come, through the french windows, but by the door. For quite a while she lay absolutely motionless, her eyes wide open, staring ahead of her. She could not imagine that she would sleep again now. Even without moving she was in some considerable pain. She would have liked to go up to the sick-room, to see what report the nurse could give. But just as she could not imagine sleeping, she could not imagine ever moving from the bed. And yet lying there, she could not think. Her mind numbed. After about an hour or so, she began to cry, but softly, in case she should disturb anyone.

The front door bell clanged very early. She was already up, though, and dressed. A little earlier she had visited the sick-room to find that Francis had rallied very slightly. He was able to move his hands a little, and had slept, as far as the nurse could tell, for quite long stretches during the night. The shutters were fastened tightly still. In the dim bedside light, Sarah had seen that he slept peacefully now.

The nurse said: "Doctor hopes that serious as it may be—if he can get through today, and make these little improvements in his condition . . ." She added, "I was glad I had not to send for Mrs. Vernor in the night."

Hearing the front door bell now, Sarah walked at once from her room, along the corridor, and through into the hall. She felt shaky and a little dizzy as one who has not been to bed at all. She was numbed too, and aching dully. A maid in crisply laundered uniform was just unbolting the front door.

Richard Ingham stepped in. His face was so drawn, so pale, in the early morning light, that she was at once moved to pity. Her dislike of him for a moment forgotten (and how could I—*now?*). He recognised her, but not immediately. I am in the wrong place, she thought. He associates me only with Downham.

She explained herself briefly. "Mrs. Ingham," she said, "she is not with you?"

The maid said, "The mistress, sir, Mrs. Vernor, I shall just fetch her, sir."

"No, thank you. I g-go straight up, please." He turned to Sarah: his voice was curt but it was the shortness of anxiety, fatigue. "Mrs. Ingham and Isabella are in t-town. I t-t-telegraphed at once, but it can be they spent last night in the country—some b-ball . . . I fear delays—" The maid stood there still. He said: "Miss Rawson will sh-sh-show me up . . ."

She did not expect that he would want to waste time in polite conversation with her. He went at once upstairs, without stopping to wash or remove his coat. At the door of Francis' room, as she was about to turn the handle, he said, his voice warmer now: "Before I see him— how b-b-bad is it?"

"I don't know," she said simply. When they went in together, Francis slept still. Richard spoke a little with the nurse, then took a seat near the bed. Without looking at Sarah, he said: "Miss Rawson, please stay—if you would. And t-tell me all that you c-c-can, of yesterday . . ." She saw that his hand, which lay over Francis', trembled with fatigue.

After a while coffee was brought in for them both, and soon after Mrs. Vernor came down. Sarah was not sure whether she should stay on in the room. She did not want to move. Also, she *did not want* to be downstairs with the Vernors—with Martin Jepson.

"Meta sleeps *very* heavily still," said Mrs. Vernor. "You have charmed her, Miss Rawson." (And your brother, thought Sarah, angrily. Does *he* sleep well?) "Breakfast will be sent up for you both. Although if Miss Rawson would rather come down now? You know that we have arranged for Communion to be brought to your son, Mr. Ingham? About ten o'clock. And the doctor calls, any moment."

Just as she left the room, Francis woke. He was conscious and seemed to recognize Richard. His eyes followed Sarah too. But he could not speak. And the improvement from yesterday seemed only temporary, for within minutes of Dr. Faber's arrival he had taken a turn for the worse. Eyes closed now, laboured breathing.

Mrs. Vernor had come in with the doctor. "It is not brain fever?" she asked anxiously. "Such hard work, such brilliance. Sometimes . . ."

"No, no," Dr. Faber said, "no, no. Some—some cerebral trouble, yes, but not that. A clot, possibly? We must have confidence—and *hope* . . ."

Throughout the morning, the breathing grew heavier and heavier. Sarah remained in the room. She felt numbed, in mind and body. Frozen. Unreal. She had not thought of going back to Newnham. Although Richard had not asked her to stay, once when she had gone out for a little and returned, he had said, unexpectedly: "Ah, I f-f-feared you had left us—"

A telegram had been received from Mrs. Ingham, that she arrived in two hours' time. It was sent from somewhere in Hampshire. Sitting there, anxiously watching for the slightest change, Sarah found her own troubles not out of mind, but dwarfed. (Alas, it *had* been real, last night. When the pains, the aches, the bruising went, would the memory? She feared not.)

When there is a right moment, she thought, I will say what occurred. She *should*, of course, tell Mrs. Vernor. Or Dorothea? Or—whom? Half of her wanted to shout it from the rooftops—this terrible thing that has been done to me . . . and yet, how could she *speak* of it? She thought with horror, what words would I use? And how can I hope to be believed? It is not likely, they would say. Gentle, silly, crazy Martin Jepson—never . . . her sense of shame too. It was very acute. Almost as if it had been in some way her fault. But in the face of the so much greater suffering here in this room, she would not, *must* not think any more of it.

It had not been possible to give Francis Communion. His condition was worsening. Dr. Faber had called again about half past ten. There was no one in the room except the nurse, Richard, and Sarah. Mrs. Vernor came in quite often, and once Meta's voice was heard outside the door. Mrs. Ingham was expected any moment.

The end was very quick. Richard had hold of Francis' hand still: he was watching his son's face anxiously when very suddenly the breathing changed. It become very soft. He gave gentle little sobs. Richard's eyes did not leave him for a second. Then Francis' lips puckered up, gathered together softly—his face suddenly that of a child. For a minute or two the soblike breaths went on. Then—nothing.

TWENTY

I look for ghosts: but none will force
Their way to me; 'tis falsely said
That there was ever intercourse
Between the living and the dead.

WORDSWORTH, "The Affliction of Margaret"

It was Kate's idea, that he should go away and take Sarah with him. "You could go to France," she said. "Anywhere but Bordeaux . . . Why not Paris? Just you and Sarah . . ."

So it had been arranged. They were to go within a week or two of Sarah's coming down from Cambridge, and were to spend all of the time in Paris. He had found Sarah on her return very shaken, naturally, by Francis' death. As he had been. He had called at the Abbey—the servants were all in mourning. He had spoken only with Richard. Kate had asked him also to take up a note of condolence. "It is from all of us," she said.

Sarah would be going back to Cambridge for about a month in the summer, to study. The Long Vacation term. Several of her friends would be there. Yes, she looked forward to it, she said, her face belying her words.

We are a pair, he thought, as they set out on their journey. He in heavy mourning still, she in part-mourning. Nor was he able to recapture with her (perhaps it had been for the moment only—but *how* it had been needed . . .) the companionship of the night in Kirsty's house, after Rose's death, after Sarah's rising from the dead. But in spite of that—it was good to be together. We shall make each other laugh, he thought, somehow . . .

Only it did not seem so. *She* was not in the mood—and then *he* . . .

Even the matter of the Valentine which he had not showed her at Easter when she came home, and which now on the eve of leaving for Paris he brought out for her—that did not help. She did not tease him, and it would not have been appropriate—but it might perhaps have helped . . .

"It seems in poor taste," she said, looking at it.

He said sadly, "But the sender . . . He—she, they do not know. As last year when I was first married and it was sent to Linden House. It is someone who knows nothing about me . . ." He took the card back from her. The same small neat hand-printed characters; a little painting of the Alps in water-colour, pasted on; and the words below:

> See the mountain kiss high heaven,
> And the waves clasp one another
> No sister flower would be forgiven
> If it disdain'd its brother . . .

But when he had put it away again he had done so strangely enough with all Rose's effects. He could think of no explanation for his action.

Rose's effects: he was still not through with tidying and sorting these. Although she had possessed relatively little—much less than most—the task had been emotionally too formidable for him. Kate had come to the house and helped: without her it would have been impossible. Some things he had kept for Bea when she should be grown up—some of the books and prayer-books (Rose's *Garden of the Soul*—he had not been able to use it), some clothes if they were timeless, lace, jewellery . . . He had had some correspondence with Sybil about all this. She had wished everything to be sent to Foxton for sorting. But distressing as he found every sad evocation of Rose—that he could not have agreed to.

And now the task was almost done (he did not expect now that the mud of the Firth of Tay would yield either Rose—or her belongings). There remained only: the diary. It terrified him still. Since that moment when he had seen it on the marble topped counter of the refreshment room, amongst the flotsam of the crash—sock, umbrella, bonnets —her bedraggled velvet bag: and inside it, the hard leather case with its brass lock, its neat initials—he had not known what to do with it. Home again, he had put it in a drawer. He was tempted sometimes, surprisingly, to send it to Foxton. Let it be *theirs,* he thought in reckless abandon, knowing that he himself could not destroy it—yet did not wish to keep it. But then at the thought of *Sybil* forcing the lock, prying into its secrets . . . Of—Nick even . . . It was not to be borne.

On the eve of going to Paris, while packing, he decided suddenly to take it with him: putting it into his portmanteau in its thick flannel wrappings, just as he had brought it back from Dundee. When I am there, in Paris, he thought, I shall decide whether to read it or not . . .

He and Sarah spent a day and night in London first (impossible not to remember the Rose of two years ago). The Channel crossing was stormy—a summer squall. Sarah was very seasick. He plied her with champagne but on arrival in Paris she was still very low. It seemed to him a bad beginning.

They stayed at the Hôtel de l'Étoile in the Rue de Saints-Pères. He wanted to take her out and about: the second evening they dined at Magny's in the Rue Mazet because he knew of its famous Dinners—in a private room, attended by Flaubert, George Sand, Turgenev, Gautier . . . But its heyday was over—it had begun to go down after the Siege of Paris. Now the proprietor was dead a year or so—and the atmosphere quite different. But eating there, Sarah livened a little. They went another night to Véfours and then, hearing that it was more fashionable to eat on the boulevards, they went the fourth night to a small restaurant on the Boulevard Poissoniere. That evening went well—tomorrow they were to go to the Opéra, and during the day he had bought for Bea the very latest in dolls—she would be far too young for it yet, but later . . . It was called a Bébé doll and could be bought only there. It moved its limbs, blinked its eyes—spoke even: "Mama, Mama . . ." Sarah had said robustly that she didn't think *that* for the best. Might not Bébé be doctored perhaps to say only 'ma'? But he was proud of his buy—so proud.

They had rooms next door to each other in the hotel and that evening she had seemed much better, more lively. Whether it was the wine or more general, he was glad only, and when they were back from the restaurant they talked in his room for nearly two hours—of anything, everything. A great deal about their childhood. She told him too of her dream about the Kissing Gate, and Edwy. He told her of his. He said, "I wonder if *other* people do? If perhaps from childhood they hear so much about it, that if they live in or are from Downham, they *must* dream . . ."

"You can't *order* it, though," Sarah had said. "I tried once . . ." She seemed almost happy when he kissed her good night: "Darlingus stupidibus, we've been a long sad way together. And it is very, *very* kind of you to bring me here, and we are going to have a wonderful time . . ."

Perhaps because he was relieved of worry about her, when she'd gone he settled himself in a chair in his dressing gown, brandy and water beside him. He lit a cigar. Then after a few moments, turning up the lamp, he crossed over to the huge walnut chest of drawers, and took out Rose's diary. The smell of weeds, salt, mud had permeated even the flannel covering. He had with him a small clasp knife and with this he broke the lock. Inside was a tooled leather volume—how many times had he not seen it? (Rose on Lake Garda: "I must write up all about lovely Sirmione, Paul . . .") He was afraid now to open it. When he did so, he turned the pages over rapidly—seeing nothing. He realised that he was trembling. *I must be brave.* Ash crumbled from his discarded cigar. He sipped from the brandy and water, then closing his eyes for a moment, he opened them again and taking up the diary, looked at the first entry.

November 1878

All my old journals, my dear old diary—all destroyed, and this is the last time I write before I shall start a new life . . . And I write now in case I should ever forget—although how *could* I forget these last months?

I am going into all this with *my eyes wide open.* For I have prayed—how I have prayed—I asked: Thy Will not mine. Because before, it had all seemed so simple—Was it not perhaps too easy for me? My soul—as a flower opens, it moved towards Thee. For me it would have been an easy life—the convent. I do not speak for others. (I saw already at school that for some it was *very* hard . . .) But for me—such peace. After the first thoughts and worries (my vocation, was it true?) that settled, I had such peace. But *not hard-won.* I was sad only for a little while—that I should have to give up children (my *own* children—not perhaps those of others . . .), family life, everyday innocent pleasures. But in return—I was to receive every blessing a hundred-fold—for had You not told us so? It came easily—it was more natural inclination than anything else, I *know that now*—and I think in my pride (I know in my pride) I mistook it. I had thought to have it all too easily. And Father Bromhead—I may write this here—he is not the person I would have chosen to speak to. Except that placed as he was in our home, his voice of course was Your Voice. He did not say—he never said to me, that he was against or for—

My sorrow then, it was only that I must wait, and that *they* did not wish me to go. Papa said little, but Mama much. And she *spoke for him,* she said. It was only Nick, my dear Nick (so restless always, so uneasy, so truly loving of me), only *he* said that he understood. He said it as a child says it. What more natural, he said, *what more natural?* (Quite the opposite of Mama—) And yet *it is not natural.* It is violence done to everything, to all that we have within us—and that planted by God.

I realised that. I came to realise that, in my turmoil—and I *must* write about it—my agitation of the spirit when suddenly that day in the garden—*he*—Paul, who is so soon to be my spouse—when he asked me, *shocked* me with his question—I think I was shocked not so much because it was unexpected (and indeed it was, it was!)—nor yet because anyone waiting as I was to enter religious life might well receive just such an offer, and count it only a temptation, or rather—a cross to bear . . .

But I had not known until *he spoke to me* that slowly over some months, certainly since Everard's death and his presence there (his helpful presence), I had accepted him—Nick's friend, another brother perhaps—as *if he were family*. I could not be with him as Elfrida was—is—so easy, so light—but I felt when I saw them together—he is *good*. And then, when Mama had said that perhaps he wished to be a Catholic, and that I must pray. And I had prayed, so hard—and now seemed about to see those prayers answered. And then—*this*.

That I did not say "No" at once (as I would have thought to have done, had anyone presented it to me as an "and *if* . . ."), that I did not —I realised meant something. I would not now go through those next few days again—Dear Lord, it was as if . . . it was not that something came from outside, and was to sweep me away—nor even that I was uprooted—but rather that *something in me* was rooted out. The upheaval, the—I knew that I must speak to Father Bromhead, but—I scarcely needed to hear what he said. He spoke only the words *spoken to me already by God*. For I knew, it was torn out of me in those few days—I knew that *for me*, the convent would be too easy. That although virginity is the higher state, as we are taught, it did not mean that *I* was called to it—or even worthy to be . . . That I should honour my parents and please them in all things that are not sin—he did not *need* to repeat any of this—

It came to me, praying in my room, and again (together with *him*) in the chapel, that I must do what appeared to be the hard thing—that I must give up what *I* wanted and that to keep it would be, against all appearances, to lay up treasure on earth . . . And I must not. I must give away, up, all, everything. I knew, by instinct, by the *grace of God*, that there—with him—I was needed. And that to give up my life in that way I would save not only my own soul (and that must not be, *never* should be our first consideration) but far far more important, I should be helping to save his—

And so—after much much thought, and *so* much prayer—I was able
—and with my parents' blessing—I said "Yes" . . .

December 1878

We fly to thy patronage, O sacred Mother of God, despise not our
prayers in our necessities, but deliver us from all dangers, O ever glori-
ous and blessed Virgin—

I have not been able to write anything for several days. First it was
the rush of the wedding and then we must travel—and also—I was
tired. But—and now I must pray about this . . . I pray—Holy Virgin of
virgins, pray for us, Most renowned Virgin, pray for us, Most powerful
Virgin, pray for us, Most merciful—

I do not know how to write this—but I *must*. I *cannot understand*.
What should happen to me now that I am married—what I was told
of, a little—what should be done to me—I cannot understand *why it
has not*—(And what too is wrong with me, that I *cannot ask*—we are
so easy together in everything else.) Yet, if this is how it is to be—it
cannot be right. I am afraid all the time that it is from some fearful
consideration for me, that I should not suffer perhaps—as I have been
warned people do—or that I am in some way holy to him and must not
be defiled . . . Tower of David, Tower of ivory, House of Gold, Health
of the weak, Refuge of sinners, pray for me—*I cannot understand.*

Now I must write also some details of what we have seen in Milan.
The Duomo . . .

9th December 1878

It has happened. I do not know how to write or what to say. It is my
soul shaken—not my body. So *this* is the secret . . . It is no wonder
that such fibs, such falsehoods, are told about it—and that it is not for
children to know what this is—*I love him so dearly*, I must write this
first—I know now that I was waiting always to love him (but that I
should have been given *this!*).

And when I had already had so much—the love of my family, the
blessings, the approval of everyone—yes everyone. All that I had dreaded
—*not* come to pass—because his sister (and how I had feared that
meeting) because she was at once lovable and loving. And his mother
also—although so angry, so sad in herself, it was *only natural* that she
should feel like this—for had I not taken Paul *and* taken him from the
God of his childhood? Such strangeness and fears it must have given
her. And indeed, she *did* at first frighten me—but then—that day when
she was in pain, when she could scarcely speak for blinding head pains,

that she should have said to me (and I had *read* to her only)—"Thank you, my dear—" And I had said "But—thank *you*—" and fallen into her arms. To love is easy—

14th December 1878

Too much—can there be too much? Too much happiness—I may not distrust it just because it comes from the body—if it brings us together as it does, again and again—if it brings us together before God—I am not ashamed, what shame can there be? Now am I not flesh of his flesh (was I not fashioned from one of his ribs?)—It is too much. Too much happiness—"a bundle of myrrh is my Beloved to me—he shall abide between my breasts—"

I have scarcely room left on the page to say that five days ago we were at Sirmione—a fine winter's day, a blue sky—and now already the dressing bell has gone . . .

The carriage clock in the room struck one in the morning. He read on, turning the pages: Now, it was Christmas—then all through the spring. Throughout, her joy at carrying the child, her quiet peace. He read of a calm sea and a prosperous voyage. But the ship had yet to come into harbour safely. And it had not. He dreaded to read of that . . .

20th September 1879

Not *one* word written for over two months—and what can I say now —what can I say that is not *darkness*? "The sorrow that is according to God worketh penance steadfast unto salvation, but the sorrow of the world worketh death—" and "sadness hath killed many and there is no profit in it"—"because," St. Francis de Sales says, "for two good streams which flow from the spring of sadness, there are six which are very evil . . . the enemy takes advantage of sadness to tempt the good—he strives to make the good sorrowful in their good works . . ." I cannot see so much as an inch before me, I cannot find a way through—"*If anyone is sad, let him pray* . . ." I cannot. How can I? "My eyes have failed for thy word—when wilt thou comfort me?" O Jesus, be to me a Jesus . . .

24th September 1879

I *cannot even love my child*—I know that I ought, but even that most natural of affections—I do not have even that . . . And yet I suffered for her—I did not know there could be such suffering in the body without death as relief—I am ashamed that I prayed to *die* . . .

And I was wicked even in that—for I would have left my child motherless, and my beloved without a helpmeet—and all for a little pain that was *as nothing* beside Christ's—

So I am alive—and yet am not, for my weakness is such that no degree of *will*—I try each day and fail again. And again. It is as if I were broken—this darkness, this dark night—the weakness of my body. I write of it only because it *is* important—for its effects on others (and most especially on *him*—). The nerve weakness that I weep when I *would not* weep—I accept it, all of it—but How long Q Lord, how long?

22nd November 1879

A whole year ago—almost! But we have nothing left—No, that is not true or just—I have a lovely child, that someone else must feed and she is happy and that is good. But *he* is not happy—already the worst is that he *regrets* that he married me. All—all which used to be such *joy* for us—all that—gone. I cannot believe it will ever happen to me again. It was *too close to Heaven*—so that I—we—might have thought we had here our Abiding City—

I grope weakly in the darkness for—no, not my safety—I know that I am safe even though I cannot *feel* it—"The Eternal God is thy Refuge, and underneath are the Everlasting Arms—" No, it is that for *him* I am a millstone, a trial, a thorn in his flesh—I irritate by what I cannot help —that is the hardest to bear. And in spite of all I know of right and wrong I would not count it a sin, would not feel it one—if *someone else* could give back to him the happiness he had (and which I gave him through the grace of God—for he was not happy before we married—).

I will suffer everything, gladly, for him. Only for him. Dear Lord give him peace and happiness and *not to need me* . . .

27th December 1879

Again the anniversary of dear Everard's death. Two years now—and today we had the Requiem Mass. But Christmas—what shall I say of *that?* except that it is good we are a family—I was sad again that Nick, my Nick was not there—he scarcely writes now, or visits—

And tomorrow I must go on a journey—one that I dread (you see, I am wanting in courage too—). But dearest Sarah is not well enough to go, so that I must travel alone—I think that it would not take much to dissuade me, except that I know *he wishes me to be there*—in spite of all, he would mind . . .

But our last words—our exchange at the very last, just before he should leave—even then I could not manage to speak as other people do, but must needs quaver—and then irritate more by these *wretched* tears (What nun spoke to us of the Gift of Tears?). I say only I wish never to cry again . . . And yet tomorrow for the slightest thing—and it will be again.

It is the boat tomorrow, the little *boat* I dread. I am not used to travel alone—if a storm should get up—what nonsense to be so *weak* . . . Be brave and resolute—Dear Lord, may I *never again* cause him such annoyance—may I show those virtues I do not feel—so that always, wherever, *whatever*, he shall *know* that I love him . . .

TWENTY-ONE

"It does not seem to have made you any happier, Sarah," said Mama. "You do not seem any the more content for having your own way."

"What own way?" Sarah asked wearily. It might have been better left. She thought of that too late.

"Even your grammar is deficient. You do not really speak any recognisable form of English. By 'own way' I mean this desire to emulate men . . . Well, you are there in a man's world, you study, just as men do—and you are not more contented. Rather *discontented*. And it is not I alone who notices. Several people—I have been most *particularly* asked this summer—'What is the matter with Sarah?'"

Sarah said, "These are people who have nothing to do with their time but remark upon other persons' facial expressions, or bearing—"

"As usual you are trying only to escape the point."

"Which is what?"

"Do not try to disconcert me, Sarah, by impudent answers. I repeat, you have now your own way—against the known wishes of your father—mine were not consulted—and yet you may be seen—all the world may see that you are none the happier for it."

"I am not bound, since the journey to the Tripos is both long and difficult, I am not bound to look *deliriously* happy for every inch of the way."

She thought that such an answer could only inflame matters further and regretted it instantly. But Mama chose to ignore it, saying only: "For the *photograph* perhaps you could look as if your own way pleases you?"

The photograph. Ah, yes. The whole family was to be taken at a studio in Leyburn, so that Uncle Jamie, Mama's brother, who had written recently from Canada and requested it, might see how they all looked. It must be done at once, for Mama was just about to leave for Scotland to spend the month of August on Loch Tay, with Kirsty and her family.

"Who will hold little Bea? She must of course be in the photograph, but not the nurse, I think. Paul would look awkward. I think as grandmother *I* shall hold her . . ."

It was not one of Mama's languid days. Once again Sarah could feel coming from her that dreadful suppressed energy which made her, Sarah, always ill at ease, fearful.

"Your uncle has not seen a picture for *fifteen* years. I want this to be a real family group. A feeling of exactly how we all are now—in the summer of 1880."

They were taken against a backdrop of Grecian temples, with real mock-marble columns for some of them to lean against. Bea, in Mama's arms, cried loudly throughout. Papa, fretting about the time, took his watch out three times.

Exactly how we are in the summer of 1880 . . . Sarah thought that forever after, in all the years to come, there, caught on the glass plate—ready for anyone to see again and recognise—would be her sick, trapped panic. Her mounting terror . . .

When had she first realised? It had been slow in coming, the truth. She wondered what sort of peculiar blindness, what shutters had come down over her normally quick mind, her robust common sense. I knew, she thought, if I was ignorant of how exactly a child comes forth, I knew at least a little of how they were made . . . *So why did I not think?* It seemed to her perhaps that in the slow, numbed days after (two shocks: Francis' death also), in her disgust, her desire to think no more about it, to *forget*, she had curtained off the truth, the real fear, the real horror.

So. Thinking nothing that month of June. Then home again and in Paris with Paul—and in her mind vaguely expecting a "visitor," as it was always called, but not concerning herself about it particularly. She had even (and to remember this!), she had even been glad that the week had passed without the inconvenience, the griping pains and malaise that she had always known—and which for some reason was often worst in the summer months. Also she had missed before: at sixteen and seventeen she had been visited only at two- or three-month intervals. She would have thought it convenient to return to that.

The month of July. That had passed too. She was back at Newnham, spending a few weeks of the Long Vacation term catching up on parts of her work which in the spring she had covered too quickly She had begun even to feel a little better in herself—some kind of animal vigour, a liveliness which hinted of a return to her old self. I feel well, she had thought one morning. Her tutor too had remarked, "You look blooming. Not a usual sight in the enervating Cambridge summer . . ." Seeing herself in the glass, she recognised that this was so. A face perhaps more rounded, the skin clearer.

Dodo was spending July and August in Cornwall with her family, so that Sarah had not the embarrassment of refusing invitations to the Vernors. They did not know she was in Cambridge. In June it had been easy for her to plead pressure of study. She could not imagine ever willingly going back to their house now—tainted as it was by the outrage committed on her *and* the wasteful and (it seemed to her) useless death of Francis (why, why, why?).

On the last Saturday before she returned home, she and Jessie had walked over the fields from Newnham to Grantchester. In the morning Jessie had visited the pastry-cook's in Little St. Mary's Lane and had now in a hamper enough food for five. She intended that they should eat it by Byron's Pool. "Sarah love, you *know* you'll be hungry by the time we've walked—" (She should have added, Sarah thought, "and I have *waddled* . . .")

The weather could not have been lovelier. After days of sultry heat there had been a storm, and now the whole countryside smelled fresh again. Although Yorkshire was her first love, and home to her, she had grown to love the country around Cambridge. Today as they walked, the thistles showed purple among the oats, the hedges were lush still—blackberries ripening fast, finches after the honeysuckle berries. Swallows and martins gathered on the tower of Grantchester Church. Walking through the village itself along the sun-dappled roadway, she saw in the gardens convolvulus, clematis, and everywhere roses full-blown, overblown. The reed thatching overhung the white-washed cottage walls.

She stood for a moment outside one cottage. Jessie, puffing, was a little way behind. Above her, doves talking quietly in the dove-cot. A blackbird, crust in beak, sped by. She noticed idly one rose, bigger than the others, vivid pink, almost blown. She leaned forward to catch its scent. As she plunged her face in, drawing in her breath—suddenly: she knew.

I am going to have a child. Then again, like some terrible litany—over and over again, I am going to have a child, I am going to have a child.

Jessie spoke to her. She knew that she did because she could hear, but could not understand or answer. She wrestled still with the new-formed sentence. *I am going to have a child* . . . She supposed that they must have walked home although she could remember nothing of it afterwards. Jessie's inconsequent prattle: she must have answered it satisfactorily, for as they walked through the front door, Jessie said with a great sigh, "Well, that *was* nice . . . And to think Miss Graham promised more *rain*."

But later that day she came into Sarah's room and after a moment, ventured: "Something is worrying you, *Sarah*." As so often she relished the name, clinging to it, a little lift of the "rah" at the end, a wrong emphasis which irritated Sarah always. "Is it those Unseens you've not done? Or is it what Miss Graham said at breakfast? Really, I don't think—"

Ah, dear God, thought Sarah, if only *they* were my worries. How I would rejoice, and thank heaven fasting . . .

At first it was impossible to realise. Just to know was enough. It paralysed her. Action, some action, any action—yes, that would be good. But what? There was no one she could tell. She thought with a backward glance of pity for herself, remembering how she had felt after the outrage, *I should have told someone then*. But she had not done so. Now certainly, before too long (before how long?) she would have to speak.

And what good would it do? It would not undo the child's conception, it would not take her back to how she had been. Her days at Newnham would be ended as effectively as if she had given herself under the willow trees to the dearest love of her heart.

The next day, Miss Clough, meeting her in the corridor said, "My dear, you look pale today—" (And certainly she had ceased to bloom: from yesterday afternoon, from that *moment*, she had ceased to bloom.) An answer came into her mind, at once. What if she should say it? Should reply: "No, I am not quite myself, Miss Clough. I expect a child in the spring of next year, all being well (and I very much fear that it will be)—and the worry of it all has quite taken the colour from my face . . ."

Instead she murmured only something about reading too much, and the summer heat. And moved on, to Miss Clough's kindly: "Well, my dear, see if you cannot go to your bed early for a night or two. And perhaps miss prayers in the morning?"

Back home again. To Mama's complaints. And the photograph. She tried to think straight. But that was the worst of it, that although she would sit very still, in strained repose, pencil and paper in hand so that she might try and write out her problem, her mind would not work at all. It raced. She would not have believed it could race so fast. Trying to list what she might do, who might help and *how* they might help, she found that after two hours she had only a blank sheet of paper—except for "? February" written at the top, and again at the bottom.

She had taken a book from her father's shelves. But it had not made sense to her. She had been too greedy, too frantic, trying to understand, digest the facts. The words swam before her eyes. The calm thinking, the application of her mind on which she set such store—all gone. Where? But then she thought: It is not to do with my mind, it does not concern it. It is to do with my body. My body only . . .

Two days after the photograph she, reluctantly, had to attend a party in Leyburn. Both her parents were there too. Dressing for it, she realised that already some of her clothes did not fit as they should, that she had to lace tighter and tighter. Soon, soon . . .

Going upstairs to the cloakroom halfway through the evening, she overheard two women talking.

". . . She's had her child, has Ada Cosgrove. There'll be some rejoicing over that. It was a *son*, you know—"

"She's taken her time, then, producing an heir. I'd rather thought it was *for* that—the match?"

"Oh it was, it was. But she lost one, you know—last winter. All her own fault too. Hunting it was, she fell at a fence. Really vexed with her, George was. And she'd been told, *I* had told her indeed—do not ride to hounds . . . One season she'd to give up, that's all. And then to jump, to risk a spill—*Well* . . ."

Sarah thought, I always knew there must be a way out, an answer. The idea, she had the idea now. She could not believe she had not thought of it before. Was not the child an invader? (Was it even now, a child? How little I know . . .) And worse, worse—might she not be nourishing, harbouring, a simpleton? As this last horror dawned on her, she thought, *I must act* . . .

But a cool mind surely was needed, and this she did not have. Once again her brain hurried and scurried, unable to settle. I do not even know, she thought, *how* a child is lost . . . She remembered very vaguely Sibby Helliwell speaking of two weeks in bed—early in the nine months or later? I do not know. *I know nothing*. That was what was so terrible. And when, a little calmer, she was able to read the book she had taken, it spoke only of treatment—and of what must be done to ensure that another "miscarriage" did not follow the first.

One will do, she thought grimly, replacing the book on the shelves. Perhaps it did not matter how it was to happen? Since by then the trouble would be over: she would no longer be having a child. I will wait to worry about all that, she thought. Sufficient unto the day . . .

On five occasions she stood at the top of the staircase at Linden House—and thought about jumping. But after only a few moments she begun to tremble, her knees to shake. She realised she could not do it—and would it anyway be enough? If it is just that I must fall . . . But from what height? And if I fall too far, if *I break my neck?*

Her nights now were largely sleepless. In the day she went riding sometimes as much as three times—causing Mama to remark on "this sudden passion for fresh air." Papa seemed pleased and thought it would blow away the cobwebs of study. Kate complained gently that she scarcely saw her (*if I could only tell Kate*—but at the very thought, a wave of shame and self-disgust came over her . . .). Paul and the baby had gone now to Foxton until September.

For four days after Mama left for Scotland, the weather would not allow her to ride. It scarcely allowed her out of doors. Gales were followed by lashing rain, and then more gales. When at last she could go, her mare was restless, full of pent-up energy. She herself felt tired, sluggish—hopeless. But if she was ever to do anything . . . It must be today, she thought.

She rode out in the morning and then again in the afternoon, this time going quite a way, up on to the moors beyond Little Grinling and then back by the tumbled down remains of Becky's home (*that* far away tale . . .). The sun was high in a clear blue sky. Larks sang. In the distance the wavy lines of the hills, blue-misted with the heat. It would have been a wonderful afternoon for happiness. As she came across the moor a flock of mountain linnets, little brown twites, scores of them, were bobbing about in the heather, chattering, twittering. A kestrel hovering overhead disturbed them, and with a rush they were off. A dog barked in the valley.

I must act. She was not likely to be easily thrown. She had a good seat on a horse. And she was afraid too of hurting her mare. She rode on, where the dry grass, flattened by the wind, was bleached, yellowed. The dry-stone wall ran alongside. She came suddenly upon quite a wide gap—the stones missing from almost half the wall. Dismounting, she checked that none lay about on the other side, moved the few that did, and came back.

She could not think clearly, could not reason at all. She shut her eyes, urged her mare on, and leapt—perfectly. Then, again The third time, her eyes open, she remained leaning forward to the jump as the mare cleared the wall. It was all it needed. Losing her balance as the mare landed she fell onto the horse's neck and then to the left, and down. She rolled over twice. Then lay still.

The pain was under her heart. She felt it the moment she tried to move, stabbing her side, high up on the left. As if a stake had been driven through it. (And up there surely was where the child lay?) She had not broken anything, she could walk, she could even remount.

With great difficulty she began the ride down. She did not know what to think. She felt frightened, and in pain. It hurt to breathe and she found she was scarcely doing so: leaning all the while forward on the mare's neck, trying to ease the pain. She came down on to the road just before Little Grinling, thinking perhaps that she might go to Kate. *Kate* would know what to do . . . But then again, I cannot, she thought.

She went on instead, by road, to Downham. It was still very hot. Her mouth felt very dry and, frightened, she trembled still. She met only two people as she went along. One of them, a farmer with a lurcher, looked at her strangely, but a waggon going by minutes later, loaded with women and children—no one seemed to notice her.

She wished that she had stayed up on the moor. The jarring of the mare's hooves on the metal road; it was very painful. As she came over the bow bridge she thought that she would turn off a moment on the Abbey road. The dark cool green of the trees round about the Kissing Gate beckoned. I will go home that way, she thought, and stop for a while in the churchyard. Sit in the cool of the church perhaps.

She hadn't thought of the difficulty of dismounting, of the pain. (But surely the stake was going right *through* her heart?) She tied up her mare: the horse shook her head, swished her tail against the late-afternoon flies. Sarah thought, I cannot wait to get to the Kissing Gate. It seemed to her some sort of talisman, a friend even. Going painfully up the steps, she leaned gratefully against it—breathing as little and as slowly as possible.

She was about to go on through when too late the thought struck her: Matthew Staveley. If she should meet *him* now . . . (And when already this month because of her worry, her shame, she had refused two invitations to luncheon, and had not yet been to give him a report on her progress.) I will go back now, at once.

But it was at that moment she felt the sudden rush, warm, between her legs. A second's rest and then—again. On and on. Now she had pain too. Not the one under her heart but a different one: that low cramping she recognised so well. She thought desperately—the "visitor." Perhaps after all . . . what I was waiting for . . . it is only that, but heavy, very, very heavy (as sometimes it had been before when long awaited) . . . I have not to worry. Her thoughts flew in all directions: I was mistaken, there was never anything. Then—but that is absurd. No, but it is true. It will be all right. If I can just get home. As best as I can, *I must get home.*

She was clinging to, not leaning against the Gate now. A fresh wave of pain came over her. Cramped up, breath held to avoid worse pain— that was why, she thought afterwards, she did not hear the sound of a horse, the wheels of a dog cart. Jangle of reins.

Her mare whinnied. She turned, clinging still to the Gate.

"Miss Rawson—Miss *Rawson.* Are you, have you—*what* is the m-m-matter?"

Of all those who should see her like this. Of all the ill fortune . . .

He had come up to her now, taken her arm. She could not meet his eyes, look at him even.

"I am all right," she said at once. "I rest—only."

"B-but—"

"I fell," she said. "I fell a little way back. Up on the moors." She spoke with difficulty. "It is my side—when I breathe. That is all. It is nothing. Nothing. I go home in a moment."

"You do not."

His voice was very firm, his grip on her arm tight. "You must c-come with me. That is your horse?"

She nodded weakly.

"S-someone shall bring it back—"

Just then she was wracked suddenly, a huge fist, a great gathering pain low down now. She clutched at the Gate as if she would drown. If I might die . . .

"One m-m-moment—" He had let go of her arm. She thought only, thank God, he goes, he is going. But in seconds he was back. She felt a rug about her shoulders. Her fingers slackened on the Gate, as she was lifted up in one movement.

Her last memory was of shame. The blood, she thought. The blood on the steps, beneath the Kissing Gate. He will see the blood . . . She opened her eyes for a moment, but the sky was darkening. It seemed to be closing in on her. It grew darker and darker—and she could remember no more.

Pain must have brought her back, because when she next knew anything, it came for her so sharply, with such a drawing, puckering feeling. As if something were about to break inside her. She moaned, caught her breath. The pain of breathing . . .

She remembered then, but only a little. That the ground had risen and fallen below her, stairs, voices, her own moaning.

She heard that sound again now, as if from someone else. A hand touched hers. She saw that she was in a bed, the curtains partly drawn, only a little light behind them.

"Miss—you're badly agin. Will I ring for t'Missus, love?" The face peering at her, white-capped, was elderly.

"Yes," she said. "Yes. Yes, please." She shut her eyes again but almost at once it seemed, someone stood by the bed.

"Miss Rawson, dear. Sarah—"

Frances Ingham, Mrs. Ingham. She remembered, I do not mind Mrs. Ingham. The figure by the bed was in heavy mourning. Francis is dead, she thought. Her son is dead.

"Yes," she said. And then, "I am sorry—"

"Sarah, dear—Dr. Wilson has been sent for. He is on his way. And your father. We are trying to find your father—"

"No," she said, between her teeth. "No, I don't want to see—" Another bout of pain.

Frances Ingham's voice was low. She took Sarah's hand in hers.

"You know that you fell, my dear, and may have done damage? You are very shocked. You fainted for quite some time."

"Am I—" She saw that she was in a nightgown.

"Mrs. Munby, here—who is a nurse from the town. She has undressed you. She was here visiting our housekeeper . . ."

"I want to go," she said. "I must go at once." It seemed to her very important that she leave this house quickly, quickly. Escape home, hide herself in her room. *Be left alone.*

"Please, ma'am, the surgeon, ma'am, he's here—"

She did not know him. It was not Dr. Wilson. A robust, matter-of-fact man. "Remove the coverings please. Mrs. Munby, is it? We have met, I think."

The shame. And the pain. Frances Ingham whispering. Going over and sitting in a chair by the window.

"Now, let us see . . ." He spoke briskly. "A *fall,* I hear? From a horse. If you could tell me, please."

She said faintly, "I jumped—we jumped, I fell awkwardly. The pain—" Her limp hand pointed under her heart. (The other pain—it was past describing . . . she could not.)

"But I understand also—there is the *bleeding?*"

"It is just what I have, it is just—the month . . ."

"Possibly a little excessive—no? It is quite possible for a shock to precipitate the discharge, of course. Or—it was due?"

"Yes."

"Now—answer my questions as best as you are able. I am going to examine you, and . . ."

The curtains were almost drawn about the bed. She cried out with pain. And the confusion—she had lied. "No, no," she tried to say. "No, no—I want to go *home*."

"We shall not go anywhere at the moment." His hands were more gentle than his voice. After he had finished it seemed all confusion again. She heard that he spoke with Frances Ingham, but she could not make out the words. She said again, very loudly, "No, no. *No*." Then another spasm took her over.

He did not address her directly again until he was about to leave. She heard his recommendations from where he stood at the table by the end of the bed, his voice brisk.

". . . thirty to forty drops of laudanum in a cold drink. Saline, please. And keep Miss Rawson cool. She must be kept absolutely quiet. Do not move her. If any great weakness—six to eight drops aromatic sulphuric acid in water. Everything—lost, to be retained, please. I shall return in the morning." He was writing, swiftly. "The cracked rib—nothing to do I think. It will of course take much longer than—the other."

He came back to the bedside. "I should have said, I am in *locum tenens* for Dr. Wilson. He visits Wales at the moment." His manner was, if not cold, expressionless, his voice flat. "If you have not already realised what is happening to you, Miss Rawson—*if*—then Mrs. Ingham will talk with you." Then a little more gently, but almost as if ashamed to be gentle: "Courage, please. Always courage . . ."

She heard him say then as he took his leave of Frances Ingham: "May I express my deepest regrets—I hear—the son of the house . . ." Then the tone changed again. "I am a London man . . . the opportunity to visit the Yorkshire dales . . ."

Pain, still more pain. Frances Ingham saying, "Mr. Ingham will offer you some fishing. I am sure that . . ."

Then more pain, and Frances Ingham stood beside her again.

"Sarah, my dear. We must speak—"

She could not believe it when all was explained. So this, this was *it*—the end result, what she had desired and aimed for. It would be all right. But at what cost? And that she could have been so *stupid*, that was perhaps the worst—did it not compound the shame?

". . . So you see that it is all a very serious matter. We have your health to consider first. That is our responsibility. You are not to be moved. Mrs. Munby is willing to stay the night . . ." She paused. "Fortunately, Isabella spends the month of August with her grandparents in Hampshire. The other girls are in the schoolroom. No one in the house shall hear of this—other than that you have had a fall. Your father I un-

derstand is in Richmond—you did not know that?—and does not return
until late—"

She interrupted with terrified vigour. "No. Nothing is to be said.
Nothing—" And she began to cry.

"Of course, my dear, of course." She spoke soothingly. A hand
touched Sarah's hot forehead. "Nothing shall be said. If that is your
wish . . . Your rib. We shall speak only of that. And that you are
bruised . . ." She paused. "He visits tomorrow of course. Dr. Rawson, I
mean. I think it almost certain that by then—what is to happen to you
—that it will be over . . ."

A blurred world of laudanum. Pain receding, then returning. Receding. Quite gone now. Cold linen compresses on her abdomen, silk
dipped in oil to plug her. She felt in the night that *all* her blood had
flowed out of her. More laudanum.

She woke thirsty, weak with thirst. But able to eat a little too. Papa
was at her bedside very early: a before-breakfast visit, the first of his
round. And saying so jovially, with such a false heartiness (if he *knew*,
she thought . . .): "So, little one, what have we been doing? And when
my back was turned. You must be more careful. Are they then to plaster this rib?"

She was awkward with him, wished the visit over. He seemed embarrassed that she should have been asked to stay at the Abbey. "You
could be moved if you wish—the rib is not so very bad. But—they press
you to stay?"

"It was fright," she said. "The fall—I had not expected to be so
shocked." She thought that she would begin to cry. She was white in
the face, she felt certain, drained. She fancied the birthmark even
drained of its vivid colour . . .

After breakfast, Frances Ingham again: "I think, my dear, if you are
well enough—do you feel that you can tell me—us—anything? I have
not said, except in the briefest of letters, how grateful I feel—we *both*
feel, for your care for Francis during those terrible hours, and in the
happier days before. Now, if I could, I would wish to help. We would
wish to help . . ."

Oh, my God, *he* did not have to know, must *he* know?

"Must Mr. Ingham? I did not wish—"

"I am accustomed to tell him everything. But any confidence—it
would be completely safe." She hesitated. "It is just—Sarah, you must
tell us a little. We should know perhaps something."

But she could not. She said only: "It was not my—I was not willing."
Then: "You believe me?"

"Of course, my dear. You do not need to ask. Only—we should know —was it here in Downham? Or as we might suppose at the University? You are not perhaps—it is not an affair of the heart? I think not from what you say. But if without naming names—we might help . . ."

"No"—she recognised in herself a fierce obstinacy—"No, I cannot. I would not say anything."

"You have suffered, Sarah—"

"But it is all *past* now. And since you believe me, that I was not willing . . ."

And there it was left. They asked, she knew, only from concern, but —how could I tell? To muddy Francis' death, it was not to be thought of. She conceded only, adding it as a rider: "It was not Downham. Or Yorkshire."

She saw that the room was full of flowers.

"We sent them up to you, Sarah, very early this morning. They are all from the Abbey gardens. Also, I forgot nearly—your Aunt Kate has sent a message. She has not been well herself—she will send fruit and flowers. She comes to see you tomorrow."

She had been allowed up and was sitting in a chair by the window when Richard came in. His visit surprised and embarrassed her— although she might have supposed he would come to be thanked. She did not know where to look, so staring out of the window across at the beeches, she said as quickly as possible, to get it over: "I have to thank you, Mr. Ingham. I was in an unhappy way. You have played well the Good Samaritan." The last thing she had intended was sarcasm. She tried to remember how she had felt as they sat together at Francis' deathbed. "I am sorry," she said, "I had not meant—"

"I understand. No one could wish to be f-found like that. It cannot be pleasant for you to s-speak of it." He was watching her carefully as he spoke (Do not let *him* ask me who it was, she thought. I cannot . . .). "Mrs. Ingham says you are much better?"

"Yes. I hope by the end of next week. As soon as Dr. Matthews advises, I shall go home. It don't seem right, taking your hospitality like this . . ."

"No, please. As long as it n-needs. We could perhaps, when you are stronger, s-speak of Francis? I have had sent to me some of his papers. Greek mainly. M-Matthew Staveley—"

The door opened. Frances came in. "Dear, I have Mrs. Rawson here. Sarah, here is your Aunt Kate . . ."

Kate looked pale. She came over at once to Sarah. Richard and she had exchanged only the coldest of greetings (They *really* dislike each other, Sarah thought), and as soon as was possible, Richard excused himself. He did not mention again Francis' papers.

Oh, but it was good to see Kate. Left alone with her, she found herself suddenly weeping uncontrollably.

"Your rib—you hurt more than that? There are other injuries, darling?" Kate leaned forward, concerned.

"No—yes. It was not as they said . . ."

It hurt to cry, to breathe deeply. She told her then—everything. The whole sad story spilt out. But Kate, when she had comforted her, said only: "Sarah, why did you not tell me *then?* That I might have suffered with you . . ." She said, "Promise me, darling, that you will not for something so important—*ever* be alone again?"

She was weak, so weak, and wept easily. And yet at the same time nervously excited as if something were about to happen. At the weekend she was visited by Laura, the youngest girl, who brought with her two large pieces of board tied with ribbon.

"This is a drawing, Miss Rawson. I have drawn you falling from your horse. If you will tell me the shade of his coat, I will colour it in . . ." She was a slight child with a large forehead and thin, light brown hair. She too had the curious blue eyes of her family.

"Cicely would not come to see you," she said. "She is very superior. But she is being silly because you are at University and she wants to learn Latin and Francis had said he would teach her. *I* think Latin silly for a girl; Papa says she may, when she is older. She is twelve and I am ten—*just* . . ."

The night before she left the Abbey, she dreamed that all of it, all the horror—she did not know how—was to happen again. I shall go in the river, she thought. I shall drown myself. She ran through the Abbey gates and along the road. She saw then that Richard came after her.

"It is no good to rescue me," she said. "It is too late." But he followed her still. "Go back," she called, "you are not needed. I shall jump in as my grandmother did. I have *to save someone*—"

She had reached the Kissing Gate. Because he was so nearly up to her, she hurried to open it, to go in—to escape him.

He said as he reached her, breathless: "It is yourself you have to save."

She said cheekily, "Why are you not *stuttering*, tell me that?"

"I do not *need* to do it, I do not do it with those I love."

"Go now," she said, from the safety of the Gate.

"But I shall not hurt you. With me it will be all right—"

"No, never," she said. "No one shall *ever*."

"Try," he said, but coming no nearer. Standing at the bottom of the steps looking up at her. "Try me, *please*. With me, it will be quite different—"

"There are no nightingales in Yorkshire," she said to him. "They do not sing in Yorkshire, you know . . ."

TWENTY-TWO

Flo said: "Patrick, please repeat after me. I shall recite it through first—

" 'Sukey, you shall be my wife
And I will tell you why:
I have got a little pig
And you have got a sty;
I have got a dun cow,
And you can make good cheese;
Sukey, will you marry me?
Say Yes, if you please . . .' "

Kate watched Patrick who with pencil grasped firmly was trying to write down some of the words as Flo said them. Seated at the elm birthday desk, he was a picture of fierce concentration: it seemed to her sometimes that all the energy his legs would have used had gone into his hands—and most especially his writing hand. His tongue peeped out between his lips, his pencil dug into the paper.

"Silly daft trying to write it. *Say* it now after me—'Sukey, you shall be my wife . . .' "

The best, Kate thought, is that one day it will be so. She will be his wife. I feel certain of it. Never have I seen two people, in a simple uncomplicated manner, more suited (I will not allow myself—now or ever —to be reminded of Richard and me. It is not the same: it is all happening so much earlier, with so much more certainty and confidence. It is not hidden and, above all, never never never shall I behave as Georgiana Ingham . . .). They had been inseparable this last summer except for the time when Will had been to Harrogate to stay with the Helliwells (just at the time when the Christy Minstrels were there. They had performed on the Stray in front of the Prospect Hotel, and by pushing himself and pleading his case, Will had been allowed to do two turns with them . . .), and Sukey coming over to Little Grinling often, had won Flo and Patrick's hearts. Best of all, though—she had won Ned's.

From their first meeting (and Ned had refused during the Easter holidays to see her at all) when Kate had brought everyone together in July of that year, all had gone well. Sukey and Will had performed together as a birthday surprise for Ned. She had a pretty little singing voice: soon Ned's flute was brought out and he was saying: "No, try this . . . I never knew *that* song . . . it's a bonny air is this one . . ."

It had been a lovely evening. Will's happiness, Ned's happiness, the affection of the younger children—and the ghost of Nanny finally laid aside by the living presence of Sukey.

> ". . . I have got a dun cow,
> And you can make good cheese,
> Sukey, will you marry me?
> Say Yes, if you please . . ."

ended Patrick, triumphantly.

Kate was already in bed when, clothes tossed carelessly over the chair, Ned climbed wearily in. The children were both asleep. Outside, a December gale tore through the trees, sighing, moaning. The windows rattled. He said carefully, head turned away—as if he must tell somebody (and of course he must, he must): "We'd another set to with Greaves today. Ugly it was. He's wanting still to be head over all—to have full charge when I'm not about. Doesn't like it I've put young Appleyard to do the overseeing—"

She said: "But he's half Greaves's age. And he wasn't even apprenticed with you. Isn't that what it's about?"

"It is—I don't doubt. But I can't give Greaves charge—not when there's days on end, especially wintertime, when he's not in at all. I told him that. But there's no reasoning with him, and never was." He paused, blew out the candle. "Anyway," he said in the darkness, "it's not that important a matter . . ."

"It will be to him," she said. "He never forgets a grudge—or misses a mischief." She remembered the evening of Paul's party . . .

"Quite a set to. Some evil things he said. It's hard not to be hard . . ."

"You should be harder."

"Ah, Kate, now. We've had that before. And you the gentlest of souls—"

"It is you think me gentle."

But that he did not seem to hear. He went on: "It was ugly enough at any rate while he spoke. I thought I might have to send him home—but then, when we'd almost done with the work, he was suddenly as pleasant as could be. As pleasant as *he* can be, that is—"

"Which is not pleasant at all. I distrust most of all his smiles—"

"Little Kate," he said it even more wearily, "little Kate—such bitterness. Such anger. If I can forgive him, for Mother's sake, why not you?" He hesitated: "Is it—after all, is it perhaps—still that sad business?"

"What sad business?" She said it warily.

His voice was full of warm concern: "You hate still because of that evil rumour, those words . . . *tainted* . . ." He shuddered as he remembered. "You hate him because it was *he* said that . . . it was he said you should never have children. That you were diseased . . ."

She did not answer.

"Come, that's true now—isn't it?"

She felt welling up in her now her own rare, but very real anger. "Ah, you think then—you really think—you imagine I would have believed anything I heard from *him,* a half-crazed millstone round our necks, that you don't know any better than to keep on at the works—you really think that"—the anger rose in her gullet now—"you think me so brainless, such an Irish half-wit, idiot—whatever . . ." She could not stop. In her anger, she repeated the words over and over again: ". . . half-wit, idiot . . ."

He was appalled: "But love, there was never—I never . . ." She could feel that he was appalled, but she could not stop the flow: the tears so many years hidden, the hate indistinguishable from sorrow, deep sorrow.

"You think it was a nobody, that I would have let someone like that—their word, that I am so *stupid* I would believe a nobody—"

"But you'd not tell us, Kate. Remember now—how you wouldn't say . . ."

". . . As if I'd believe something from *him.* When I was told on the best of authority. When I was told that John knew. She said, 'John knows'—she said that . . ."

"Ah, *she.* My love, it is a she now. It was women gossiping after all . . ." He had put out a hand and was stroking her hair gently. "My little love—"

She thought: it will be over in a moment. The whole sad business put away again. But then—his voice, firm, insistent.

"Who *was* the gossip, then—they'd no right. There's little we can do now. But they'd no *right*—"

She said, suddenly weary: at the same time loving all those women in

Downham who had said nothing, who whatever their gossiping had not spread that foul rumour: "It was none of them."

"*Who*, then?"

"No, none of them." Then she let it out like a sigh. "It was her. Mrs. Ingham. Georgiana Ingham—"

His astonishment. "Why? Why her? Katie, why *her?*"

She was surprised at her own calmness. "That I might not marry her son . . ."

In the darkness she sensed again his astonishment.

". . . Georgiana Ingham? That you might not marry her son . . . Kate—*what's this?*"

She said, her mouth dry: "Richard and I—we wished to marry—"

But then, it seemed that she had shocked him. That it should have been there all those years—that knowledge so important to him, to them both, should have lain hidden. For a while he did not speak at all. His hand, still on her hair, was tense. Outside the wind rose again, moaning.

"This is a new tale," he said at last, but hesitantly, "we'd not . . . did anyone know of this?"

"No." She buried her face in his arm: "Leave it all be. It's long ago, and—" But then when he said nothing: "I did no wrong," she said.

"It's not—I'd no thought wrong was done. It's—" he said it with a mixture of sadness and anger—"it's—the life you had, that I knew nothing of, that you went through all that and—I couldn't help. That you never asked . . ."

(Walter, she thought. All that too. He never knew of *that* either. And she remembered Sarah-Mother saying: "Never let Ned know, never let him know, he'd kill his brother . . .")

She was silent, thankful for the darkness. Then his voice, very firm again: "Mrs. Ingham, *she* said that, told you that?"

"Yes, Ned. Yes. Yes."

"You weren't much more than a bairn. And you believed her." He repeated it sadly: "And you believed her." Then he hesitated, "But Richard—could *he* not see it for the wicked nonsense it was? Surely *he* —Kate, I cannot understand . . ."

"He did not know," she said in a low voice. Then when Ned said nothing, she added, "And he *does not* know."

"There's wickedness—there's been wickedness, eh?" The well-loved voice from childhood, asking, probing. "Kate, Kate, what's all this . . . what *is* all this?"

She shook her head, the tears gathering, filling her throat, a great lump. I do not want to look there, I *do not want to look back* . . .

"And you'd not tell me—even now?"

The tears spilled over. In the safety of his arm, she wept.

"Katie—you could tell me . . ."

And then, she did. Perhaps, she thought, I had always wanted to tell him. Perhaps I had always needed to. At the end, when she had finished her tale, he said only, over and over again: "My poor love, my pretty Katie, my little cockyolly bird . . . that folk could be so *wicked.*"

She said in a small voice, "But you see, darling, as I said—so many years, is it not, and Richard long since happily married? And, too—how would I have dared, Ned? *She* did not think me fit. Like should marry like—"

"Daft," he said, "that's daft." Indignant on her behalf: "There's no place too high for you, no place wouldn't be the better for you in it. The Queen herself, for one of *her* sons . . ."

"Ned, that's fond nonsense—"

"No," he said, "no. You'd have managed. Why nowadays there are actresses even, marrying lords and earls and whatever."

She said again: "It's all so long ago, Ned."

". . . That they should have insulted you like that. I spoke only of that. But as for the *other*—"

"Yes," she said, "yes, for the other, that *was* very wicked . . ." She felt a leaden pain from the stirring of memory. "I hate her," she said. "I fear that—I hate Mrs. Ingham."

She felt his arm tighten about her. "You and I," he said, "you and I, we've no cause to love that family . . ."

"I have tried—not to hate."

His only answer was to draw her closer to him.

"Please forget it all. It is all behind us, Ned. Gone. Long ago." She talked to herself. She realised that it was Kate she told, Kate she reassured. "Quite forgotten, Ned."

When he did not speak, she thought at first he had slipped into sleep. She lay very still, fearful of moving his arm even a little.

And then suddenly, he turned towards her. His remembered hunger —it was as if she forgot every time, only to learn again. Not so often now, not as it had been once, but every time the same: he was so hungry for her, searching, always searching—so that now between her breasts, now in her hair, now in the sudden eager thrust, the gasp of happiness so long before journey's end. His joy just that she was his. His exploring, searching hands. She must give him her mouth too, pressed against his: this was how she could give to him, show her gratitude. A body after all which had lived now twenty years without Richard, borne three children . . . Ned known, Ned welcomed, again and again. I owe him so much, too much—the burden is almost too great. Only by giving like this . . .

Then in a great shuddering, his joy, Ned's joy. He said once again, as how many many times before: "Such happiness," he said. "Such happiness. You make me so happy."

In that is my peace.

Ned called round at Linden House. Kate had been there only fifteen minutes. She had come in with him early, as it was market day. Flo and Patrick were with Mrs. Cowley. Later they would go for their lessons. On the journey in, perhaps because of last night, Ned had been especially tender. Now, coming in where she sat with Catriona, he stood there, white-faced.

"You'll have to see," he said. "You'd best come and see . . ."

Greaves had no key to the works. He had never been given one (yet another of his complaints). But it had not last night deterred him. He had broken into the building—it could, they supposed, have been in the very early morning—but by the time anyway that Ned had arrived, followed a few moments later by Appleyard, the damage was complete—and Greaves nowhere in sight.

Kate, looking at it all, could hardly believe it. The work of a madman—some anger out of all proportion. He is worse, she thought, worse even than we had imagined.

He had been busy with a knife. Every rope slashed, torn, strewn about, every bale of jute, cotton, hemp, pulled from its place, cut through, twisted. A great mess of confused, hacked-at yarns lying entangled with the finished, destroyed ploughlines, halters, snares . . . Confusion absolute. And then, as if that had not been enough, as if he had not used sufficient energy, he had laid about him—presumably with an axe. The wheel of the rope-walk, the frames, everywhere splintered wood, wood with great crevices . . .

Catriona had not come with them. Kate found herself trembling. "The constable," she said. "Did you—"

"No," he said shortly. "No, I'll not. It's *him*, though, right enough—he's left a note." He handed Kate a piece of torn envelope, scrawled across it in an uncertain hand: "i het you rawson al rawsons." She did not want to look at it. "He's wrong in the head—he'll have to go. No doubt of it. But police, that's another matter. Mother—she'd not have wished that, Kate. Never."

"When he's done damage like this?"

"You don't remember Hannah," he said. "It was before your time. What was done to Hannah . . ."

TWENTY-THREE

Mother was wearing the locket with the painted miniature of Tarley. He thought: My thirty-year-old elder sister, Charlotte Rawson—except that she would surely be married by now. Would she ever have defied or crossed Mother? We shall none of us know . . .

"What are you staring at?"

"I dreamed. I was thinking merely . . ." He turned his eyes away from the small smiling face with its surround of black curls.

"You remind me of Ned," she said sharply. "That far-away look . . ." She took up her letters from the table. "He is the best of the Rawsons."

A throw-away remark—and where did it place Father?

"He is also the most foolish," Catriona said. "You have heard what that disagreeable and plainly crazed Greaves has done?"

But he had heard nothing, knew nothing of it. She explained briefly, saying at the finish: "And Ned did not call the constable . . . He has not spoken with the police at all. He has merely visited Greaves himself and members of his family—the upshot being that Greaves who of course will never work there again (or anywhere) is to be looked after by a sister of his and her family, the other side of Leyburn. It is not far enough. I had rather—and your father feels the same—that he had been apprehended as a lunatic-at-large. We cannot have people behaving like that . . . Ned was ever too tender-hearted. Old mad women—and now misshapen mad men—"

"One only," Paul said.

"One is enough. There has been folly from the beginning with that Greaves. It was a legacy from your grandmother—she wished him upon the rope-works. And then the death-bed promise . . . It is all nonsense. Such a promise *cannot* be binding in these circumstances . . ."

She changed the subject then. "Your Christmas—you go definitely to Lancashire?"

"Yes."

"Then we have just Sarah here . . . and *she* of course has not yet decided what to do with all that expensive education. It will soon be summer and finis . . . I must say, Paul, I hope that you think your money
well spent?"

He said tiredly: "We are not to start that again?"

"Start what?"

"Acid asides—references to an arrangement that was between Sarah
and me only—"

"Och, you may be as foolish with your money as you wish. It is yours
. . . And you have now Almeida House, that you have made no decision about. What of that? I think really that you should get yourself
quite together—decide what you will do with it—be firm with the
Straunge-Laceys, that they shall not make you come running at their
smallest bidding—and that you will bring Bea up as *you* wish. Rose
would have wanted it so . . ."

Once she must have had a pretty voice, he thought: because now
sometimes he could hear it behind the present one—or on the rare occasions when he would think—she is happy!—when he would hear behind
the voice, a hint of something lighter, prettier . . .

"Last Christmas—*that* Christmas, was with the Straunge-Laceys—"

"Perhaps you would kindly allow me to run—even to ruin my own
life? If the Straunge-Laceys seem to interfere—what is it that you do?
You say that I am to do as I wish, and then tell me what it is *you* wish
. . . I shall decide."

"Oh, you make me tired," she said, getting up from the table. The
locket banged against her bodice. "*Everything* makes me tired . . ."

Sybil wrote, on thick black-bordered paper: ". . . so happy that you
will be present for the Requiem on dear Everard's anniversary—and
then that other, still so fresh a sorrow in our hearts, on the 28th . . .
Yet again we shall have to forgo Nicholas' presence—so fond of Austria
and things Austrian has he become . . . Otherwise little Bea will have
all her aunts and uncles about her! (Hubert enters the Novitiate in
January—we are so proud.) Hermione and the new baby are here already. Dolly will follow. Ivo is a dear little man and can talk now—he
has a lisp which is quite enchanting . . . I think it is so important that
we keep a sense of *family* for little Bea's sake. I pray for you daily.
There will be a Mass for you on your birthday—I count on you to stay
until then! I plan also a children's party on the Feast of the Holy Innocents, for the little ones living hereabouts (and of course Bea, and Ivo!)
—I think this is how dear Rose would have liked her anniversary kept

. . . Mr. Straunge-Lacey is well but has been worried about the arboretum—he has lost two valuable trees—a Pride of India and I *think* a
Drooping Juniper. An expert will come to see about it—Hermione's
new baby has the *dearest* blue eyes . . ."

He had not seen Elfrida since the death of Rose: a whole year. She
had been either at Princethorpe or, as in the summer, staying away with
cousins. In that short space of time—she had grown up. Because he had
not seen her it seemed to him that it had happened overnight. She had
left the convent this last term, and was to come out next summer. She
did not seem very pleased about this, and was lectured at by Hermione.
("You cannot imagine how I was longing and longing at your age to
leave the schoolroom . . . Life is not *there*, you know.") But Elfrida
seemed wanting in animation, compared with the child he remembered.

Christmas went well enough, though, and much as he mourned Rose,
he found that somehow here at Foxton, where he thought it would
have been worst, his guilt was less . . .

Elfrida too seemed brighter as the days wore on. He took her down to
dinner each evening: usually he complimented her on her appearance—
the leggy Elfrida corseted now, curling chestnut hair as thick as ever
but tamed—thinking that she might lack confidence. On the night after
Christmas there was a party, with Guess the Face (holes in newspaper)
and Hide and Seek. Paul was stabbed by the thought: in Guess the
Face, seeing only Nick's eyes staring through the newspaper—would I
have told Nick from Rose? Elfrida grew very excited that he had not—
that *no one* had discovered her place in Hide and Seek. "*Do* you know
the story of the Mistletoe Bough?" she cried, the old Elfrida. "It was
not as dangerous as that—but *very* secret all the same . . ." He enjoyed too the Holy Innocents' party—Bea was admired excessively by all
the visiting children, and their parents (Ivo's, or rather Hermione's,
nose quite put out of joint . . .). He burst with pride. Elfrida was helping with the tea, rushing about with jellies and trifle, looking her old
tomboy self. Imp had been sat in a chair with a napkin about him,
where he behaved beautifully, provided the titbits arrived regularly.

The weather was unusually mild, and damp. It did not really suit
Foxton, overlaying its beauty with a forlorn, desolate aspect. He was
not as much outdoors as other times. The day after his birthday party,
meeting Elfrida on the stairs after luncheon, he said: "You are not to
practise that infernal piano this afternoon—"

"But it's the very *sumnabulation* of my accomplishments, and
though I do not *care* to do it—"

"Oh, fetch Imp," he said. "And take a walk with me . . ."

She came downstairs ready. She had the dog in her arms.

"Where?" he asked.

"Oh, the lake," she said. "Let's go by the lake."

She had not said the arboretum. But when they had been walking a little, she said to him: "I don't care for the arboretum in winter. I know there are evergreens—but the *whole* is not right. For me it is a summer place. No, I can't explain—"

"I understand."

"I am so full of odd feelings, you know. It is not very nice."

"It is very strange . . . Lacey—"

"Dear Paul—" She put a hand on his arm.

As they walked towards the lake they spoke of last night's party. ". . . And that we must always ask that *dreadful* confloption Reginald —did he not spoil it for you?"

"No—but only because no one could. It was an evening, a party fit for a prince. I could not *but* enjoy it . . ." He remembered Elfrida, flushed with pleasure, animation, when they had led the dancing—a little hampered, a little awkward in her tight, sheathlike evening dress.

". . . He was quite obfuscated, you know. But Mama is quite blind— because he is Catholic, I think. And also the family is as old as ours . . ."

They were standing now by the lake, a little back from it where some silver birches grew in a clump. A very slight wind had got up, stirring the branches. He said: "You are looking forward to London? . . . All the excitement—"

Imp sniffed about at the water's edge. "Oh no, not at all," she said. "I am—not at all."

"Elfrida—that is not my Elfrida," he said lightly. "All that fun . . . Hermione . . . And look too, that was how she met Dolly."

"I don't want to meet Dolly—"

"Well, not Dolly exactly—but *someone* . . ." He said, half-smiling: "Speaking just the two of us—someone better, of course. You *deserve* better than Dolly—"

"No." She took one of the fringes from the end of her scarf and twisted it round her gloved finger. "No."

He was surprised at the savageness of her answer. He said gently, guessing what it was he had stumbled on: "You want to be a nun—isn't that it?" And when she didn't answer, he went on: "They cannot mind that—surely? A Catholic family. I know how it was—with Rose. But they would not make you wait like that. It was only that Rose—"

"Oh, *Rose*," she said, "Rose. God was good to Rose—"

"Elfrida—love. And when God—when He allowed her to die. You cannot want—Elfrida . . ." Because she appeared so distressed, he put an arm about her shoulder, lightly.

The violence of her reaction. Turning, she all but fell against him. Then freeing herself suddenly, she trapped his face between her gloved hands. And then—a shower of kisses. Face, moustache, eyes, her cold lips brushing his surprised ones, his chin, his nose. Cold, cold against his cold cheeks.

She was crying. "I'm sorry," she said, as she broke away. "I'm *sorry*. Young ladies . . . I know, no *lady* would do that. I did not think . . . I never would have . . ." She had turned her head away from him. "What can you think of me? That I should—"

"It is all right," he said. "It is all right."

"No, how can it be," she cried, "how can it be when I love you so, when I love you so much and nothing can come of it—and then you ask me—tell me how wonderful it will be in London . . . I want none of that—how could I, how could I when all I want is *you?*"

Imp ran in small circles about her, made anxious, excited by her crying. But she did not notice him.

"Rose . . . God was good to her, you see. He gave her you. And she had not even asked. I ask—I pray *so much*—you cannot think how I pray . . . some way in which . . . All this year—it was after the accident, after the bridge—I thought of you all alone and how Rose could not help you and how I liked you so much and was so fond of you—and then I realised it *wasn't that*—at all. It was quite, quite different, something quite else . . . *I love you*—"

She had taken off her tammy—some hair escaping fell forward over her cheek. She did not brush it back.

"I didn't . . . I know it will *never* never go, and that I shall always be unhappy, but I want you, please, darling Paul, to be happy again . . . I *do* mean that . . . I dreamed so often—I know it is bold and wrong, but I dreamed so often that you kissed me, as I have just kissed you . . . that you *rained* kisses on me—I did not know I could behave as I have just done . . . perhaps I have in me still some of the wine from last night? What do you think, Paul? You see, I thought last night, all through your party—what happiness—what *torture* . . ."

He could think of nothing to say, and cursed himself for his silence. Her tears were running down still when he said: "I am not worth all that . . ."

"That is not for you to decide—how can you decide? *You* do not know . . . And then—*how can you say such a thing?*"

The January sky was dark already, the light across the lake was misty. Water slapped the sides of the rowing boat moored at the edge. It was growing very cold, and dank.

He said: " 'The sedge is withered from the lake, and no birds sing . . .' "

"You will not want me to come and stay in Downham," she said in a small voice. "To be with Bea. I have thought so often of Downham— and all you had told us that first time. Do you remember that summer, when Nick brought you, and you said then all the stories of the Kissing Gate—I found it so exciting, I liked it because it was superstitious and because it was to do with a church but not *holy* . . . I wanted to come when Rose lived there . . . only I did not—and now it is too late. If only I had loved then. I would not have been so wicked then—when you belonged to Rose . . ."

He said gently: "You know—it could not be, even if . . . Rather, it *cannot* be . . . the law of England. The Act, the Deceased Wife's—"

"I know," she said soberly. "I know that it is not possible . . ."

He said, and wondered if he spoke wisely: "You make of me something I am not. I think if you knew me—"

"No," she said, "no. It is not that kind of love. I love *you*, so that it does not matter what you do or what you are . . ." She turned again towards him, pulling on her tammy, slightly askew. She said: "Would you kiss me—just once? Please. Then I shall never, never, never ask again. Ever . . ."

When he had kissed her—her lips were cool still, and tasted of fruit: "Thank you, darling Paul," she said.

Back in Downham, he felt very flat. Cold weather set in, and then snow, ice. For some days at the end of January they were cut off from Leyburn and Little Grinling. At the beginning of February, Mother told him that Kate was "in a certain condition . . . She expects, you see, at the end of the summer. At her age—some risk, of course. I thought that you should know, so that you may take greater care—so that you do not abuse her good nature. She is too willing always to give of her time . . ."

And I am guilty, he thought. When he went into Mass in Leyburn, he prayed especially for Kate. His Kate. That Patrick should not happen again. That she should be delivered safely of a live child . . .

On the twentieth of February he received his fourth Valentine. It was addressed still to Linden House. A painting of the sea, pasted on as before. A quantity of expensive ribbon, and the other half of last year's verse:

> And the sunlight clasps the earth
> And the moonbeams kiss the sea
> What are all these kissings worth
> If thou kiss not me?

TWENTY-FOUR

"Line a hundred and sixty-six," Sarah said patiently. "Here . . . Although it's literally 'she hopes,' it must mean 'she *thinks*, that wild beasts killed the poor infant . . .' After all, Dodo, she *is* the mother, and loves her child—"

"Really," said Dorothea, giving a great sigh, pushing the text across the table, "really I am no good, and never shall be. It is hard enough to make out what Euripides said literally—without having to bring *further* thinking to it. I am tired—"

"And I. But I help you just with this last line. Two ambiguous accusatives—but what was suggested at the Supervision, was that we should take as the *subject* . . ."

Outside the sun shone. June 1881 and only one more term until she finished, at Christmas, her time in Cambridge. A year now since that terrible night at the Vernors'. The room that she had this summer—it was not so well placed for the nightingales: she did not think she could have borne many nights of their song. Not yet. But she was not able to avoid them altogether. Two nights ago, waking, hearing one, she had dived under the bedclothes, hands over ears, and stayed there till morning. It has come to a fine pass when a twenty-seven-year old woman must needs hide from nightingales . . .

But she supposed also, if she was honest, that it was something to do with Richard, as well. I, Sarah Rawson, who was to remain heart-whole, always and for ever. Who was to have had more *sense* . . . But in those weak days last August and September, it was as if she had been caught defenceless. At any other time—I *would* have been strong, she told herself, I would have been. But then feeble, grateful, vulnerable, she had dreamed of the Kissing Gate. The dream about Edwy had spoken the truth—so must this, whatever form the truth took. It is to be a hopeless love, she said (for how could it ever be other?), and I am to learn to live with it.

But oh, it was hard. For early March of this year had brought death to the family. Mama widowed, and she, Sarah, without a father. John had died from a stroke, following soon after a fall from his horse—he had been riding on a treacherously icy road, late at night. It had all happened before she could be summoned home (they had not thought the fall itself serious enough to send for her). That she had not been in time to see him alive had added much to her grief, and her regrets. Regrets that she had not somehow, in some way, been able to help him recover from the upset of the trial. She thought often, if that wicked girl *knew* the harm she had done . . .

Paul had been to see her here in Cambridge at the beginning of May, staying for a week. If it was possible to be happy at the moment, then those had been happy days. He told her that Mama, although still shocked, was a lot better. That she was leaning heavily on Uncle Ned, who went now up to Linden House every day for his dinner hour; and that Kate, although only two months now away from the birth of her baby, had been wonderful. "It is she and Ned who have done all the sorting, and tidying of papers and effects . . ."

Dorothea's voice came through to her, despairing. "I intend to give up. It is not as if I am in for the Tripos like you. And outside—it is *summer*, you know."

". . . this line—you had as well get it right. Then you may put everything away with a clear conscience. It is of course an accusative of *respect* here . . ."

"Sarah—"

Sarah looked up. Dorothea was standing her pencil on the table, knocking it over, standing it up again . . . "Sarah," she said. "There is something not very nice I should tell you. I would rather not—but if you are to come to Aunt Vernor's again (and you must, you shall—you cannot be always refusing), then it is best you are told. If you should ask perhaps where Mr. Jepson is—you are certain you saw nothing in the newspapers?"

Sarah raised her eyebrows. "The Cambridge *Gazette?* I have not had the time, Dodo—"

"It has been there, I think. Or somewhere. He has, you see—it appears that he is even less all right than we thought. That he is—not quite *safe*, Sarah. The incident—I do not know what I am to call it—it was out at Grantchester. Some poor woman, Sarah, that was just walking there—he did, or tried to do, I am not certain, something—I *cannot* say it—"

"Indecent assault," Sarah said. "I think that is the term. And they caught him?"

"Oh yes, yes. And he may not go out freely—he is quite confined now. I thought just that you should know . . . If you should come to us. It is very difficult, you know, to speak of these matters, when it is one's *own relations* . . ."

"Yes," Sarah said wearily. "I have a little experience of all this. And now—have we not promised ourselves an afternoon, a whole afternoon, in a punt?"

Apart from Dorothea, it was still Jessie she saw the most of. Jessie Hudson's burning interest—apart from food—was teaching. Above all, as she had said that first evening, she wanted to own her own school. Her plans after next term were to secure the best teaching post available, and then to begin immediately saving money. "It is not very practical, or probable, Sar*ah*," she said. "But it is by little beginnings . . . And who knows, eh?" Often in the evenings, if Sarah was at home, she would bring in her books, finish up all Sarah's biscuits, then fetch from her own room a horrid brew of cocoa, always too strong and gritty for Sarah, which she would sit over and talk. She had every idea for the perfect school—she wanted only the occasion to put them into action. Her enthusiasm fired Sarah's so that often Sarah found herself excited, and involved—and happy to argue some of the night hours away.

This year, still in mourning for Papa, she did not expect or want to have much to do with the May Week festivities. She refused politely a handful of parties: sitting instead in her room, she wrote Matthew Staveley a long detailed account of her work. His letters, and he never wrote less than three or four times a term, had always been a great comfort to her.

On the second Tuesday of May Week, when there were to be several College Balls in the evening, she was sitting a little after lunch in her room—deciding that if she could only summon the energy, she would write *Paul* a very long letter. (She hoped always that his, as those of Matthew, might have in them news of Richard . . .)

A maid knocked on the door. "You have a visitor, miss. Visitors—"

She could not believe it when she saw them. It was as if she had forgotten to pray—and yet her prayers had been answered. Richard had with him his sister, whom she recognised, but did not really know. Julia Ingham, she had been once. She was very fine looking, with dark lively eyes. Kate had spoken of her always with affection. And Francis—she remembered Francis too, at one of those Vernor tea parties, speaking of her. He had told her that his uncle had died.

"We have come to ask, Miss Rawson, if we may take you out to dinner? My brother and I—we could not let another person from Downham go unvisited. And we have had each other's company all day for two days now—fresh blood, please . . . We should like it so much, seriously, if you would join us?"

She wondered that Richard could bear it—to visit Cambridge at this time of all times. But it appeared that he was guardian now to Julia's sons, and Edmund, the eldest, was now at the end of his first year here. They had come up together to see his Tutor: there were some problems, not very serious, but she thought it best that someone *in loco patris*, as Richard put it, should do the talking. And they had enjoyed the opportunity of being together in such a beautiful place, in perfect weather. Edmund, Julia said, would not be there this evening, since he was of a party for a May Ball.

During dinner, which they ate in the Bull Hotel, near St. Catharine's College, she talked too much. Far, far too much. It was a form of nervousness—but she was unable to stop. She drank some wine with the meal, to calm herself as she thought, but it only set her tongue going faster. But there must have been some sort of blessing on the evening— for they did not either of them seem to mind. She told them excitedly of the Graces of last February—a triumph for women at the university, since the Tripos examinations were now formally opened to them.

"But we may still only attend lecture and lab classes with gracious permission of the lecturers . . ."

They spoke of Richard's daughters—a little of Francis. She mentioned the papers, Greek she thought, which he had spoken of in the summer. "I should like still to see those—"

"If you would t-truly be interested?"

How to say that even were she *not*? But she was, of course. Memories of Francis, affection and interest for and about him—they were all part of her love for Richard.

The feeling of a party, of excitement, was everywhere. Eating strawberries and cream, she saw all around groups who were evidently something to do with one or other of the College Balls—although most people would be eating in their rooms. Richard spoke movingly to her of Papa, and how he had been loved in Downham.

"I could not, you see," she explained, "be part of all this just this term. And I would not want to be. But an outing such as this—I am very grateful . . ."

When they had finished dining, the light outside was only just going. Some flares were being lit. In the huge elm trees outside "Cats" College, the rooks cawed still.

Back in her room—they had engaged a fly to take her direct to Newnham—she hoped only that she would not be disturbed. The wine had made her brave. She thought even that she might bear the nightingales . . .

Just before climbing into bed, she fetched once more from its hiding place the words Matthew Staveley had written for her, that first October. I have courage, she told herself. I shall be all right.

"A man should consider a voyage from the land, to see if he would be able and would have the skill; but when he has come upon the deep, he must needs run with the wind there is . . ."

TWENTY-FIVE

Presentiment is that long shadow on the lawn
Indicative that suns go down,
The notice to the startled grass
That darkness is about to pass.

EMILY DICKINSON

So cold outside. November cold. But inside it was as comfortable as
ever. The long room of the cottage at Little Grinling. It wanted only
Paul, that most frequent of visitors, to complete the scene.

Instead, though, Ned was there: he had been at home nearly three
weeks with bronchitis, which was only just now mending (and the
month before that, when the baby was born, he had been ten days with
a heavy cold and fever). He coughed still a great deal. Flo was at this
moment, with Kate's guidance, making him a cough mixture. Treacle,
honey, vinegar, aniseed—they were simmering now over a slow fire.
Laudanum and ipecacuana wine waited on the side to be added when it
was cold.

"I shall have to test it," Flo said. "As soon as it is done. Patrick
may not."

"Shall—"

"Shan't," she told him. "Because there is *laudanum* in it . . . ." She
was very proud of herself because she was doing all the cooking that
day. Irish stew had been over the fire for an hour already, and there was
pepper cake in the oven, with some big apples ready to be baked.

Patrick chanted, "A governess is coming next week and she shall
sleep in the step-house, a governess is coming next week and . . ." Sitting at the desk made by Sukey's father, he was cutting out scraps for
Flo, who was making a scrap screen. She handed him the sheets from

the fashion magazine, did the pasting, and in every way had the last word. In between pasting, directing, and cooking, she rocked the baby's cradle, which lay between her and Kate.

Ned said affectionately, "I know someone who will have forgotten all her lessons if the governess doesn't come soon."

"*I* haven't forgotten anything," said Patrick, his tongue curling over his lip as his scissors worked round the feathers on a lady's bonnet.

But it was on account of him that they would have a governess now. It had been all right for Flo to share, but the difficulties and inconvenience of wheeling Patrick to and fro—it was thought better that the step-house should be divided up into a bedroom and a schoolroom. Will, when he came home, would sleep in the village.

Ned was seized by coughing again. It seemed to Kate that he looked not just tireder but suddenly older. He had taken John's death hard. And Catriona, unwilling perhaps to ask too much of Kate in the way of love and support, because the baby was only a few months away, she had leant on him. In the first few days after the shock she would see no one else.

For herself, she was surprised at how much less it had affected her than she would have thought. Sad, yes. Too sudden, yes. Too young: only fifty-five. But it had seemed to her often in the last four or five years that John had not wanted really to go on. The spring had gone out of his step, the laughter out of his voice. He smiled seldom. It was as if he had looked into the future and did not like it. That dreadful girl had done for him (and yet he would never speak against her . . .).

What a pair they are, she thought, he and Ned, with their misplaced loyalties. John unnecessarily gallant, Ned refusing to prosecute Greaves "because Mother would not have wished it . . ." Although the havoc at the works had shaken him more, she thought, than he perhaps realised.

"It's proved costly," was all he had said, though.

"Was there no insurance?"

"Not the right kind—"

"But you would not take it any further?"

"No," he had said obstinately. And it was enough, she supposed, that Greaves's sister and family the other side of Leyburn had now the care of him. Certainly the Rawsons had paid their debt to Hannah. And it was one unpleasantness the less when visiting the rope-works.

"Agree then," she said to Ned, "agree that it goes better without him . . ."

"Yes," he had said, half-smiling now, "yes. It goes better." Then he had added, but with a full smile: "And we have not him to quarrel over now—eh, Kate?"

"Ah," she had said, kissing him, "*we* do not quarrel . . ."

Flo said now, "I shall serve the dinner at *half* after three." She was looking anxious again. "If you are back then from the dressmaker's?"

"Yes, darling, yes. Yes, I shall be . . ." Flo taking so seriously the work which Mrs. Cowley did for them daily. Had not Mrs. Cowley (like everyone else it seemed, there being so many colds and bad chests about) been ill, then Flo would have been allowed to help only—not to fuss so. "I leave soon, my love."

She had had her dressmaker, Mrs. Thackray, for fifteen years now. Although she lived only in the village, she was a cripple, so that Kate went to her always. She had not been since the baby. She needed half-mourning now for John—a dress that would fit her figure, altered by childbirth and feeding. And the visit must be arranged to fit in with the feeds. If she went soon and was back at half past two, the baby, just fed a little while ago, would not wake.

She looked now where Flo rocked the cradle—turning the magazine pages at the same time. Johnnie (the name had been Ned's wish), only two months, but already so much a part of the family—as if a place had been kept waiting specially for him. Flo's pride and delight. Ned, surprised out of his mourning for John. A perfect body too, so that part of her wept for Patrick. ("I want to see its legs, let me see its *legs* . . .") She had feared something sad, some mischance, right up until the wonderful moment when she had heard: "Eh, but he's *bonny* . . ." The undisguised delight in the midwife's voice. Johnnie slept now but in his dreams his lips worked at the nipple. Thin skin, fair hair, downy on the tiny skull beneath its cotton cap. She longed for the moment when he should be unbound, when he was washed by the fire. The "little small" fingers, as Flo called them, clenched tight then spreading open wide their perfection. Even the crying in the night—she did not mind. It would not be for very long. And it was only she with her breasts who could make him better . . .

"Will wrote to me," Flo said. "Does Papa know that? He's making up a song of his own that's to be funnier than 'Captain Cuff.'" Pasting glue on a scrap, she added resignedly, "But you can be sure Sukey's had a *much* longer letter . . ."

"Flo, your *linctus*," said Kate. "It will quite boil away—"

> "Sukey, you shall be my wife
> And I will tell you why:
> I have got a little pig . . ."

sang Patrick.

Between coughs, Ned said, "Kate," turning suddenly to her: "Kate, remember?" He sang, his voice cracking all the time with the cough:

"I peeped through the window,
I peeped through the door,
I saw pretty Katie
A-dancing on the floor.
I cuddled her and fondled her,
I set her on my knee,
I says, Pretty Katie,
Won't you marry me?"

"Yes, yes. I had forgotten . . ."
"Yes, yes, I *like* that," said Flo.
"Yes, yes," said Patrick. "Yes, yes, yes. Yes yes, yes. Yes. Sing it again . . ."
Kate shivered. Suddenly, gooseflesh, cold. So much so that she started. In a moment she was right again. But Ned had noticed.
"What is it?"
"Someone walked over my grave. Only that—" She thought that perhaps it was her milk about to come in. Sometimes, just before—a strange feeling. "I must go," she said. "I should have left."
"Listen to this," said Flo, "it says here 'what shall we say of a dress trimmed with cats' heads, ditto her bonnet and muff?' Do you think they are *real*? And—*and* this ballgown here—with mice running up and down it . . ."
"I don't know, I don't know, my little one."
She was really going, really leaving now. Kisses. Hugs. "Patrick, you are to stop cutting, and read for Ned . . ." She was almost away. A quick kiss on Ned's forehead, a handclasp. "My love." Then just as she had the door open and was almost through it, Flo's anxious cry: "What do I do if the carrots aren't boiled enough?"
Oh, but really I cannot, she thought, smiling, closing the door behind her, as if she had not heard.

It was very cold. Frost rimed the gate still as she laid her gloved hand on it. In the chill air rooks soared one after the other into the high elms behind the village green. Just before Mrs. Thackray's cottage she had to pass a farm. In the yard there on the frost-hardened ground, finches and sparrows and tits searched for grain in the trodden mud and chaff. There were few people about there, or in the village. She saw only two children and a man from the farm leading a donkey.

Mrs. Thackray lived with her sister and family. The cottage was scarcely large enough. Part of one room was curtained off for Mrs. Thackray's clients, but even then the nieces and one of the nephews ran in continually.

"Give over—you disturb the lady. You're disturbing Mrs. Rawson . . ."

Mrs. Thackray asked always after Patrick first: "How's the little small one? Plucky is he still? Same as ever?" And today: "None of the bairns are badly? Mr. Rawson and his chest—is he nicely now? . . . And the new one, then? If I could see *him* . . . Mrs. Rawson, ma'am, if you could think to perhaps fetch him up this way . . ."

"He is to be christened this month," Kate said.

"Is he now? And the comic turns—how are they going like? He's a big lad for his age—Will . . . and I don't doubt he'll stretch out more before he's done growing . . ."

She chattered all the time, through a mouthful of pins. The dress was to be a day-dress for best, to see Kate through the winter. It was black and white, half-mourning. The matching jacket was astrakhan lined with quilted silk.

Kate was pressed to drink a cup of tea before she left. She refused: "No, no. No, thank you. We eat soon—"

It seemed to her suddenly very dark in the room. She thought that she was going to faint. She put out a hand . . .

"Mrs. Rawson—Ma'am, are you fit?"

"It is nothing," she said. She added: "I should have eaten. I have been too long without food. The child—"

"And you'll not take a bite, then—nor even a sup?"

"Thank you, yes—I *am* thirsty . . ." Not tea, she refused the tea again. She drank instead a long glass of water. And almost immediately the milk came in—pressing against her breasts, hardening them. She imagined always that the baby sensed—as if some cord still attached them. "I must hurry," she said. "Thank you, thank you. I come back in one week—and you shall have the dress ready. Your work—as always, I am delighted with it . . ."

She thought of Will and how when she had first fed him, it had brought back everything. Ireland. The time *before John* . . . She was hurrying as she went: for although it was not far to home, she had been longer than she meant. The light was going fast—it must be nearing four. As she walked up the path to the cottage, she saw that they had put up the shutters already.

She lifted the latch, saying: "Darlings, I am—"

But there was no one there. The long room was deserted. She ran through, towards the kitchen. Only one lamp was lit. She could not see well. She called: "Flo—Ned . . ." Then in the half-light she stopped.

The shock thickened her tongue. She tried to scream and could not. She half fell and half knelt, groping before her. Flo. She had Patrick clasped to her. But—his head . . . God, oh my God . . . the sticky bloody mess. Both. She could not tell which was what. The bodies tangled. Flo's arms, his legs, her legs . . .

Ned lay, not quite in the doorway. She tripped, fell almost, over his spread-eagled body. Mouth open, he stared upward bloodily. She began then to run forward, backward, in circles, stumbling—banging against door posts, walls. Always soundlessly screaming. A sweet fatty smell of the stew on the range. Darkness coming over her, waves of it as she blundered about, unbelieving. Dry-mouthed terror. Flailing her arms.

"God, God help me—God, where is God? *God help me*—" But she could not see. I am blind. I am blind. She crashed into a table. Sent cakes flying. A clattering tray. "Help . . . Help . . . *I must have help* . . ."

She could not find the cradle. Then—yes, there it was. Her foot banging against it, sent it rocking.

It was empty. "God help me, *help me* . . ." She rushed upstairs, crawling, stumbling. Crashing from room to room.

"My baby, my baby, *my baby* . . ." Then she was downstairs again. She was back in the kitchen. She was out in the passageway, and through, opening the back door. It swung wide open—out onto the empty darkening path and the beck running by.

"My baby, oh, dear God, *where is my baby?*" Inside the cottage again now—pulling at cupboard doors. Sobbing. Running out now towards the larder. She pulled savagely at the latch. The light was poor inside. Her feet clattered on the flagstones.

A great milk jug stood on the stone slab. Johnnie had not quite fitted in. Feet upwards. Shoulders wedged. "*My baby, where is my baby?* . . ."

Lifting him out with desperate tenderness. Stumbling, screaming, running out of the back. Into the pathway. "My baby . . ." she called. "My baby . . ." A man bringing his donkey down to the field below. His mouth, opening in horror as she rushed to him.

"See my baby, here is my baby . . ." Milk. Blood. "*Here is my baby* . . ."

For weeks she lay so ill that she could not speak at all. In the first days, her reason was feared for.

The constables had been called at once. But they were busy already. Summoned to the Kissing Gate—where two frightened boys had discovered the figure of Greaves: crouching against the wall and behind the gate. Dishevelled, bloodstained clothing. Most of it strewn around him. In the twilight he had shouted and threatened. His strength frightened them—and later the constables.

No one recalled meeting him between Little Grinling and the Kissing Gate. The axe he had used was found later in the beck a little way up from the cottage. It was thought he had almost certainly struck Ned first and that he had come in through the back door. The terrified children, trying to escape—Flo dragging Patrick—had been trapped in the kitchen. Johnnie . . .

Formalities: apprehension of a lunatic-at-large. Horror in the town. Visiting journalists. A paragraph in the Yorkshire *Gazette*. Rather more in the Wensleydale *Advertiser*.

It was Paul who did the most for Kate—who became suddenly a man of action. He who dealt with police, with Greaves's family—who did all that John would have done. He travelled to Richmond to bring Will back: took on the task of breaking it to him.

Kate had been taken to Linden House. Catriona slept with her. "*Lag na fola*," Kate cried, waking in the night. "*Poll an churtha, poll an churtha . . .*"

Her nightmares were continual. Some days she could not be certain whether she had woken, or slept still. The agony of her breasts which filled and refilled with callous regularity. Laudanum, valerian, spirits of ammonia, tepid sponging, extract of henbane, camphor. The Inghams sent hothouse flowers—the room was full of them. Will stood by her bedside and wept.

"*Lag na fola*," she called insistently in the night. It was winter, the winter of the dead. "*Lag na fola . . .*" Catriona, beside her in a moment. "*Poll an churtha . . . lag na fola . . .*"

TWENTY-SIX

The governess agency sent Paul half a dozen hopefuls in the January of 1884 (it was *they* did the hoping, he thought grimly). He did not relish the idea of the interviews, although he was used enough now to engaging servants. He was not quite sure how to go about this, and did not think it a task for his housekeeper. He could of course ask for Sarah's help. She was still on Christmas leave from her teaching post in Manchester. But he feared that she might be in one of her "managing" moods, and perhaps frighten away someone suitable. And also—he was proud. I shall deal with these matters myself . . . He read *Jane Eyre* to see how Mr. Rochester had conducted his interview—but found that it had been done by correspondence with the housekeeper . . .

Kate. *Kate* would have been the best. That he did not ask her was only because since the terrible events two years ago, he had felt strongly that she must no longer be the one on whom everybody leaned. They had all done it, they were all guilty, but it must not be so now.

She had recovered from the tragedy, certainly. And it had not made her hard or bitter. She was still for him anyway the same lovely Kate (and *who else* should I love?). She had made a life for herself in Downham, living in the Rawson house on Hillside, with Will, to whom the house belonged now. Jane Helliwell lived there too: she was now a semi-invalid. Aunt Eliza had died, of pneumonia, last winter. Now Kate did many of the good works that she and Jane had once done. (Matthew Staveley had remarked to Paul that "in Mrs. Rawson the sick and lonely and bereaved of Downham have their greatest friend . . .") Will, all she had left of her family, was eighteen now and planned soon to marry his Sukey. Strangers had bought the rope-works. Will was articled to a solicitor in Leyburn, although his heart was still on the stage. But, Paul thought, becoming a family man would alter all that.

"Whenever are you arranging for that governess for Bea, Paul dear?" Sybil had said at Christmas. And he had had the satisfaction at least of saying that he was doing something about it. *The Morning Post* she had thought would be better than an agency—but he had not been able to face the prospect of all those eager, anxious letters. I would send away the suitable, he thought, I should never be able to judge.

Sybil had been pressing about it first in the summer, saying at least three times, "Bea is *four* now—and we must really see about her education. These first years are *so* important, Paul dear—when I think of some of these nursemaids, and the *wicked* religious heresies that come from their lips . . . I know that they know no better, but often they are the chief woman's influence in a child's life . . . You know what the Jesuits say? 'Give me a child for the first seven years . . .' You had not thought to have a Catholic nursemaid?" (He had not.) "I am surprised. But for the governess, you must promise, Paul dear. She may be Beatrice *Rawson,* but she is still part of the Straunge-Lacey family—of dear Rose."

He stayed at Foxton never less than three times a year, sometimes even five. Hermione was often there at the same time. They were good friends now in an easy-going way: he liked her ability to take or leave the Straunge-Laceys. Her own family was large now—four and another on the way this spring. Hubert was in the Jesuit novitiate still. Benoit was said to be something of a ladies' man, even (that new word) a "masher," so exaggerated had become his style of dress. Elfrida he had not seen for some time: although she wrote to him long friendly, studiedly nonchalant letters from the "Les Oiseaux" convent school in Paris to which she had gone at her own request. She would come back this summer.

Nick. He saw Nick two times out of three now. On the surface they were scrupulously polite to each other, Nick exaggeratedly so. But they seldom addressed a word to the other that they need not—and were never alone. Paul thought, I have grown a thick enough skin over it all. It was a long time ago. In another life.

The woman at the agency said it would be possible, when he asked for a Roman Catholic governess, but she had sighed. "They will all be *Irish,*" she told him. Out of the six she had sent him, one of them most particularly wanted the post—he could not now remember which—but as to being Irish only one, a Miss O'Driscoll, was obviously so. In fact the first of the two coming today was from Scotland, with a name to suit.

She sat with hands laid on her knees, which were slightly spread. There seemed a profusion of jet trimming on her dress. He judged that she could not be less than forty-five, possibly fifty.

"Miss McIntosh—"

"Flora McIntosh, uh-uh. Now, I'm from Edinburgh—you'll see it there on my papers—and the first thing I wish to say, Mr. Rawson, is that I'm used to unruly bairns, so you need have no fear. It is *she* will have the fear. The fear of the Lord—"

"I'm not sure that I want—" he began.

"You'll be wondering how I am a Catholic? My mother, God grant her peace, was Irish and kept the Faith against all difficulties. I'll not give any cause for complaint there . . . uh-uh. Do you know Edinburgh at all, uh-uh, you do? Then you'll know it for a fine place, a fine place." She looked around the room. "Now if you will just tell me, Mr. Rawson, what my duties will be?"

He did not seem to be doing very well. "I am not—"

"Uh-uh. I shall expect a free hand with arranging the wee one's studies. At four years of age—she has her letters?"

"I am not certain."

"Uh-uh. And her prayers?"

"Some prayers. Little ones only . . ."

She looked all around again with a dissatisfied air. "Is there no lady of the house?" she asked.

"I thought I had told the agency—"

"Uh-uh. No matter at all. It is no bad thing there is no one to come between the bairn and me. Your housekeeper, Mr. Rawson, she seemed a pleasant enough body—she does not interfere?"

Flora McIntosh was at least pleased with Flora McIntosh, he thought. He wondered how he was ever to fit in the words "No, thank you," or at least "May I let you know?"

"Are you accustomed to use the *rod*? It is the only language, you know. They understand that fine. Lasses too. Uh-uh. Never fear, Mr. Rawson, we'll soon have a wee one that can read *and* say her prayers *and* do her numbers . . ."

How to be rid of her? He had not expected that it would be *he* who was interviewed. (His imaginary problem had been, what should he ask, how should he avoid lengthy awkward silences . . .) On impulse now he said: "Was it *you* particularly asked for this post, Miss McIntosh?"

"It was not!" For some reason the question caused great indignation. "I'm not accustomed to ask. This is the first post where I've not been asked *for*. Bespoken. I was with Catholics in Glasgow, and Dundee— from one family to another, always *begged* for . . . It was a wee thought I had when visiting Yorkshire—that I might like a post in the countryside and not in a city." She rose suddenly, gathering up her large velvet bag. "But I have considered it all, and on *second* thoughts— uh-uh—I don't think you would suit me at all." She came horribly near, too near him: "You've just to thank me for coming, Mr. Rawson. Uh-uh. And I'll be away . . ."

Paul was not in a good mood to see the next hopeful who, he gathered, had been waiting here some time already. He was prepared to be frightened of her too. She was much, much younger. Probably no more than twenty-five. Not very tall, dressed in black, very simply except for her hat, which with its sharply peaked brim he recognised as fashionable. Beneath it showed a quantity of ash blond hair. Her voice was attractive, assured. She said very early in the interview (and it was he interviewing this time): "It is very important to me that I have this post." She did not speak anxiously, but as one stating a fact. But he found himself embarrassed by it and said clumsily:

"You are—without means?"

"It is not a question of charity. I have a post at the moment in York, with the Massinghams. Before that I was with a Catholic family in Norfolk—"

"Miss Hurst," he said carefully, "you—"

"*Mrs.* Hurst." But she corrected him gently.

"I am sorry—"

"I am a widow," she said.

"I am sorry," he said again, "I had not looked carefully. It is— recent?"

"Four years ago. Captain Hurst was in the Indian Army. I was out there too. He was killed in a border skirmish."

"I take it there were no children?"

"One boy. He died two months after. An epidemic—"

"I am sorry," he said yet again. And was wondering what next to ask, when the door was pushed open suddenly and Bea, followed by her nurse, burst in on them.

"Aunt Sarah, my Aunt Sarah's here!" Then catching sight of Miss Hurst, she stood still for a moment and then, running towards her, pulled at her chair arm.

"*Come* here, Miss Beatrice," called the nursemaid from the doorway.

"Who are you, may I kiss you, your hair is like Bébé's. Bébé's my dolly from Paris, Papa bought her . . . She says 'Ma . . .' like a sheep . . . Papa, Aunt Sarah's come to tea, come to tea, come to tea . . ."

The nursemaid apologised. "Miss Beatrice, she *would* come, sir."

"No, that is all right." He was always glad to see her, but particularly so now. It broke up the formality. She had climbed onto Mrs. Hurst's knee and was playing with a cross which hung round her neck.

"Do you wish to hold it? It is silver from India, Beatrice."

"Give me."

"Please—Beatrice."

"*Please.* Now—give me . . ."

Watching Bea and Miss Hurst, Paul thought the young woman might well say, "This child is in need of discipline . . ."

But she did not. Although in the weeks that followed he felt certain that she administered it . . .

He engaged her immediately, that afternoon. They had had tea first, with Sarah there. She had given her approval straightaway, after the meal, saying to him: "The blond widow, the blond *cendré*—I should certainly employ her. She will lighten your life—"

"If we are to have puns of *that* order . . ."

"No, but I am serious. You must settle for her. She is not *too* good-looking—her skin is bad. She has had a child, which is the most important—and will know how to act with Bea . . ."

And it did seem to him that he had made the right decision. For Bea was immediately happy—and good, although not too much so. She and Mrs. Hurst talked sometimes of her son. He overheard them once:

"What did you call him?"

"Harry. I told you—before."

"And how old was he?"

"Three. Just. You ask only that I shall say it all again—"

"What did he *look* like?"

"He did not have curls as you do, but straight hair—"

"When I learn a *new* prayer, can it be for him?"

If she had a fault at all it was that she was too earnest, perhaps a little too serious. He thought that it might be because she was so anxious to please—although she seemed assured enough. When he did in fact glimpse that she had a sense of humour, it was in the most unlikely circumstances.

They were in the train going to Foxton. It must have been February. It was her first visit there. She was talking to Bea about her doll, which went everywhere with her. ". . . and soon you will learn some French and then you will see that Bébé is *your* name in French—twice. For the letter *B* is said by them *Bay* . . . not *Bea*. If you wait, we shall get out some letter cards . . ." She reached into her bag and brought out a small leather case.

For some reason—he did not know why (if I *knew*, he thought, I would not have said it)—the case, although much smaller, reminded him of Rose's, with the diary.

"I loved my wife," he said suddenly, into the silence. And then stopped, horrified.

But happily Bea did not notice. Mrs. Hurst said only, her voice perhaps deliberately light: "I am sure that you did—"

He was looking still at the case, trying to hide his discomfort. It had on the corner small gold initials, "M.E.N." She saw that he was staring at it, and putting it away again, she said hastily, as if embarrassed herself: "I am sorry"—she had coloured—"I know what it spells." Then she smiled: "I fear my father was not really thinking . . . Such a pity, such a missed opportunity. He had only to have put, say, 'Agnes' in front—and I would have been, would I not, truly edifying? We should think always of these things, Mr. Rawson . . ."

TWENTY-SEVEN

"Sarah—"

"Yes, Mama."

"I should like to speak to you—*if you can spare the time*."

Why, oh why, Sarah thought, laying down the pile of books, taking up another—*why* cannot she ask me without sarcasm? ("Five minutes," she said now. "I shall be with you in five minutes . . .") It spoilt everything. It made what was surely going to be a tart exchange into an argument, a disagreement almost—before it had begun . . . And it will none of it ever change: another twenty years and we shall be still at each other's throats—a crabbed old maid, a bitter widow.

But at least, she thought, at least I no longer have to live with her. After the next few weeks *that* will all be over. No longer shall I have to spend the long, long school holidays doing and saying the wrong thing —and being reproached for it . . .

Paul's surprise was five months old now. It had been her Christmas present for 1883. Almeida House. For her very own. It was like Newnham—the present of Newnham all over again. "Darlingus stupidibus . . . *a whole house*—" She had not been able to believe it: the card under the Christmas tree with the lovely drawing in black and white showing Almeida House just as she had always known it—except that just above the gate was a board, and written on it in large letters, the word "SCHOOL" . . .

"Darling," he kept saying, when she protested, as protest she did, "darling, it is for *me* to apologise—that I should have been so long in thinking of it. That I did not *immediately* decide—Sarah must have Almeida for her school! Have you not always wanted—well, for years now, have you not wanted a school?"

Yes, yes, yes. Oh thank you, yet again. It had been only to work out a term's notice in Manchester, to write excitedly to Jessie (for she needed a partner, and who better? Yorkshire food was plentiful and nourishing and the produce of Wensleydale very attractive—Jessie would not suffer, although she might increase . . .), and then to begin her plans. She was in the midst of them now—every day more busy than the next, if she was to open by the autumn. Perhaps in fact, Mama rather resented this—that she should have so much that was so meaningful and that *must* be done. Although surprisingly Mama had not, at least of late, seemed displeased with the whole idea. She had said even that she felt glad, reassured, that Sarah should have so secure a future . . .

"My school may fail—"

"Hardly. With the ghost of Old Jacob about? You are fortunate, Sarah, that you cannot remember him at all clearly—but I can assure you that failure, of a financial nature at any rate, was not in his book. And I have no doubt that you will have inherited some at least of his hard head for business. And your grandmother too, your namesake, in her own way, she too was able." She had paused before adding: "Your maternal grandfather—James Dunbar. *His* talents, albeit misused, were quite extraordinary in that direction . . ."

Hurrying now to go and speak to Mama, to be within the five minutes she had promised, Sarah reflected that had it not been for the sad, sad news about Will's Sukey, life generally was beginning to improve for the Rawsons. Paul and Bea and that most excellent governess seemed content enough; Kate, her same sweet self, and as courageous as ever. And she, Sarah, about to have her very own school which would keep her here in Downham, purposefully, all the year round—and as near to Richard as circumstances would ever allow. (*That* love, she thought—I shall just have to live with it. I suspect even that I may have to die with it. Just as I cannot imagine anything ever coming of it, nor can I picture a time when it will leave me . . .)

If there is any nonsense with Mama, she thought, walking across the hall, I shall tell her—in case she has not heard—the news about Sukey. We shall be rid at once then of whatever trivia she wishes to discuss . . .

She did not wait to see in fact, but opened the conversation herself by saying: "Mama—about Sukey . . ."

"What? What of Sukey?" Catriona's voice was sharp. "Kate told me of some illness—a fever, a cough. What is it you know?"

Sarah told her briefly: Sukey had been found to have consumption. The variety known as "galloping." "If you had not been away several days, Kate would, I am sure, have told you. A consultant has confirmed the verdict. There seems—no hope. An aunt had it, you know. A little while ago. It is perhaps hereditary."

To her surprise, Mama's eyes filled with tears. But then, as if recollecting herself, she said: "And I—I also, had some news. But I should I think—as soon as possible—be with Kate. How is Will?"

"I go there this afternoon—to Hillside. I shall spend the evening. He, as far as I know—he is at the Rawcliffes' most of the time . . ."

There was an awkward silence. I should have said that better, Sarah thought. She is distressed, as I am distressed, at yet more trouble for Kate, and hers . . . But when after another few moments, nothing was said, she ventured, but politely: "You wanted me for something? Because, if not—" Already she was working out in her mind how much she could get done before going to Kate's, so that she was surprised, because only half-listening, when Mama said: ". . . I learned too, you see —in Leeds, that for me also—there is no hope."

"Hope?" She caught desperately at the last word, not understanding, not wanting to understand . . . "Hope? How do you mean? What—"

"I had not wanted to tell you like this. In my mind—I had thought, imagined perhaps a grander, even a more delicate way of telling you. And you are the first, other than the consultant, to know . . ."

Sarah shut her eyes. I shut them for very shame, she thought. "Please tell me—if you would." Her voice came out small, and colder than she intended.

"I had, have had for some time—various symptoms. I saw a consultant in Leeds a little while ago, and then—just now. He confirmed for me what we had both suspected. I have a growth—of quite the wrong sort, and for which they can do absolutely nothing. It will be a matter only of time . . ."

Even the word "Oh"—she could not say that. She could not speak at all. "I am sorry, sorry, sorry . . ." she kept saying in her mind—but she could not voice it.

"Please—don't say . . . I would rather not have conventional expressions of sympathy . . ."

"I had not—" She had found her voice now. But if this was all she was to say with it . . . She could think only: but we have never loved each other, and now it is too late. She scarcely heard that Mama was speaking still.

". . . I shall stay here only as long as it needs to comfort Kate, and to arrange my affairs. I have written out in draft a letter to the Clarendon Crescent Dunbars . . ."

But what was this? It was too many shocks at once; she could make nothing of it. "You are—leaving?" She felt, and knew she sounded stupid.

"I made the decision yesterday, and thought out all the details in the night—sleep evaded me. Hardly surprisingly. I have been pondering on all this for some time—that since you are now independent, and have a home of your own, I need not worry, nor feel responsible for you. And that what I should like to do in the time remaining to me—is to go back *where I belong*. I did not *really*, I suppose, care for Edinburgh so much as Wester Ross—at one time. But over the years, because of certain circumstances, that changed. Now, when I think of happiness, and belonging, and ending my days, it is *Edinburgh* that comes to mind . . ."

"But who will care for you, what shall you do, where may you live? It is all so—"

"Robbie—the friend known as Mr. Buchanan, whom I have known all my life—he is a great medical figure there. He will look after me. And Kirsty, she will come to me. I shall not be lonely . . . I shall stay only at Clarendon Crescent to begin with, until something else can be arranged. I have, you see, reasonable health at the moment. And little pain. I want only—I cannot *wait* to be back in Scotland. It is simply that . . ."

Again the silence. "I am glad," Sarah began. "I am glad that for the moment—you are well enough. And that you can go where you would wish most to be . . ." Her voice trailed away.

"Sarah," Mama said. "I have not been a good mother." The words came out in a rush—but decisive, deliberate, as if rehearsed. Sarah, taken aback, did not answer.

"I want now—before it is too late—to ask"—she hesitated—"I suppose I should call it *forgiveness* . . . It is difficult for me—to be frank, you know and I know, that because I lost Tarley, and was left with you, I punished you for it. That was wickedness . . . I think that it has not gone unnoticed—by God, and by others. But I am what I am. So that I can only say, which for me is very difficult—*I am sorry*."

Sarah said at once, "But no—it is I have been the difficult daughter. Always arguing, discontented—you have had trouble with me always—"

"Others have not. In the darker hours of the night, I came to realise that. And that I have been very wrong. *I* was never reconciled with *my* mother—she was angry with me to the end. That I did not marry some wretched ageing laird—I forget now even his name—that I did not spend more time with her, that I spoke of railroads . . . There was no end to it. And I did not understand her—that she suffered, that our family disgrace was for her something *beyond bearing*. It is not for us, you see, Sarah, to decide how much others can or cannot bear. My own life—it has been three quarters disappointment. I say no more. But now that it is almost over, I think that I *need* that we should part friends . . ."

And so we shall, Sarah thought later that day. For they had kissed—awkwardly enough. But nevertheless, they had kissed. A kiss other than a dutiful one. A kiss of peace. She did not suppose that they would get through the remaining days, or weeks, in Downham without some form of sparring. And that was so. But it was not the same: the edge had gone from it. On Mama's part it was half-hearted. On Sarah's, it was tinged with sadness—and real anger. Anger about the might-have-been. We *could* have been friends, she kept thinking. For she is far, far more like me than she knows . . .

All through June and July there were workmen at Almeida House. Since it was to be at least partly a boarding school, there were dormitories to be built—in a new small wing. Classrooms too to be arranged. And a smart new front entrance facing on to the market square—the very one which Old Jacob had spoken of so often, and done nothing about . . .

Warm water (not hot, Sarah learned that they must not be hot) pipes in the corridors and schoolrooms. For ventilation she was advised to install a system called "Tobin's tubes . . . which supply continuous streams of air without draught . . ." Jessie was in charge of everything to do with the kitchen, including the engaging of a good cook. She had joined Sarah at the end of May, just after Mama's departure, and would stay now through until the school's opening. A prospectus was out already, and most of the teaching staff engaged. Every day it seemed brought fresh excitement: Paul was over often, to admire progress—and to pay the bills. "Is it too much?" she would ask anxiously. "You are the major shareholder of course—but it will be *so long* before we see profits . . ."

He was only proud, though, and quite, quite unworried. Downham generally regarded her with a mixture of admiration and caution. And not a little interest. Parents who came to bring their daughters, or visit would want perhaps to stay overnight in Downham—or at the least to take refreshment, to buy goods from the shops. The numbers would not be great—but the folk would be well-to-do, quality . . .

Such busy days that really, for Sarah, much of her sadness—about Mama, about Sukey—was masked. There were scarcely enough hours in the day: and then in the evenings there were books to be studied and plans to be drawn up They must read both of them about class management, about syllabuses, examinations, about other schools and where *they* had gone wrong. Must study educational science generally. Both of them would sit with their copies of Bain: *Education as a Science*—making notes, comments, arguing. Sometimes, and especially when Jessie brewed the hated cocoa, it was like being back at Newnham . . .

In late July, she was surprised one morning to receive a visit from Richard. Caught wearing a working apron, with bits of fallen plaster in her hair, she was almost rude to him—not because of her looks (there is no hope there, she thought), but because she resented not being able to savour the joys of anticipation, to prepare what she might say, how she might behave. If I had only *known* . . .

He had come about Cicely and Laura—his two younger daughters. Would she, could she, would it be p-p-possible to take them as p-pupils? Sarah saw Jessie stare at him as he stuttered, and felt immediately a wave of protective anger.

Hoping that he would stay a little—wanting him never to go away ever—she persuaded him to drink some wine with them: sending out immediately. She hoped too that after a while Jessie would find something urgent to call her away. And she was lucky—for even before the wine came, Jessie remembered that she had an appointment to arrange about supplies of butter and cheese to the school . . .

"Laura of course I know already—and her lively drawings . . . Cicely, I recall, wished to learn Latin . . . I shall be teaching Classics myself— a little, but Mr. Staveley"—she stopped, and smiled at the memory— "he is on our prospectus as Visiting Professor . . . he will teach several times a week, as his work permits—"

"I had heard. He t-told me. It is *his* idea Cicely and Laura should come . . ."

When they had spoken of all the practical arrangements, she said— wanting him to stay on, but all the same meaning what she said: "Those papers of—Francis'. We spoke of them once, and then again when I dined with you, in Cambridge. I should like still to see them . . ."

He was delighted. He had not thought her interested. It was so easy, he said, when it was one's own children, to suppose everything to be of interest to others—when it was not.

"And Isabella," she said. "It is only Isabella now that I have not met."

"She is in London, for the s-s-season. My sister, whom you met in Cambridge—Isabella is with her. B-b-but she returns today. This very evening. She has been, I hear, quite a s-s-success . . ." He smiled: "Once again, I p-p-praise my children . . ."

That evening, she was standing in the gateway of Almeida House. She should have eaten about an hour before but she had only just finished directing the workmen, and now wanted to see about the small board which was to be fastened to the gates. Looking about her for a moment before going back in, she saw a carriage approaching—coming towards the market square from the Abbey side of Downham.

She watched it a little before realising that it was in fact the Ingham carriage. *Perhaps he is in it.* Trying to look without staring rudely, she watched as it passed by. But she saw only kindly Frances Ingham, sitting alone. She goes to meet Isabella, Sarah thought. It will be that. Isabella back from London—a success. Thinking of Richard that morning, remembering him, Sarah smiled.

She heard the news very early the next morning. She was surprised she had heard nothing the night before: there had evidently been quite a commotion in Downham, although the accident had actually happened nearer to Leyburn.

The coach, with Frances and Isabella and the maid who had travelled with her, had been coming back to Downham when suddenly, quite without warning, the pole of the carriage had broken. They were going downhill and before the coachman could stop the horses, Frances Ingham, panicking, had jumped from the carriage. Followed by the maid. Isabella had stayed calm. And safe. The maid had suffered severe bruising and grazes, together with a broken arm. But Frances Ingham, although lifted at once carefully to the roadside, and then carried into the nearest house—had died within the hour.

TWENTY-EIGHT

The autumn of 1885, and Kate thought: I have settled into sadness. It is a way of life. And so long as I do not make others suffer through my sorrow . . . I must think rather of the happiness I have had (and I have had so much), of the happiness I can yet give . . .

But it seemed that blow only succeeded blow. That her troubles would never be over. All about me, she thought: death—or departure. Will: that he should have gone was only natural, she could not have expected otherwise. And Catriona's death, almost ten months ago now, that was only partly a sadness, since if she had lived she would surely have suffered. But she had died quickly, and peacefully, from heart failure. Apparently the growth was thought to have pressed on her heart. She had been fit though, until a day or two before—out and about in her beloved Edinburgh.

But Sukey's death . . . Ah that, Kate thought, *that* I cannot accept. When Will had lost already so much: a father, two brothers, a sister (and in such terrible circumstances). Sukey's family history of consumption—an aunt who had died of it while living with them, other relatives—it did not make the sheer waste of it any the less. Or lighten her own pain at Will's departure . . .

He had waited some seven months before making his decision. She knew it had not been a light one. "I'm so sorry—*darling* Mother, I am sorry, sorry. Only I *must*. I can't—there's no way of staying in Downham . . ." (And she could not really, had she *ever* been able to imagine him as a solicitor? A *solicitor*—her singing and dancing Will?) He was twenty, and very talented: she would not worry about him—only miss him very, very much. "I'll be all right," he had told her. "You'll see . . ." And so far that had indeed been true. He had been in work almost continuously. News came to her from Youdon's Alexandra Hall at Sheffield, The Star at Bradford, The Parthenon at Liverpool, even The

Scotia—Glasgow . . . She had travelled to Leeds to watch him at Thornton's. In the summer months there had been a road show: the latest was that he performed at The Argyle, in Birkenhead. Next year, or the year after, he spoke of his own concert party. *She* thought that sooner or later, probably sooner, he would be topping the bill somewhere (and perhaps he thought that too, for his last words to her just before he left Downham were: "I'm a toff, I'm a toff," kissing her, holding her hands very tight, "I'm *immensikoff* . . .").

The letter from Walter was addressed to Number Three, Hillside, to the Rawson Family. It arrived late on the fourth of November—Mischief Night. She saw it not so much as an omen but rather as some horrid trick: that Walter had actually *arranged* its arrival . . .

It came from America, from somewhere in Oregon. It was ill written, in a hand she could just recognise, on rather grubby lined paper. It was not, fortunately, very long. Its main purpose seemed to be a plea for money, albeit a slightly half-hearted one. Reading it though, Kate trembled. God forbid, she said to herself, over and over again, as she skimmed through it quickly, God forbid that he wishes to return here . . .

But she did not need to worry. As she read it again, more carefully, she thought: I am the only Rawson left alive who *knew* Walter (and he has the power still, after all these years, to distress me . . .). He had had his fiftieth birthday at the end of last year, and it had been that which had prompted him to write. "I could not let my half-century go by without acquainting you all of it since the fact will have escaped your noses . . ." He had grown pompous and heavy-humoured, she thought; the words seem out of place with the scratchy pen and cheap paper.

She looked in vain for a few pleasant words—anything which might redeem him in her memory. But each sentence was more self-satisfied than the one before. The passage of thirty years had only confirmed his character. She liked least of all the final paragraph, with its postscript . . .

". . . I am enclosing an address not mine where you may mail money which is always welcome as I said earlier in the letter. If anyone's dead in the family as they must be by now has anyone any solicitors tried to find me, I could do with my rightful shares of everything, I have not communicated with any of you because none of you loved me not even Mother, it is a good thing that the ladies here are accommodating if you know where to go—do not misunderstand me, I am a success. P.S. What happened to that little Irish cuckoo?"

She showed the letter to Sarah the next day, when she came to sit with her after the fireworks party at the school. "We were finished by half past seven," Sarah told Kate, "and they are all safely bedded—if not asleep. Miss Hudson is very lenient about Lights Out . . ."

She found the letter amazing. "After all these years . . . Shall you send money?"

"Perhaps," Kate said. "Perhaps. I am that sort of person. And Ned would have wished it—I think . . ."

"But that he should have started in Australia, and ended in America —it is a long way. Did not some man years ago come begging to us— when Paul was still at Oxford—saying he had fought alongside Walter?" She held the paper to the light. "It's such crabbed difficult writing. The Dixie Greys, is it? In 1861—anyway as far as I can make out he seems to have changed sides after becoming a prisoner. That sounds in character . . . How he is living now, it is rather hard to discover. I like this: 'I have a finger or two in a number of prosperous pies . . .' Kate, I imagine him somehow grown *very* fat."

But Kate did not want to imagine him at all. She wanted only to forget that he had come back into their lives, even if only by letter. Sarah said now: "Let me keep it, as a curiosity. When Bea is a little older— *she* will find it fascinating."

"And Will," Kate said reluctantly. "When he is next with us . . ." She did not want to be reminded continually of loved ones absent. I must learn to be alone—just as Richard, too, must be learning. Nearly fourteen months now since the coaching accident, and Frances' death. Her first thoughts then had been for Richard—and the children. She had wanted the very day she heard, to rush to the Abbey, to take them all under her wing—to console Richard, to *explain*. But then common sense had prevailed, and habit, and she had written instead a letter—as warm and sympathetic as she dared, but conventional, proper: her condolences joined to those of the Rawson family . . .

She asked Sarah now, because she loved to speak of them, how Cicely and Laura fared in their second year at Almeida House.

Sarah, it seemed, wanted to speak of them too. She was obviously more than a little proud of them—that they should be doing so well, that Richard should be so pleased he had sent them there. "It is only," she said, "only—their continuing grief. What more natural? But I cannot suffer it *for* them. Time will help—Cicely manages the best. She has more of her mother's nature (and yet, Kate—*you* must have thought this—how could someone so placid, as I remember her, have panicked so? If she had but sat still in the carriage . . .)."

"Yes," Kate said thoughtfully. "Yes." Thinking to herself, how often we suddenly, unexpectedly, act unlike ourselves. And just when it matters most . . . "We shall never know," she said. "Her thoughts in those few seconds—how *sensible* her action may have seemed to her."

When she looked over at Sarah next, it was to see her with head bowed, hands clasped together. She said quickly, "Are you all right, darling? You have not worked *too* hard—you spend perhaps too much time—"

"No," Sarah said. "No. It is something I wish to tell you. To *ask* you—" She looked up now. "I have wanted for a long time to say something of this—to discover what you think. It is *your* advice I would want, that I would respect and abide by. Your consolation perhaps—for I have not much hope . . ."

But why should I think, Kate told herself, when Sarah's tale was done, why should I think that only *I* may love Richard hopelessly? Is it not my wonder really that every woman does not want what I may not have? But try as she might, she could not listen calmly. She felt as if a knife twisted her heart. It takes so little always, to awake everything.

She knew, Sarah said, that he had been happily married, that while Frances had lived she must never, never allow even the *thought* to pass through her mind. But now that he was a widower, with motherless daughters, and without a son to carry on the family—did Kate think that ever, *ever*, after a decent interval of time, there was *any* chance at all for her?

"I love him so," she said, the tears trembling. Strong Sarah, who had dismissed Edwy so easily all those years ago. In the light of the gas lamp, as always when she was agitated, the birthmark looked darker than ever . . .

But of course she had a chance, Kate told her. For she *had*. Kate felt certain of that. Richard was, surely, a marrying man. And Sarah was doing so much already for Cicely and Laura. She could counsel only patience. Perhaps because of her pain she went too far, giving her too much hope. She trusted she had not . . . But Sarah, kissing her, had said, "No one could have been *more* help. Darling Kate. I know you do not like him too well—but I, I love him *so* . . ."

She spent a sleepless night. The house, full of memories, seemed full also of weird rustlings and creakings, sighs. There was little wind outside. When she opened the bedroom window, the road was quiet, deserted. All the Bonfire Night celebrations long since over.

Perhaps it is a mistake to live here, she thought. But Little Grinling —that would have been quite impossible. Now, with Catriona gone, and Will, and Sukey . . .

Sarah loves Richard. The letter from Walter, together with Sarah's revelation, and their talk together: it had brought everything back. Richard, Walter—the experiences jostling together. Richard had healed Walter: *then*. But now it was all like yesterday, as if it had been only yesterday Walter's clumsy fingers in the little bedroom under the eaves —here in this house.

The summer after Richard first came back from school. It happened then. Walter hated me so. And we were so innocent, were we not— Richard and I, and Julia and even Hetty, standing round the piano with Miss Hooper.

> "Sing sing what shall I sing?
> The cat's ran away with the pudding string,
> Do do what shall I do?
> The cat has bitten it quite in two . . ."

TWENTY-NINE

"Save us, O Lord, waking, and keep us sleeping, that we may watch with Christ, and rest in peace . . ."

"Amen," Paul said, trying to keep his eyes from wandering round the cold stables-chapel. Usually it was kept warm enough, but these, the first night prayers since his arrival, were cold indeed Benoit, next to him but one, was ostentatiously holding his hands over a lighted candle . . .

"Preserve us as the apple of thine eye and protect us under the shadow of thy wings. Vouchsafe, O Lord, to keep us this night without sin."

"Amen." It looked to be a cold Christmas in every sense, he thought. Since their arrival in the late afternoon, Sybil had behaved very coolly, very oddly towards him. He had tried desperately to think in what way he might have offended (but he sent news regularly of Bea, brought her to Foxton more often than he cared to, was at least outwardly if not inwardly a devout Catholic . . .). Her expression was if anything wounded, and when she looked at him (which she appeared to avoid) it was more sorrowfully than angrily. He had wanted to ask if Mrs. Hurst, or Emily as he thought of her, might sit with them at dinner. It seemed to him that it would be all right, and not embarrassing, and that she would fit in well. But he had found himself unable to mention it at all.

"I confess to Almighty God, to blessed Mary, ever a Virgin, to blessed Michael the Archangel, to blessed John Baptist, to the holy apostles Peter and Paul and to all the saints, that I have grievously sinned in thought, word and deed, through my fault, through my fault, through my exceeding great fault . . ."

Fortunately he had not had to see Nick yet, although he was in England and had been at Foxton until yesterday. He would return either tomorrow or at least by Christmas Eve. Elfrida, sadly, he would not see at all. She was with Hermione and her family (six children now).

"Of these and all my other sins, I most earnestly repent, and am heartily sorry . . ." The time for examination of conscience had come and gone while he was dreaming. He turned the pages forward of his prayer-book, and read:

> N.B. When you are in bed and cannot sleep, employ your thoughts in some spiritual exercise, or in saying the beads . . . Or else you may think on those uneasy beds which the souls have in hell or purgatory. If you chance to awaken in the dead of night, forthwith imagine yourself to be present among the choirs of saints and angels, and with sudden acclamation cry out with them in the words of the hymn which they incessantly sing: saying . . .

"God the Father bless me, Jesus Christ defend and keep me," prayed Father Bromhead, "the virtue of the Holy Ghost enlighten and sanctify me this night and for ever . . ."

"Amen."

"Paul," said Sybil Straunge-Lacey, as they left the chapel. "Paul, I wish to speak to you."

"Where—" he began, taken by surprise. Usually her summons were at tea-time.

"Now. At once. In my room, please." Her voice was cold, her tone that of a grown person to a naughty child. He did not like it at all.

He liked it even less when, going up the stairs together, without speaking, they arrived in her room. The door was no sooner shut, than she began to weep. At first silently, then with noisy gulps. He did not know what to do. Was not sure whether to sit or stand, to comfort her, or to behave as if nothing were wrong . . .

Recollecting herself very suddenly, she said: "Do not sit down, please. Come away from that chair. I have something to say to you which I should wish you to hear *standing up*. Something so—" She broke off, a catch in her voice again. "Excuse me," she said, then with icy politeness, "I intend first to light a candle here at the statue of the Sacred Heart—that He may watch over my tongue. And that He may purify it from the *filth* which I shall have to utter . . ."

He could not understand and was afraid now. He thought, while she is lighting it I shall escape. And too: I will not be spoken to in this manner.

"Mrs. Straunge-Lacey," he began, his own voice cold.

But as if he had not spoken, she cut in at once: "Nicholas is from the house today—I feel this is the time to speak to you, before his return. But"—again the catch in her voice—"my God, and I do not blaspheme, my God, that I should have to use such words. The *deed* of course, but the words alone. So odious . . . my mouth is full of filth."

He stood already indicted—but of what? *What have I done?*

"Tell me," he said. "Kindly tell me what all this *is about*—"

Ignoring him still, she instead asked a question: "The jewels in a mother's crown," she said. "I entrusted you with her, did I not? Entrusted you with my daughter?"

"Yes, but—" He was not now surely to be blamed for the collapse of the Tay Bridge?

"And Our Lord will ask me, Jesus will say to me, what did you *do* with that jewel, your own little flower, were you not able to *protect her?* In her innocence, her purity . . . I loved her—as only a mother can love."

The air in the room was heavy. The fire burned brightly in the grate. Above on the mantel amongst the bric-a-brac, the ornaments, the faded cards, the photographs, Rose gazed at him: thirteen, fourteen, white-veiled for First Communion, solemn, her mouth a little open. I loved her too, he wanted to say. At the same moment, as if following his look, Sybil crossed over and took down the photograph in its velvet frame. Holding it in one hand, she thrust it at him—close, too near for him to see.

"Yes, Rose. *She.* It was she I entrusted to you. She who was to have belonged only to God. Who was to have been the Bride of Christ . . ." Then before he could protest, snatching it away again, she reached for a small miniature of Nick. So hasty was she that a flutter of cards fell after, lying on the carpet near the fire.

"Look at *this* now. Hold it," she said passionately, "yes, hold it in your hand. Look at his face. Twelve years of age, and this is the face of innocence. Is it not? *Is it not?*"

He stood dumbly, holding it, not wanting to look. She had moved away, and was weeping again.

"For everything to depend on Benoit," she cried, "as it does, as it does . . . You have seen what seriousness we have *there*. How can we depend? Nicholas' promise, to me, to Mr. Straunge-Lacey—yes, look at Nicholas' picture, look at it, he is not married, is he, nor ever likely to be . . . Look, look, look at that picture again in *all its purity* . . . And then ask what sword of sorrow pierces my heart . . ."

Then, "*No!*" she said as he stepped forward to lay down the miniature. "No, do not come near me. Please, do not come nearer." Her voice sharp. In her agitation she was pacing up and down; wisps of hair escaping her bun gave her a wild appearance. She spoke between sobs.

". . . this vagabond's life, this never settling, wandering . . . at first I thought it does not matter, he waits only *to be certain* . . . Alice, you see, it was to be Alice. But she, long ago, someone else—two children now . . . I—we have worried, we have worried. Yes. And I have spoken to him, how many times? Never an answer. Always 'soon, it will be soon' . . . I thought then it was only to wait. But yesterday, only yesterday—and all our hopes shattered. 'Why do you not marry?' I reproached him, for the twentieth time, 'Why do you not marry?' And then he said—" She glanced around wildly. "And then he said, 'I cannot. I am—'" She choked on the words. "He said, '*I am such a one as should not marry . . .*'"

She was silent for a few moments, taking out a handkerchief, dabbing savagely at her eyes. "He said then—he said then: 'And it is *he* has made me so . . .' And then he cried. Yes, he wept, Paul. *As I am weeping now . . .*"

Paul was silent. All words seemed to have been taken from him. What was to come next? What could be worse?

"Then he told me. He was so ashamed—such shame that he could not utter the words. And nor can I, nor can I . . . Our Lady of Sorrows, be with me now . . . he told me then something of your—beastliness. Of *what was done to him* . . ." She turned in her tracks and suddenly faced Paul.

"You polluter of young men—that have brought your *filth* into this house. No, do not dare to look me in the face. Avert your eyes . . . Yes, Nicholas trusted me with his secret, his secret sorrow, he told me *all*. We wept, we wept together. 'How,' I asked him, 'how, *why*?' . . . And then, 'I was seduced,' he said. 'Mother,' he told me, 'Mother—I speak to you as a young girl might, as a *maiden*—I was seduced by one *versed in the ways of the world—*'"

He could not believe what he heard. Now he was less able to speak than ever. Words attributed to Nick continued to flow from her—held together by calls on Our Lady, on St. Aloysius. Unlike Nick as they were, granted that the words had first to pass through Sybil's brain, the reported words were just recognisably Nick at his most melodramatic. In sudden cold anger, he said, interrupting her: "*Those* were his words? Did he use *those* words?"

She chose to ignore him. ". . . And then, ah *then* when you had muddied him, rubbed him in all the filth of your beastliness—you *tired of him* . . . Yes, I know that too . . . Nothing would do for you but you must look for another fresh flower, another to despoil—and this time, this time, it is no less than Our Lord's own Bride. Only *that* is good enough for you, only there is there innocence enough for your depraved tastes—that like some beast or animal we see in the field cannot tell if he lies with man *or* woman. Bringing with you God alone knows (for Our Lady does not, Her Son would not allow that she should . . .), *God alone knows* what disease and dirt from your manner of living . . . No! No, no, do not try to *speak*, I do not hear you . . . Do you think I did not notice *how* our daughter was at the end? Weak, nervously prostrate, deeply sorrowing, without any joy left in life . . . She knew, *she knew*—I am certain of that. *And* knew that she must spend the rest of her life with something foul that she could not understand, could not even name. I thank God, to think that I should have to *thank God that she did not live—*"

"You speak what you will regret," he said, raising his voice above hers. "You lie—"

"Who are *you* to speak of lies? Hypocrite—what did Christ say—'not that which goeth into the mouth, defileth a man, but that which cometh out of the mouth . . .' No, no, do not now try to justify yourself . . . There is nothing to be said, nothing that *can* be said—Oh, my dear God, I think now of the Seven Sorrows of Our Lady, it is only in thinking of those that I can, *shall* bear mine—"

"Listen to me now—that I should be allowed to speak—" He sought for words that would arrest her. But his own distress—he could not. "What you *say* that I have done—"

"Dear God, Mother of Divine Grace, Mother inviolate, Mother *undefiled*—pray for us . . . I cannot—that these matters should even be *spoken* of . . . I cannot tell Mr. Straunge-Lacey. It would kill him, it would kill him. The shock. And you—" Her voice rose and rose. He feared that she would become quite out of control.

"And, and you have care of *our grandchild*—what suffering do you think *that* is to me now? And I can do nothing about it. Nothing. Confession, the Sacrament of Confession—have you been to Confession?"

Taken aback, still shaking, he said: "That is not your affair—"

"As I thought, as I thought—there is to be no repentance, and you have *care of a child*—Refuge of Sinners, Comfort of the afflicted, *pray for me*—Nicholas, I can forgive Nicholas, innocence is so vulnerable, but remember this, *remember the words of Jesus*—'Whoso shall offend one of these little ones which believe in me, it were better that a millstone were hanged about his neck, and that he were drowned in the depth of the sea . . .' "

He had to get out. He was afraid now that, made forcibly silent, he might use his anger in action. That he would shake her, *demand* that she listen . . .

"I see that you try to escape. Go, go, you may go. *You* do not care—" As he put his hand on the doorknob, she made one last attempt.

"You killed my daughter," she cried, "you have ruined my son . . ." Then, her voice turning almost to a wail, " 'Is it nothing to you, all ye that pass by? Behold and see if there be any sorrow like unto my sorrow . . .' "

There were three days to go before Christmas. Nick would return tomorrow. He passed a sleepless night—he had not expected anything else. In the morning before breakfast (which he scarcely dare attend) he was brought a note from Sybil Straunge-Lacey. It said only:

"In future it would be better if you did not visit us. I cannot forbid you the house naturally, but I should be grateful if you would in future send Beatrice to stay accompanied only by Miss—" then she had crossed this out—"*Mrs.* Hurst. You may give the child any explanation you wish. Elfrida, I thank God (and Our Lady who has surely watched over her) is not here. She *may not* come to stay with you. Although she is of an age to make her own decisions, she will of course do as I wish. I shall not tell her why a visit is forbidden.

"While I may regret in the light of day some of the *manner* of my speaking last night, I do not regret *what* I said. They remain my true thoughts. I wish for as little as possible to do with you now, and in the future. Except in public and where politeness requires, I shall not speak to you . . .

"In deepest sorrow, and disgust, I remain yours,

"Yours

"Sybil Straunge-Lacey"

He did not know how to get through the day. He felt like a criminal, and could think only of how soon Nick would arrive. He was expected in time for dinner.

Benoit, rising very late, was to be seen extravagantly dressed. "Utterly mashy" as Elfrida had said in her last letter. His dress coat was strikingly tight-waisted, so that his claims to be corseted rang true. His trousers, cut very close, had the bottoms well up to show fancy buttoned boots. His waistcoat was embroidered with silk flowers. For the first time he affected a monocle. Had Paul been less distressed he would have found it amusing.

The weather had turned colder still. But he knew that whatever it was like, if at all possible Bea and Emily always took a walk (that was

why, Emily said, "she has now so many roses in her cheeks . . ."). He
said to Emily: "May I join you?"

She appeared surprised, but pleased. They talked on the way—Bea
running just a little ahead, her unused muff dangling round her neck.
Imp, eight now but as active as ever, rushed out to join them. Emily
insisted they go back for a ball, so that Bea might throw it for him.

They walked in the direction of the lake (scene of Everard's death, of
Elfrida's declaration . . .).

She said suddenly: "You are not happy, Mr. Rawson."

"Are you?"

"Yes," she said simply. "In so far as I can be now. I have at least
something of what I wanted—"

"Which was?"

"A home," she said. "A small child to care for. Bea, you see, is the
age Harry would be . . . But," and she turned to him, "why do we
speak of *me?* You answered me Scotch fashion just now. I ask you
again—is something perhaps not—right?"

"Nothing," he said, suddenly afraid that if he told her only a little,
however small, he would tell *all* . . . "Nothing, there is nothing. Fatigue only—"

"Bea!" called Emily, "Bea, you do *not* run near the water. Not near
the water, *please* . . ."

Dinner was a torment. Nick had arrived after the dressing bell. Paul
did not see him until they came down. There were then too many people present for him to say anything. The meal itself seemed unending.
Only a day or two later and it would have been a fast day dinner, and
the more quickly over . . . Benoit's talk was all of the stage door. Father Bromhead watched him but said nothing. Nick urged him on,
pleading ignorance, wanting everything explained, described. Only
Aunt Winefride seemed thoroughly to enjoy it—listening avidly, popping eyes on Benoit and not her soup. Augustus Straunge-Lacey, in a
dour mood, said little. Sybil was icily polite to Paul. Nick she treated as
one just returned from hospital, or a hazardous journey. "You look
unusually tired," she told him twice.

"I want to speak to you—alone," Paul said, at the first opportunity
after the meal. "Now. In your room." He felt already tired and dizzy
from emotion and lack of sleep. He feared he sounded like Sybil last
night . . .

"Alone? Really—what is this? Sudden *brotherly* love?" He was smiling, although his voice was light and nervous. He threw an arm about
Paul's shoulders. Paul shook him off angrily.

"Now," he said, "upstairs. At once—"

He could hardly wait. Going up the wide staircase, he felt the words tumbling through his head, angry, bitter, righteous. Once in the room— in two minutes he had spilled out everything. He stood there shaking.

Nick too stood. Smiling. Paul could not believe that he smiled. He said to Paul: "But what is the *fuss?* It will all pass . . . If she has not the chance to excite herself again. She is like that. A person just for the moment. I was not too serious. It was what she wanted and needed, that I should tell her something of that sort—it has given her a great deal of excitement. Coloured her life in vivid hues for *days* to come . . ."

"Damn all that, damn it. Damn you that you are never serious. *This* was serious, *is* serious—" He grew confused, could not think now what Nick had said. "You were not serious, damn you, bloody damn you? Never serious—"

"Look, dear Paul—and language, language, these walls are not *accustomed*, you know . . . Look, it is not as you think. I am a very serious person. Very serious—"

"Those words, those absurd words, phrases—'maiden, seduction, unversed in the ways of the world,' all those"—he was shouting now. Nick raised his hand and, humiliated, Paul lowered his voice: "You spoke those absurd phrases, truly?"

"But of course—"

"For fun. When you did not mean them? For a bloody lark—"

"But *of course I meant them.*" He sounded genuinely astonished. "Language does not alter content. Of course they were meant—"

"*Now* what am I to believe? And when you *smile—*"

"Yes, I meant them all." He shrugged his shoulders. "At the time."

"Damn all that too—indeed, did you, indeed—"

"Yes, but yes. *At the time* . . ." He crossed over to the bureau by the fireplace. Coming back with a box of cigars, he offered Paul one. "No? Are you certain? The R.O. has his fangs drawn these days . . ."

"You tell me you are serious, and you fool around damnably. *Will you be serious*—damn you that thinks you may say what you please to whom you please."

"Yes. I *may* say what I please. And do what I please too. I always have. And God can forgive me. God will."

"And that, that is the sin of presumption—"

"Ah, we are grown quite the little theologian. It cannot be already seven, *eight* years since it was I so carefully explaining these little points . . No, I tell you, God understands. He can see into the secrets of men's hearts—"

"Then he must see that you have told *foul lies*. Calumny—not detraction but *calumny*—mock my theology if you wish, but that I *know*. And you *will not discuss it*—damn you, you *will not discuss it seriously* . . ."

He said casually, "Why did you not betray me then? Why not?" His voice was light still, but he was not smiling. "Perhaps there were no thirty pieces of silver, eh? Was that why? Nothing to be gained—"

"Everything to be gained. Everything. My good name. My—my . . . Of course I did not betray you. And that you knew, that I would not. That I never would." To his horror, he had begun to cry. Now he would be powerless, at Nick's mercy. "I would not—and it is *Rose* I think of . . ."

"Ah, *Queen Rose of the Rosebud garden of girls, Come hither, the dances are done, In gloss of satin and glimmer of pearls—*" His voice broke. "Damn you, now I say damn *you* . . . She spoke the truth, the Wise Woman—no bloody false accusation there. As surely as you killed her with your own hands, you killed Rose—"

Paul struck him. The blow glancing off Nick's jaw, knocked him back for a moment. Then righting himself, he said shakily, "Yes, yes, I say it again." He too had begun to cry. "Queen lily and rose in one. If you had not taken her away, *stolen* her from us, our treasure—she would be safe now. In her convent. Praying . . . And instead you—" He broke down completely. He said angrily, "I lost Franz, you know. This autumn. I lost him—and someone must pay . . ."

"Why should it be I? What have I to do—"

"You betrayed me, you know. You did betray me. When you took Rose. Now—what does it matter *what* I say, so long as I have done with you. And that you are *punished* . . . Where is she now, my Rose, that was to save me? Deflowered. And by you. Gone. Killed, by you . . ."

"You dare to call me a murderer—"

"I do. I do." His mouth, in repose so beautiful, had become square, ugly. He shouted now: "You are, you *are*. A *murderer* . . ."

And he could be. If he stayed, he would be. (How could he ever have been afraid of what he might do to Sybil?) Here he could, might kill. The anger rising and rising in him. Shaking his head with it, he shouted at Nick.

He could not remember afterwards what he said. What Nick said in return. The shouting went back and forth. There was nothing new. The old was enough, and pain enough.

When very suddenly he left, he went clumsily, noisily down the small staircase, not caring if anyone heard him, if anyone met him. He went straight outside into the grounds, seeing on the way only a startled Benoit. "I say—what's the hurry . . ."

He made straight for the arboretum. In the darkness he was scarcely aware of where he was. An icy rain was falling, and the wind had got up. There was little or no moon. He did not mind that soon he was lost. He blundered about from avenue to avenue. Sometimes knocking against a tree trunk. His face was scratched. His hands, which he put out for protection, grazed by the bark.

He had put on no coat. As the night wore on, he found that he could not stop crying. He cried for Kate. After three or four hours, perhaps more, he made his way back to the house. The main door was shut. He discovered a side window unlocked and climbed in. Then he crept upstairs and, shivering, into bed.

Again, he did not sleep. At first light, he packed his bags, leaving on a table all the Straunge-Lacey Christmas presents. He wrote a note for Emily, explaining that he had received an urgent message late last night. "Family and business affairs . . . please console little Bea." He enclosed money for their journey back. "You are to stay until the festivities are over . . ." Another, very curt, note for Sybil.

He came downstairs very early. Kissing boughs hung in the hall, ready for Christmas. Holly and ilex were massed, dark green. He felt cold still, and could not stop shivering. Going outside, he told a startled coachman, barely up, that he must leave on the first train.

"Queen lily and rose in one . . ." He tossed from side to side of the bed. He thought at first he was at home, then was not certain. "Come hither the dances are done, are done, are done, are done . . ." Such a throbbing in his head, he thought it would burst. He heard voices too. But when painfully he lifted his head all about him was black. Darkness everywhere. "Cedar of Lebanon, Cedar of Lebanon, Cedar of Lebanon . . ." How long have I been here? He could not remember coming home—if I *am* home . . . He was hot. Very, very hot. Hotter than he had ever been. And he could not breathe. "*Rosa mystica, Rosa mystica, ora pro nobis . . . ora pro nobis . . .*" He thought as he tried to rise and fell back again, that he must get water. Water. Water. He was thirsty, so very thirsty . .

But when he looked again there was water all about him. I am at sea . . . The icy cold waves, he thought they would engulf him. Now he was cold again. He could not breathe. Hot, I am so hot . . .

A voice cried, "The bridge is doon!" Then again, and again. He knew there was something he must do—but the waters, they were about to cover him. "Where's ma bairn? *Where's ma bairn . . .*" If only he hurried he could yet save everyone. But he saw then that it was too late . . . ". . . and ye shall be left few in number . . . because thou wouldst not obey the voice of the Lord thy God . . . There is no peace saith the Lord unto the wicked . . . unto the wicked . . . unto the wicked . . ."

The wreckage was strewn all about in the water. Cushions, planks, iron stanchions, combs, window frames: light or heavy—all bobbed upon the water. Ghastly flotsam. He thought there were bodies. He did not want to see bodies, but they would not go away. He was searching for Rose now. Floating on the water was a leather case—he saw the initials in the corner—"M.E.N." . . . "I will rescue that," he called out, ". . . bring it to Emily . . . look what I have rescued for you, Emily."

But the water had come right up to the edge of the Kissing Gate. The steps were quite covered. He saw then that Nick was standing at the Gate. Opening it a little, then swinging on it . . . He tried to call out, but now he was too parched. The Gate made a creaking noise—whenever he tried to breathe. The effort was painful. Nick, swinging to-and-fro, wouldn't speak but only smiled.

"I've done with you," he called out to Nick, but when he looked again, it was Alan Dunbar. "You drunken sot," he said to Paul, "you know me—bloody drunken sot . . ."

Rose came for him. She was dressed for her wedding. "In gloss of satin and glimmer of pearls," he said dully, over and over again. But she didn't hear him. Kate would help him. He heard that he was weeping. He cried out for Kate . . .

"Drink this," said the voice.

"No . . . No . . ."

"Drink this."

A very long time later, he awoke and said: "Why are *you* here?"

"This is my home now," she said. "You employ me. And you have been very ill. You *are* very ill . . ."

It seemed to be only minutes later when she said: "Today you must try to eat something . . ."

"How long have I been here?"

"Two weeks. But you are going to be all right . . ."

"What *happened?*"

"You closed the house for Christmas, sent all the servants home. You told no one in Downham that you had returned. I imagine you must have been ill from the night of your arrival . . . By and by, I expect you will remember more . . . When *we* arrived you were very ill indeed. Delirium, fever . . ."

"And you—when were you here? Why did I come alone?"

"Business affairs summoned you back—whatever they were they have had to take their chance—and you wrote to me to bring Bea back early in the New Year. I had your letter, but I took the liberty of interpreting it my way. I told the Straunge-Laceys you had said 'the day after Christmas.' After much grumbling and some unpleasantness, we left on that day. I anticipated that you might be angry. But I think what we have is the Hand of God . . ." She laid a glass by the bed. "And now, so that you may return to sleep, I shall read to you . . ."

The next day she said: "Would you like your sister, Miss Rawson, to visit you? I have not allowed you anyone as yet—but today, I could permit her to see you . . ."

He wondered how Sarah would have reacted to such authoritativeness. "And she—what does she say?"

"There has been no trouble. We are not persons very alike, but we are at one in our concern for you . . . And your aunt, Mrs. Rawson—she shall come too . . ."

"You would allow it?" he asked mockingly. "I am permitted *two* visitors?"

But she did not notice. She said very seriously: "I think so—now. Before I would not have. I have had to be very strict." In the same tone of voice, she said, "You were not expected to live, you know."

At that moment, Bea rushed into the room.

"No one shall stop me—darling Papa, say you will be well, Mrs. Hurst cried about you, I wanted to come in . . . and *look*, I have made you a scrap picture, it has taken me *two whole days* . . . no, don't send me away, please please please . . . Listen to this, I just learned it and it is *very* very difficult . . . 'O would I were where I would be! There would I be where I am not: For where I am would I not be, and where I would be I can not . . .'"

THIRTY

The things that are really for thee gravitate to thee. You are running to seek your friend. Let your feet run but your head not. If you do not find him, will you not acquiesce that it is best you should not find him? For there is a power, which, as it is in you, is in him also, and could therefore very well bring you together if it were for the best . . .

EMERSON

The note for Sarah from Richard said only that he wished her to come and see him. ". . . it is about Laura—again. If you would care also to stay to luncheon? Although it will be dull company—both girls, as you probably know, stay with my sister over Easter . . ."

Easter already—and the school at Almeida House more than halfway through its second year. So far she and Jessie had had much to congratulate themselves on: the place ran smoothly, the atmosphere was good, and amongst the girls there seemed to be a spirit almost of adventure. The school had a full quota of pupils now of whom nearly half were boarders. This summer they hoped to have three sitting for the Cambridge Senior Locals (it would have been four if one of the parents had not raised horrified hands at the very notion), one of whom would be Cicely Ingham. For the Junior Locals there would be as many as eight.

They had put on the prospectus: ". . . Almeida House School . . . affording facilities for a thorough education in Classics, Modern Languages, Mathematics, Science, etc., meeting at the same time the most rigid requirements of parents in regard to accomplishments . . ." They had stressed too, "Modern methods throughout . . ." Sarah had wondered at first if she and Jessie had not promised more than they could produce, but as they had been more than usually fortunate in obtaining staff to the standard they required (and that in spite of their being far from any large city), all seemed to be working well. The main problem seemed to be that although many of the girls were interested in using their brains, it was often their parents who complained that proper importance was not being given to "accomplishments."

"Those *accomplishments*—the word will be written on my heart when I die," Jessie said on the last day of term. "Here's *six* complaints come in . . . Miss Attwater's Mama: 'My daughter has no head for arithmetic and I should be grateful if you would arrange immediately for her to spend each arithmetic lesson doing *vocal music*—singing will be of *much* greater use to her . . .'; and Miss Mortimer's: '. . . we are not at all impressed with either manners *or* deportment and can only conclude, as Mr. Mortimer fears, that you think learning to be more important than ladylike behaviour . . .'—and Sarah—we have Mrs. Ettisley: '. . . her papa too notices that she is reading *much more* than before—we are *very concerned*, since her mental powers *must not be strained*—we count on you to put a stop to all this . . .' And so on. Shall I tell them they have chosen the wrong school?"

Sarah thought, the evening before going over to lunch at the Abbey: I should not have favourites. But she had found it in the end impossible not to feel the most (but secretly—though she would defy anyone to discover) for Cicely and Laura. Laura the first, because she had known her before perhaps, but both of them because they were Richard's daughters. Cicely would be eighteen in the summer—she hoped to go on to Bedford College, in London. By her own choice. She said that she did not want Cambridge but would not give a reason. Sarah had wondered if it was to do with Francis' death—about which she never spoke. It was to have been him to teach her some Latin . . . Her mother's death she seemed, after the first shock, to have taken very resignedly. She had inherited her mother's placid, calm nature.

It was Laura rather who was not recovering. Now, nearly two years after, she still spoke of Frances Ingham in the present tense. "Oh, Mama likes *those* . . ." she would say of something, or "*Mama* always says that we should . . ." It was a tense little face, hers—and sometimes when Sarah saw her, pen gripped tightly, bent over her exercise book, she would be reminded suddenly, shockingly, of anxious little Flo . . .

It was that night, before going to Richard's, that Sarah had the idea. An idea of such simplicity—so *obvious*—that she could not think why she had it for the first time only now. Except that . . . any earlier, it would not have been seemly. It is not really seemly now, she thought.

Richard held up the drawings. "You have seen these, or ones like them?" He was standing by the window. The sun had just come out after a shower; it gleamed on the wet trunks of the great beeches.

She came nearer to look at what he held. To be so close to him . . . And she could not help but think of the idea she had had. She trembled. She did not trust her hand to take the drawings from him.

"This first one," he said. It was in pen and ink and showed a stage-coach of perhaps fifty years earlier. The coach was full both inside and out but—every person and all the horses too, were upside down. A pair of top boots poked from the window where a head might be expected. The horses in their traces lay and kicked . . . The second picture, more conventional, showed a post chaise in full gallop: the only unusual feature, a Grecian robed woman standing arms outstretched on the roof, as if to leap . . .

She forgot about herself then at once. Felt ashamed. In the name of their easy friendship, she said: "I am so sorry. Truly sorry. I had thought Laura improving. She *seems* often happy enough . . ." She paused. "At the beginning of this term, I had wondered. We have five—like those. I had shown you one, I think? They are not in the drawing class of course—the master who comes for that wants only perspective and drawing from the class—they may not choose a subject. But these—of Laura, they have been found in of all places, her geography exercise book—and another at the end of her English composition. Two, very small, miniatures almost, in between two arithmetic problems . . . After showing you the first, I had thought to say nothing more—"

He said sadly, "I think there is n-not anything to d-do. We must let her—if it helps . . . And perhaps with t-time . . ."

"Oh, but I understand your distress. It is—as if my niece, if Bea were to draw the Tay Bridge breaking . . . Accidents. Accidents—" then remembering Francis—"which is not to say that *illness* and death don't have as bad an effect. The death of her brother . . . she has had so much. Cicely, she is of stronger material—although I fancy there that Francis is still much mourned." She wanted to say: "Laura is like you, I think—" After a moment, as he was putting away the drawings, she did say it—but she could not add, as she wished to: "And *that* is why I love her so dearly . . ."

He did not comment though, but said only, "She was very c-close to her mother. And thirteen, f-fourteen, it was not a good age that it should happen—"

He showed her to a seat. She wondered how far away he would sit. If I am to speak, she thought . . . When she had arrived she had been kept waiting for perhaps twenty minutes or more, which had given her time to become more than usually self-conscious in his presence.

"I am *so* s-sorry," he had said, when at last he came in. "My m-mother —she has some indisposition. I had just now to spend some time with the d-doctor. We shall, I think, have to have in a c-consultant."

"Then it is serious?" she had asked. "I am—"

"No—just puzzling. Unexplained. She k-keeps to her room, but is d-dressed and up . . ."

Now he had rung for a drink. He was talking again about Laura.

"I have to thank you, for everything. Almeida House, it has been more than a s-school for her. I am more than g-grateful. You have been k-kind to me in trouble now twice . . . In C-Cambridge . . ."

She noticed that he did not mention the terrible event in her own life—his role in it. She would do so.

"And you to me. It is *I* to be grateful . . ."

Silence. She did not know if she had embarrassed him. She thought not, for he raised his eyebrows only and half-smiled. She burst out suddenly: "It was an assault you know. What happened to me. I had no choice—or chance. I should have reported it, at once—if only to save others. And later when . . . I should have told you both, you and Mrs. Ingham—but I did not see then any point. I do not now. I should perhaps not be saying any of this—" But she could not stop now. She had wanted to for so long, that he might not think ill of her: "It was some sort of misplaced loyalty—to that family. The family where— Francis was taken ill . . . It was the uncle, who was not quite . . ." She talked on, and as she told the story, it was as if a great load were lifted.

She ended: "I am of course quite over it—so long ago . . . and I am very strong as to mind and body. The scars of the mind, they are quite healed. And as to—the other, I understand there was no lasting damage . . . But still, you know, I am in your debt. *Your* rescue—Mrs. Ingham's kindness . . ."

He had flushed. "That—it was what anyone . . . But about—the other. I am so s-sorry. So very v-very sorry . . ."

She could not remember afterwards how they had seemed to move quite easily—or perhaps not so easily? from that to everyday topics.

"It is agreed you stay to luncheon? Yes, of course. I had hoped that Matthew Staveley would join us—but he must p-parochialise as he calls it and has not the t-time today."

"The weeks before Easter," she said. "It is always busy. And—he does so much for us at Almeida House. The girls he takes for classes—they all look forward to his visits. And that he does it—teaching them—when he doesn't believe in it . . . that I particularly admire."

The time was passing. If she was to make real her idea of the night—then it must be soon. Already she had found that she was *almost* not alone with him for luncheon. *I must speak now* (only it was so outrageous, the idea: coming to her in the middle of the night so that when she had tried, in vain, to sleep again she had wanted, hoped to dream of the Kissing Gate. To know if she did right . . . She remembered the time in Paris with Paul, when they had told each other of their dreams about the Gate. "You can't order it, though . . ." she had said).

"You—take a holiday, Miss Rawson?"

"Not this time, I think. There was a question perhaps—that I might accompany my brother and niece. They are at the sea, you know. He convalesces still . . . And then my aunt, Mrs. Rawson—she would have liked me to join her in Harrogate—she will be there over Easter. But there is so much to be done . . ." I am talking on, she thought, for the sake of *not* speaking. *I must speak.*

Instead she said, with a rush of her old aggressive manner: "You are not I think very kindly disposed towards my aunt? No—say nothing . . . I *see* your face when she is mentioned. And your cold tone . . . Do not think I have not noticed. And it will not do. There is *no one* must dislike her. Laura, who has met her at the school—she reads there you know—she worships her. She said, 'Mrs. Rawson is the kindest person I ever met in my *whole* life . . .' Everyone loves Kate—and yet you . . ." She poked at the carpet with her boot, stubbing in the toe: "But there is always someone," she said in more even tones, "there is always someone we dislike" (And for me, once, it was *you* . . .). "We cannot help it. Childhood memories. Perhaps it is not good to be in the schoolroom together? Childish rivalries—and who knows what?"

She was amazed at herself. He too. He appeared shocked. She was not able to say anything more than trivialities for the next half hour—and wondered in fact if she should not apologise . . .

Then towards the end of the meal—they were alone, and the cloth had been taken away for dessert—she thought suddenly: *now* . . .

"I should like to ask you something . . ."

"Yes?" He had cut into an apple. She stared at it, watched as the stalk fell off. The skin of the apple was russet, wrinkled.

"I wish to say, Mr. Ingham . . . I know that what I shall ask . . . that it is wrong, quite out of place for me to . . . except that it is only custom. That alone . . ." Her voice was not very firm—to give herself confidence she spoke a little too loud: "There is nothing in the Bible," she almost shouted, "nothing that *I* can find. Or in the law of the land . . . The rule that I may not—is custom only—"

"What is?" he asked. He looked patiently surprised. "What is c-custom only?"

Now she would say it: ". . . That a gentleman should ask—that it should always be *he* who asks a lady . . ."

"Yes, Miss Rawson, b-but . . ." He had paused, knife in hand, the apple barely touched. His expression was puzzled. He smiled: "Ask what?"

She saw that what she said had not been taken personally. But it *must* be . . . In a great rush, she said now:

"I know that it is only two years since, and that you cannot . . . that you still . . . I *know* that you feel the loss of Mrs. Ingham still . . . it is not that I am unaware but what I am asking is—if you could, if you would—ever consider—marrying me?"

It was said . . . And not a word of it was as she had planned in the night (but for men it could not be easy either. She remembered now with a pang of conscience, Matthew Staveley . . .). It had seemed to her then so simple, such a splendid plan. She had worked it all out.

There was a very, very long silence. This time she did not look at him at all but stared straight ahead at the gargoyles in the fireplace. And they stared back.

"What," he said, "what d-does one say?" She thought but could not be certain that he sounded—it could not be—amused . . . "I am not certain, you s-see, how a l-lady is accustomed to b-behave—in these matters . . ."

The colour had flooded her face. She felt that the birthmark too—as ever, spreading, deepening. *I am ugly*, she thought.

But he waited now surely that she should say something else? He had said—I do not know how to answer. Closing her eyes tight shut, she plunged again.

"I love you. I dare to say that. I love you. I have loved you ever since —that day. Or soon, soon after . . ." The words tumbled out: "I would be mother to Laura—and to Cicely if she would let me. Isabella is married and would not need me . . . I am thirty-two and I know that there are at least a dozen perhaps fourteen years between us—but they are not of great importance. And—" she paused a moment—"I can—if you wished . . . if you would want, I could, I *would* give you a son . . ."

Then she burst into tears.

He was perturbed at once: getting up, putting an arm about her shoulders. She said, "I don't play the man's part very well . . ."

"No," he said, "you are not very m-manly—" But once started she could not stop. He said, "You must come back in the drawing-room— and we will d-discuss it . . ."

Fifteen minutes later, quite calm again, she sat on the sofa, a glass of brandy beside her. He had not said "yes"—but certainly, most certainly, he had not said "no" . . . And because she had stopped crying, she had been able to explain herself. To say that she knew of course he did not love her—yet. But one day, perhaps? And that it was not good for man to be alone . . . and, and . . . every thought from the night-watches.

"And the Abbey," she said proudly, "I would not worry that I am not born to it, I should manage very well. These matters, they do not worry me—"

"Before I s-say anything myself," and he smiled: "I s-should have to ask—the b-business of Almeida House—what of *that?*"

"Oh, but I have thought of all that—and was to have said it right at the beginning. You would see—I should keep the school . . . Miss Hudson is a more than equal partner. I can do *both*—be Mrs. Ingham at Downham Abbey *and* joint headmistress of Almeida House . . ." The brandy lent fire to her tongue. "You would see. Too much to do is anyway better than too little—it is not as if I should try to be, say, a parson's wife and also run the school—that would be difficult. But anyway too much to do is better than too little. Most people are not using up a tenth part of the energy they have. My mother . . . I remember. It is too little not too much to do that kills . . ."

"B-bravely spoken—all of it," he said. "And now—"

"I should manage very well," she interrupted. "You would not have cause for complaint. Although people might say—"

Now it was his turn to interrupt. "People—p-people, we are not to c-concern ourselves about them. The Inghams, they have b-been here m-many years—they do always just as they p-please . . . No more of that, M-Miss Rawson—"

But now, soon, the moment would come when she would have to leave. When he would have to give an answer . . . She finished her brandy, refused another—and waited.

He told her then what an honour it had been, and how he could not but be moved, and was *not at all* shocked (". . . since there m-must be a f-first of everything, and even if you are first only in D-Downham . . ."), that it should have been *she* who asked. But—and again he smiled: "Allow me to b-behave perhaps as a l-lady would in s-such circumstances—and ask for t-time to think . . ."

But yes, of course. (Had she not done the same herself to Matthew Staveley?) And such a decision, to think that it might be made on the spot—when, as he said, he had not so much as *suspected* . . . So this is how men feel, she kept telling herself, when *they* propose where they know it to be unexpected . . .

He held one of her hands in both of his. It was the longest touch she had ever had. She could only think, standing there: the *dreams* I have had . . . The colour flooding her face again.

"I shall t-tell you to your f-face. I would not b-believe in doing such a thing by l-letter . . . You would perhaps c-come to luncheon again? N-next week?"

That evening back at Almeida House, the last thing before going to sleep, she took from her drawer the old faded daguerreotype of Grandmother Sarah, Big Sarah, Sarah-Mother as Kate had called her. The face, so like her own, looked straight at her. I even *feel* like her, she thought—as if I had inside me (as indeed I have) some part of her . . .

"Would *you* have done what I did today?" she asked the picture. "Would you have been so bold—defied convention, cocked a snook at custom? For that is what I have done—and *I am not ashamed* . . . Would you have done it?"

No. Definitely no. But when she asked, "And would you have been *shocked?*" she felt that perhaps she would not—that she would have understood . . .

It was a very long week. Paul wrote from Filey and a postcard came too from Kate in Harrogate. She was well and much stronger . . . "I am out every day—some beautiful gardens are to be laid here, the Valley Gardens, in time for the Royal Jubilee next year . . ." Sibby sent fond love.

When the day came at last, she was too nervous almost to dress. Walking past the Kissing Gate on her way, she thought of every superstition—good or evil—to do with the Gate. If it would do any good, *I could believe them all.* Why had she not thought of burying a charm bag—something, anything of hers, of Richard's? I could do *even that* . . .

The Abbey seemed to be in some confusion: when she was admitted, servants were scurrying through the hall. A voice called from the top of the stairs, out of sight: "You've to send up when doctor arrives—eh? Quicksticks . . ." But she had waited only a couple of minutes in the drawing-room—when Richard came in.

Crossing the room, he took both her hands again in his, and said: "I wanted to s-see you at once—to s-say—that I have been thinking a g-great d-deal, that I have not c-come to a d-decision lightly—"

"I am sure you have not . . ." (O hands joined together—may we never never be separate again.)

". . . and that I think it would indeed be p-possible. So that I answer you t-today—with a 'yes' . . ." But before she could reply, he was saying quickly, apologising: "If I appear n-now d-distracted, it is that—you see, my m-mother's illness. She has t-taken a grave turn for the worse—last n-night, this m-morning. I d-did not wish to put you off . . ." He paused. "And—you will understand—that we m-may agree between our-selves, c-consider that we are engaged—but that as yet there c-can be no announcement—"

"But of course not . . ."

"The s-situation is very g-grave. We had thought it only weakness b-before, from some t-trouble inside. The consultant I spoke of last week —he was cheerful on his v-visit. But s-since, there has been internal b-bleeding, D-Doctor says . . . It is affecting now her m-mind. She wan-ders and is no longer quite c-clear . . ."

Torn between the sudden unbelievable rush of happiness—and her concern for him, she said: "Should I not leave?"

"No. Please, no." He managed to smile, "If you are to b-be of the household then you c-cannot escape with such ease . . ." Then more seriously: "If you would afterwards p-perhaps visit her with me?"

They were only just beginning the meal when a maid came rushing in—not waiting to pass the message through a manservant: "Mr. Ingham, sir, Nurse says as how t'old Mistress is shouting—and naming you, sir, an' miscalling folk—an' ye mun come, sir . . ."

Sarah said, "I shall come too." She knew that he wanted her to. And even though it looked as though Georgiana Ingham would not live to be her mother-in-law, she would wish to be there now.

The room was full of spring flowers—early narcissi, daffodils, a few vi-olets. But they could not mask the oppressive sick-room smell. Al-though the weather outside was quite chill, the large fire burning in the grate seemed to overheat the room.

In the four-poster, curtains drawn back, her once pretty face stretched, hawklike almost, Georgiana Ingham turned her head from side to side. She muttered only. The nurse told them that a few mo-ments ago only the shouting had stopped.

"She keeps fancying she sees Mr. Ingham—and then she's shouting, sir, because he's crossed her, or vexed her . . ." Her mind apparently was clear now for shorter and shorter periods.

Sarah sat by the bed, not far from Richard.

"Read to me . . ." The voice although weak was one used to com-mand.

"Read to me now—" She looked around the faces. "No—not you," she said to Richard. "My son stutters," she announced. "He stutters, stutters, stutters you know—" She tossed her head on the pillow: "Charles—bad father—son stutters. Charles laughs . . ." Then the expression on her face changed. She looked suddenly lucid.

"*Read to me.*"

"What would you like?" Sarah asked.

There was a pile of books by the bedside. She picked them up, skimmed the titles: *Amor vincit* by Mrs. Herbert Martin, *Dr. Caesar Crowl, Mind-Curer* by Paul Cushing, *Romola* by George Eliot, *Sex to the Last* by Percy Fendall . . .

She chose the George Eliot. She could feel herself watched. Mrs. Ingham asked to be propped up a little . . .

" 'Chapter One,' " Sarah read, " 'The Shipwrecked Stranger.

" 'The Loggia de' Cerchi stood in the heart of old Florence, within a labyrinth of narrow streets behind the Badia, now rarely threaded by the stranger, unless in a dubious search for a certain severely simple doorplace, bearing this inscription: *Qui nacque il divino poeta.* To the ear of Dante—' "

"Can't hear. Can't hear . . ."

Sarah raised her voice: " '. . . To the ear of Dante, the same—' "

"*Can't hear.* And don't know you, don't know you . . . Who are you?"

"Miss Rawson. From the school. Almeida House—"

"Never heard of it—no school here. No *school* here . . ."

Sarah began again. " '. . . To the ear of Dante, the same streets rang with the shout and clash of fierce battle between rival families; but in the fifteenth century . . .' "

"Who *are* you? I don't know you, don't know . . ."

Richard said patiently, "It is M-Miss Rawson, Mother—"

" '. . . but in the fifteenth century, they were only noisy with the unhistorical quarrels and broad jests of woolcarders in the cloth-producing quarters of San Martino and Garbo—' "

"Rawson—*she* is not Miss Rawson . . ."

Sarah closed the book. She said, "To read—I am not sure it is for the best—"

But Georgiana Ingham was growing very agitated: "Rawson . . . not Miss Rawson . . . that's not Miss Rawson . . . hair very red . . . red hair—"

Sarah said at once, "She thinks of my aunt. She is thinking of *Mrs.* Rawson . . ."

"No, no—not *Mrs.* Rawson. Red hair, bad girl, Miss Rawson . . ." She was slipping a little down the pillows.

Richard said nothing. She noticed his face very drawn—he looked almost frightened. She thought that it must upset him very much to be here.

"*She's* not Miss Rawson . . . Get her out of here . . . Out, get out . . . want *Miss Rawson* . . ."

Trying to soothe her, Richard stroked her hand.

"Want Miss Rawson . . . must tell her . . . bad . . . bad . . . *Richard* . . . Where's Richard?"

"Here—I am here . . ."

"Must tell Miss Rawson. Wicked . . . I have been wicked . . . *Is she there?* Must see her . . ." She had begun to cry, beating her free hand up and down on the coverlet. "Can't see . . . it's *black* . . . Can't see . . . *Is she there?*"

"Yes, yes. I am here," Sarah said, hoping it would help. "Miss Rawson is here . . ."

"Got to forgive—tell her. Miss Rawson—girl Kate, little Kate . . . can't marry my son . . . won't have it, *won't have it* . . . Georgiana always gets own way, own way . . ." The crying turned for a moment to a sort of laugh. She sounded pleased. "Got own way . . . *got own way* . . . Richard hand . . . take hand again . . . Miss Rawson—*hand* . . . give."

Sarah, confused, disturbed—put out a hand, felt it grasped, twisted—the sudden strength of a dying woman. Whatever this is about, she thought, I shall have for now to be Kate—for Richard's sake . . .

"Tell can't marry son, that's right . . . tell wicked lie, meant for best . . . can't let son go to *her* . . . Irish rubbish . . . rubbish . . . honour, has *honour*, foolish girl do anything for Richard . . . Easy"—she laughed again. "*Easy.*" The hand that held Sarah's pulled, clutched. "Tell her she's famine child . . . easy . . . tell her she's foul, tainted, ugh . . ." Her voice changed suddenly. It became for a few moments loud, and very clear.

"Miss Rawson, you are foul, riddled with it . . . unmentionable disease . . . tainted . . . *you should not ever give birth* . . ." Her voice weakened again: "Go on . . . do it . . . pretend doctor says . . . fine pair of legs John has . . . tell her John knows truth, brought her back from Ireland . . . secret disease, no marrying Inghams . . . Promise, Miss Rawson, promise . . . won't tell Richard . . . tell him anything, get rid of him . . . don't tell truth Richard's sake . . . give him *bad* children . . ."

Suddenly her voice rose: "Wicked . . . I was *wicked* . . . God . . .

tell me God forgives . . . meant well . . . saw Richard crying then . . . saw son crying . . . lost her, lost his Kate . . . did what I told her . . . *She did what I said* . . . yes . . . now must get Richard wife, quick, quick . . . Julia's beau, nice girl . . ."

Sarah, cold in spite of the heat in the room, was appalled, frightened too. And the expression on Richard's face . . . *What is all this?* she wanted to cry out.

"Good girl, Frances, make good match there . . . forget what I did . . . No, am *wicked* . . . I forget what I did . . . God can't punish if can't remember . . . only little lie . . . Kate sad, don't mind Kate sad— see Kate sad long, long time . . . don't care . . . God forgive me . . . *God forgive me* . . ." Suddenly, pulling her hands from theirs, she began to thrash about in the bed. Wildly, arms, legs, and all the time shouting, "God forgive me, must forgive . . . *must forgive!*"

Richard had leaned over her at once. The nurse was there too. Very soon, as soon as they could calm her enough, she was given another draught. After what seemed a very long while, she lay for the moment still—only her head tossing to-and-fro on the pillows, to-and-fro.

"I think," Sarah said, "that you must explain to me. It is—I think that, after all, we—are not to be married . . ." (*I shall not weep*, she thought.) "Please—you are to forget anything you may have said to me. You are not committed. You did not give me your word then or at any time . . . You must consider yourself, that you are—and *I* am too," she said defiantly, proudly (*I shall not weep*), "that we are both quite, quite free . . ."

He looked still too shocked to speak. Tea had been brought for them into the drawing-room. Gradually when he had drunk a little, and sat very quiet, she saw a little colour come into his face, that he looked calmer.

"And now," she said, reaching out, taking his hand, "and now . . ." She felt suddenly not thirteen, fourteen years younger but older, older by far.

"Richard dear, now—please—tell me everything . . ."

THIRTY-ONE

Elfrida's letter was forwarded when Paul and Bea and Emily had been at the seaside, in Filey, already two weeks. She wrote:

". . . I heard only the other day how ill you had been, Paul dear. (And only because Sarah wrote me a little note.) I hope from the bottom of my heart that you are in splendiferous health again—did you go abroad to convalesce? I expect too that is why you have not been to see us. But *why not* for Easter next week? You were always used to—

"Now, I should not have written that, because it sounds like a *reproach* and *it is not*—But dear Paul, I know that something is wrong since Mama will not speak about you *at all* and says only that Mrs. Hurst may perhaps bring Bea in July, but that you are not able to come. Of course I do not believe her. Hermione hinted that there was some kind of upset or 'words' at Christmas, and that you were in disgrace and had to absquatulate (do you remember how we used to wish just that for that horrid Franz Monkey-face, years and years ago when I was young?—I am *twenty-one* now . . .).

"I am only lately back from Hermione's (sadly, she lost a baby in February—that is why I stayed on) and am not sure now *what* I shall do or where I shall go. Perhaps France? I have a number of friends there from schooldays, and one of them is organising a group of women who will help especially women 'unfortunates'—it could be that I could do some good there. I would not want to stay at home . . . (Paul, I thought of coming up to see you unannounced, but that would not be fair, or right. Not just because Mama forbids it, but also because I think I must learn now really to Renounce you—Only, and I know that you do not mind my saying this—*Oh how I miss you—*)

"Well, the news is: about Hermione, I told you. Hubert progresses in the Novitiate, and has become a *little* solemn—not unlike my memory of Everard. Next, some very important Balkan professors came to see

the arboretum! Apparently there are trees in there which are *very* special—perhaps unique—

"About Nick—he has just left for Austria where he is to spend the
summer. He has just equipped himself *totally*—more if that is possible
—for mountaineering, which is the latest craze (he who used to mock
poor Everard now peppers his talk with grappling irons and crevasses
and bergschrunds . . .).

"And last of all, because it is the best and *happiest* news—Benoit is
to marry!! In June or July, I think. It is all very very sudden. À *mon
avis*, she is rather a confloption—and very young (only seventeen this
month), but he is head over heels—*and* she is quite outrageously suitable. She is a third cousin and the family—he is in the diplomatic corps
—have been in St. Petersburg till last year. Magdalen came to stay for a
party in January and I hear that it was *coup de foudre*—and that Benoit
has talked of nothing else since (unless it is clothes, that she may admire him the more—). He does not care to play the corker so much
since—and all that "stage-door" talk is gone. It was only for effect, I
think. Mama *and* Papa are of course absolutely delighted. So—happy
endings? Some people are indeed fortunate that they love where it is
permitted, and are loved in return—

"Does that sound bitter? Dear Paul, it is not meant like that. En *pas-
sant*—I am still utterly mashed on you . . . No, how *could* I write in
that sort of language? I am ashamed. It is not you that I do not take *au
serieux*, it is myself. I am afraid perhaps to put on paper *real* words like
—I love you, Paul, so very much. And I *always shall*. There—I promise
never to say it again!

"I pray for you every day. Please pray for me. From your loving
friend and sister,

"Elfrida Straunge-Lacey"

Twice in the first week at Filey, Emily was mistaken for Bea's
mother. "It is the hair," she said in explanation, adding with a smile,
"it cannot be the complexion . . ." And certainly Bea had the pinkest
possible cheeks to accompany her blond curls. When out with her, Paul
could not fail to be proud. It was her eyes only which recalled Rose—
and Nick. (The curls and waves might be Elfrida's, except that he
remembered Father had had strong, although dark curls. Tarley
too . . .)

Bit by bit, now that he was recovered, Paul was piecing together the
missing hours, and days, of his life. Emily, he found, had had words
with Sybil—rather stronger ones than she had at first admitted to.

"I held my ground," she said. "It was nothing."

"But," he said, "I cannot have it that you should be—shouted at in this manner. These matters, they were nothing to do with you. *You* were not the one at fault—"

"Your concerns, the *child's* concerns I should say rather, they are mine . . . And anyway," she said in firm tones, "I was brought up by a difficult aunt. I recognise bluster, and how far it may be challenged. Mrs. Straunge-Lacey . . . I had seen it all before, you know." She hesitated then. "It is not my place to say, Mr. Rawson—since I am employed only to teach and care—but it seems to me that you forget sometimes it is *you* in authority over Bea. She is your child. She is not and never will be the property of the Straunge-Laceys. Nor can I believe, from what you have told me, that her mother would have wished so. When I argued the point at Christmas, I stood proxy for your authority only, and the expression of your wishes—"

"Which were—"

"Yes." She smiled. "I was not on very strong ground there. But I had made the decision to leave early—it had been impulsive, I know—" She looked suddenly vulnerable. "But—instinctive. And it was not such a bad decision, was it?"

"If you had not made it, I would not be here to applaud it . . ."

He was able now to remember more and more of the illness. It came back to him like a dream remembered. He said to her one day: "You sent for a priest, did you not?"

"Yes," she said. "Yes, you had Extreme Unction. You were as grave as that. Two days delirious in an unheated house—it was not pretty . . ."

His recovery, though, had been very slow. Even when he grew a little stronger physically, he found that he was not captain at all of his thoughts, or his emotions. Tears were the order of the day. Morbid imaginings, depression, weakness. He wept, too late, for Catriona. Allowed to go out for short walks, he would cross and recross the market square, looking at Linden House—now occupied by a Dr. Goodall and his large family. He had bought it from Dr. Marriott, Father's successor, a Bradford man who had felt isolated and cut off in Downham.

Determined as ever not to lean on Kate, he went too far the other way, so that she reproached him gently: "You are never seen these days —when you walk out, why not call here? I see more of Bea than you, and I am only *great*-aunt to her . . ." But he was afraid. Once alone with her, he might spill out all his grief—and for that, how would he forgive himself? And yet, and yet, he thought, awake once in the watches of the night, is she not perhaps lonely? Do I not—again—do wrong?

It had been recommended that he go abroad to convalesce, as soon as he was strong enough. In March perhaps. He thought of the South of France, or Italy—so long as it was not Lake Garda—but he had been wanting in the energy to arrange it. In the end he had instead taken a house by the sea for the months of April and May, so that Bea too might have the benefit. He had thought also of asking Kate to join them, but by then he had heard that she was to join Sibby Helliwell and family in Harrogate . . .

He did not know Filey. Kate, who had been companion there many years ago, spoke well always of it. The wide stretch of beach promised to be very suitable for Bea. Five miles of clean sands could hardly be bettered. There was the attraction too of the Brigg. A mile-long natural pier of sandstone, with caves and gullies made by the sea, and a great deal to interest the naturalist—he fully intended some serious study. The Brigg was dry for several hours before and after low tide, and the rock pools left were reputed to be full of interest. They would not be far from the sea either, as the house they had taken was in the beautiful Crescent which wound round the cliff top, overlooking the wide bay.

He had reckoned without the weather. For the first ten days or so it was so bitterly cold as almost to send him home again. But by going out to walk, however stiff the wind, he gradually made himself stronger, until he finally began to welcome Filey Brigg with the northeast wind blowing, and the breakers crashing against the rock, higher and higher, drenching him with spray. Sometimes when he climbed down amongst the great boulders he felt that it might be dangerous. But he took no care.

They had servants with them and Bea's nurse. Their days soon took on a routine. Bea had her lessons with Emily every morning. He would go out and walk, or study and write up his finds of the day before. If the weather allowed all three of them would go out together in the afternoon. If not—and one afternoon it snowed—Emily would play games or read with Bea. Bea was almost seven now. Emily remarked one day, her voice almost deliberately light: "I have to say in honesty—and I would rather not—that in another three or at the most four years, Bea will need much more than I can provide."

The ground beneath him. Suddenly it was no longer firm. It was as if he had just begun to trust it—and then . . . Although he could not suppose she would stay forever. He had not even thought that he wished it.

"She could go to Almeida House," Emily continued. "That would seem to me an excellent idea . . . And since it would be by the day only, there would be no religious problem. Miss Rawson would be delighted, would she not?"

"She would scarcely take her so *young*," he said quickly. "And I cannot see what is the haste. Are you not happy with us? If that is the case, I would prefer honesty . . ."

They were all three in the pony carriage going down the steep hill from the Crescent to the sands. Seated opposite her, he could not miss the expression on her face. She had flushed, and there was a tremor of her cheek. But she replied coolly enough: "Honesty is precisely what I gave you. I am not accustomed to behave or speak deviously, unless some great occasion warrants it. And this was not such a one. You did wrong, I think, to question my sincerity . . ."

He knew that he should not have spoken as he had, but he was unable now to apologise. She had gone on immediately to talk to Bea, as if nothing had happened.

". . . and this afternoon we shall look especially for a starfish that has grown new arms. As Papa explained, when one is lost, another forms at once—so that we may perhaps see a little stump. Would it not be fine if we too could grow new limbs like that?"

He wished suddenly, desperately, that he could from somewhere conjure up another daughter, a son, who would need her. Or better still, that time, arrested, would allow the three of them to go on just as they were: here in Filey—lessons in the mornings, outings in the afternoons —such order to their days—forever and ever Amen . . .

". . . the hermit crab, Bea, has armour only on the front of his body —the soft part underneath he must protect by living in a shell that another has abandoned. He will adapt his body so that it fits the shell. For other habits of this crab—you must ask Papa . . ."

For the first fine day they had planned a very ambitious expedition. And at the beginning of the third week the weather changed for the better, and after two afternoons had been hot and sunny—the bitter March-like winds forgotten—they decided the next day should be the outing. The idea was to go to Flamborough Head, the great chalk cliff sticking out into the North Sea—scene nine hundred years before of a Viking invasion, and now the haunt of guillemots, puffins, kittiwakes. Even more and better birds were to be found on the cliffs above Bempton. Their plan was to ride over first by carriage and then to walk along the cliff top path between Bempton and Flamborough Head. On a clear day they were promised a spectacular view of Filey and its Brigg, and even beyond to Scarborough. *And*—an army of sea birds lining the cliffs . . .

He woke early. The whole sky above the sea was a deep rose colour. The sun was just coming up, and when daylight appeared the air prom-

ised to be warm and dry. And indeed when they set out, beneath a clear
sky, it was hot enough for June.

Bea was a good walker and had promised to stay always the far side
of Paul away from the cliff edge. She was very good and obedient that
afternoon—although she had sulked for about ten seconds a little earlier, because she might not bring Bébé with her . . . They were half
way along the cliff path when the sky darkened. It was very sudden.
They had not seen storm clouds gathering. But now this menacing grey-
black, all the time lowering. It had grown chill too.

At first sight he had thought it would be only an April shower, but
he realised now from the sudden stillness, the electric air, that they
could not now avoid a storm. Almost at once the rain began. A wind
with it too. He began at once to hurry them—so that they should be
down the cliff path and to safety before it worsened. But perhaps the
whole outing had been too ambitious for him because, although haste
and worry enabled him to move quickly now, he was at the same time
overwhelmed by sudden fatigue. The weakness of the convalescent. He
wondered seriously whether he might not fall by the wayside. For weeks
now, with his fatigue, he had suffered from sudden attacks of *déjà vu*.
He had one now. All the way down, hurrying them, helping them to
safety, the rain blinding him, running in rivulets—Emily pale and tense,
Bea exhilarated and loving it—he felt: I have been here before. Below
them, barely visible now, the water frothed, crashing angrily against the
rocks . . . He was afraid even to glance downwards.

I have been here before. I have been here before . . .

They could not drive back at once but had, all dripping as they were,
to take shelter in an inn near Bempton. After they had had a warm
drink, a lull in the rain allowed them to make the drive back. But they
were so wet, and the storm clouds so obviously about to break, that the
journey was a misery. Emily was very game, glad only that they were
safe—it was he weak-kneed, fearful still. She was concerned that he
might have activated his illness. She spoke of what must be done for
him as soon as they returned: "I did not nurse you for all those weeks
so that you might have licence to begin all over again. We have been
foolhardy that we did not ask locally how the weather might be . . ."
She did not seem much worried for Bea, who was continuing to enjoy
the excitement. *Her* first thoughts had been not for Paul but for Bébé.
"How good that I *didn't* bring her, Papa—to think how she might have
been blown away over the cliff side . . ." And then, "Shall we have a
storm, do you think? A real storm? Say, please, that we shall have
thunder and thunder and *thunder*—may I stay awake for it?"

He would not have thought she would have much choice . . . but when they were back and she had had her supper, tucked up in bed, she fell asleep almost at once. He had been reading *The Princess and Curdie* to her and, looking up for a moment, saw that she no longer listened. Emily, who had seemed very tired, had gone already to her room. Fires had been lit upstairs—she said that if he would excuse her, she would have her supper up there.

The storm had begun in earnest. Although all the shutters were fastened, the wind rattled them so and the rain sounded so violent beating against the skylight that he could not settle at all. Each clap of thunder seemed to him louder than before. He had not wanted to eat, and sat now in the long drawing-room facing the Crescent. Out there, beyond, below, the sea raged. Storms, angry waters tumbling, boiling—he had indeed been here before . . . Rose, Rose—whom he could not have saved. And yet . . .

The shutters rattled so violently that he leaped to his feet, certain someone was at the window. When he sat down again, foolish, he felt not relief but more fear. He thought of trying to smoke quietly, to re-collect himself—but the more he tried the more his panic grew. *I cannot be afraid of a thunderstorm* . . . He thought then that he was certainly becoming ill again. Now he could not breathe. His panic grew. I am child again and afraid of the storm. *Then*—Kate would comfort me. He thought suddenly: Bea, the very age now when sheltering from the thunder and lightning I slept with Kate, and was comforted . . . At the very idea that she, his daughter, might be suffering the same, his weakness and panic left him.

He rushed upstairs to see that she was all right. A lamp was on, turned down very low. There was no sound. By its light he saw that, mouth slightly open, she slept the heavy sleep of the physically tired. Her breathing was even. One arm lay outside the coverlet, the other was clasped tight round Bébé. For a while he watched her. It seemed even to calm him a little. But he was no sooner downstairs again than the panic returned.

When his hand would not keep still even to strike a lucifer, he abandoned the idea of smoking. I am going to be very ill, he thought again. Then he thought: why do I not ask Emily for something—a draught, a powder?—she is the keeper of the medicine chest. He knew he deceived himself—that he was afraid, and must talk to someone. But, he thought, she will understand.

He knocked at her door (God allow that she is still up, still awake. That she has not thought nine o'clock a proper bedtime).

"Come in," her voice said.

She was kneeling before the fire. She wore a peignoir of blue velvet.

When she turned he could barely see her face for the cloud, the mass of fair hair which hanging almost to her waist she tried to push back.

She appeared flustered. "I am so sorry—I thought it was Bea's nurse. She brings in often some sewing . . . I would not have had you see me like this—"

"But—" he began.

"It had, you see, to be rinsed and dried. All the salt and the spray—I had not realised how it was until I came in here." Now that he could see her face—her cheeks, perhaps from the fire, were high-coloured. "In one moment—I shall have it fastened . . ."

"Please. *Please.* No, it is for me to apologise. I was looking in on Beatrice and—"

"Half an hour since, I visited her. She sleeps very well. The storm has not—"

"Will you marry me?" he said. Afterwards he could not remember planning the words. They sprang from him. When she said nothing but just stood there quite still, he repeated: "Will you marry me—Emily?"

He could not think why he had not said it before. It seemed so natural. And it was this, not fear of the storm which had brought him to her room. *I should have asked months ago . . .*

"Will you, Emily?"

"I—"

"Forgive me," he said hurriedly, "I should not have spoken in that manner without any sort of preamble. I have surprised you, alarmed you . . ."

"No, no," she said. "It is only that—"

He said to her: "I loved my wife."

She smiled then. "You said—just that on a train journey once . . . As I told you"—she was smiling still—"it is not in question—"

But he did not know why he had said it. Just as last time. Blurted out as if spoken for him. And she found it amusing . . . But his proposal— she still had not answered that . . . He forgot that he was rushing her, that he had but just apologised for causing alarm.

"Now . . . please say—*will you?*"

"Oh, my dear, it is not that I would not, it is not that—" He thought, seeing her usually calm face puckered, dismayed, that she was going to cry. Her voice too was uncertain. "If I could . . . I cannot think of a greater . . . if you knew how *much* I . . ."

"*Will you or will you not?*"

"This is not like you, Mr. Rawson, that you should be so—peremptory. I am only trying to say that I *do* want . . ."

"Sit down," he said, "oh, please sit down—where you were—any-where. By the fire . . ."

"And you?"

"Yes—I shall sit beside you. And . . . Emily, darling Emily, you are saying 'yes'—is that not right?"

He thought, felt certain that she was about to come into his arms. Now he was so near . . . But she had turned her head away. Her voice was small, a little cold.

"I would have to . . . I could not accept . . . there is something you should know, *must* know first. And—"

He felt that he began to shake. "It is that you are married already. You are still married. Not a widow . . ."

"No," and he saw that she smiled again. "No, I am—quite free. It is only that—" her voice wavered. "You should know who I am. Without telling you that, I could not accept . . ."

He sat too on the hearth rug, like a boy again: knees drawn up, chin resting on them. He said carefully: "Very well—I am not sure that I understand . . . I know you to be—Mrs. Emily Hurst, widow—"

"Look at me," she said. "No—*look* . . . You never saw me before?"

He shook his head. "You tease me—"

"Before the interview, I mean. Never? You are *certain*?"

"Yes, yes. Emily, *what is this*?"

"I stall only for time," she said. "I . . . do you remember the leather box I have at home and how once we joked? M.E.N. . . ."

"Or better still, and more edifying—A.M.E.N.—" He tried to keep his voice steady because he did not know where this was leading—and because she appeared to him distressed. "We had thought to add *Agnes* . . ."

She did not laugh. "M.E.N.," she repeated. "I thought at the time, that perhaps you would . . . Mabel Emily Nugent . . . Now, does *that* mean nothing?"

For a moment it did not. Then it all came back. He felt that she had hit him. Looking at her—but he could not. He turned away at once . . .

"You see—you *do* remember . . ."

"You are—" He shuddered. Felt cold suddenly with the realisation. "That woman. You are *that* girl—the girl of the railway carriage." He didn't know why he did not say "court case" or "trial" or even "scandal" . . .

"Yes. I—"

"And you *dare*," he said, emotion overwhelming him, "you have *dared* to come into my house—to be with my child—to . . . to . . ." He was shaking his head to-and-fro, he banged against his knees: "You have dared . . . What do you *do* here, with us? Tell me that? Had you not damaged the family enough? If you knew how we had felt. If you knew . . ." To his horror he realised that he was weeping. The illness, he thought, it is that makes me so weak still.

"My father," he was shouting now, "my poor father, who was never the same again. *He* was not able to forget. You may have been—and indeed you walked from the court scot free, and *that* was not right . . . that was not right, *was it?* But my father, *he* bore you no grudge. *He* was able to forgive. *I* cannot . . . and then you think to come and—and . . ." He was blustering now, the words tumbling over each other. His sense of outrage confused him.

Perhaps he had really frightened her. She was quite silent. He did not care to look up.

"And why—why do you have to tell me this? I do not want to hear it. I never wished to meet—*that* girl. Miss *Nugent* . . ."

But her voice was not very frightened. Only a little quieter. And he, it had been he, to shout . . . She said quite firmly: "I had to say it. Because of what you just asked me. You forget that, I think . . . You have made it clear that you do not wish to hear—anything I might have to say." She paused. "There is more. That is not all, you see . . ."

What—what could be worse? I shall get up and go, he thought. Tomorrow she can pack her bags. She need explain no more . . .

"I do not wish to hear. Anything further—it is only to do more damage. The sooner everything is ended, without discussion . . ." He had thought to get up, but sat there still. He did not trust his shaking knees.

Now her voice was very cool, very assured. She is detestable, he thought.

"I think in fairness to me that you must—that you should listen . . ."

"*I* do not owe you any fairness. You were not fair—" Then when there was no response, he added, his voice aggressive, belligerent even: "Well? *Well?*"

"It was not true," she said quietly.

"*What* was not true? Certainly as you yourself acknowledged, admitted, *too late*, your indictment of my father—no, it *was not* true. That you should mention it . . ."

"No—no. It was the other. It was my confession."

"What do you mean?" He grew frightened again.

"My confession. It was that that was not true . . ."

But he could make nothing of any of it. He did not want even to understand. "I don't know what you are saying . . ." He shouted again: "*Have you not done enough damage?*"

She stood up. As she rose he saw her lift the great mass of hair, pushing it, thrusting it back, tossing her head. "I could go," she said. "I could leave you, and forget it all. Or try to . . ." Her voice was quite calm. "I could just allow everything to be as it was before. I could go out of your life—let the truth remain where it is . . . Hidden." Only then her voice faltered: "But I *shall not* . . . I have not the courage. That sort of courage. I—*love* you too much . . ."

But he was angry, so angry. "Oh, love. Love. What is love?"

"Indeed—indeed. What is love? If I had not loved you . . . and *at first sight*—for what else was it? If I had not, then I should not be here . . . and we would not—" Her voice trailed away. There was a moment's silence. Then, "I cannot tell you," she said.

"Tell me what you will," he said. "I shall not believe it . . ."

"If . . . I shall *try* . . . I speak of the day of the trial. The Assizes. The morning—"

He said coldly, "You can bear to look back? To that time. I should have thought—"

"Why not? Why should I not? *I* did not do wrong—"

"Come, come—*really*, Mrs. Hurst . . ."

"You sound now like the judge—*he* was not pleased with me that day. I made . . . there were many difficulties. I think perhaps . . ." Then her voice very incisive: "Will you please allow me to tell you? Whether you believe me or no—whatever . . ."

"Go forward. Please do not allow a Doubting Thomas to interfere with or hamper your tales of the fantastic. I should like to hear what you might invent . . ."

"The truth is—only the truth. I shall tell you, and you will listen . . . I came early that day, the day of the trial—or else, I came to the wrong place, I do not recall . . . but I was in the anteroom, went through it, and my cousin that was with me, she said: 'That is he—the son of your . . . your . . .' She used I think some strong word (they were then very much for me, as was only natural) '. . . that is *his* son.' You were pointed out to me—and . . . I do not know how to say this, because really it is not modest. Not at all. But I looked, and looked. And it was as if . . . it had never happened to me before but they call it I think *coup de foudre*. I had thought myself, *think* myself a calm person, but I was . . . it was as if I were possessed. And I *do not regret it* . . . And then, when I had to appear in court, and was in the box, I saw you again of course. I could see you all the time. You did not look at me at all— much of the time your head was bowed. I was distressed for you, for your father. Yes, for him too. For you *all*. It overwhelmed me completely—that, and . . . how I felt. It is not possible really to explain. I *try* only . . . You would allow me to continue?" She sounded but only very slightly hesitant.

"I would not . . . Yes, yes, of course. You are free to speak." He did not trust his voice, if *he* should try to talk.

"I thought then, could only think of what I would be doing—to *all* of you. That it would bring down your family, that your father would be ruined, that you—*you* would suffer on my account. While I . . . I had—*have* no family to speak of. I was a nothing. I could disappear . . . And so . . . you will remember what happened next—that I made a decision. A very sudden one. I am not usually a creature of impulse— but then . . . *that* time it was the complete impulsive gesture. Only a little thought before—as I have described to you. And then . . . it was done, and no going back. I cannot pretend, you see, Mr. Rawson, I cannot pretend that I *never* regretted it. Now—no. But how many times in the past? It was a pure impulse, but it did not stay pure. There were, have been, many times . . . It was the action of a saint perhaps—but it was done, you see, by a sinner . . ."

He forced himself to say, for he wanted only to give in now, to say . . . but what?

"I am to believe you?" he said. "That you tell the truth now? When you lied, under oath . . ."

"Perhaps a Jesuit might allow—it would be a Jesuitical point, who knows? Casuistry, purely. But . . . Yes, I went to Confession. I confessed, you see, what I had done."

He tried to keep his voice and his manner offhand. "And what did your priest say?"

"What you might expect. Or not . . . That I was very wrong, *very* wrong to lie under oath. But that God would allow for my motives, that I had *tried* to do good . . . but that we may not take God's name in vain, sin so seriously on *our own judgment*. That it was for God to decide in these matters, that we may not play God and that I sinned through pride. And that the end does not justify the means . . ." She smiled now. "I am sure that you know the rest."

After a moment's silence he said, his voice shaky: "Then . . . it really happened? The assault . . . all that—" He could not really take it in.

"Yes," she said simply. "Yes. I am afraid so."

"Tell me," he said. "Tell me. I think that I shall have to hear. Not, please, in the manner in which you spoke in court—and I tried then, not to listen—but just simply, as you would speak to—" he hesitated— "as you would speak to a—friend . . ."

He could see that she did not wish to. She said so too. "I would rather not. But yes, I see that I should. That I owe it to you . . ."

"You had begun with only conversation? And then—I cannot believe . . . I must believe—"

"Yes," she said simply. "Yes, at the beginning we spoke together. It seemed natural that we should. Two travellers, enclosed in what would have made a very small room, for the length of a not very interesting journey. And we enjoyed our conversation, and each other's company— and why not, since he is *your* father (and see how well you and I talk together, and are at ease with each other . . .). It was all so easy and pleasant. And my book—it lay untouched on my lap, after that first half hour. I am not by the way an *aficionada* of Rhoda Broughton—it had been a friend's suggestion, and I had soon become bored . . ."

"What did you speak of? What *kind* of conversation was it? I recollect only pleasantries, and poor jokes—"

"To begin with, yes. But then we had discussed more—about our families (You were spoken of. His hopes for you. His pride. Sarah— even mention, I think, of her birthmark . . . We were quite at our ease, quite natural). He asked me then, if I were not *Scotch*. I told him not at all. He said that his wife was from Scotland but that it was of someone else I reminded him. A look, he said, only a look. An expression perhaps. 'And then your name—*Ellie*.' But that was not my name, I told him. He had misheard. For I had given away my name, you see. We had laughed together—just as you and I did—at my initials: M.E.N. And I had told him that I used in fact my middle name 'Emily.' He coloured then. 'I had thought you said Ellie. Forgive me.' And all the while, you know, he watched me—and it was with frank admiration. I can say that now. Now that I am older, and wiser. I was not used to too much attention, and had not been taught or led to think that I looked well. For someone so much older and, it seemed to me, distinguished looking, to wish to look at me all the while we spoke . . ."

Paul said, "If you do not wish to tell—the rest. I would prefer it, that you should. But if you do not wish . . ."

"I was much to blame I now see," she said. "Both then, and later. I was young and did not think. Did not *know*, really. Although everything happened suddenly, I could have stopped it. For in a manner of speaking, I had begun it—" She was silent a moment or two. Then she continued: "It was a brooch I had—a very intricate affair, with jagged claws at the top. I wore it to one side, just near where my bodice fastened. I thought, after we had been talking awhile, that I would fetch from my portmanteau some photographs and drawings that I thought would interest him . . . As I reached up for it, he rose at once to help me. We collided. My brooch caught the fabric of his jacket—perhaps even the buttonhole. I cannot recollect. But for a few seconds we were —very close. And then, the next thing that I knew, he was kissing me. If I had moved away then, perhaps expressed displeasure . . . But I did not. I was both shocked—and pleased. I was flattered, you see. No one had ever—it had never happened to me . . . But then, for him— because I returned his kiss—it was not enough. How could it have been? He was breathing then very deeply, holding me so tightly that I could scarcely move. I grew suddenly very frightened—but you see, *I could not stop what I had started.* That is why I feel I am so much to blame . . . that a woman more versed in the ways of the world would have known what to do . . . From that moment, in my memory, it is of panic only. Mine *and* his. I felt that my dress was torn, there in the front. And he was calling me then 'Ellie, Ellie.' He seemed scarcely to know what he was doing . . . I was forced back on the seat. His hand . . . I was afraid, both because of his strength and because of where his hand was . . . I saw then that he was—as I said in the statement—un- undressed . . . I thought then of trying to open the door, that I *must* escape. I think that I might have . . . I knew so little, you see. I knew so little that, unwittingly, I was able to provoke and also to assume that because he touched me—there . . . that I was lost. That he would do— everything. You see, a girl is taught only about the greatest dangers— not perhaps what you might call—and I must make a railway joke here —the stations in between . . ."

"But your mistake," Paul said. "If it was a mistake, it was natural enough." He realised now that he was championing her. "You are not to take the blame."

"But yes. Partly, yes. I do not know how it would have ended . . . but then, the train, it began slowing down. He released me then, before the train drew into York. I could see at once, that he was very distressed. Distraught even. But so was I . . . He said to me, 'I should not—you will not say anything?' He pleaded with me almost. 'You will not?' But I was too shocked. I could not speak at all. I turned away. And then as the train halted, he pulled down his luggage and was away —at once. It may have been that he was not—properly dressed. I stayed awhile in the carriage, until I felt able to walk, to compose myself a lit- tle. But in fact I became if anything more upset. It was then I ran out, and spoke to the first woman I saw . . ."

"You could not have done otherwise," he said.

"Who knows? After the first hearing, I did not wish to go through with it. But my relations—everyone urged me. I *must* prosecute. They felt certain that I had averted danger only because the train had drawn into York . . . The frenzy around me was kept up. I even began to believe myself some of the comments I read in the paper—some of the inventions . . . And then—the day of the trial. My feelings that day. I have told you . . . I *could* not do it. I could not ruin your family, you, your father—whom after all I had *liked*. But I was so frightened, knew so little. And so, I gave the evidence you heard. The invention. I was in my own way not displeased with it. I fancied that it rang true—precisely because it was not the truth . . ."

He said, "But—if you had been prosecuted?"

"Exactly what I thought. Too late. Had I been a better person, more pure in motive, perhaps I would not have worried. But I did. For quite some time. Until I heard that—all was to be well."

"In the courtroom—you did not show it . . ."

"An orphan, Mr. Rawson, must be accustomed to containing her emotions—often there is no one to whom . . . many times it is not advisable, you see, to show them . . .

"Afterwards, when I had done it, when the judge had rebuked me, when I was in absolute disgrace—I realised what it would mean. They were bad days. I received—because there was no one to look first through my post—I received some letters that even now . . . I cannot . . . that I would rather not remember. That people should have such minds . . . My cousin, he had no patience with me. I got through the summer as best I could. In September I had an invitation from another, distant cousin in India—in a Punjab regiment. I did not know whether they had read newspapers out there—I did not take the risk, but went out in October for the cold weather . . . using my cousin's surname. By Christmas, I was married. I told Captain Hurst—the truth. But no one else. And from then on anyway, I was Emily Hurst. The Mabel I had by the way never liked or used . . . The next autumn Harry was born. I was happy, or almost so. I loved, although I was not in love. And I was much loved in return. And I had my child . . . Life might have gone on that way—for who knows how long? Perhaps I would have brought Harry back to England when he was seven or eight—for schooling. But I would not have stayed. My life was out there. And it was a good life . . . until, suddenly—like a puff of smoke . . . all gone. The Piffers, his regiment, always in action on the North-West Frontier—a border skirmish, and I was widowed. A cholera epidemic the next summer and I am lucky to survive. My child did not. After that—I did not want to stay. I think, perhaps, that I could have married again. I am certain . . . but I returned—to safe anonymity."

"Here . . . but how do you come here? How are you in Downham?" He heard already that his voice was gentle.

"Ah, that. You see, I had not forgotten you. Not quite. And I had read, you know (a long time after the event) of your wedding. In India. And I had been glad for you—interested too, that you should have become Roman Catholic. But later—and I had read first of Bea's birth—I saw about the Bridge. *Her* name was there, a short paragraph . . . You will remember . . . I almost wrote to you then, anonymously. So that you should *know* of my sympathy. Of course then I had not had my troubles . . . Then when I was back in England and had taken a post— the only one I could think of—as governess, it was then that Chance or Destiny or the Hand of God, call it what you will . . . I was on holiday, and at the home of some very remote acquaintances for a week or ten days. At dinner one evening—and we were many miles from here— two guests who were from Yorkshire mentioned your name. They spoke of the motherless Bea, and how well you managed. She was to have a governess, one of them said. 'And I have told him,' she went on, 'I have told him to go to Mrs. Burrows' Agency, in York. Quite the best. Quite the best. Especially as he requires a Roman Catholic—*most* difficult . . .'"

"I cannot think," Paul said, "who she might have been. There are two persons in Leyburn, who could have told me . . . But I cannot recollect—"

"At first I thought I would try to speak with the Yorkshire guest— about you. But it was not possible. And she left the party early. I was not certain either what I should say . . . But the idea had come to me. I felt that it was meant—that I *must*. I did not see myself even with a choice in the matter. And I became determined then, to secure the post . . . You see, I *am* impulsive. As at the trial . . . And I wanted to see if what I had felt for you then, in passing, could have—*would* have, more depth . . ."

He said: "Yes?"

"Yes," she said. "You know that it did . . . I see—God in it all. That I should have gone straight to the Agency, that *indeed* you should have applied there. And . . . but you know the rest. How I came to Downham, how I wanted the post—so much. How Bea so sweetly ran into my arms . . ."

The fire which had been burning so brightly when he came into the room, was glowing only now. And the storm, the raging storm—while he had not been noticing, it had died down.

She said: "And here endeth my tale . . ."

He looked up at her. "The Valentines—" he began.

"Yes. Oh—yes . . ."

"I suddenly knew," he said. "When you spoke just now. But . . . if it was you, then—how?"

"Just a foolish—a romantic idea. When I was at my lowest ebb, just before I left for India, I passed a few days preparing—four, five was it? and gave them to a girl friend, from schooldays, in Portsmouth. She was to post them each year . . . She is of a romantic disposition, and confessed to having thoroughly enjoyed it. But I—I regretted it when I saw to what bad taste it led. When you were widowed . . . And I had not the wit to write to her that she should send no more. I fancied anyway, that she was not likely to remember . . ."

"I have to say—they were not always *exact* as to the date . . ."

"There. You see."

"But—almost always—they gave pleasure. And the guessings, the false accusations . . . The most unlikely suspects. Ah this, I cannot forgive."

"I see," she said smiling. "I see that you do not forgive me."

" 'I love,' " he said, " 'and he loves me again, Yet dare I not tell, Who . . .' "

" 'Yet if it be not known, The pleasure is as good as none . . .' "

"Your hair," he said, "it reminds me—" But he could not say about Kate. One day. With time perhaps. But not yet.

She said: "Please. I ask you now. You do—believe me?"

He nodded because he could not speak. He put out a hand towards her.

"Oh, my dear," she said. "Oh, my dear."

THIRTY-TWO

Long years apart—can make no
Breach a second cannot fill—
The absence of the Witch does not
Invalidate the spell—

The embers of a Thousand Years
Uncovered by the Hand
That fondled them when they were Fire
Will stir and understand—

                    EMILY DICKINSON

It had rained without cease the whole journey from Harrogate. Now as the train drew near Leyburn, Kate could not make out the countryside at all. The windows were wet and steamed, and a gale more like March than April sent the rain thudding against the glass. Only by her watch could she tell that they had almost arrived.

Sarah had telegraphed yesterday, and Kate had replied at once—and given the time of her train. But even though the message, or part of it, was "Good news imperative urgent you return home immediately . . ." she could not completely trust it. That it was something to do with Will—some triumph of his—was the most likely. When she knew, really *knew*, then of course she would rejoice, but inured as she was now to disaster (and have not all of us, just these last years, had more than our share? Sukey—did *she* have to die?), she had come even to expect it. So—until I have seen Sarah, and spoken with her . . .

Walking down the wet platform—how like me, she thought, to have chosen the far end of the train; her luggage wheeled before her, she looked round anxiously for Sarah.

Instead she saw Richard, just coming from the ticket barrier. Ah no, she said to herself, now there is *him* to avoid. She tried to compose her face, to look a little into the distance—beyond him. But because it was Richard it was not possible. Never possible.

And anyway—he was coming straight towards her. Almost blocking her way. She said: "Good evening, Mr. Ingham—" not looking at him.

"*Kate*—"

Oh no, she thought. What is this? Her heart drummed. I grow no better—I shall never be cured. She said quickly, still without looking at him: "Perhaps you have seen Miss Rawson? I—"

"Did you expect her?"

She said coolly, "I—it is possible. Yes, she has sent for me—"

But something was wrong. Even as she spoke, he had hold of her arm. "I am to b-bring you. The carriage. Out here . . ."

She did not speak at all then until they were inside, and her luggage stacked. She did not know that she could be so calm—in the face of what she felt certain must be some disaster. And it is *he* sent to tell me . . .

When the carriage door was shut, he said then, in a great rush: "Kate, Kate—" She saw that he trembled.

"*Yes?*" Now she trembled too.

"I m-must tell you . . ."

She did not believe it—when she was told. She could not at first. It was too much happiness. The shock as great as a disaster. She was trembling still.

"Oh, but yes," she had to say to him, "yes, yes, indeed it is all true. It happened all of it, exactly like that . . ."

She was afraid too at first of his touch. Nothing altered, nothing altered. It was as yesterday. When she still could not stop trembling, he held her more closely. The journey back to Downham—it seemed it would go on forever. It *must* go on forever.

"I had thought—some disaster. And that Sarah was to break it, but softened first with something happy, or good—I was uncertain. Only fearful, always fearful—"

But he was telling her already (as if he knew, as if anyone knew . . .) that she would never suffer again. He would not allow it. They would never, never be apart again.

"You do not stutter. See, you are not stuttering—" But it was she crying . . .

"I am not used to stutter with you. You remember, it was not often, and n-never with your name. Kate, Kate, Kate . . ."

And then it seemed that, so much explaining was there to do, that it was each vying with the other.

"That I should have b-believed you. Anything so unlike you—that were so good, so gentle—"

"And I, and I—that I should have been so stupid . . . To believe her. If I had not *believed* . . ."

"I thought, you see—and I had been used to my father, who was one moment smiles and then again, b-blows. And Mother too—you saw how, for just a little, the sun would go in . . ."

"That I should have mocked you, that I had to—that I *could*, when I loved you so much . . ."

Later, he said: "You knew about Sarah?"

"No—"

"Oh," she said when he told her. Then with a smile: "Oh, but how like Sarah—that she must be a New Woman. She is so dear. But—" And then it seemed to her terrible that she should be so happy at Sarah's expense. "Does she—is she—"

"She understands—everything."

She was afraid even for a moment to let go of his hand. It was as if, for all the years they had not touched . . .

"And my mother. Do you—can you forgive her?"

"Yes. Yes—I have had to try and forgive Greaves. That was such an exercise as never. After that, after that—" She shuddered. "And I could do it. *Just.* So after that—your mother. It is not so very difficult."

"I c-cannot. Yet."

But terrified still by her happiness, she had thought, when he told her about Sarah, of her age: "I am—I cannot give you a son, darling."

"My l-love, such obstacles you raise—that have had the greatest obstacle knocked down at one blow. We must not—"

"But a *son*. It is more important, is it not, than perhaps for others? The Inghams, the Abbey—it has meaning in Downham . . ."

"Indeed. And *that*," he said, his mouth stopping hers. Then when they had finished, "*That* is what I think of your objections." He said more gravely, "My d-darling, all your love, all my love cannot bring Francis back . . . I had long ago thought what it was I should do. B-before Sarah—I had a plan made, and shall now carry it out. I had m-made my will. Julia's Edmund—he is to have everything. If he wishes he m-may change his name to Ingham. But it is not important. Julia knows. He d-does not."

They would soon be coming into Downham. She was to go straight to the Abbey, have dinner there. In three days it would be Georgiana's funeral. "You will come?"

The wedding, it could not be at once. "I think because of her—we must wait a little . . ."

And Kate did not say, he did not say: because of her, we have waited already twenty-seven years . . .

They were not the same people. She wondered how it would be, and knew it would be all right. They spoke, or tried to speak now only of the future. But the past returned again and again—sometimes happy, sometimes sad. Later that evening, they spoke of the Squire's old room with the painted walls.

". . . we are not the same people," she was saying, half in jest, "we cannot be lying about all day in decorated bedrooms—"

"We shall be *m-much* time doing that."

"But, but—"

"It is for me to b-bluster and stutter," he said. "I silence you—like this . . ."

"We must repeat our p-pledge at the Kissing Gate—"

"But we shall look so foolish," she protested.

"We are foolish." But then he added, "No, no, we have *b-been* foolish. Think only—think only, how foolish we *have been* . . ."

Later he said, "We shall meet there, at the Gate. Very early. That is b-best."

"How early? Just as the sun is rising?"

"Just as the sun is rising . . ."

"Stand there . . . the other side of the G-Gate. If someone should pass—let them see, let them see . . . And now s-say, 'I, Katharine Rawson.'"

"I, Katharine Rawson . . ."

"'. . . pledge my troth to Richard Ingham—that we shall always be one and never twain that only d-death can part us . . .'"

"I, Katharine Rawson . . ."

"I, Richard Ingham . . ."

"I love you," he said, again and again.

Then we were both the other side of the Gate. We stood back, under the oak tree. Its leaves were tinged with russet. There, almost hidden from the road, we kissed to seal our pledge.

THIRTY-THREE

Sarah was putting some flowers—late September roses—on Francis' grave (some too on his mother's), when turning, she saw Matthew Staveley behind her.

"Good day," he said smiling.

Always glad to see him, she smiled back. The churchyard was almost empty except in the far corner near the copse, where an elderly man tended a grave.

"I was just now in the church," he said, "and came for a moment to the porch—and saw you."

"I am glad that you did. I am only here a minute—"

"You go back into Downham?"

"No—on up to the Abbey. I stopped—just for the graves. I go to see Mr. and Mrs. Ingham—"

He said, "I did not know they were back?"

"Three days. It appears that it rained without cease in Galway . . . but that they saw it *could* be beautiful—and when we have had days of autumn sun here! Dublin was drier, I understand . . . But all in all—a success. She wanted, you know, to see Connemara . . ."

"Yes, of course . . . But little Laura—you find her improved?"

"Yes. Very much. Much better, much happier. And Cicely—"

"Is very clever. She will make the best advertisement for your school possible. You must be proud."

She smiled. "I was to have said before you interrupted—that she is happier too. But does she, *has* she ever studied as hard as I, those months with you—I blush now for the mounds of paper I set before you . . ."

She remembered then: it had been the time also of his proposal. Wanting to move on quickly, she said, "You continue visiting professor

—as we call you on our prospectus—all this academic year? You are not too busy?"

"Someone must organise the Golden Jubilee here—so there will be somewhat. But the roasting of an ox in the market square—someone else may see to that. I shall be able to plead higher things—such as Almeida House . . ."

"Thank you." She took up her gloves, which she had laid by the grave. Yellowing leaves from the lime tree nearby lay scattered. She said, "I want to thank you, that you work so hard for us—when you cannot and do not agree with us, or our aims . . ."

"I do not need to agree or to approve," he said, "in order to *admire*. Almeida House is quite an achievement." He paused. "You would accept admiration?"

"With pleasure—"

She made as if to go, but to cover the awkwardness of the moment, she said lightly: "Summer is almost quite gone. The swallows—I saw yesterday, they will leave soon—"

When he said nothing, she told him: "And now I must go . . ."

"I also. But—you will let me walk you there, to the Abbey?"

"I would not hear of it—" She laughed. "It is only a few yards and—you are busy."

"As far as the Gate then?"

They walked down the path together. Thistle beards floated by the edge of the grass. He said smiling: "You came *in* by the Kissing Gate, of course?"

"Of course—"

"It dies hard, does it not? But—I have never preached against it, and think now that I shall not. If people *wish* to walk the long way round . . . happily I am exempt . . . I think anyway they will go, gradually—the superstitions. This next generation. Or the one after. They will know better." He turned: "But you yourself, you do not *believe*?"

"No—but I dream. I have had dreams of the Kissing Gate. And I am not alone—"

"I too," he said. "Strangely enough, I dreamed once."

"And you would not tell me your dream?"

He smiled. "No," he said. "It was too happy. I could not—"

They had reached the Kissing Gate. As he opened it, he said, " 'The iron gate ground its teeth to let me pass . . .' Yes?"

"Mr. Browning, 'Serenade at the Villa,' " she said promptly. "We are used to more obscure Browning, you and I . . ."

As she was about to go through the Gate: "You are sure," he said, "I shall not go with you?"

"No, no. Thank you. I walk alone. Really. It is for the best."

"I see you then in two weeks' time at Almeida House?"

"Do you remember?" she said: "'A man should consider a voyage from the land, to see if he would be able and would have the skill; but when he has come upon the deep, he must needs run with the wind there is . . .' I wanted now to thank you—"

"Yes," he said. "Yes."

She walked towards the Abbey. Just before the archway she turned. Matthew Staveley, leaning on the Kissing Gate, watched her still.